Buffy
the vampire slayer™
OMNIBUS

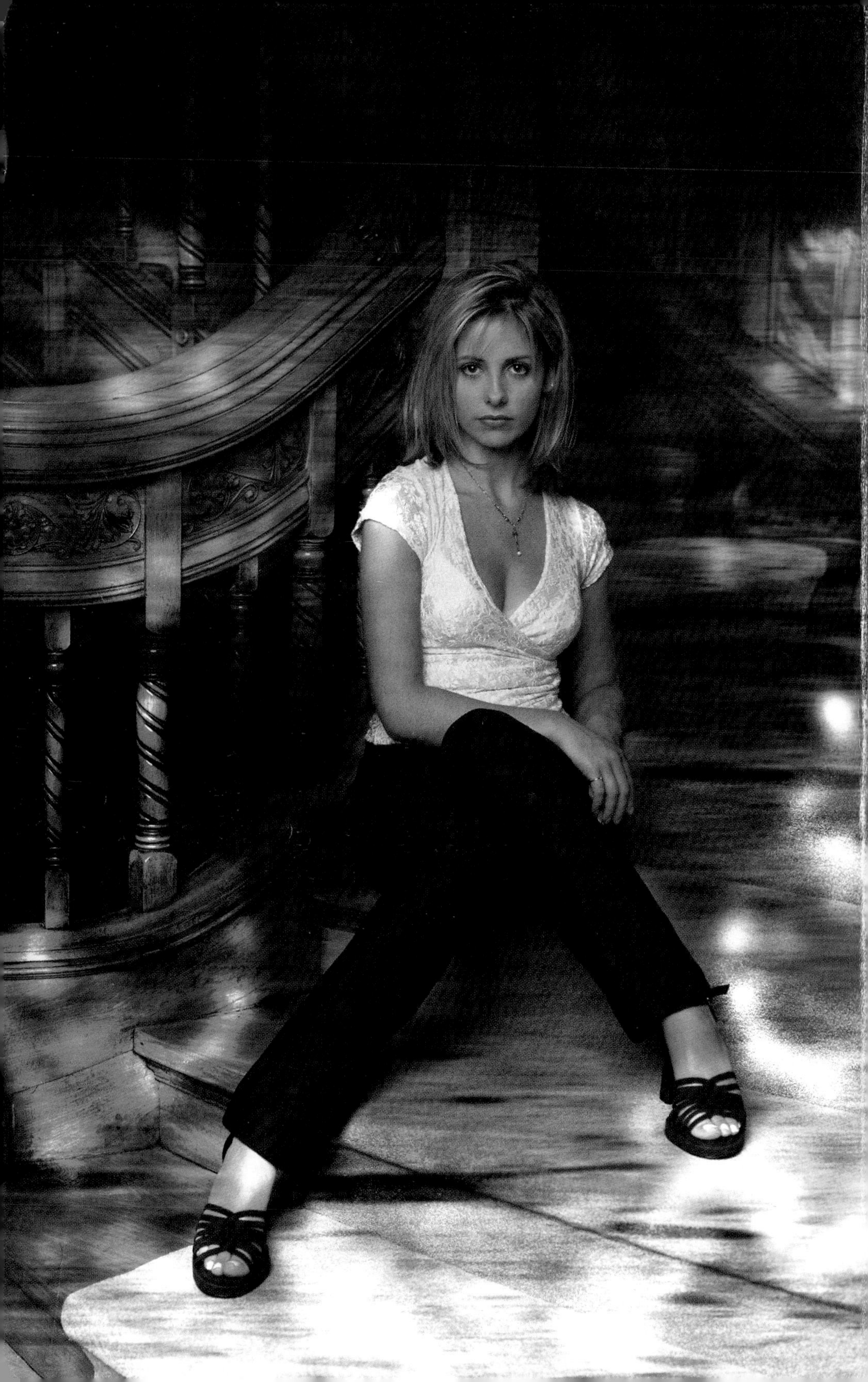

Buffy the Vampire Slayer™

OMNIBUS

VOLUME 2

DAN BRERETON
CHRISTOPHER GOLDEN
HECTOR GOMEZ
BRIAN HORTON
PAUL LEE
SCOTT LOBDELL
JAMES MARSTERS
JEFF MATSUDA
FABIAN NICIEZA
DOUG PETRIE
CLIFF RICHARDS
LUKE ROSS
RYAN SOOK
JEN VAN METER

Based on the television series created by Joss Whedon.

These stories take place before Buffy the Vampire Slayer *Season One and through early Season Three.*

DARK HORSE BOOKS®

Publisher MIKE RICHARDSON
Editor SCOTT ALLIE
Assistant Editor KATIE MOODY
Assistant Editors on Original Series MATT DRYER, BEN ABERNATHY, MIKE CARRIGLITTO & ADAM GALLARDO
Collection Designers LIA RIBACCHI & HEIDI FAINZA
Cover Illustration PAUL LEE & BRIAN HORTON

Special thanks to Debbie Olshan at Twentieth Century Fox, David Campiti at Glass House Graphics, and Michael Boretz, Caroline Kallas, and George Snyder.

BUFFY THE VAMPIRE SLAYER™: *OMNIBUS* VOLUME TWO
Published by Dark Horse Comics, Inc., 10956 SE Main Street, Milwaukie, Oregon 97222.

This volume reprints
"Angels We Have Seen on High", originally published in *Reveal*, November 2002;
Buffy the Vampire Slayer #60–63, originally published August through November 2003;
"MacGuffins", originally published in *DHP Annual*, August 1998;
Buffy the Vampire Slayer: Spike & Dru–The Queen of Hearts, originally published October 1999;
Buffy the Vampire Slayer: Ring of Fire, originally published August 2000;
Buffy the Vampire Slayer: Spike & Dru–Paint the Town Red, originally published April 1999; and
Buffy the Vampire Slayer: The Dust Waltz, originally published October 1998;
all from Dark Horse Comics.

Published by Dark Horse Books
A division of Dark Horse Comics, Inc.
10956 SE Main Street
Milwaukie, OR 97222

darkhorse.com

To find a comics shop in your area, call the Comic Shop Locator Service toll-free at (888) 266-4226.

First edition: September 2007
ISBN: 978-1-59307-826-3

10 9 8 7 6 5 4 3
Printed in Canada

INTRODUCTION

In 1998, Dark Horse launched a series based on Joss Whedon's *Buffy the Vampire Slayer*, which proved to be one of our most popular and enduring comics. The book ended in late 2003, shortly after the TV series. The seven stories in this second Omnibus show what we were up to at the very beginning and at the very end of the run, as well as a defining stretch in the middle that helped to get us on the right track.

The pre-Season One "Angels We Have Seen on High" and *A Stake to the Heart*, the first stories in this volume, were done at the end of the original comics series. They display two notable stylistic departures, with Jeff Matsuda's cartoony depictions of the characters, and Brian Horton's paints over longtime penciller Cliff Richards. These stories also reflect a narrative choice that met with some skepticism. When, near the end of the series, I decided to set stories early in Buffy's career, I chose to include Dawn—who, of course, wouldn't have been there. I felt that we could add something valuable to the Buffy mythos, reflecting what an older Buffy would *remember* about her early adventures. As we move into stories written before Michelle Trachtenberg's first appearance on the show, expect not to see Dawn in this Omnibus series again until the fifth or sixth volume.

From these pre–Season One stories, we leap into the only story set during—or rather, immediately after—Season One. "MacGuffins" was the first Buffy comics story, published in *Dark Horse Presents*, the legendary anthology that launched such Dark Horse series as *Concrete* and *Sin City*. While the Spike and Dru stories collected here take place around the same time, we don't catch up to Buffy again until after Angel has turned evil, toward the end of Season Two, with *Ring of Fire*. And the next time we see Buffy, Angel's good again, and it's Season Three, with *The Dust Waltz*. The flow may get rocky through the book, but you get some truly historic moments in the history of our comics.

Ryan Sook remains one of the most controversial artists to have worked on Buffy. Some hardcore fans of the show hated his work. Many comics fans felt it was the high point of the series. I snuck Ryan in on the first Spike and Dru comic, *Paint the Town Red*, because I thought he was perfect for a horror story. Joss loved Ryan's work on the title, which was one of the first positive comments I got from the man himself, way back when I had no direct contact with him.

The writers with whom Ryan worked are perhaps more important to the history of the series than Ryan himself. That first Spike and Dru comic was the brainchild of Christopher Golden, arguably the definitive *Buffy* novelist, who wrote dozens of comics for me. Chris brought in James "Spike" Marsters, whom he'd met while working on the first *Watcher's Guide* for Pocket Books. While it never led to more work with James—note that *Queen of Hearts* is just Chris—it did a lot to validate the series in the eyes of fans.

And Ryan's work validated the series with comics purists, including Doug Petrie. Doug approached me shortly after that first Spike and Dru comic, proposing a series about Buffy and Angelus, head to head, with Ryan drawing. This required Ryan to meet Sarah Michelle Gellar's approval, about which I had my doubts. But it worked, and we had a creative coup with the first *Buffy* comic written by a writer from the show. More would follow, ultimately leading to Joss himself writing Season Eight.

So pardon our shoddy continuity, and enjoy this look at the beginning of Buffy's career, when you never knew whether her lover would prove good or bad—but you certainly knew he wouldn't be Spike.

Scott Allie

ANGEL
WE
HAVE
SEEN
ON
HIGH

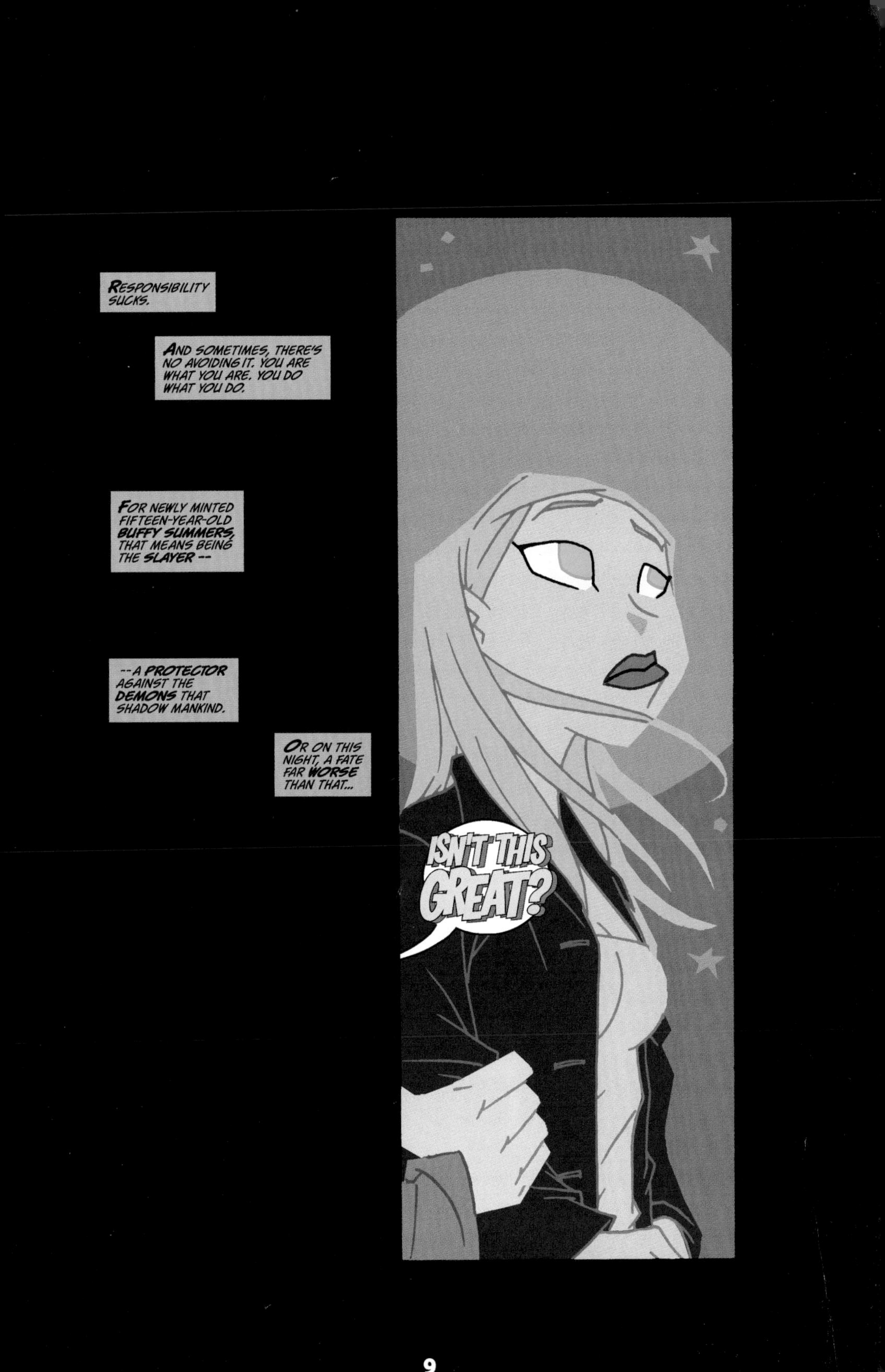
RESPONSIBILITY SUCKS.
AND SOMETIMES, THERE'S NO AVOIDING IT. YOU ARE WHAT YOU ARE. YOU DO WHAT YOU DO.
FOR NEWLY MINTED FIFTEEN-YEAR-OLD BUFFY SUMMERS, THAT MEANS BEING THE SLAYER --
--A PROTECTOR AGAINST THE DEMONS THAT SHADOW MANKIND.
OR ON THIS NIGHT, A FATE FAR WORSE THAN THAT...
ISN'T THIS GREAT?

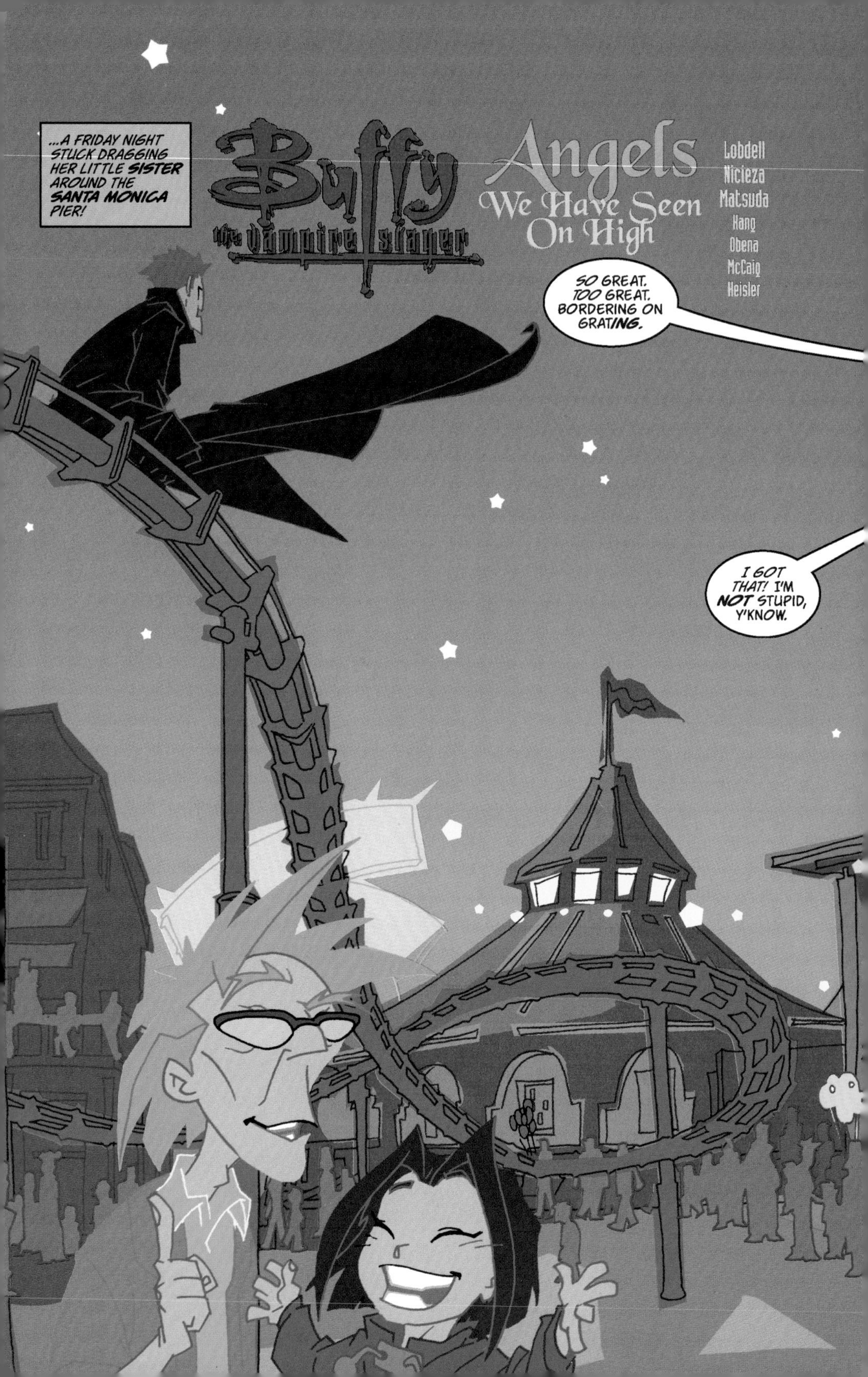
...A FRIDAY NIGHT STUCK DRAGGING HER LITTLE SISTER AROUND THE SANTA MONICA PIER!
Buffy the Vampire Slayer
Angels We Have Seen On High
Lobdell
Nicieza
Matsuda
Hang
Obena
McCaig
Heisler
SO GREAT. TOO GREAT. BORDERING ON GRATING.
I GOT THAT! I'M NOT STUPID, Y'KNOW.

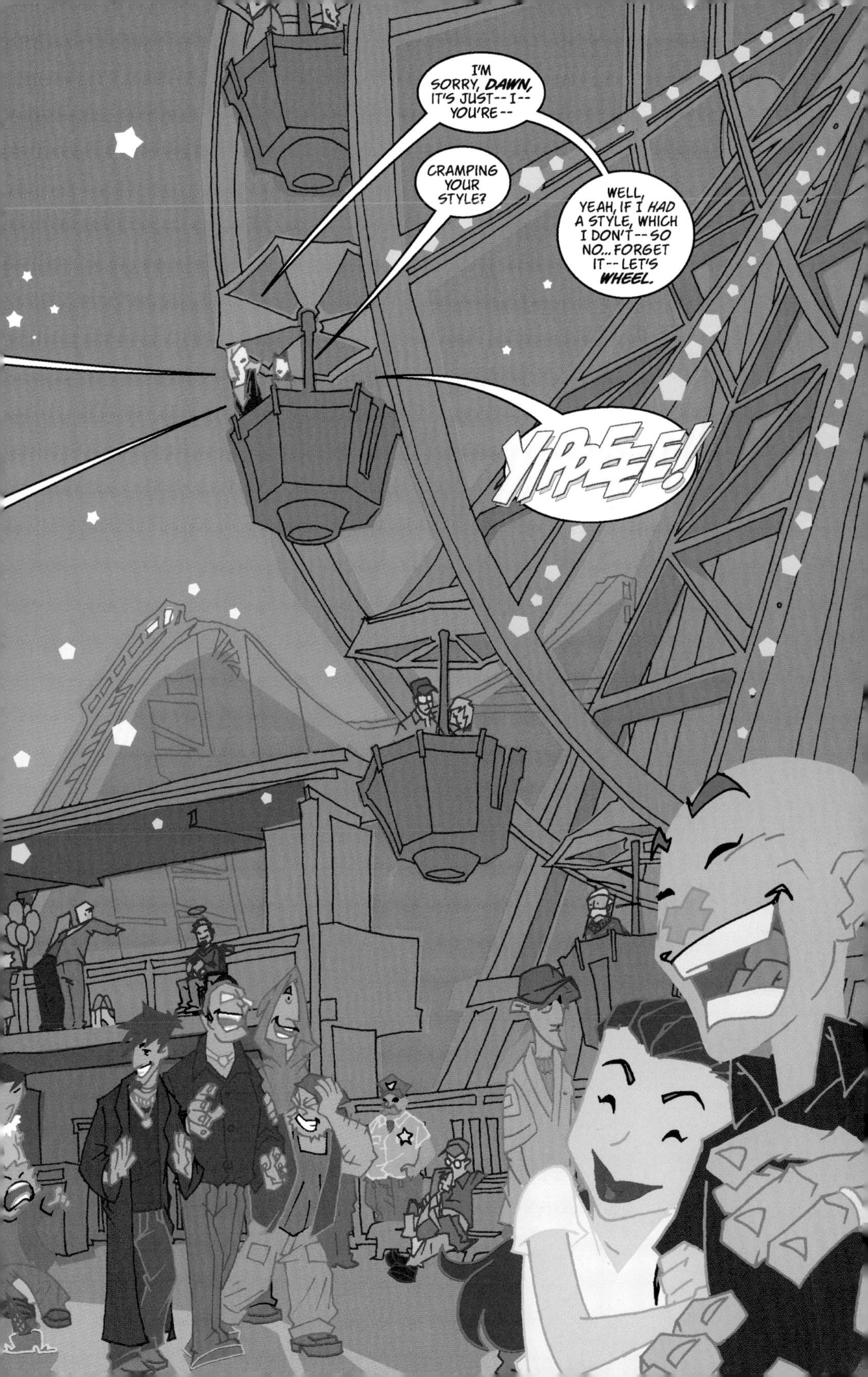

I'M SORRY, **DAWN,** IT'S JUST-- I-- YOU'RE--
CRAMPING YOUR STYLE?
WELL, YEAH, IF I *HAD* A STYLE, WHICH I DON'T-- SO NO... FORGET IT-- LET'S **WHEEL.**
YIPEEE!

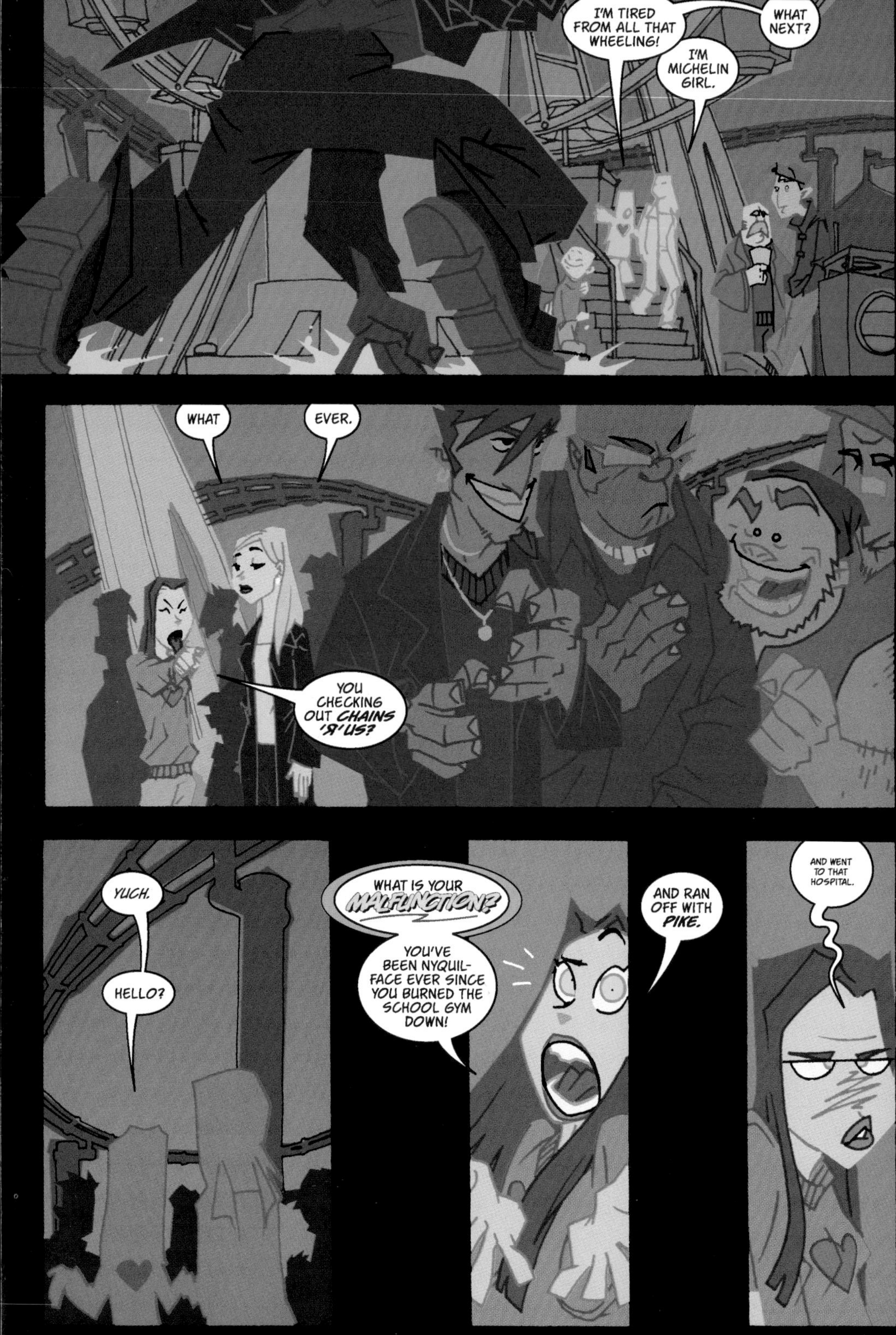
I'M TIRED FROM ALL THAT WHEELING!
WHAT NEXT?
I'M MICHELIN GIRL.
WHAT
EVER.
YOU CHECKING OUT CHAINS 'R' US?
YUCH.
HELLO?
WHAT IS YOUR MALFUNCTION?
YOU'VE BEEN NYQUIL-FACE EVER SINCE YOU BURNED THE SCHOOL GYM DOWN!
AND RAN OFF WITH PIKE.
AND WENT TO THAT HOSPITAL.

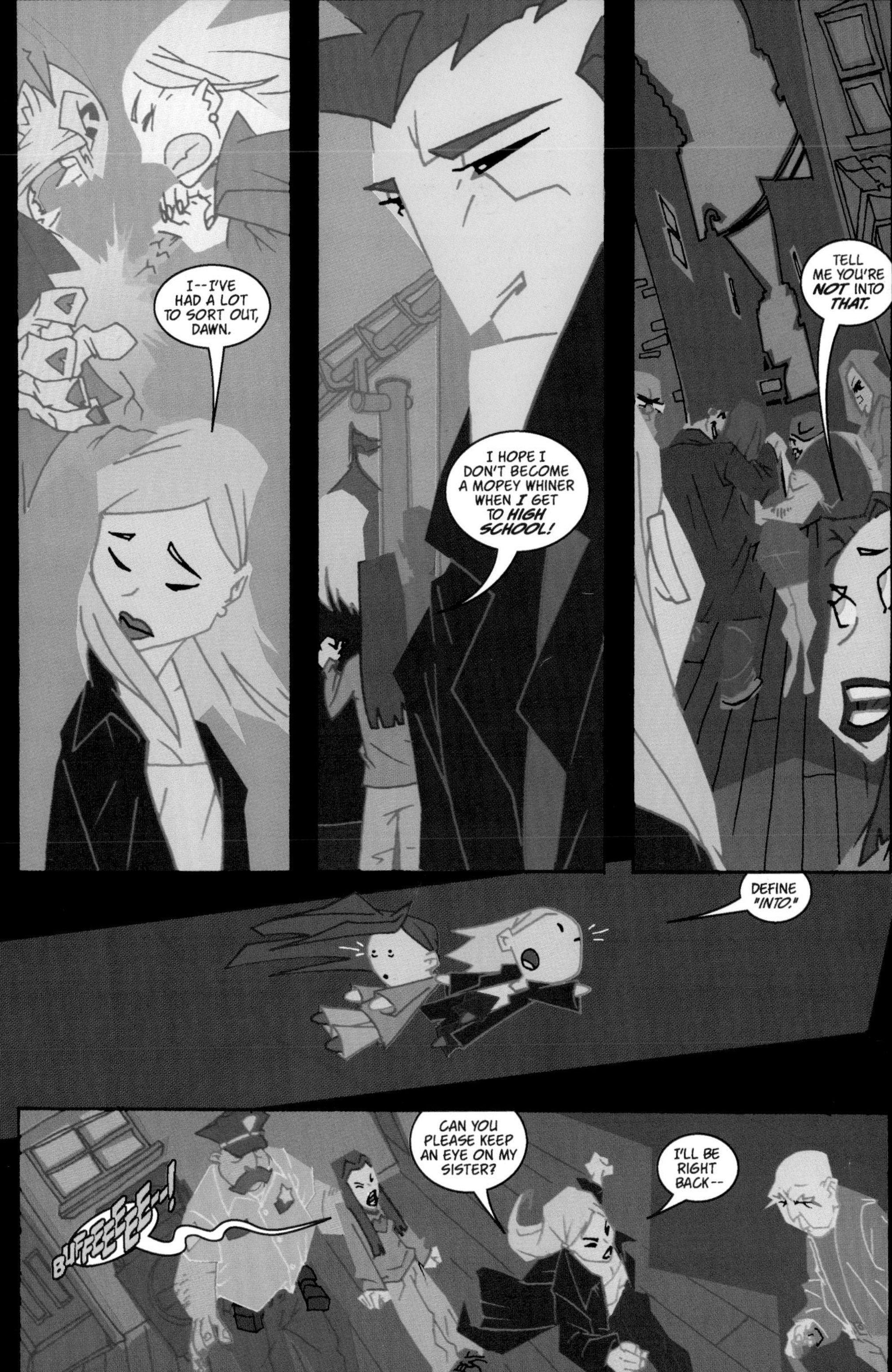
I--I'VE HAD A LOT TO SORT OUT, DAWN.
I HOPE I DON'T BECOME A MOPEY WHINER WHEN I GET TO HIGH SCHOOL!
TELL ME YOU'RE NOT INTO THAT.
DEFINE "INTO."
BUFFEEEEEE--!
CAN YOU PLEASE KEEP AN EYE ON MY SISTER?
I'LL BE RIGHT BACK--

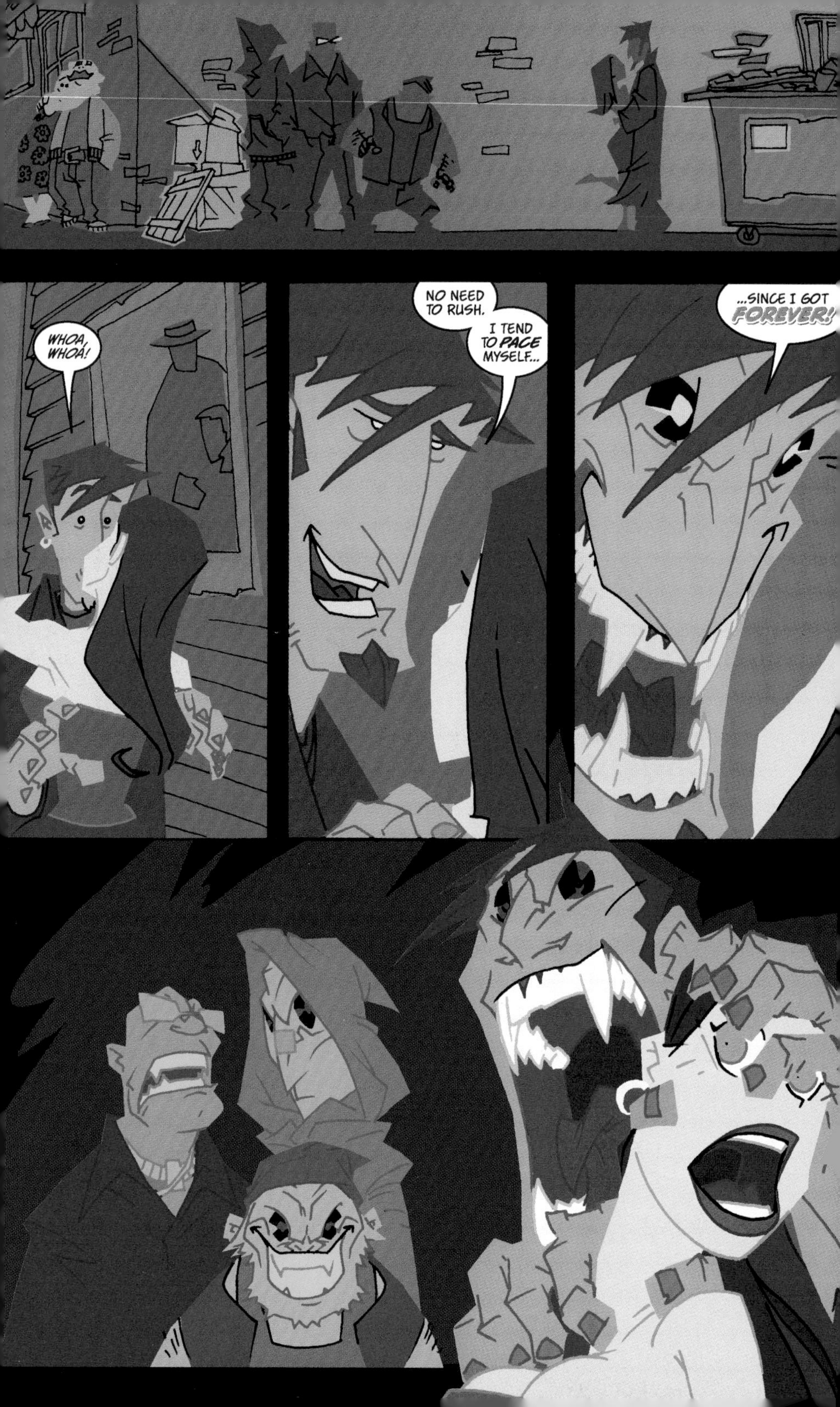
WHOA, WHOA!
NO NEED TO RUSH.
I TEND TO PACE MYSELF...
...SINCE I GOT FOREVER!

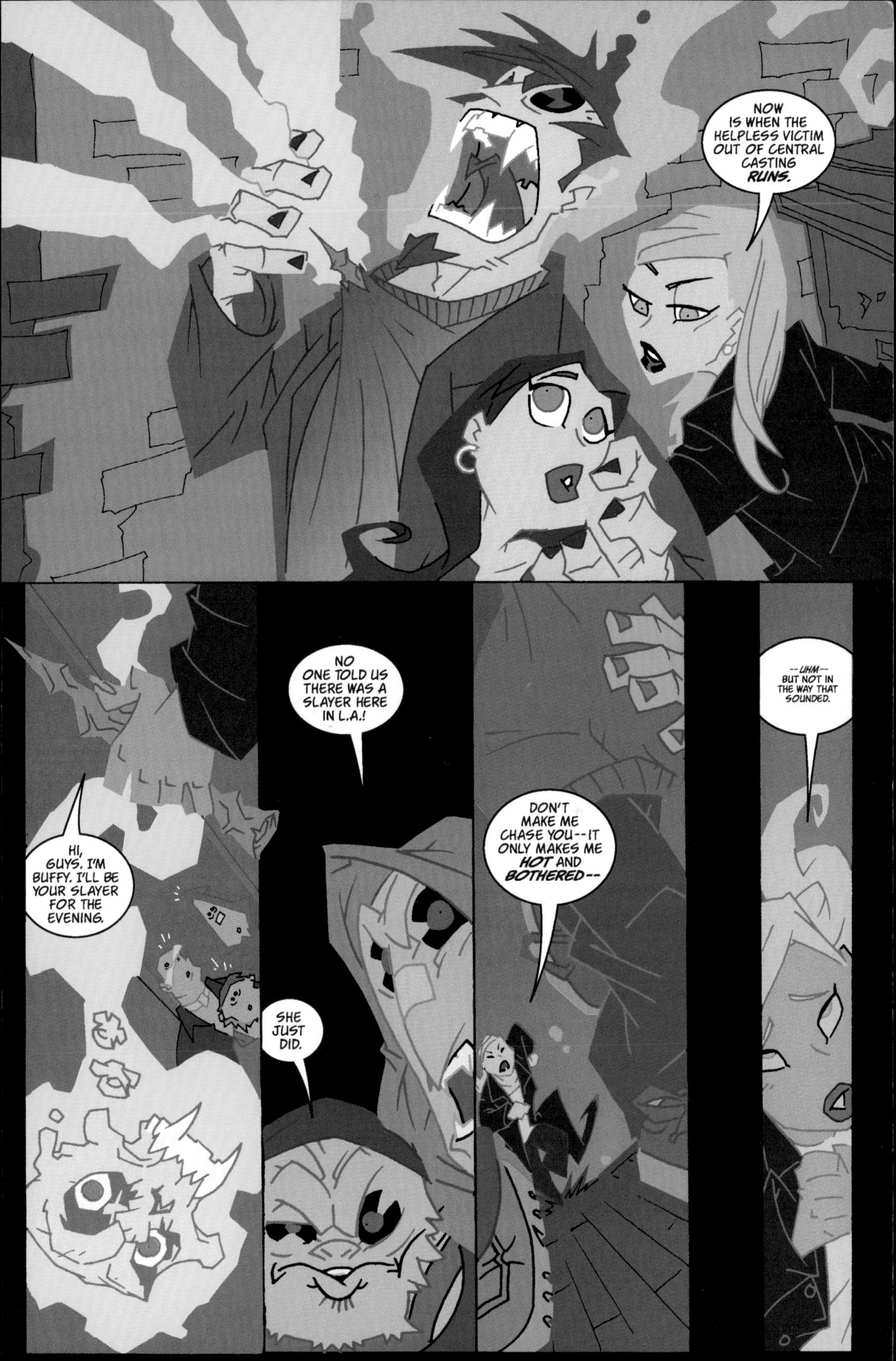
NOW IS WHEN THE HELPLESS VICTIM OUT OF CENTRAL CASTING *RUNS.*
HI, GUYS. I'M BUFFY. I'LL BE YOUR SLAYER FOR THE EVENING.
NO ONE TOLD US THERE WAS A SLAYER HERE IN L.A.!
SHE JUST DID.
DON'T MAKE ME CHASE YOU--IT ONLY MAKES ME *HOT* AND *BOTHERED*--
--*UHM*-- BUT NOT IN THE WAY THAT SOUNDED.

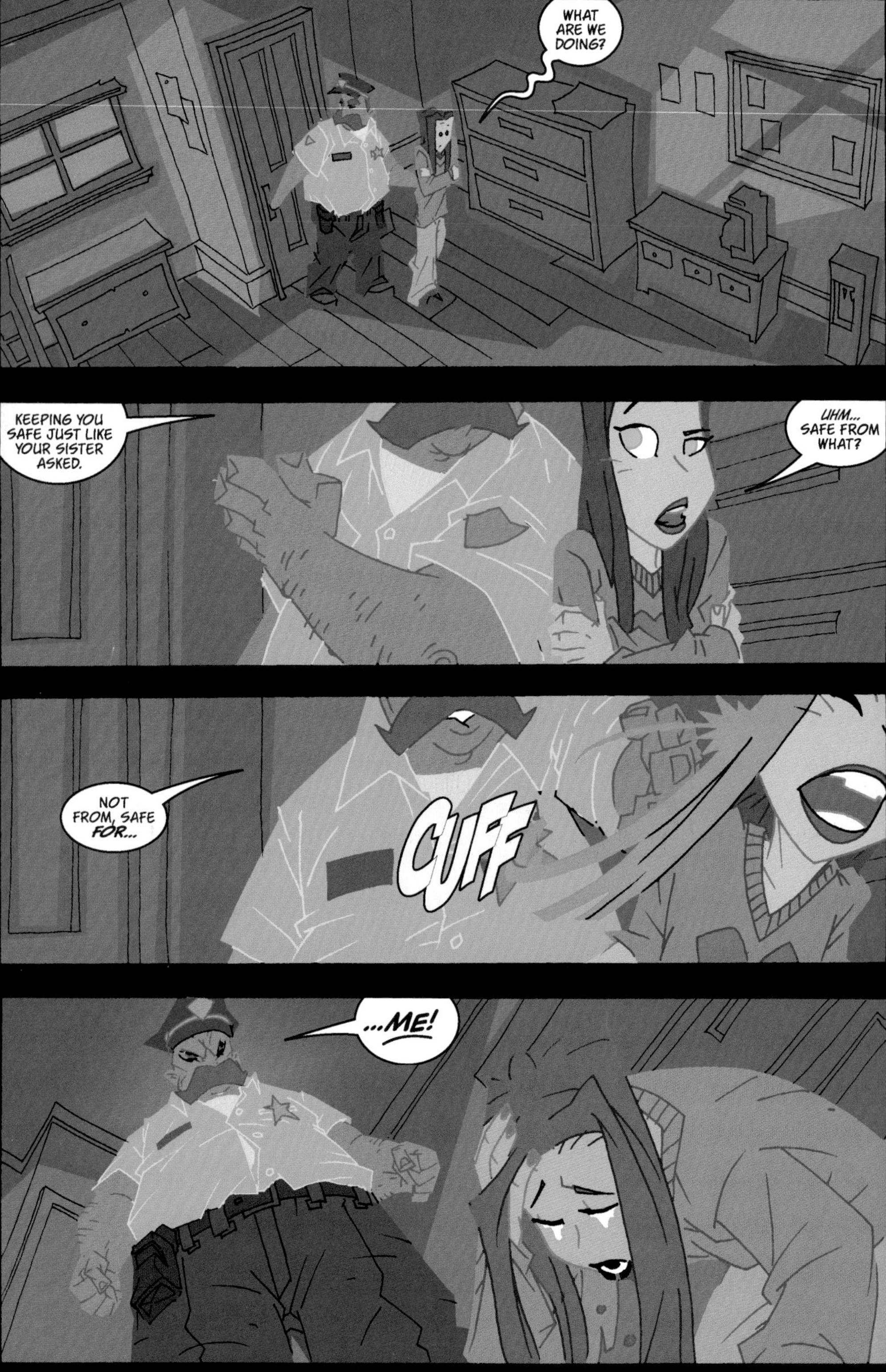
WHAT ARE WE DOING?
KEEPING YOU SAFE JUST LIKE YOUR SISTER ASKED.
UHM... SAFE FROM WHAT?
NOT FROM, SAFE *FOR*...
CUFF
...*ME!*

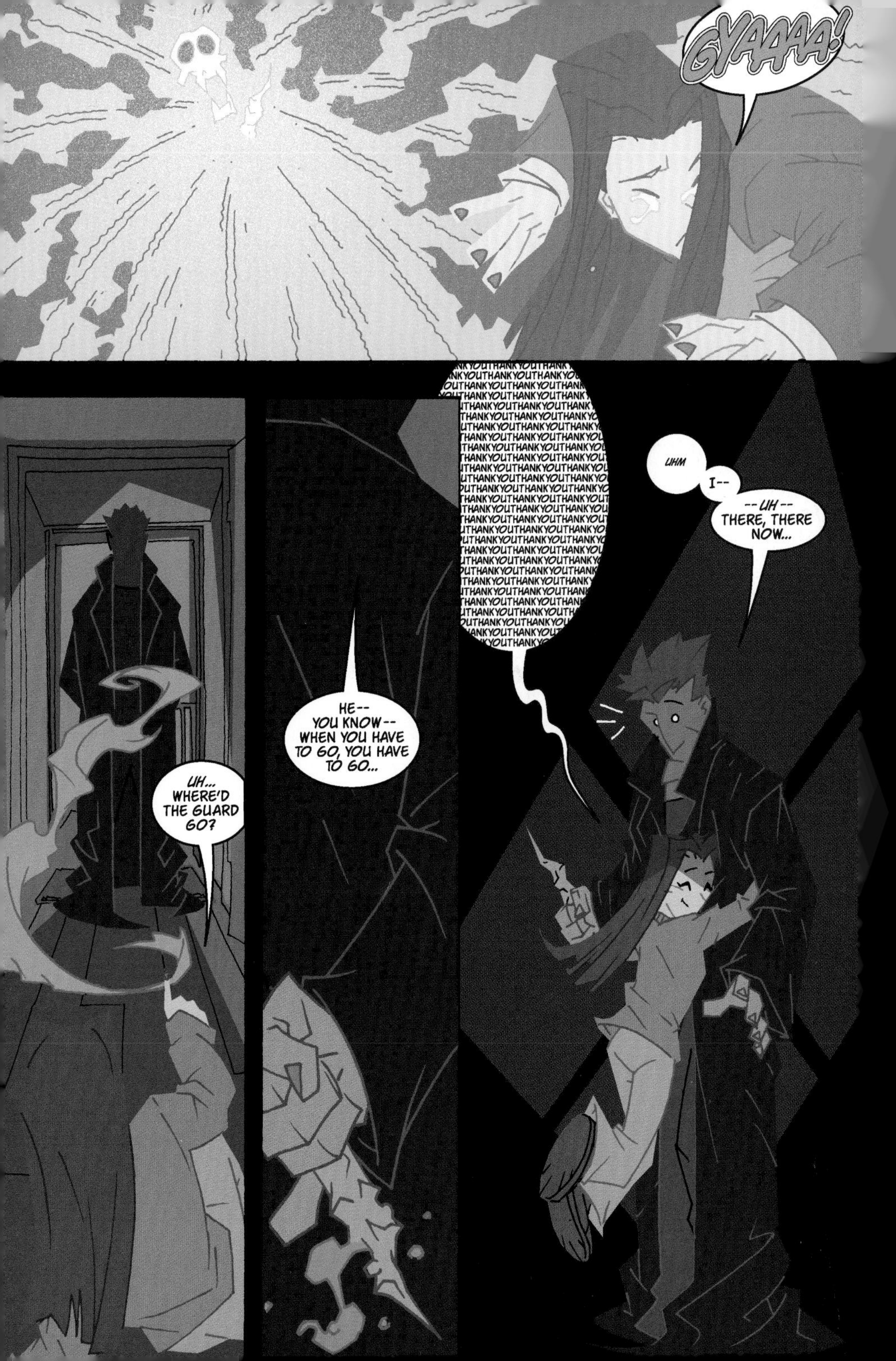
GYAAAA!
UH... WHERE'D THE GUARD GO?
HE-- YOU KNOW-- WHEN YOU HAVE TO GO, YOU HAVE TO GO...
THANKYOUTHANKYOUTHANKYOU
UHM
I--
--UH-- THERE, THERE NOW...

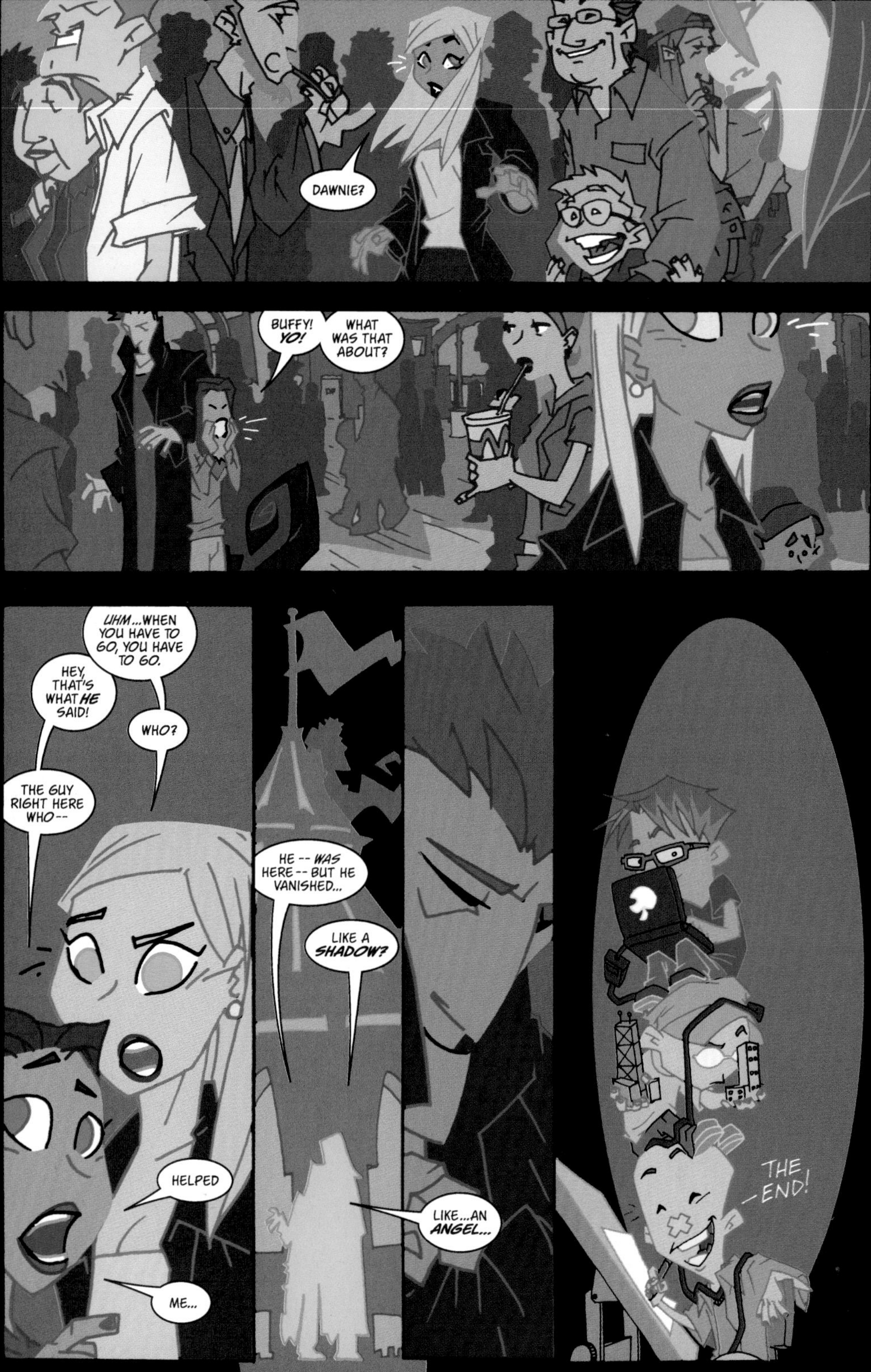

DAWNIE?
BUFFY! YO!
WHAT WAS THAT ABOUT?
UHM...WHEN YOU HAVE TO GO, YOU HAVE TO GO.
HEY, THAT'S WHAT HE SAID!
WHO?
THE GUY RIGHT HERE WHO--
HELPED
ME...
HE -- WAS HERE -- BUT HE VANISHED...
LIKE A SHADOW?
LIKE...AN ANGEL...
THE END!

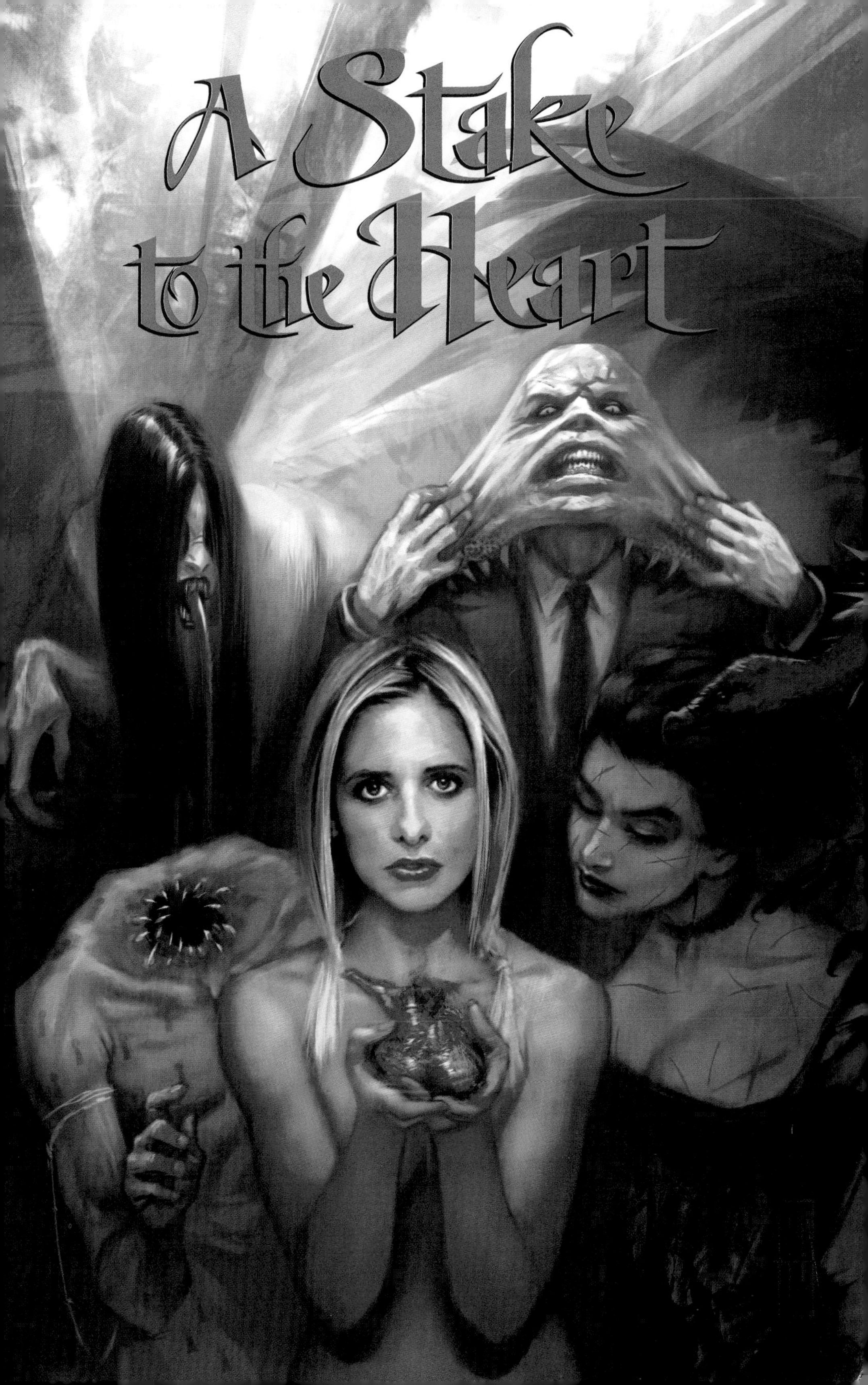
A Stake
to the Heart

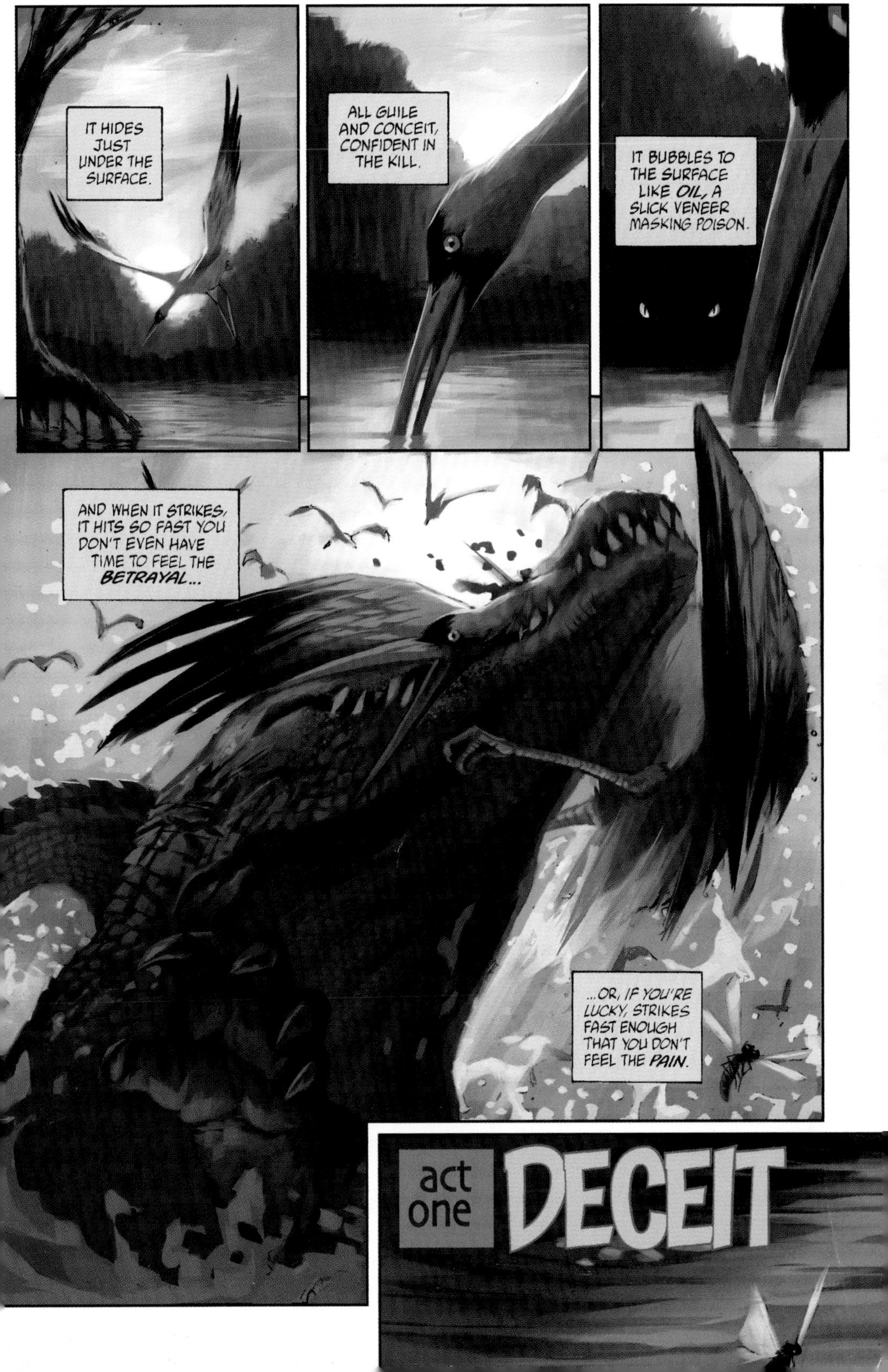
IT HIDES JUST UNDER THE SURFACE.
ALL GUILE AND CONCEIT, CONFIDENT IN THE KILL.
IT BUBBLES TO THE SURFACE LIKE OIL, A SLICK VENEER MASKING POISON.
AND WHEN IT STRIKES, IT HITS SO FAST YOU DON'T EVEN HAVE TIME TO FEEL THE BETRAYAL...
...OR, IF YOU'RE LUCKY, STRIKES FAST ENOUGH THAT YOU DON'T FEEL THE PAIN.
act one DECEIT

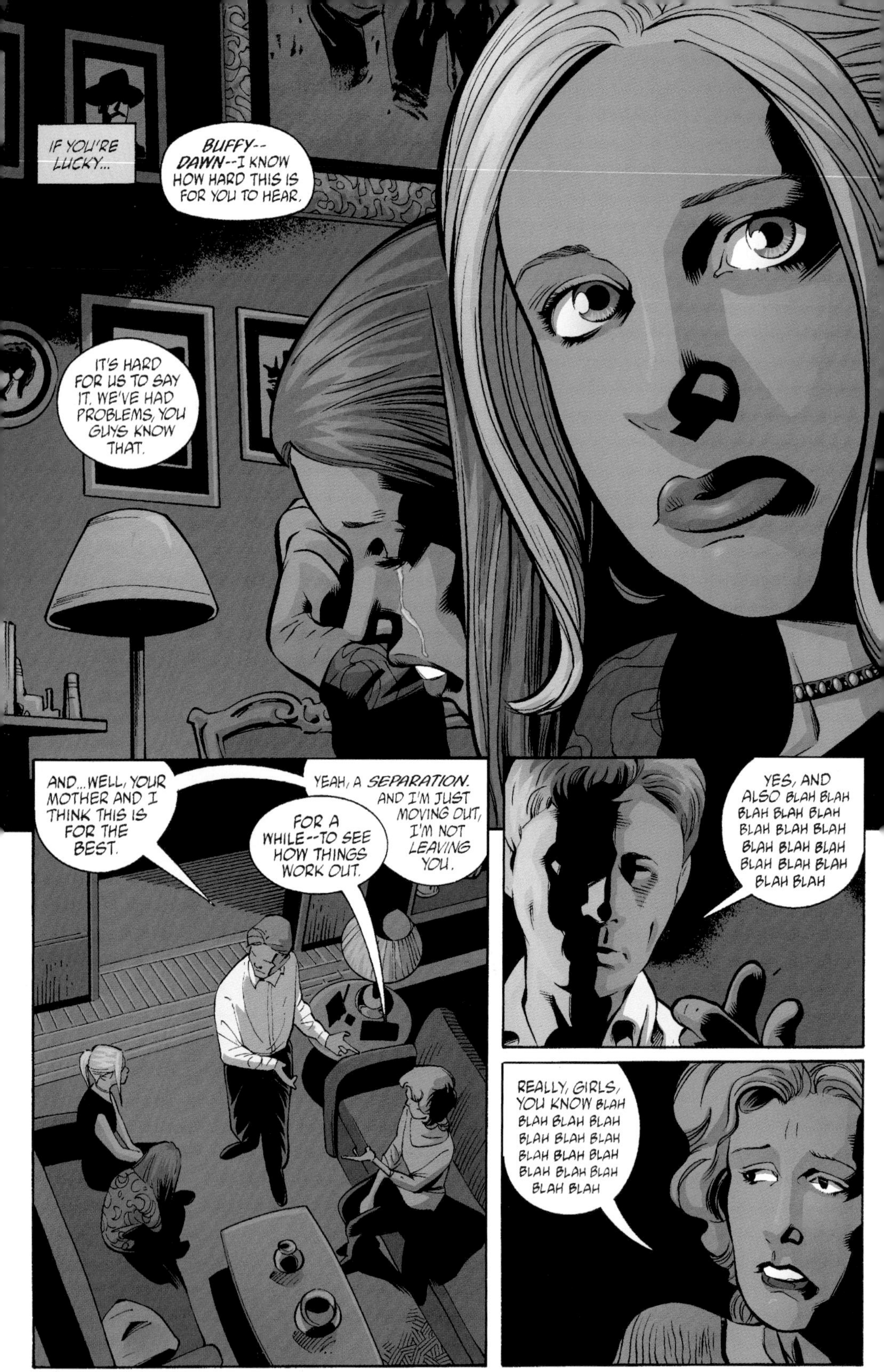

IF YOU'RE LUCKY...
BUFFY--DAWN--I KNOW HOW HARD THIS IS FOR YOU TO HEAR.
IT'S HARD FOR US TO SAY IT. WE'VE HAD PROBLEMS, YOU GUYS KNOW THAT.
AND...WELL, YOUR MOTHER AND I THINK THIS IS FOR THE BEST.
YEAH, A SEPARATION.
FOR A WHILE--TO SEE HOW THINGS WORK OUT.
AND I'M JUST MOVING OUT, I'M NOT LEAVING YOU.
YES, AND ALSO BLAH BLAH BLAH BLAH BLAH BLAH BLAH BLAH BLAH BLAH BLAH BLAH BLAH BLAH BLAH BLAH BLAH
REALLY, GIRLS, YOU KNOW BLAH BLAH BLAH BLAH BLAH BLAH BLAH BLAH BLAH BLAH BLAH BLAH BLAH BLAH BLAH

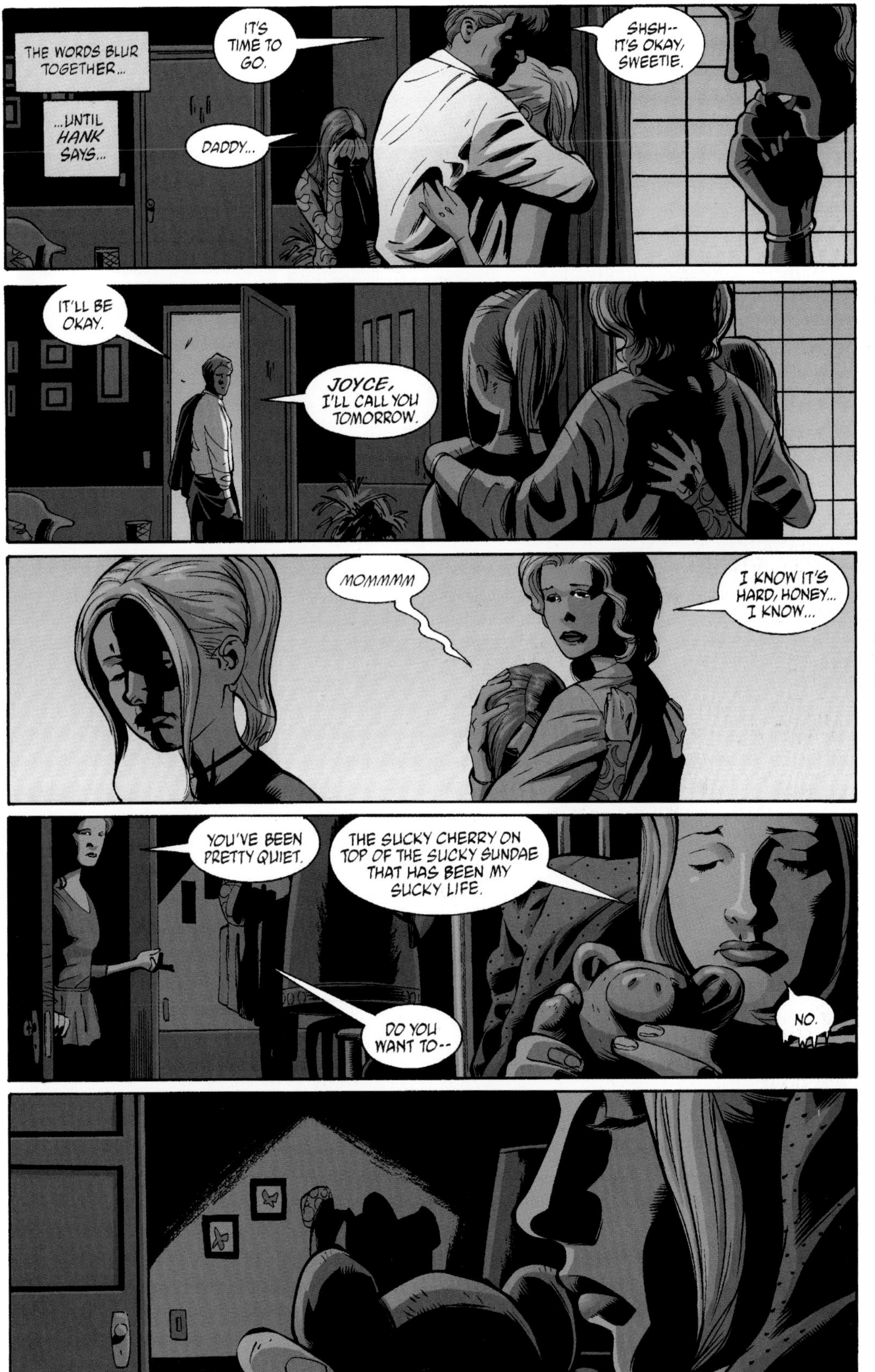
THE WORDS BLUR TOGETHER...
...UNTIL HANK SAYS...
IT'S TIME TO GO.
DADDY...
SHSH-- IT'S OKAY, SWEETIE.
IT'LL BE OKAY.
JOYCE, I'LL CALL YOU TOMORROW.
MOMMMM
I KNOW IT'S HARD, HONEY... I KNOW...
YOU'VE BEEN PRETTY QUIET.
THE SUCKY CHERRY ON TOP OF THE SUCKY SUNDAE THAT HAS BEEN MY SUCKY LIFE.
DO YOU WANT TO--
NO.

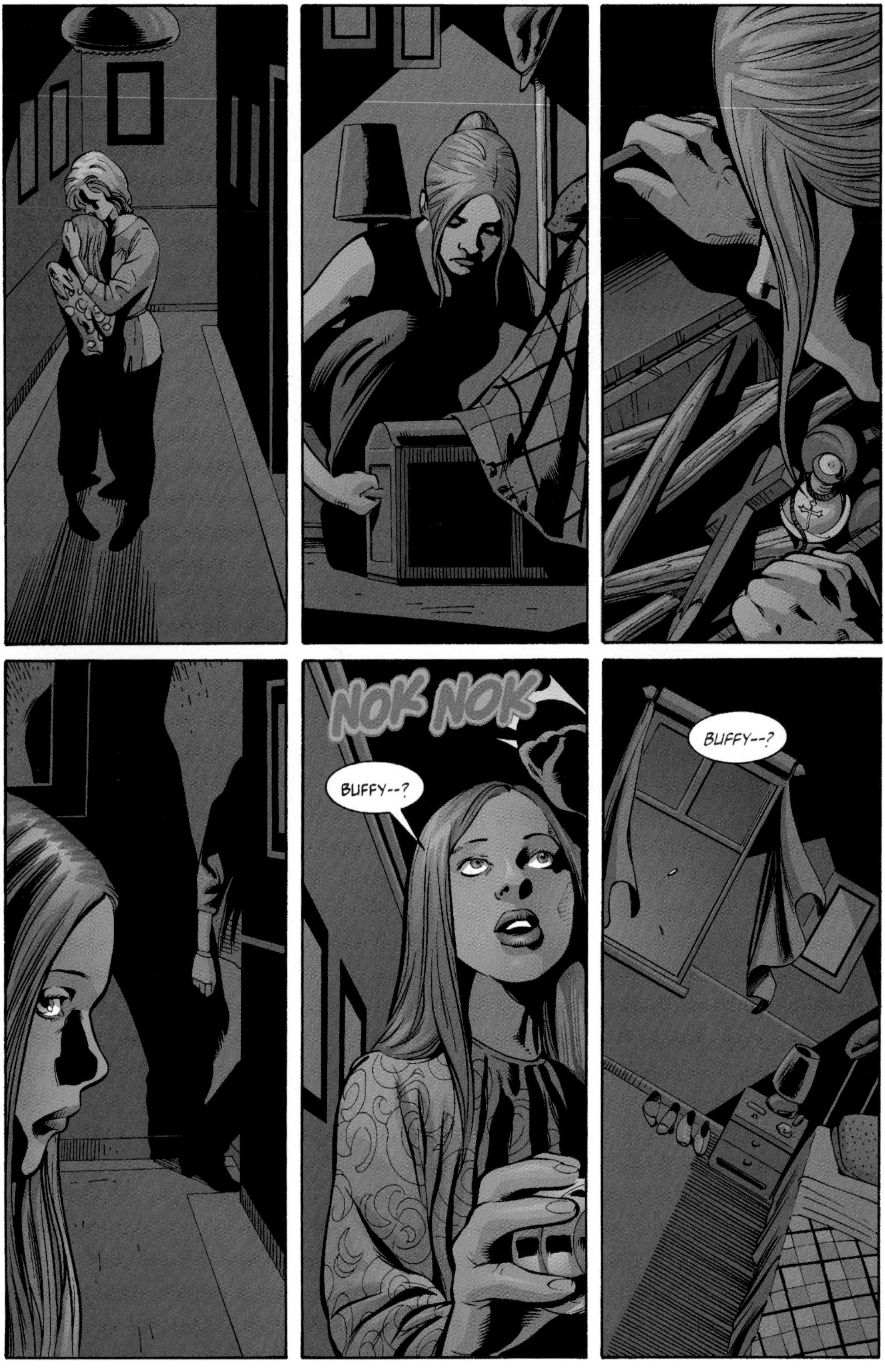
NOK NOK
BUFFY--?
BUFFY--?

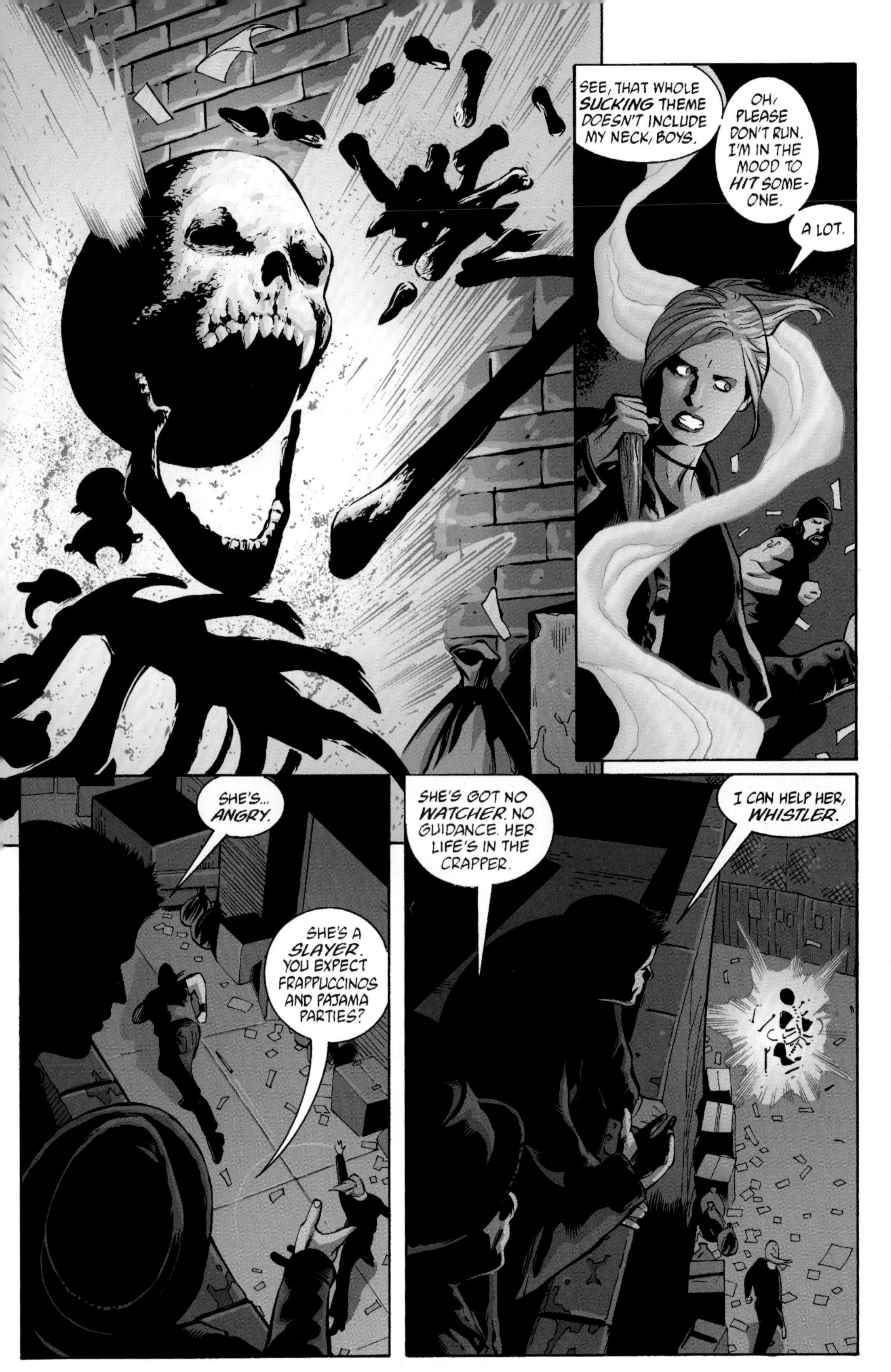
SEE, THAT WHOLE SUCKING THEME DOESN'T INCLUDE MY NECK, BOYS.
OH, PLEASE DON'T RUN. I'M IN THE MOOD TO HIT SOME-ONE.
A LOT.
SHE'S... ANGRY.
SHE'S A SLAYER. YOU EXPECT FRAPPUCCINOS AND PAJAMA PARTIES?
SHE'S GOT NO WATCHER. NO GUIDANCE. HER LIFE'S IN THE CRAPPER.
I CAN HELP HER, WHISTLER.

ANGELUS, YOU CAN BARELY HELP YOURSELF.

DON'T CALL ME THAT.

IT'S YOUR NAME. IT'S WHO YOU ARE. AIN'T IT? I MEAN... YOU'RE THE BIG BAD VAMPIRE, AIN'TCHA...?

IN LAS VEGAS...* I HAD TO DO IT-- TURNING HIM WAS THE ONLY WAY TO FREE OURSELVES FROM THAT TIME-TRAP, BUT...

...I CAN STILL TASTE HIS BLOOD IN MY MOUTH.

*SEE VIVA LAS BUFFY

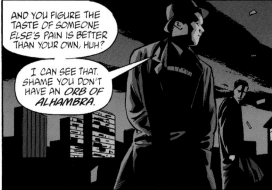

AND YOU FIGURE THE TASTE OF SOMEONE ELSE'S PAIN IS BETTER THAN YOUR OWN, HUH?

I CAN SEE THAT. SHAME YOU DON'T HAVE AN ORB OF ALHAMBRA.

THAT WOULD DO THE TRICK...

I AIN'T PAYIN' FOR THAT.

YEAH, THIS IS GONNA WORK OUT WELL...

HE SAYS WE CAN GET ONE FROM A LAW FIRM?

KRASH

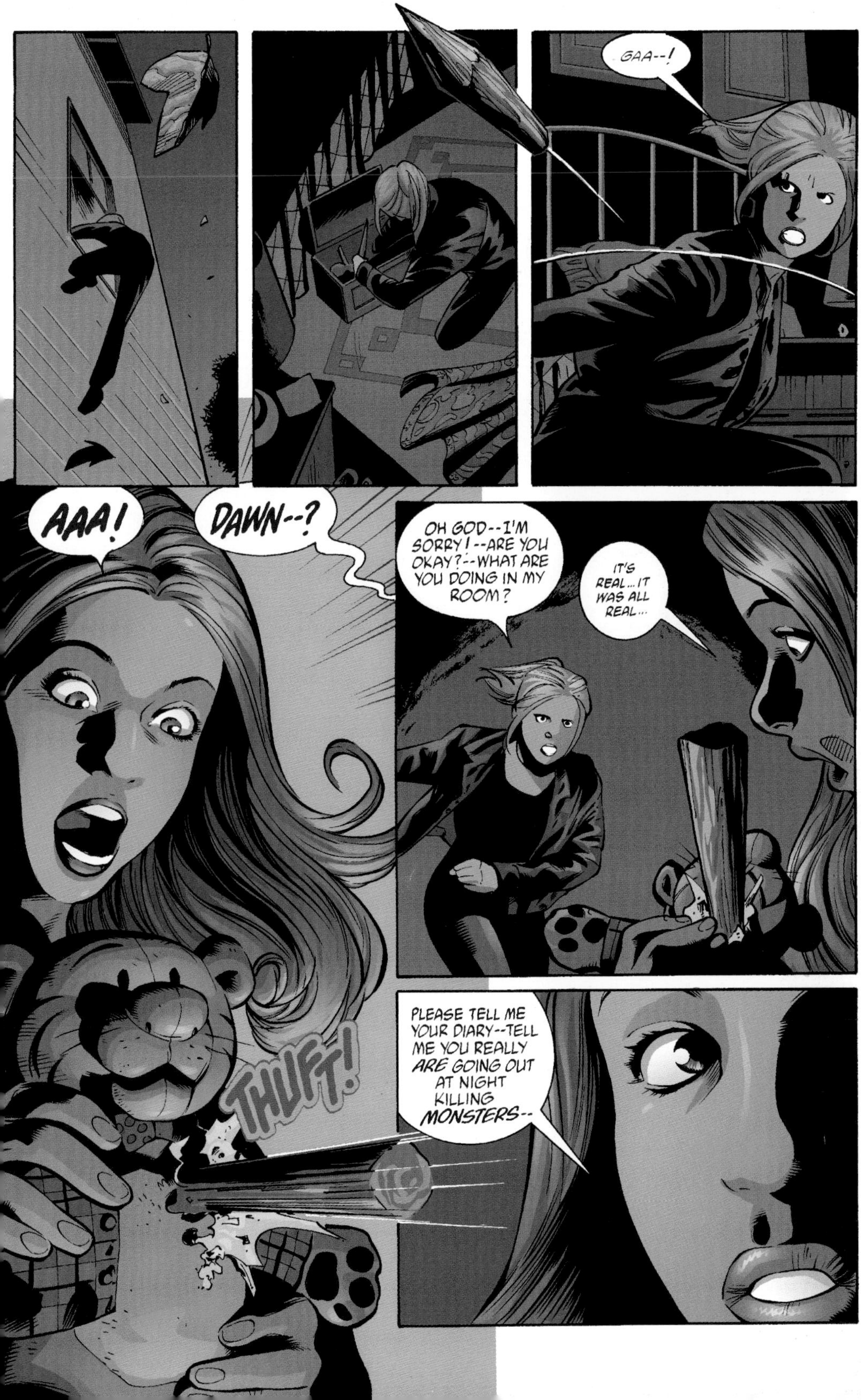
GAA--!
AAA!
DAWN--?
THUFT!
OH GOD--I'M SORRY! --ARE YOU OKAY?--WHAT ARE YOU DOING IN MY ROOM?
IT'S REAL... IT WAS ALL REAL...
PLEASE TELL ME YOUR DIARY--TELL ME YOU REALLY ARE GOING OUT AT NIGHT KILLING MONSTERS--

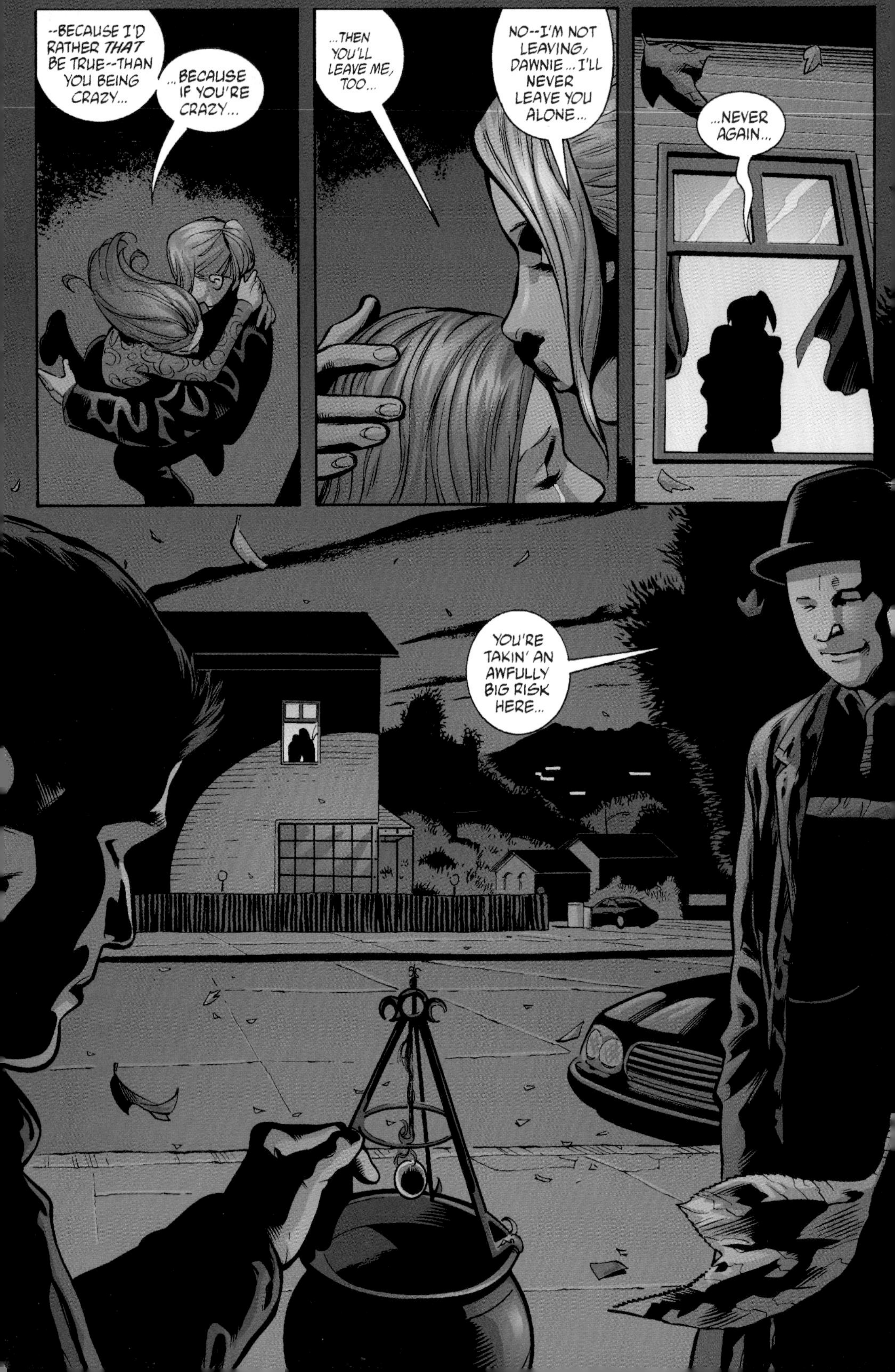
--BECAUSE I'D RATHER *THAT* BE TRUE--THAN YOU BEING CRAZY...
...BECAUSE IF YOU'RE CRAZY...
...THEN YOU'LL LEAVE ME, TOO...
NO--I'M NOT LEAVING, DAWNIE... I'LL NEVER LEAVE YOU ALONE...
...NEVER AGAIN...
YOU'RE TAKIN' AN AWFULLY BIG RISK HERE...

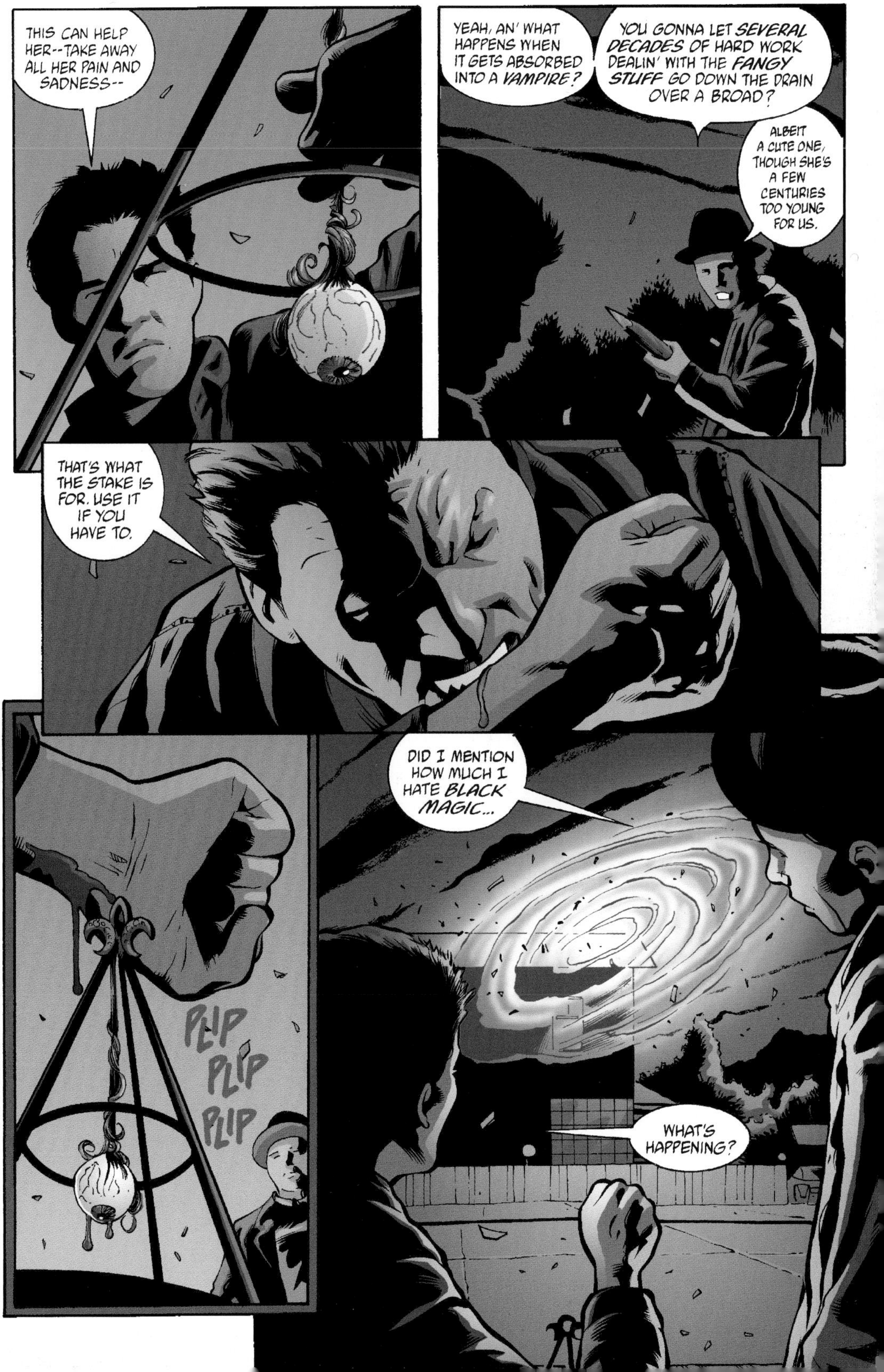
THIS CAN HELP HER--TAKE AWAY ALL HER PAIN AND SADNESS--
YEAH, AN' WHAT HAPPENS WHEN IT GETS ABSORBED INTO A VAMPIRE?
YOU GONNA LET SEVERAL DECADES OF HARD WORK DEALIN' WITH THE FANGY STUFF GO DOWN THE DRAIN OVER A BROAD?
ALBEIT A CUTE ONE, THOUGH SHE'S A FEW CENTURIES TOO YOUNG FOR US.
THAT'S WHAT THE STAKE IS FOR. USE IT IF YOU HAVE TO.
PLIP PLIP PLIP
DID I MENTION HOW MUCH I HATE BLACK MAGIC...
WHAT'S HAPPENING?

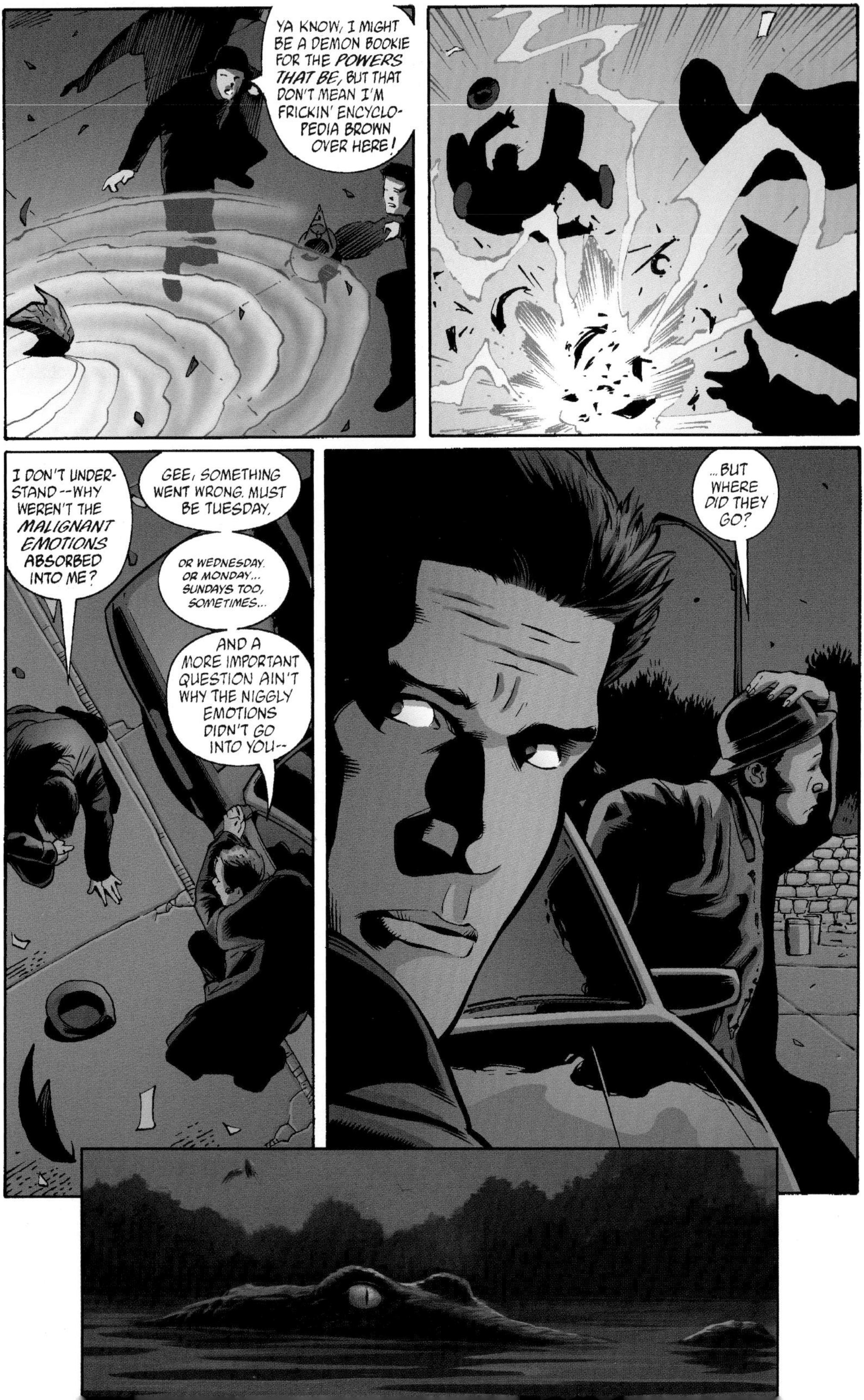
YA KNOW, I MIGHT BE A DEMON BOOKIE FOR THE POWERS THAT BE, BUT THAT DON'T MEAN I'M FRICKIN' ENCYCLOPEDIA BROWN OVER HERE!
I DON'T UNDERSTAND--WHY WEREN'T THE MALIGNANT EMOTIONS ABSORBED INTO ME?
GEE, SOMETHING WENT WRONG. MUST BE TUESDAY.
OR WEDNESDAY. OR MONDAY... SUNDAYS TOO, SOMETIMES...
AND A MORE IMPORTANT QUESTION AIN'T WHY THE NIGGLY EMOTIONS DIDN'T GO INTO YOU--
...BUT WHERE DID THEY GO?

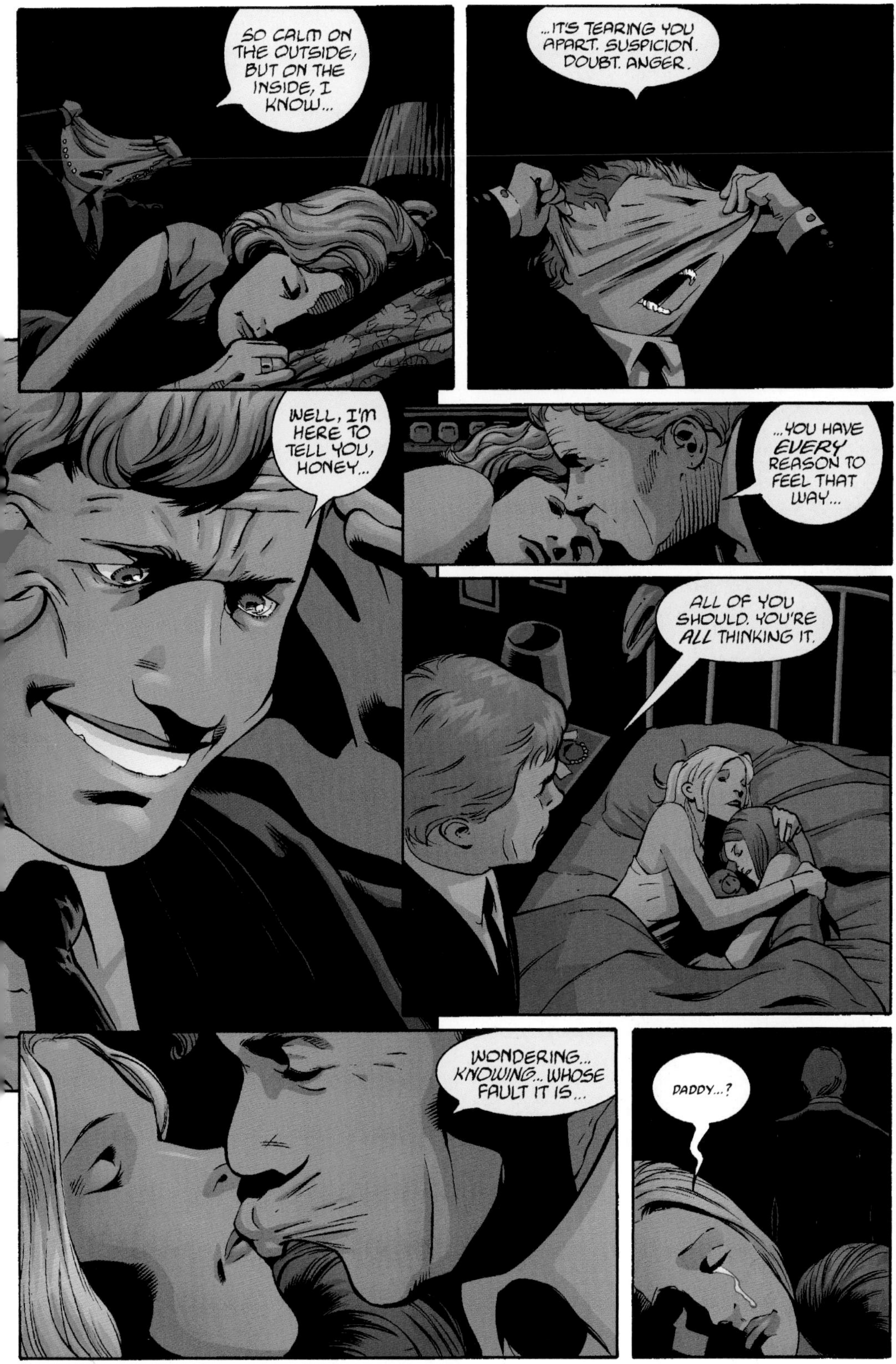
SO CALM ON THE OUTSIDE, BUT ON THE INSIDE, I KNOW...
...IT'S TEARING YOU APART. SUSPICION. DOUBT. ANGER.
WELL, I'M HERE TO TELL YOU, HONEY...
...YOU HAVE EVERY REASON TO FEEL THAT WAY...
ALL OF YOU SHOULD. YOU'RE ALL THINKING IT.
WONDERING... KNOWING... WHOSE FAULT IT IS...
DADDY...?

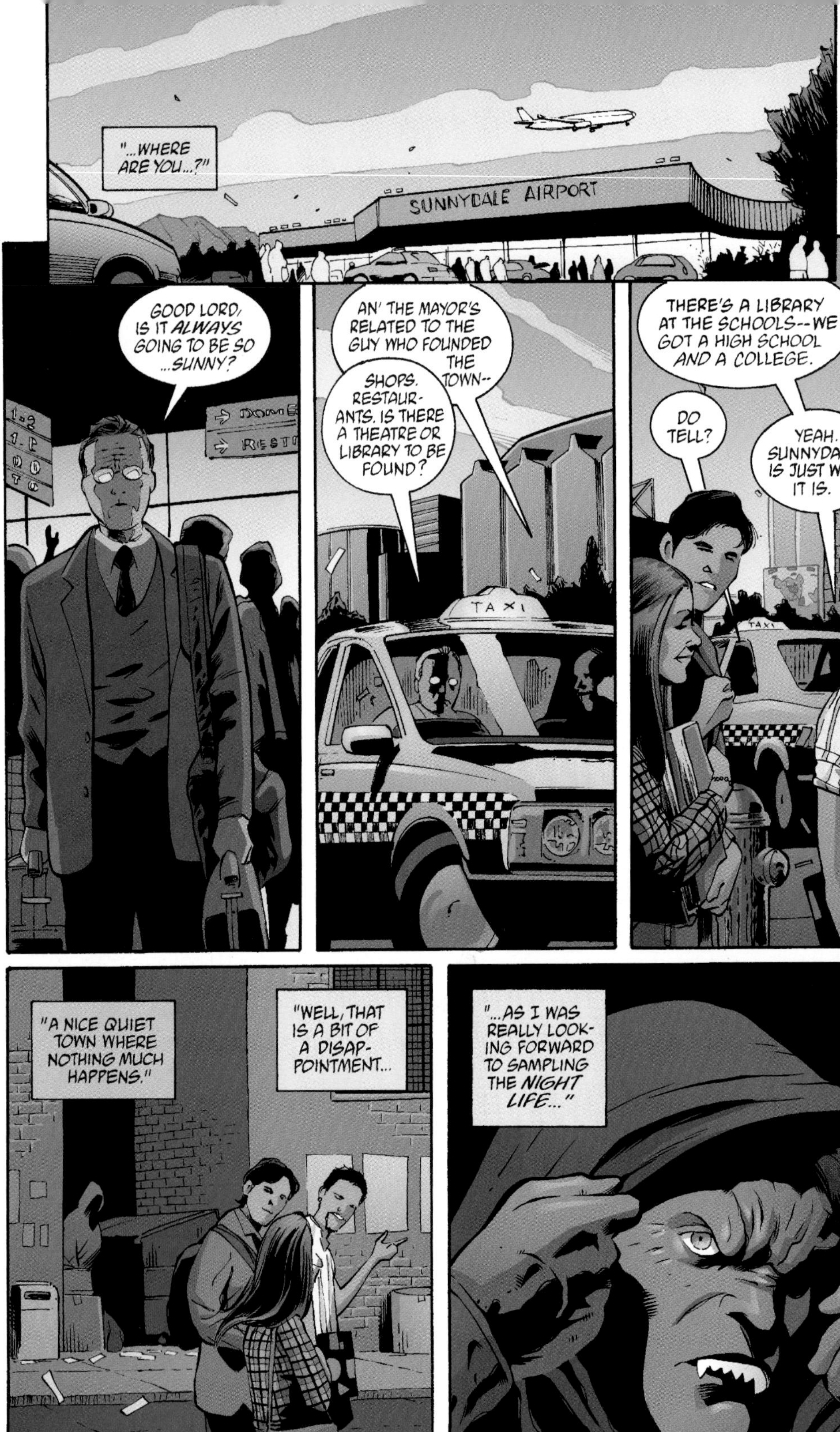
"...WHERE ARE YOU...?"
SUNNYDALE AIRPORT
GOOD LORD, IS IT *ALWAYS* GOING TO BE SO ...SUNNY?
AN' THE MAYOR'S RELATED TO THE GUY WHO FOUNDED THE TOWN--
SHOPS. RESTAURANTS. IS THERE A THEATRE OR LIBRARY TO BE FOUND?
TAXI
THERE'S A LIBRARY AT THE SCHOOLS--WE GOT A HIGH SCHOOL AND A COLLEGE.
DO TELL?
YEAH. SUNNYDALE IS JUST WHAT IT IS.
"A NICE QUIET TOWN WHERE NOTHING MUCH HAPPENS."
"WELL, THAT IS A BIT OF A DISAPPOINTMENT...
"...AS I WAS REALLY LOOKING FORWARD TO SAMPLING THE *NIGHT LIFE*..."

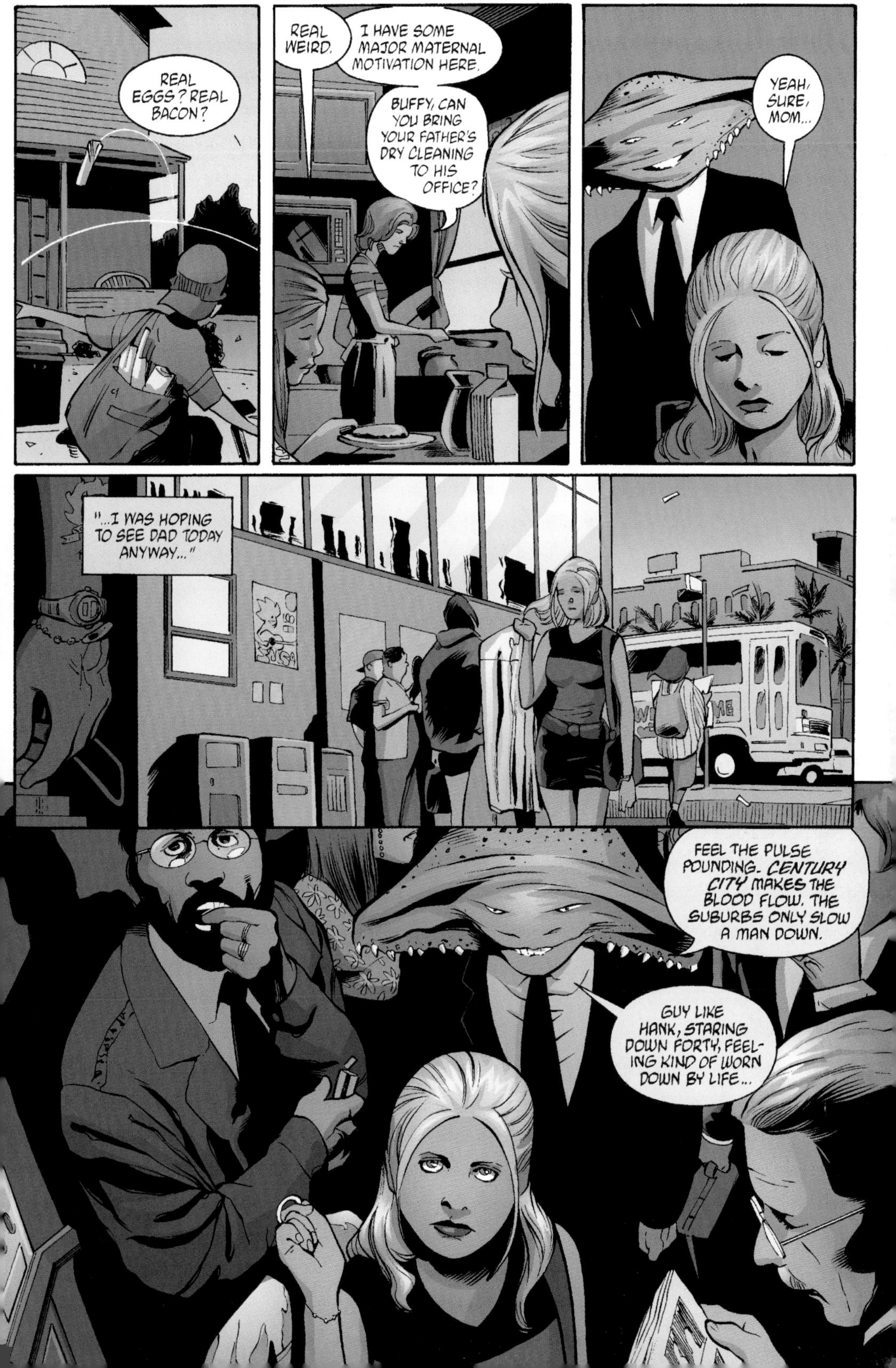
REAL EGGS? REAL BACON?
REAL WEIRD.
I HAVE SOME MAJOR MATERNAL MOTIVATION HERE.
BUFFY, CAN YOU BRING YOUR FATHER'S DRY CLEANING TO HIS OFFICE?
YEAH, SURE, MOM...
"...I WAS HOPING TO SEE DAD TODAY ANYWAY..."
FEEL THE PULSE POUNDING. CENTURY CITY MAKES THE BLOOD FLOW. THE SUBURBS ONLY SLOW A MAN DOWN.
GUY LIKE HANK, STARING DOWN FORTY, FEELING KIND OF WORN DOWN BY LIFE...

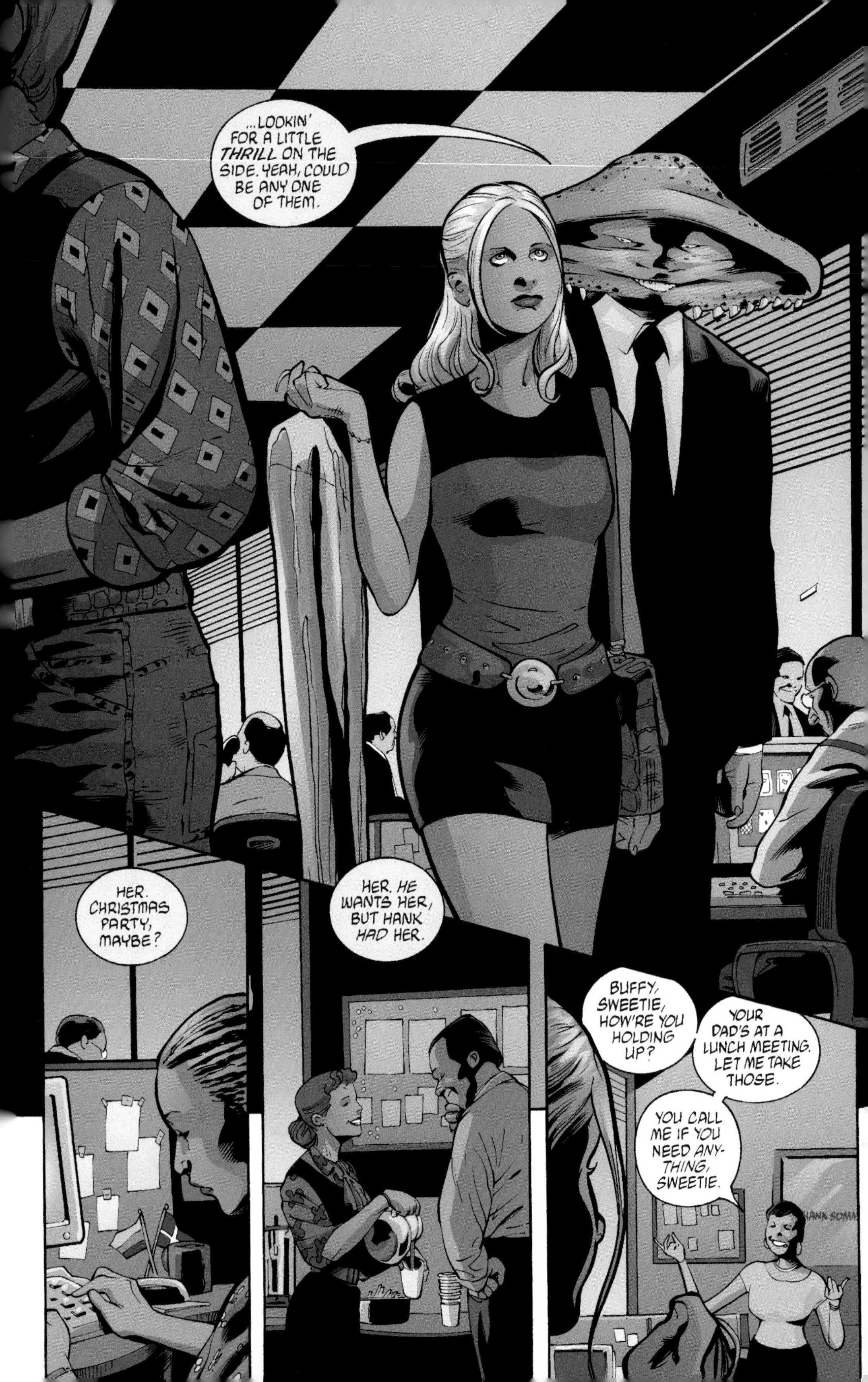
...LOOKIN' FOR A LITTLE THRILL ON THE SIDE. YEAH, COULD BE ANY ONE OF THEM.
HER. CHRISTMAS PARTY, MAYBE?
HER. HE WANTS HER, BUT HANK HAD HER.
BUFFY, SWEETIE, HOW'RE YOU HOLDING UP?
YOUR DAD'S AT A LUNCH MEETING. LET ME TAKE THOSE.
YOU CALL ME IF YOU NEED ANY-THING, SWEETIE.

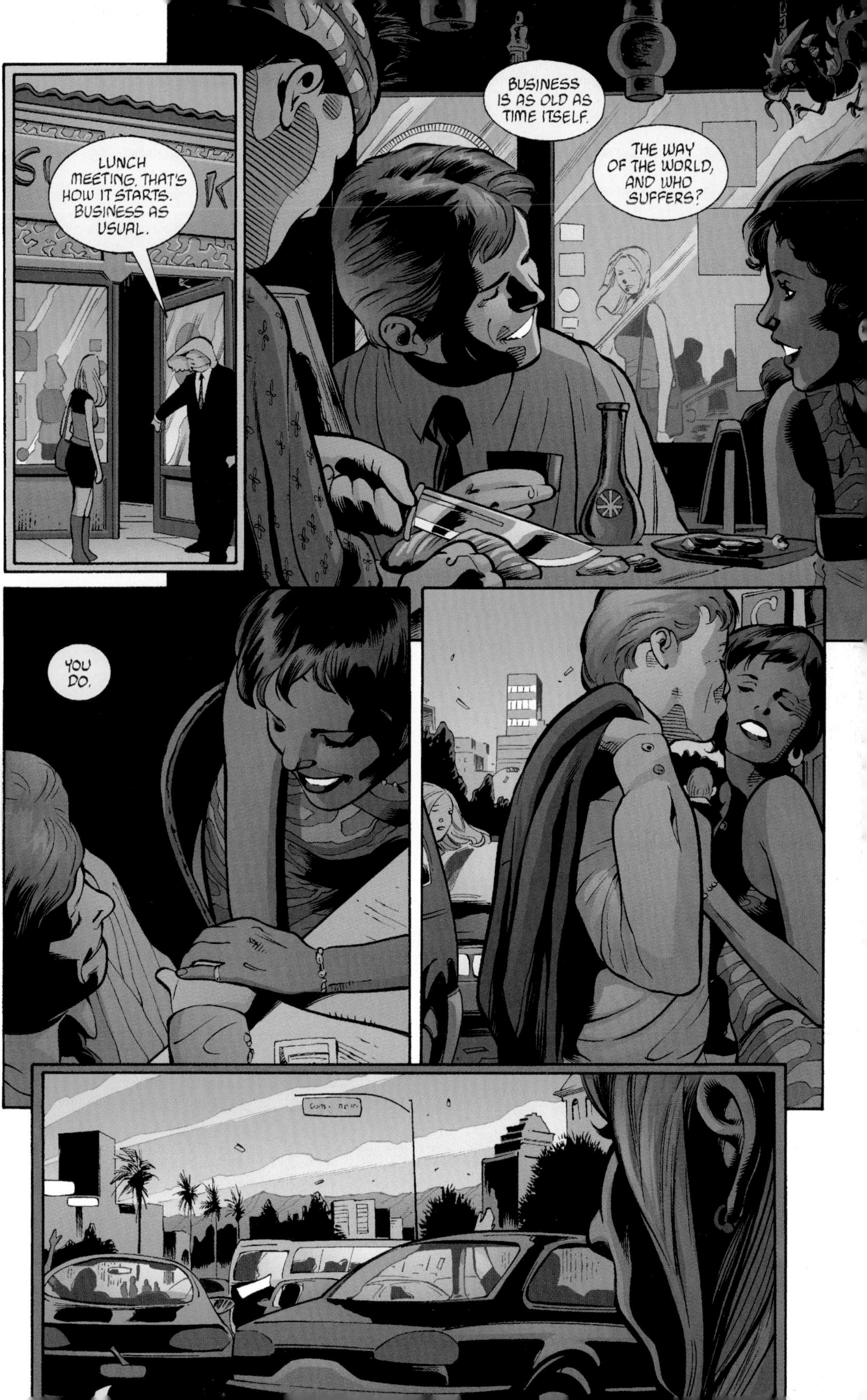
LUNCH MEETING. THAT'S HOW IT STARTS. BUSINESS AS USUAL.
BUSINESS IS AS OLD AS TIME ITSELF.
THE WAY OF THE WORLD, AND WHO SUFFERS?
YOU DO.

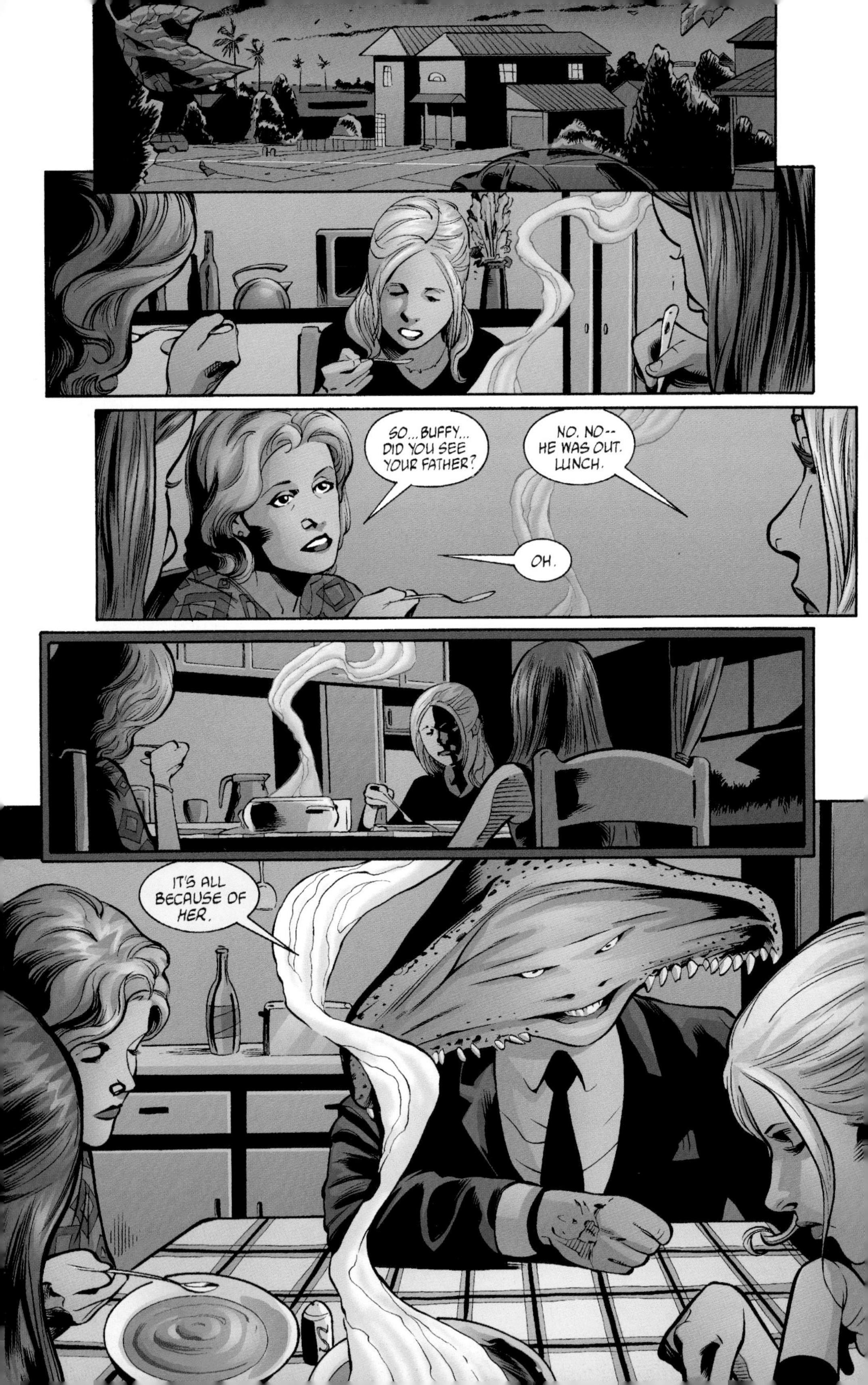
SO... BUFFY... DID YOU SEE YOUR FATHER?
NO. NO-- HE WAS OUT. LUNCH.
OH.
IT'S ALL BECAUSE OF HER.

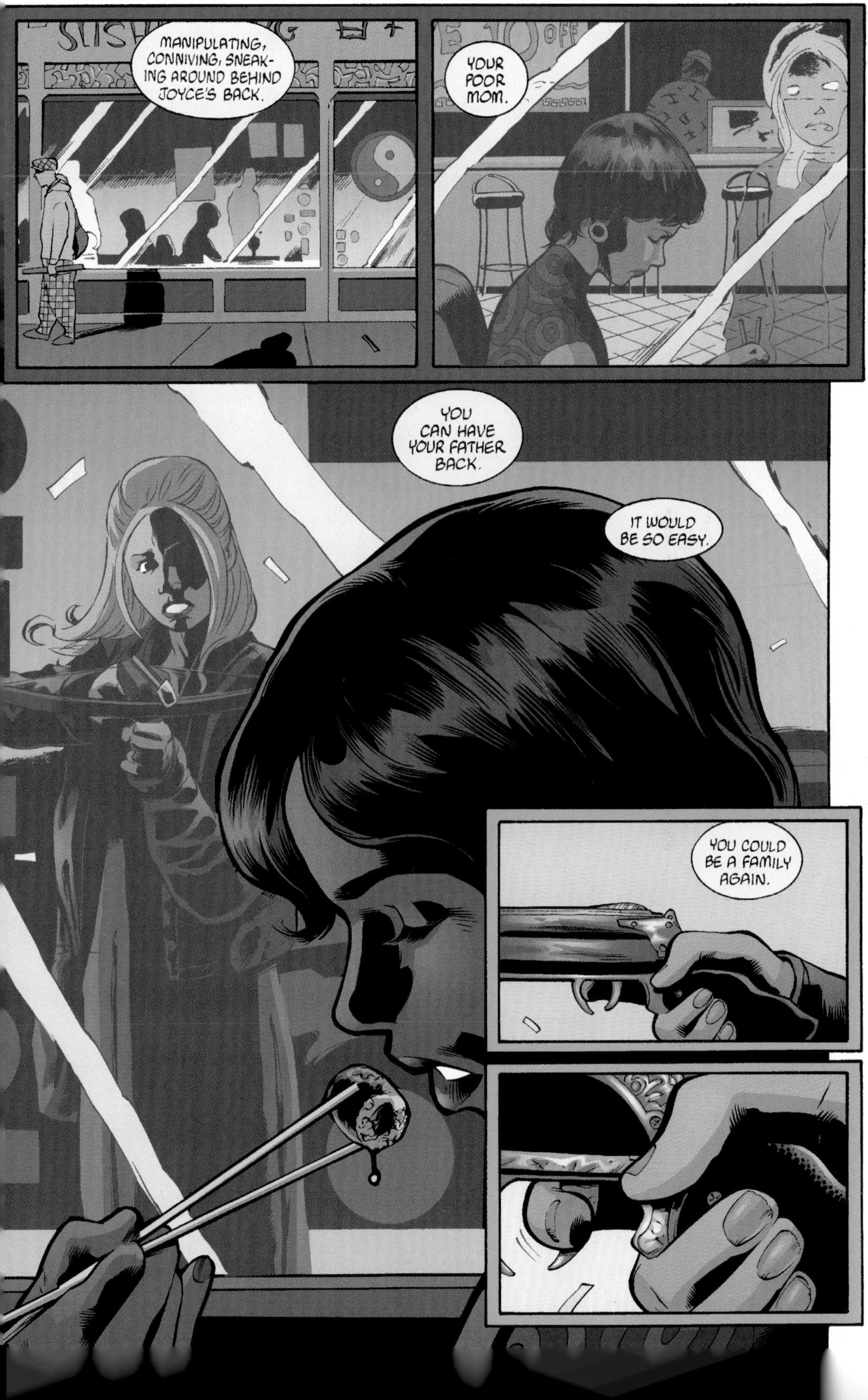
MANIPULATING, CONNIVING, SNEAKING AROUND BEHIND JOYCE'S BACK.
YOUR POOR MOM.
YOU CAN HAVE YOUR FATHER BACK.
IT WOULD BE SO EASY.
YOU COULD BE A FAMILY AGAIN.

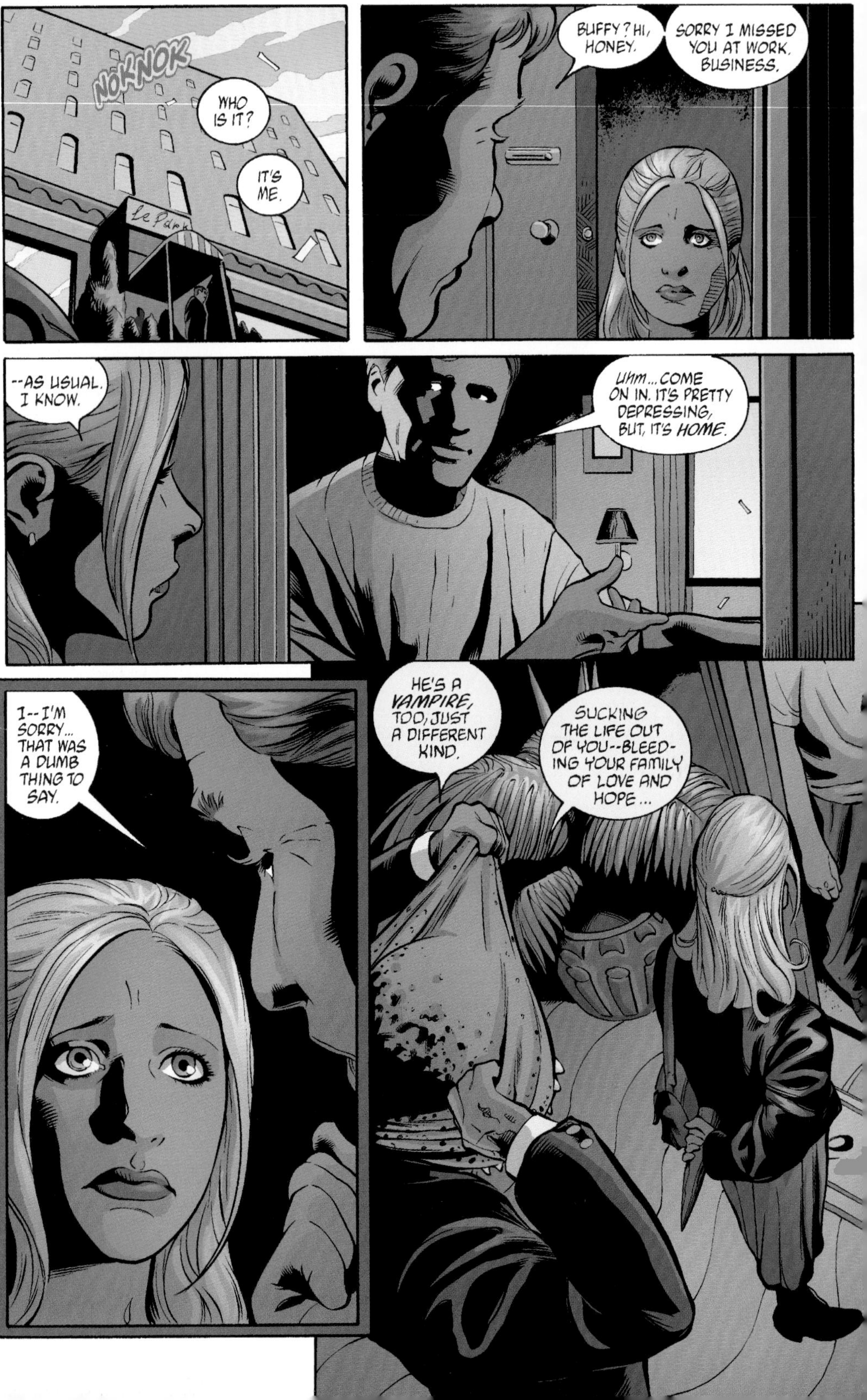

NOKNOK
WHO IS IT?
IT'S ME.
BUFFY? HI, HONEY.
SORRY I MISSED YOU AT WORK. BUSINESS.
--AS USUAL. I KNOW.
UHM... COME ON IN. IT'S PRETTY DEPRESSING, BUT, IT'S HOME.
I--I'M SORRY... THAT WAS A DUMB THING TO SAY.
HE'S A VAMPIRE, TOO, JUST A DIFFERENT KIND.
SUCKING THE LIFE OUT OF YOU--BLEEDING YOUR FAMILY OF LOVE AND HOPE...

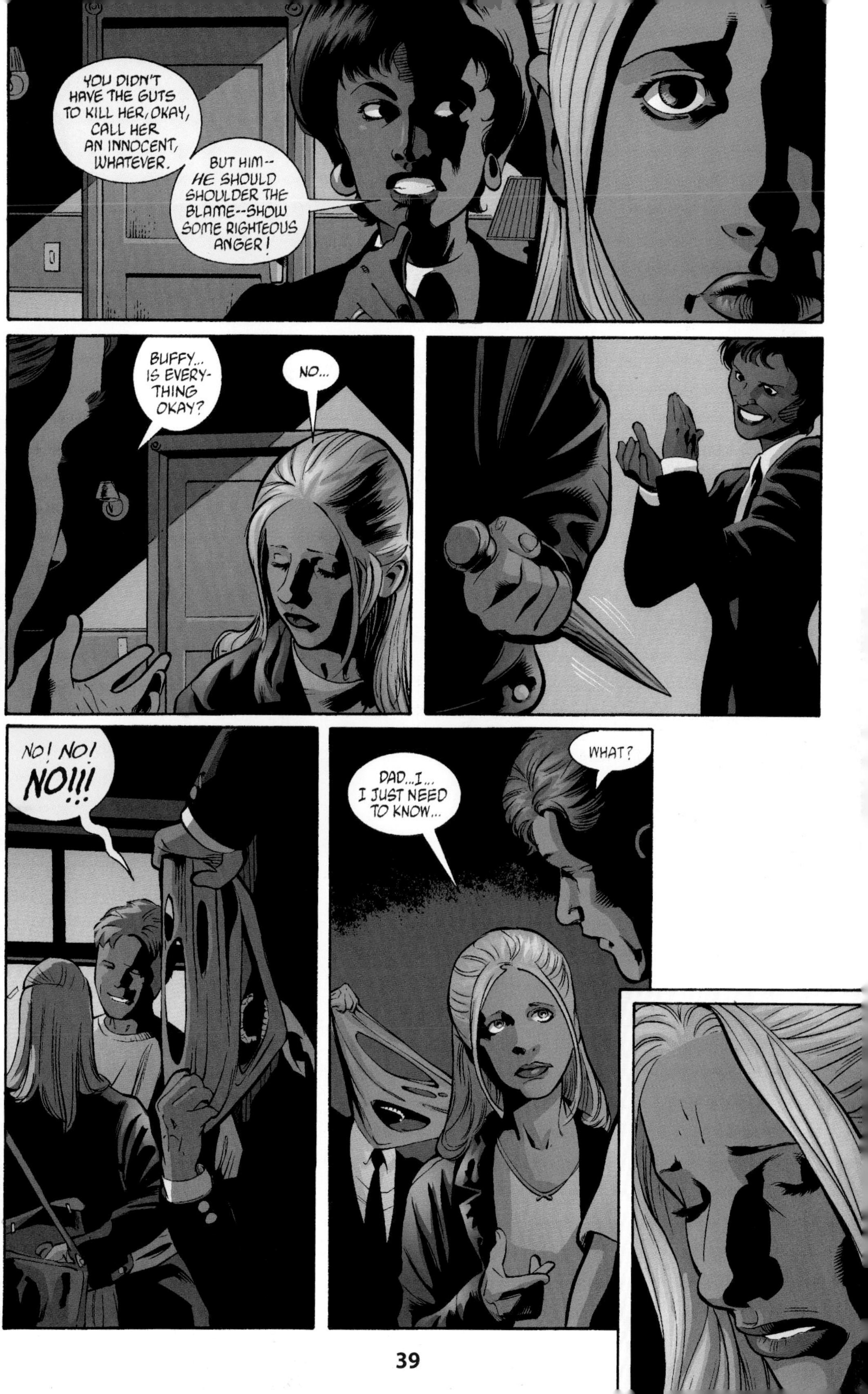
YOU DIDN'T HAVE THE GUTS TO KILL HER, OKAY, CALL HER AN INNOCENT, WHATEVER.
BUT HIM-- HE SHOULD SHOULDER THE BLAME--SHOW SOME RIGHTEOUS ANGER!
BUFFY... IS EVERYTHING OKAY?
NO...
NO! NO! NO!!!
DAD...I... I JUST NEED TO KNOW...
WHAT?

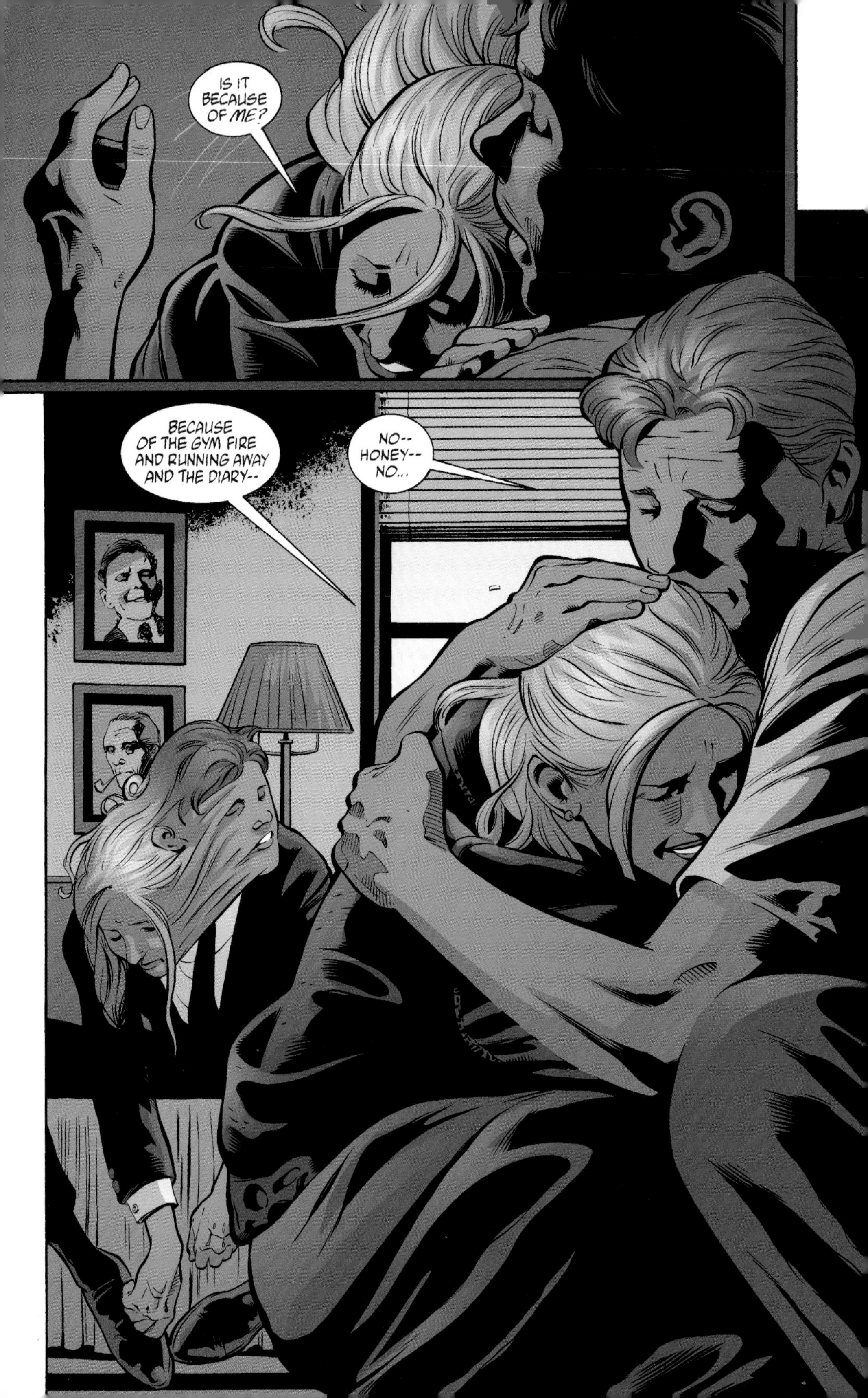
IS IT BECAUSE OF *ME?*
BECAUSE OF THE GYM FIRE AND RUNNING AWAY AND THE DIARY--
NO-- HONEY-- NO...

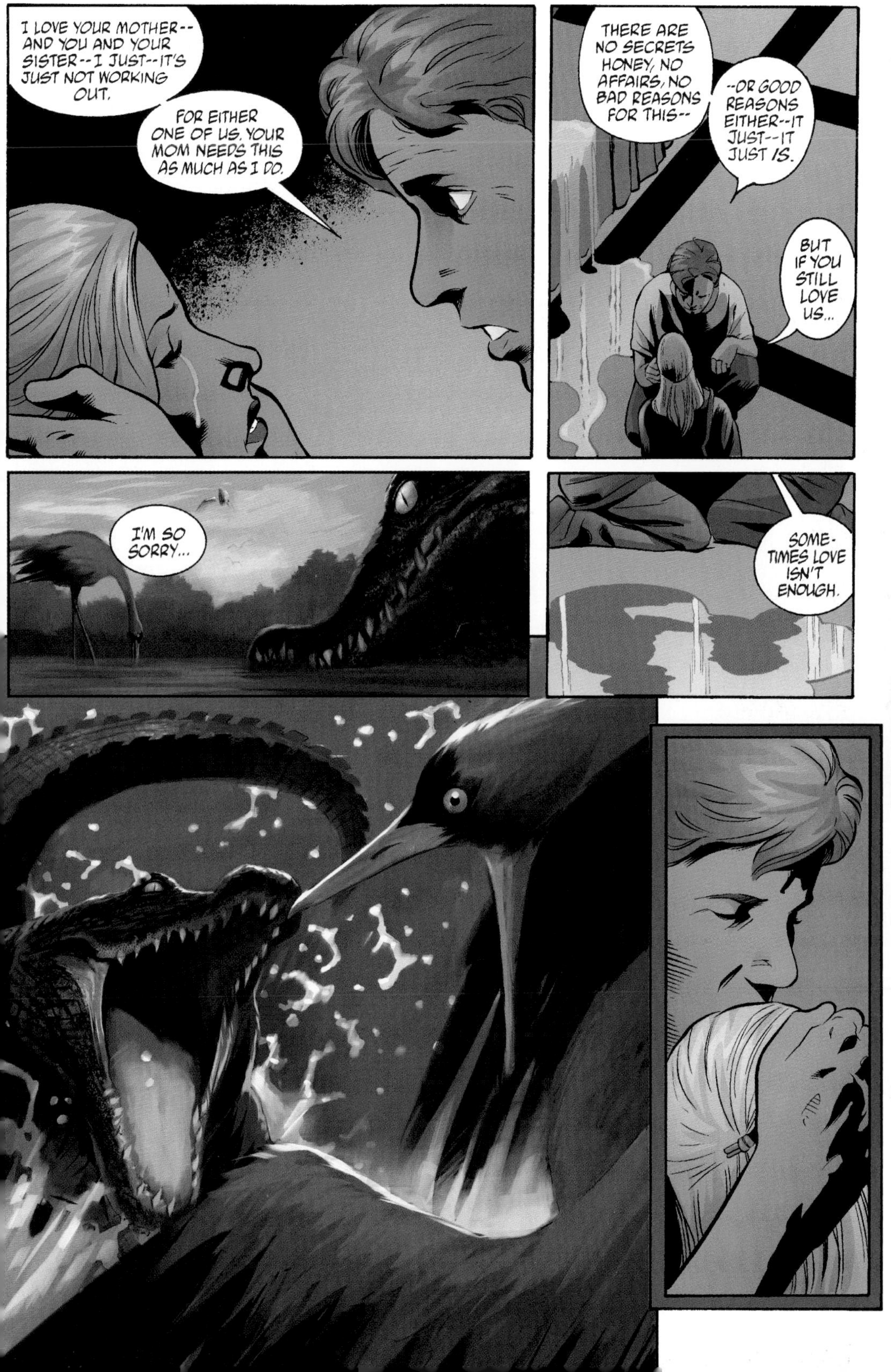

I LOVE YOUR MOTHER-- AND YOU AND YOUR SISTER--I JUST--IT'S JUST NOT WORKING OUT.
FOR EITHER ONE OF US. YOUR MOM NEEDS THIS AS MUCH AS I DO.
THERE ARE NO SECRETS HONEY, NO AFFAIRS, NO BAD REASONS FOR THIS--
--OR GOOD REASONS EITHER--IT JUST--IT JUST *IS*.
BUT IF YOU STILL LOVE US...
I'M SO SORRY...
SOME-TIMES LOVE ISN'T ENOUGH.

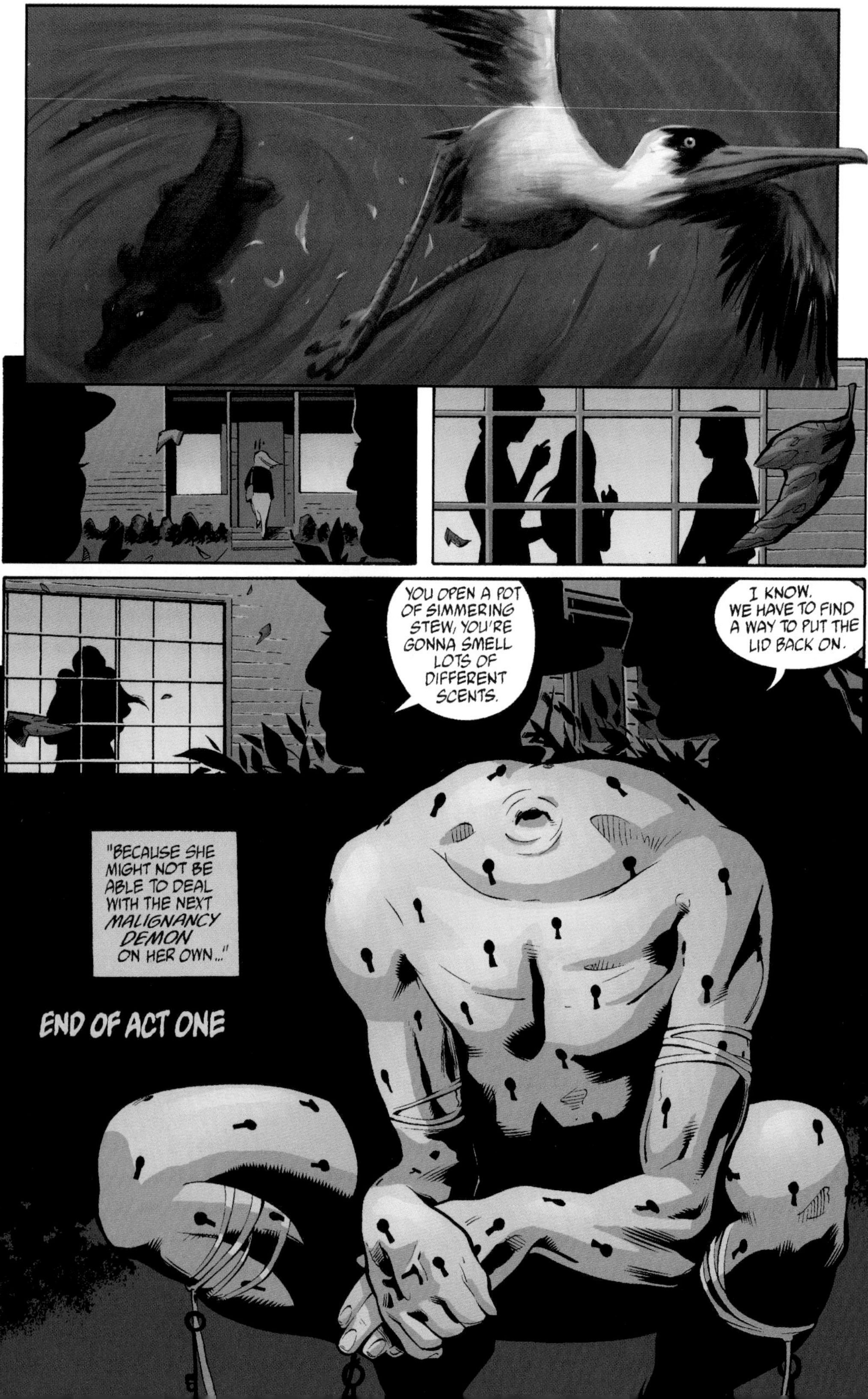
YOU OPEN A POT OF SIMMERING STEW, YOU'RE GONNA SMELL LOTS OF DIFFERENT SCENTS.
I KNOW. WE HAVE TO FIND A WAY TO PUT THE LID BACK ON.
"BECAUSE SHE MIGHT NOT BE ABLE TO DEAL WITH THE NEXT MALIGNANCY DEMON ON HER OWN..."
END OF ACT ONE

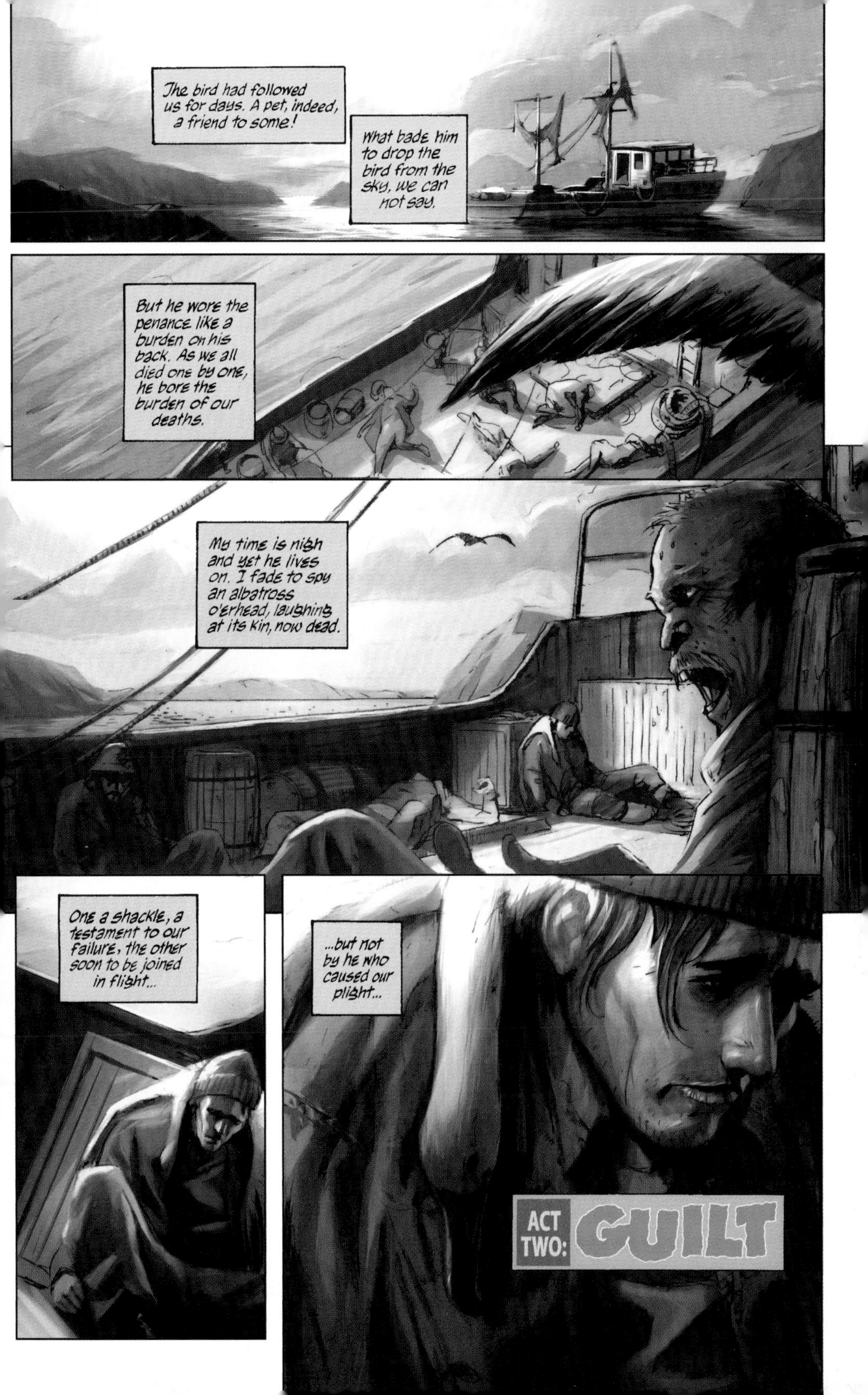
The bird had followed us for days. A pet, indeed, a friend to some!
What bade him to drop the bird from the sky, we can not say.
But he wore the penance like a burden on his back. As we all died one by one, he bore the burden of our deaths.
My time is nigh and yet he lives on. I fade to spy an albatross o'erhead, laughing at its kin, now dead.
One a shackle, a testament to our failure, the other soon to be joined in flight...
...but not by he who caused our plight...
ACT TWO: GUILT

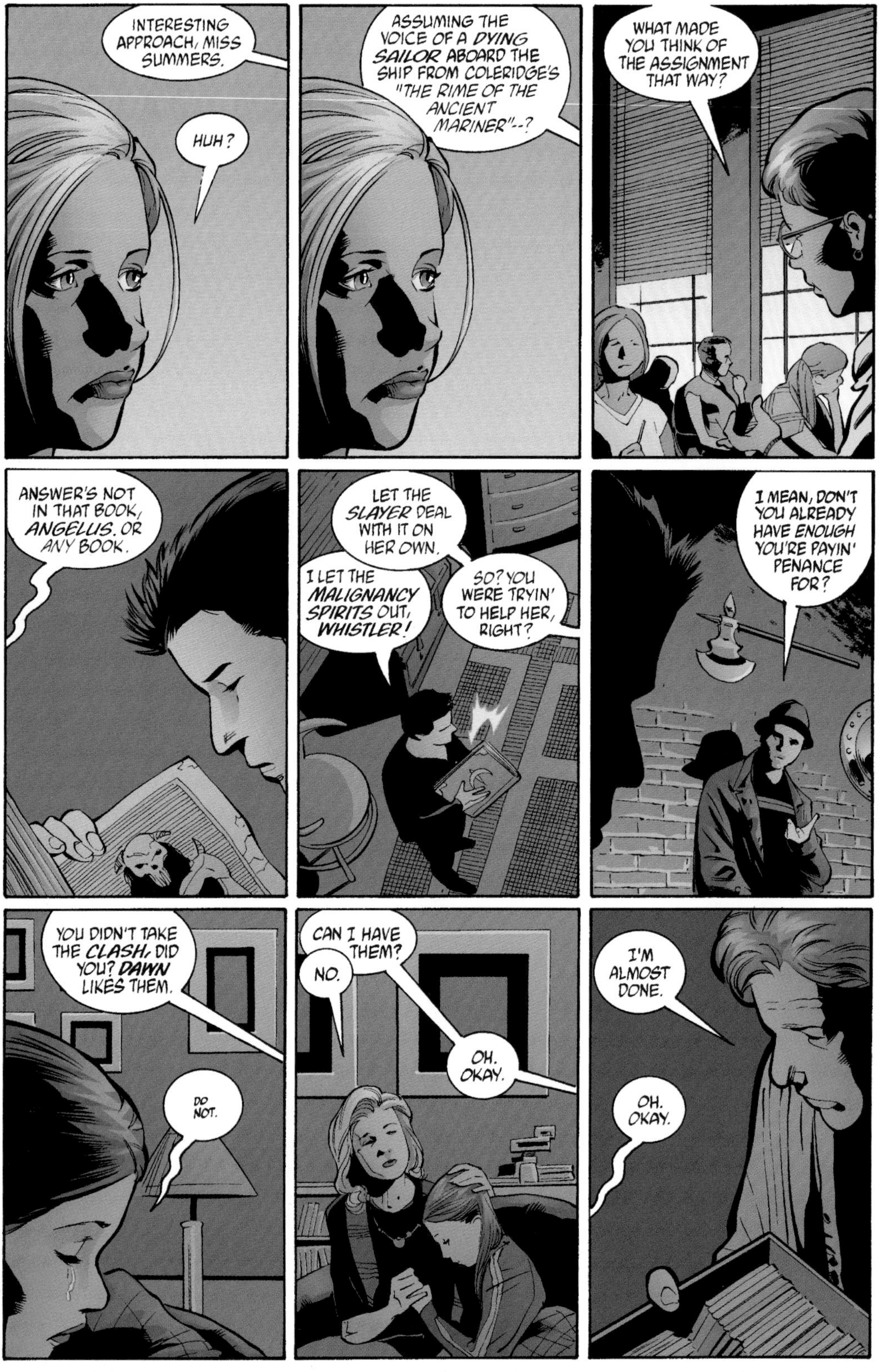
INTERESTING APPROACH, MISS SUMMERS.
HUH?
ASSUMING THE VOICE OF A DYING SAILOR ABOARD THE SHIP FROM COLERIDGE'S "THE RIME OF THE ANCIENT MARINER"--?
WHAT MADE YOU THINK OF THE ASSIGNMENT THAT WAY?
ANSWER'S NOT IN THAT BOOK, ANGELUS. OR ANY BOOK.
LET THE SLAYER DEAL WITH IT ON HER OWN.
I LET THE MALIGNANCY SPIRITS OUT, WHISTLER!
SO? YOU WERE TRYIN' TO HELP HER, RIGHT?
I MEAN, DON'T YOU ALREADY HAVE ENOUGH YOU'RE PAYIN' PENANCE FOR?
YOU DIDN'T TAKE THE CLASH, DID YOU? DAWN LIKES THEM.
DO NOT.
CAN I HAVE THEM?
NO.
OH. OKAY.
I'M ALMOST DONE.
OH. OKAY.

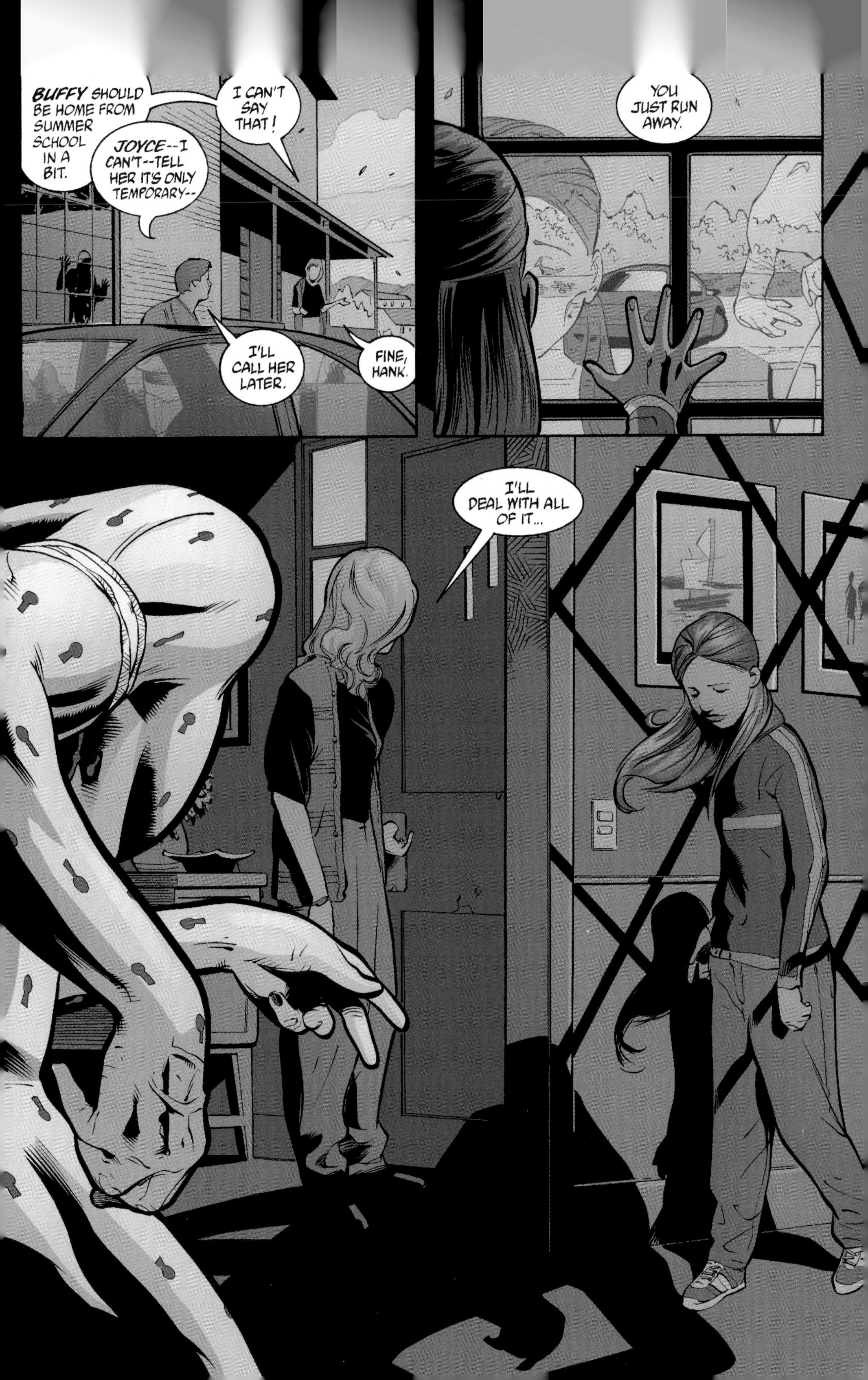
BUFFY SHOULD BE HOME FROM SUMMER SCHOOL IN A BIT.
I CAN'T SAY THAT!
JOYCE--I CAN'T--TELL HER IT'S ONLY TEMPORARY--
I'LL CALL HER LATER.
FINE, HANK.
YOU JUST RUN AWAY.
I'LL DEAL WITH ALL OF IT...

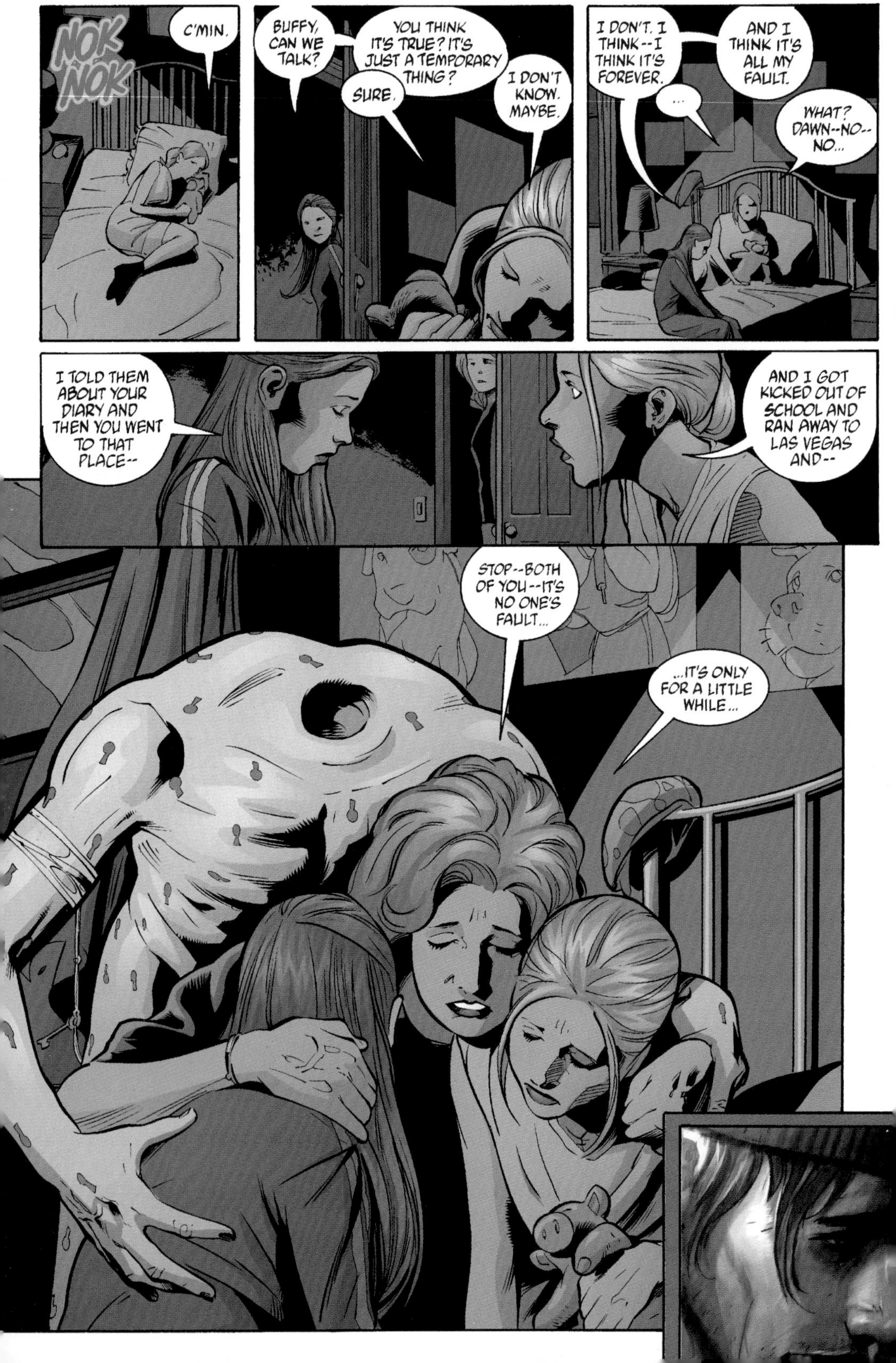
NOK NOK
C'MIN.
BUFFY, CAN WE TALK?
SURE.
YOU THINK IT'S TRUE? IT'S JUST A TEMPORARY THING?
I DON'T KNOW. MAYBE.
I DON'T. I THINK--I THINK IT'S FOREVER.
...
AND I THINK IT'S ALL MY FAULT.
WHAT? DAWN--NO--NO...
I TOLD THEM ABOUT YOUR DIARY AND THEN YOU WENT TO THAT PLACE--
AND I GOT KICKED OUT OF SCHOOL AND RAN AWAY TO LAS VEGAS AND--
STOP--BOTH OF YOU--IT'S NO ONE'S FAULT...
...IT'S ONLY FOR A LITTLE WHILE...

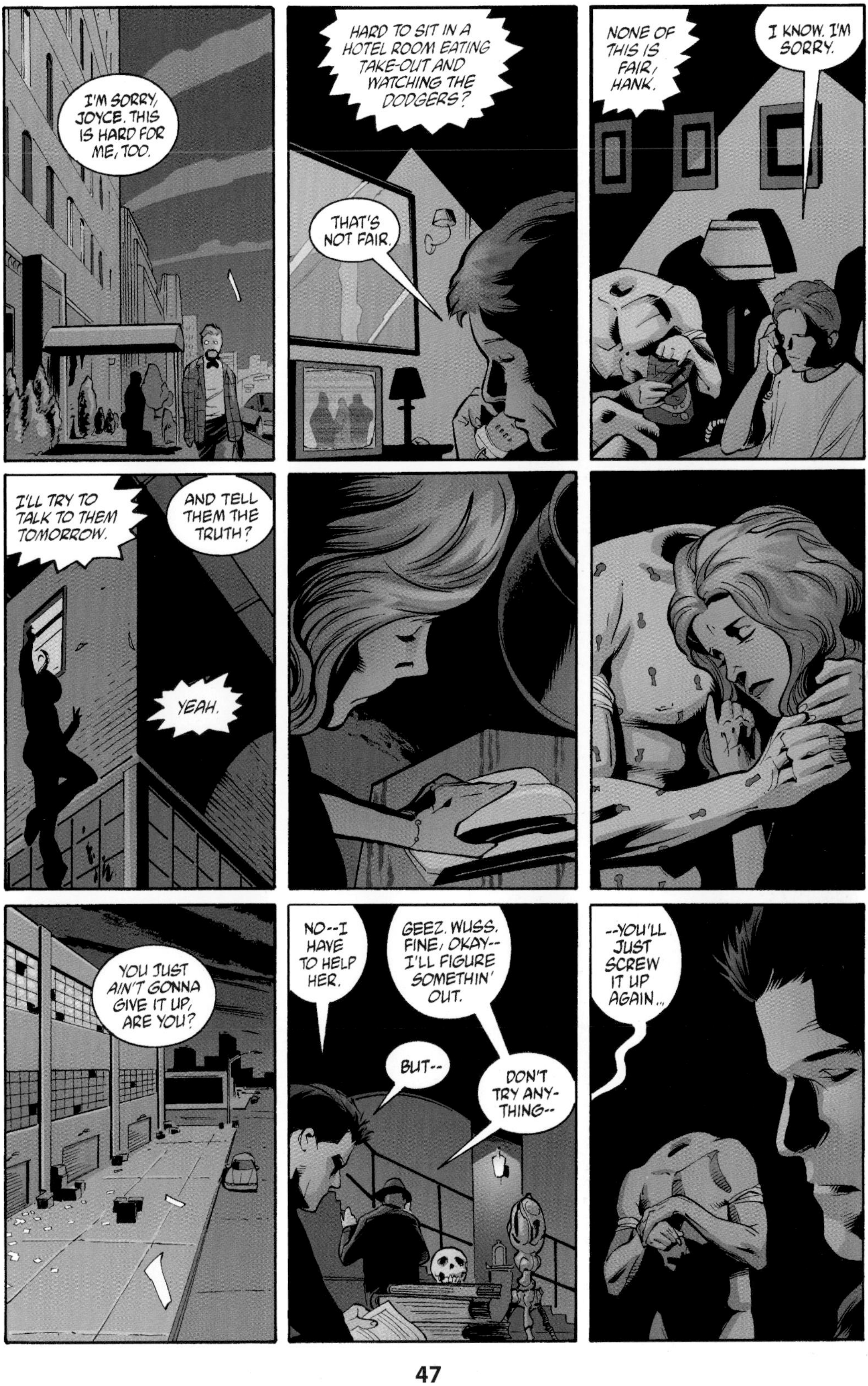
I'M SORRY, JOYCE. THIS IS HARD FOR ME, TOO.
HARD TO SIT IN A HOTEL ROOM EATING TAKE-OUT AND WATCHING THE DODGERS?
THAT'S NOT FAIR.
NONE OF THIS IS FAIR, HANK.
I KNOW. I'M SORRY.
I'LL TRY TO TALK TO THEM TOMORROW.
AND TELL THEM THE TRUTH?
YEAH.
YOU JUST AIN'T GONNA GIVE IT UP, ARE YOU?
NO--I HAVE TO HELP HER.
GEEZ. WUSS. FINE, OKAY-- I'LL FIGURE SOMETHIN' OUT.
BUT--
DON'T TRY ANY-THING--
--YOU'LL JUST SCREW IT UP AGAIN...

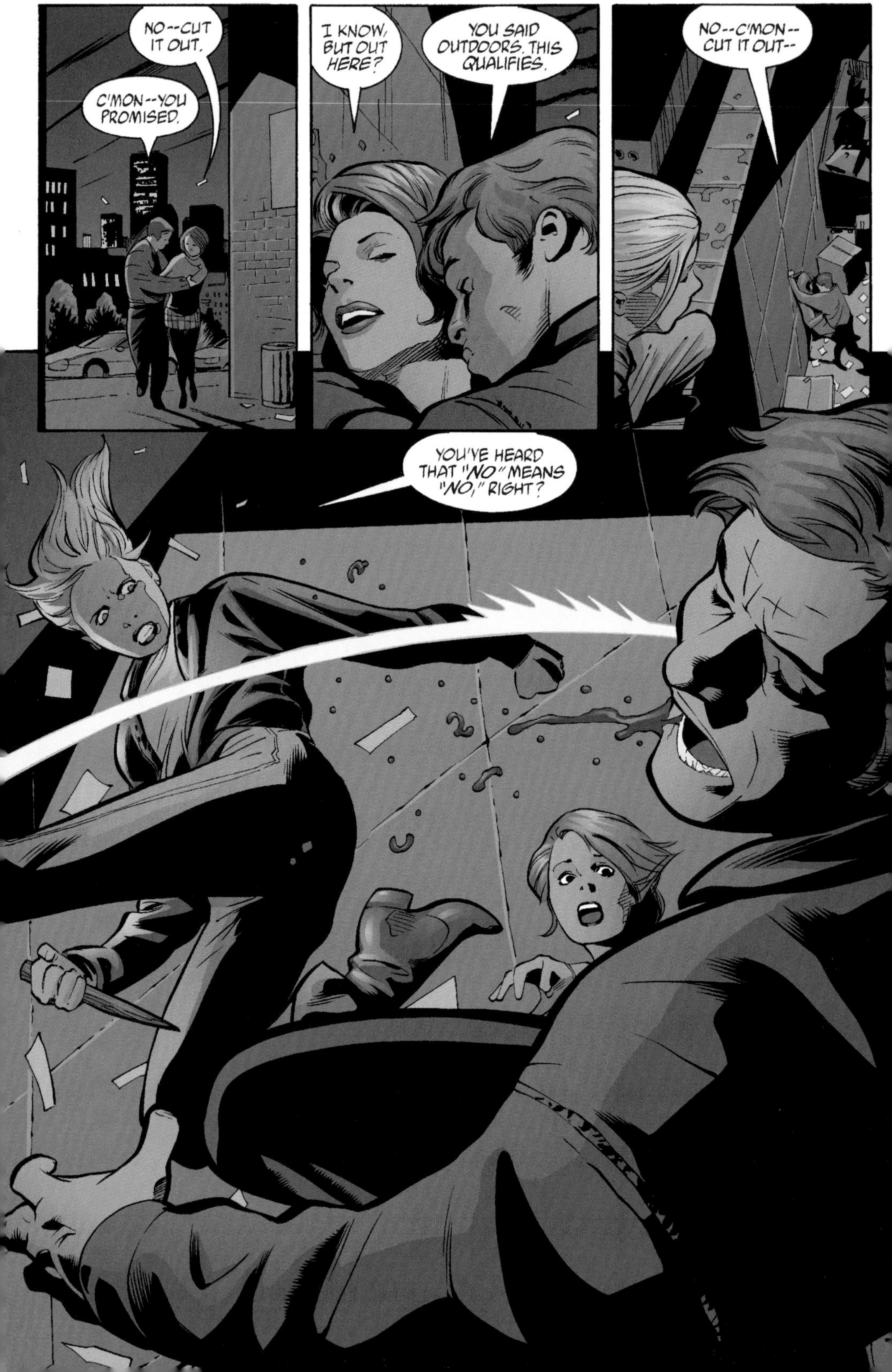
NO--CUT IT OUT.
C'MON--YOU PROMISED.
I KNOW, BUT OUT HERE?
YOU SAID OUTDOORS. THIS QUALIFIES.
NO--C'MON--CUT IT OUT--
YOU'VE HEARD THAT "NO" MEANS "NO," RIGHT?

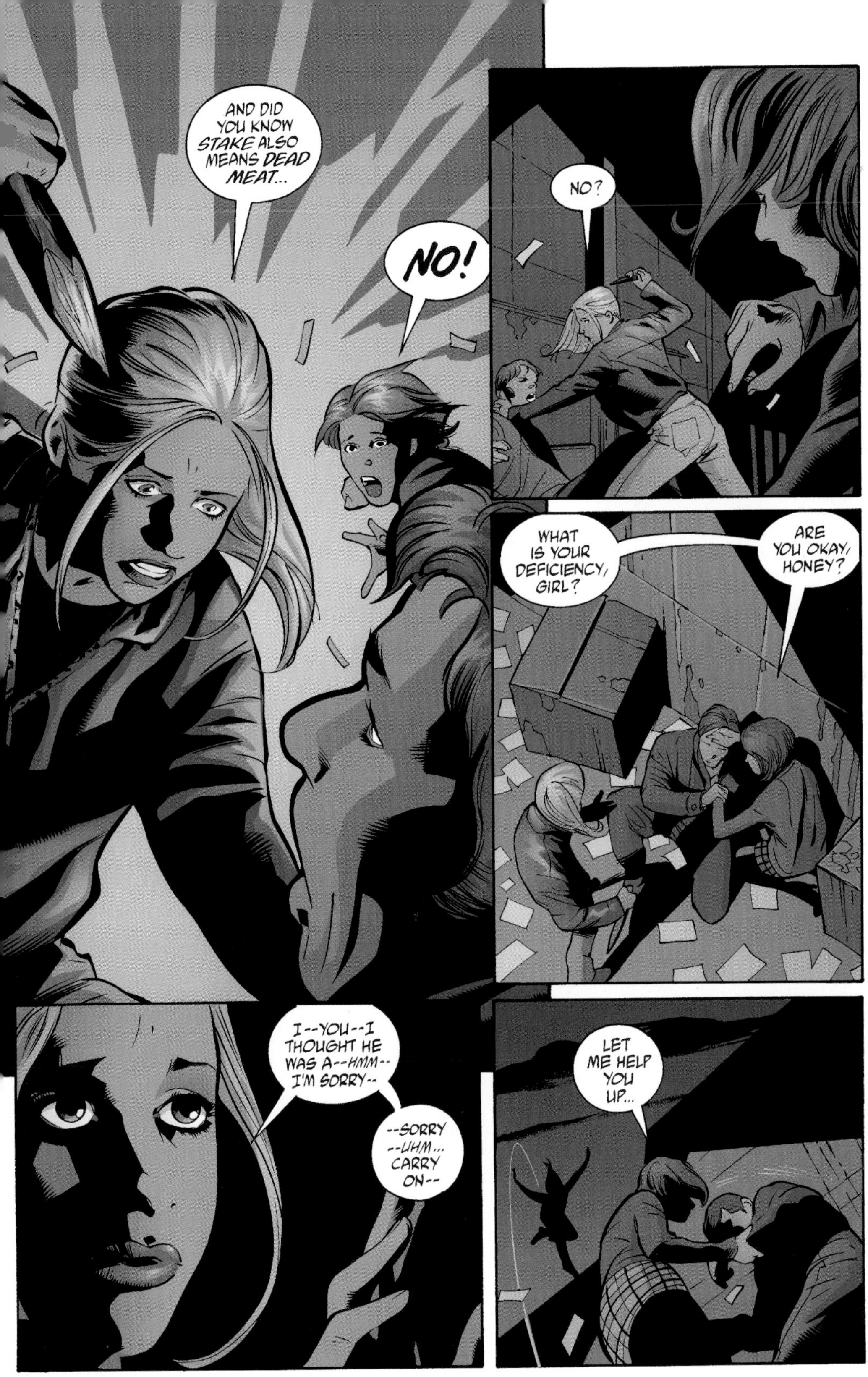
AND DID YOU KNOW STAKE ALSO MEANS DEAD MEAT...
NO!
NO?
WHAT IS YOUR DEFICIENCY, GIRL?
ARE YOU OKAY, HONEY?
I--YOU--I THOUGHT HE WAS A--HMM-- I'M SORRY--
--SORRY --UHM... CARRY ON--
LET ME HELP YOU UP...

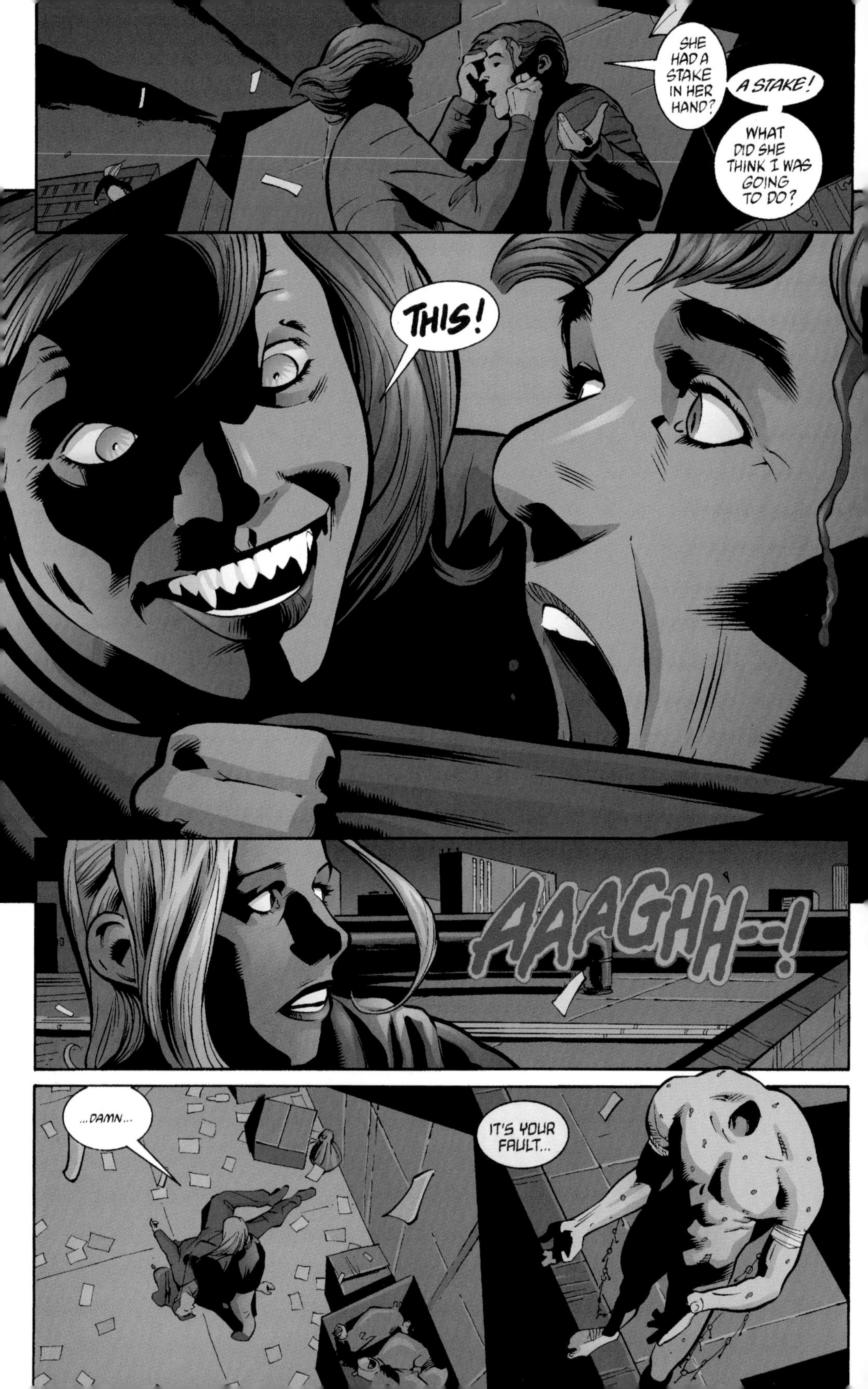
SHE HAD A STAKE IN HER HAND?
A STAKE!
WHAT DID SHE THINK I WAS GOING TO DO?
THIS!
AAAGHH--!
...DAMN...
IT'S YOUR FAULT...

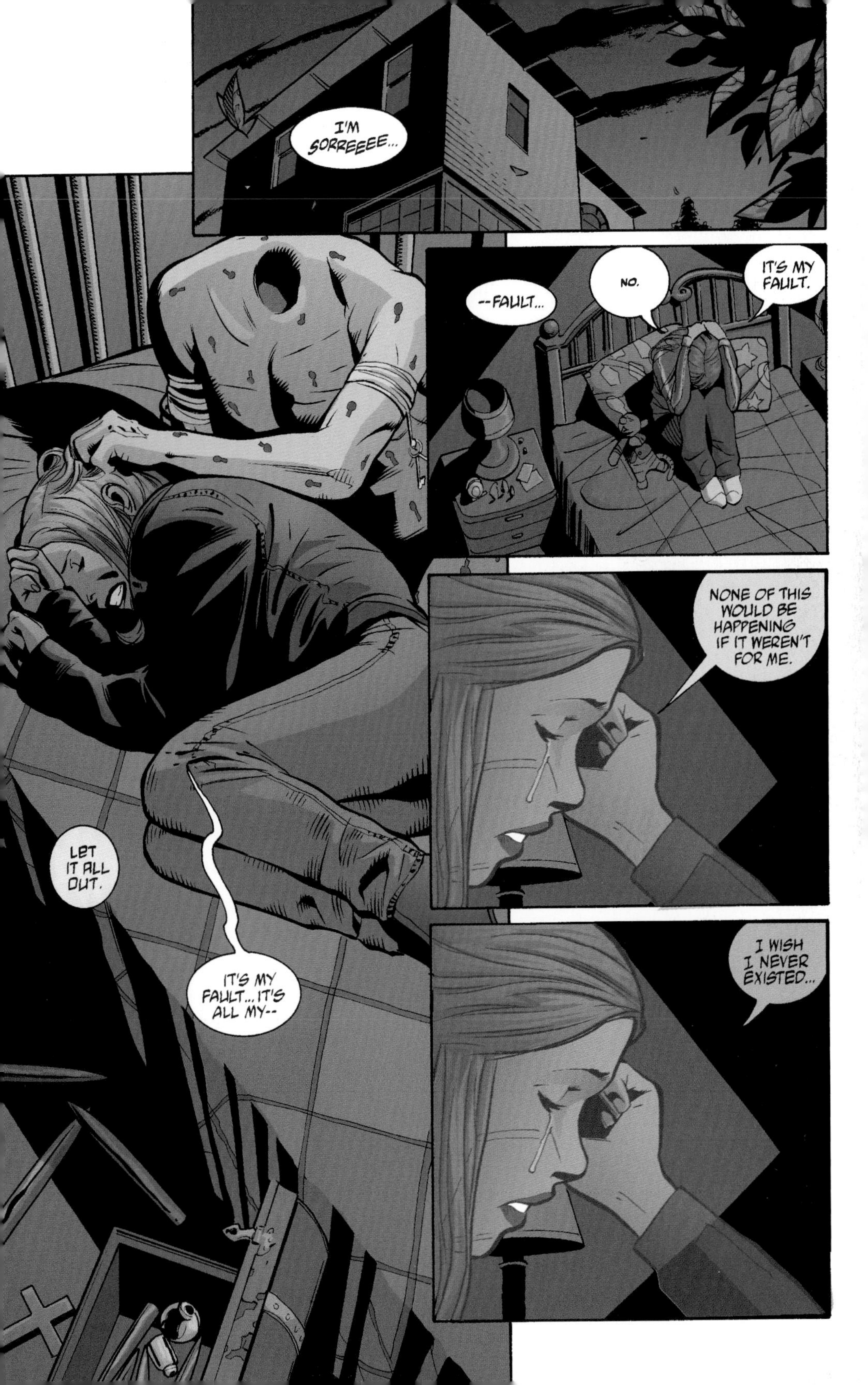
I'M SORREEEEE...
--FAULT...
NO.
IT'S MY FAULT.
NONE OF THIS WOULD BE HAPPENING IF IT WEREN'T FOR ME.
I WISH I NEVER EXISTED...
LET IT ALL OUT.
IT'S MY FAULT... IT'S ALL MY--

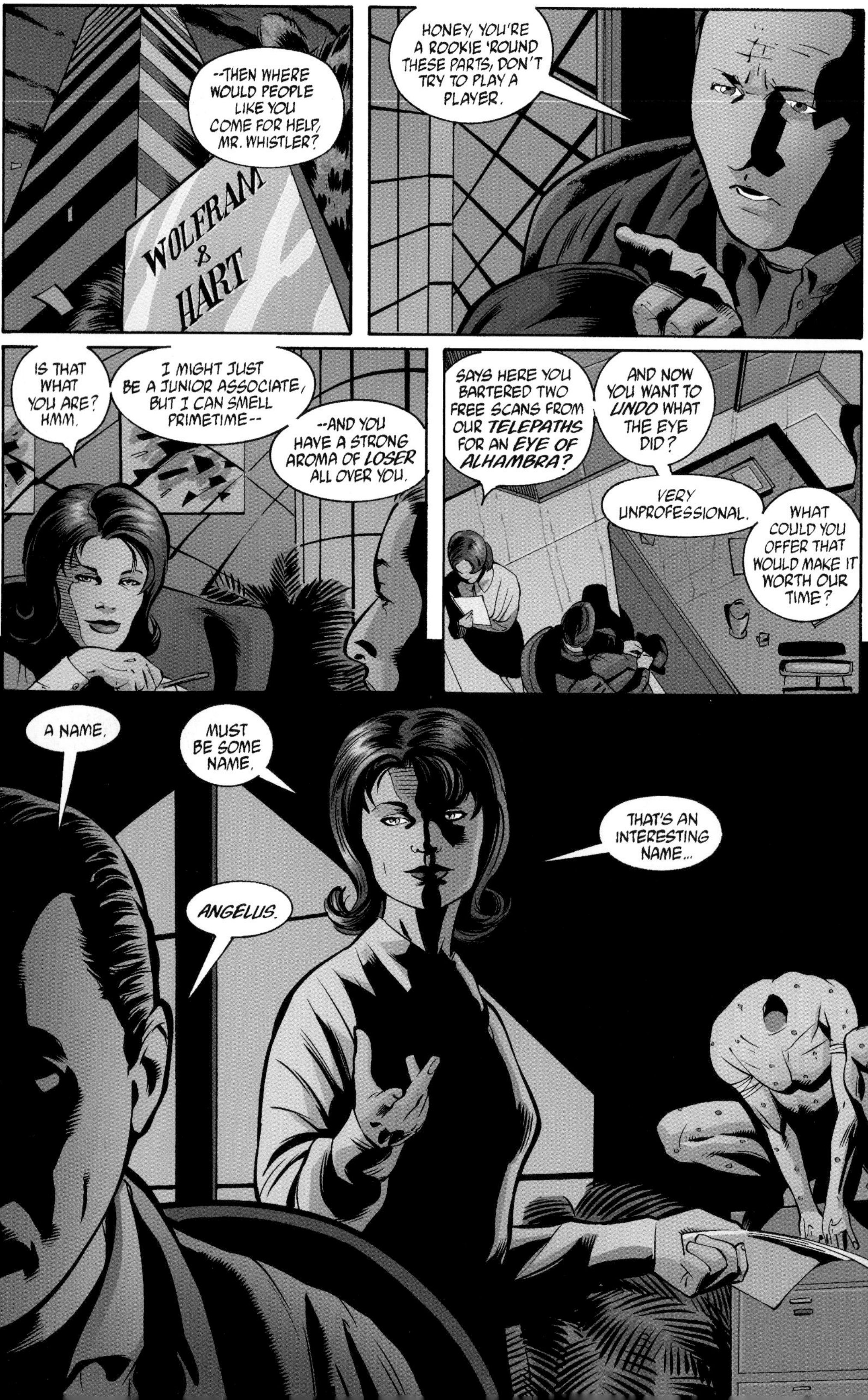
--THEN WHERE WOULD PEOPLE LIKE YOU COME FOR HELP, MR. WHISTLER?
WOLFRAM & HART
HONEY, YOU'RE A ROOKIE 'ROUND THESE PARTS, DON'T TRY TO PLAY A PLAYER.
IS THAT WHAT YOU ARE? HMM.
I MIGHT JUST BE A JUNIOR ASSOCIATE, BUT I CAN SMELL PRIMETIME--
--AND YOU HAVE A STRONG AROMA OF LOSER ALL OVER YOU.
SAYS HERE YOU BARTERED TWO FREE SCANS FROM OUR TELEPATHS FOR AN EYE OF ALHAMBRA?
AND NOW YOU WANT TO UNDO WHAT THE EYE DID?
VERY UNPROFESSIONAL.
WHAT COULD YOU OFFER THAT WOULD MAKE IT WORTH OUR TIME?
A NAME.
MUST BE SOME NAME.
ANGELUS.
THAT'S AN INTERESTING NAME...

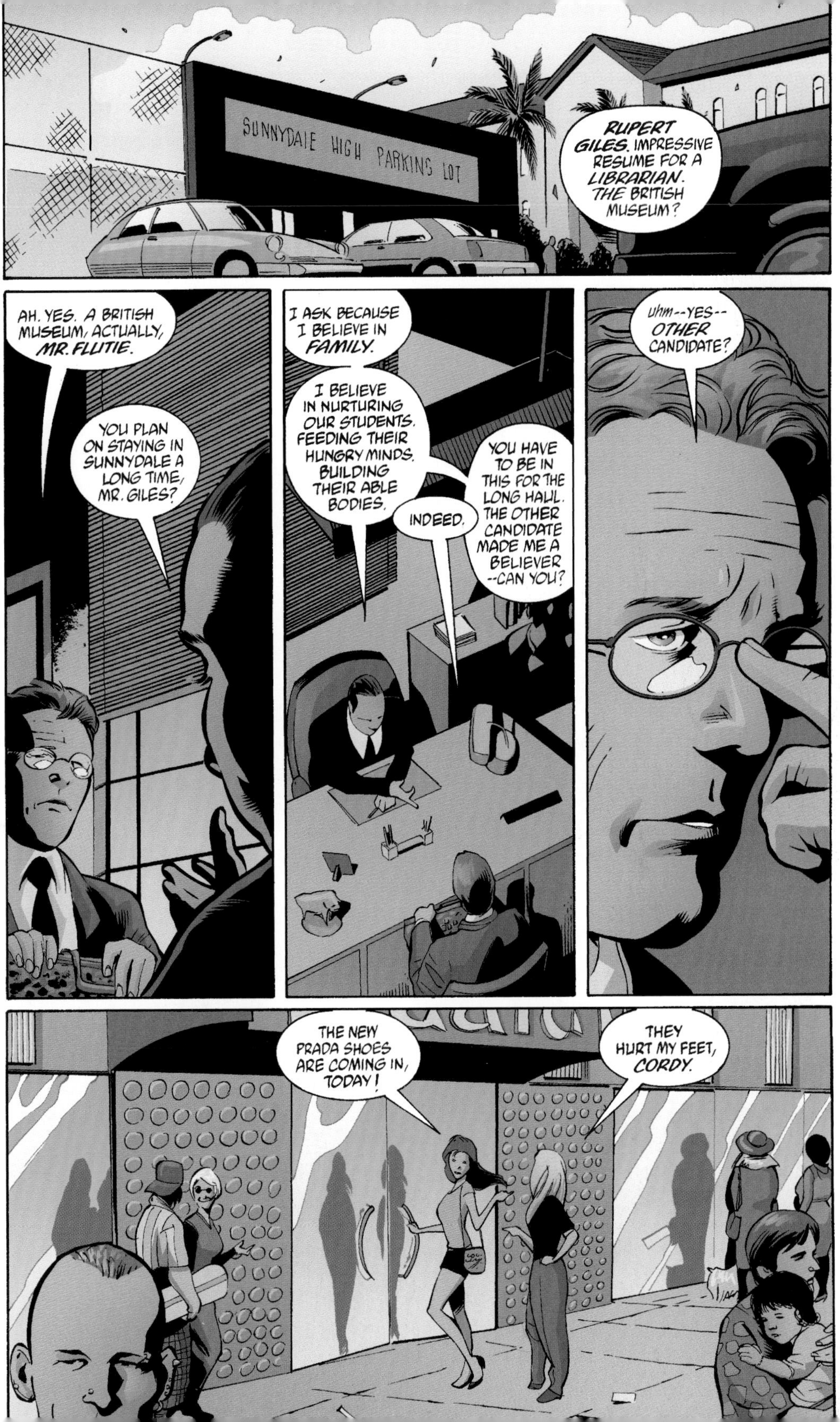
SUNNYDALE HIGH PARKING LOT
RUPERT GILES. IMPRESSIVE RESUME FOR A LIBRARIAN. THE BRITISH MUSEUM?
AH. YES. A BRITISH MUSEUM, ACTUALLY, MR. FLUTIE.
YOU PLAN ON STAYING IN SUNNYDALE A LONG TIME, MR. GILES?
I ASK BECAUSE I BELIEVE IN FAMILY.
I BELIEVE IN NURTURING OUR STUDENTS. FEEDING THEIR HUNGRY MINDS. BUILDING THEIR ABLE BODIES.
INDEED.
YOU HAVE TO BE IN THIS FOR THE LONG HAUL. THE OTHER CANDIDATE MADE ME A BELIEVER --CAN YOU?
uhm--YES--OTHER CANDIDATE?
THE NEW PRADA SHOES ARE COMING IN, TODAY!
THEY HURT MY FEET, CORDY.

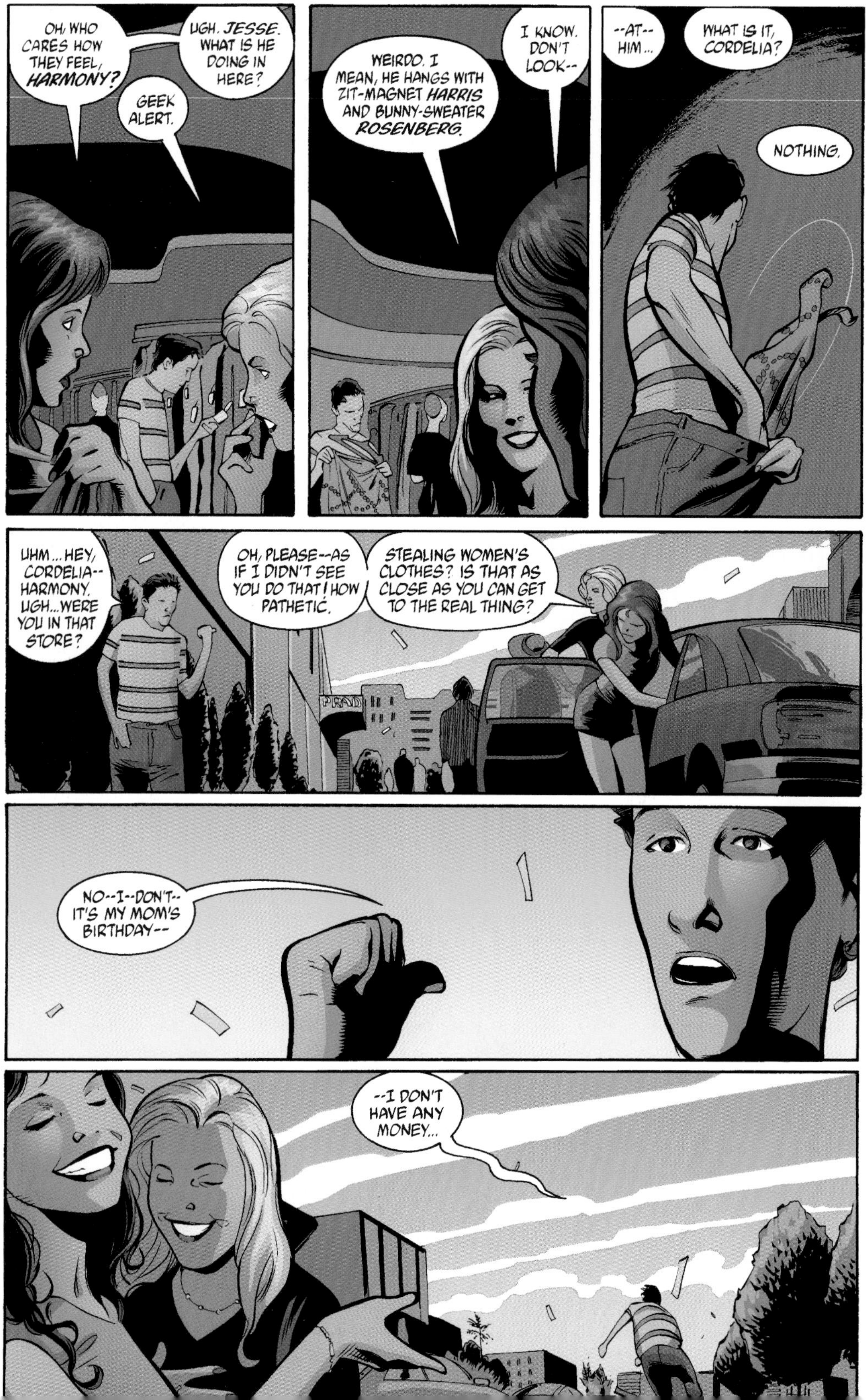
OH, WHO CARES HOW THEY FEEL, HARMONY?
UGH. JESSE. WHAT IS HE DOING IN HERE?
GEEK ALERT.
WEIRDO. I MEAN, HE HANGS WITH ZIT-MAGNET HARRIS AND BUNNY-SWEATER ROSENBERG.
I KNOW. DON'T LOOK--
--AT-- HIM...
WHAT IS IT, CORDELIA?
NOTHING.
UHM... HEY, CORDELIA-- HARMONY. UGH...WERE YOU IN THAT STORE?
OH, PLEASE--AS IF I DIDN'T SEE YOU DO THAT! HOW PATHETIC.
STEALING WOMEN'S CLOTHES? IS THAT AS CLOSE AS YOU CAN GET TO THE REAL THING?
NO--I--DON'T-- IT'S MY MOM'S BIRTHDAY--
--I DON'T HAVE ANY MONEY...

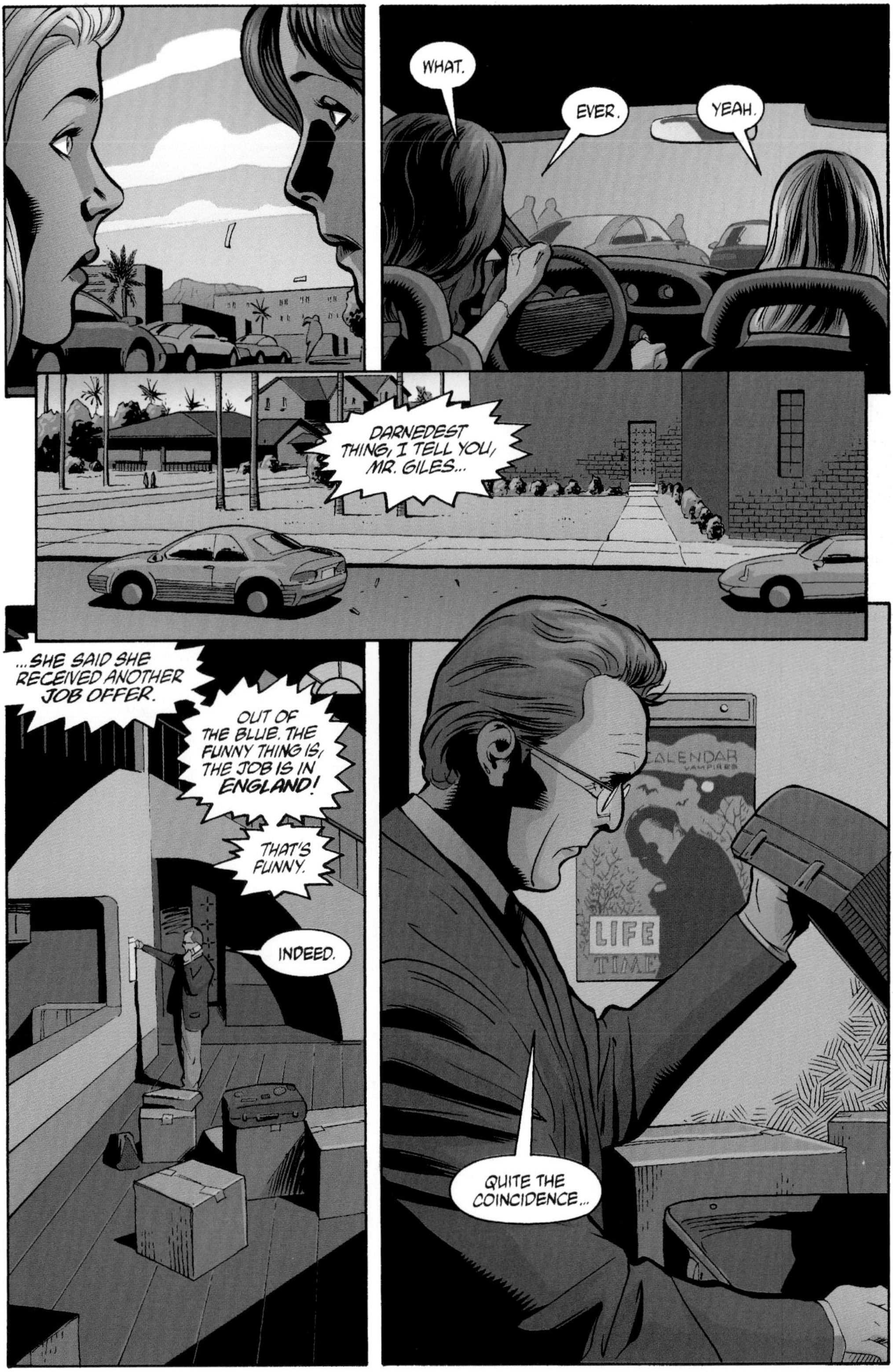
WHAT.
EVER.
YEAH.
DARNEDEST THING, I TELL YOU, MR. GILES...
...SHE SAID SHE RECEIVED ANOTHER JOB OFFER.
OUT OF THE BLUE. THE FUNNY THING IS, THE JOB IS IN ENGLAND!
THAT'S FUNNY.
INDEED.
CALENDAR
VAMPIRES
LIFE
QUITE THE COINCIDENCE...

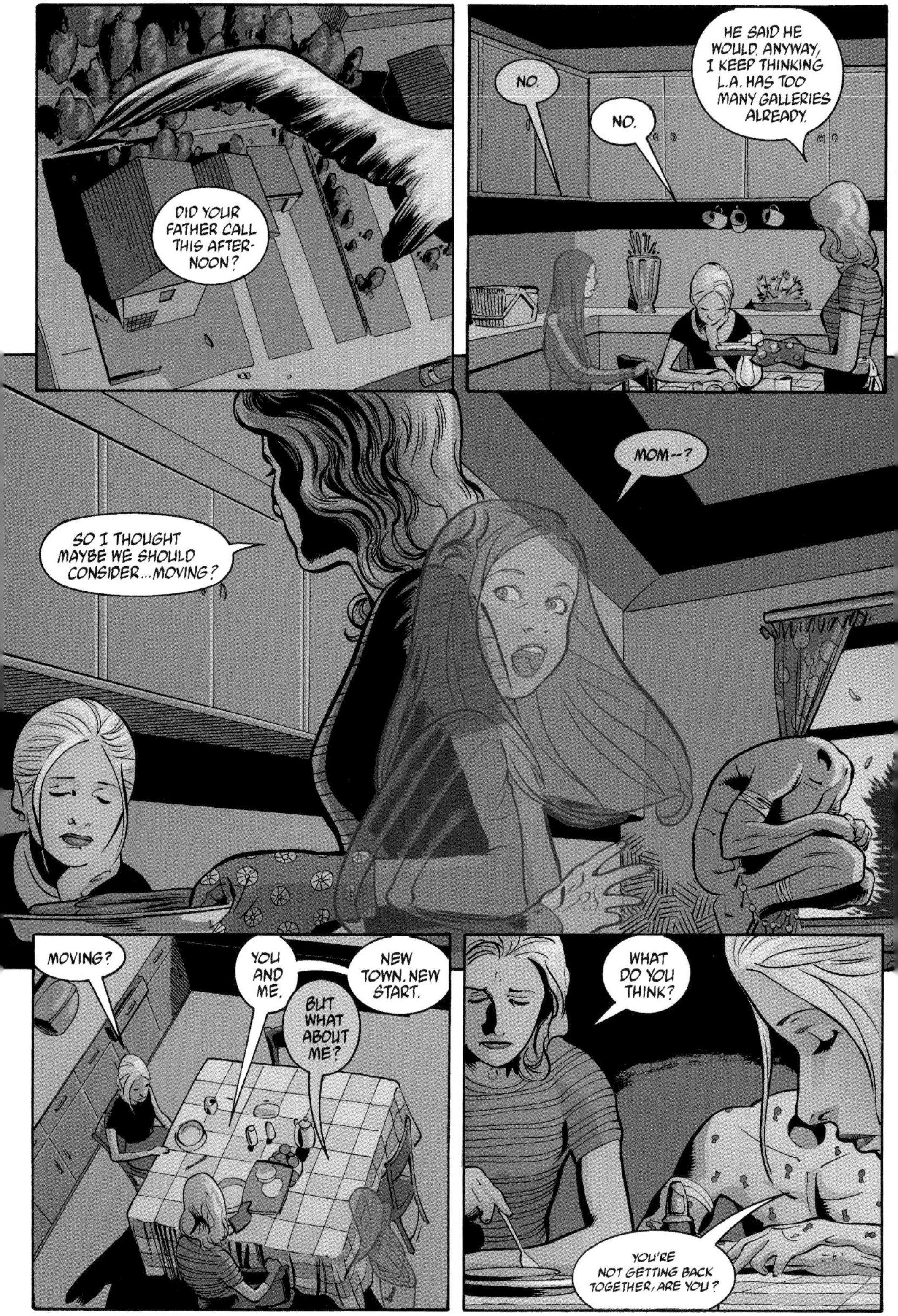
DID YOUR FATHER CALL THIS AFTER-NOON?
NO.
NO.
HE SAID HE WOULD. ANYWAY, I KEEP THINKING L.A. HAS TOO MANY GALLERIES ALREADY.
SO I THOUGHT MAYBE WE SHOULD CONSIDER...MOVING?
MOM--?
MOVING?
YOU AND ME.
NEW TOWN. NEW START.
BUT WHAT ABOUT ME?
WHAT DO YOU THINK?
YOU'RE NOT GETTING BACK TOGETHER, ARE YOU?

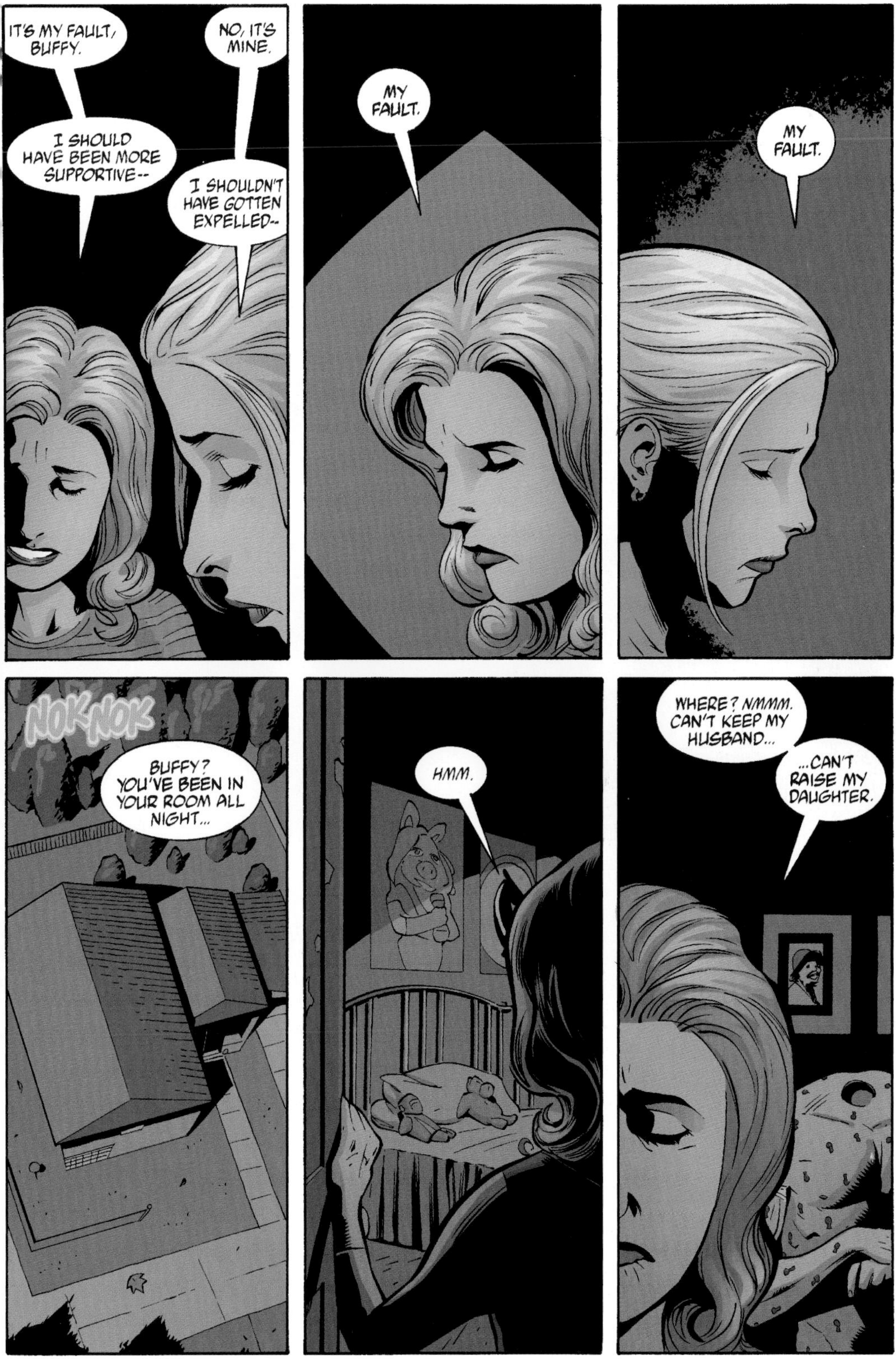
IT'S MY FAULT, BUFFY.
I SHOULD HAVE BEEN MORE SUPPORTIVE--
NO, IT'S MINE.
I SHOULDN'T HAVE GOTTEN EXPELLED--
MY FAULT.
MY FAULT.
NOK-NOK
BUFFY? YOU'VE BEEN IN YOUR ROOM ALL NIGHT...
HMM.
WHERE? NMMM. CAN'T KEEP MY HUSBAND...
...CAN'T RAISE MY DAUGHTER.

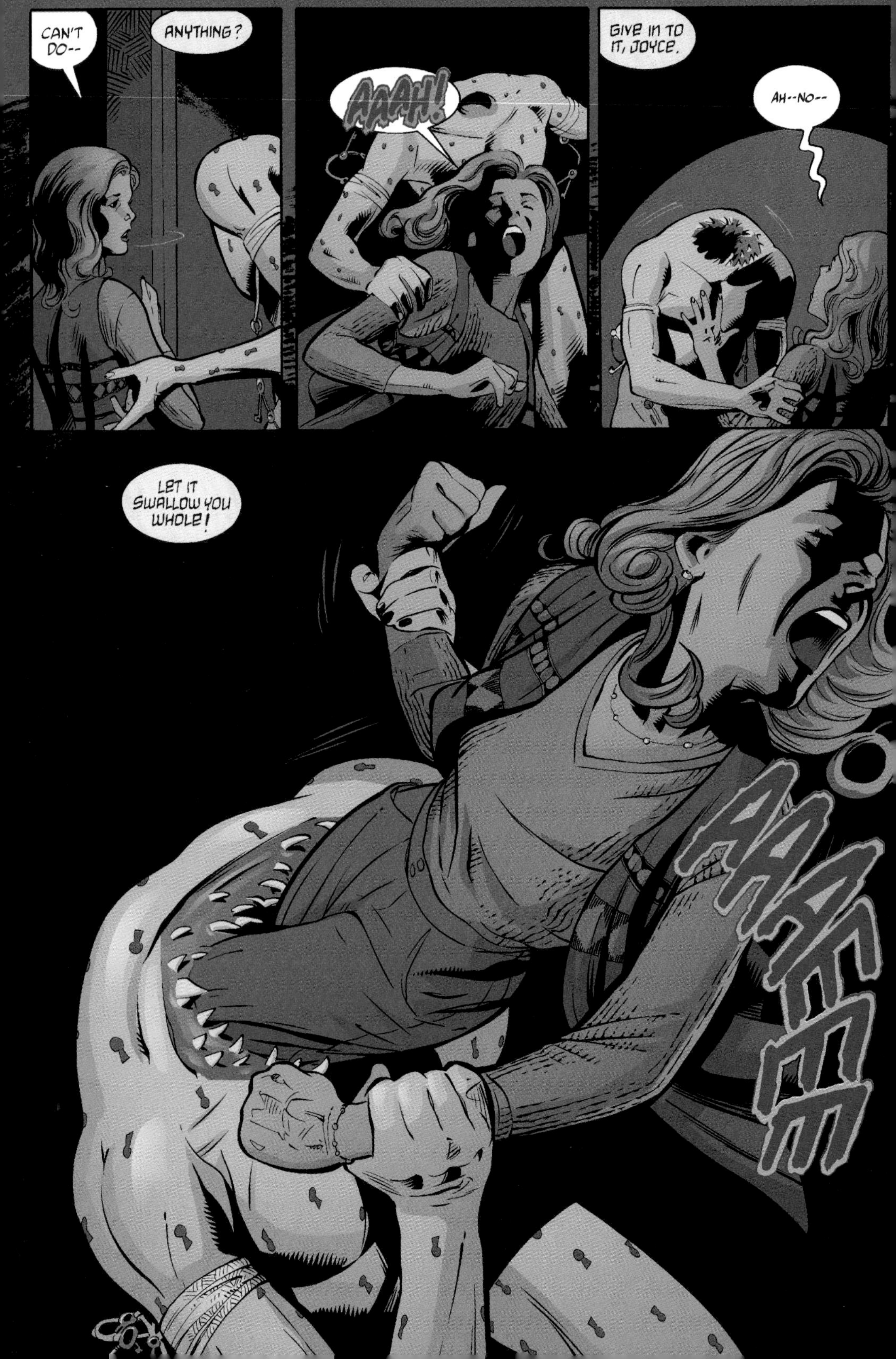
CAN'T DO--
ANYTHING?
AAAH!
GIVE IN TO IT, JOYCE.
AH--NO--
LET IT SWALLOW YOU WHOLE!
AAAEEE

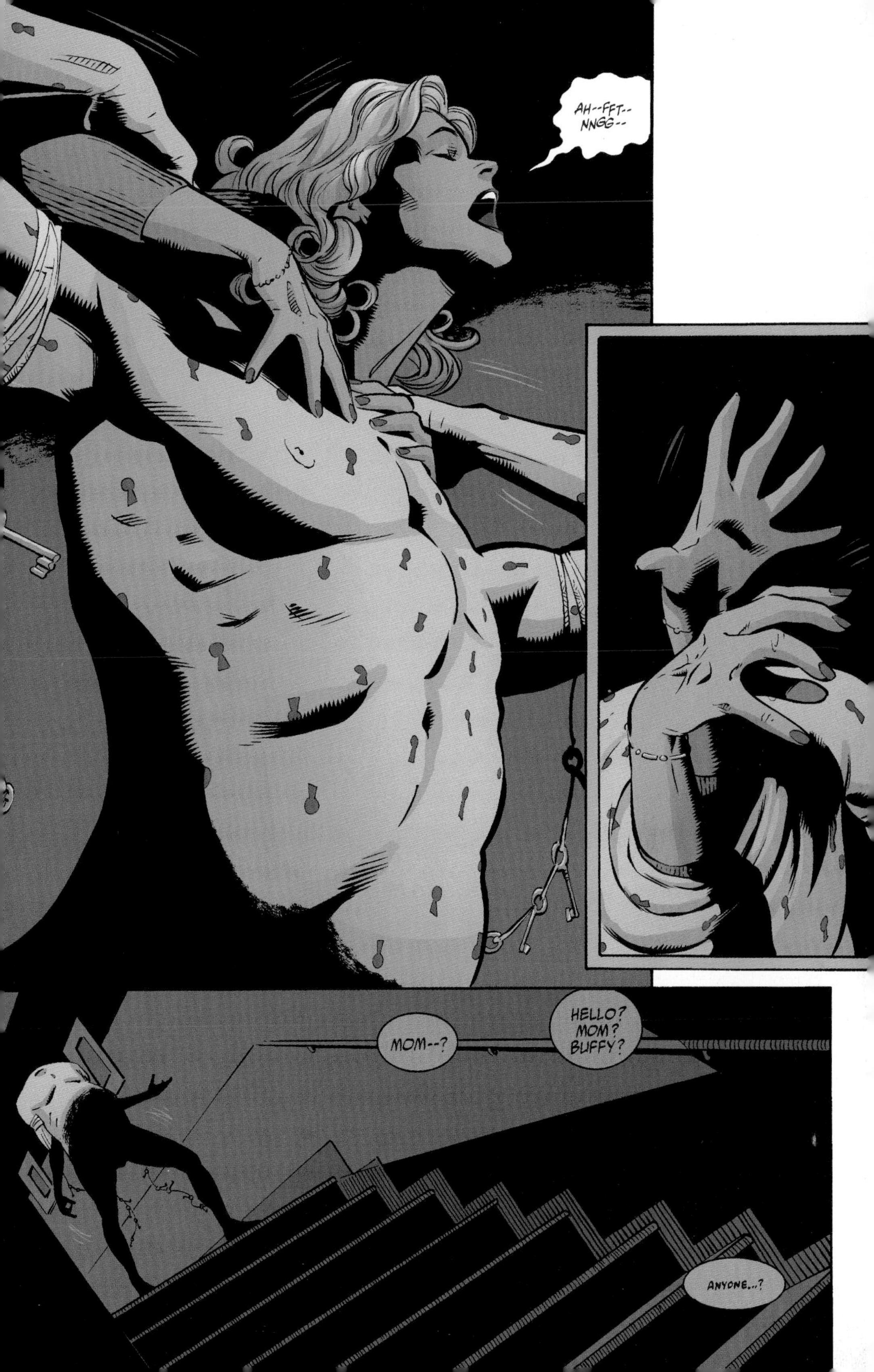
AH--FFT--
NNGG--
MOM--?
HELLO?
MOM?
BUFFY?
ANYONE...?

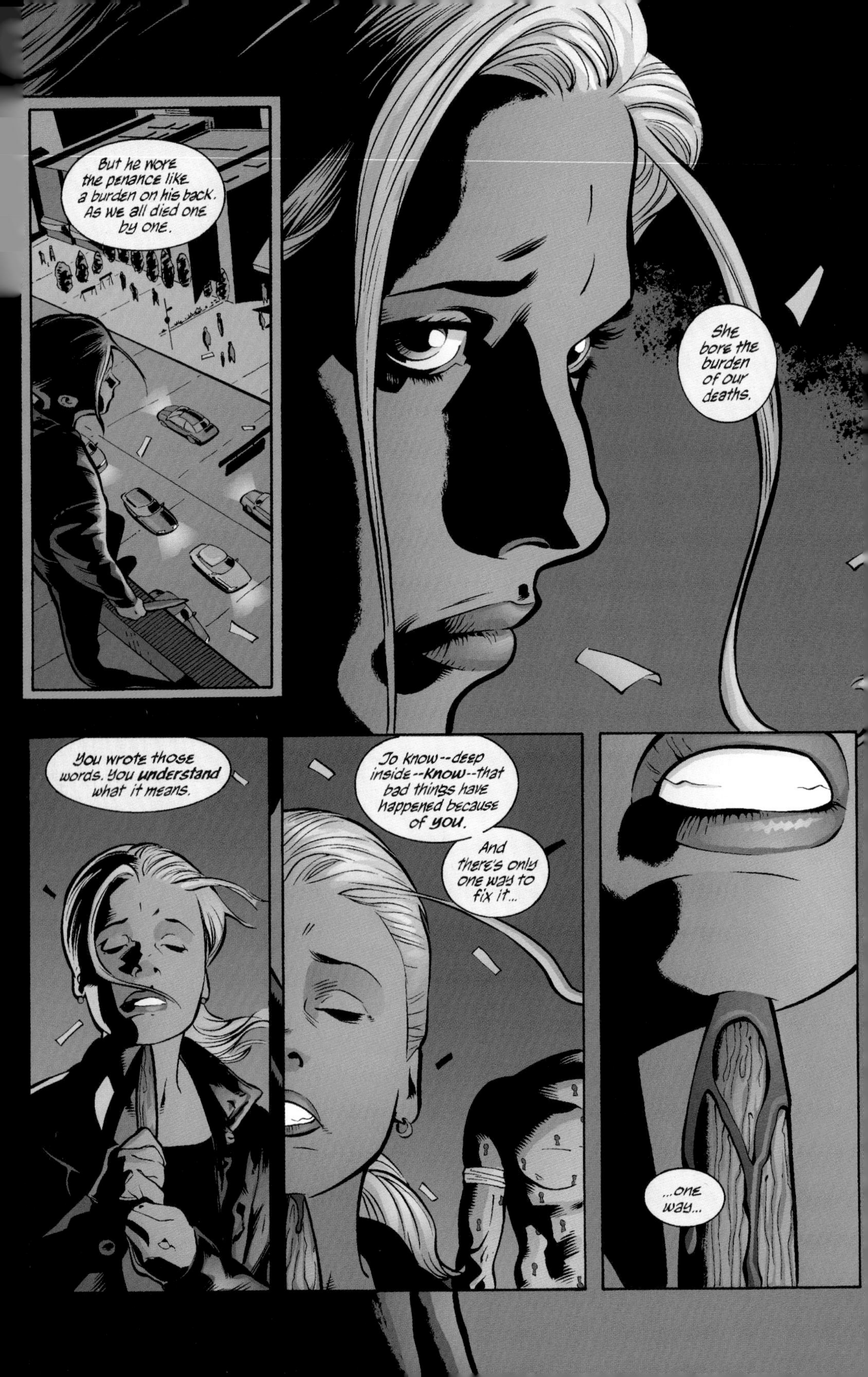
But he wore the penance like a burden on his back. As we all died one by one.
She bore the burden of our deaths.
You wrote those words. You **understand** what it means.
To know--deep inside--**know**--that bad things have happened because of **you**.
And there's only one way to fix it...
...one way...

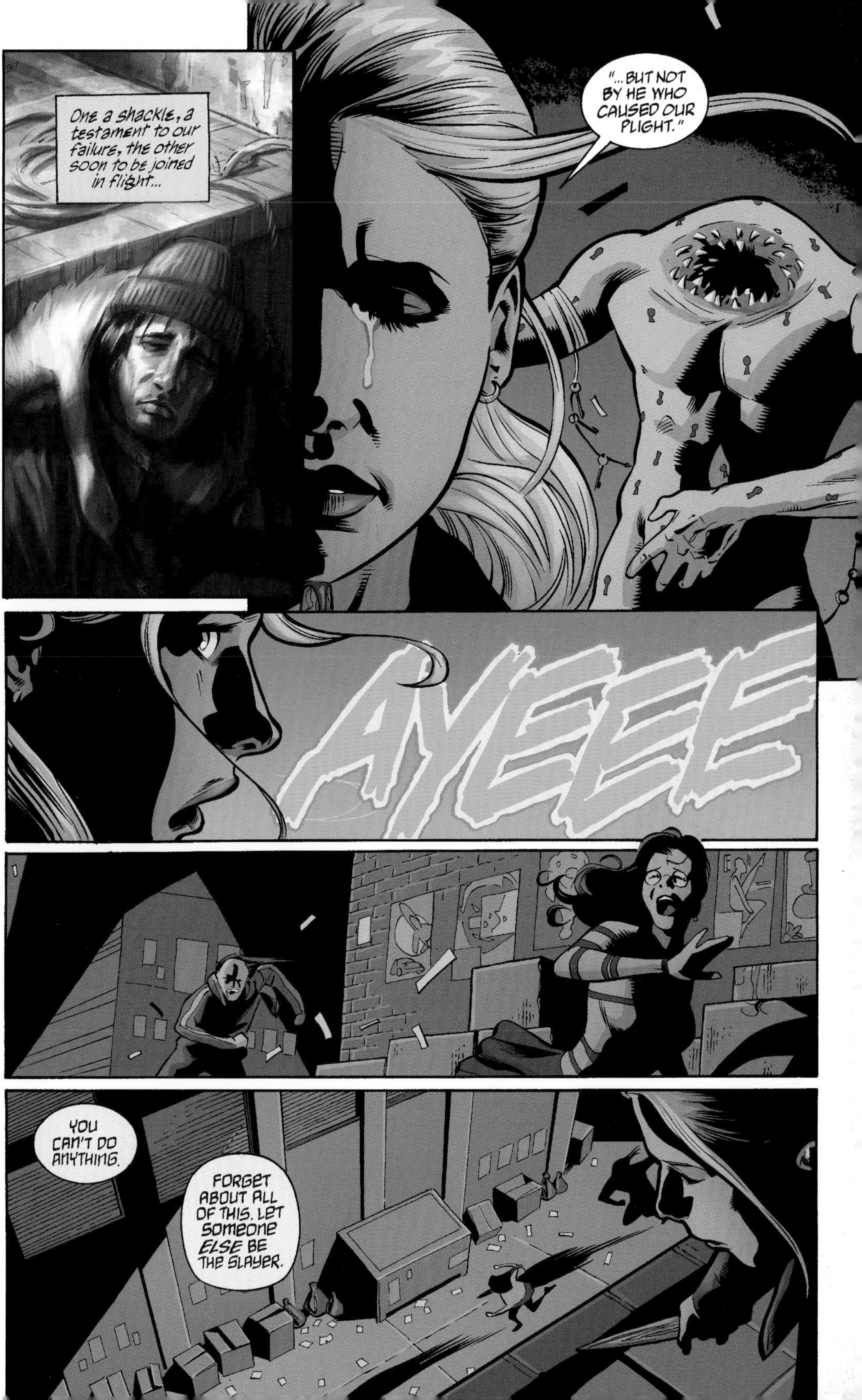
One a shackle, a testament to our failure, the other soon to be joined in flight...
"...BUT NOT BY HE WHO CAUSED OUR PLIGHT."
AYEEE
YOU CAN'T DO ANYTHING.
FORGET ABOUT ALL OF THIS. LET SOMEONE ELSE BE THE SLAYER.

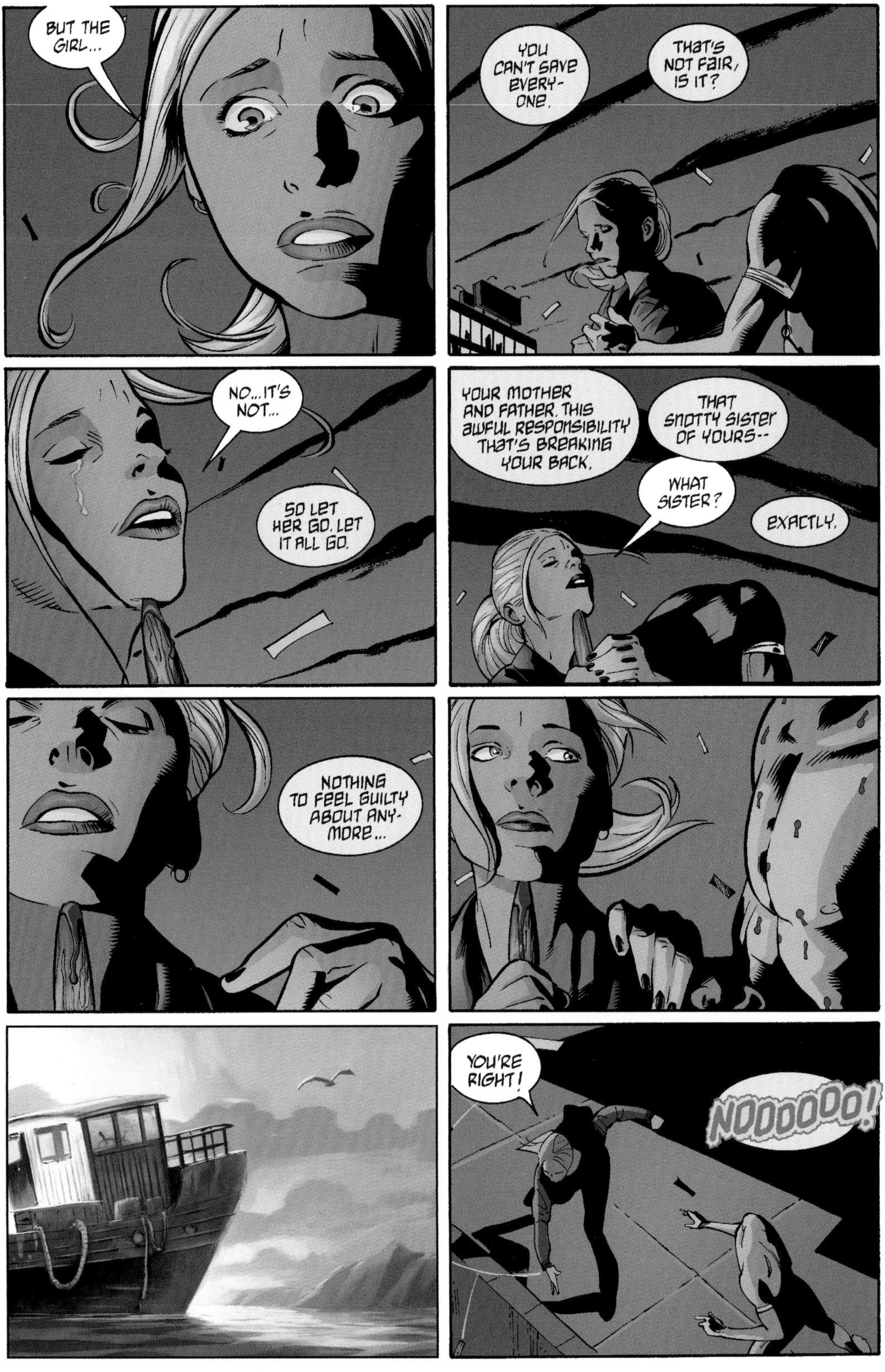
BUT THE GIRL...
YOU CAN'T SAVE EVERY-ONE.
THAT'S NOT FAIR, IS IT?
NO...IT'S NOT...
SO LET HER GO. LET IT ALL GO.
YOUR MOTHER AND FATHER. THIS AWFUL RESPONSIBILITY THAT'S BREAKING YOUR BACK.
THAT SNOTTY SISTER OF YOURS--
WHAT SISTER?
EXACTLY.
NOTHING TO FEEL GUILTY ABOUT ANY-MORE...
YOU'RE RIGHT!
NOOOOOO!

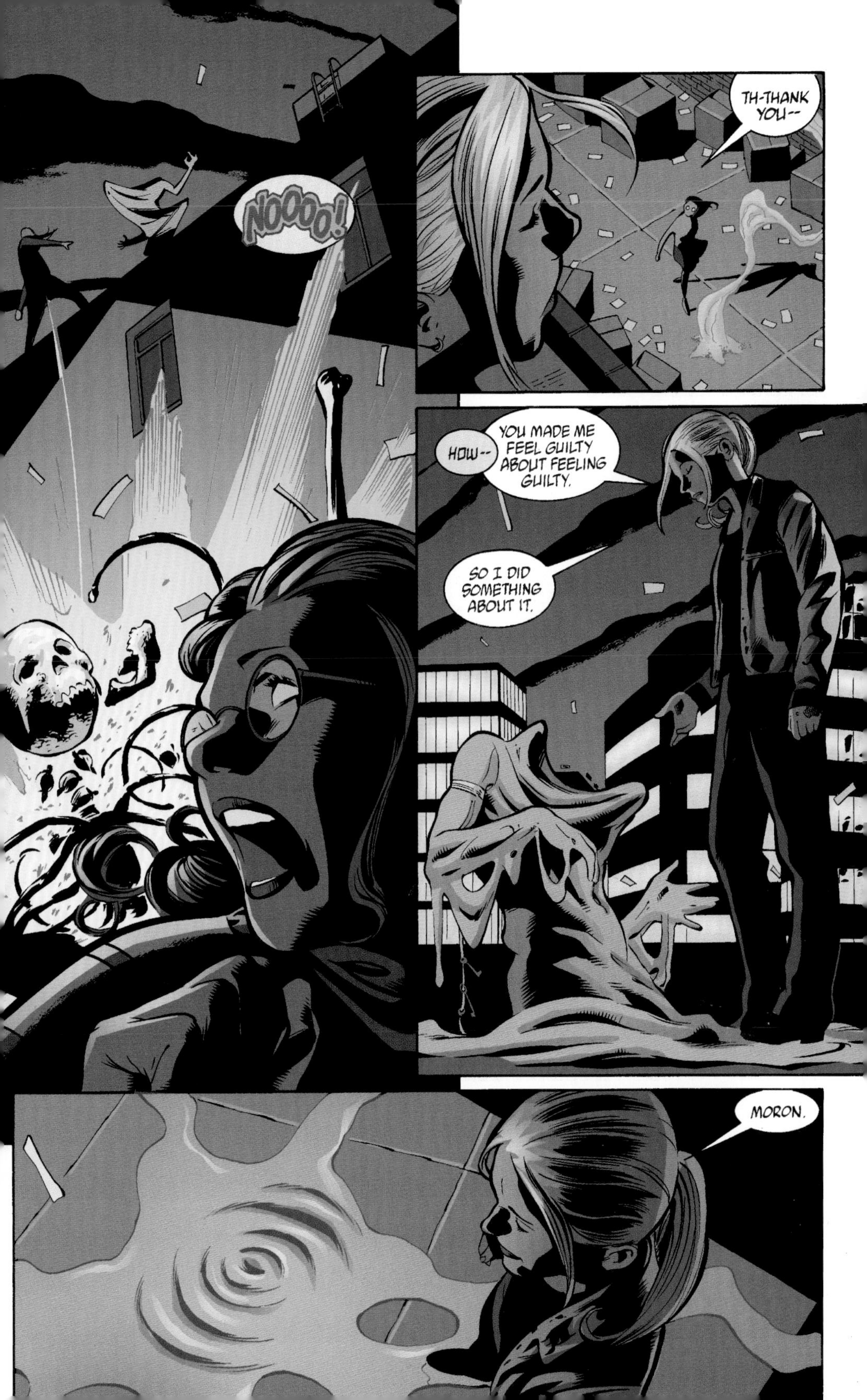
NOOOO!
TH-THANK YOU--
HOW--
YOU MADE ME FEEL GUILTY ABOUT FEELING GUILTY.
SO I DID SOMETHING ABOUT IT.
MORON.

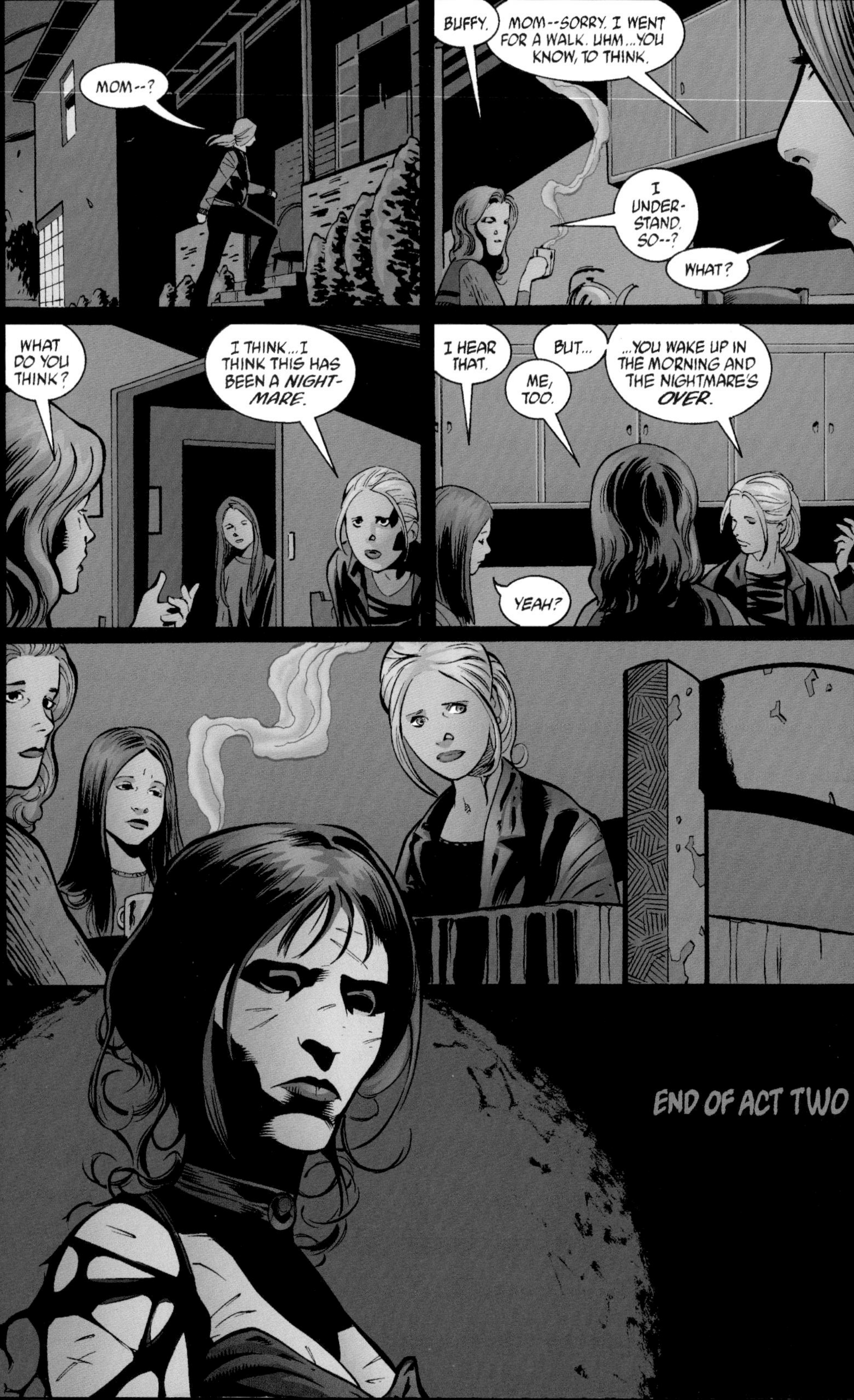
MOM--?
BUFFY.
MOM--SORRY. I WENT FOR A WALK. UHM...YOU KNOW, TO THINK.
I UNDER-STAND. SO--?
WHAT?
WHAT DO YOU THINK?
I THINK...I THINK THIS HAS BEEN A NIGHT-MARE.
I HEAR THAT.
ME, TOO.
BUT...
...YOU WAKE UP IN THE MORNING AND THE NIGHTMARE'S OVER.
YEAH?
END OF ACT TWO

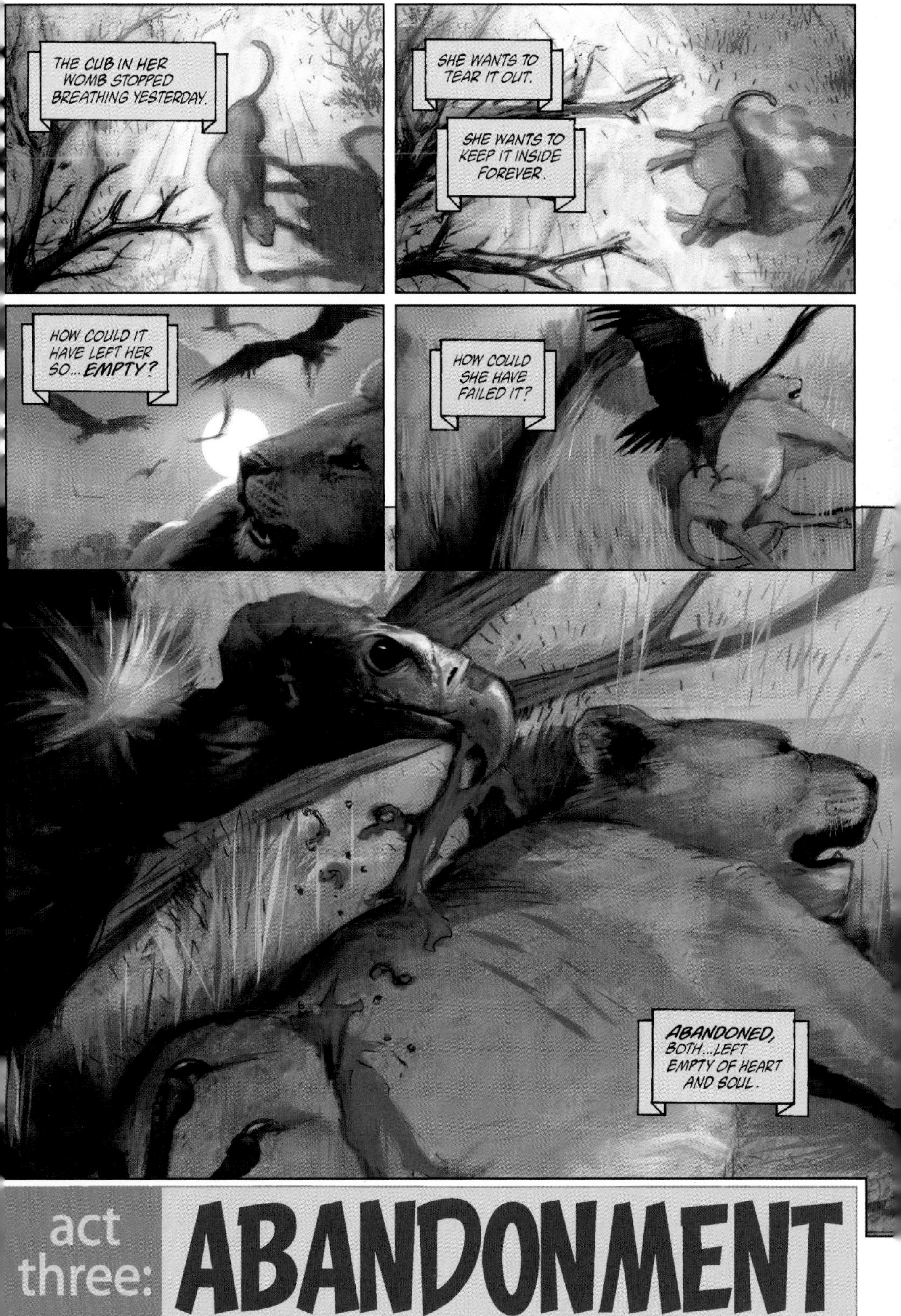
THE CUB IN HER WOMB STOPPED BREATHING YESTERDAY.
SHE WANTS TO TEAR IT OUT.
SHE WANTS TO KEEP IT INSIDE FOREVER.
HOW COULD IT HAVE LEFT HER SO... EMPTY?
HOW COULD SHE HAVE FAILED IT?
ABANDONED, BOTH...LEFT EMPTY OF HEART AND SOUL.
act three: ABANDONMENT

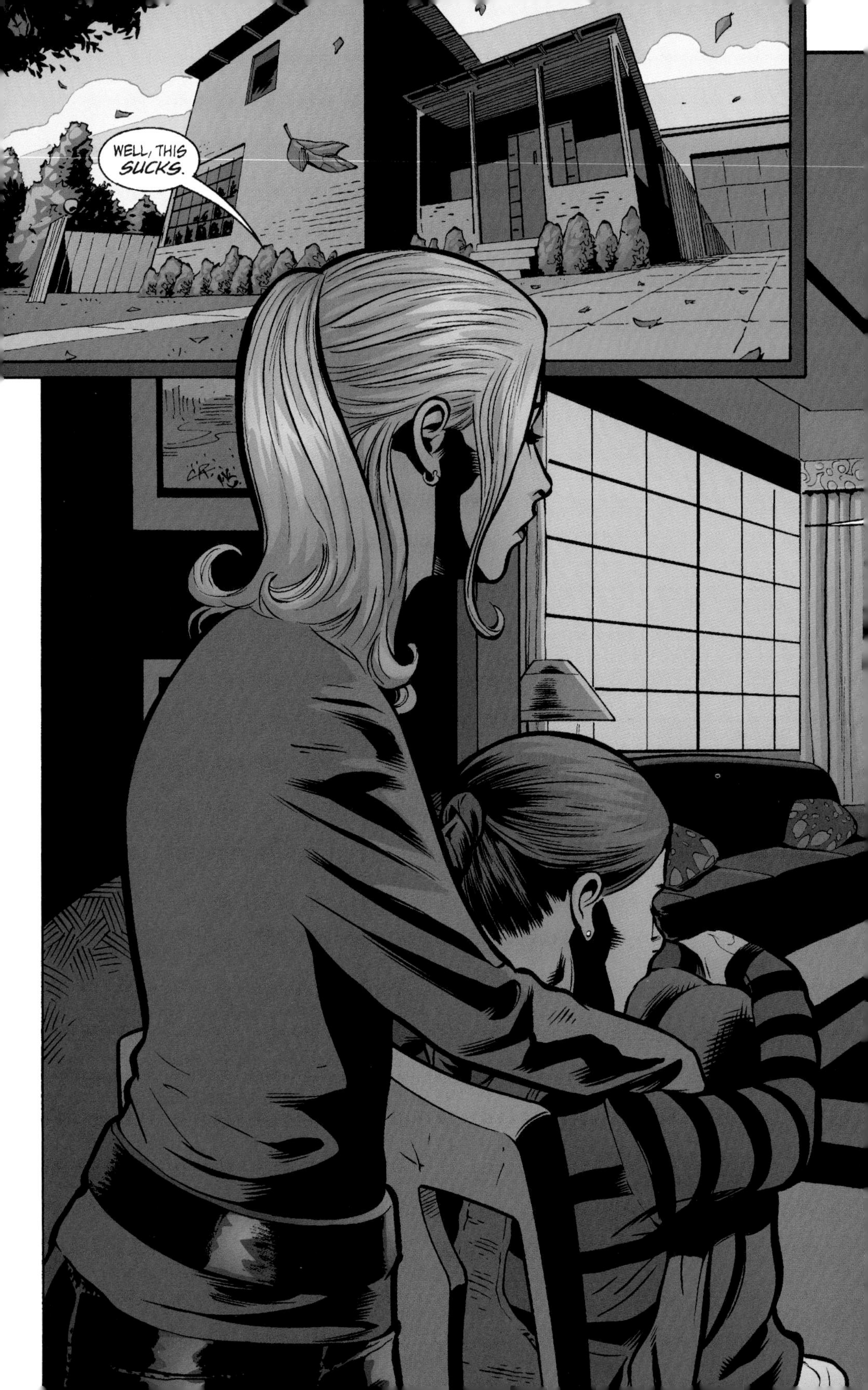
WELL, THIS SUCKS.

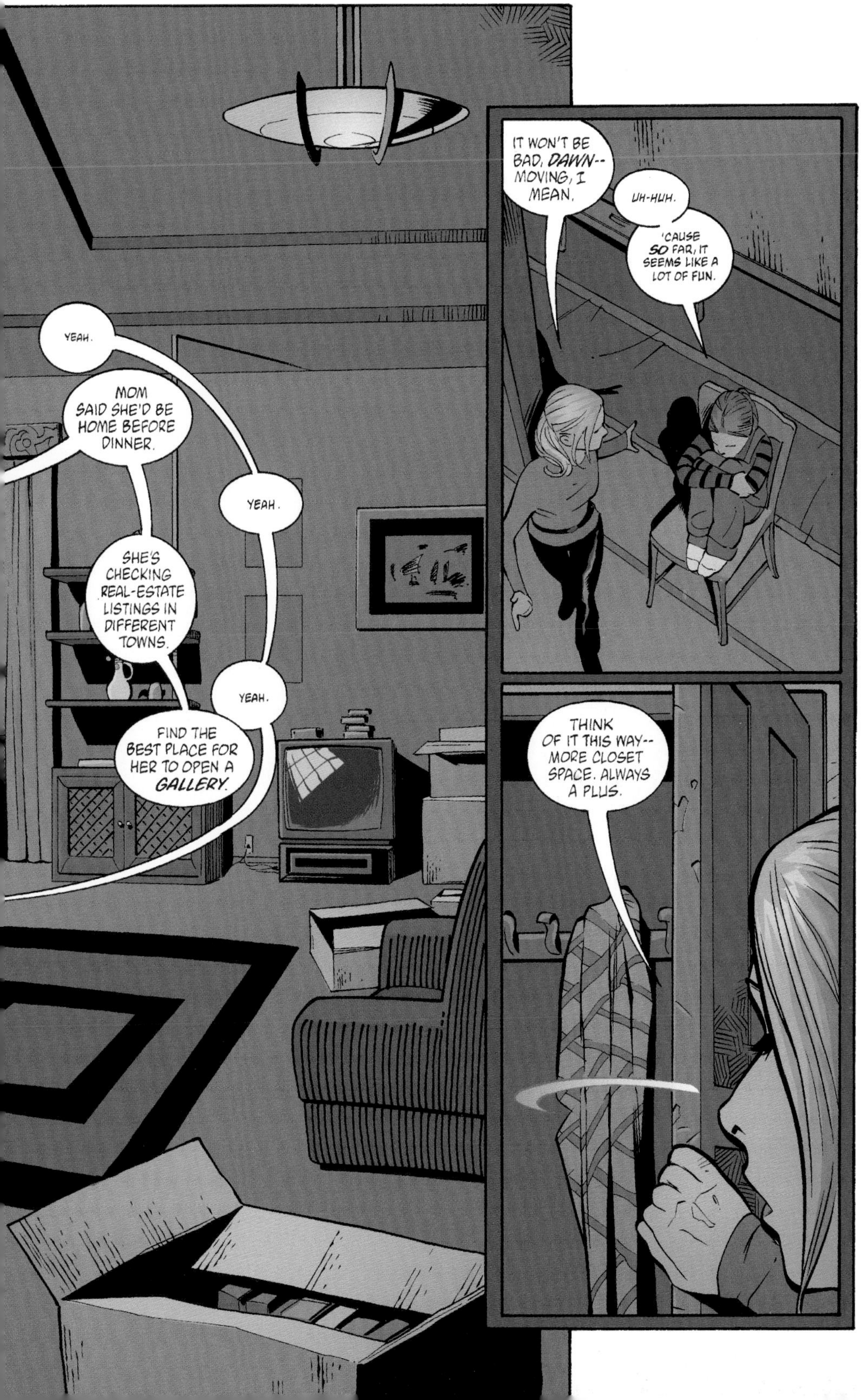

YEAH.
MOM SAID SHE'D BE HOME BEFORE DINNER.
YEAH.
SHE'S CHECKING REAL-ESTATE LISTINGS IN DIFFERENT TOWNS.
YEAH.
FIND THE BEST PLACE FOR HER TO OPEN A GALLERY.
IT WON'T BE BAD, DAWN-- MOVING, I MEAN.
UH-HUH.
'CAUSE SO FAR, IT SEEMS LIKE A LOT OF FUN.
THINK OF IT THIS WAY-- MORE CLOSET SPACE. ALWAYS A PLUS.

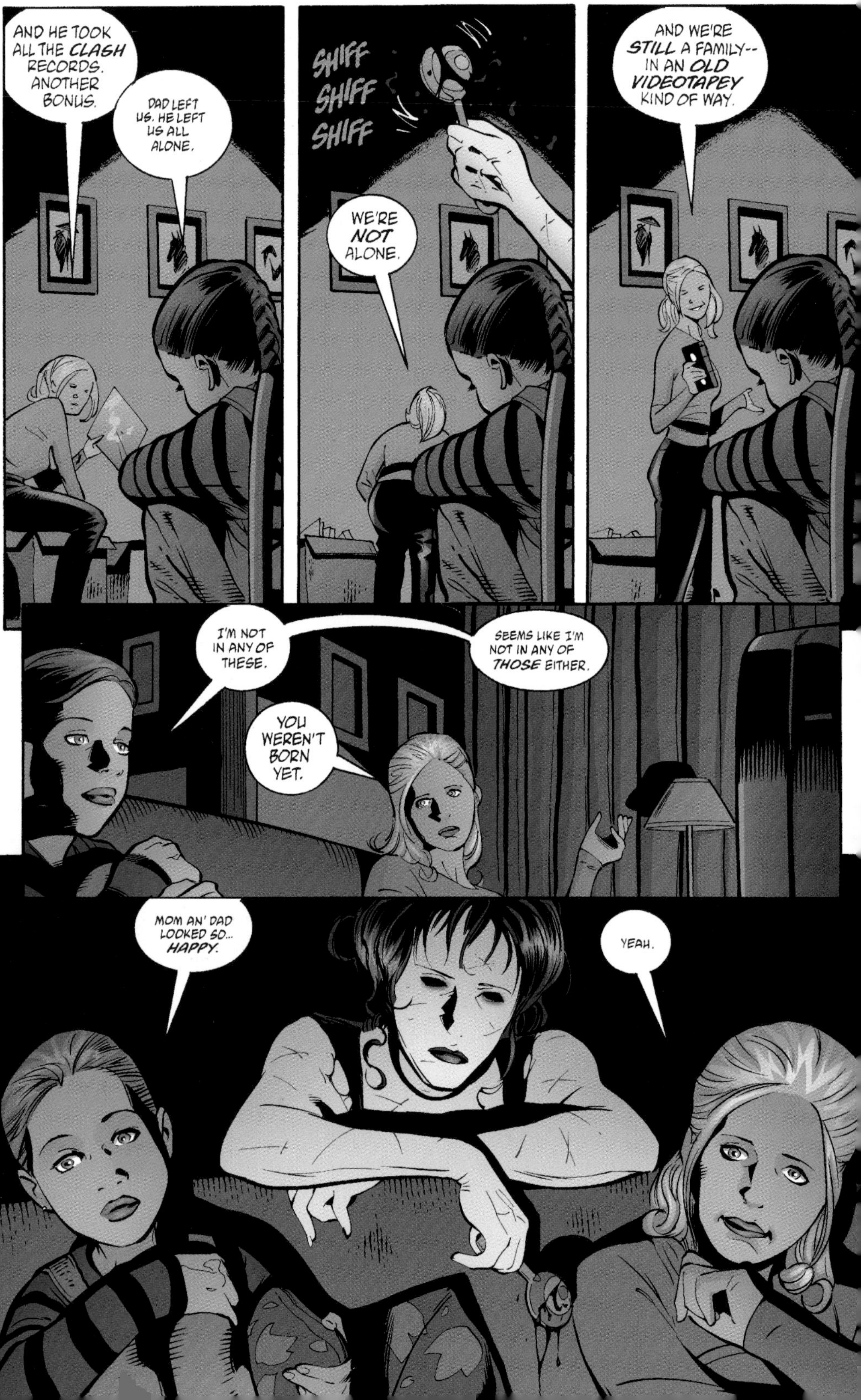
AND HE TOOK ALL THE *CLASH* RECORDS. ANOTHER BONUS.
DAD LEFT US. HE LEFT US ALL ALONE.
SHIFF SHIFF SHIFF
WE'RE *NOT* ALONE.
AND WE'RE *STILL* A FAMILY-- IN AN *OLD VIDEOTAPEY* KIND OF WAY.
I'M NOT IN ANY OF THESE.
SEEMS LIKE I'M NOT IN ANY OF *THOSE* EITHER.
YOU WEREN'T BORN YET.
MOM AN' DAD LOOKED SO... *HAPPY*.
YEAH.

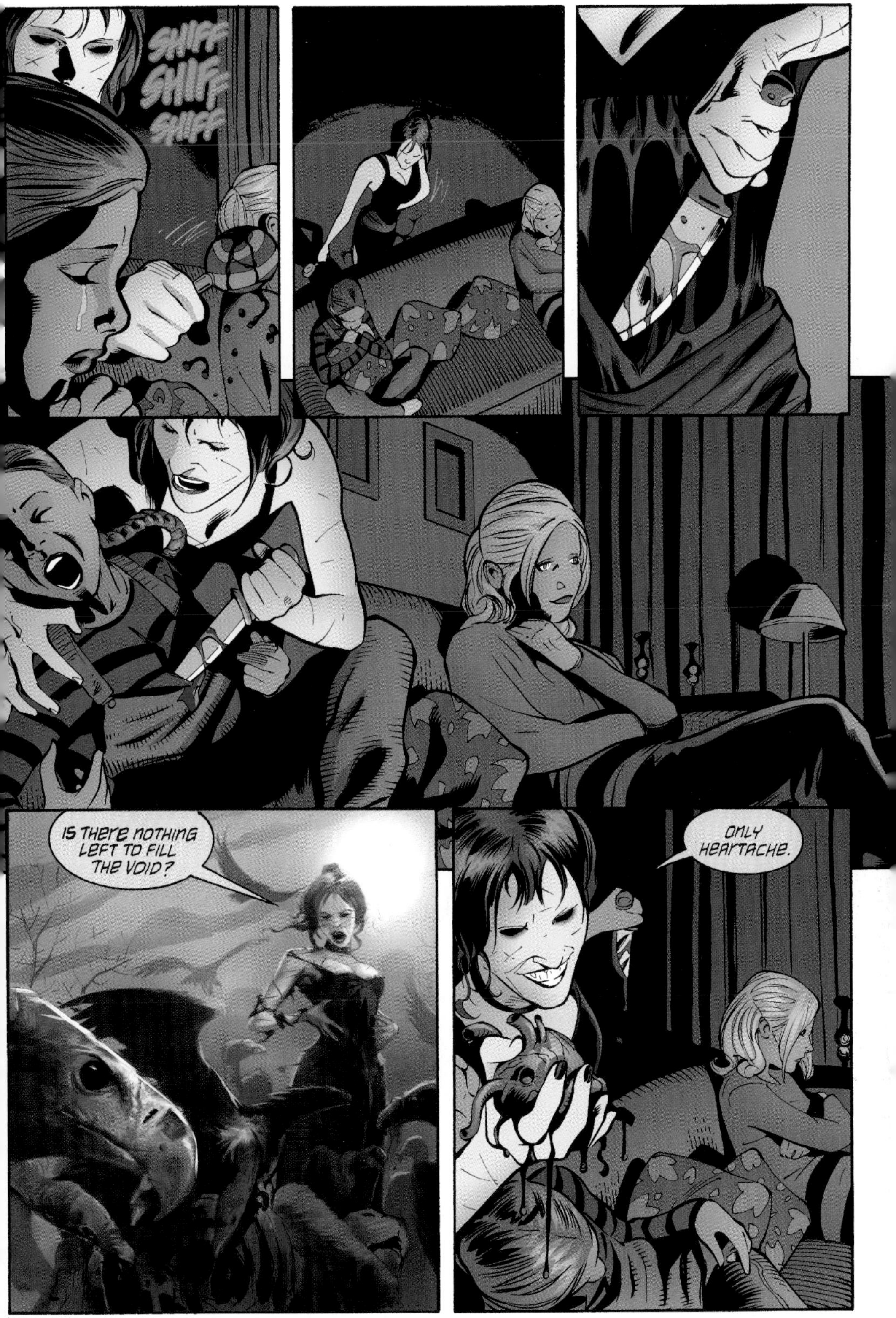
SHIFF
SHIFF
SHIFF
IS THERE NOTHING LEFT TO FILL THE VOID?
ONLY HEARTACHE.

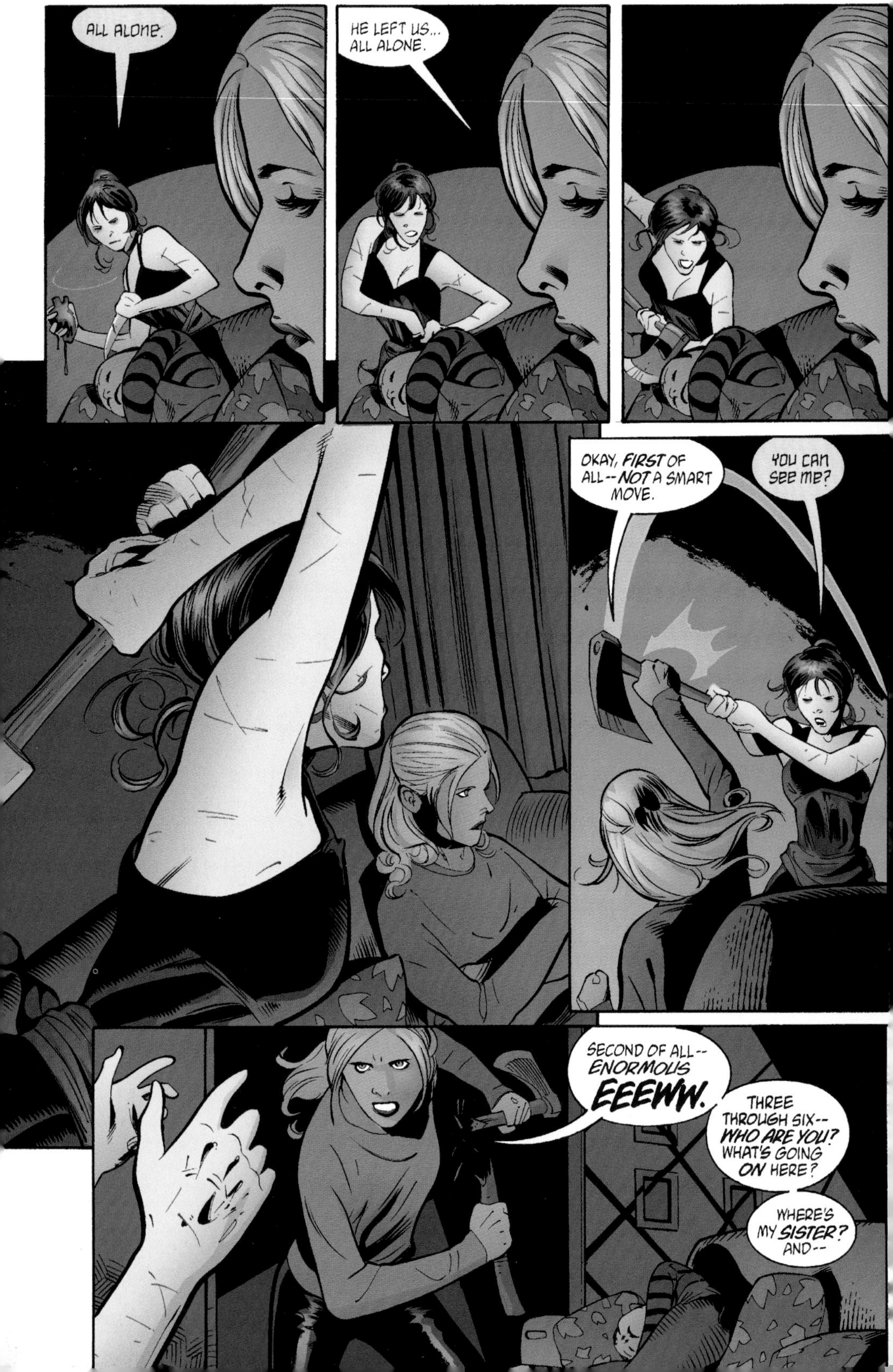
ALL ALONE.
HE LEFT US... ALL ALONE.
OKAY, FIRST OF ALL--NOT A SMART MOVE.
YOU CAN SEE ME?
SECOND OF ALL-- ENORMOUS EEEWW.
THREE THROUGH SIX-- WHO ARE YOU? WHAT'S GOING ON HERE?
WHERE'S MY SISTER? AND--

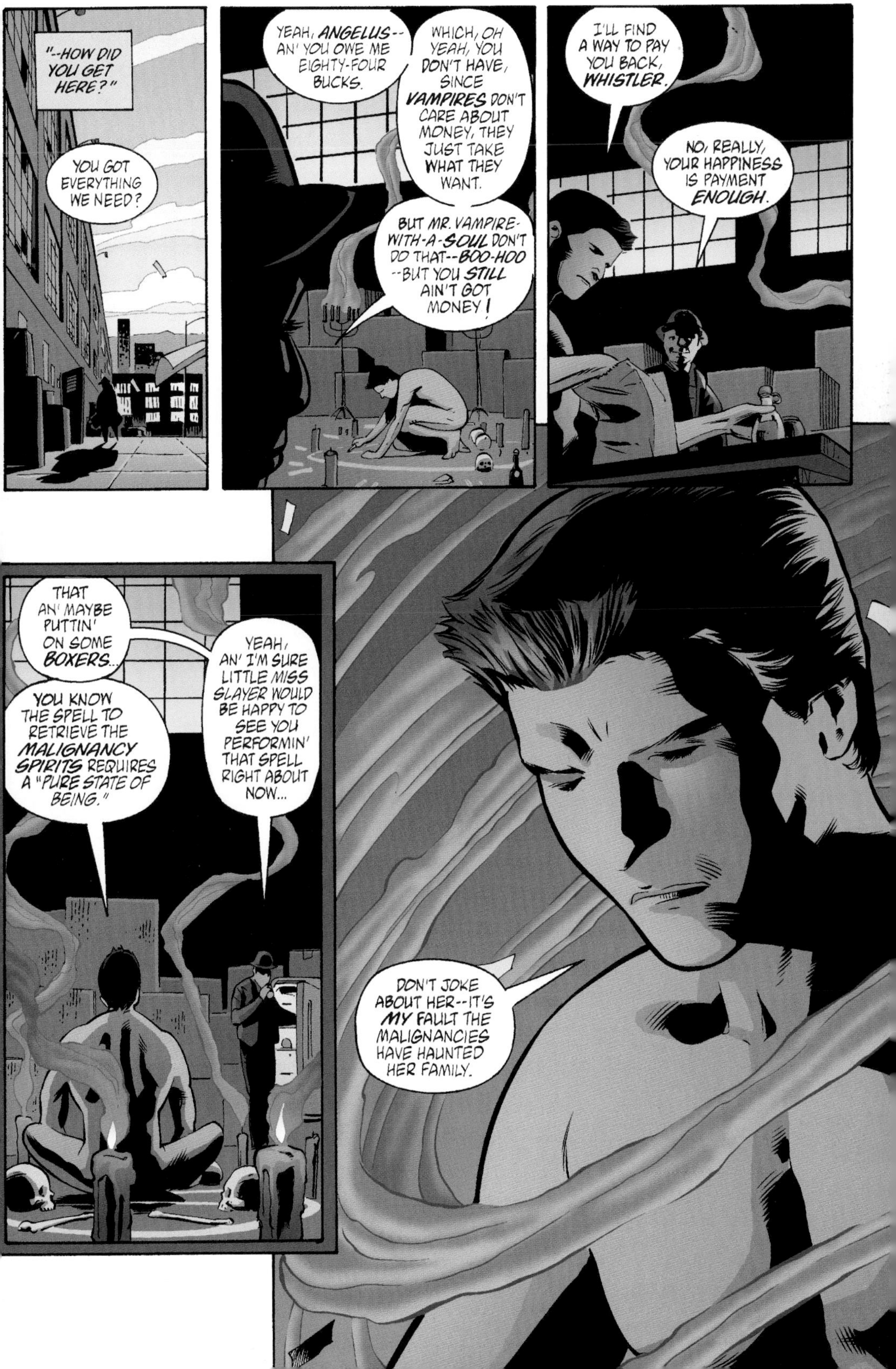
"--HOW DID YOU GET HERE?"
YOU GOT EVERYTHING WE NEED?
YEAH, ANGELUS-- AN' YOU OWE ME EIGHTY-FOUR BUCKS.
WHICH, OH YEAH, YOU DON'T HAVE, SINCE VAMPIRES DON'T CARE ABOUT MONEY, THEY JUST TAKE WHAT THEY WANT.
BUT MR. VAMPIRE-WITH-A-SOUL DON'T DO THAT--BOO-HOO --BUT YOU STILL AIN'T GOT MONEY!
I'LL FIND A WAY TO PAY YOU BACK, WHISTLER.
NO, REALLY, YOUR HAPPINESS IS PAYMENT ENOUGH.
YOU KNOW THE SPELL TO RETRIEVE THE MALIGNANCY SPIRITS REQUIRES A "PURE STATE OF BEING."
THAT AN' MAYBE PUTTIN' ON SOME BOXERS...
YEAH, AN' I'M SURE LITTLE MISS SLAYER WOULD BE HAPPY TO SEE YOU PERFORMIN' THAT SPELL RIGHT ABOUT NOW...
DON'T JOKE ABOUT HER--IT'S MY FAULT THE MALIGNANCIES HAVE HAUNTED HER FAMILY.

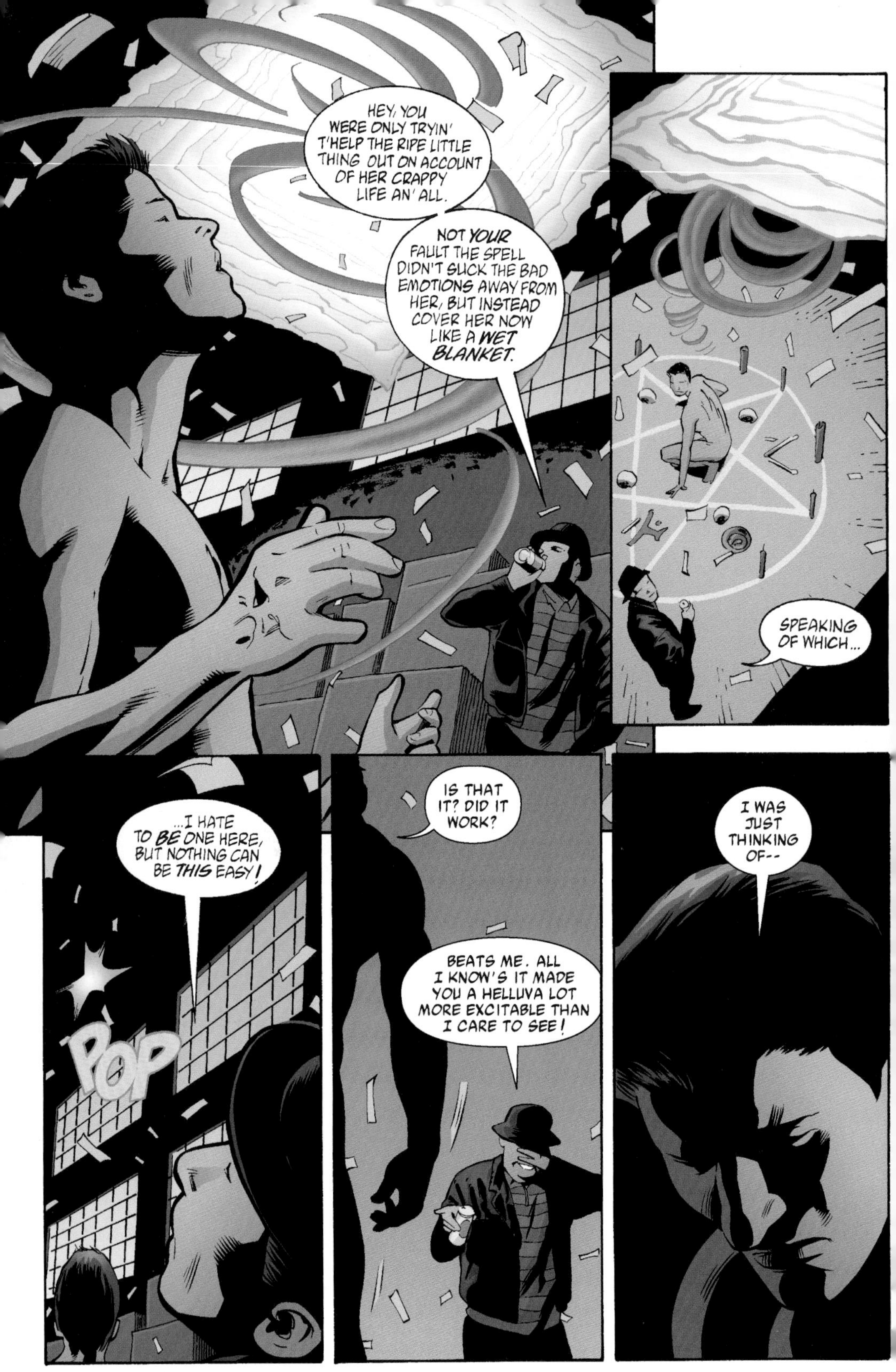
HEY, YOU WERE ONLY TRYIN' T'HELP THE RIPE LITTLE THING OUT ON ACCOUNT OF HER CRAPPY LIFE AN' ALL.
NOT YOUR FAULT THE SPELL DIDN'T SUCK THE BAD EMOTIONS AWAY FROM HER, BUT INSTEAD COVER HER NOW LIKE A WET BLANKET.
SPEAKING OF WHICH...
...I HATE TO BE ONE HERE, BUT NOTHING CAN BE THIS EASY!
POP
IS THAT IT? DID IT WORK?
BEATS ME. ALL I KNOW'S IT MADE YOU A HELLUVA LOT MORE EXCITABLE THAN I CARE TO SEE!
I WAS JUST THINKING OF--

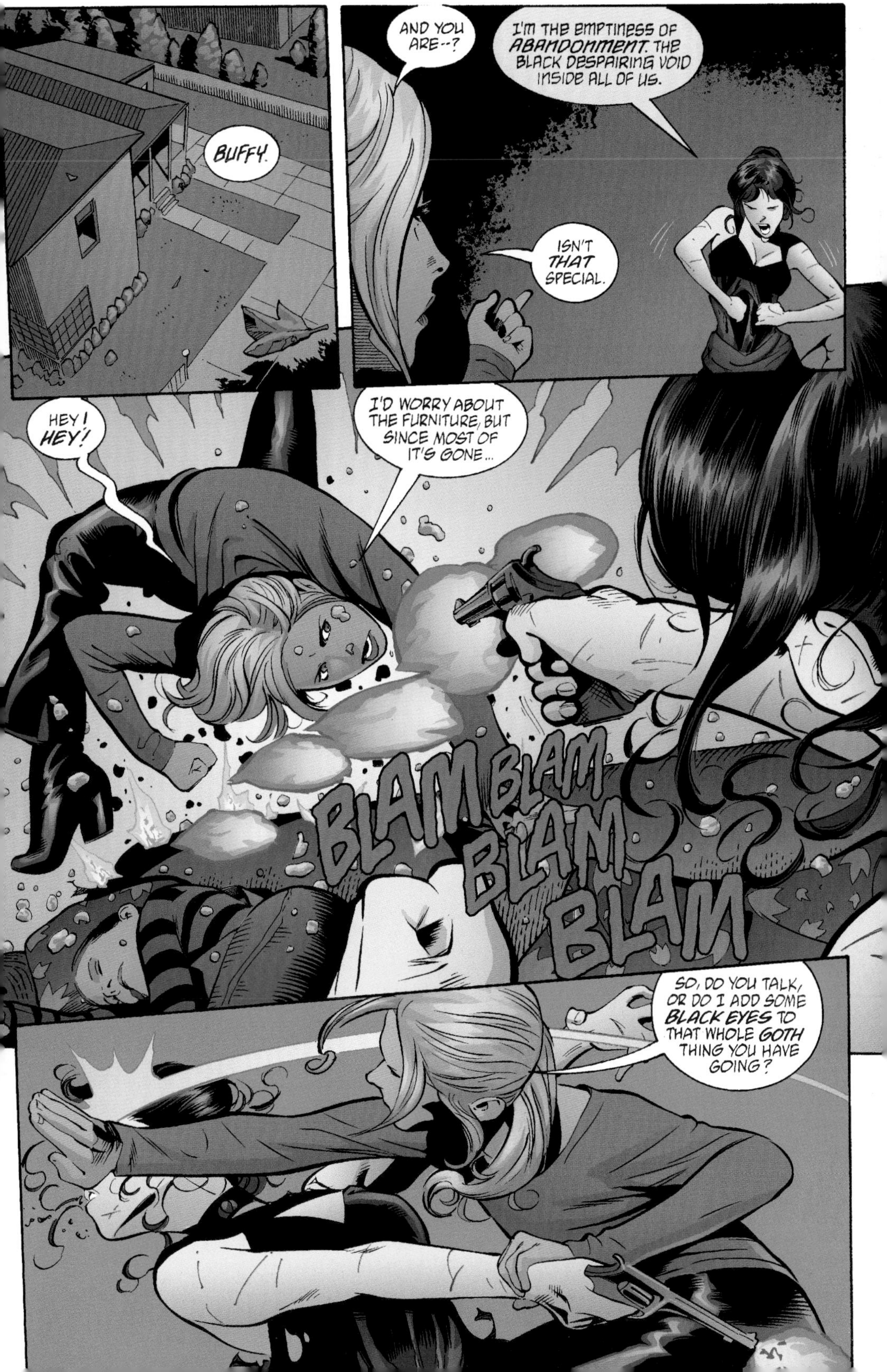
BUFFY.
AND YOU ARE--?
I'M THE EMPTINESS OF ABANDONMENT. THE BLACK DESPAIRING VOID INSIDE ALL OF US.
ISN'T THAT SPECIAL.
HEY! HEY!
I'D WORRY ABOUT THE FURNITURE, BUT SINCE MOST OF IT'S GONE...
BLAM BLAM BLAM BLAM
SO, DO YOU TALK, OR DO I ADD SOME BLACK EYES TO THAT WHOLE GOTH THING YOU HAVE GOING?

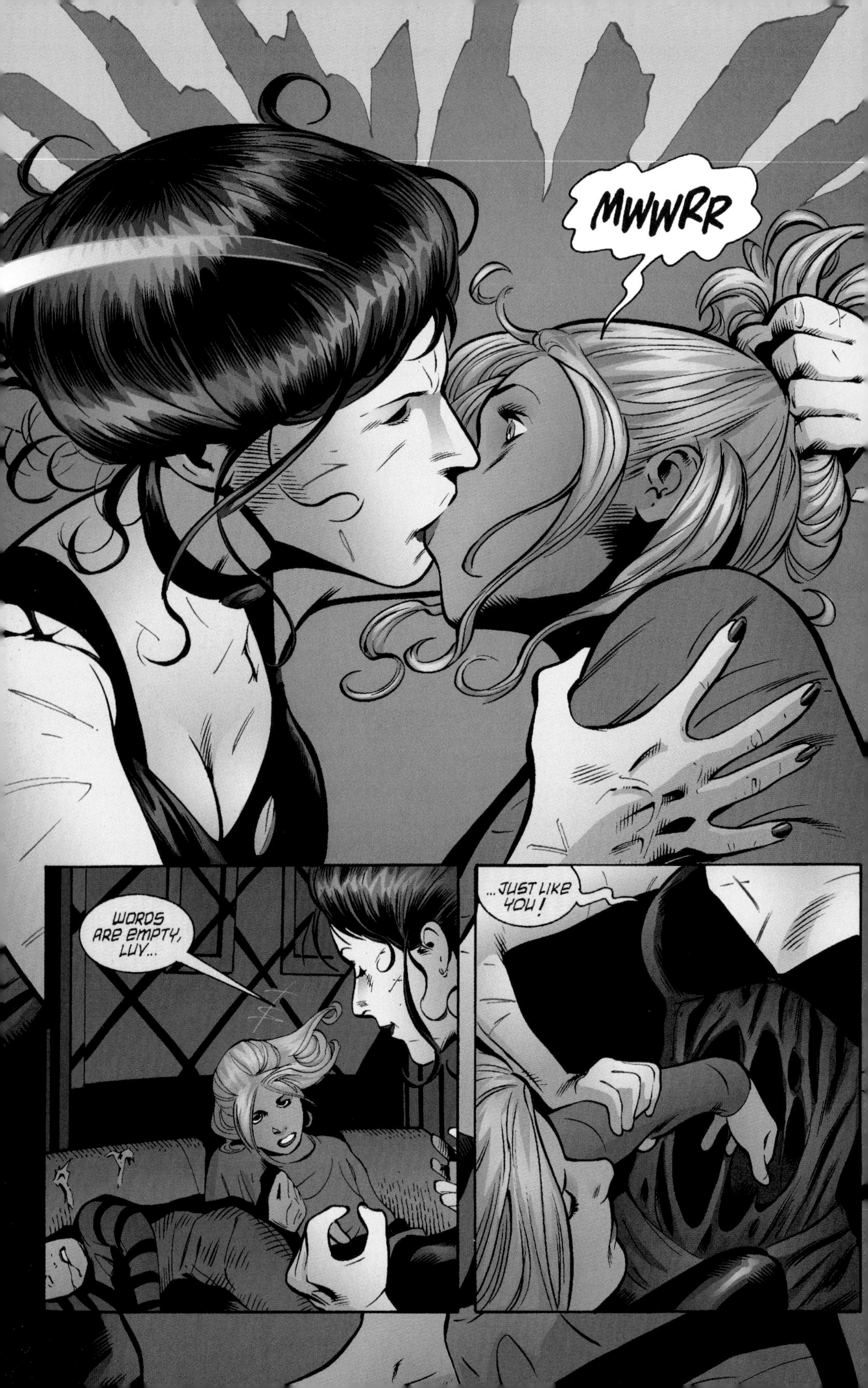
MWWRR
WORDS ARE EMPTY, LUV...
...JUST LIKE YOU!

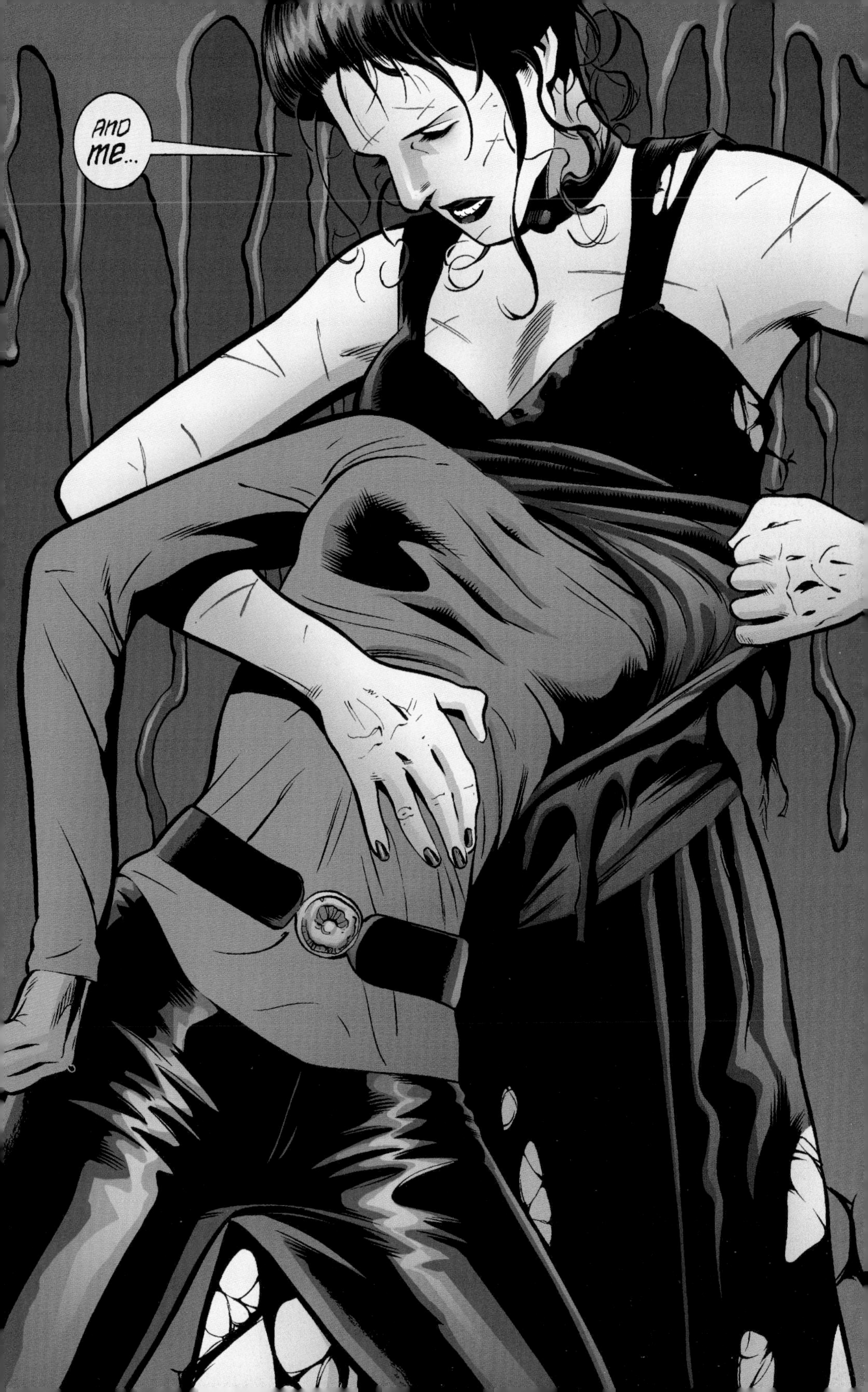
AND ME...

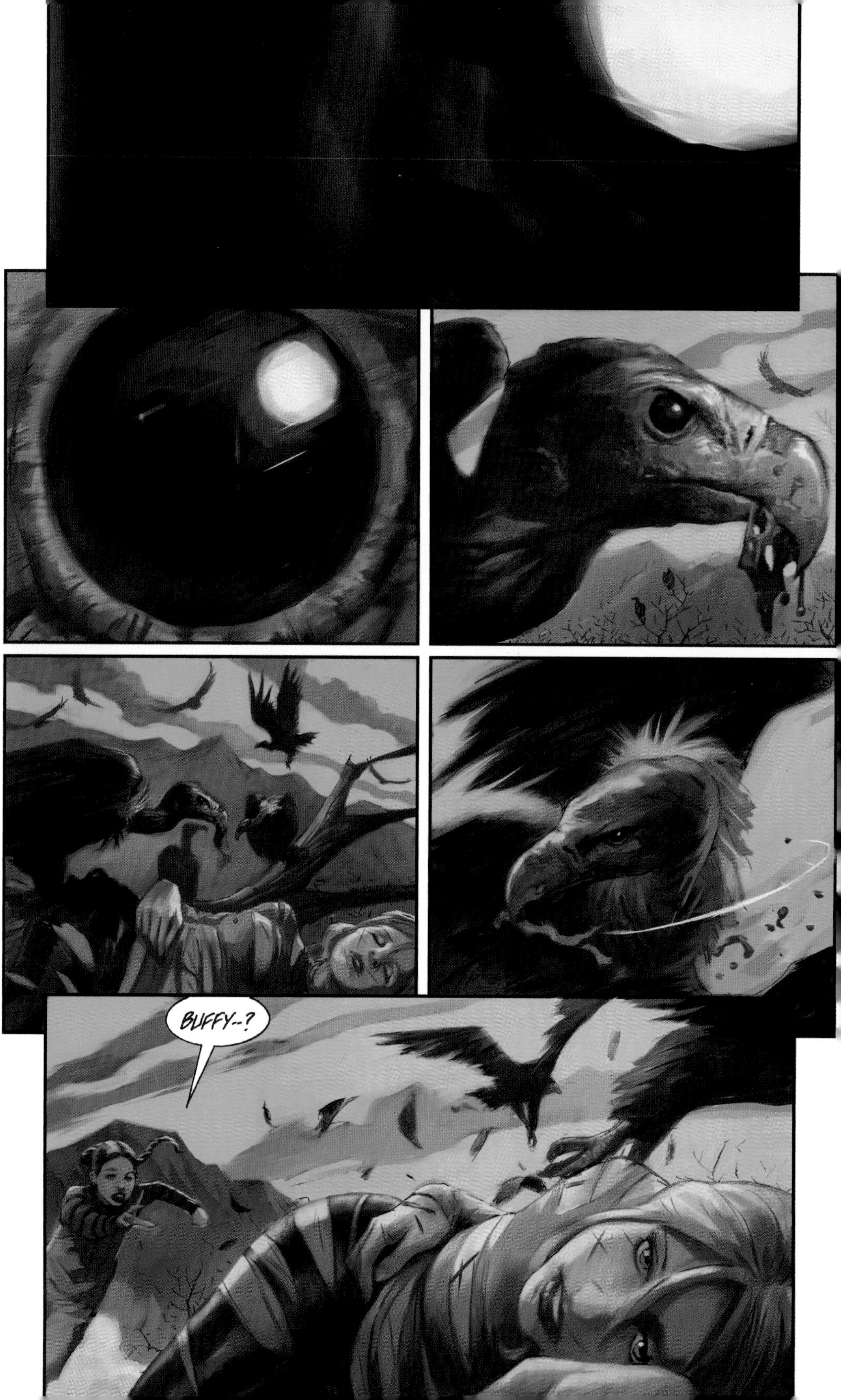
BUFFY--?

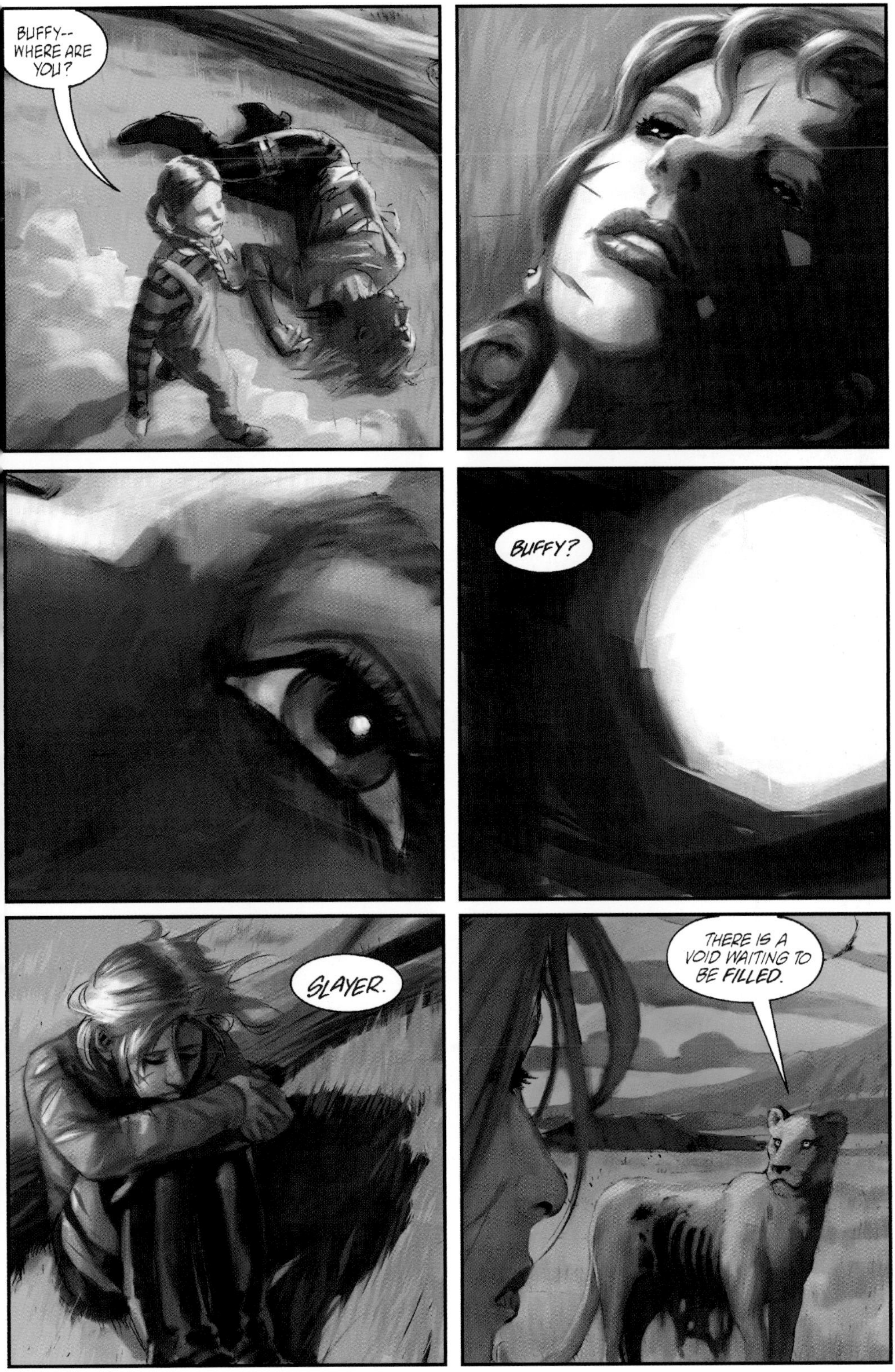
BUFFY-- WHERE ARE YOU?
BUFFY?
SLAYER.
THERE IS A VOID WAITING TO BE FILLED.

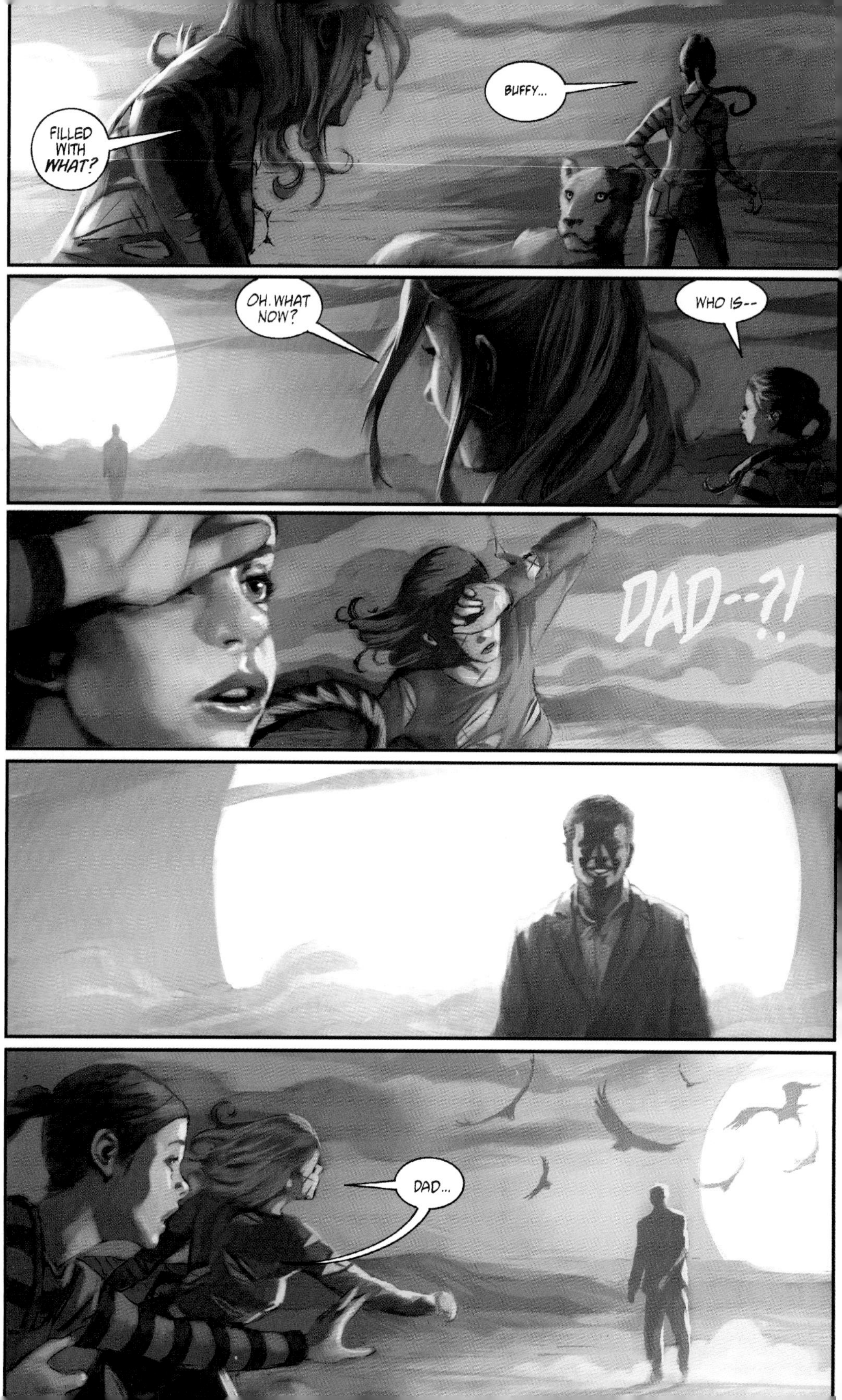
FILLED WITH WHAT?
BUFFY...
OH. WHAT NOW?
WHO IS--
DAD--?!
DAD...

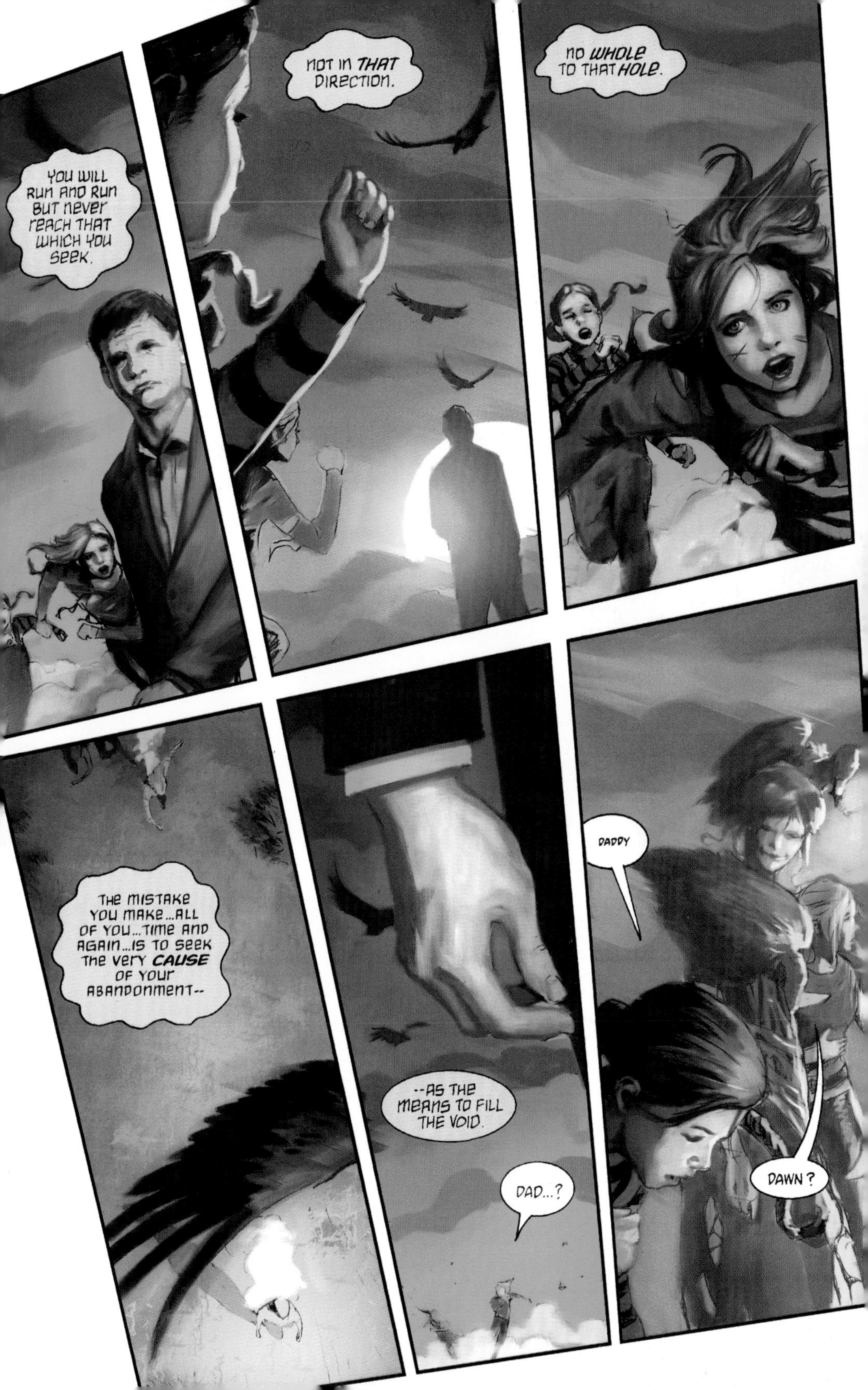
YOU WILL RUN AND RUN BUT NEVER REACH THAT WHICH YOU SEEK.
NOT IN THAT DIRECTION.
NO WHOLE TO THAT HOLE.
THE MISTAKE YOU MAKE...ALL OF YOU...TIME AND AGAIN...IS TO SEEK THE VERY CAUSE OF YOUR ABANDONMENT--
--AS THE MEANS TO FILL THE VOID.
DAD...?
DADDY
DAWN?

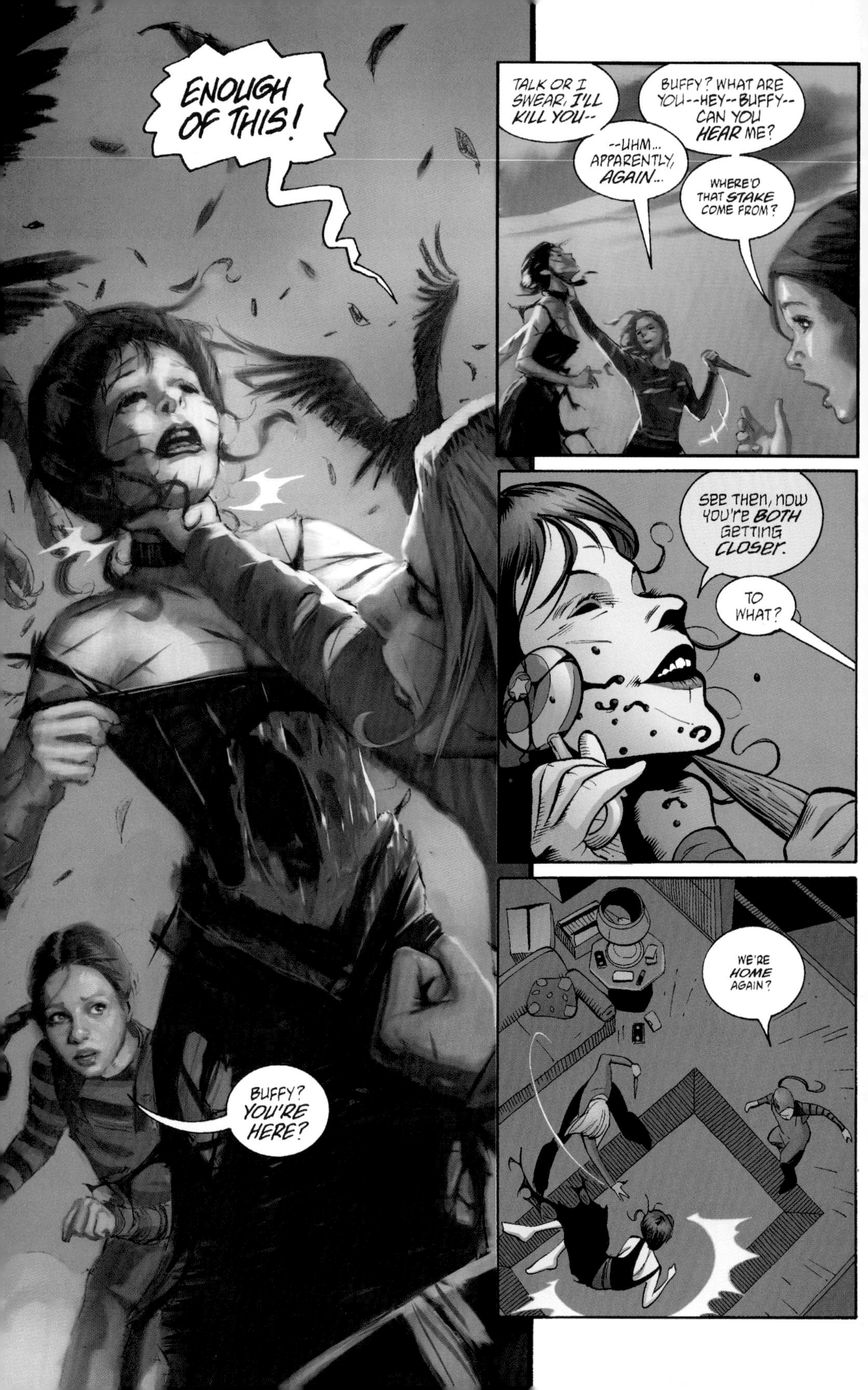
ENOUGH OF THIS!
TALK OR I SWEAR, I'LL KILL YOU--
--UHM... APPARENTLY, AGAIN...
BUFFY? WHAT ARE YOU--HEY--BUFFY--CAN YOU HEAR ME?
WHERE'D THAT STAKE COME FROM?
SEE THEN, NOW YOU'RE BOTH GETTING CLOSER.
TO WHAT?
BUFFY? YOU'RE HERE?
WE'RE HOME AGAIN?

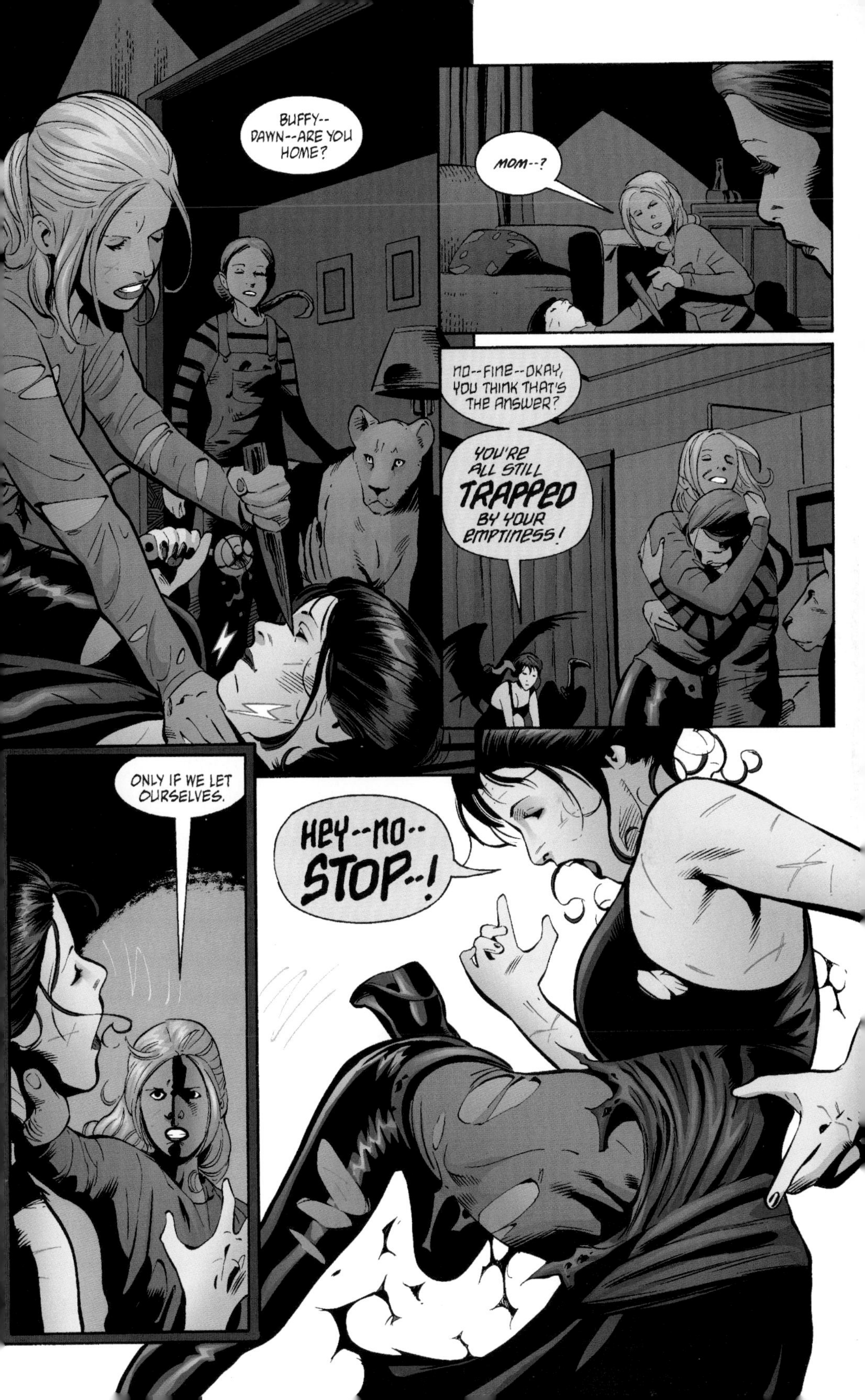
BUFFY--
DAWN--ARE YOU
HOME?
MOM--?
NO--FINE--OKAY,
YOU THINK THAT'S
THE ANSWER?
YOU'RE
ALL STILL
TRAPPED
BY YOUR
EMPTINESS!
ONLY IF WE LET
OURSELVES.
HEY--NO--
STOP--!

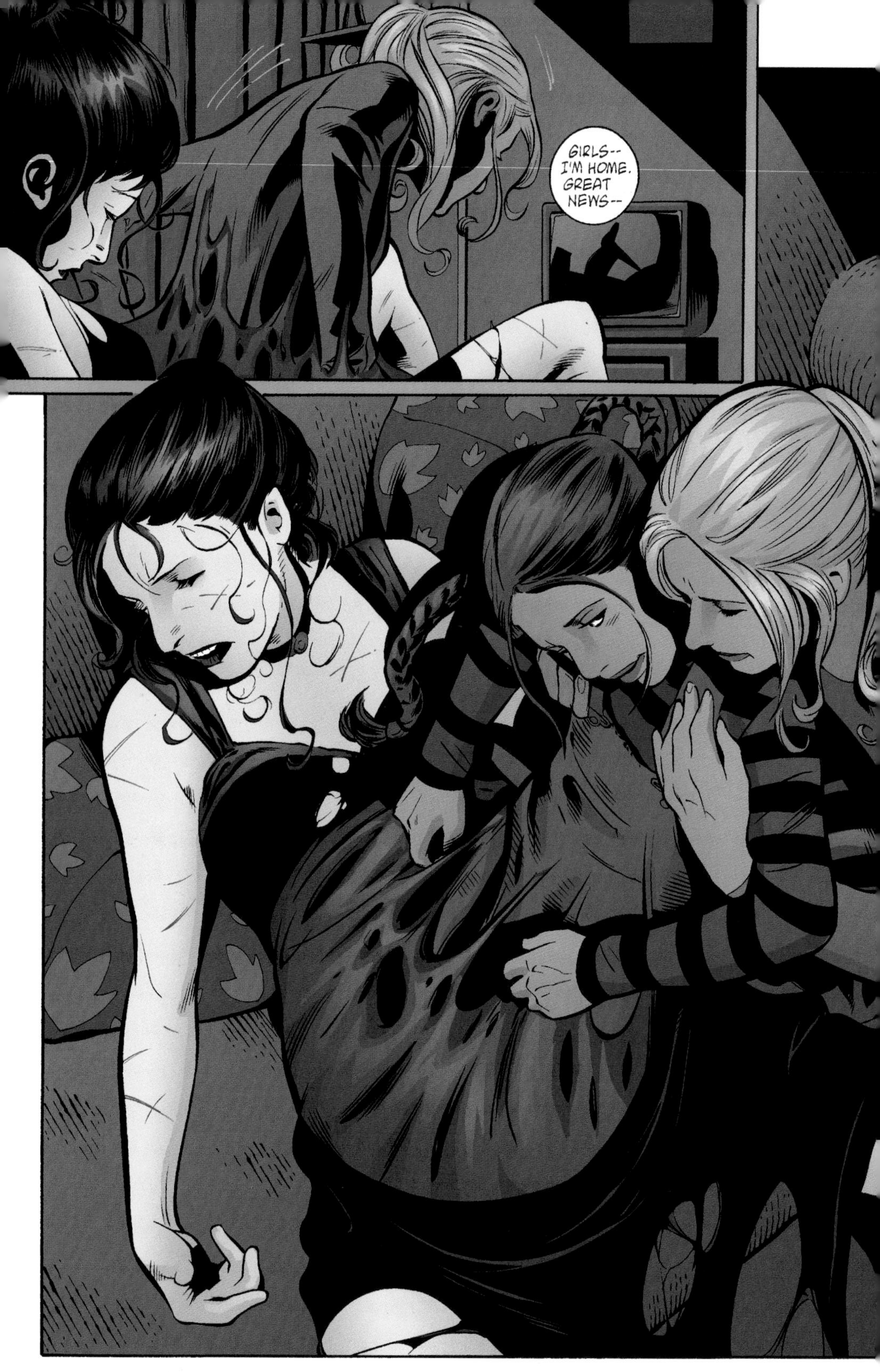
GIRLS-- I'M HOME. GREAT NEWS--

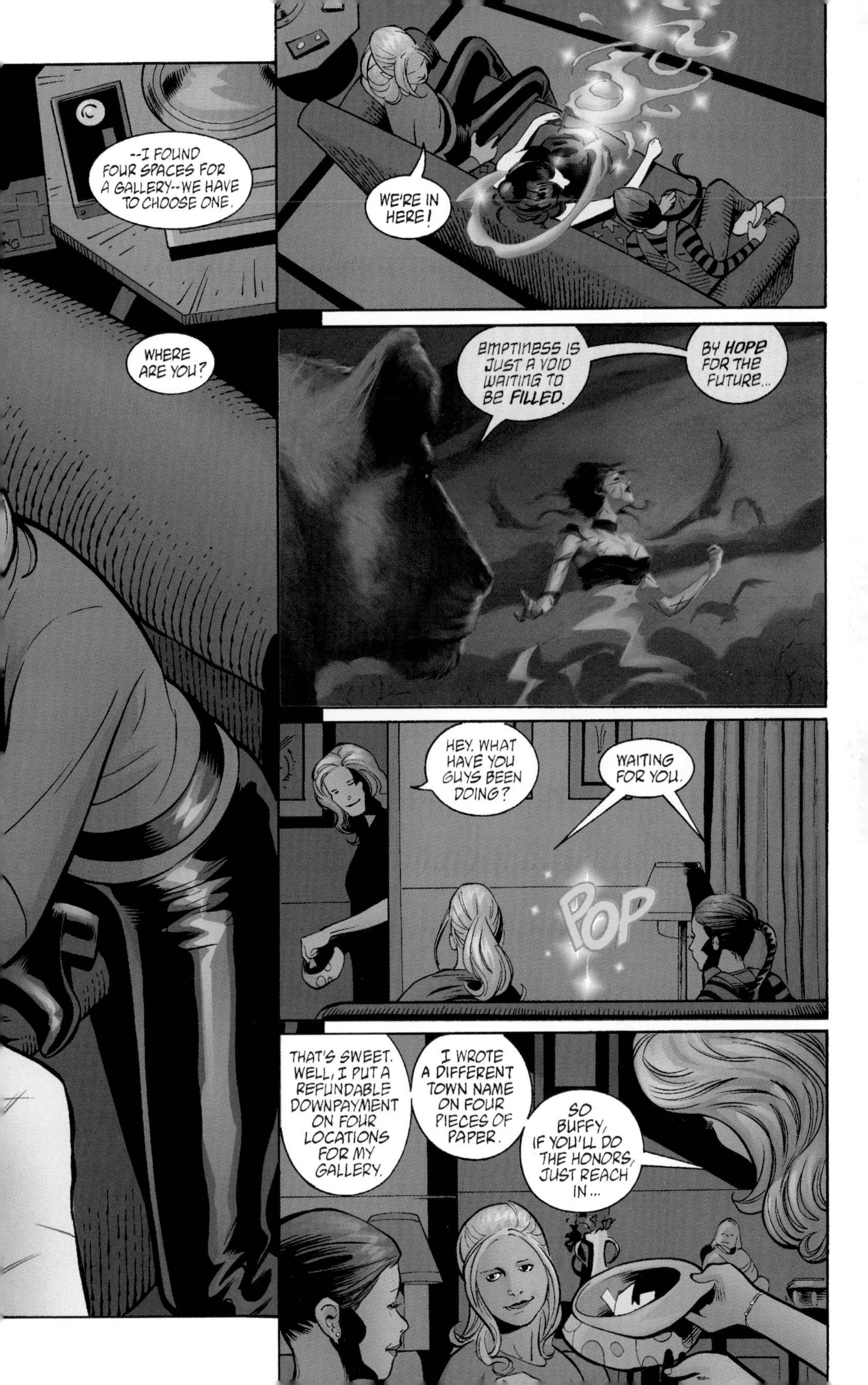
--I FOUND FOUR SPACES FOR A GALLERY--WE HAVE TO CHOOSE ONE.
WE'RE IN HERE!
WHERE ARE YOU?
EMPTINESS IS JUST A VOID WAITING TO BE FILLED.
BY HOPE FOR THE FUTURE...
HEY. WHAT HAVE YOU GUYS BEEN DOING?
WAITING FOR YOU.
POP
THAT'S SWEET. WELL, I PUT A REFUNDABLE DOWNPAYMENT ON FOUR LOCATIONS FOR MY GALLERY.
I WROTE A DIFFERENT TOWN NAME ON FOUR PIECES OF PAPER.
SO BUFFY, IF YOU'LL DO THE HONORS, JUST REACH IN...

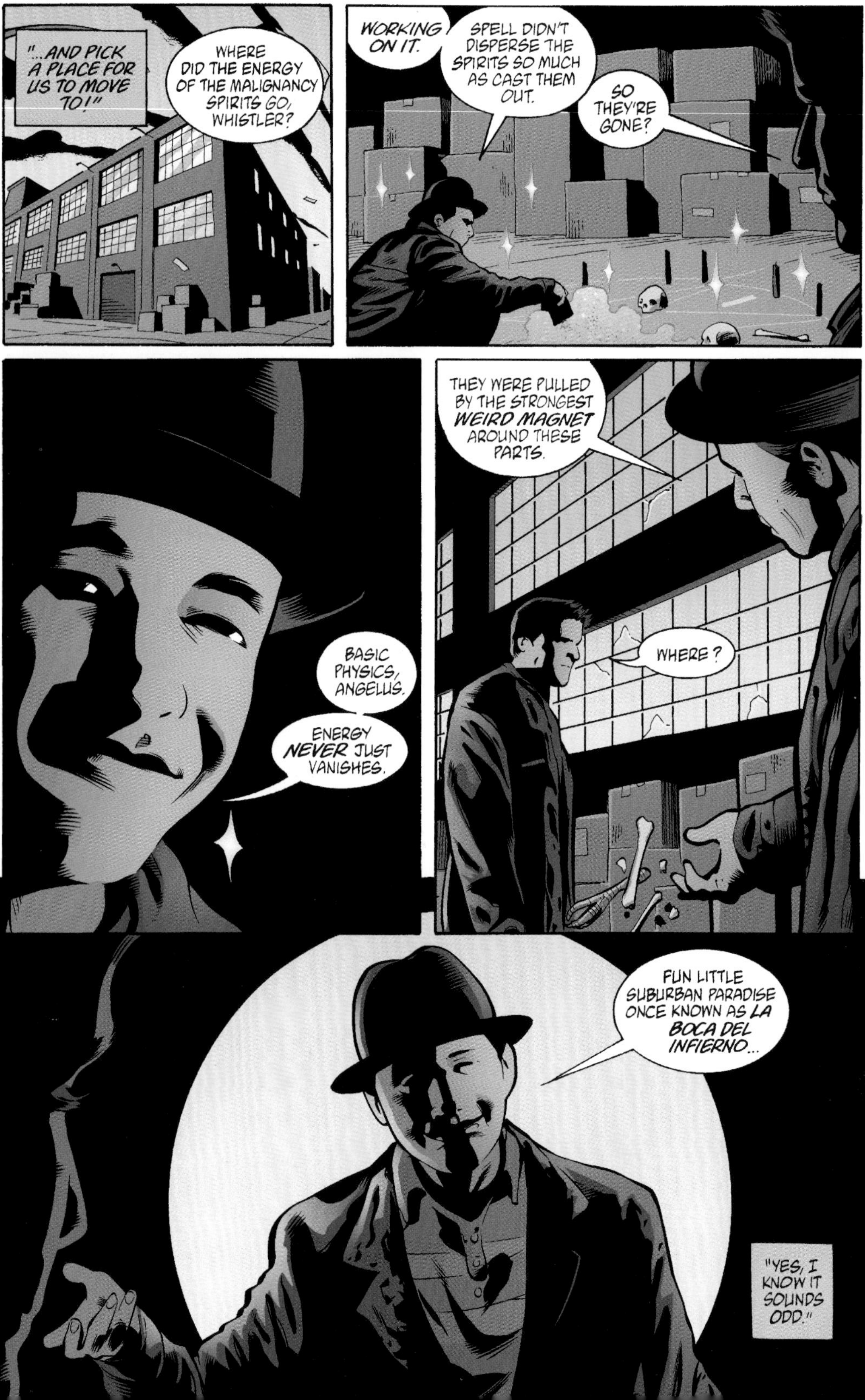
"...AND PICK A PLACE FOR US TO MOVE TO!"
WHERE DID THE ENERGY OF THE MALIGNANCY SPIRITS GO, WHISTLER?
WORKING ON IT.
SPELL DIDN'T DISPERSE THE SPIRITS SO MUCH AS CAST THEM OUT.
SO THEY'RE GONE?
BASIC PHYSICS, ANGELUS.
ENERGY NEVER JUST VANISHES.
THEY WERE PULLED BY THE STRONGEST WEIRD MAGNET AROUND THESE PARTS.
WHERE?
FUN LITTLE SUBURBAN PARADISE ONCE KNOWN AS LA BOCA DEL INFIERNO...
"YES, I KNOW IT SOUNDS ODD."

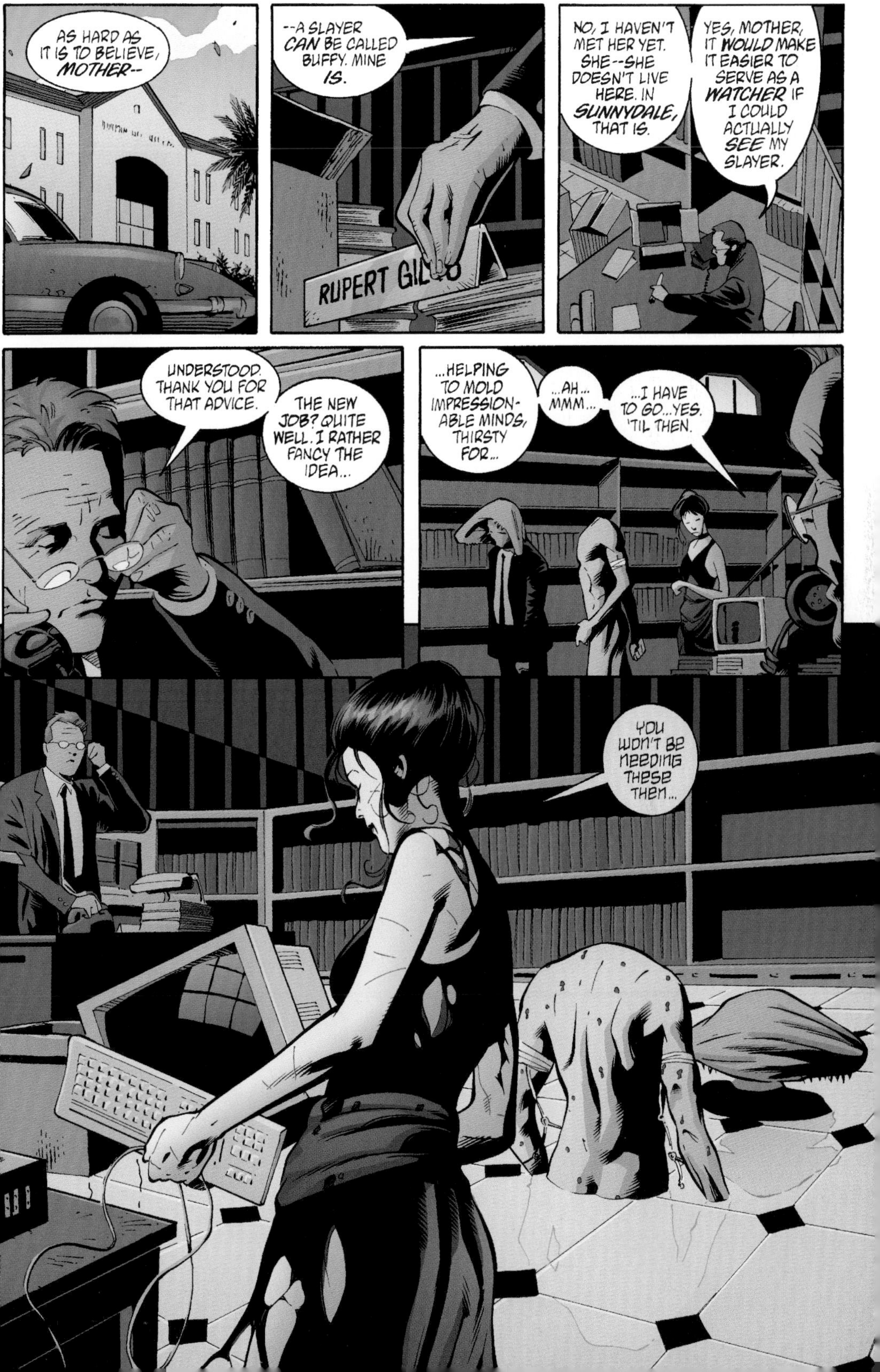

AS HARD AS IT IS TO BELIEVE, MOTHER--
--A SLAYER CAN BE CALLED BUFFY. MINE IS.
RUPERT GILES
NO, I HAVEN'T MET HER YET. SHE--SHE DOESN'T LIVE HERE. IN SUNNYDALE, THAT IS.
YES, MOTHER, IT WOULD MAKE IT EASIER TO SERVE AS A WATCHER IF I COULD ACTUALLY SEE MY SLAYER.
UNDERSTOOD. THANK YOU FOR THAT ADVICE.
THE NEW JOB? QUITE WELL. I RATHER FANCY THE IDEA...
...HELPING TO MOLD IMPRESSION-ABLE MINDS, THIRSTY FOR...
...AH... MMM...
...I HAVE TO GO...YES. 'TIL THEN.
YOU WON'T BE NEEDING THESE THEN...

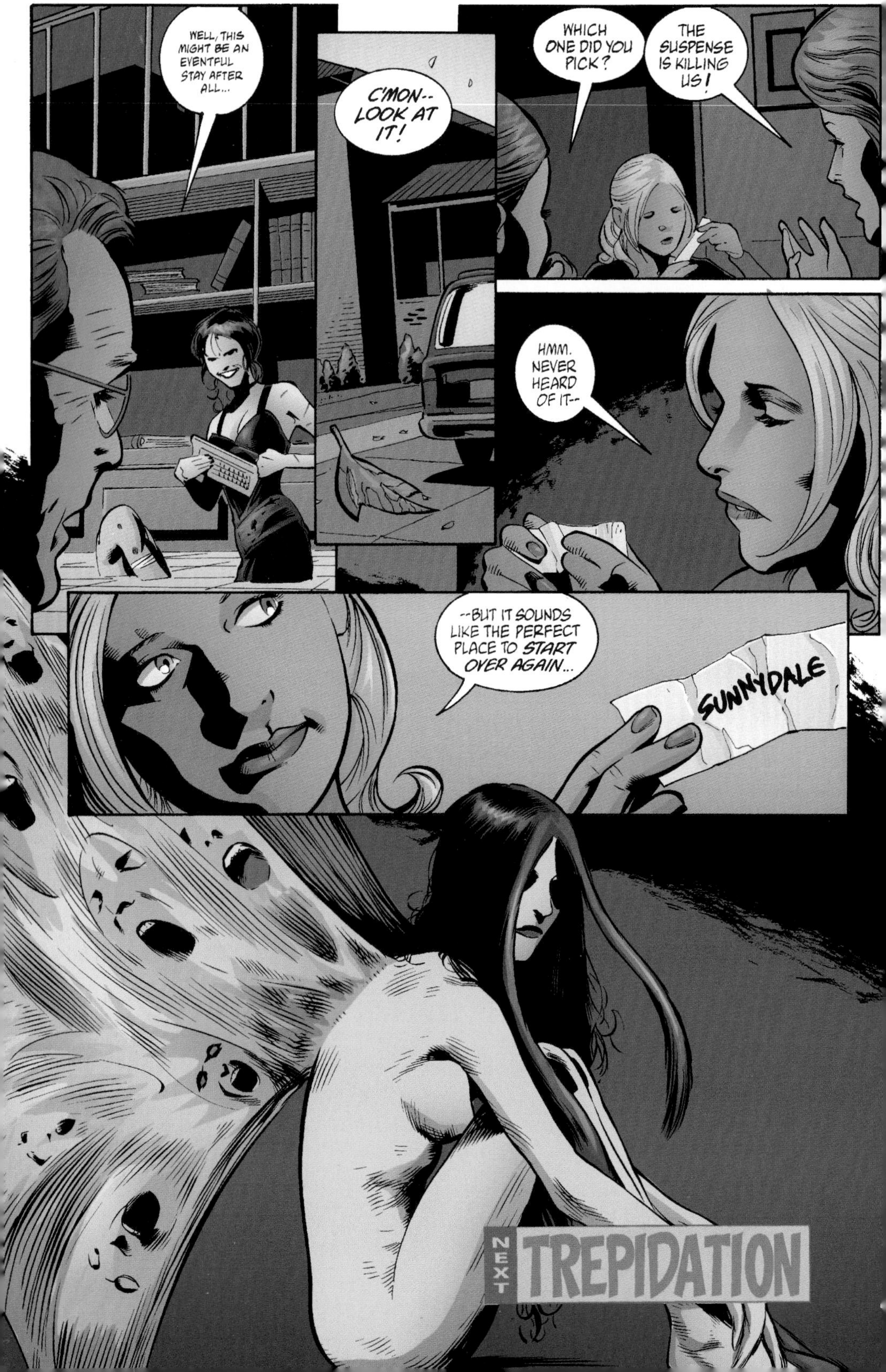
WELL, THIS MIGHT BE AN EVENTFUL STAY AFTER ALL...
C'MON-- LOOK AT IT!
WHICH ONE DID YOU PICK?
THE SUSPENSE IS KILLING US!
HMM. NEVER HEARD OF IT--
--BUT IT SOUNDS LIKE THE PERFECT PLACE TO START OVER AGAIN...
SUNNYDALE
NEXT
TREPIDATION

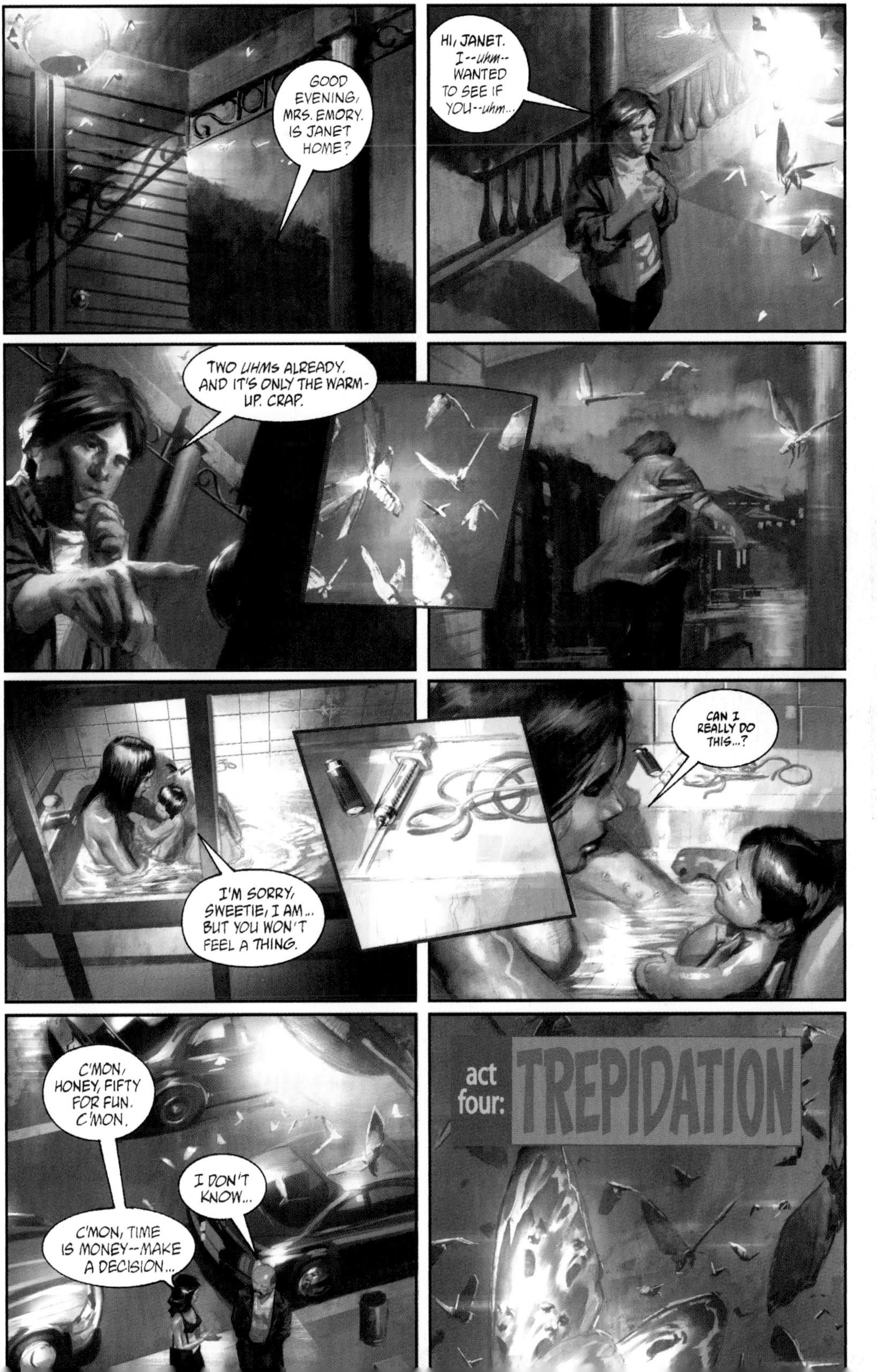
GOOD EVENING, MRS. EMORY. IS JANET HOME?
HI, JANET. I--uhm--WANTED TO SEE IF YOU--uhm...
TWO UHMS ALREADY. AND IT'S ONLY THE WARM-UP. CRAP.
I'M SORRY, SWEETIE, I AM... BUT YOU WON'T FEEL A THING.
CAN I REALLY DO THIS...?
C'MON, HONEY, FIFTY FOR FUN. C'MON.
I DON'T KNOW...
C'MON, TIME IS MONEY--MAKE A DECISION...
act four: TREPIDATION

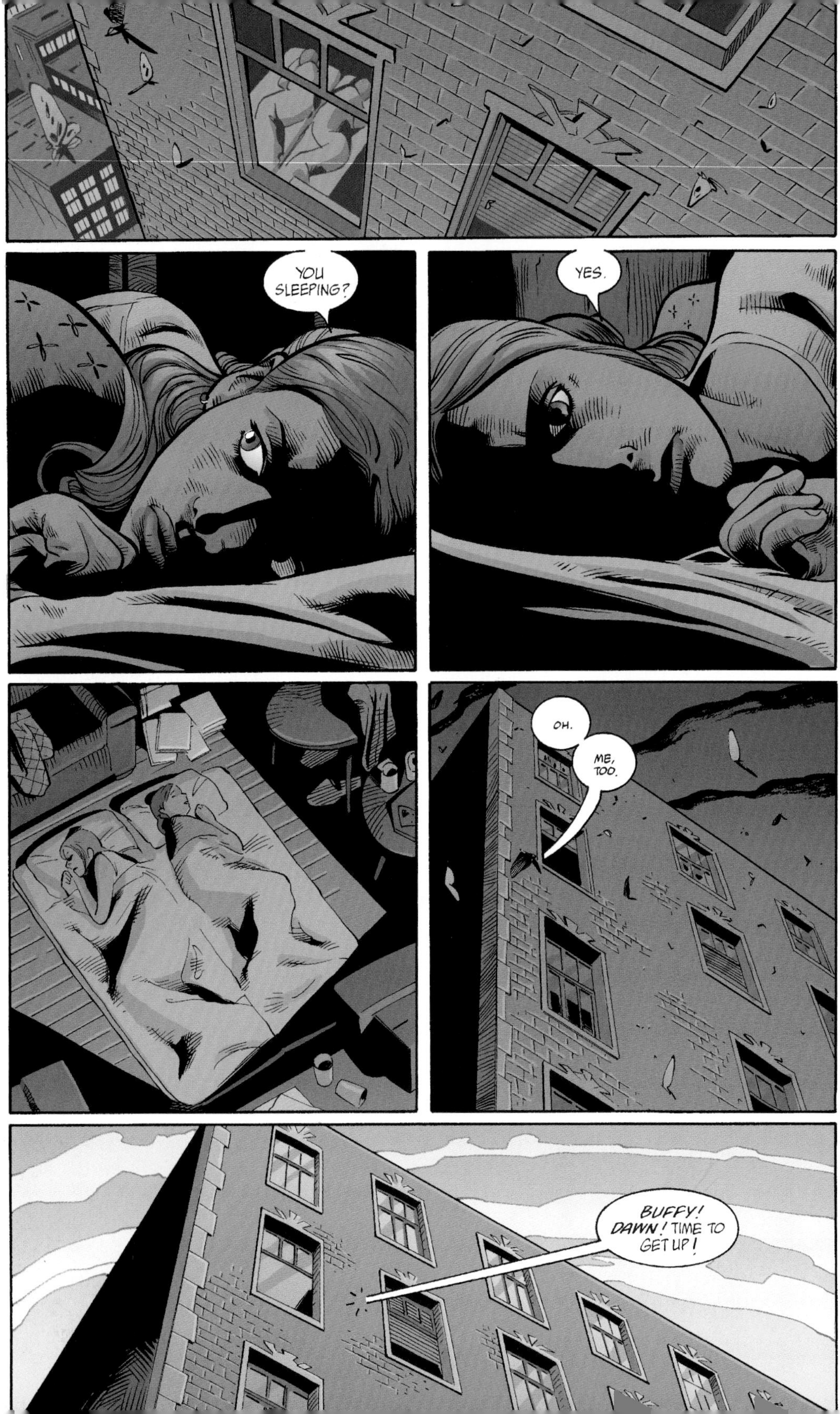
YOU SLEEPING?
YES.
OH.
ME, TOO.
BUFFY! DAWN! TIME TO GET UP!

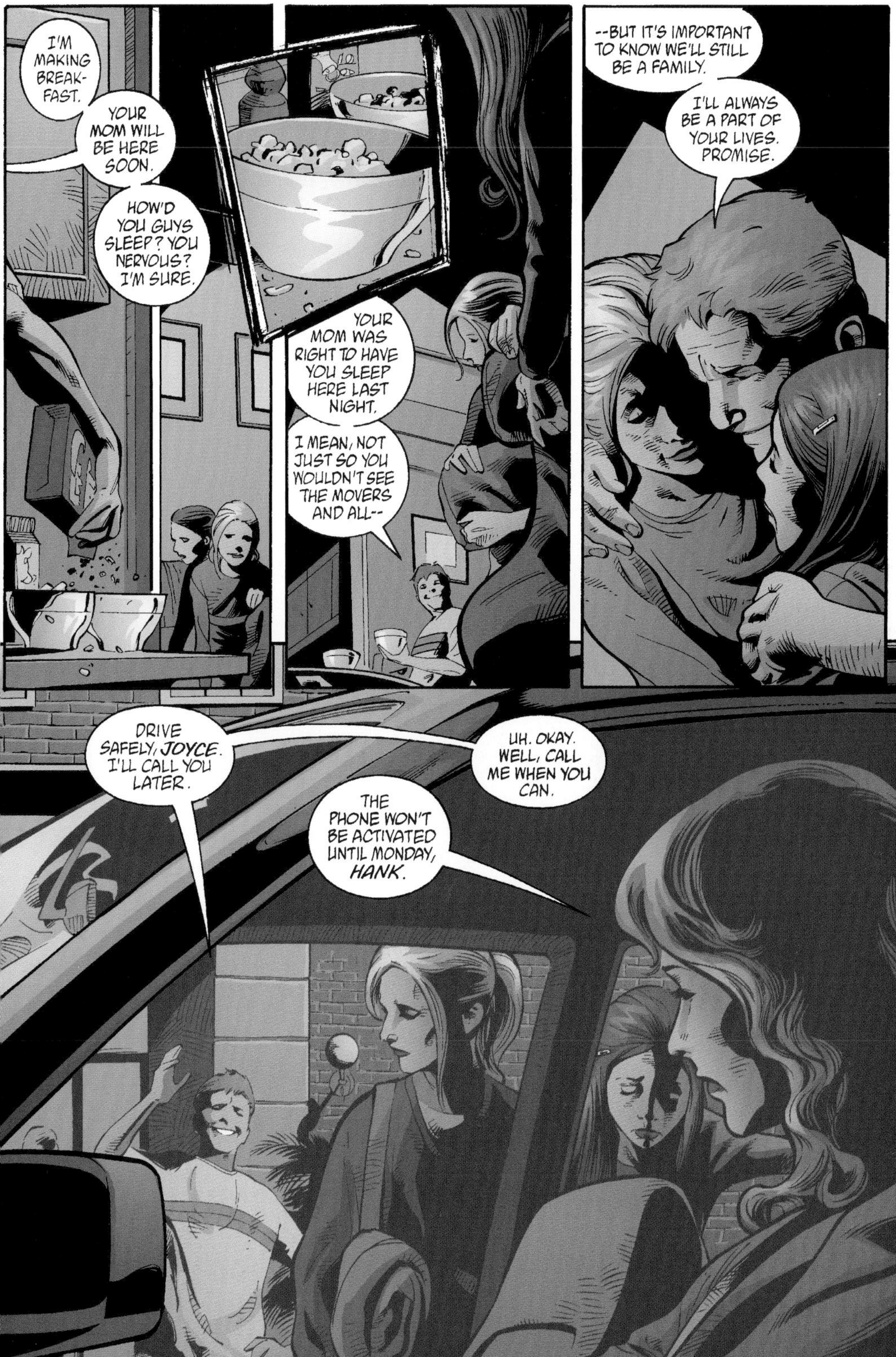
I'M MAKING BREAK-FAST.
YOUR MOM WILL BE HERE SOON.
HOW'D YOU GUYS SLEEP? YOU NERVOUS? I'M SURE.
YOUR MOM WAS RIGHT TO HAVE YOU SLEEP HERE LAST NIGHT.
I MEAN, NOT JUST SO YOU WOULDN'T SEE THE MOVERS AND ALL--
--BUT IT'S IMPORTANT TO KNOW WE'LL STILL BE A FAMILY.
I'LL ALWAYS BE A PART OF YOUR LIVES. PROMISE.
DRIVE SAFELY, JOYCE. I'LL CALL YOU LATER.
UH. OKAY. WELL, CALL ME WHEN YOU CAN.
THE PHONE WON'T BE ACTIVATED UNTIL MONDAY, HANK.

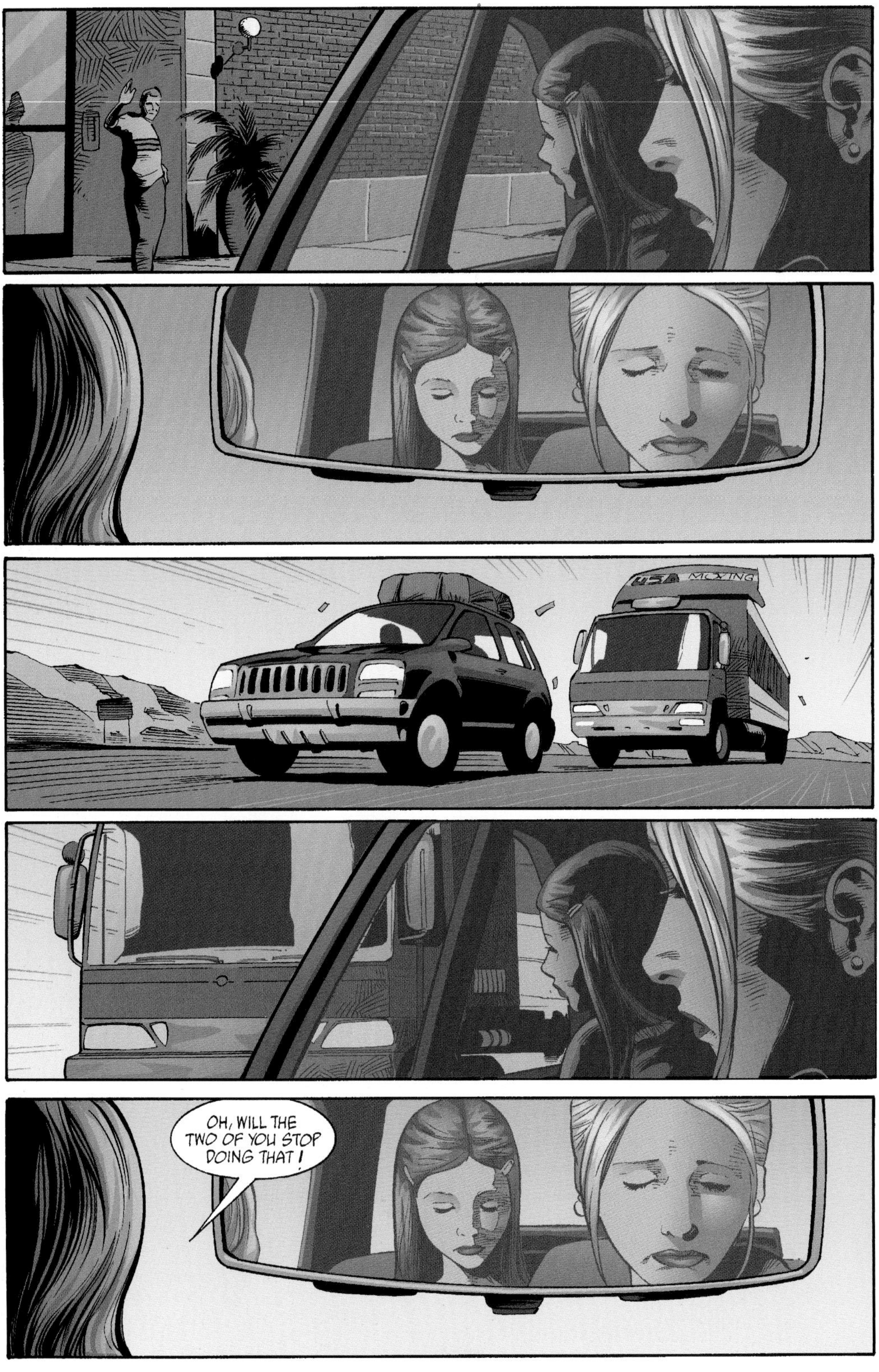
OH, WILL THE TWO OF YOU STOP DOING THAT!

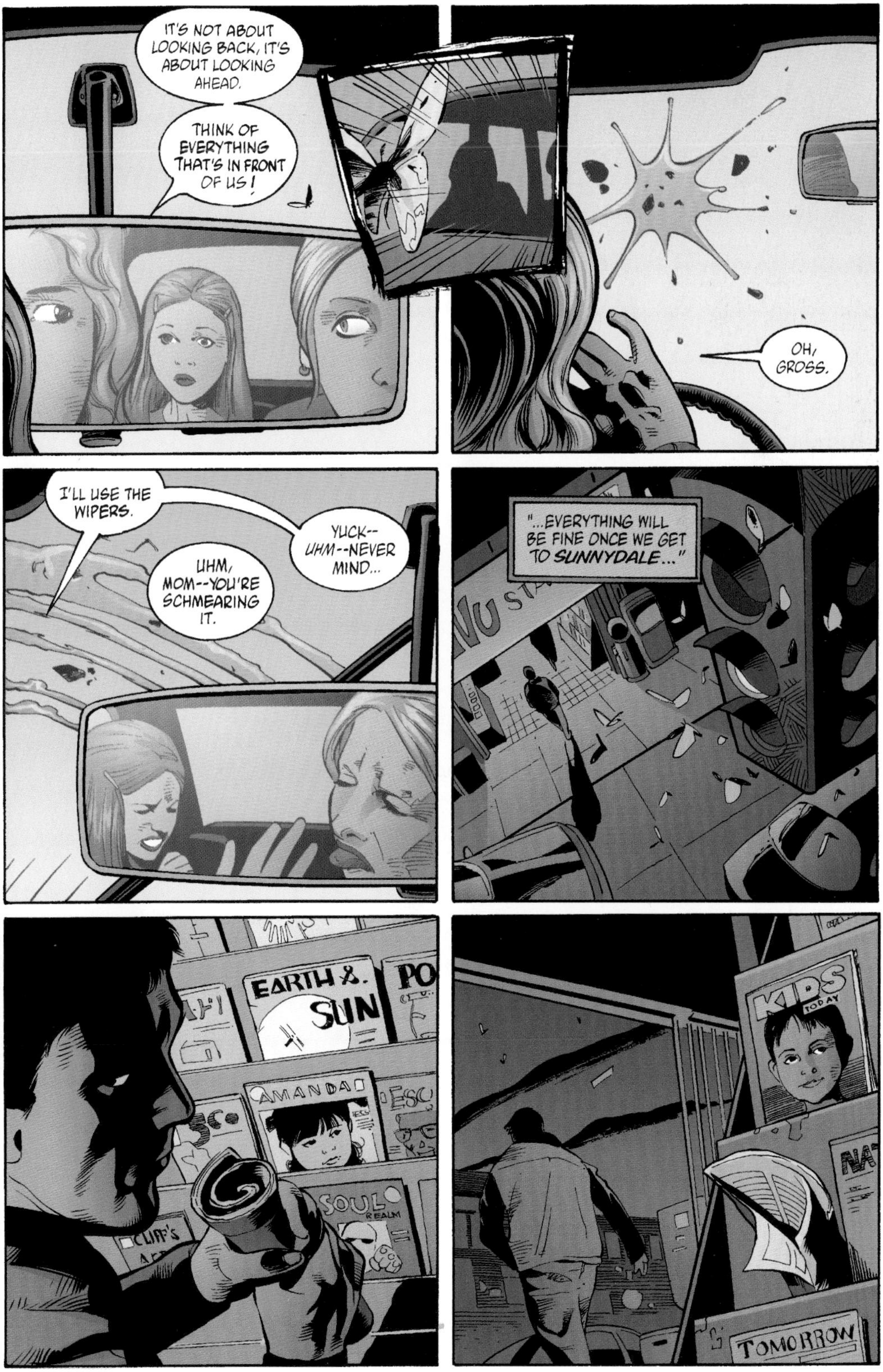
IT'S NOT ABOUT LOOKING BACK, IT'S ABOUT LOOKING AHEAD.
THINK OF EVERYTHING THAT'S IN FRONT OF US!
OH, GROSS.
I'LL USE THE WIPERS.
UHM, MOM--YOU'RE SCHMEARING IT.
YUCK-- UHM--NEVER MIND...
"...EVERYTHING WILL BE FINE ONCE WE GET TO SUNNYDALE..."
EARTH &. SUN
AMANDA
SOUL REALM
KIDS TODAY
TOMORROW

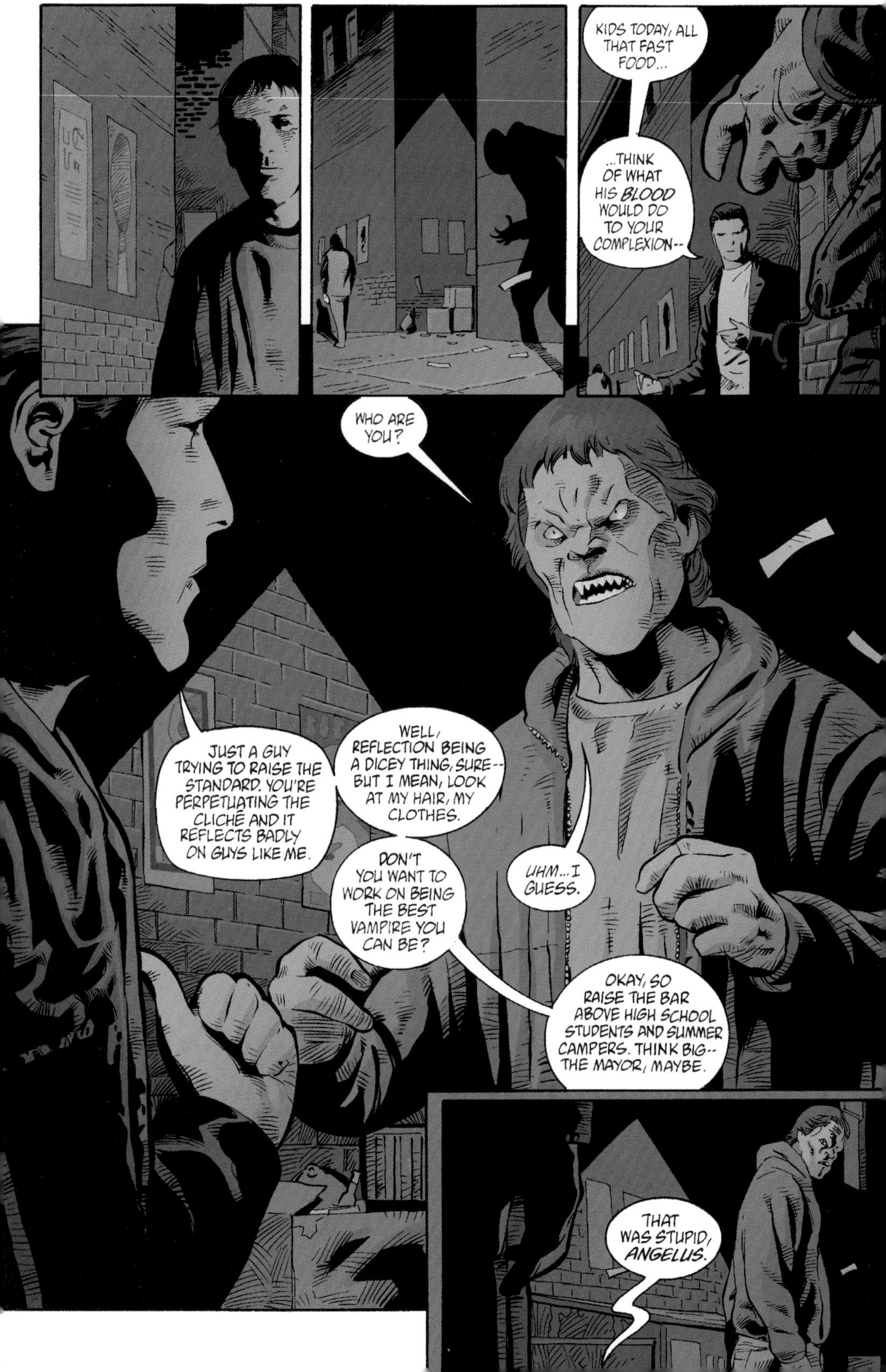
KIDS TODAY, ALL THAT FAST FOOD...
...THINK OF WHAT HIS BLOOD WOULD DO TO YOUR COMPLEXION--
WHO ARE YOU?
JUST A GUY TRYING TO RAISE THE STANDARD. YOU'RE PERPETUATING THE CLICHÉ AND IT REFLECTS BADLY ON GUYS LIKE ME.
WELL, REFLECTION BEING A DICEY THING, SURE--BUT I MEAN, LOOK AT MY HAIR, MY CLOTHES.
DON'T YOU WANT TO WORK ON BEING THE BEST VAMPIRE YOU CAN BE?
UHM... I GUESS.
OKAY, SO RAISE THE BAR ABOVE HIGH SCHOOL STUDENTS AND SUMMER CAMPERS. THINK BIG--THE MAYOR, MAYBE.
THAT WAS STUPID, ANGELUS.

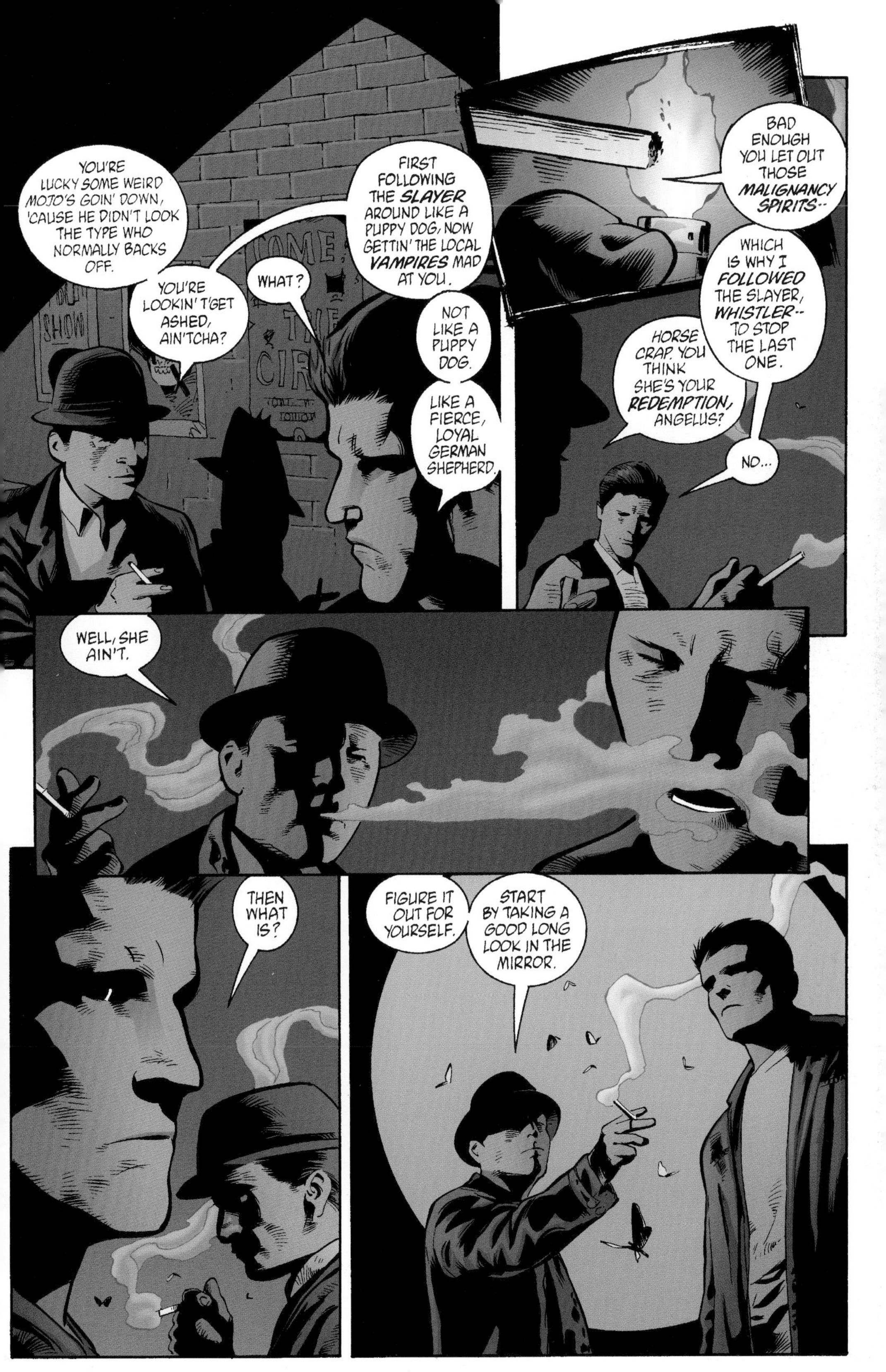
YOU'RE LUCKY SOME WEIRD MOJO'S GOIN' DOWN, 'CAUSE HE DIDN'T LOOK THE TYPE WHO NORMALLY BACKS OFF.
YOU'RE LOOKIN' T'GET ASHED, AIN'TCHA?
WHAT?
FIRST FOLLOWING THE SLAYER AROUND LIKE A PUPPY DOG, NOW GETTIN' THE LOCAL VAMPIRES MAD AT YOU.
NOT LIKE A PUPPY DOG.
LIKE A FIERCE, LOYAL GERMAN SHEPHERD.
BAD ENOUGH YOU LET OUT THOSE MALIGNANCY SPIRITS--
WHICH IS WHY I FOLLOWED THE SLAYER, WHISTLER--TO STOP THE LAST ONE.
HORSE CRAP. YOU THINK SHE'S YOUR REDEMPTION, ANGELUS?
NO...
WELL, SHE AIN'T.
THEN WHAT IS?
FIGURE IT OUT FOR YOURSELF.
START BY TAKING A GOOD LONG LOOK IN THE MIRROR.

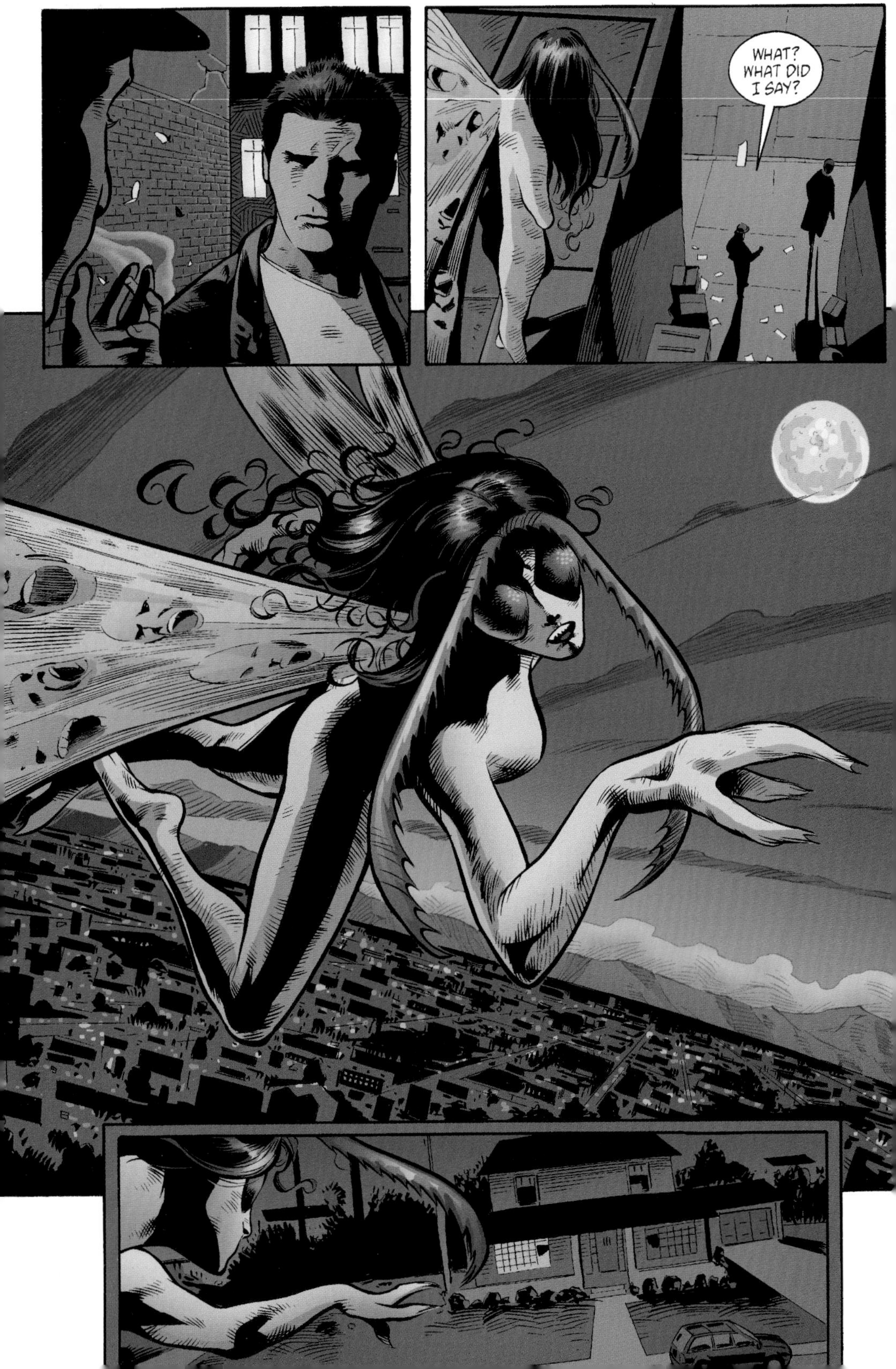
WHAT? WHAT DID I SAY?

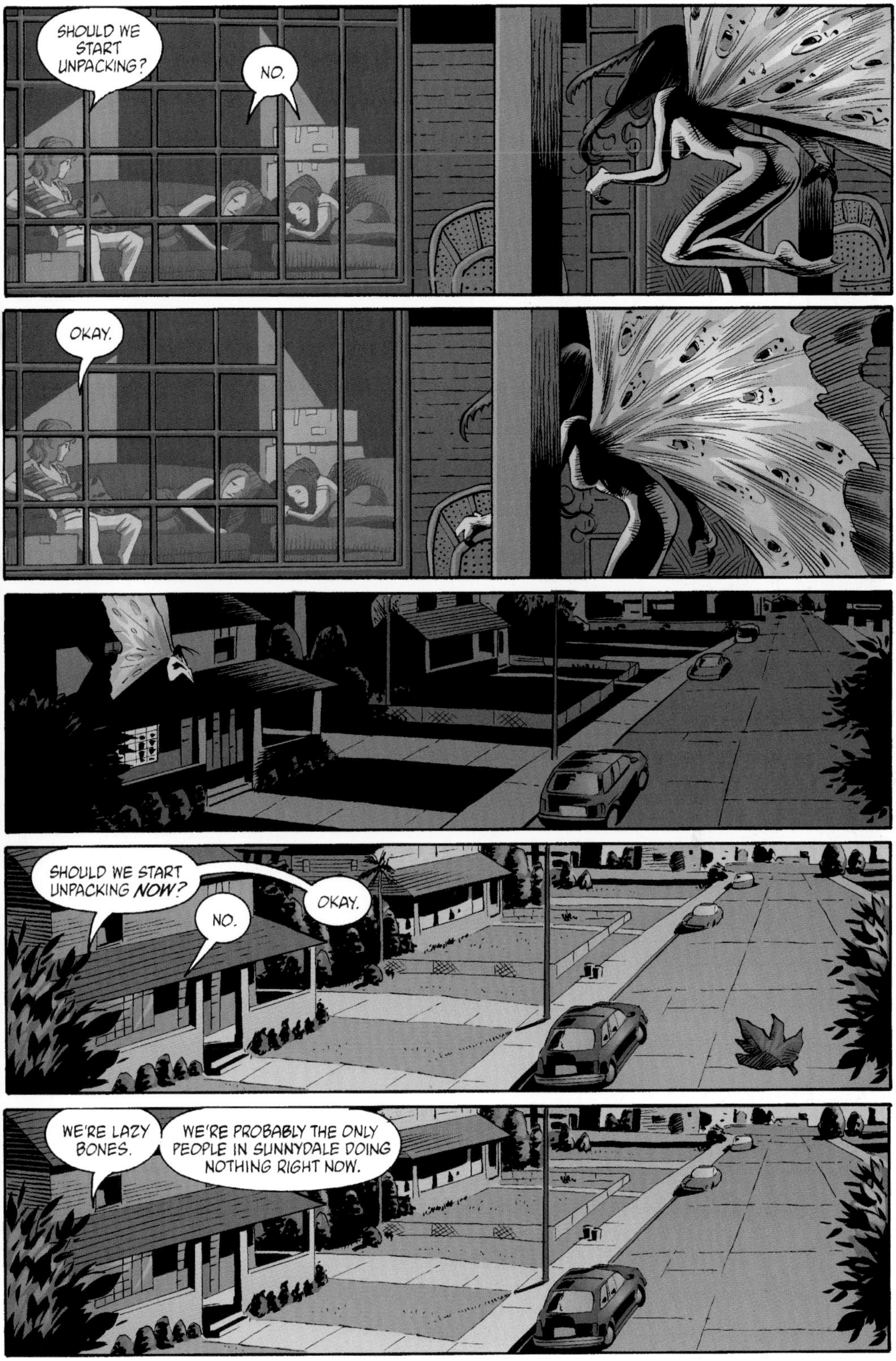
SHOULD WE START UNPACKING?
NO.
OKAY.
SHOULD WE START UNPACKING *NOW?*
NO.
OKAY.
WE'RE LAZY BONES.
WE'RE PROBABLY THE ONLY PEOPLE IN SUNNYDALE DOING NOTHING RIGHT NOW.

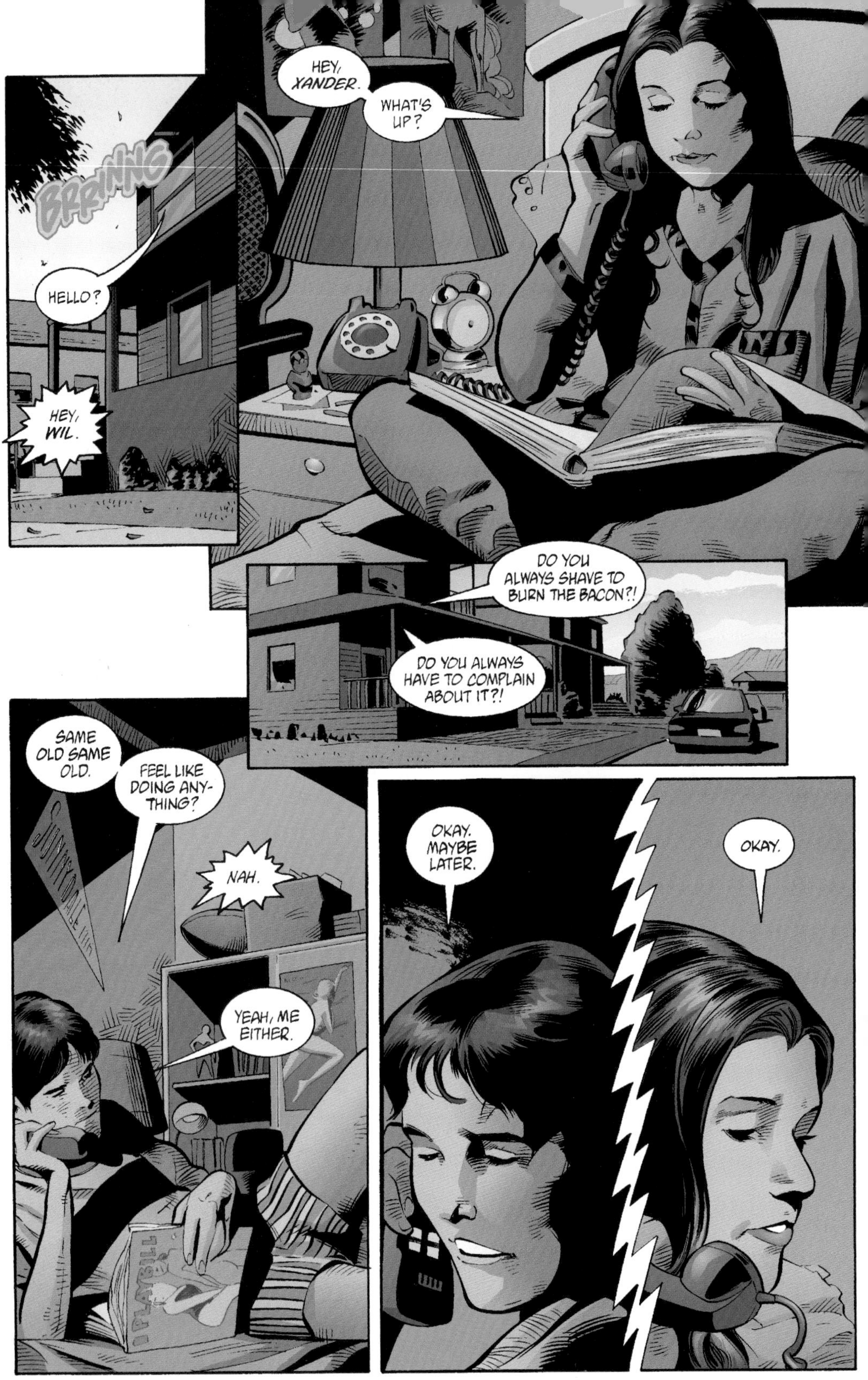
BRRINNG
HELLO?
HEY, XANDER.
WHAT'S UP?
HEY, WIL.
DO YOU ALWAYS SHAVE TO BURN THE BACON?!
DO YOU ALWAYS HAVE TO COMPLAIN ABOUT IT?!
SAME OLD SAME OLD.
FEEL LIKE DOING ANY-THING?
NAH.
YEAH, ME EITHER.
OKAY. MAYBE LATER.
OKAY.

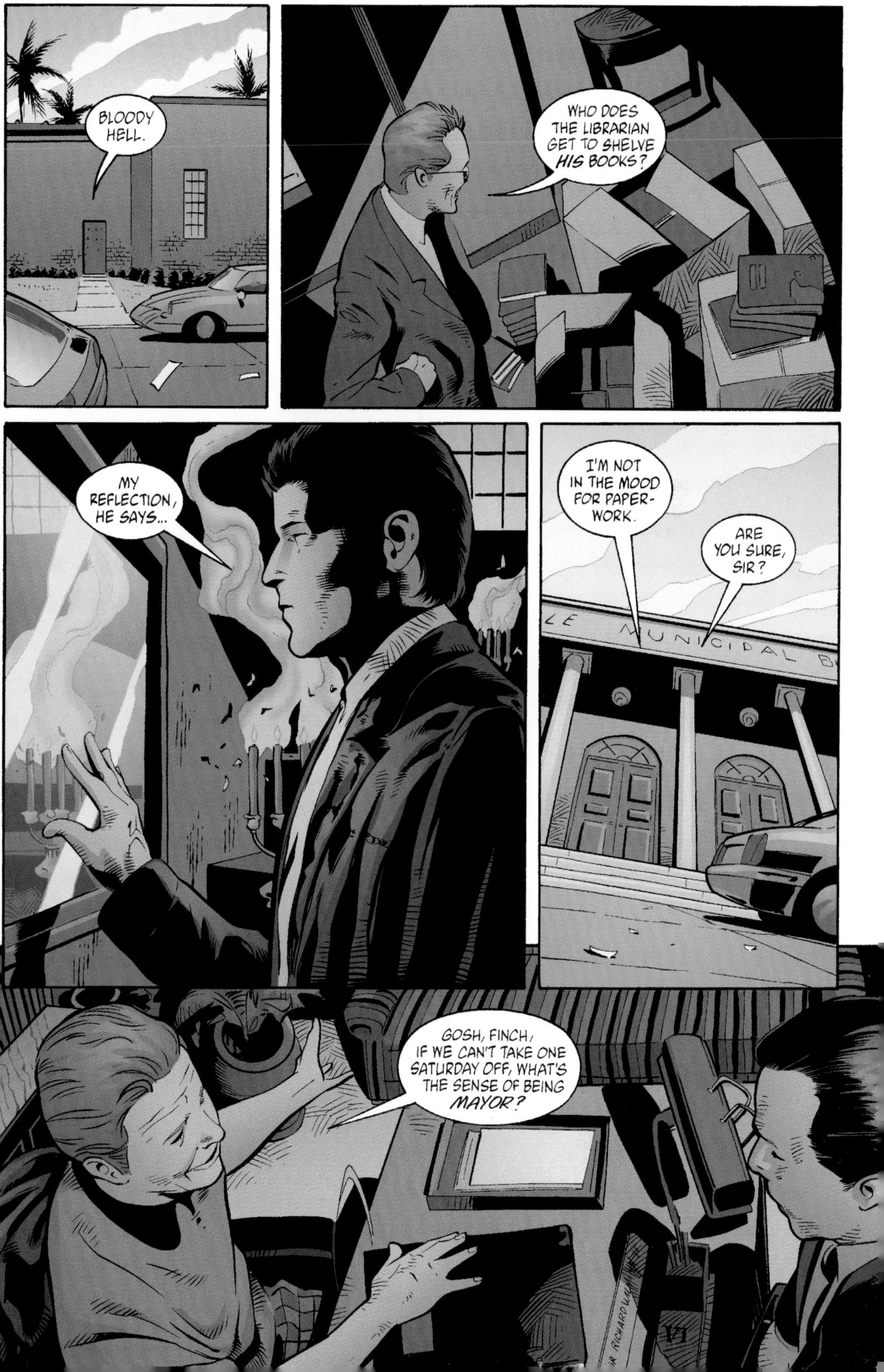
BLOODY HELL.
WHO DOES THE LIBRARIAN GET TO SHELVE *HIS* BOOKS?
MY REFLECTION, HE SAYS...
I'M NOT IN THE MOOD FOR PAPER-WORK.
ARE YOU SURE, SIR?
GOSH, FINCH, IF WE CAN'T TAKE ONE SATURDAY OFF, WHAT'S THE SENSE OF BEING *MAYOR?*

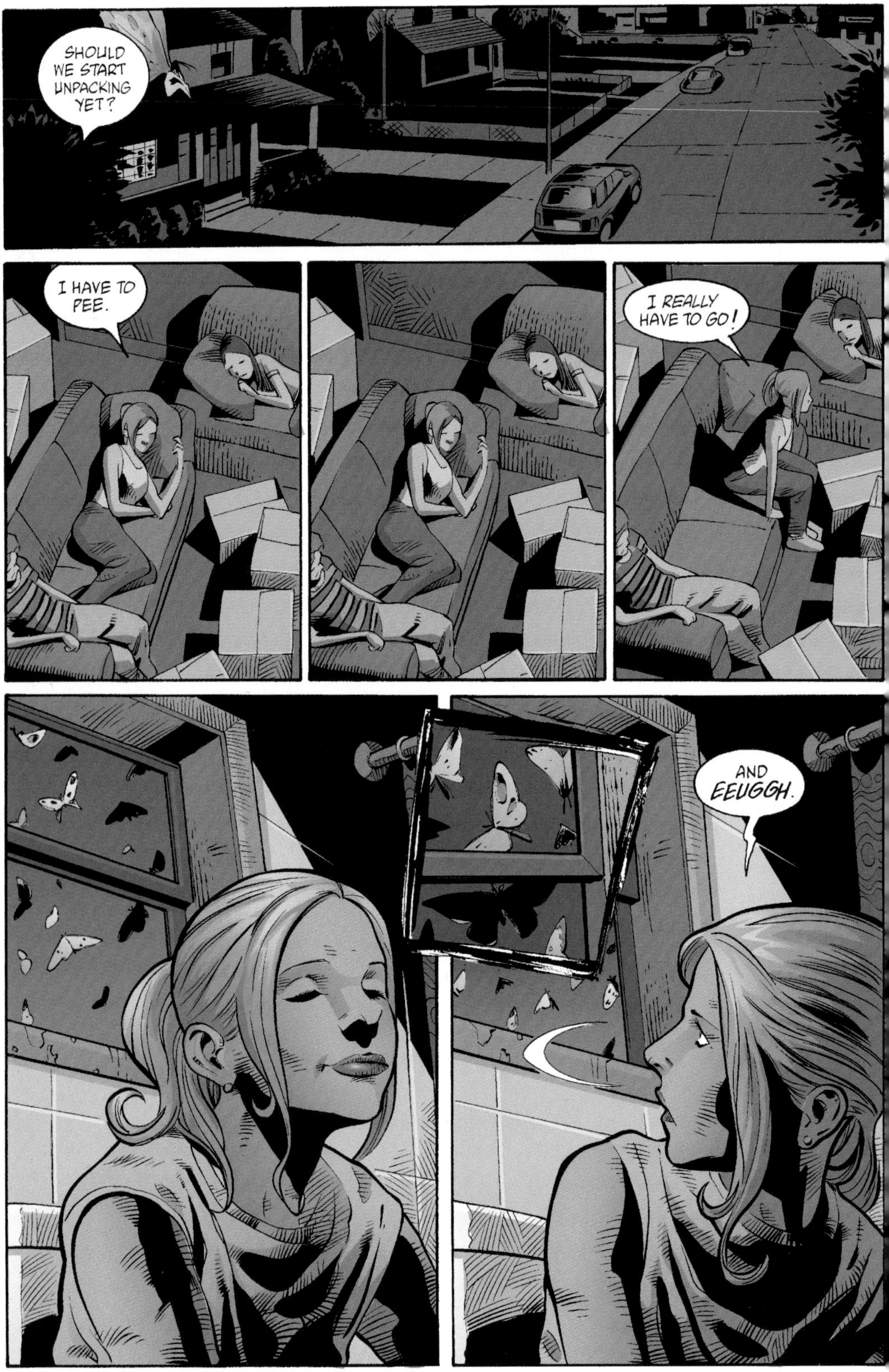
SHOULD WE START UNPACKING YET?
I HAVE TO PEE.
I REALLY HAVE TO GO!
AND EEUGGH.

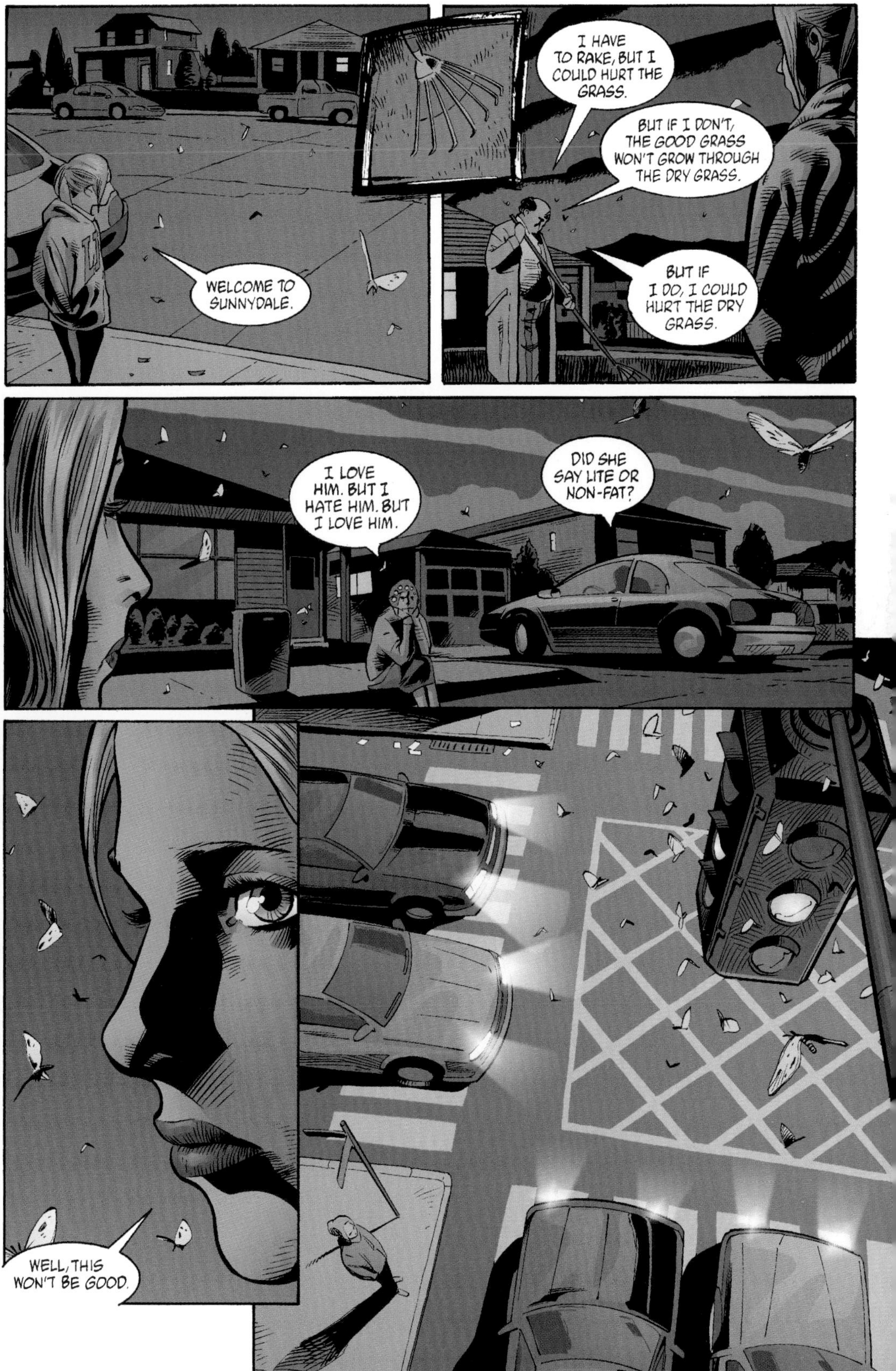
WELCOME TO SUNNYDALE.
I HAVE TO RAKE, BUT I COULD HURT THE GRASS.
BUT IF I DON'T, THE GOOD GRASS WON'T GROW THROUGH THE DRY GRASS.
BUT IF I DO, I COULD HURT THE DRY GRASS.
I LOVE HIM. BUT I HATE HIM. BUT I LOVE HIM.
DID SHE SAY LITE OR NON-FAT?
WELL, THIS WON'T BE GOOD.

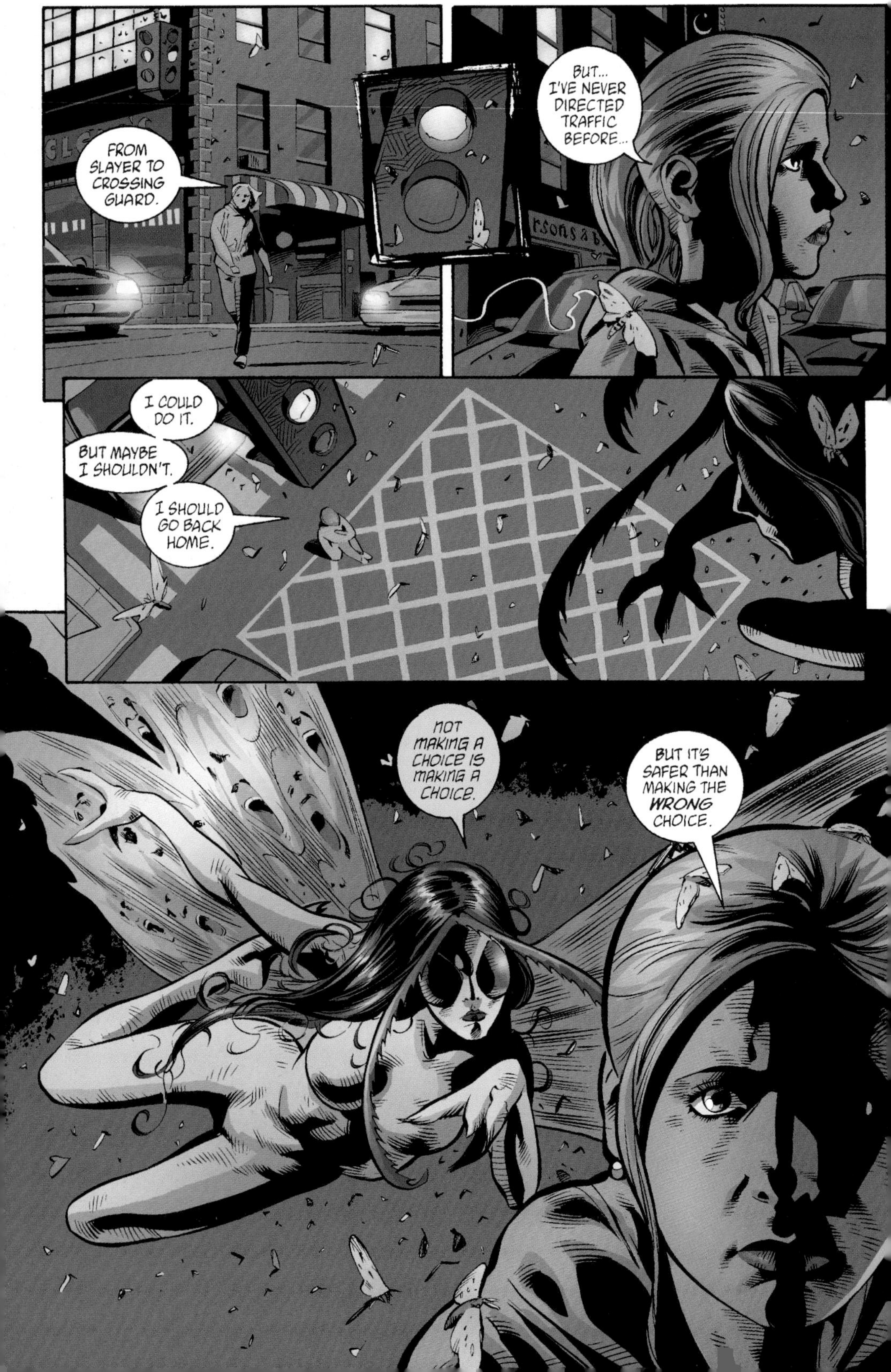

FROM SLAYER TO CROSSING GUARD.
BUT... I'VE NEVER DIRECTED TRAFFIC BEFORE...
I COULD DO IT.
BUT MAYBE I SHOULDN'T.
I SHOULD GO BACK HOME.
NOT MAKING A CHOICE IS MAKING A CHOICE.
BUT IT'S SAFER THAN MAKING THE WRONG CHOICE.

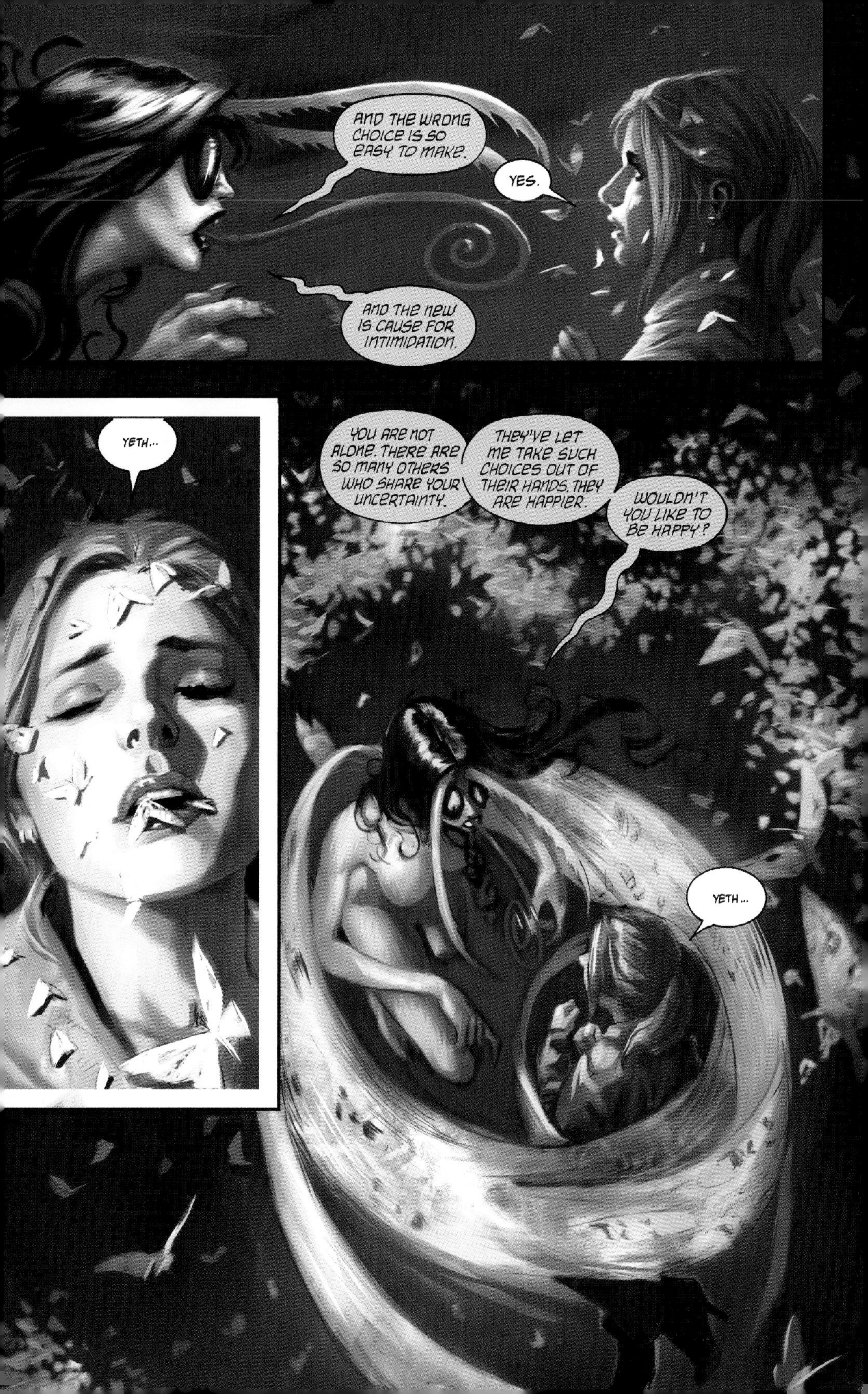
AND THE WRONG CHOICE IS SO EASY TO MAKE.
YES.
AND THE NEW IS CAUSE FOR INTIMIDATION.
YETH...
YOU ARE NOT ALONE. THERE ARE SO MANY OTHERS WHO SHARE YOUR UNCERTAINTY.
THEY'VE LET ME TAKE SUCH CHOICES OUT OF THEIR HANDS. THEY ARE HAPPIER.
WOULDN'T YOU LIKE TO BE HAPPY?
YETH...

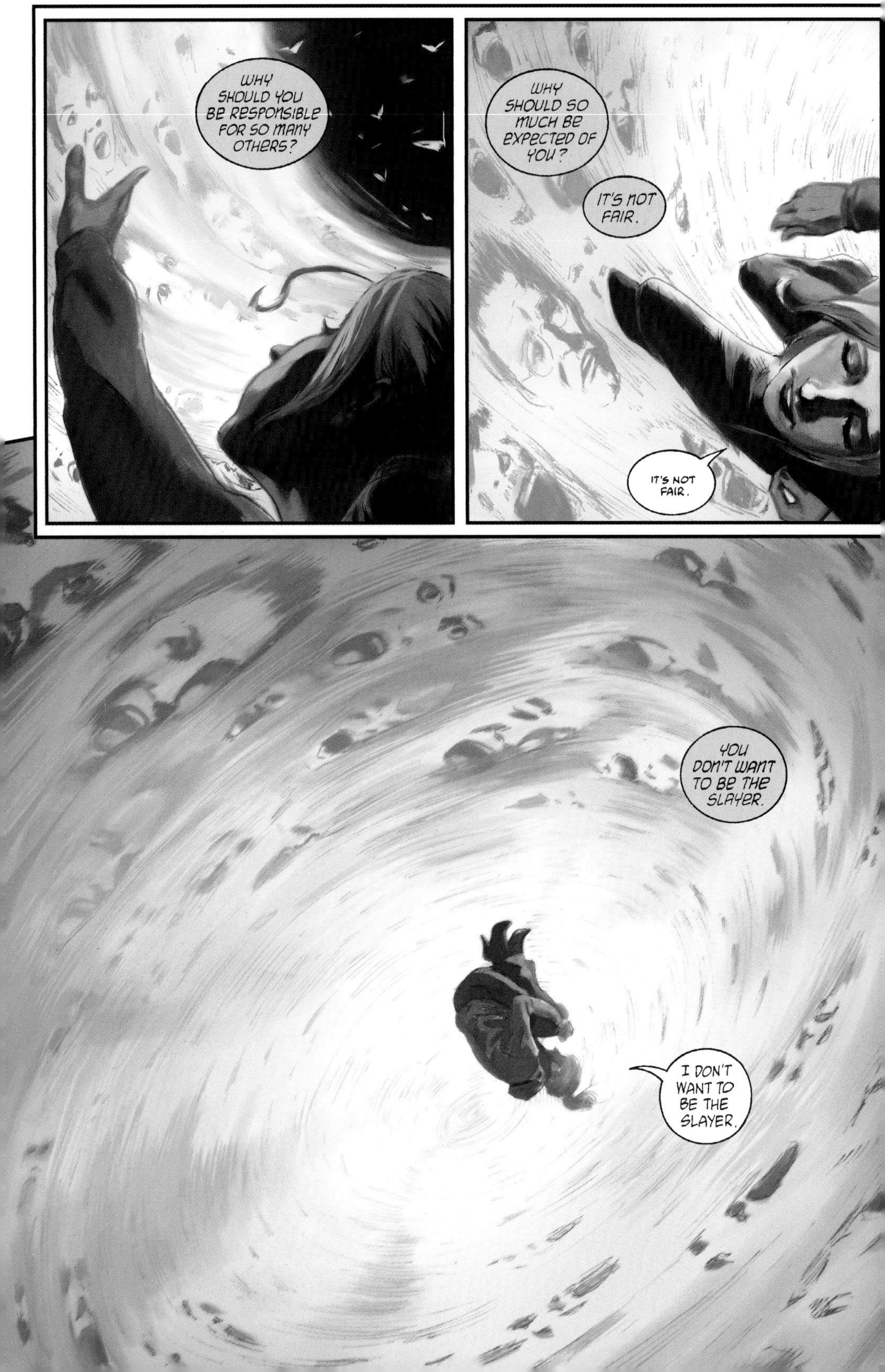

WHY SHOULD YOU BE RESPONSIBLE FOR SO MANY OTHERS?
WHY SHOULD SO MUCH BE EXPECTED OF YOU?
IT'S NOT FAIR.
IT'S NOT FAIR.
YOU DON'T WANT TO BE THE SLAYER.
I DON'T WANT TO BE THE SLAYER.

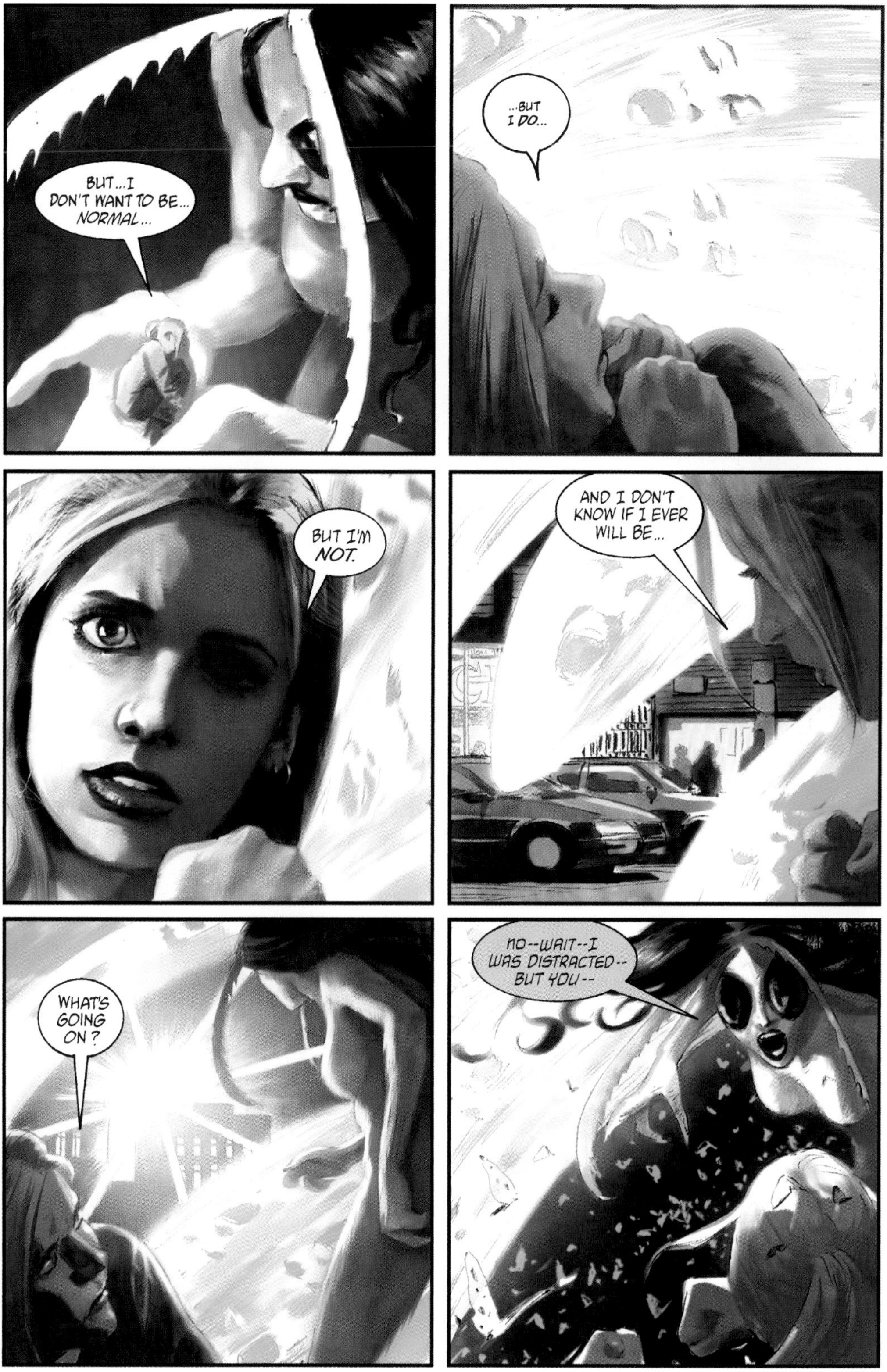
BUT...I DON'T WANT TO BE... NORMAL...
...BUT I DO...
BUT I'M NOT.
AND I DON'T KNOW IF I EVER WILL BE...
WHAT'S GOING ON?
NO--WAIT--I WAS DISTRACTED-- BUT YOU--

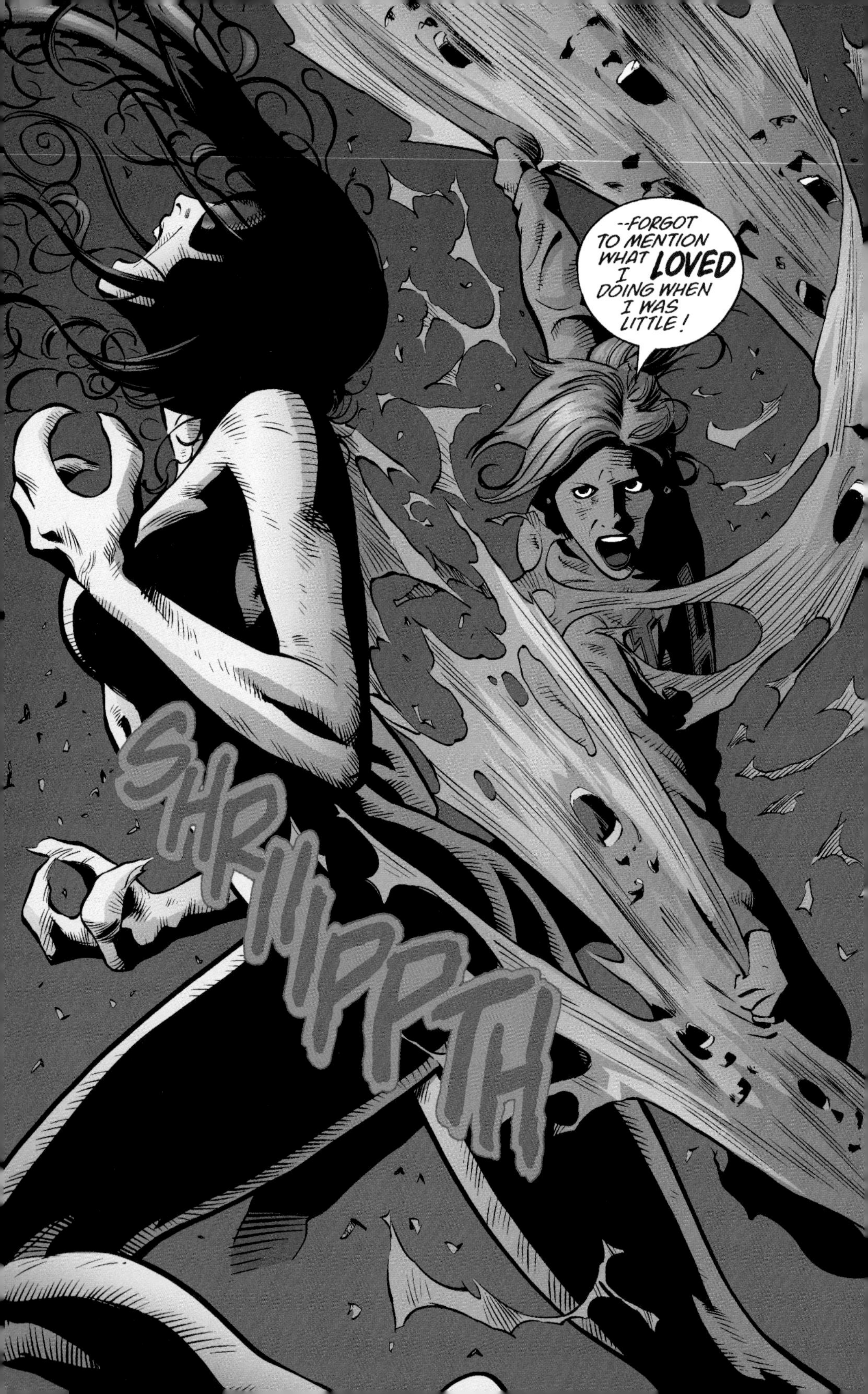
--FORGOT TO MENTION WHAT I LOVED DOING WHEN I WAS LITTLE!
SHRIIPPTH

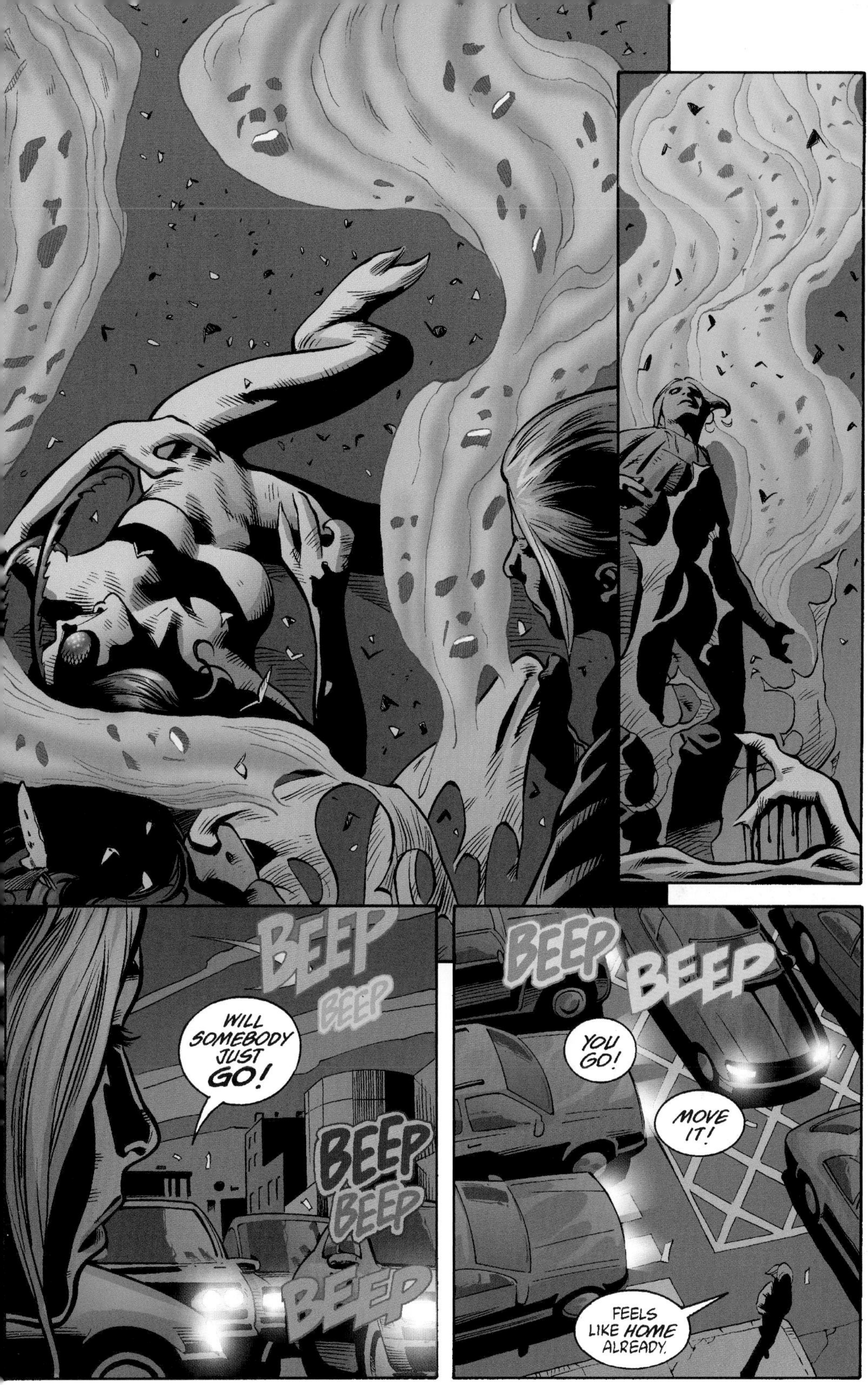
BEEP
BEEP
WILL SOMEBODY JUST GO!
BEEP
BEEP
BEEP
BEEP
BEEP
YOU GO!
MOVE IT!
FEELS LIKE HOME ALREADY.

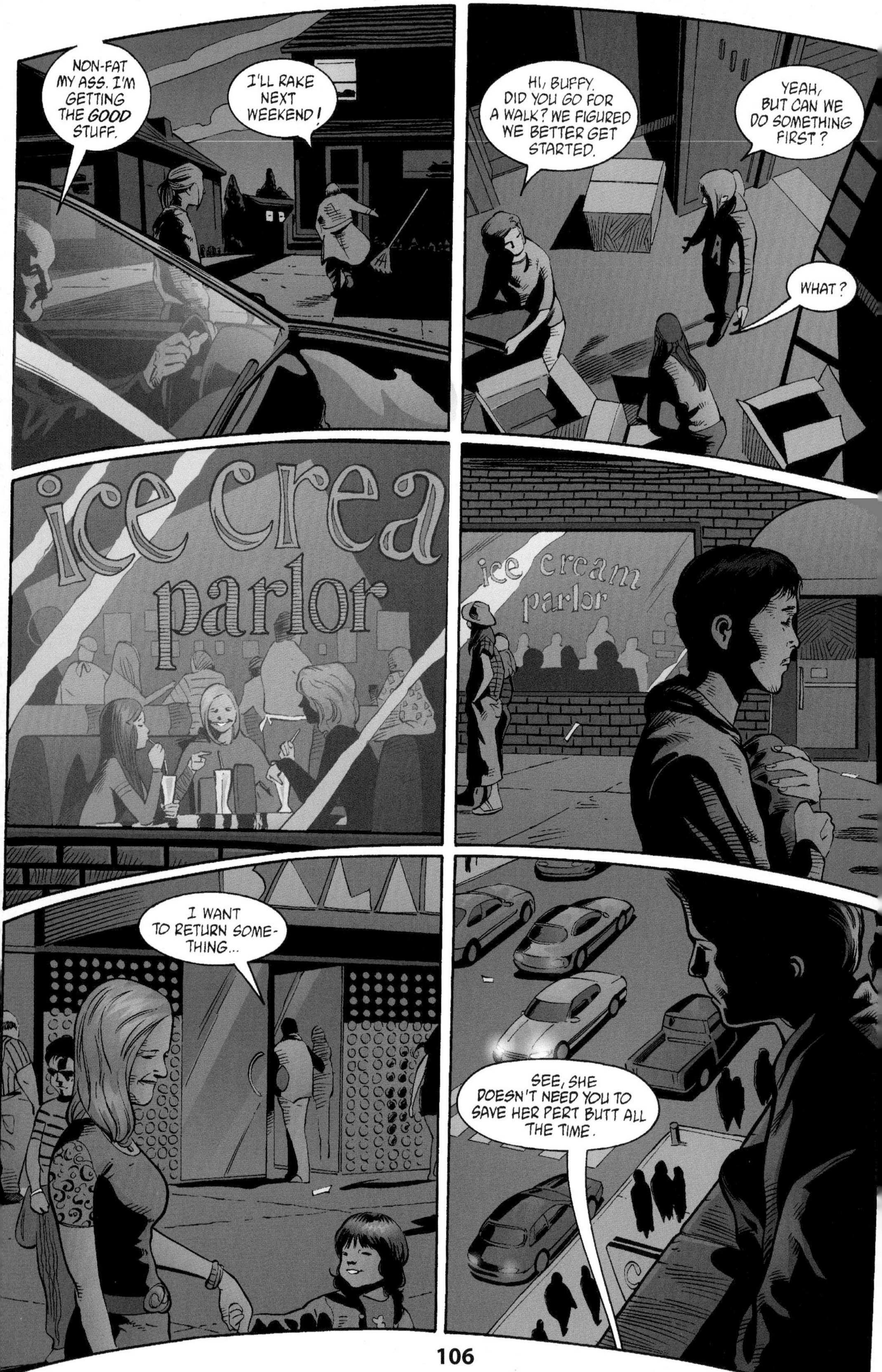
NON-FAT MY ASS. I'M GETTING THE GOOD STUFF.
I'LL RAKE NEXT WEEKEND!
HI, BUFFY. DID YOU GO FOR A WALK? WE FIGURED WE BETTER GET STARTED.
YEAH, BUT CAN WE DO SOMETHING FIRST?
WHAT?
ice crea
parlor
ice cream parlor
I WANT TO RETURN SOME-THING...
SEE, SHE DOESN'T NEED YOU TO SAVE HER PERT BUTT ALL THE TIME.

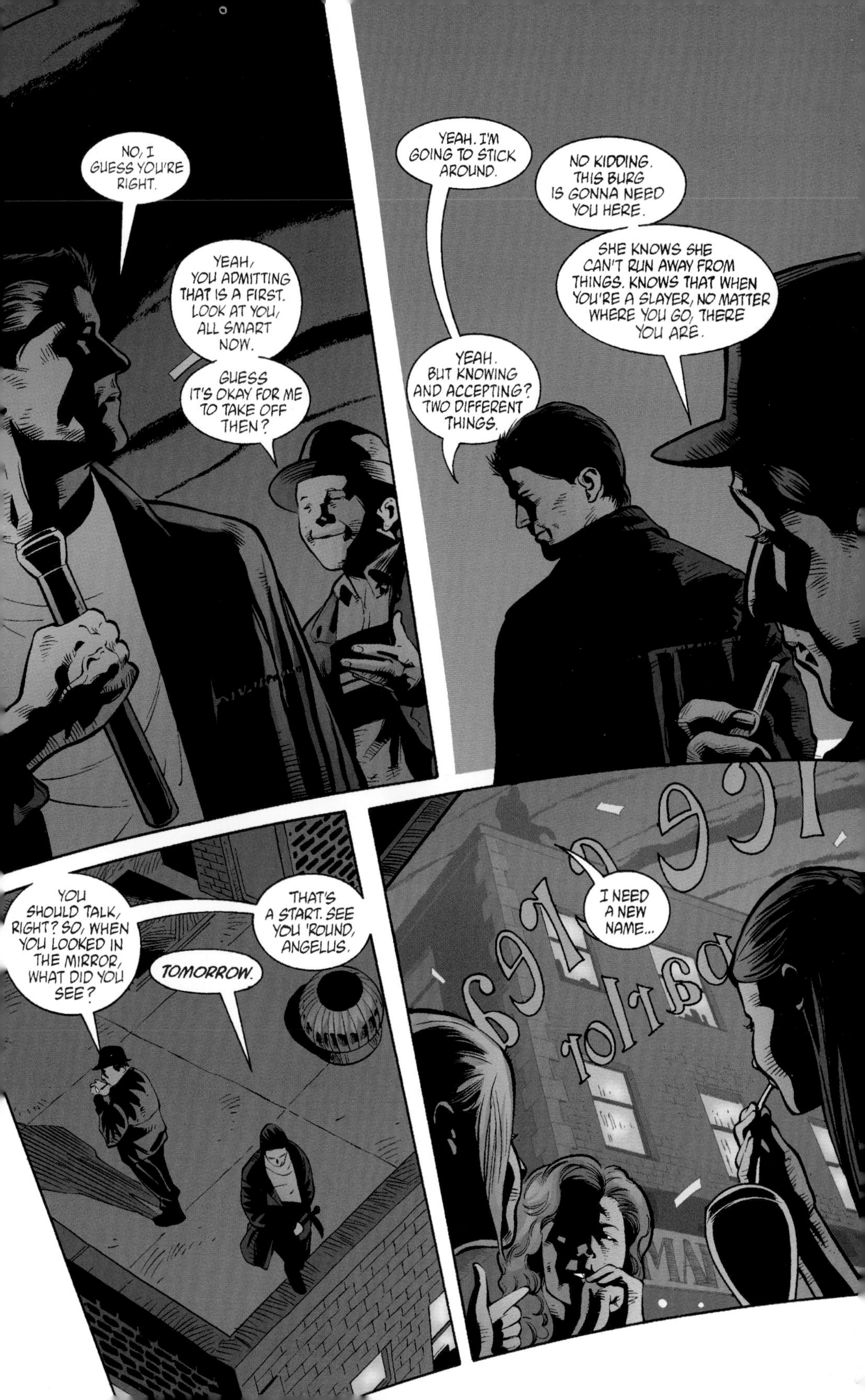
NO, I GUESS YOU'RE RIGHT.
YEAH, YOU ADMITTING THAT IS A FIRST. LOOK AT YOU, ALL SMART NOW.
GUESS IT'S OKAY FOR ME TO TAKE OFF THEN?
YEAH. I'M GOING TO STICK AROUND.
NO KIDDING. THIS BURG IS GONNA NEED YOU HERE.
SHE KNOWS SHE CAN'T RUN AWAY FROM THINGS. KNOWS THAT WHEN YOU'RE A SLAYER, NO MATTER WHERE YOU GO, THERE YOU ARE.
YEAH. BUT KNOWING AND ACCEPTING? TWO DIFFERENT THINGS.
YOU SHOULD TALK, RIGHT? SO, WHEN YOU LOOKED IN THE MIRROR, WHAT DID YOU SEE?
TOMORROW.
THAT'S A START. SEE YOU 'ROUND, ANGELUS.
I NEED A NEW NAME...

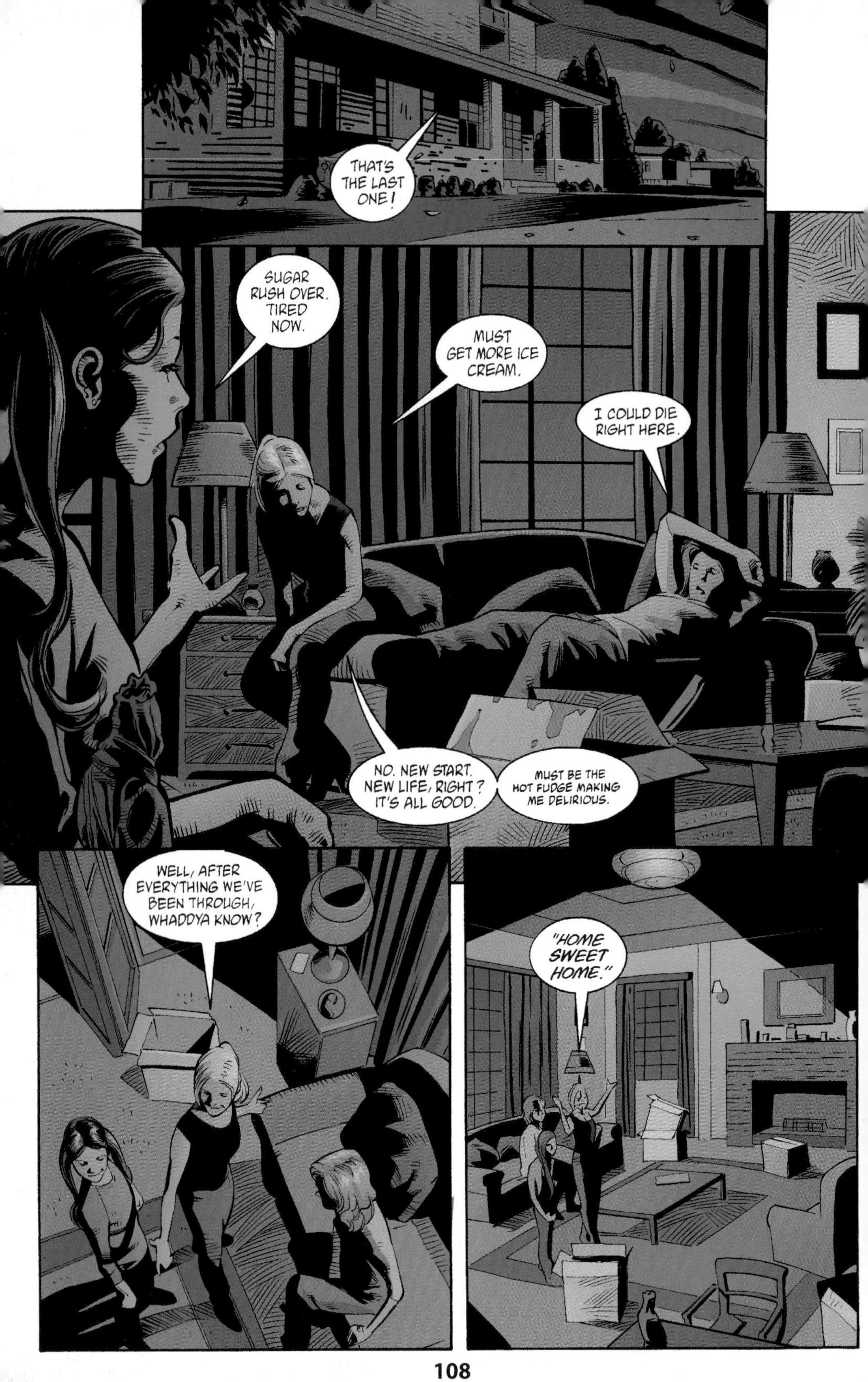
THAT'S THE LAST ONE!
SUGAR RUSH OVER. TIRED NOW.
MUST GET MORE ICE CREAM.
I COULD DIE RIGHT HERE.
NO. NEW START. NEW LIFE, RIGHT? IT'S ALL GOOD.
MUST BE THE HOT FUDGE MAKING ME DELIRIOUS.
WELL, AFTER EVERYTHING WE'VE BEEN THROUGH, WHADDYA KNOW?
"HOME SWEET HOME."

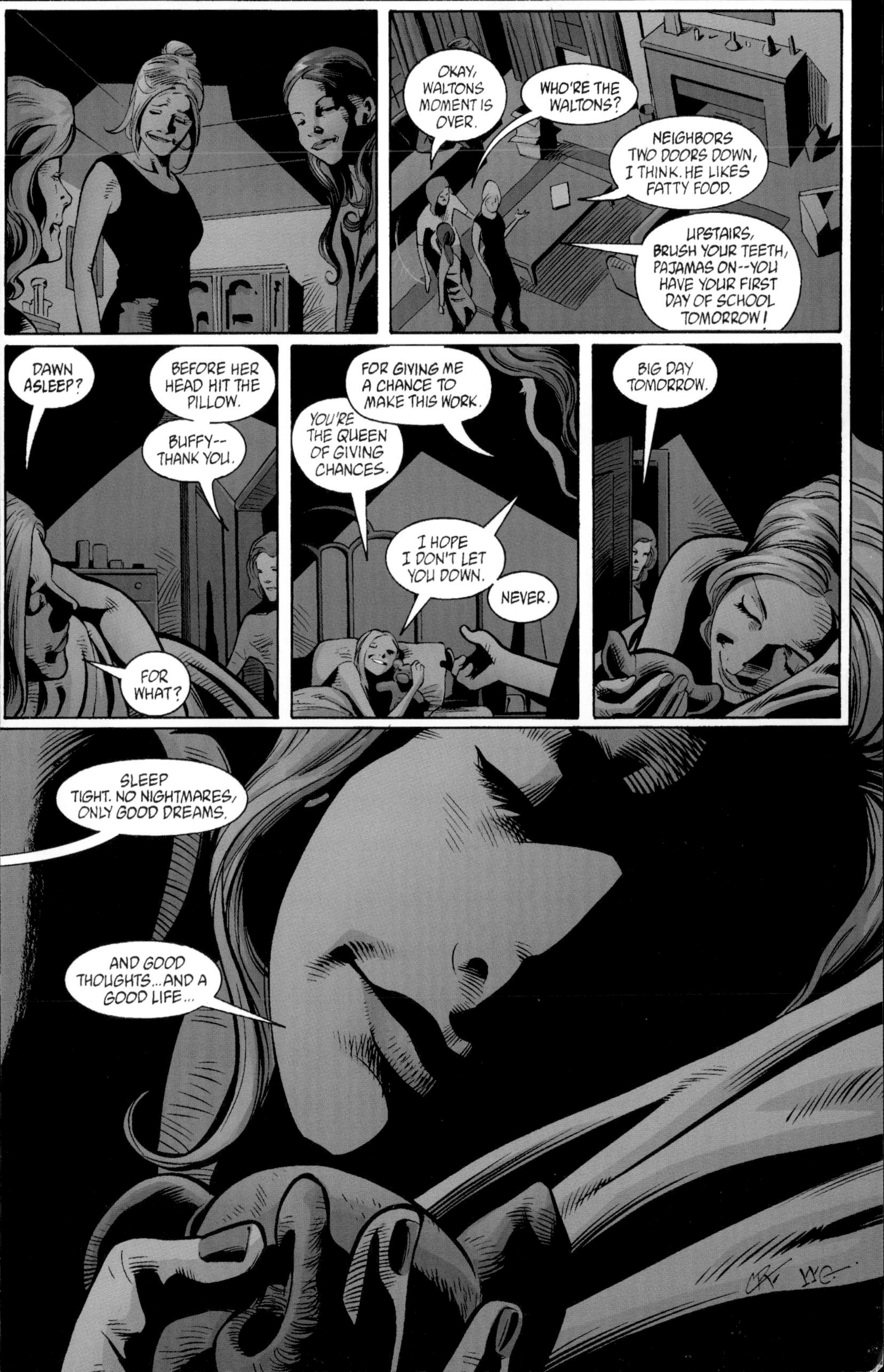
OKAY, WALTONS MOMENT IS OVER.
WHO'RE THE WALTONS?
NEIGHBORS TWO DOORS DOWN, I THINK. HE LIKES FATTY FOOD.
UPSTAIRS, BRUSH YOUR TEETH, PAJAMAS ON--YOU HAVE YOUR FIRST DAY OF SCHOOL TOMORROW!
DAWN ASLEEP?
BEFORE HER HEAD HIT THE PILLOW.
BUFFY-- THANK YOU.
FOR WHAT?
FOR GIVING ME A CHANCE TO MAKE THIS WORK.
YOU'RE THE QUEEN OF GIVING CHANCES.
I HOPE I DON'T LET YOU DOWN.
NEVER.
BIG DAY TOMORROW.
SLEEP TIGHT. NO NIGHTMARES, ONLY GOOD DREAMS.
AND GOOD THOUGHTS...AND A GOOD LIFE...

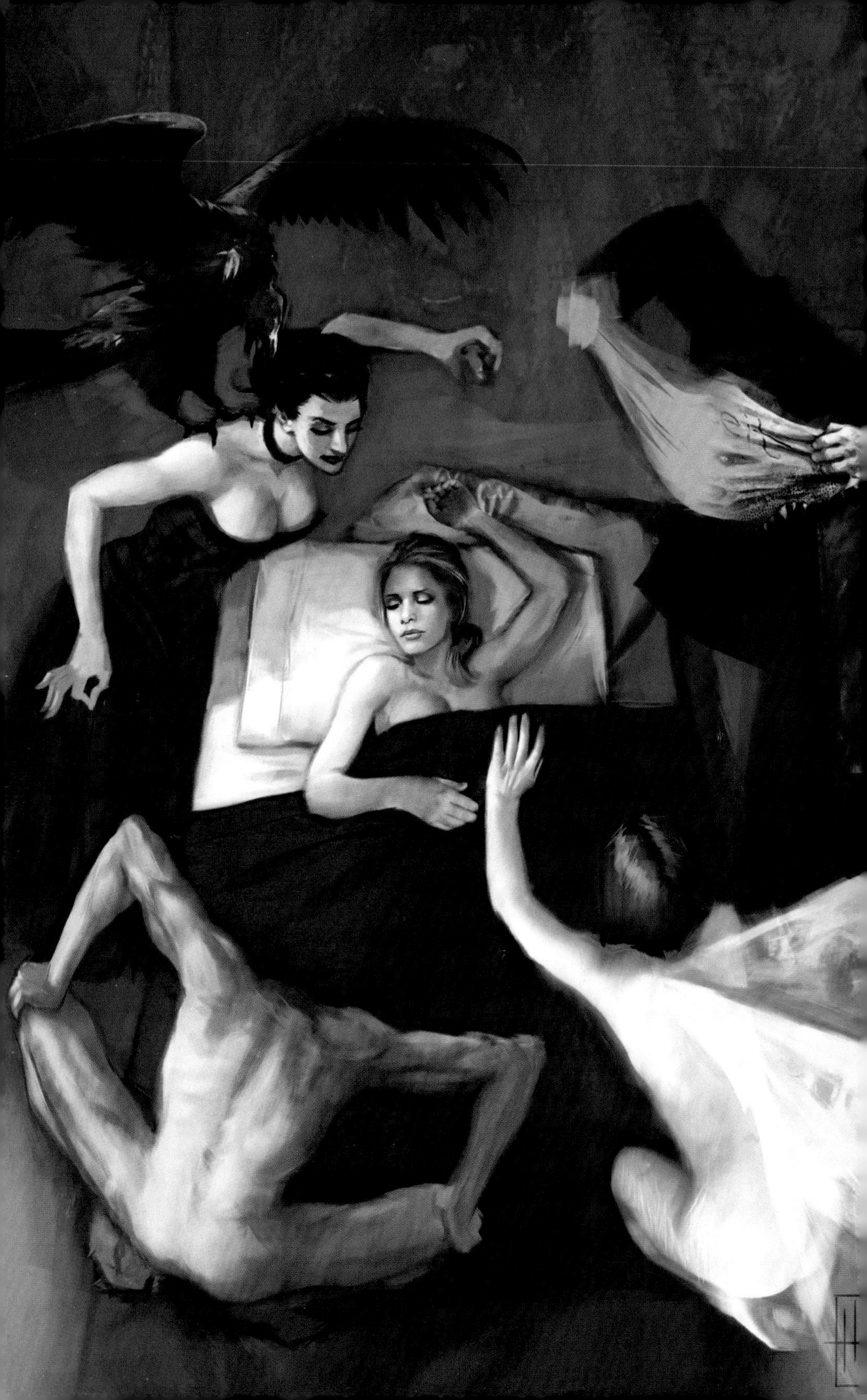

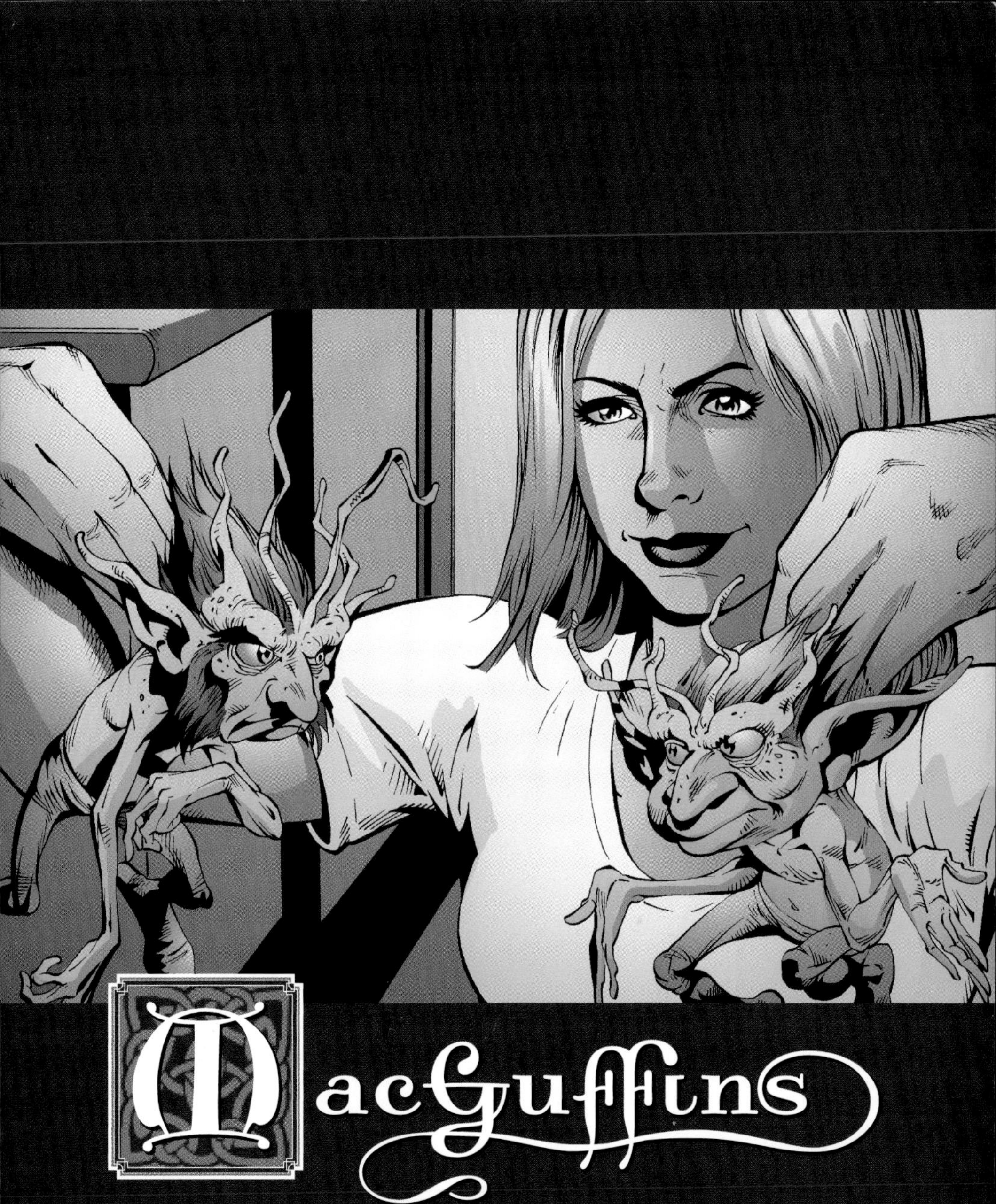

MacGuffins

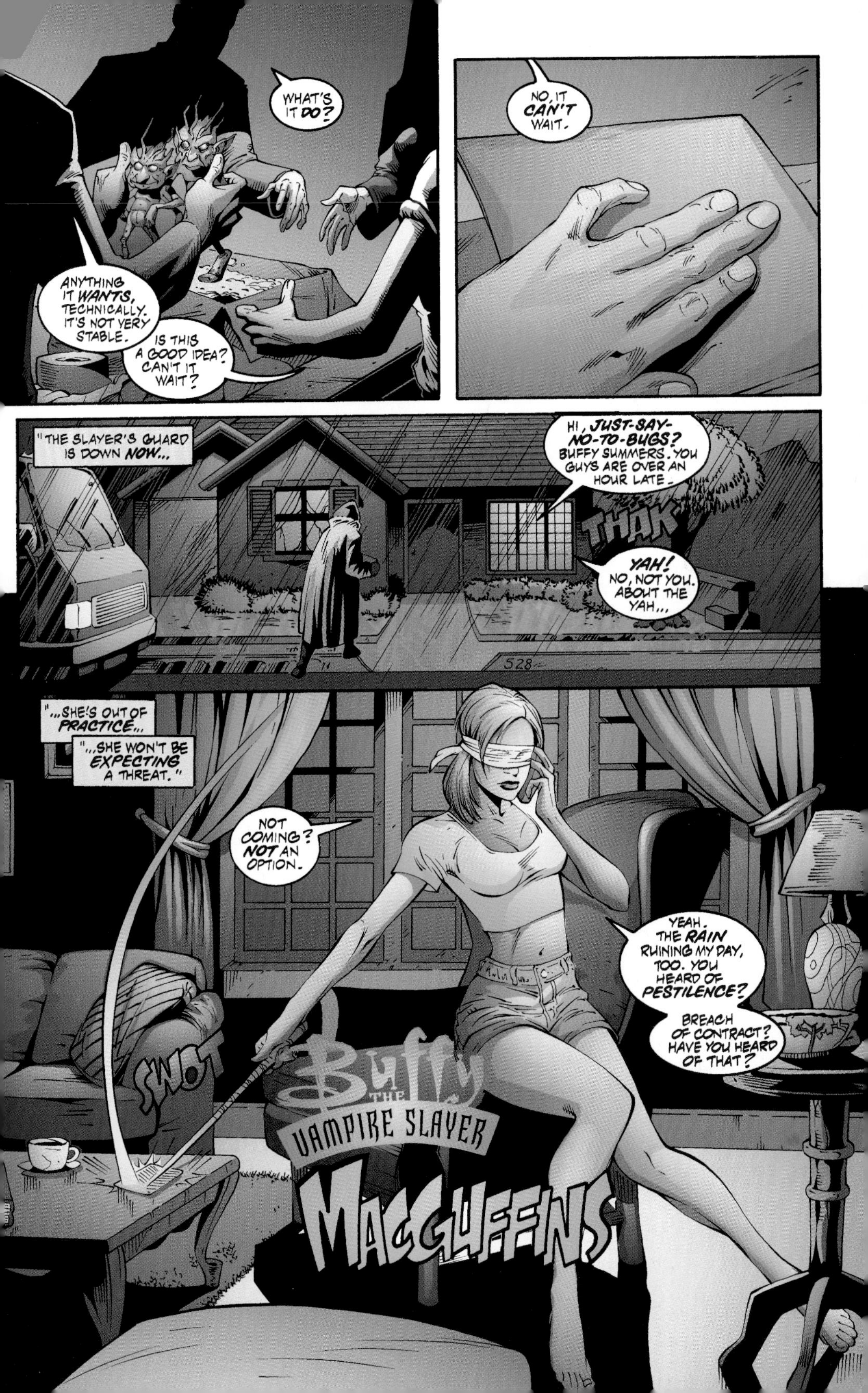
WHAT'S IT DO?
ANYTHING IT WANTS, TECHNICALLY. IT'S NOT VERY STABLE.
IS THIS A GOOD IDEA? CAN'T IT WAIT?
NO, IT CAN'T WAIT.
"THE SLAYER'S GUARD IS DOWN NOW...
HI, JUST-SAY-NO-TO-BUGS? BUFFY SUMMERS. YOU GUYS ARE OVER AN HOUR LATE.
THAK
YAH! NO, NOT YOU. ABOUT THE YAH...
528
"...SHE'S OUT OF PRACTICE...
"...SHE WON'T BE EXPECTING A THREAT."
NOT COMING? NOT AN OPTION.
YEAH. THE RAIN RUINING MY DAY, TOO. YOU HEARD OF PESTILENCE?
BREACH OF CONTRACT? HAVE YOU HEARD OF THAT?
SWOT
Buffy THE VAMPIRE SLAYER
MACGUFFINS

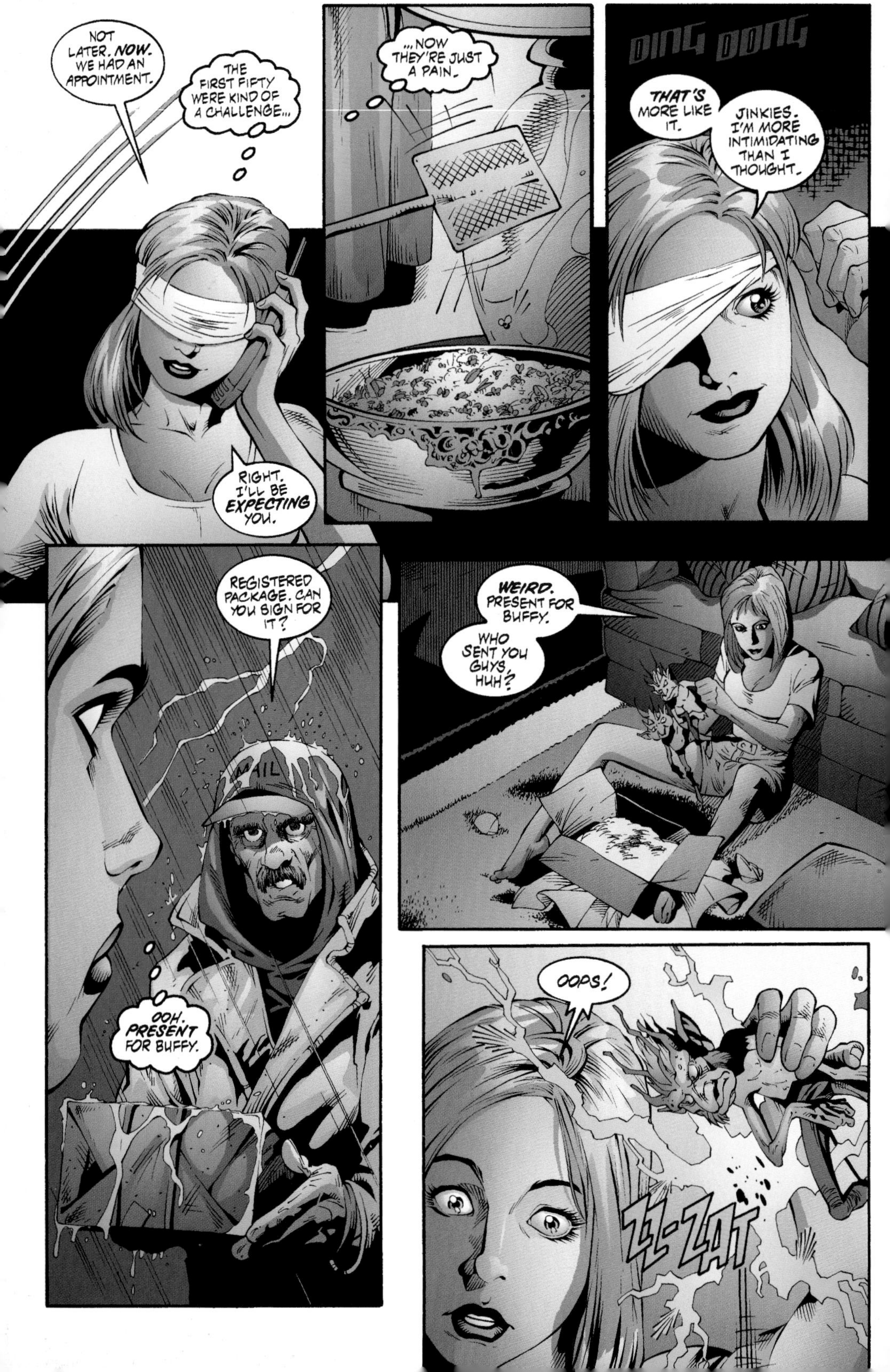
NOT LATER. NOW. WE HAD AN APPOINTMENT.
THE FIRST FIFTY WERE KIND OF A CHALLENGE...
RIGHT. I'LL BE EXPECTING YOU.
...NOW THEY'RE JUST A PAIN.
DING DONG
THAT'S MORE LIKE IT.
JINKIES. I'M MORE INTIMIDATING THAN I THOUGHT.
REGISTERED PACKAGE. CAN YOU SIGN FOR IT?
MAIL
OOH. PRESENT FOR BUFFY.
WEIRD. PRESENT FOR BUFFY.
WHO SENT YOU GUYS, HUH?
OOPS!
ZZ-ZAT

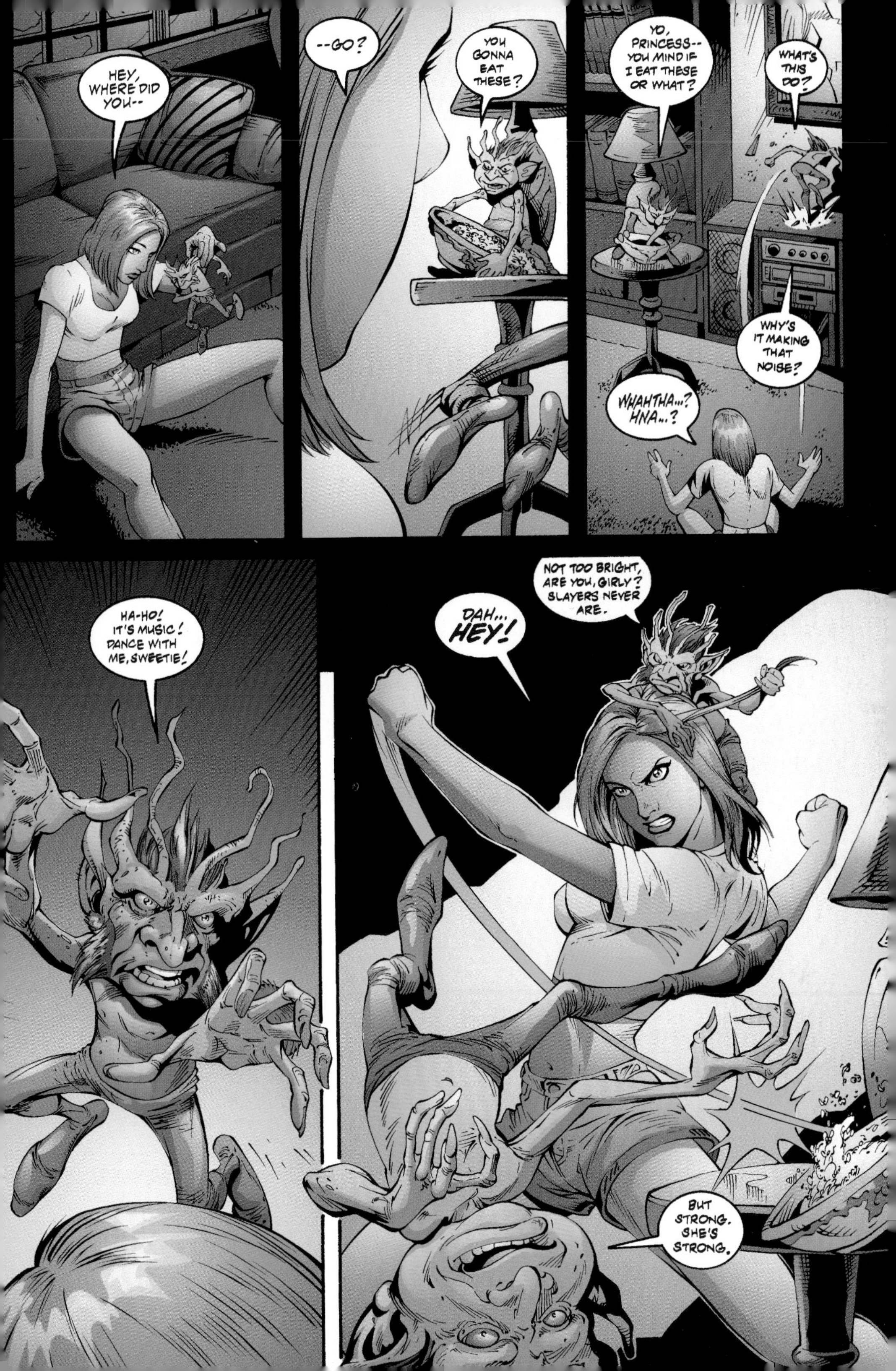

HEY, WHERE DID YOU--
--GO?
YOU GONNA EAT THESE?
YO, PRINCESS-- YOU MIND IF I EAT THESE OR WHAT?
WHAT'S THIS DO?
WHY'S IT MAKING THAT NOISE?
WHAHTHA...? HNA...?
HA-HO! IT'S MUSIC! DANCE WITH ME, SWEETIE!
NOT TOO BRIGHT, ARE YOU, GIRLY? SLAYERS NEVER ARE.
DAH... HEY!
BUT STRONG. SHE'S STRONG.

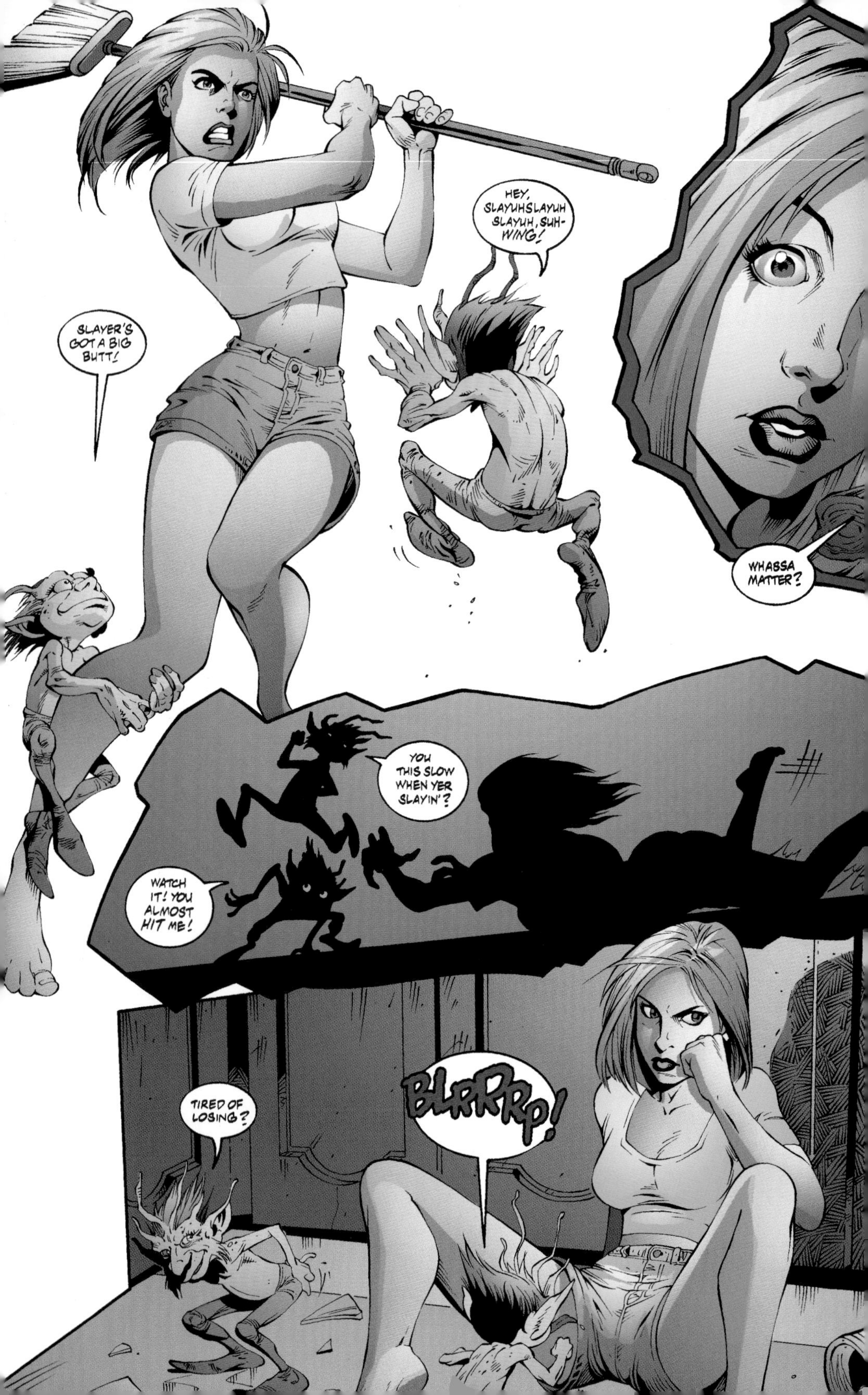
SLAYER'S GOT A BIG BUTT!
HEY, SLAYUHSLAYUH SLAYUH, SUH-WING!
WHASSA MATTER?
YOU THIS SLOW WHEN YER SLAYIN'?
WATCH IT! YOU ALMOST HIT ME!
TIRED OF LOSING?
BLRRRRp!

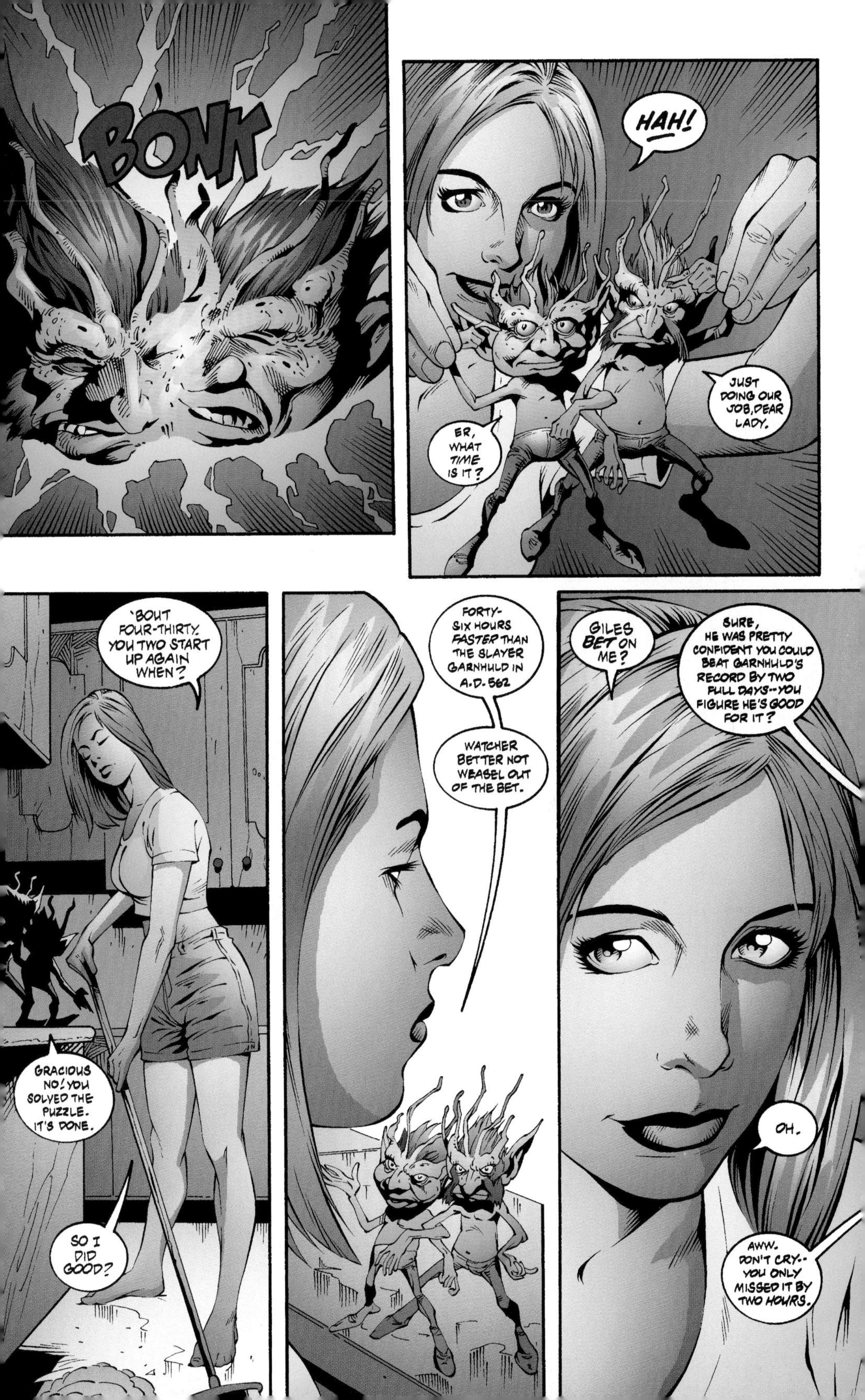
BONK
HAH!
ER, WHAT TIME IS IT?
JUST DOING OUR JOB, DEAR LADY.
'BOUT FOUR-THIRTY. YOU TWO START UP AGAIN WHEN?
GRACIOUS NO! YOU SOLVED THE PUZZLE. IT'S DONE.
SO I DID GOOD?
FORTY-SIX HOURS FASTER THAN THE SLAYER GARNHULD IN A.D. 562
WATCHER BETTER NOT WEASEL OUT OF THE BET.
GILES BET ON ME?
SURE, HE WAS PRETTY CONFIDENT YOU COULD BEAT GARNHULD'S RECORD BY TWO FULL DAYS--YOU FIGURE HE'S GOOD FOR IT?
OH.
AWW. DON'T CRY-- YOU ONLY MISSED IT BY TWO HOURS.

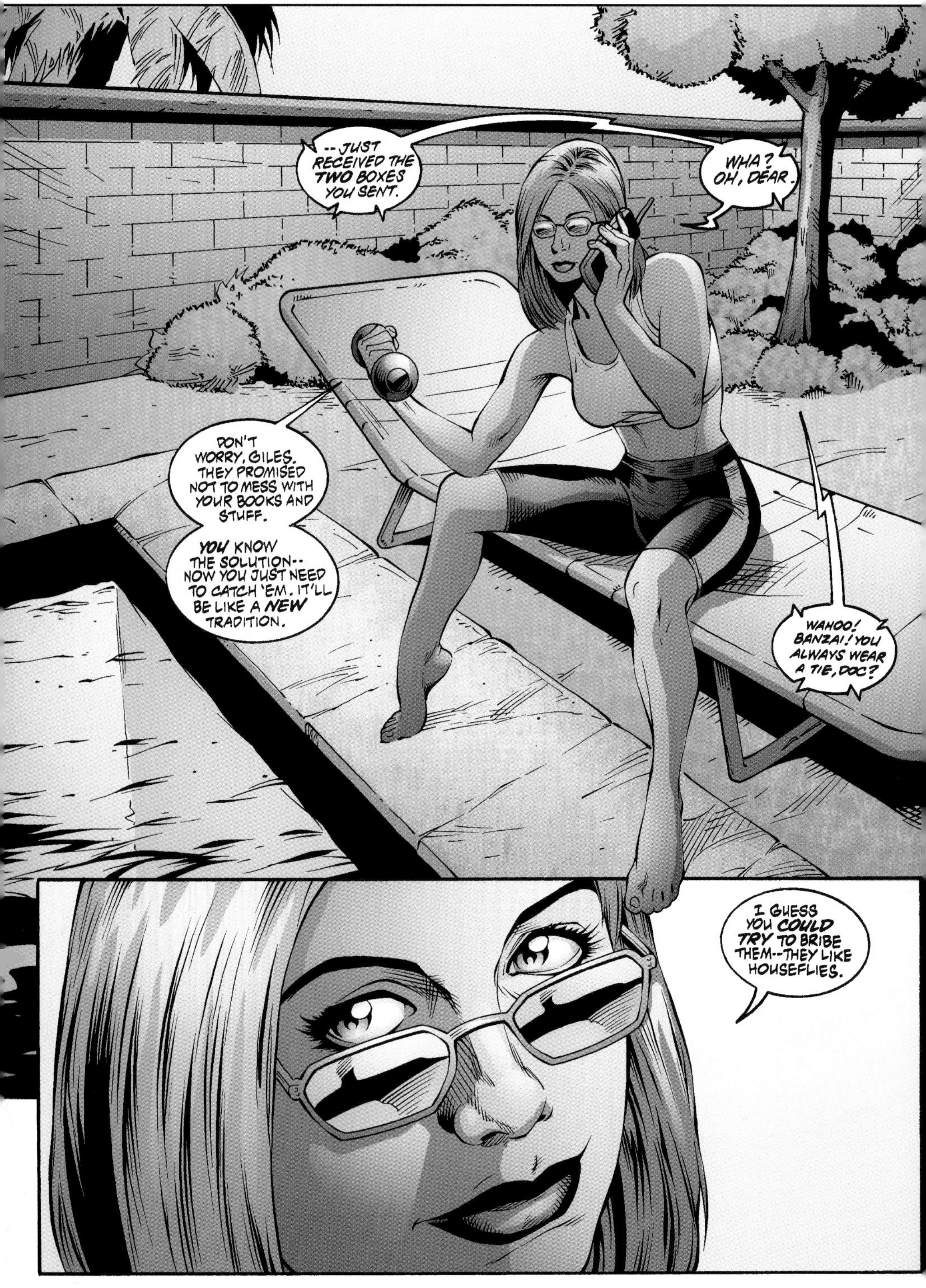
--JUST RECEIVED THE TWO BOXES YOU SENT.
WHA? OH, DEAR.
DON'T WORRY, GILES. THEY PROMISED NOT TO MESS WITH YOUR BOOKS AND STUFF.
YOU KNOW THE SOLUTION-- NOW YOU JUST NEED TO CATCH 'EM. IT'LL BE LIKE A NEW TRADITION.
WAHOO! BANZAI! YOU ALWAYS WEAR A TIE, DOC?
I GUESS YOU COULD TRY TO BRIBE THEM--THEY LIKE HOUSEFLIES.

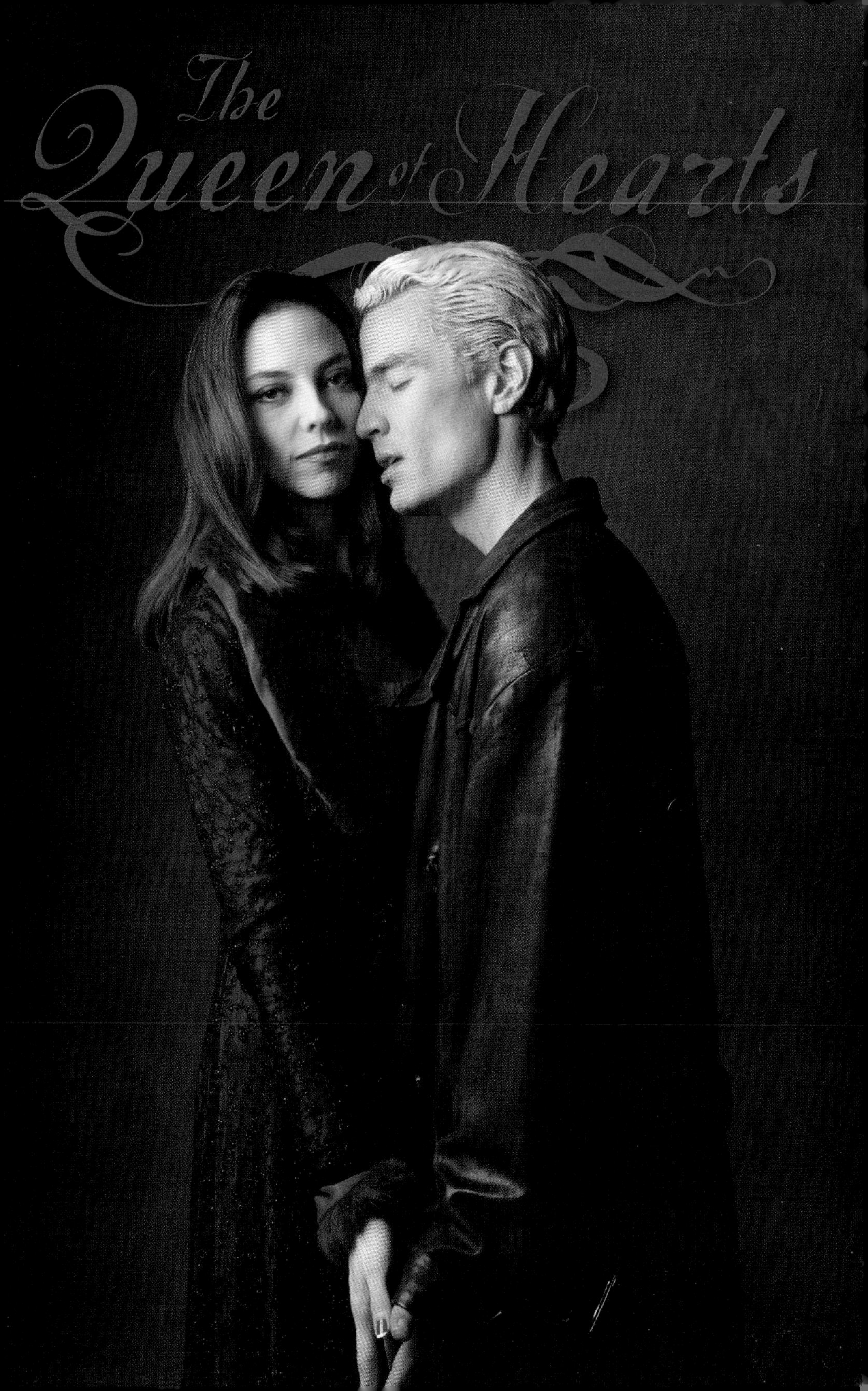
The Queen of Hearts

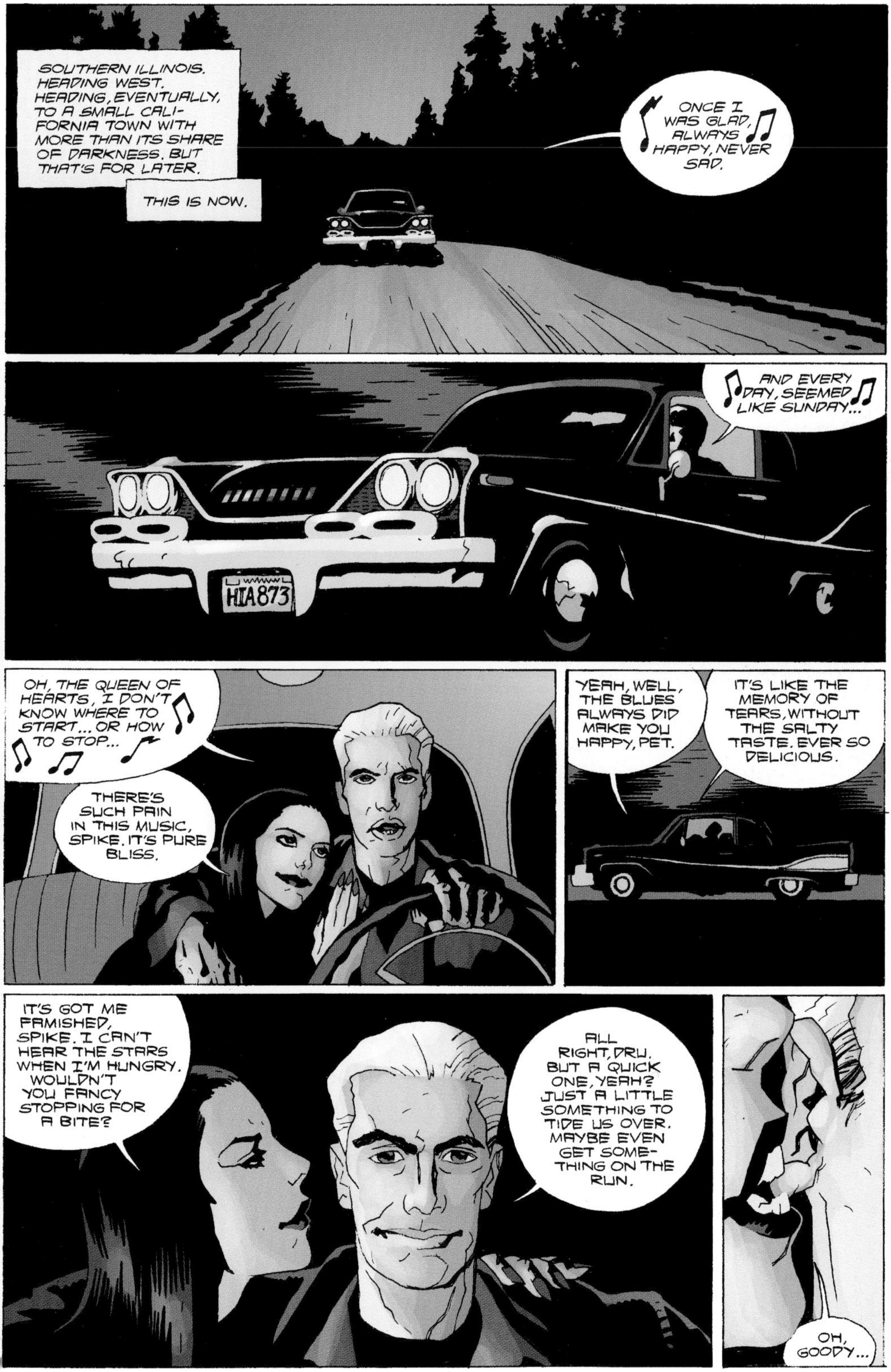
SOUTHERN ILLINOIS. HEADING WEST. HEADING, EVENTUALLY, TO A SMALL CALIFORNIA TOWN WITH MORE THAN ITS SHARE OF DARKNESS. BUT THAT'S FOR LATER.
THIS IS NOW.
ONCE I WAS GLAD, ALWAYS HAPPY, NEVER SAD.
AND EVERY DAY, SEEMED LIKE SUNDAY...
HIA873
OH, THE QUEEN OF HEARTS, I DON'T KNOW WHERE TO START... OR HOW TO STOP...
THERE'S SUCH PAIN IN THIS MUSIC, SPIKE. IT'S PURE BLISS.
YEAH, WELL, THE BLUES ALWAYS DID MAKE YOU HAPPY, PET.
IT'S LIKE THE MEMORY OF TEARS, WITHOUT THE SALTY TASTE. EVER SO DELICIOUS.
IT'S GOT ME FAMISHED, SPIKE. I CAN'T HEAR THE STARS WHEN I'M HUNGRY. WOULDN'T YOU FANCY STOPPING FOR A BITE?
ALL RIGHT, DRU, BUT A QUICK ONE, YEAH? JUST A LITTLE SOMETHING TO TIDE US OVER. MAYBE EVEN GET SOMETHING ON THE RUN.
OH, GOODY...

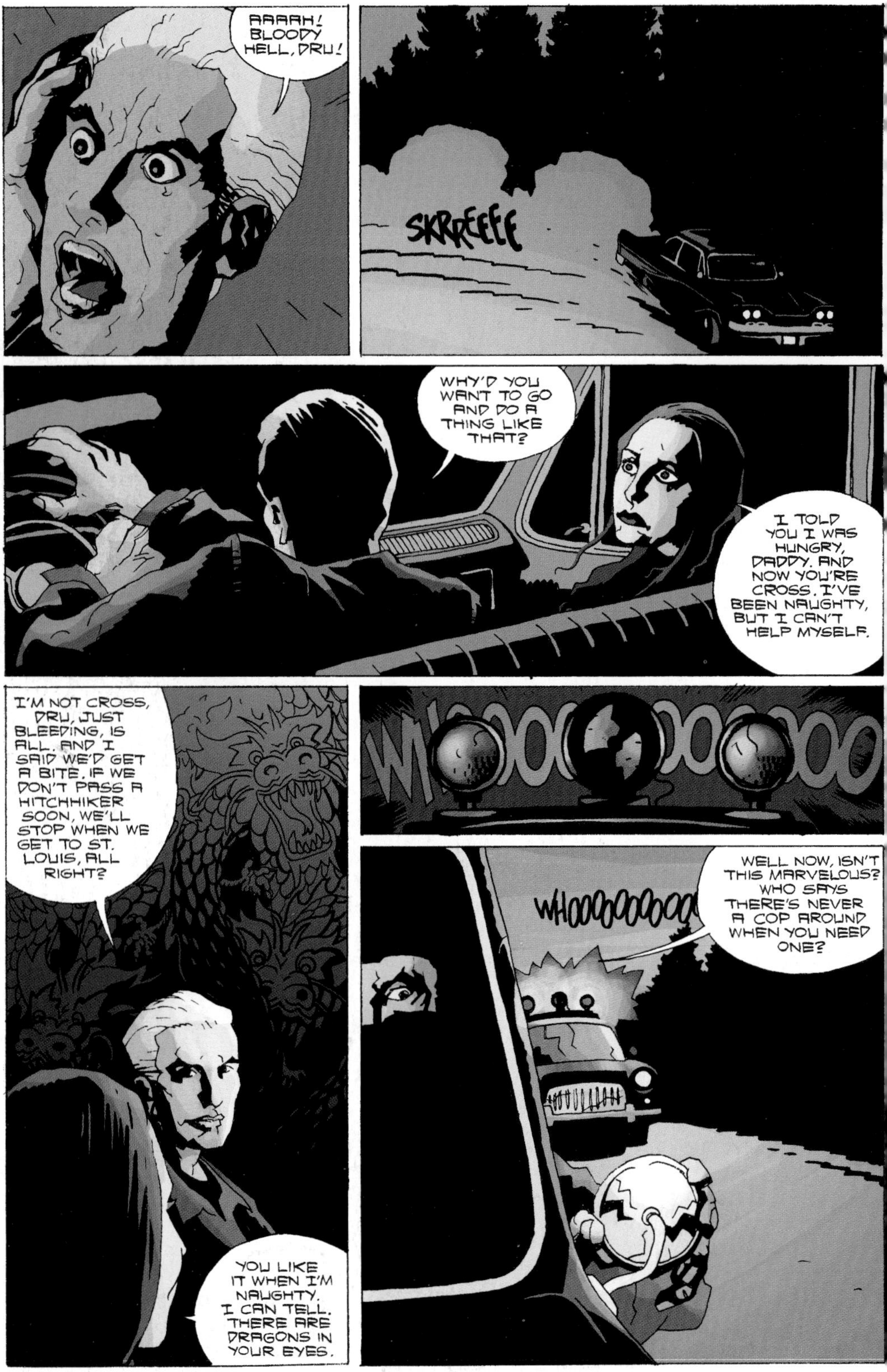
AAAARH! BLOODY HELL, DRU!
SKRREEEE
WHY'D YOU WANT TO GO AND DO A THING LIKE THAT?
I TOLD YOU I WAS HUNGRY, DADDY. AND NOW YOU'RE CROSS. I'VE BEEN NAUGHTY, BUT I CAN'T HELP MYSELF.
I'M NOT CROSS, DRU, JUST BLEEDING, IS ALL. AND I SAID WE'D GET A BITE. IF WE DON'T PASS A HITCHHIKER SOON, WE'LL STOP WHEN WE GET TO ST. LOUIS, ALL RIGHT?
YOU LIKE IT WHEN I'M NAUGHTY. I CAN TELL. THERE ARE DRAGONS IN YOUR EYES.
WHOOOOOOOOOOOOOO
WHOOOOOOOOOOOO
WELL NOW, ISN'T THIS MARVELOUS? WHO SAYS THERE'S NEVER A COP AROUND WHEN YOU NEED ONE?

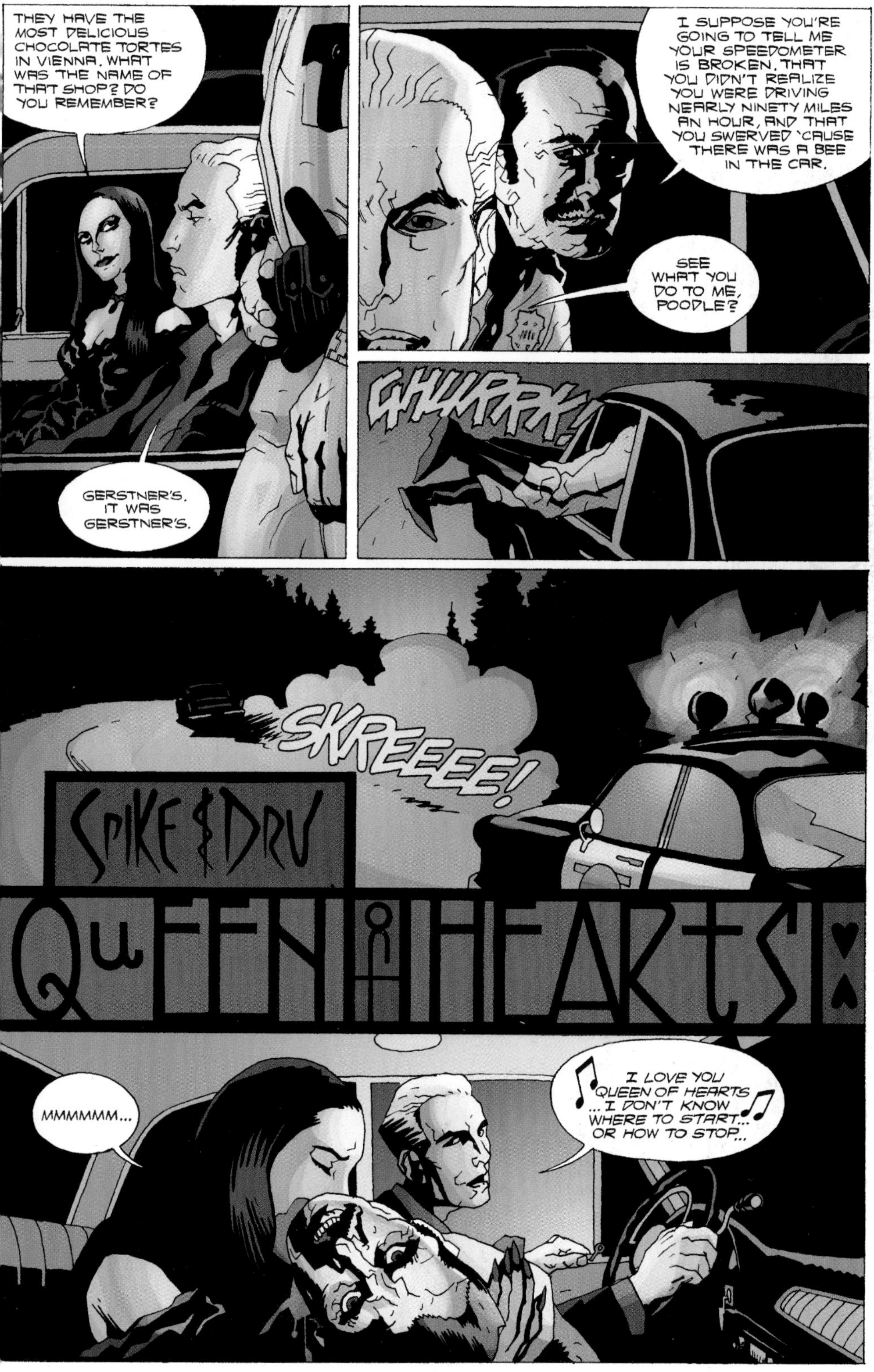
THEY HAVE THE MOST DELICIOUS CHOCOLATE TORTES IN VIENNA. WHAT WAS THE NAME OF THAT SHOP? DO YOU REMEMBER?
GERSTNER'S. IT WAS GERSTNER'S.
I SUPPOSE YOU'RE GOING TO TELL ME YOUR SPEEDOMETER IS BROKEN. THAT YOU DIDN'T REALIZE YOU WERE DRIVING NEARLY NINETY MILES AN HOUR, AND THAT YOU SWERVED 'CAUSE THERE WAS A BEE IN THE CAR.
SEE WHAT YOU DO TO ME, POODLE?
GHURRK!
SKREEEEE!
Spike & Dru
QUEEN of HEARTS
MMMMMM...
I LOVE YOU QUEEN OF HEARTS ...I DON'T KNOW WHERE TO START... OR HOW TO STOP...

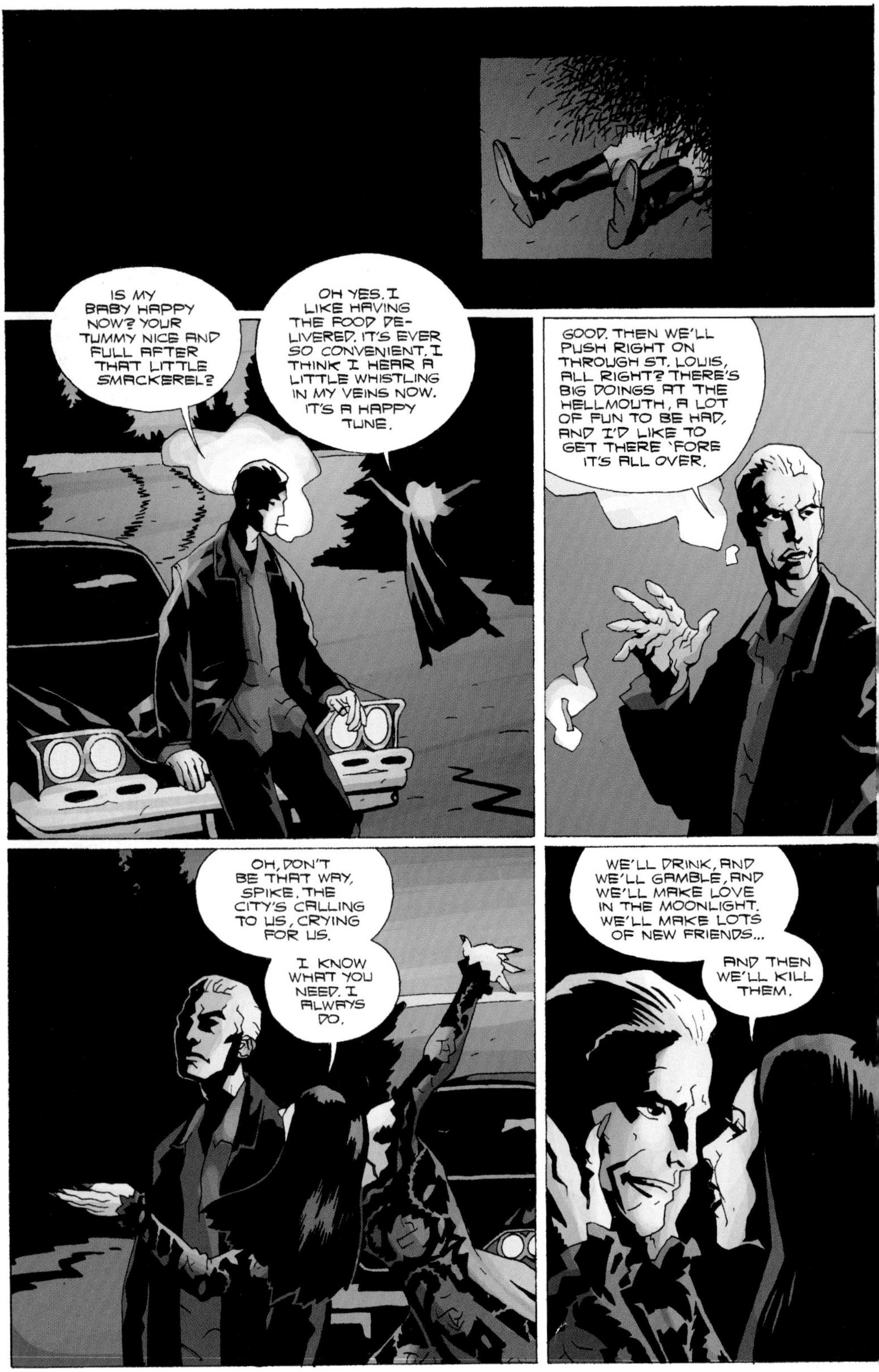
IS MY BABY HAPPY NOW? YOUR TUMMY NICE AND FULL AFTER THAT LITTLE SMACKEREL?
OH YES. I LIKE HAVING THE FOOD DE-LIVERED. IT'S EVER SO CONVENIENT. I THINK I HEAR A LITTLE WHISTLING IN MY VEINS NOW. IT'S A HAPPY TUNE.
GOOD. THEN WE'LL PUSH RIGHT ON THROUGH ST. LOUIS, ALL RIGHT? THERE'S BIG DOINGS AT THE HELLMOUTH, A LOT OF FUN TO BE HAD, AND I'D LIKE TO GET THERE 'FORE IT'S ALL OVER.
OH, DON'T BE THAT WAY, SPIKE. THE CITY'S CALLING TO US, CRYING FOR US.
I KNOW WHAT YOU NEED. I ALWAYS DO.
WE'LL DRINK, AND WE'LL GAMBLE, AND WE'LL MAKE LOVE IN THE MOONLIGHT. WE'LL MAKE LOTS OF NEW FRIENDS...
AND THEN WE'LL KILL THEM.

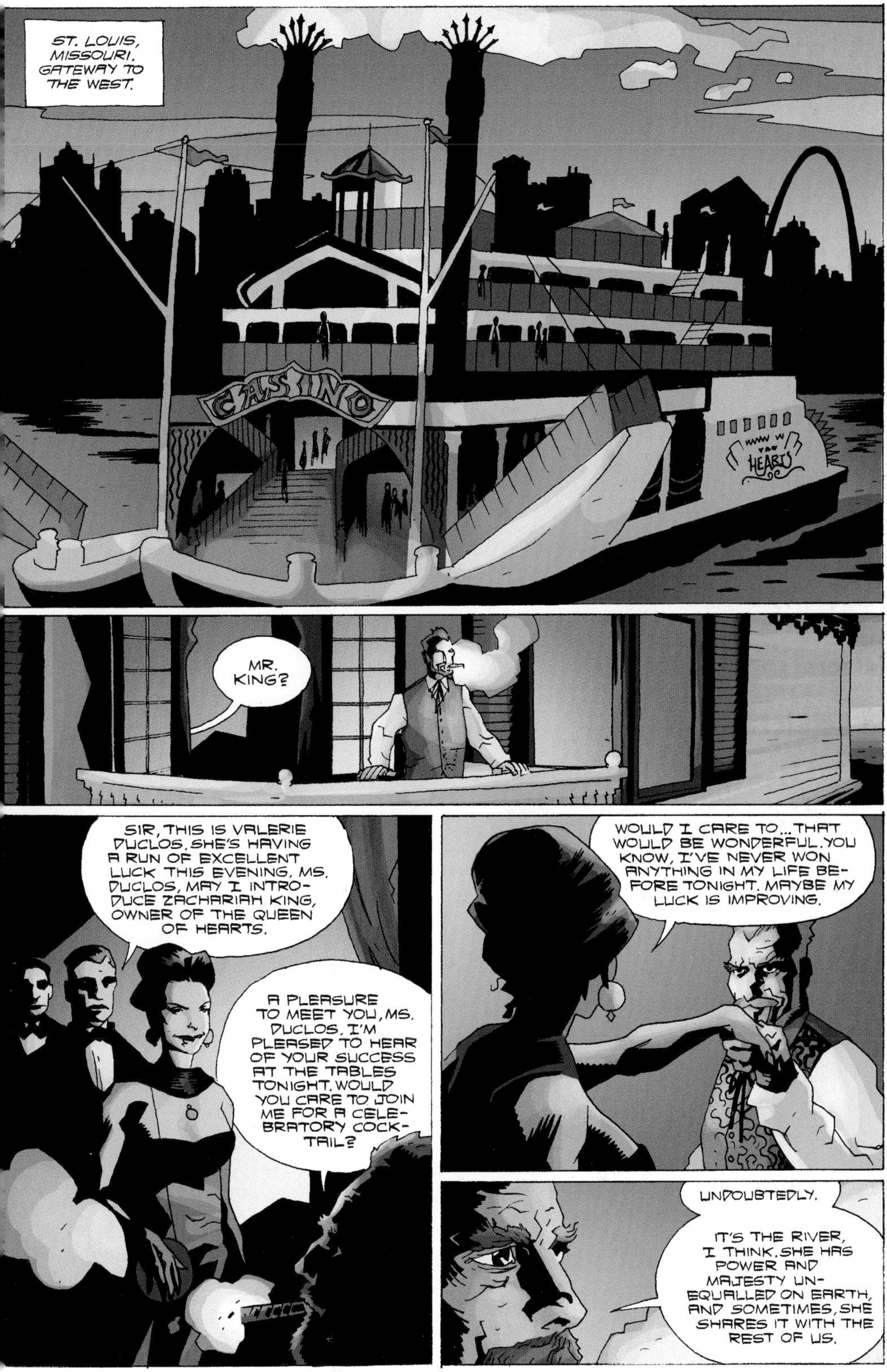

ST. LOUIS, MISSOURI, GATEWAY TO THE WEST.
CASSINO
QUEEN OF HEARTS
MR. KING?
SIR, THIS IS VALERIE DUCLOS. SHE'S HAVING A RUN OF EXCELLENT LUCK THIS EVENING. MS. DUCLOS, MAY I INTRODUCE ZACHARIAH KING, OWNER OF THE QUEEN OF HEARTS.
A PLEASURE TO MEET YOU, MS. DUCLOS. I'M PLEASED TO HEAR OF YOUR SUCCESS AT THE TABLES TONIGHT. WOULD YOU CARE TO JOIN ME FOR A CELEBRATORY COCKTAIL?
WOULD I CARE TO... THAT WOULD BE WONDERFUL. YOU KNOW, I'VE NEVER WON ANYTHING IN MY LIFE BEFORE TONIGHT. MAYBE MY LUCK IS IMPROVING.
UNDOUBTEDLY.
IT'S THE RIVER, I THINK. SHE HAS POWER AND MAJESTY UNEQUALLED ON EARTH, AND SOMETIMES, SHE SHARES IT WITH THE REST OF US.

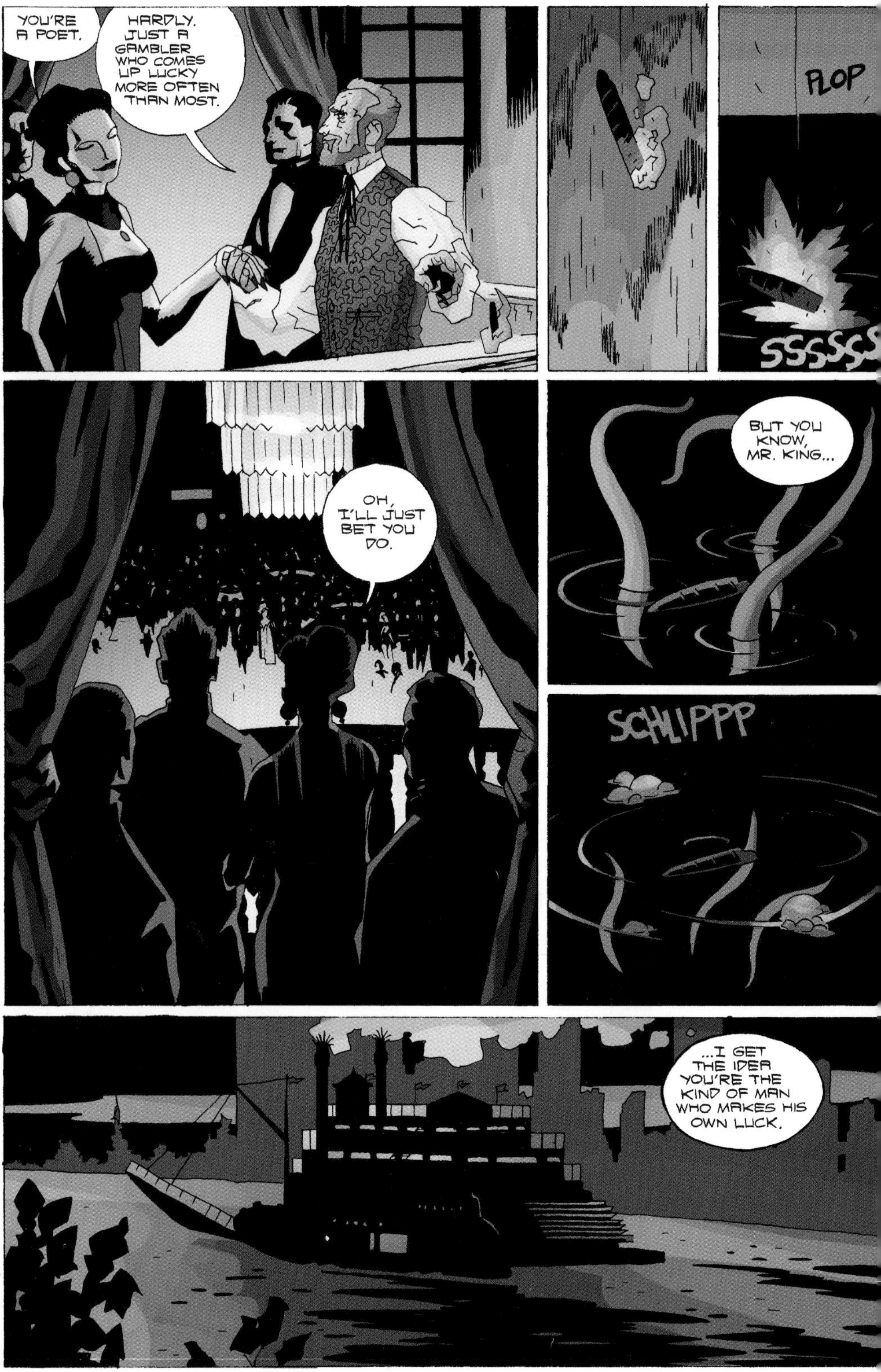
YOU'RE A POET.
HARDLY. JUST A GAMBLER WHO COMES UP LUCKY MORE OFTEN THAN MOST.
PLOP
SSSSSS
OH, I'LL JUST BET YOU DO.
BUT YOU KNOW, MR. KING...
SCHLIPPP
...I GET THE IDEA YOU'RE THE KIND OF MAN WHO MAKES HIS OWN LUCK.

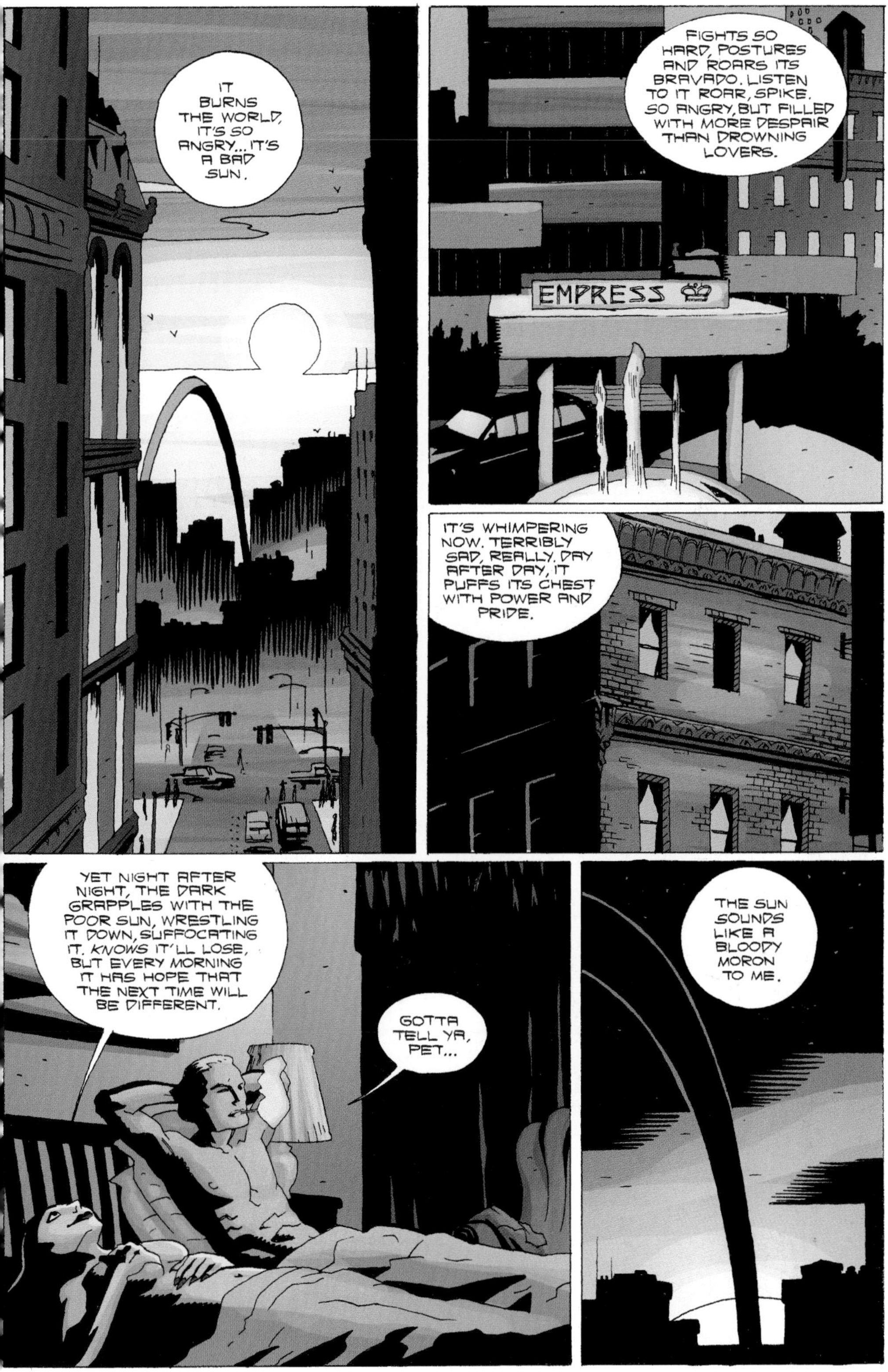
IT BURNS THE WORLD, IT'S SO ANGRY... IT'S A BAD SUN.
FIGHTS SO HARD, POSTURES AND ROARS ITS BRAVADO. LISTEN TO IT ROAR, SPIKE. SO ANGRY, BUT FILLED WITH MORE DESPAIR THAN DROWNING LOVERS.
EMPRESS
IT'S WHIMPERING NOW. TERRIBLY SAD, REALLY. DAY AFTER DAY, IT PUFFS ITS CHEST WITH POWER AND PRIDE.
YET NIGHT AFTER NIGHT, THE DARK GRAPPLES WITH THE POOR SUN, WRESTLING IT DOWN, SUFFOCATING IT. *KNOWS* IT'LL LOSE, BUT EVERY MORNING IT HAS HOPE THAT THE NEXT TIME WILL BE DIFFERENT.
GOTTA TELL YA, PET...
THE SUN SOUNDS LIKE A BLOODY MORON TO ME.

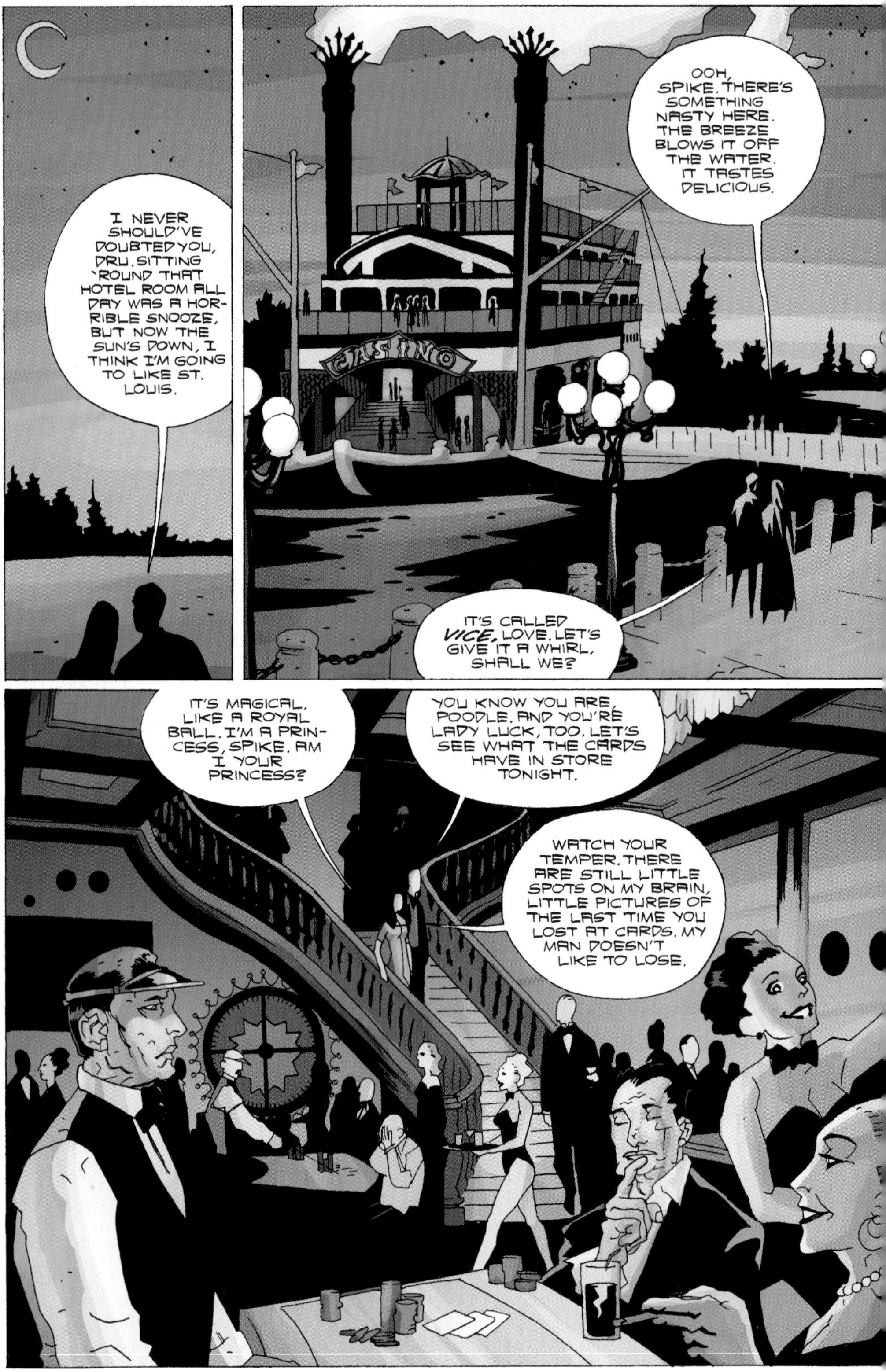
I NEVER SHOULD'VE DOUBTED YOU, DRU. SITTING 'ROUND THAT HOTEL ROOM ALL DAY WAS A HORRIBLE SNOOZE, BUT NOW THE SUN'S DOWN, I THINK I'M GOING TO LIKE ST. LOUIS.
OOH, SPIKE. THERE'S SOMETHING NASTY HERE. THE BREEZE BLOWS IT OFF THE WATER. IT TASTES DELICIOUS.
CASINO
IT'S CALLED *VICE*, LOVE. LET'S GIVE IT A WHIRL, SHALL WE?
IT'S MAGICAL, LIKE A ROYAL BALL. I'M A PRINCESS, SPIKE. AM I YOUR PRINCESS?
YOU KNOW YOU ARE, POODLE. AND YOU'RE LADY LUCK, TOO. LET'S SEE WHAT THE CARDS HAVE IN STORE TONIGHT.
WATCH YOUR TEMPER. THERE ARE STILL LITTLE SPOTS ON MY BRAIN, LITTLE PICTURES OF THE LAST TIME YOU LOST AT CARDS. MY MAN DOESN'T LIKE TO LOSE.

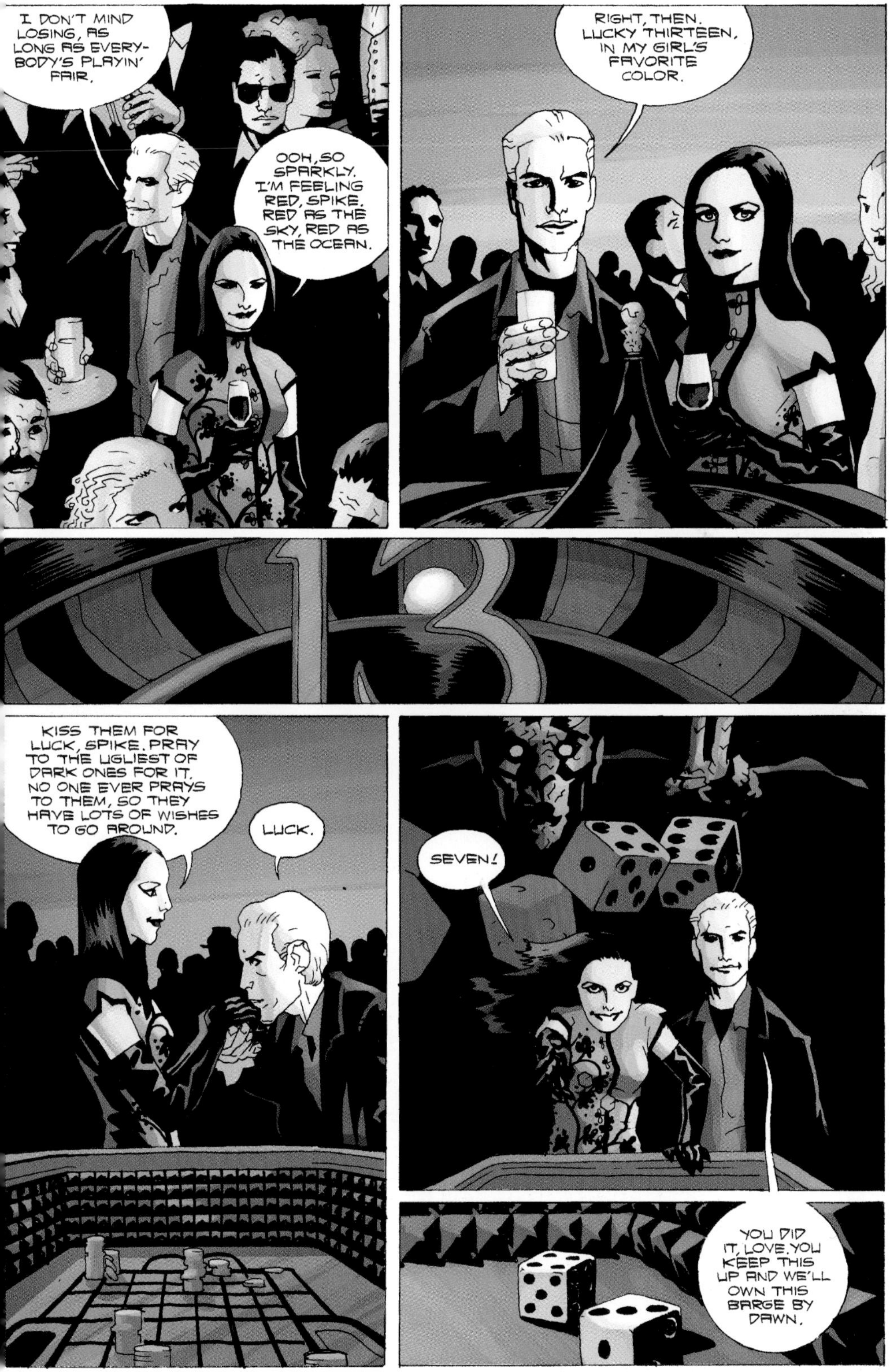
I DON'T MIND LOSING, AS LONG AS EVERY-BODY'S PLAYIN' FAIR.
OOH, SO SPARKLY. I'M FEELING RED, SPIKE. RED AS THE SKY, RED AS THE OCEAN.
RIGHT, THEN. LUCKY THIRTEEN, IN MY GIRL'S FAVORITE COLOR.
KISS THEM FOR LUCK, SPIKE. PRAY TO THE UGLIEST OF DARK ONES FOR IT. NO ONE EVER PRAYS TO THEM, SO THEY HAVE LOTS OF WISHES TO GO AROUND.
LUCK.
SEVEN!
YOU DID IT, LOVE. YOU KEEP THIS UP AND WE'LL OWN THIS BARGE BY DAWN.

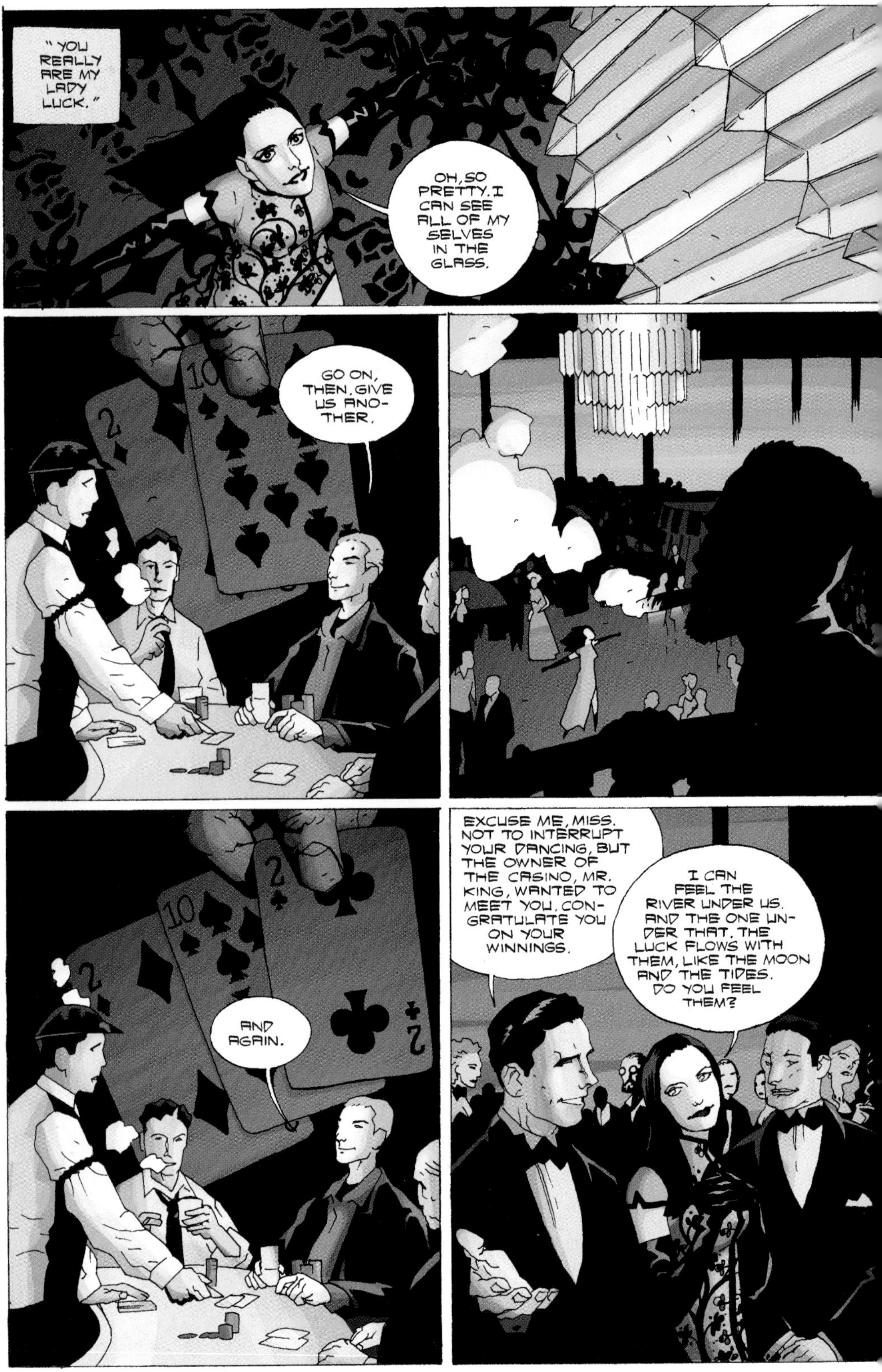
"YOU REALLY ARE MY LADY LUCK."
OH, SO PRETTY. I CAN SEE ALL OF MY SELVES IN THE GLASS.
GO ON, THEN. GIVE US ANOTHER.
AND AGAIN.
EXCUSE ME, MISS. NOT TO INTERRUPT YOUR DANCING, BUT THE OWNER OF THE CASINO, MR. KING, WANTED TO MEET YOU. CONGRATULATE YOU ON YOUR WINNINGS.
I CAN FEEL THE RIVER UNDER US. AND THE ONE UNDER THAT. THE LUCK FLOWS WITH THEM, LIKE THE MOON AND THE TIDES. DO YOU FEEL THEM?

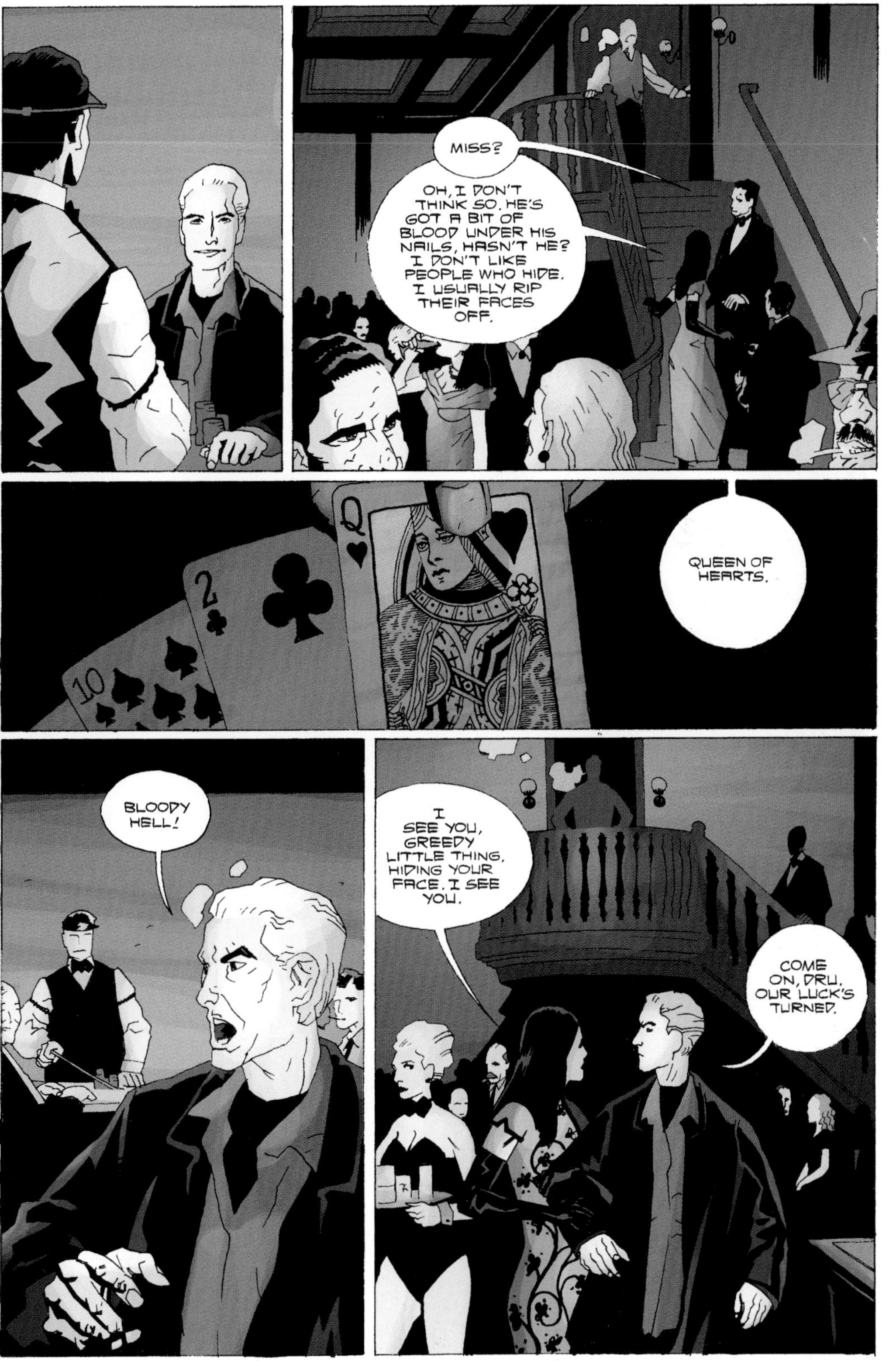
MISS?
OH, I DON'T THINK SO. HE'S GOT A BIT OF BLOOD UNDER HIS NAILS, HASN'T HE? I DON'T LIKE PEOPLE WHO HIDE. I USUALLY RIP THEIR FACES OFF.
QUEEN OF HEARTS.
BLOODY HELL!
I SEE YOU, GREEDY LITTLE THING, HIDING YOUR FACE. I SEE YOU.
COME ON, DRU, OUR LUCK'S TURNED.

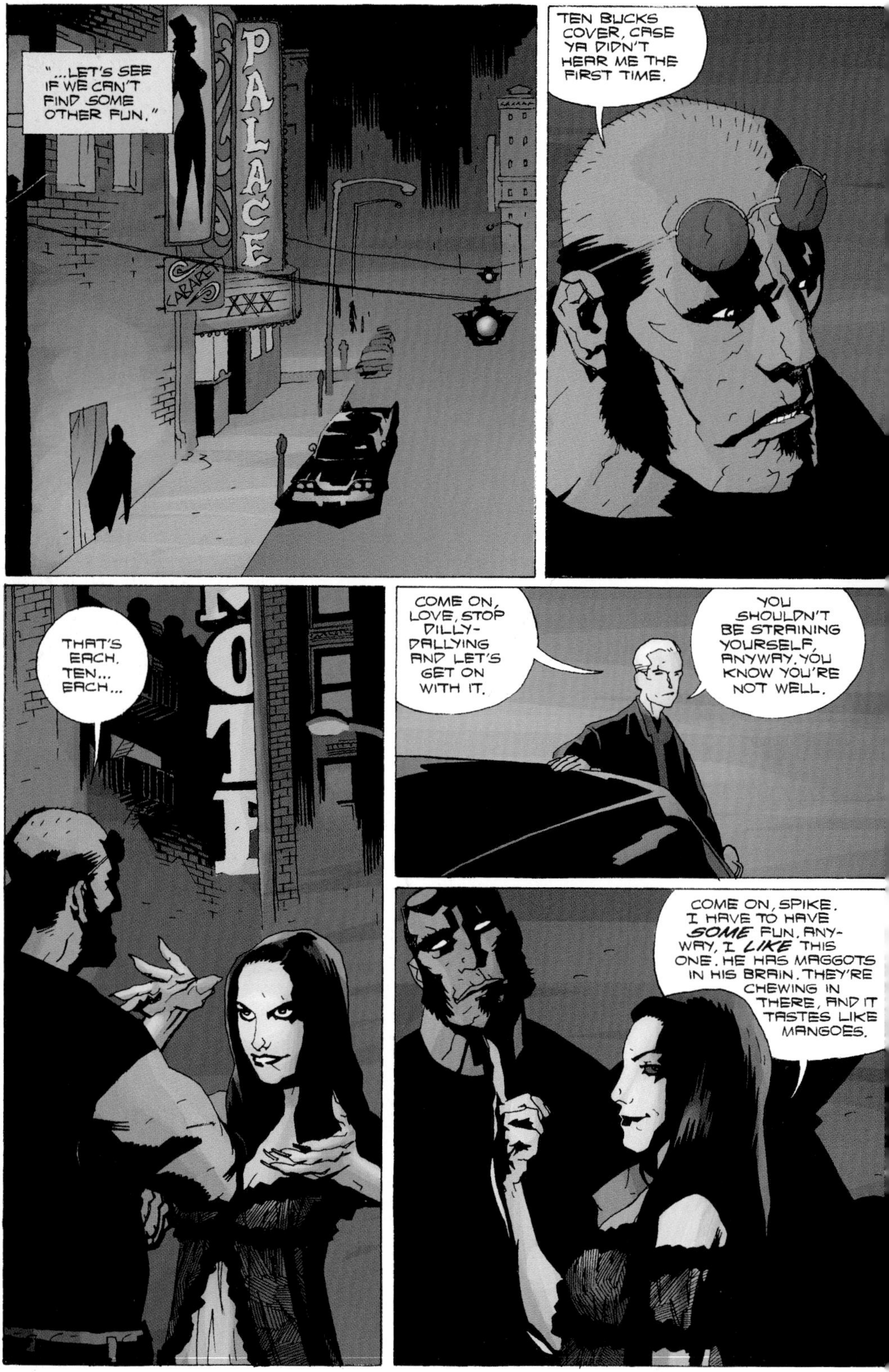
"...LET'S SEE IF WE CAN'T FIND SOME OTHER FUN."
PALACE
CABARET
XXX
TEN BUCKS COVER, CASE YA DIDN'T HEAR ME THE FIRST TIME.
THAT'S EACH. TEN... EACH...
COME ON, LOVE, STOP DILLY-DALLYING AND LET'S GET ON WITH IT.
YOU SHOULDN'T BE STRAINING YOURSELF, ANYWAY. YOU KNOW YOU'RE NOT WELL.
COME ON, SPIKE. I HAVE TO HAVE *SOME* FUN. ANYWAY, I *LIKE* THIS ONE. HE HAS MAGGOTS IN HIS BRAIN. THEY'RE CHEWING IN THERE, AND IT TASTES LIKE MANGOES.

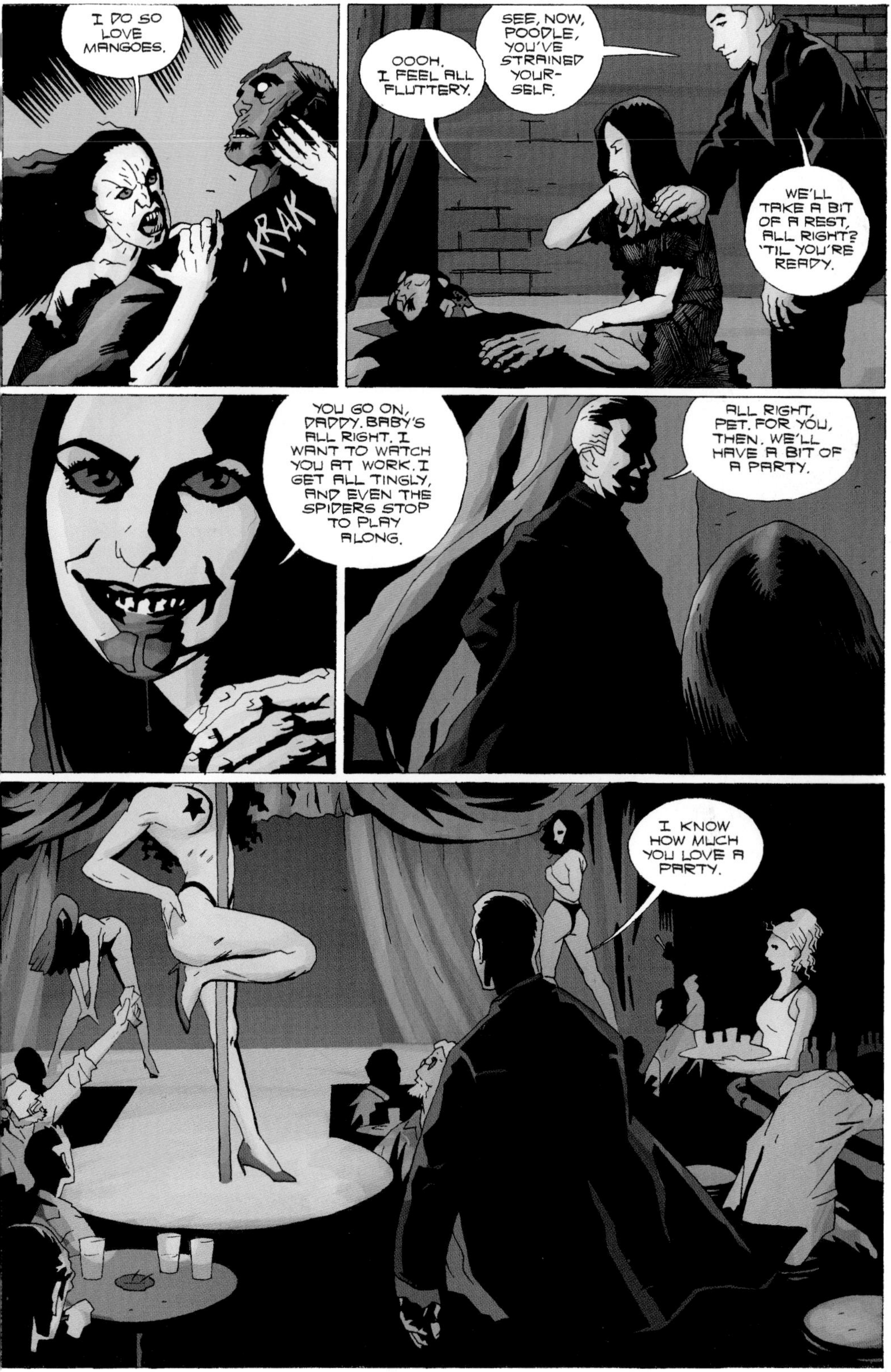
I DO SO LOVE MANGOES.
KRAK
OOOH. I FEEL ALL FLUTTERY.
SEE, NOW, POODLE, YOU'VE STRAINED YOURSELF.
WE'LL TAKE A BIT OF A REST, ALL RIGHT? 'TIL YOU'RE READY.
YOU GO ON, DADDY. BABY'S ALL RIGHT. I WANT TO WATCH YOU AT WORK. I GET ALL TINGLY, AND EVEN THE SPIDERS STOP TO PLAY ALONG.
ALL RIGHT, PET. FOR YOU, THEN. WE'LL HAVE A BIT OF A PARTY.
I KNOW HOW MUCH YOU LOVE A PARTY.

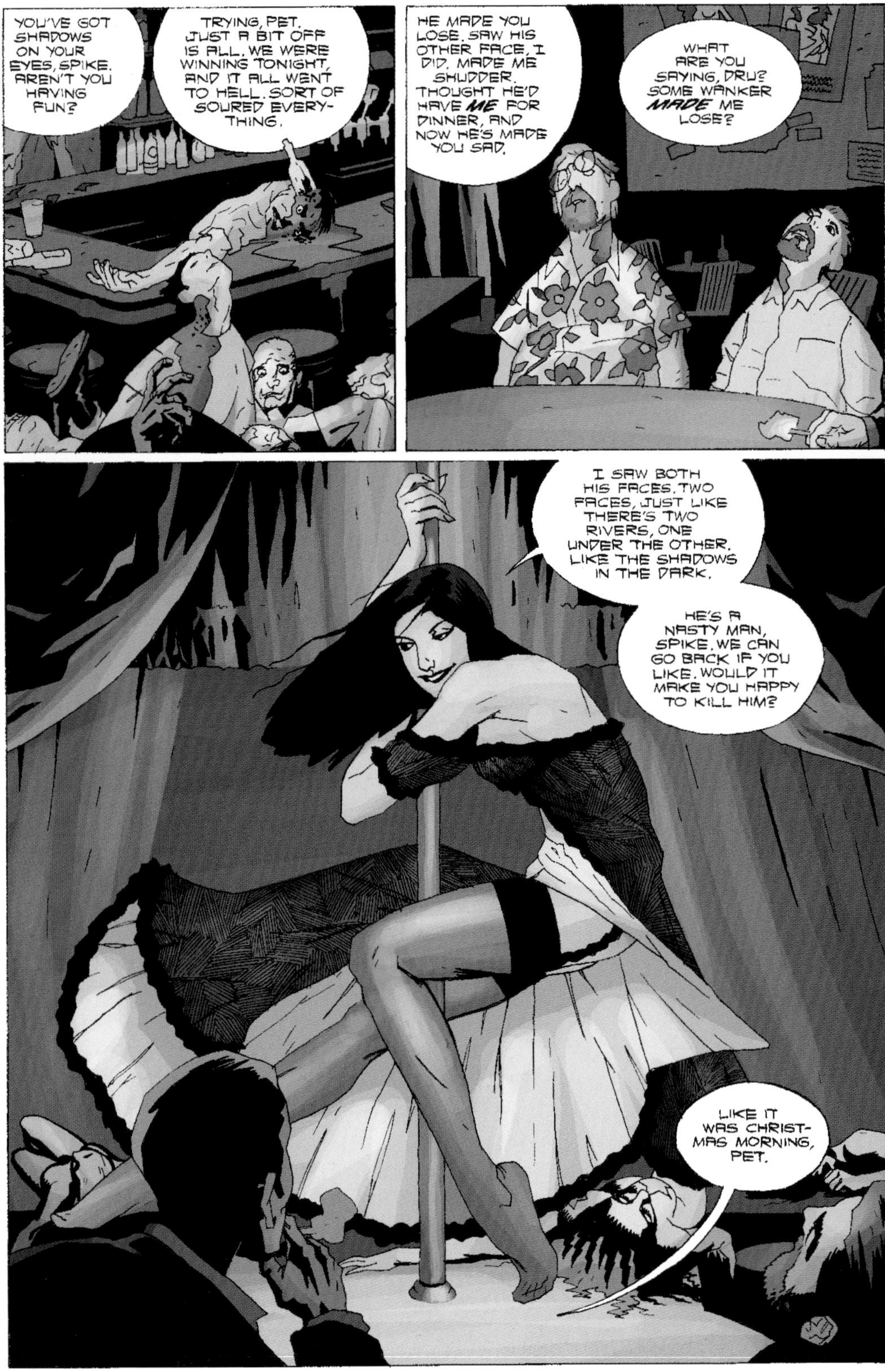
YOU'VE GOT SHADOWS ON YOUR EYES, SPIKE. AREN'T YOU HAVING FUN?
TRYING, PET. JUST A BIT OFF IS ALL. WE WERE WINNING TONIGHT, AND IT ALL WENT TO HELL. SORT OF SOURED EVERYTHING.
HE MADE YOU LOSE. SAW HIS OTHER FACE, I DID. MADE ME SHUDDER. THOUGHT HE'D HAVE ME FOR DINNER, AND NOW HE'S MADE YOU SAD.
WHAT ARE YOU SAYING, DRU? SOME WANKER MADE ME LOSE?
I SAW BOTH HIS FACES. TWO FACES, JUST LIKE THERE'S TWO RIVERS, ONE UNDER THE OTHER. LIKE THE SHADOWS IN THE DARK.
HE'S A NASTY MAN, SPIKE. WE CAN GO BACK IF YOU LIKE. WOULD IT MAKE YOU HAPPY TO KILL HIM?
LIKE IT WAS CHRISTMAS MORNING, PET.

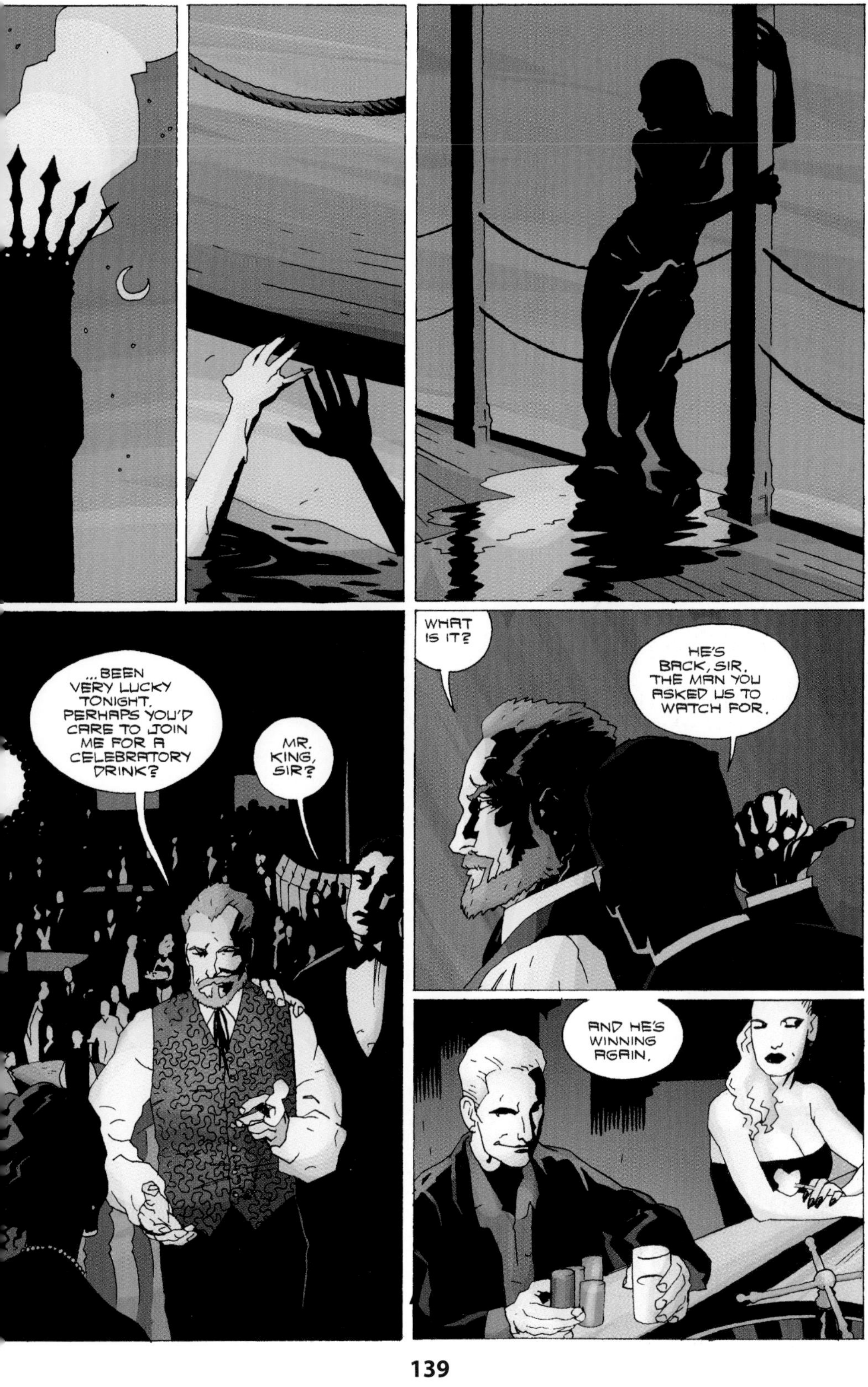
...BEEN VERY LUCKY TONIGHT. PERHAPS YOU'D CARE TO JOIN ME FOR A CELEBRATORY DRINK?
MR. KING, SIR?
WHAT IS IT?
HE'S BACK, SIR. THE MAN YOU ASKED US TO WATCH FOR.
AND HE'S WINNING AGAIN.

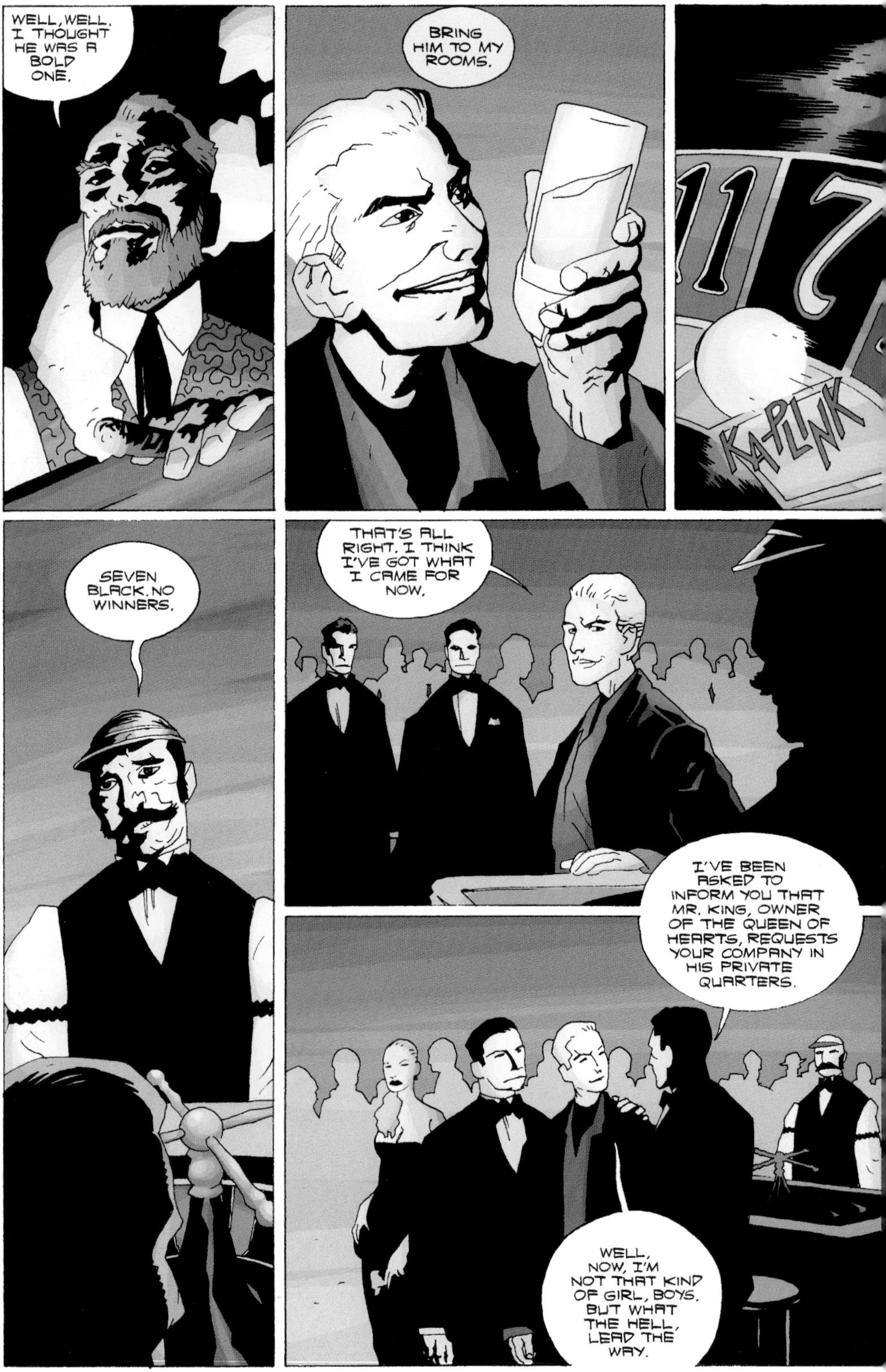
WELL, WELL. I THOUGHT HE WAS A BOLD ONE.
BRING HIM TO MY ROOMS.
KA-PLINK
SEVEN BLACK. NO WINNERS.
THAT'S ALL RIGHT. I THINK I'VE GOT WHAT I CAME FOR NOW.
I'VE BEEN ASKED TO INFORM YOU THAT MR. KING, OWNER OF THE QUEEN OF HEARTS, REQUESTS YOUR COMPANY IN HIS PRIVATE QUARTERS.
WELL, NOW, I'M NOT THAT KIND OF GIRL, BOYS. BUT WHAT THE HELL, LEAD THE WAY.

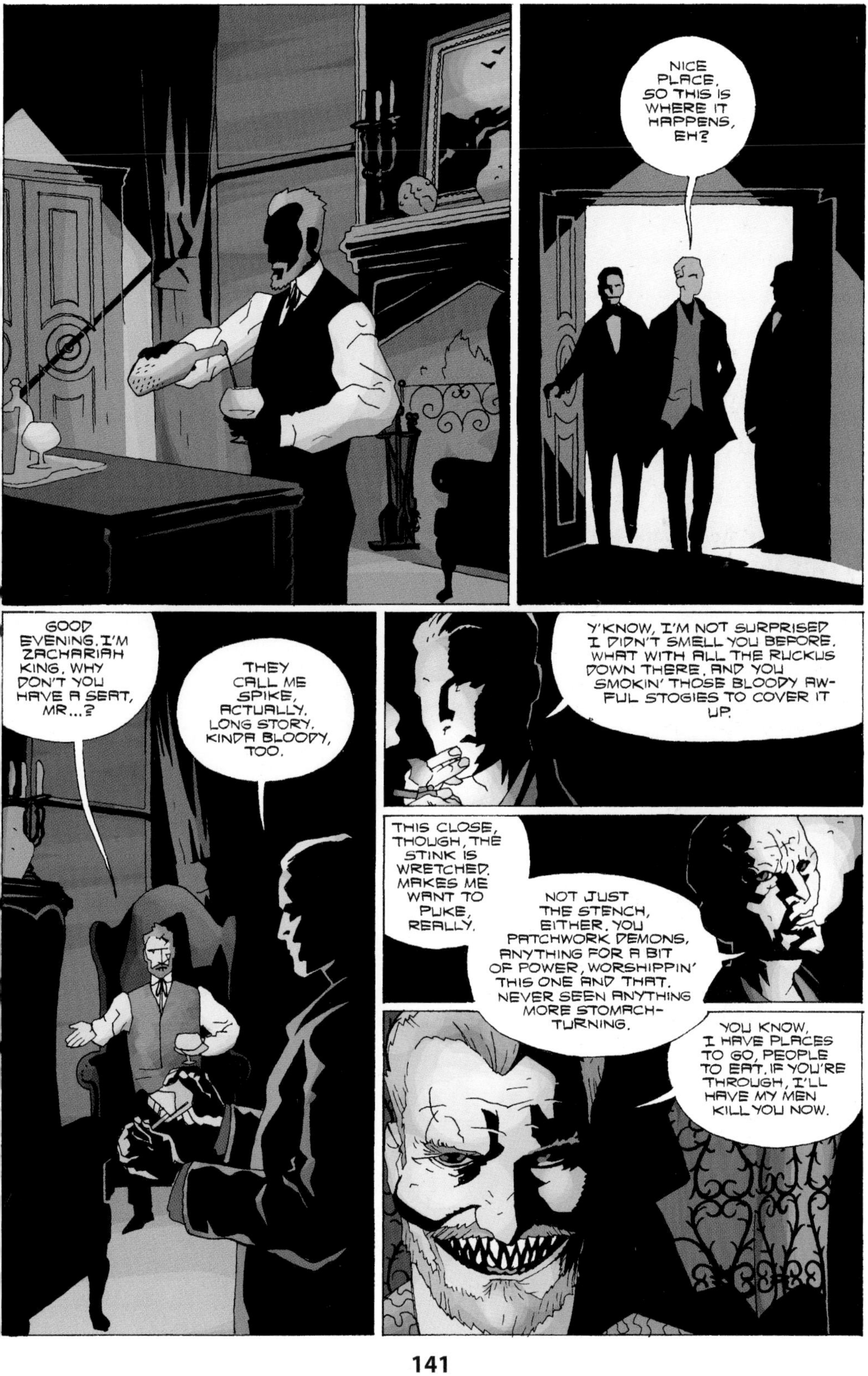
NICE PLACE. SO THIS IS WHERE IT HAPPENS, EH?
GOOD EVENING. I'M ZACHARIAH KING. WHY DON'T YOU HAVE A SEAT, MR...?
THEY CALL ME SPIKE, ACTUALLY. LONG STORY. KINDA BLOODY, TOO.
Y'KNOW, I'M NOT SURPRISED I DIDN'T SMELL YOU BEFORE. WHAT WITH ALL THE RUCKUS DOWN THERE, AND YOU SMOKIN' THOSE BLOODY AW-FUL STOGIES TO COVER IT UP.
THIS CLOSE, THOUGH, THE STINK IS WRETCHED. MAKES ME WANT TO PUKE, REALLY.
NOT JUST THE STENCH, EITHER. YOU PATCHWORK DEMONS, ANYTHING FOR A BIT OF POWER, WORSHIPPIN' THIS ONE AND THAT. NEVER SEEN ANYTHING MORE STOMACH-TURNING.
YOU KNOW, I HAVE PLACES TO GO, PEOPLE TO EAT. IF YOU'RE THROUGH, I'LL HAVE MY MEN KILL YOU NOW.

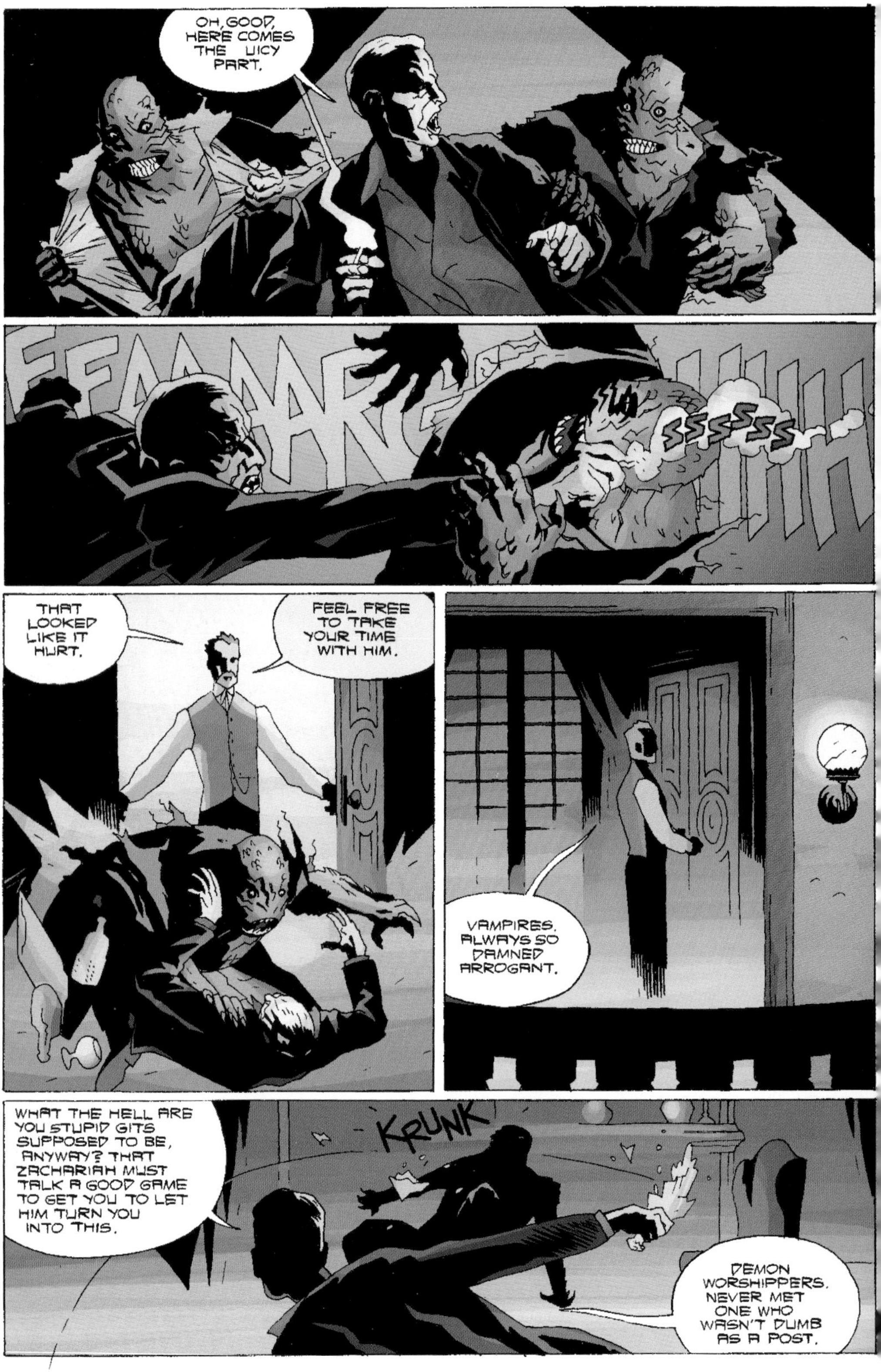
OH, GOOD, HERE COMES THE UICY PART.
SSSSSS
THAT LOOKED LIKE IT HURT.
FEEL FREE TO TAKE YOUR TIME WITH HIM.
VAMPIRES. ALWAYS SO DAMNED ARROGANT.
WHAT THE HELL ARE YOU STUPID GITS SUPPOSED TO BE, ANYWAY? THAT ZACHARIAH MUST TALK A GOOD GAME TO GET YOU TO LET HIM TURN YOU INTO THIS.
KRUNK
DEMON WORSHIPPERS. NEVER MET ONE WHO WASN'T DUMB AS A POST.

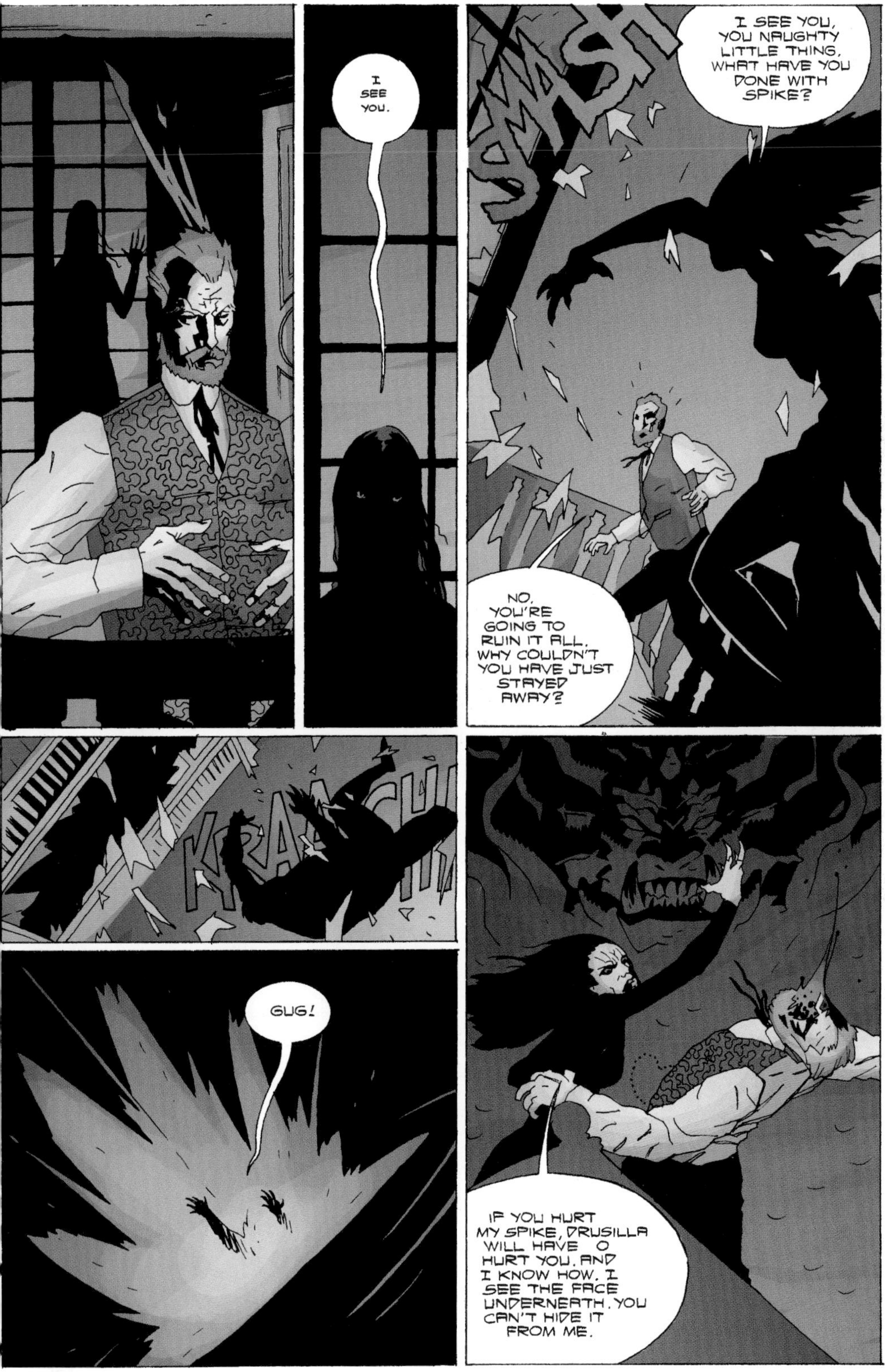
I SEE YOU.
I SEE YOU, YOU NAUGHTY LITTLE THING. WHAT HAVE YOU DONE WITH SPIKE?
NO. YOU'RE GOING TO RUIN IT ALL. WHY COULDN'T YOU HAVE JUST STAYED AWAY?
GUG!
IF YOU HURT MY SPIKE, DRUSILLA WILL HAVE O HURT YOU. AND I KNOW HOW. I SEE THE FACE UNDERNEATH. YOU CAN'T HIDE IT FROM ME.

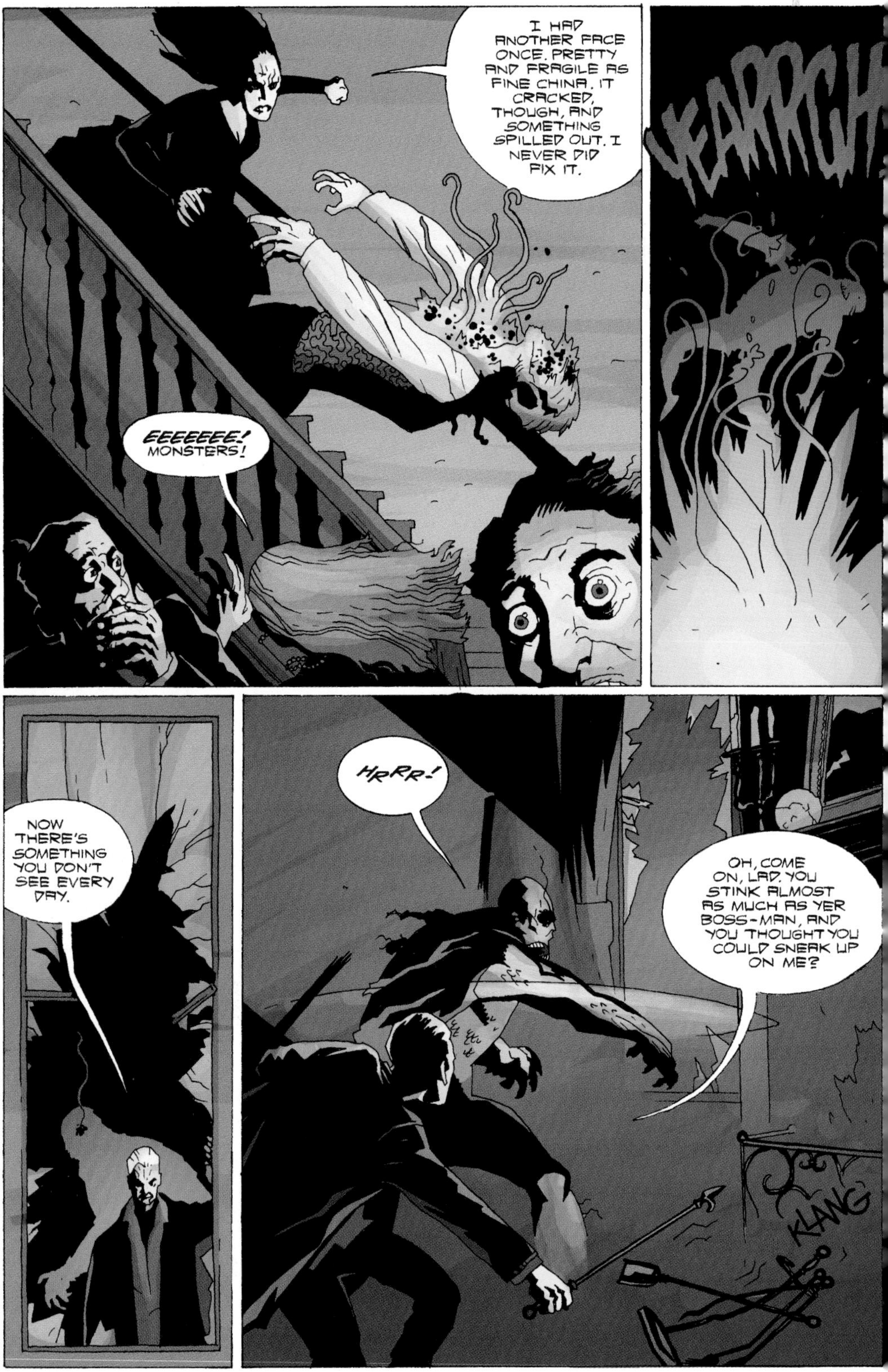
I HAD ANOTHER FACE ONCE. PRETTY AND FRAGILE AS FINE CHINA. IT CRACKED, THOUGH, AND SOMETHING SPILLED OUT. I NEVER DID FIX IT.
YEARRCH
EEEEEEE! MONSTERS!
NOW THERE'S SOMETHING YOU DON'T SEE EVERY DAY.
HRRR!
OH, COME ON, LAD. YOU STINK ALMOST AS MUCH AS YER BOSS-MAN, AND YOU THOUGHT YOU COULD SNEAK UP ON ME?
KLANG

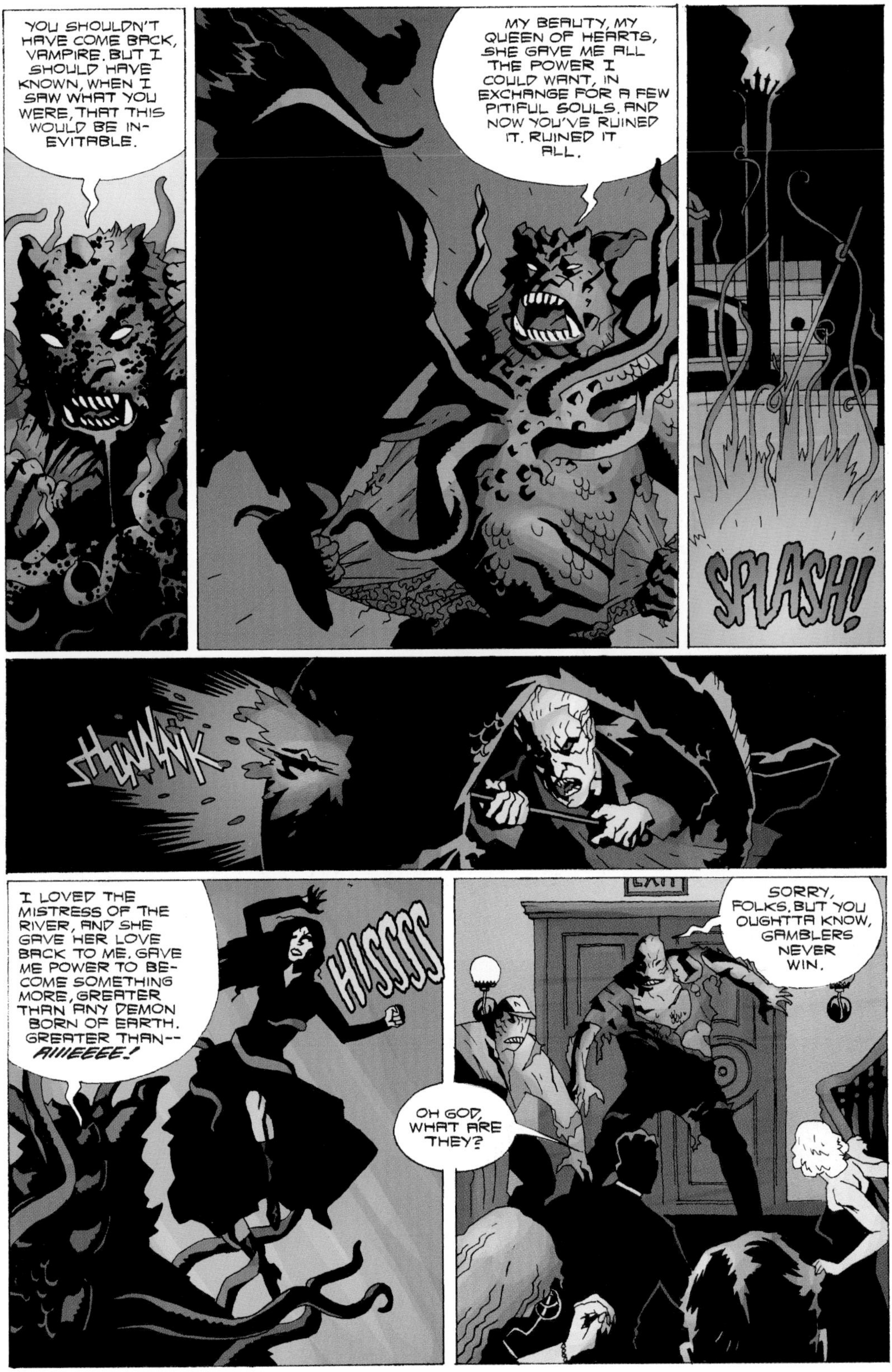
YOU SHOULDN'T HAVE COME BACK, VAMPIRE. BUT I SHOULD HAVE KNOWN, WHEN I SAW WHAT YOU WERE, THAT THIS WOULD BE IN-EVITABLE.
MY BEAUTY, MY QUEEN OF HEARTS, SHE GAVE ME ALL THE POWER I COULD WANT, IN EXCHANGE FOR A FEW PITIFUL SOULS. AND NOW YOU'VE RUINED IT. RUINED IT ALL.
SPLASH!
SHWNNK
I LOVED THE MISTRESS OF THE RIVER, AND SHE GAVE HER LOVE BACK TO ME. GAVE ME POWER TO BE-COME SOMETHING MORE, GREATER THAN ANY DEMON BORN OF EARTH. GREATER THAN-- AIIIEEEE!
HISSSS
SORRY, FOLKS, BUT YOU OUGHTTA KNOW, GAMBLERS NEVER WIN.
OH GOD, WHAT ARE THEY?

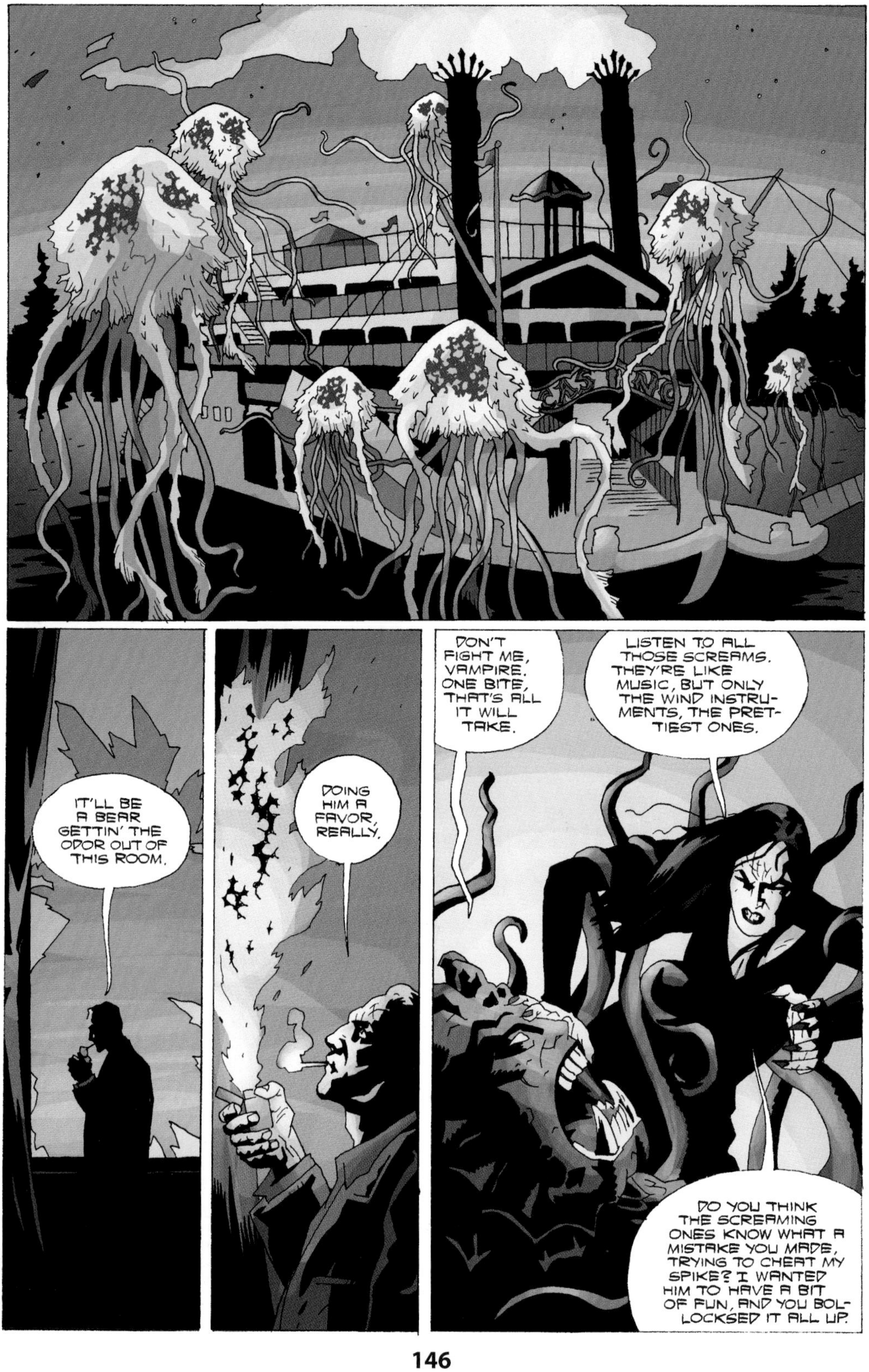
IT'LL BE A BEAR GETTIN' THE ODOR OUT OF THIS ROOM.
DOING HIM A FAVOR, REALLY.
DON'T FIGHT ME, VAMPIRE. ONE BITE, THAT'S ALL IT WILL TAKE.
LISTEN TO ALL THOSE SCREAMS. THEY'RE LIKE MUSIC, BUT ONLY THE WIND INSTRU-MENTS, THE PRET-TIEST ONES.
DO YOU THINK THE SCREAMING ONES KNOW WHAT A MISTAKE YOU MADE, TRYING TO CHEAT MY SPIKE? I WANTED HIM TO HAVE A BIT OF FUN, AND YOU BOL-LOCKSED IT ALL UP.

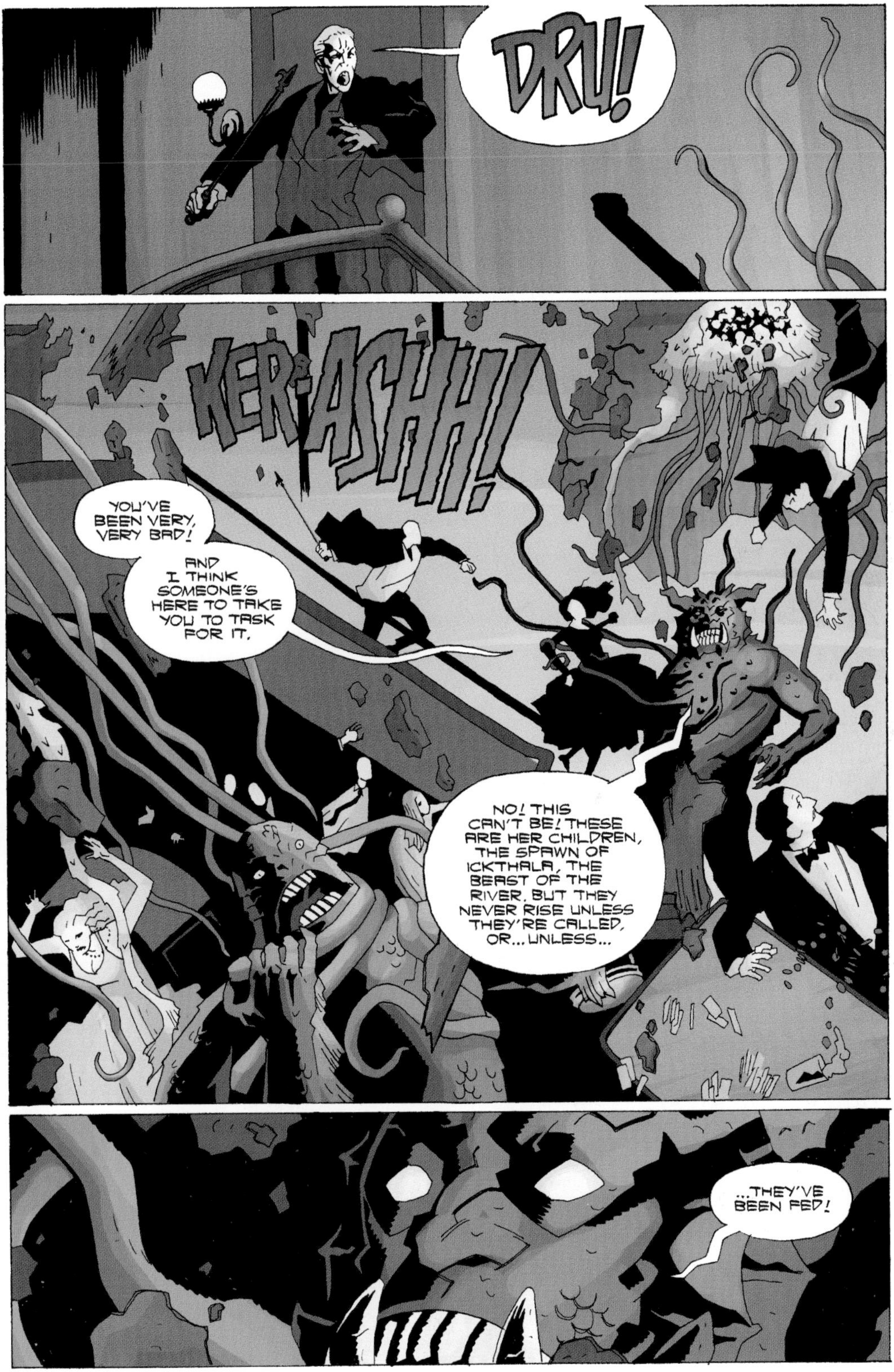
DRU!
KER-ASHH!
YOU'VE BEEN VERY, VERY BAD!
AND I THINK SOMEONE'S HERE TO TAKE YOU TO TASK FOR IT.
NO! THIS CAN'T BE! THESE ARE HER CHILDREN, THE SPAWN OF ICKTHALA, THE BEAST OF THE RIVER. BUT THEY NEVER RISE UNLESS THEY'RE CALLED, OR... UNLESS...
...THEY'VE BEEN FED!

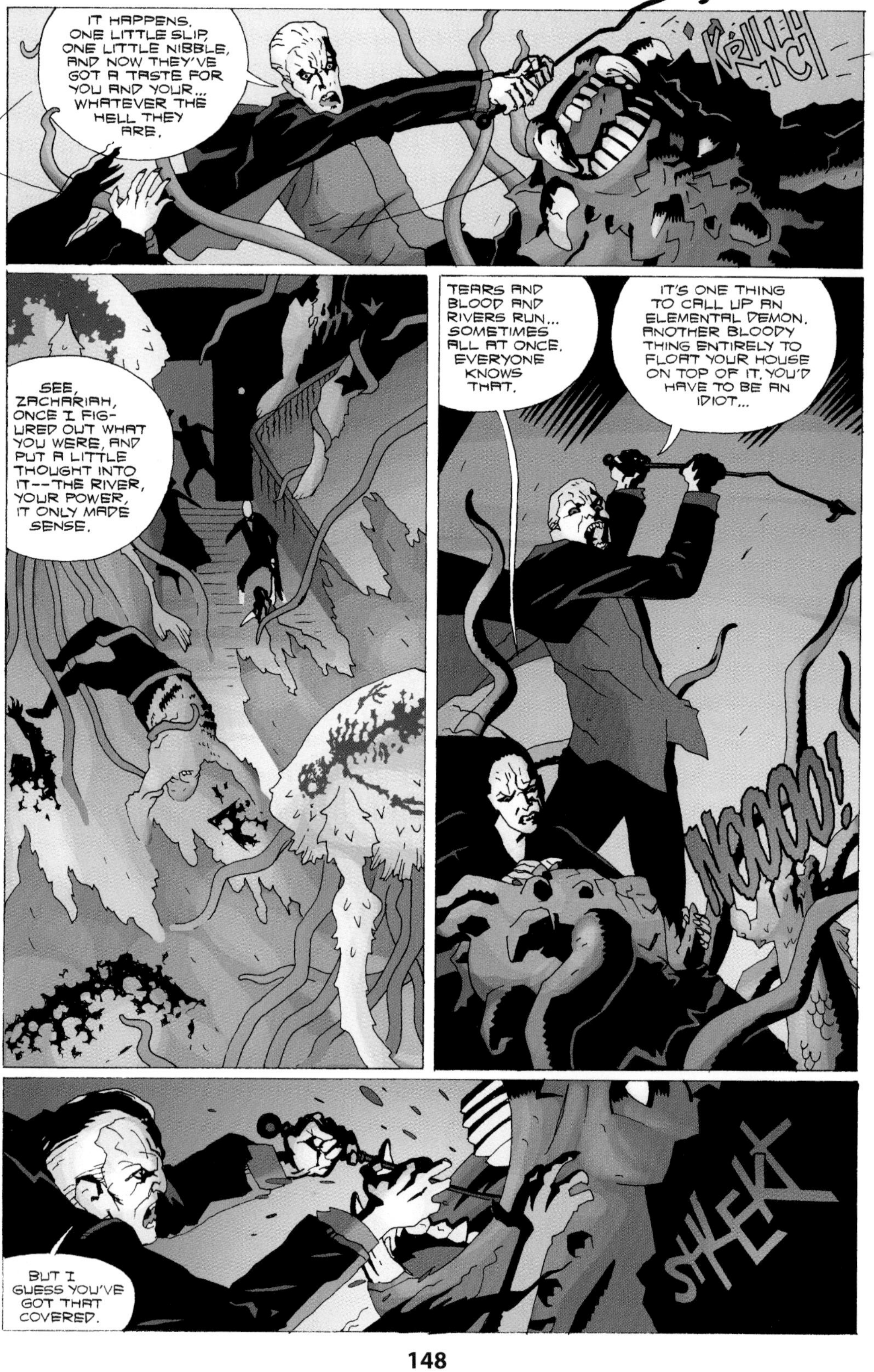

IT HAPPENS. ONE LITTLE SLIP, ONE LITTLE NIBBLE, AND NOW THEY'VE GOT A TASTE FOR YOU AND YOUR... WHATEVER THE HELL THEY ARE.
KRUNCH
SEE, ZACHARIAH, ONCE I FIGURED OUT WHAT YOU WERE, AND PUT A LITTLE THOUGHT INTO IT--THE RIVER, YOUR POWER, IT ONLY MADE SENSE.
TEARS AND BLOOD AND RIVERS RUN... SOMETIMES ALL AT ONCE. EVERYONE KNOWS THAT.
IT'S ONE THING TO CALL UP AN ELEMENTAL DEMON. ANOTHER BLOODY THING ENTIRELY TO FLOAT YOUR HOUSE ON TOP OF IT. YOU'D HAVE TO BE AN IDIOT...
NOOOO!
SHEK
BUT I GUESS YOU'VE GOT THAT COVERED.

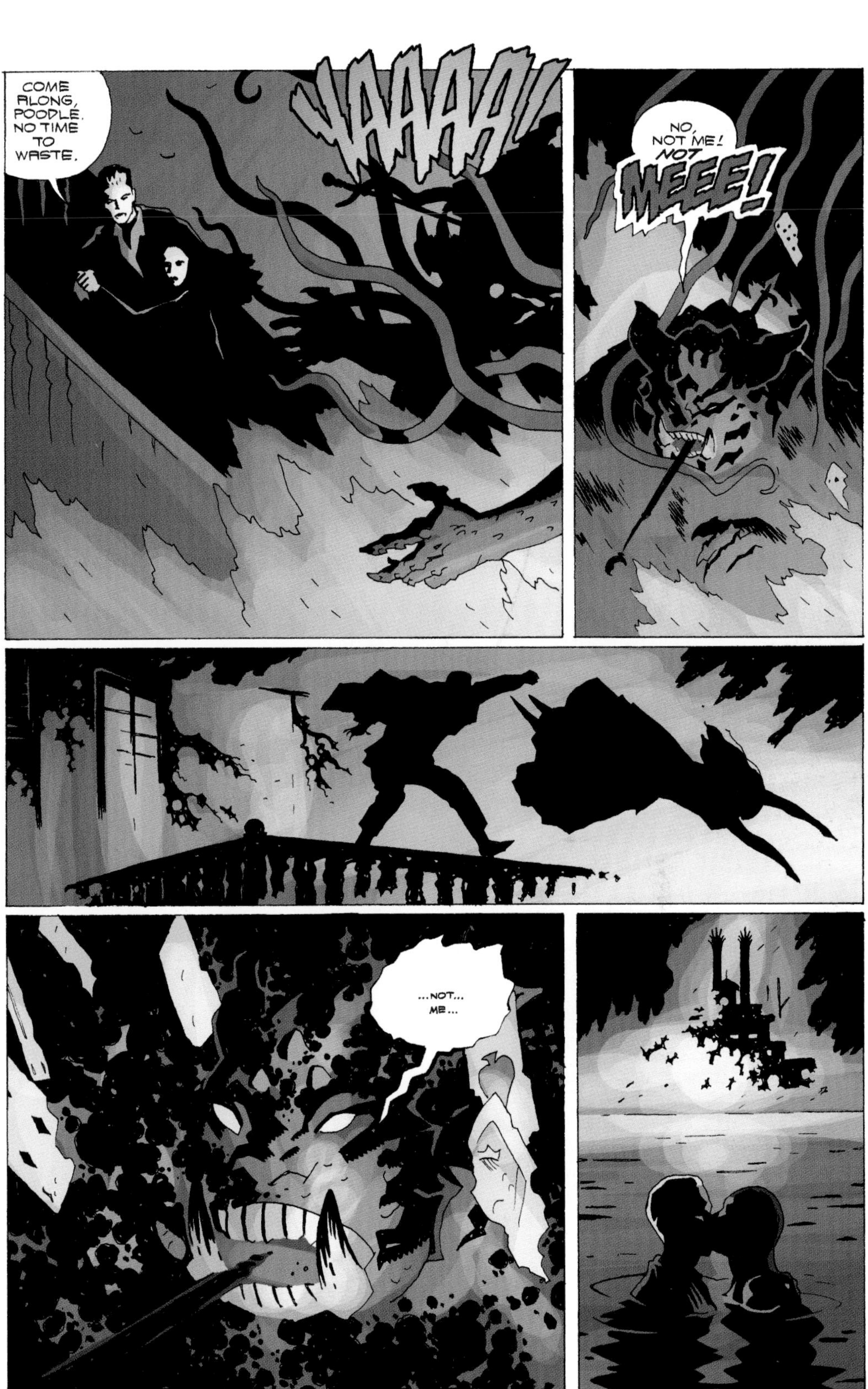
COME ALONG, POODLE. NO TIME TO WASTE.
YAAAA!!
NO, NOT ME! NOT MEEE!
...NOT... ME...

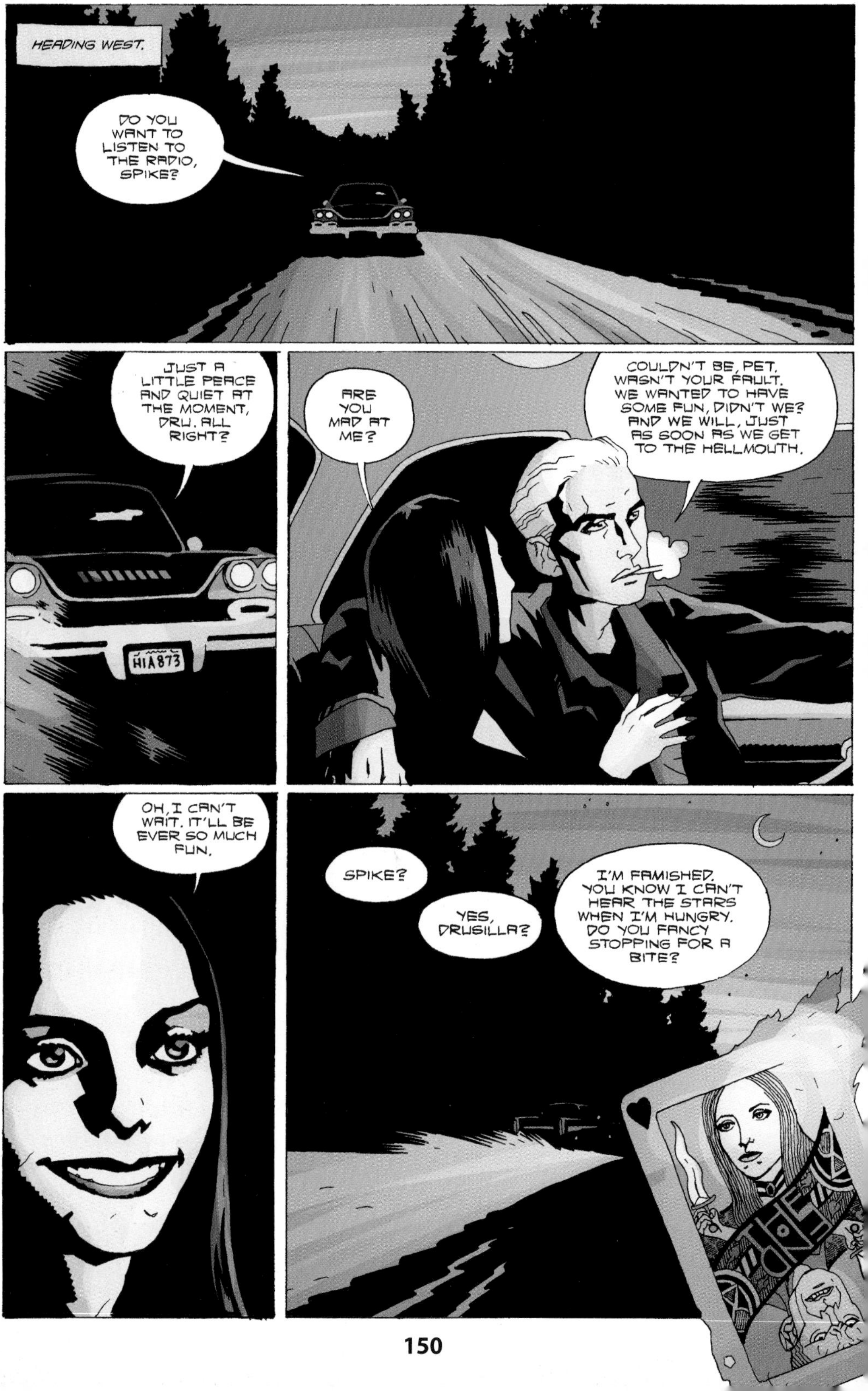
HEADING WEST.
DO YOU WANT TO LISTEN TO THE RADIO, SPIKE?
JUST A LITTLE PEACE AND QUIET AT THE MOMENT, DRU. ALL RIGHT?
HIA873
ARE YOU MAD AT ME?
COULDN'T BE, PET. WASN'T YOUR FAULT. WE WANTED TO HAVE SOME FUN, DIDN'T WE? AND WE WILL, JUST AS SOON AS WE GET TO THE HELLMOUTH.
OH, I CAN'T WAIT. IT'LL BE EVER SO MUCH FUN.
SPIKE?
YES, DRUSILLA?
I'M FAMISHED. YOU KNOW I CAN'T HEAR THE STARS WHEN I'M HUNGRY. DO YOU FANCY STOPPING FOR A BITE?

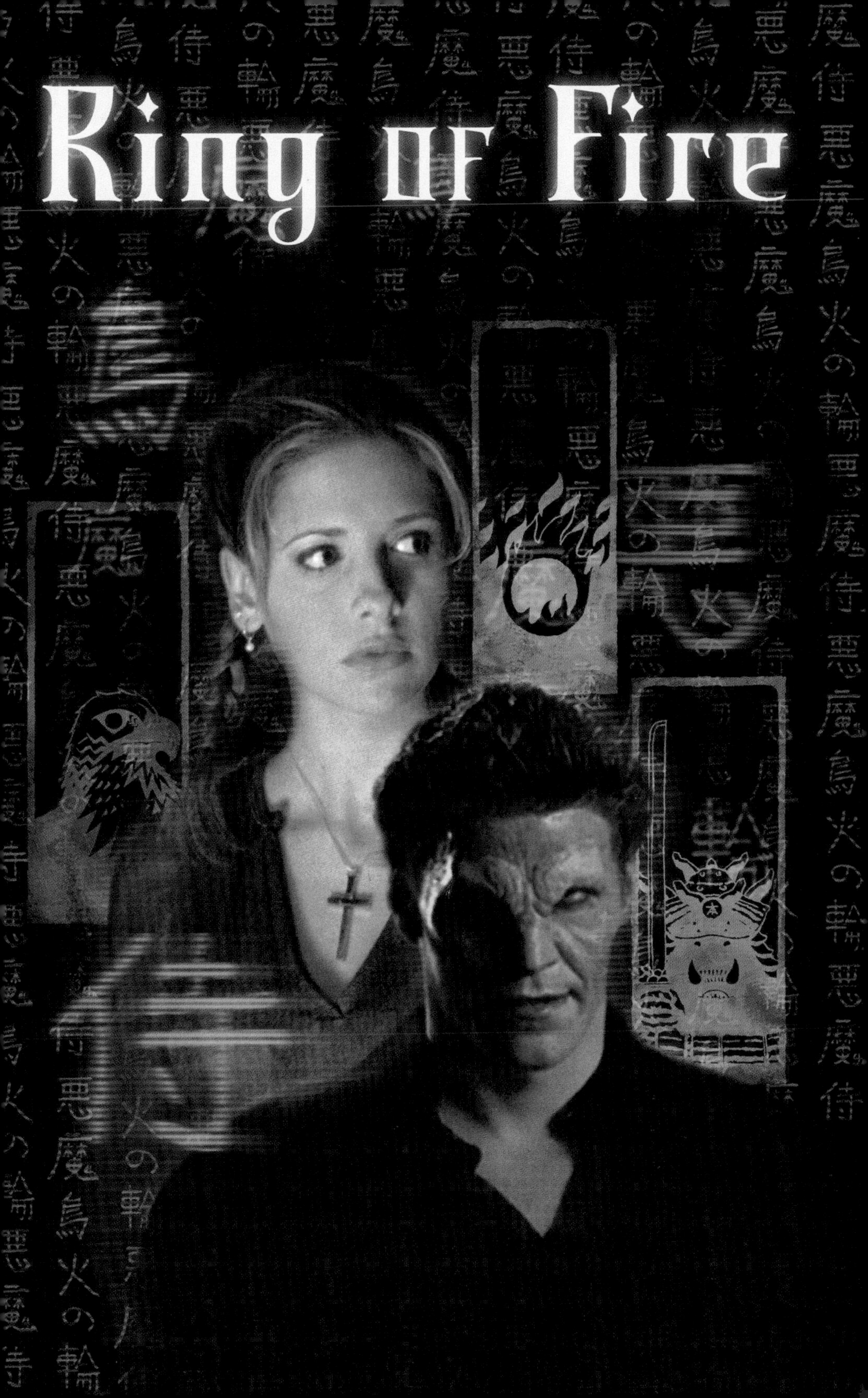
Ring of Fire

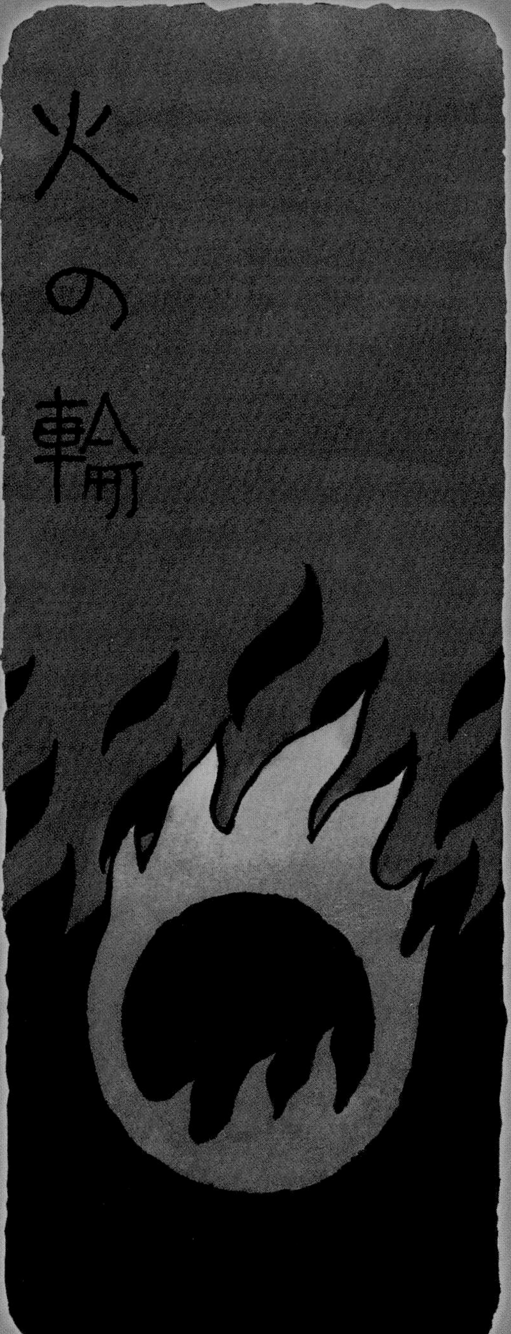
火の輪

The Rising

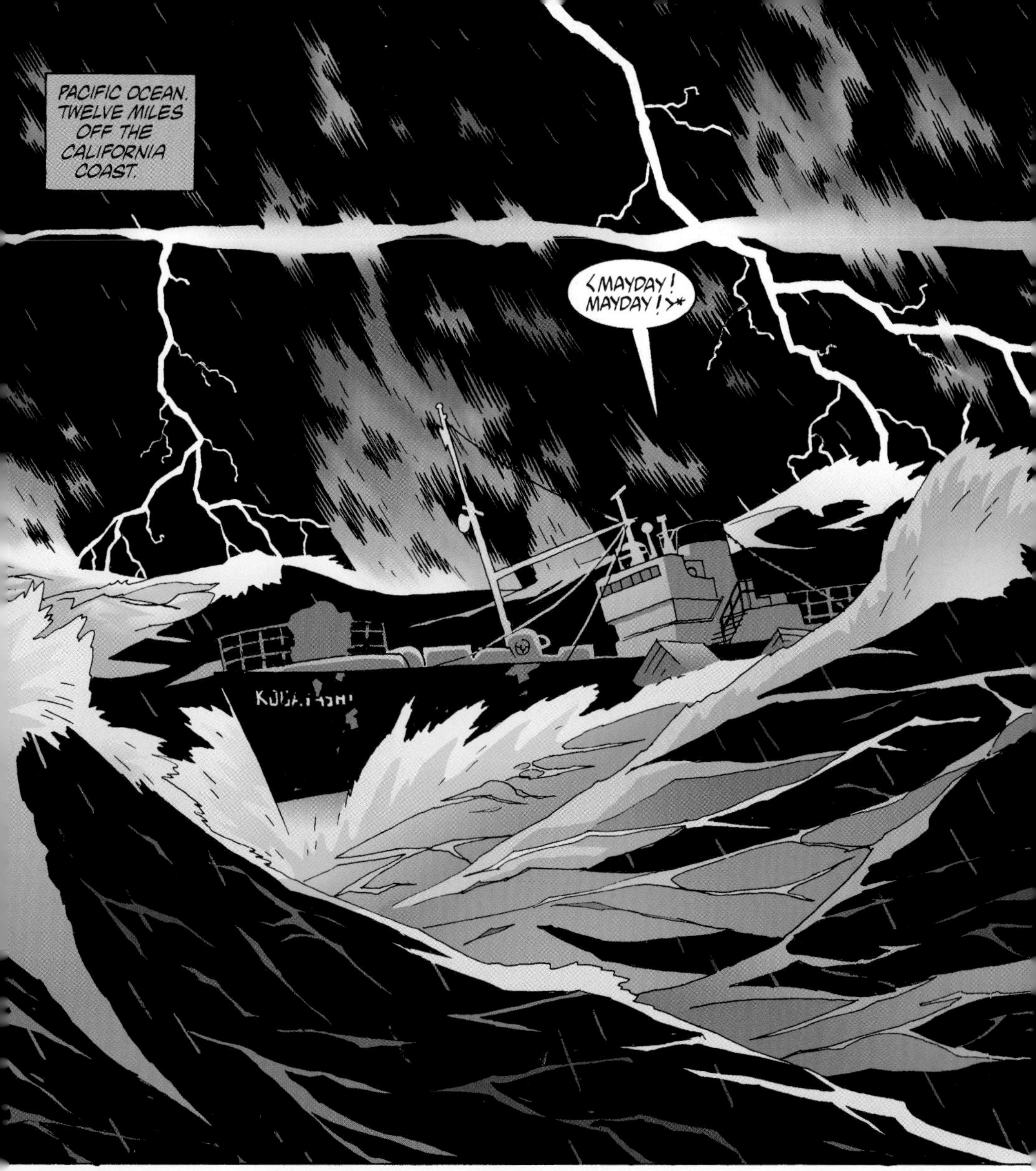
PACIFIC OCEAN. TWELVE MILES OFF THE CALIFORNIA COAST.
<MAYDAY! MAYDAY!>*
KOBAYASHI

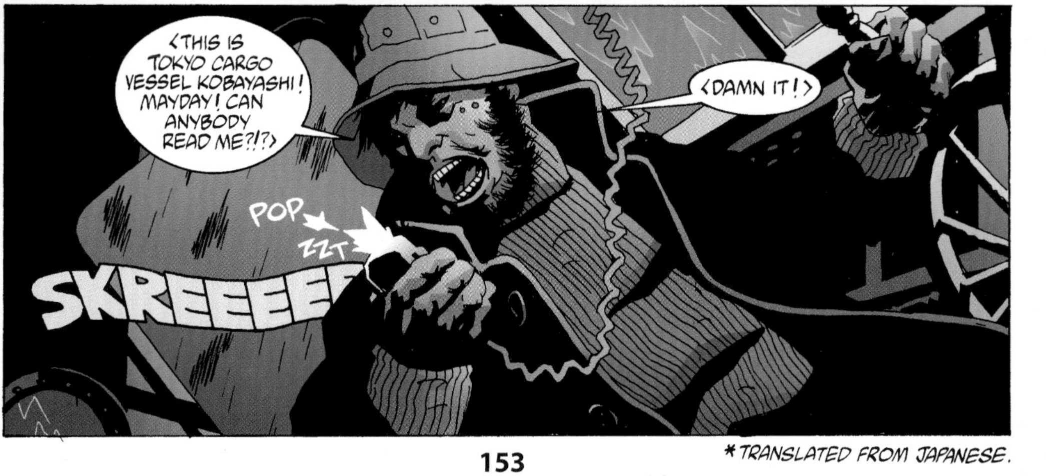
<THIS IS TOKYO CARGO VESSEL KOBAYASHI! MAYDAY! CAN ANYBODY READ ME?!?>
<DAMN IT!>
POP
ZZT
SKREEEEE

*TRANSLATED FROM JAPANESE.

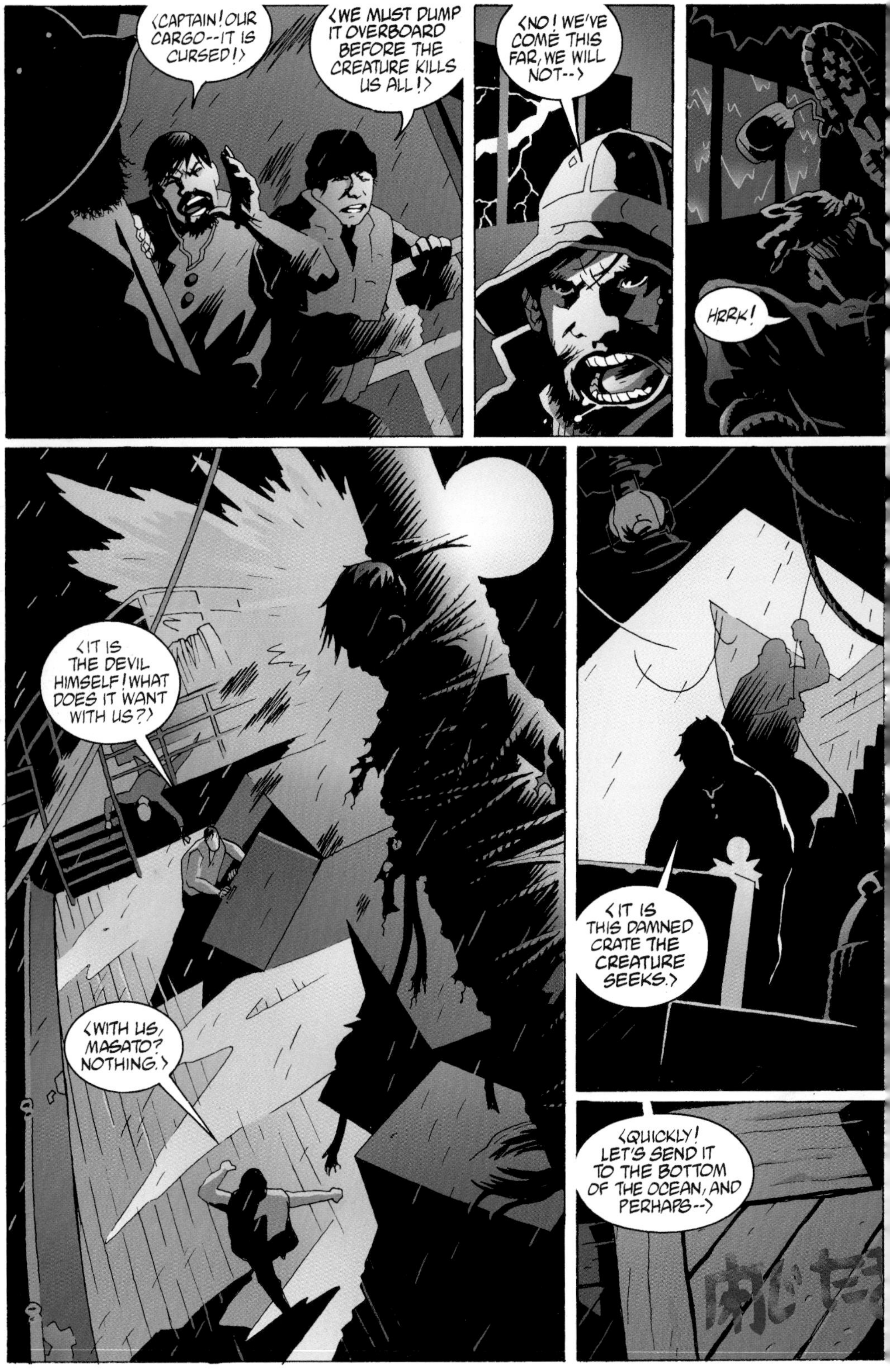

<CAPTAIN! OUR CARGO--IT IS CURSED!>
<WE MUST DUMP IT OVERBOARD BEFORE THE CREATURE KILLS US ALL!>
<NO! WE'VE COME THIS FAR, WE WILL NOT-->
HRRK!
<IT IS THE DEVIL HIMSELF! WHAT DOES IT WANT WITH US?>
<WITH US, MASATO? NOTHING.>
<IT IS THIS DAMNED CRATE THE CREATURE SEEKS.>
<QUICKLY! LET'S SEND IT TO THE BOTTOM OF THE OCEAN, AND PERHAPS-->

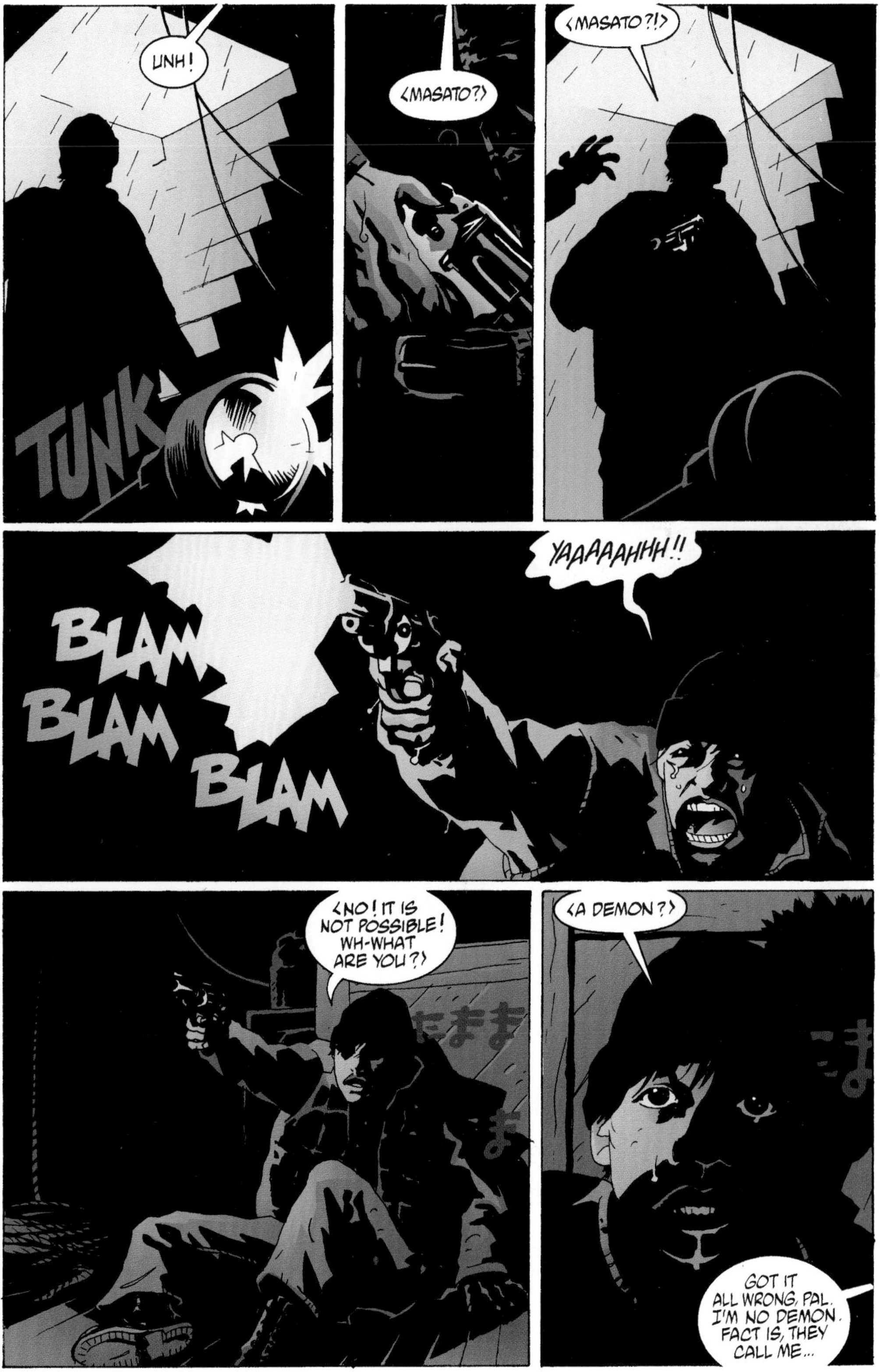
UNH!
TUNK
<MASATO?>
<MASATO?!>
YAAAAAHHH!!
BLAM
BLAM
BLAM
<NO! IT IS NOT POSSIBLE! WH-WHAT ARE YOU?>
<A DEMON?>
GOT IT ALL WRONG, PAL. I'M NO DEMON. FACT IS, THEY CALL ME...

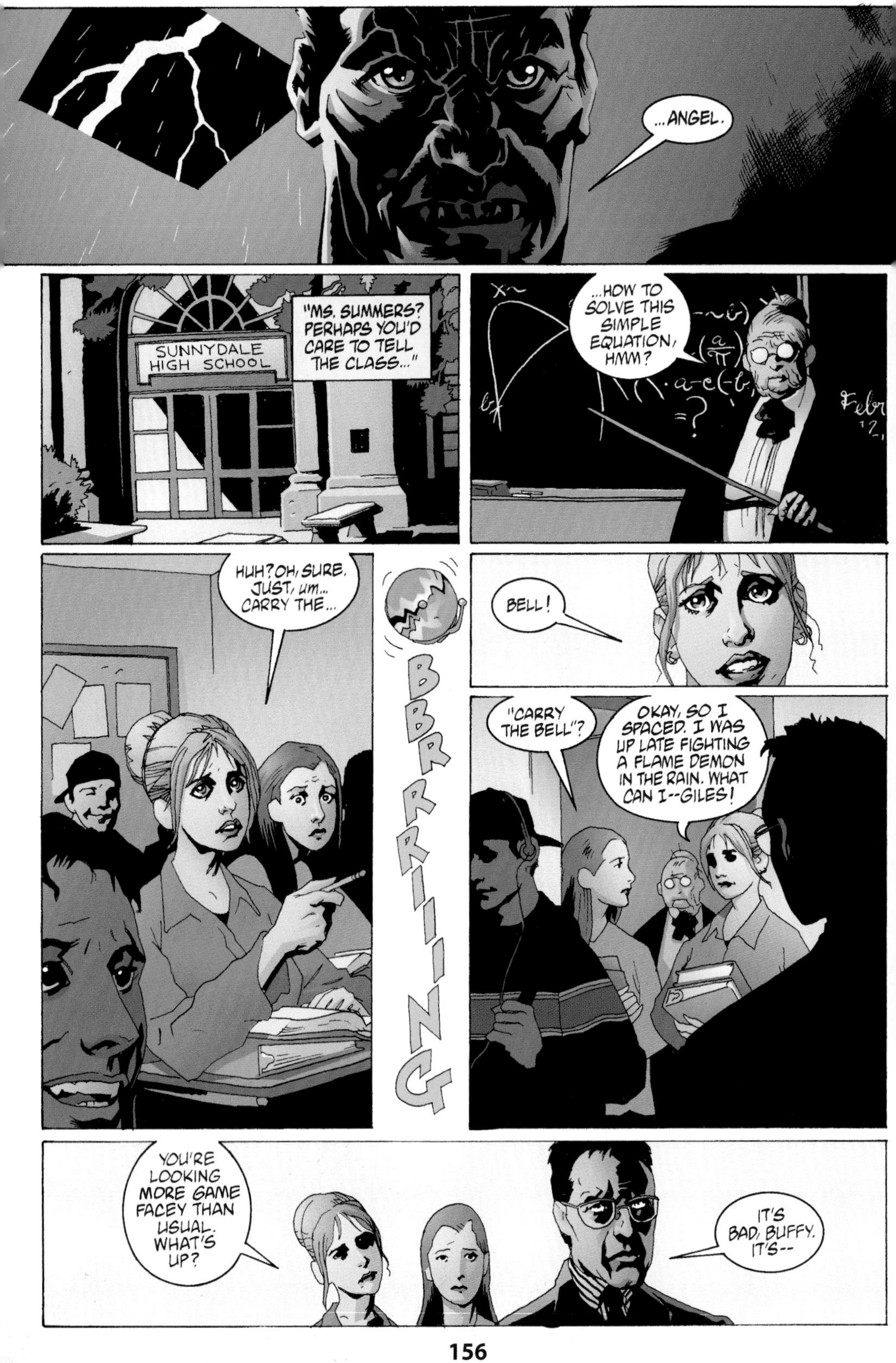
...ANGEL.
SUNNYDALE HIGH SCHOOL
"MS. SUMMERS? PERHAPS YOU'D CARE TO TELL THE CLASS..."
...HOW TO SOLVE THIS SIMPLE EQUATION, HMM?
HUH? OH, SURE. JUST, UM... CARRY THE...
BBRRRIIIING
BELL!
"CARRY THE BELL"?
OKAY, SO I SPACED. I WAS UP LATE FIGHTING A FLAME DEMON IN THE RAIN. WHAT CAN I--GILES!
YOU'RE LOOKING MORE GAME FACEY THAN USUAL. WHAT'S UP?
IT'S BAD, BUFFY. IT'S--

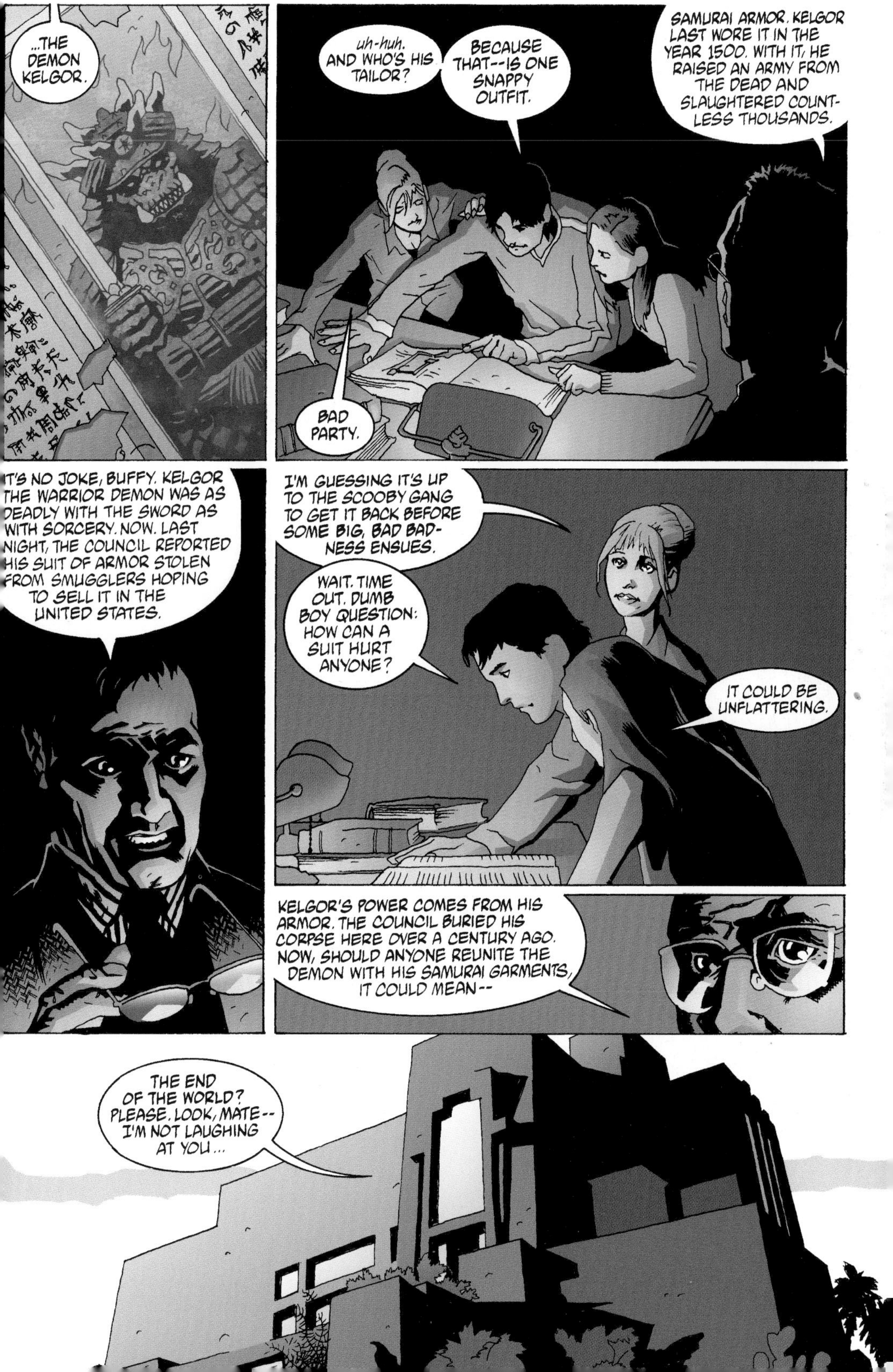
...THE DEMON KELGOR.
uh-huh. AND WHO'S HIS TAILOR?
BECAUSE THAT--IS ONE SNAPPY OUTFIT.
SAMURAI ARMOR. KELGOR LAST WORE IT IN THE YEAR 1500. WITH IT, HE RAISED AN ARMY FROM THE DEAD AND SLAUGHTERED COUNTLESS THOUSANDS.
BAD PARTY.
IT'S NO JOKE, BUFFY. KELGOR THE WARRIOR DEMON WAS AS DEADLY WITH THE SWORD AS WITH SORCERY. NOW. LAST NIGHT, THE COUNCIL REPORTED HIS SUIT OF ARMOR STOLEN FROM SMUGGLERS HOPING TO SELL IT IN THE UNITED STATES.
I'M GUESSING IT'S UP TO THE SCOOBY GANG TO GET IT BACK BEFORE SOME BIG, BAD BADNESS ENSUES.
WAIT. TIME OUT. DUMB BOY QUESTION: HOW CAN A SUIT HURT ANYONE?
IT COULD BE UNFLATTERING.
KELGOR'S POWER COMES FROM HIS ARMOR. THE COUNCIL BURIED HIS CORPSE HERE OVER A CENTURY AGO. NOW, SHOULD ANYONE REUNITE THE DEMON WITH HIS SAMURAI GARMENTS, IT COULD MEAN--
THE END OF THE WORLD? PLEASE. LOOK, MATE--I'M NOT LAUGHING AT YOU...

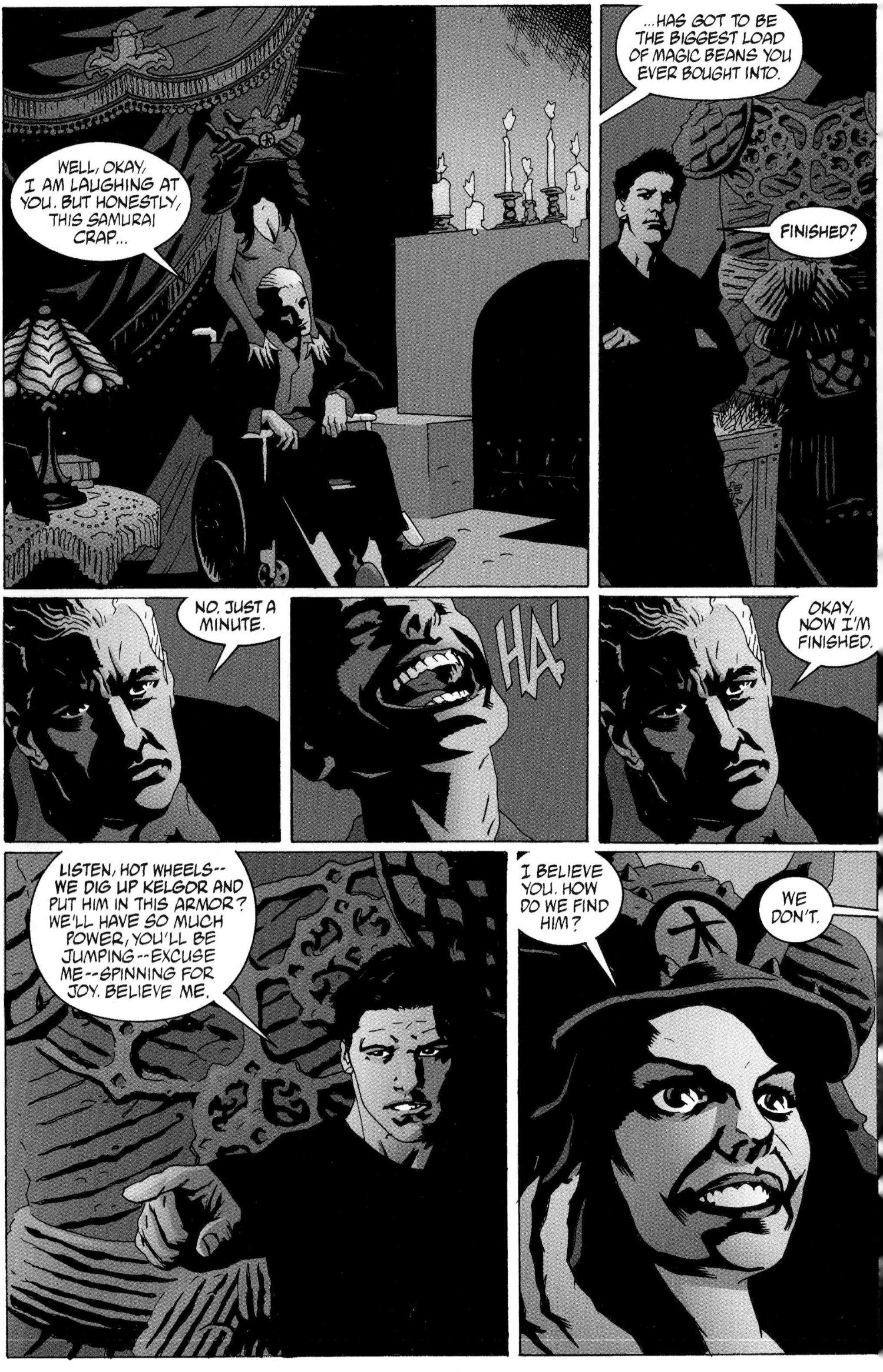
WELL, OKAY, I AM LAUGHING AT YOU. BUT HONESTLY, THIS SAMURAI CRAP...
...HAS GOT TO BE THE BIGGEST LOAD OF MAGIC BEANS YOU EVER BOUGHT INTO.
FINISHED?
NO. JUST A MINUTE.
HA!
OKAY, NOW I'M FINISHED.
LISTEN, HOT WHEELS-- WE DIG UP KELGOR AND PUT HIM IN THIS ARMOR? WE'LL HAVE SO MUCH POWER, YOU'LL BE JUMPING--EXCUSE ME--SPINNING FOR JOY. BELIEVE ME.
I BELIEVE YOU. HOW DO WE FIND HIM?
WE DON'T.

"BUFFY DOES."

OKAY. THERE'S THE SHIP...

SKRUNCH

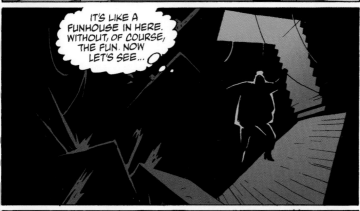

IT'S LIKE A FUNHOUSE IN HERE. WITHOUT, OF COURSE, THE FUN. NOW LET'S SEE...

...WHAT I CAN...

CLICK

SQUEAK SQUEAK SQUEAK

...FIND--

OH MY GOD!

159

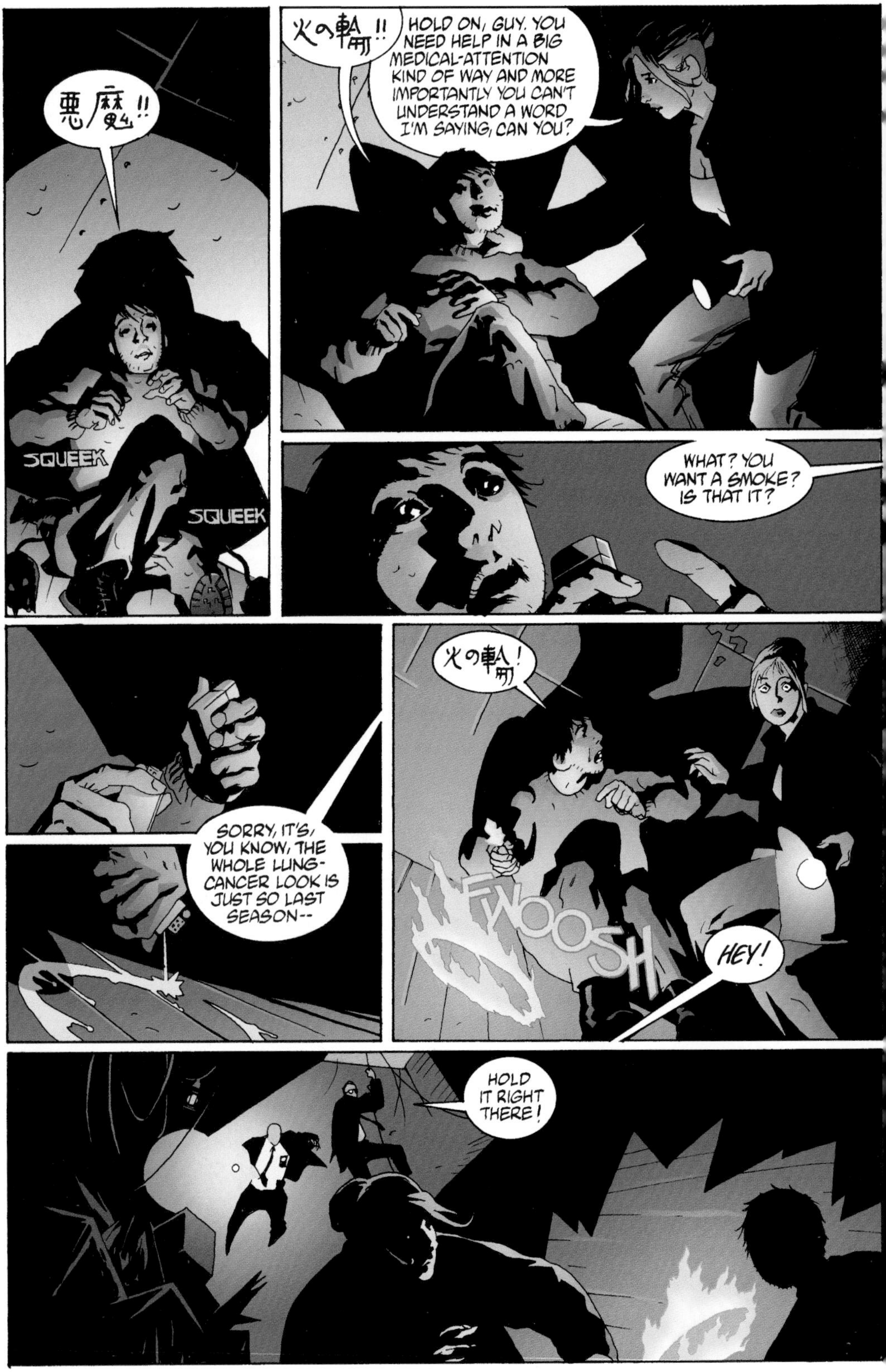
悪魔!!
SQUEEK
SQUEEK
火の輪!!
HOLD ON, GUY. YOU NEED HELP IN A BIG MEDICAL-ATTENTION KIND OF WAY AND MORE IMPORTANTLY YOU CAN'T UNDERSTAND A WORD I'M SAYING, CAN YOU?
WHAT? YOU WANT A SMOKE? IS THAT IT?
SORRY, IT'S, YOU KNOW, THE WHOLE LUNG-CANCER LOOK IS JUST SO LAST SEASON--
火の輪!
FWOOSH
HEY!
HOLD IT RIGHT THERE!

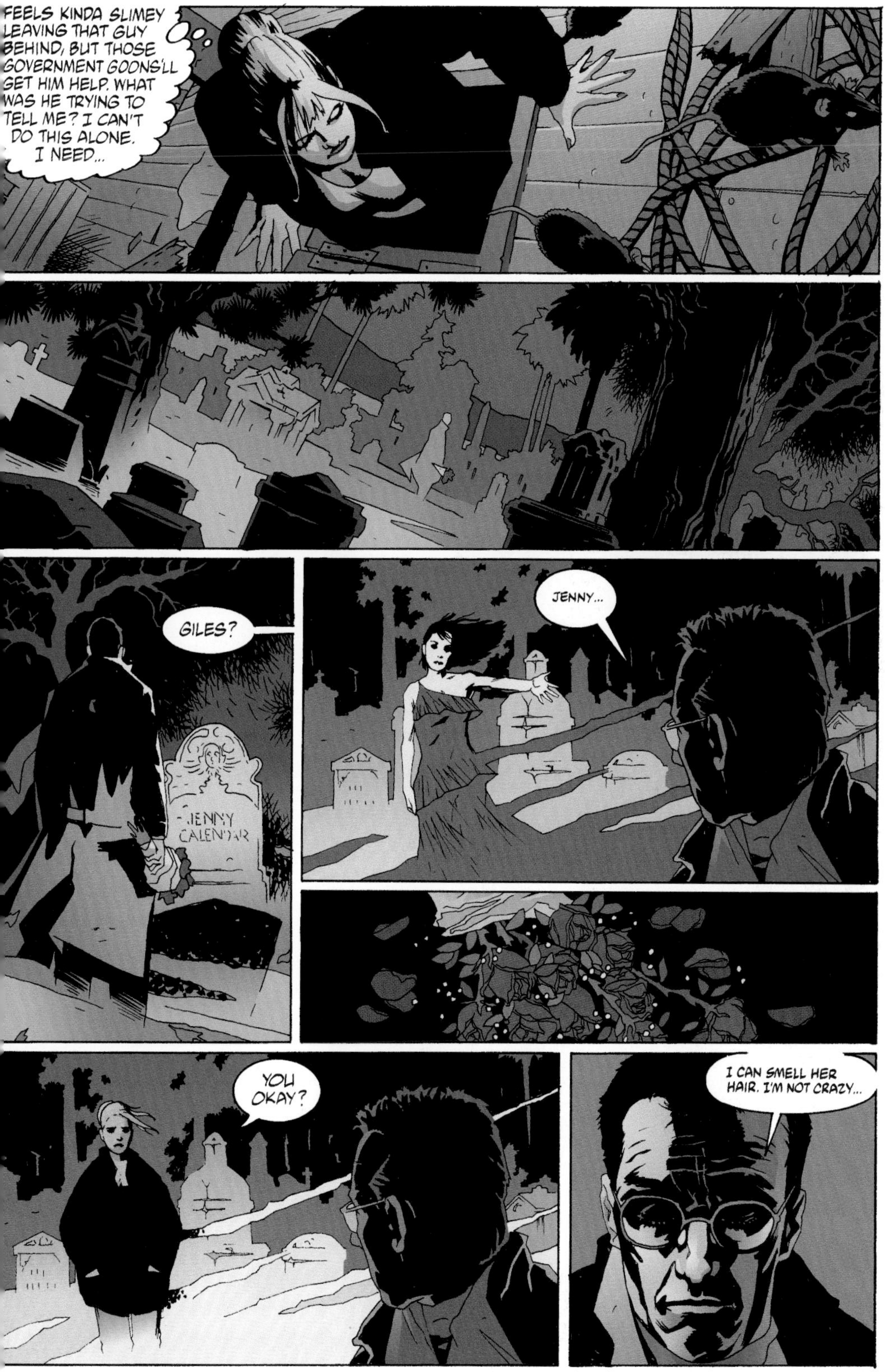
FEELS KINDA SLIMEY LEAVING THAT GUY BEHIND, BUT THOSE GOVERNMENT GOONS'LL GET HIM HELP. WHAT WAS HE TRYING TO TELL ME? I CAN'T DO THIS ALONE. I NEED...
GILES?
JENNY CALENDAR
JENNY...
YOU OKAY?
I CAN SMELL HER HAIR. I'M NOT CRAZY...

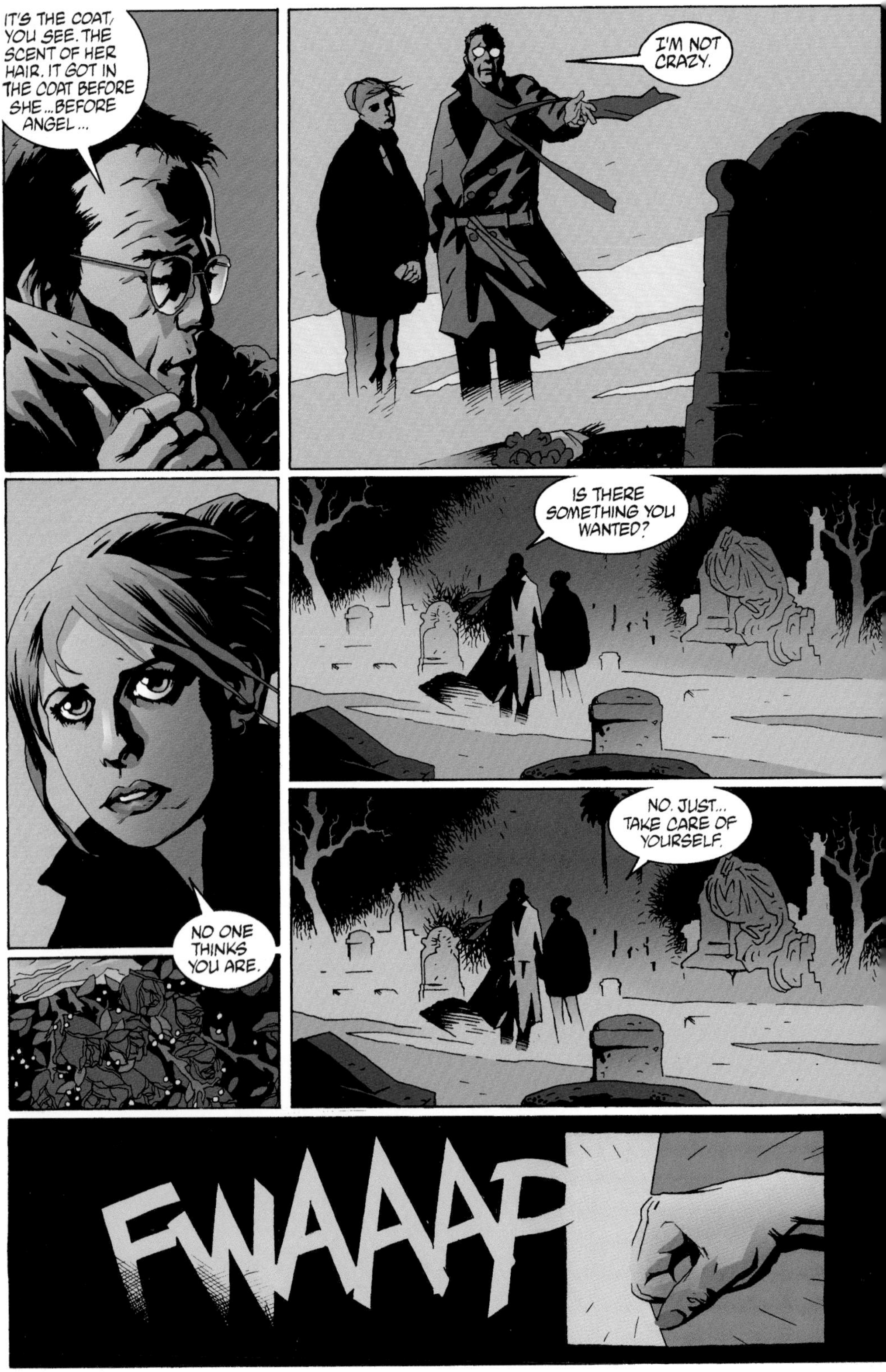
IT'S THE COAT, YOU SEE. THE SCENT OF HER HAIR. IT GOT IN THE COAT BEFORE SHE...BEFORE ANGEL...
I'M NOT CRAZY.
NO ONE THINKS YOU ARE.
IS THERE SOMETHING YOU WANTED?
NO. JUST... TAKE CARE OF YOURSELF.
FWAAAP

GOTTA TELL YOU GUYS, I'M WORRIED.

WITH THAT JAB? RELAX, CHAMP.

YEAH, LET KELGOR SWEAT IT.

DEMONS I CAN HANDLE. BUT GILES... HE'S STILL HOLDING IN A LOT OF FEELINGS OVER JENNY'S MURDER.

THINK HE MIGHT BURST?

DUNNO.

BUT WE BETTER HANDLE RESEARCH WITHOUT HIM, RIGHT NOW, HE'S IN NO SHAPE TO BE WATCHER-GUY.

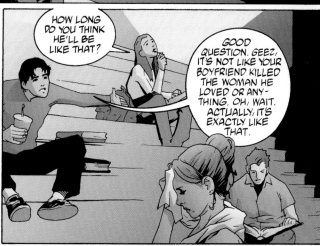

HOW LONG DO YOU THINK HE'LL BE LIKE THAT?

GOOD QUESTION. GEEZ, IT'S NOT LIKE YOUR BOYFRIEND KILLED THE WOMAN HE LOVED OR ANYTHING. OH, WAIT. ACTUALLY, IT'S EXACTLY LIKE THAT.

THANK YOU, XANDER. AND IF THERE'S A WAY YOU CAN BE LESS SENSITIVE, I'LL CALL.

YOU KNOW THAT "NOT WORRYING ABOUT KELGOR" PART OF THE PLAN?

WELL, SPEAKING FOR MYSELF...

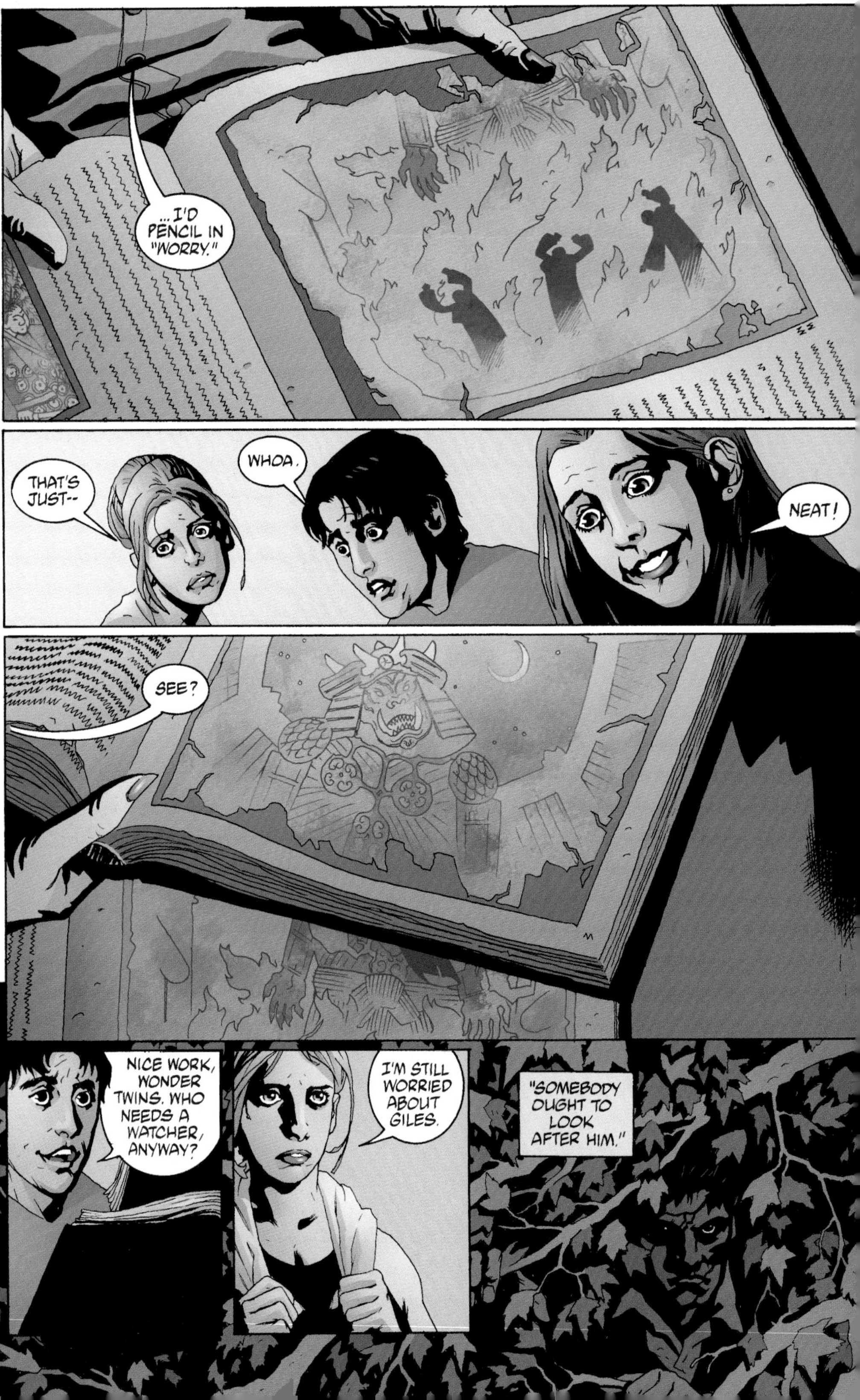
...I'D PENCIL IN "WORRY."
THAT'S JUST--
WHOA.
NEAT!
SEE?
NICE WORK, WONDER TWINS. WHO NEEDS A WATCHER, ANYWAY?
I'M STILL WORRIED ABOUT GILES.
"SOMEBODY OUGHT TO LOOK AFTER HIM."

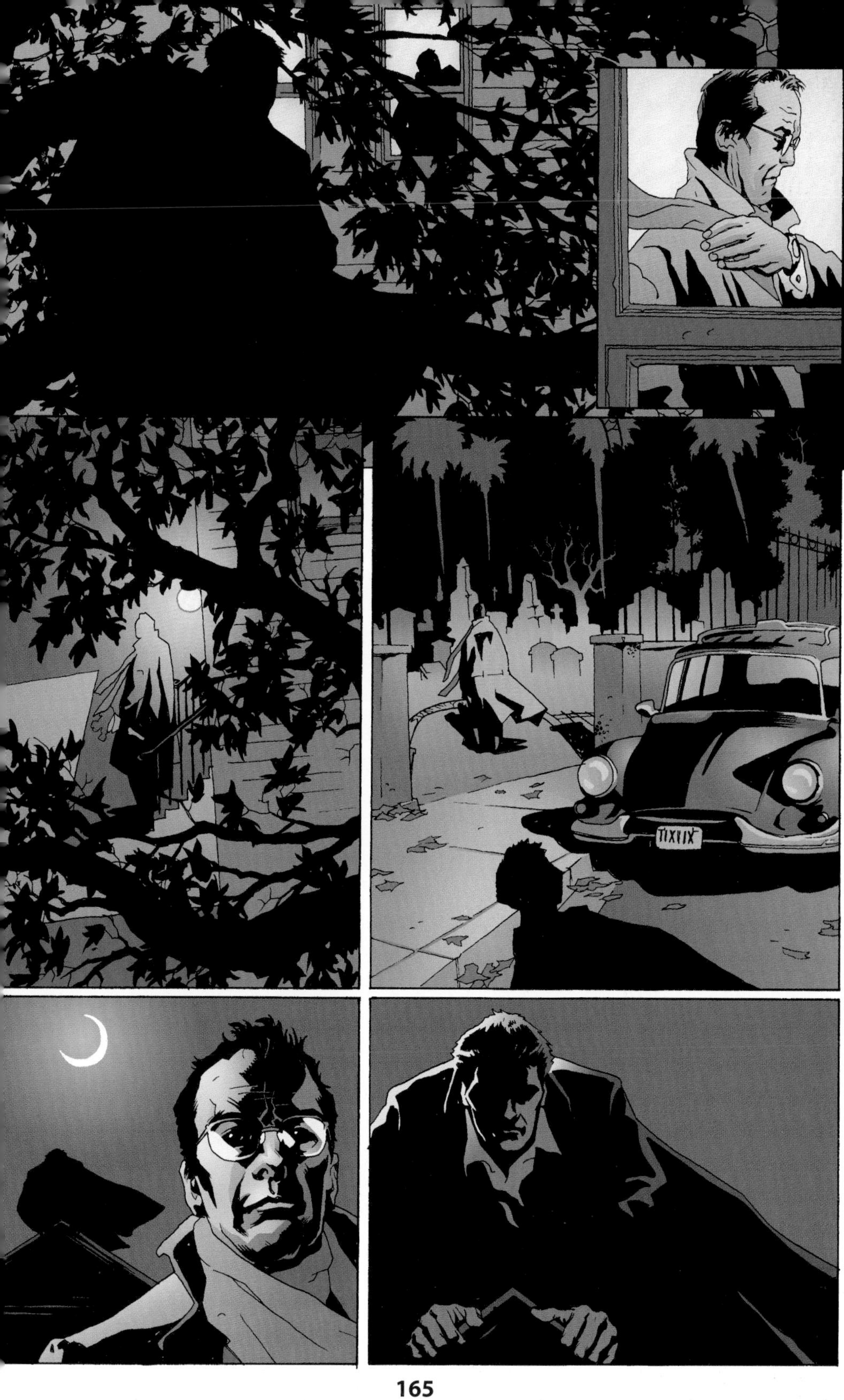

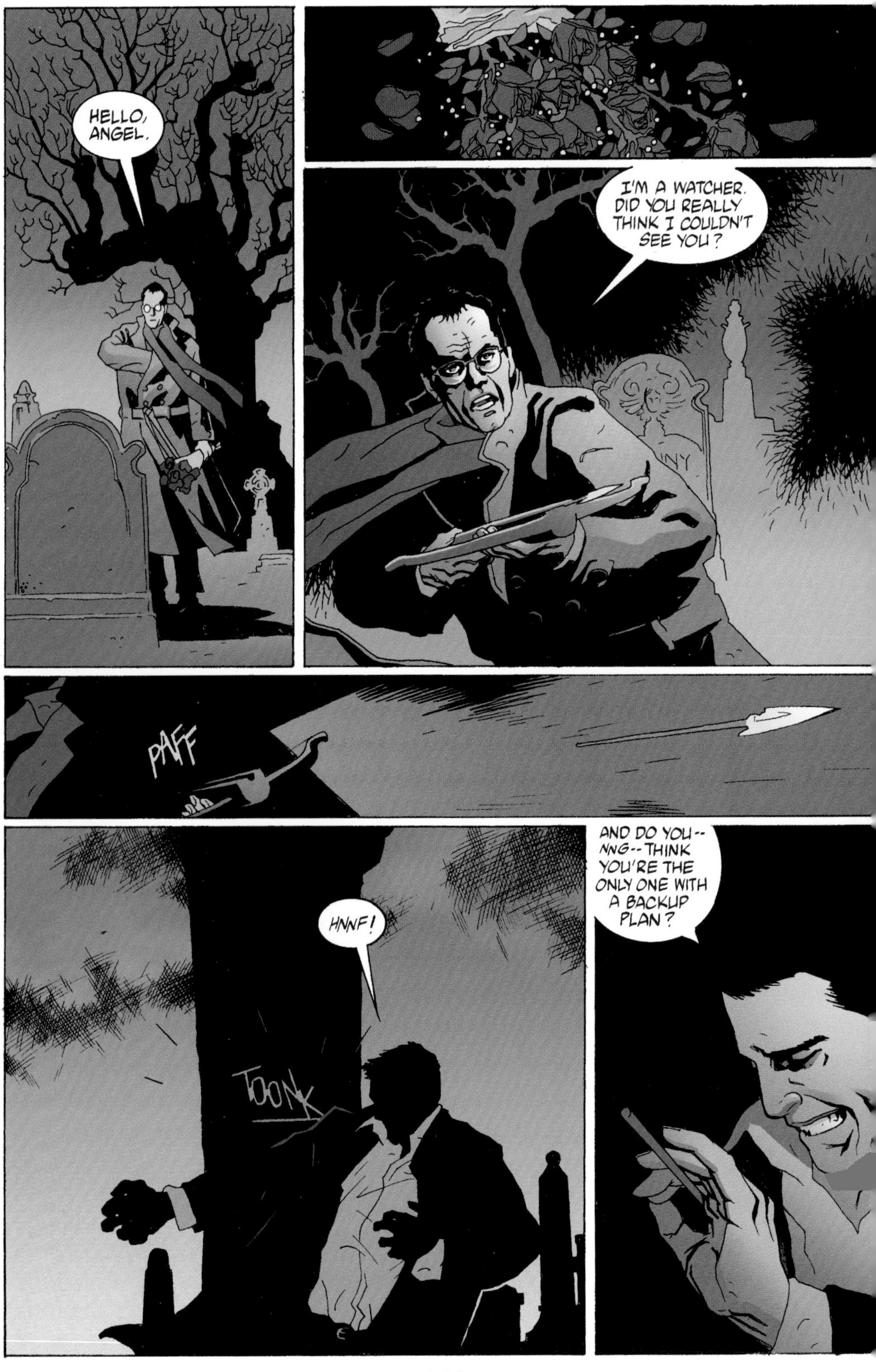
HELLO, ANGEL.
I'M A WATCHER. DID YOU REALLY THINK I COULDN'T SEE YOU?
PAFF
HNNF!
TOONK
AND DO YOU-- NNG--THINK YOU'RE THE ONLY ONE WITH A BACKUP PLAN?

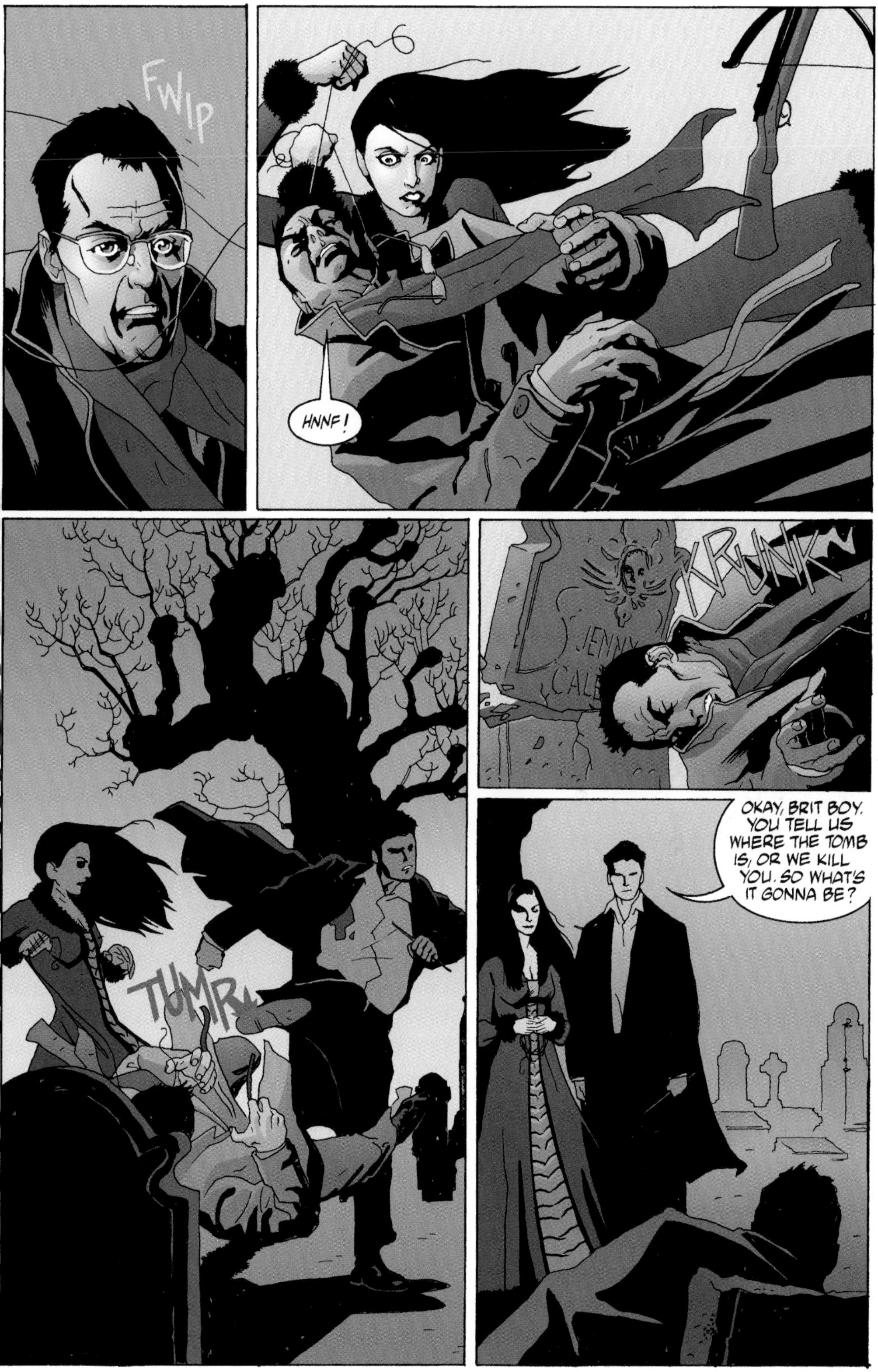
FWIP
HNNF!
KRUNK
OKAY, BRIT BOY. YOU TELL US WHERE THE TOMB IS, OR WE KILL YOU. SO WHAT'S IT GONNA BE?

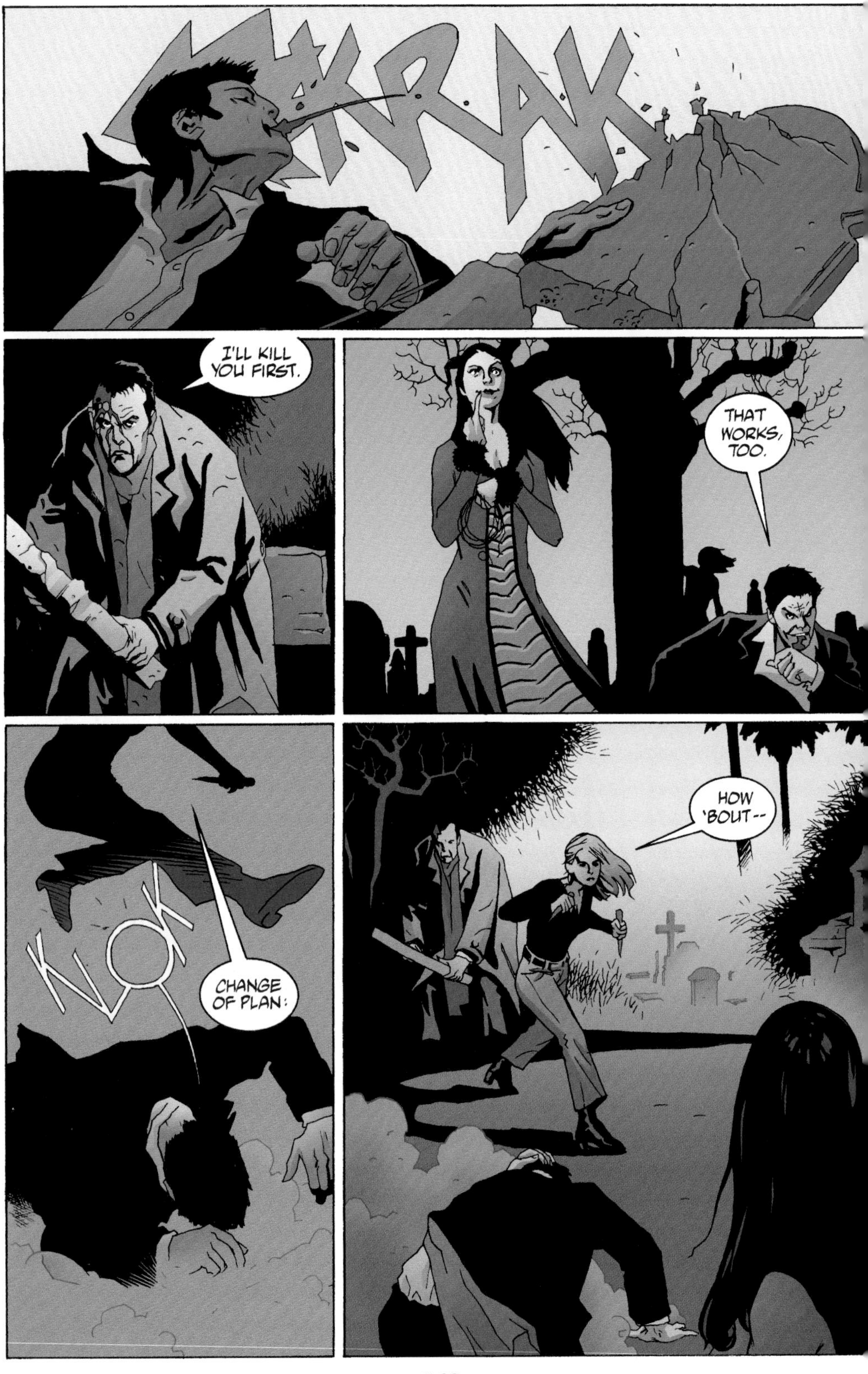
KRAK
I'LL KILL YOU FIRST.
THAT WORKS, TOO.
KLOK
CHANGE OF PLAN:
HOW 'BOUT--

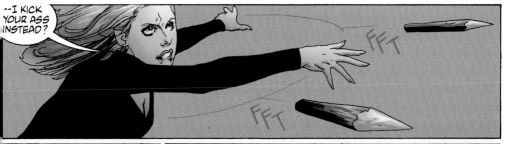

--I KICK YOUR ASS INSTEAD?

FFT

FFT

OKAY...

...THIS MUST BE THE PLACE.

HOMEY.

YEAH, A REAL BLOWER-UPPER OPPORTUNITY.

WE SET UP A PROTECTION SPELL AND NOBODY CAN IGNITE THE RING OF FIRE.

THE THING I LOVE THE MOST ABOUT THESE OLD TOMBS? TWO WORDS--

WHEELCHAIR.

ACCESSIBLE.

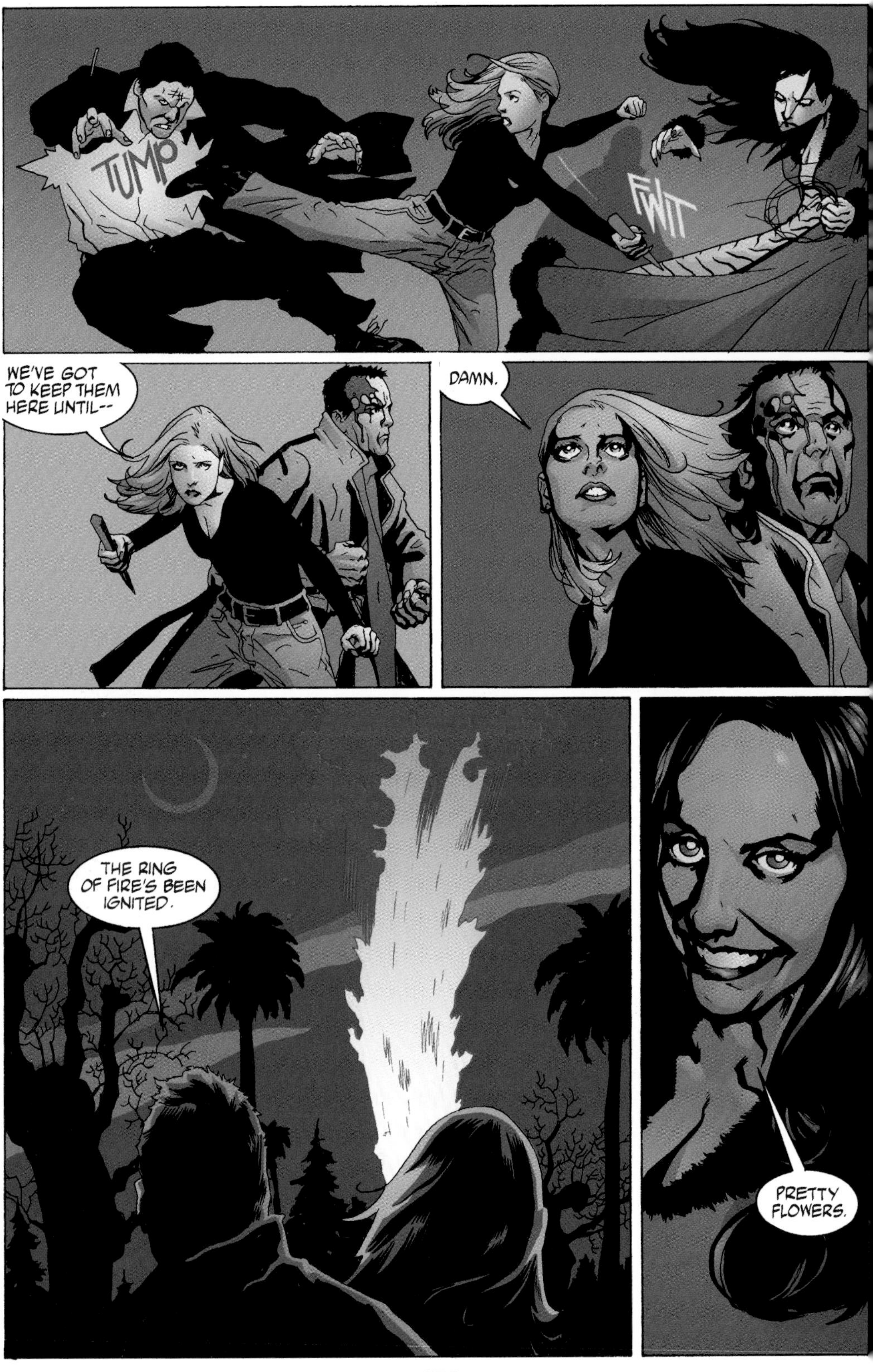
TUMP
FWIT
WE'VE GOT TO KEEP THEM HERE UNTIL--
DAMN.
THE RING OF FIRE'S BEEN IGNITED.
PRETTY FLOWERS.

SPIKE MUST'VE TRAILED THE OTHERS. I BETTER BOLT.

YES...

YOU OKAY?

I'M FINE.

GO.

GILES LOOKS PRETTY ROCKED. WISH I COULD STAY, BUT I BETTER TAKE CARE OF SLAYER BIZ...

...INSIDE.

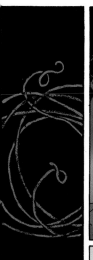

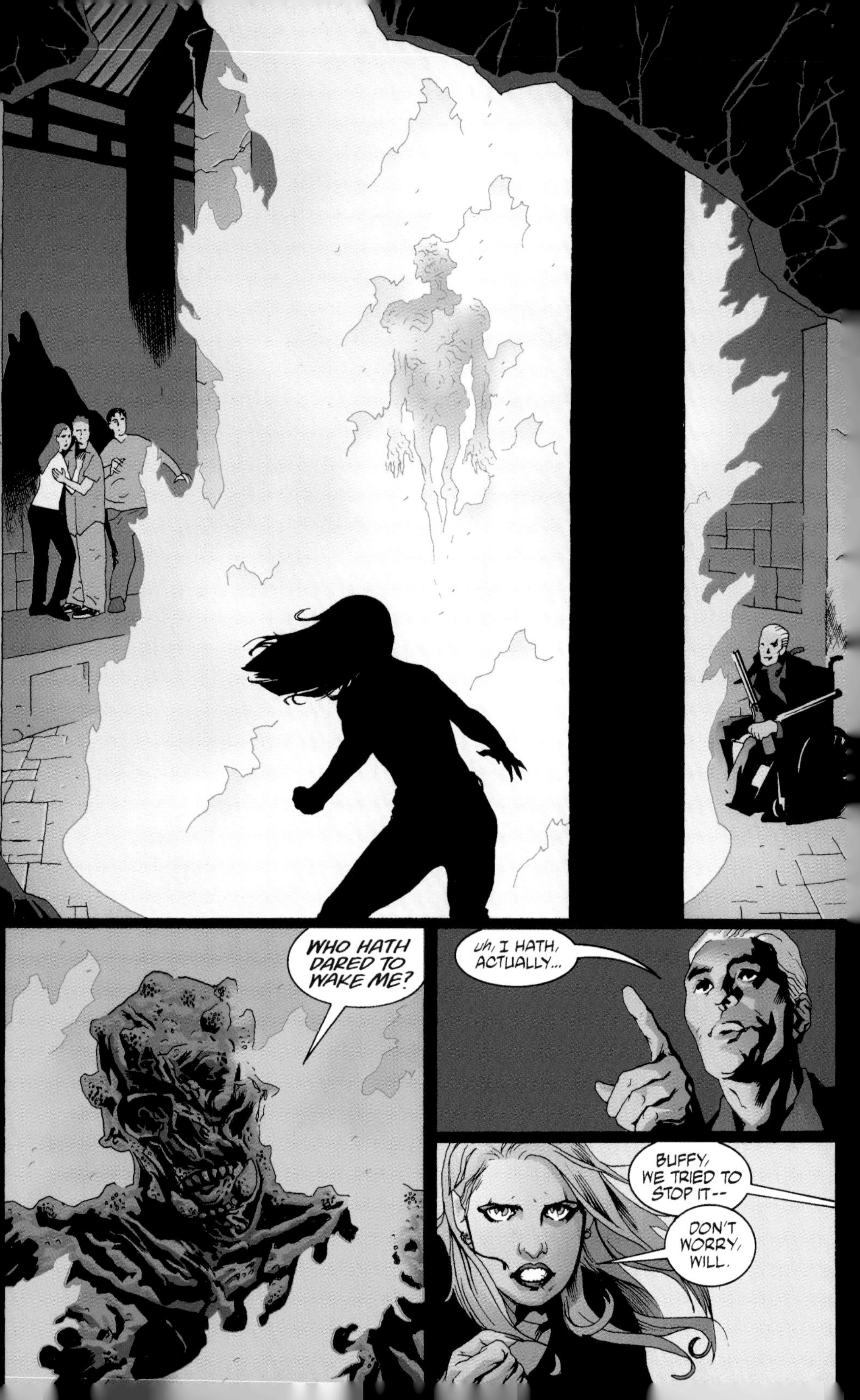
WHO HATH DARED TO WAKE ME?
uh, I HATH, ACTUALLY...
BUFFY, WE TRIED TO STOP IT--
DON'T WORRY, WILL.

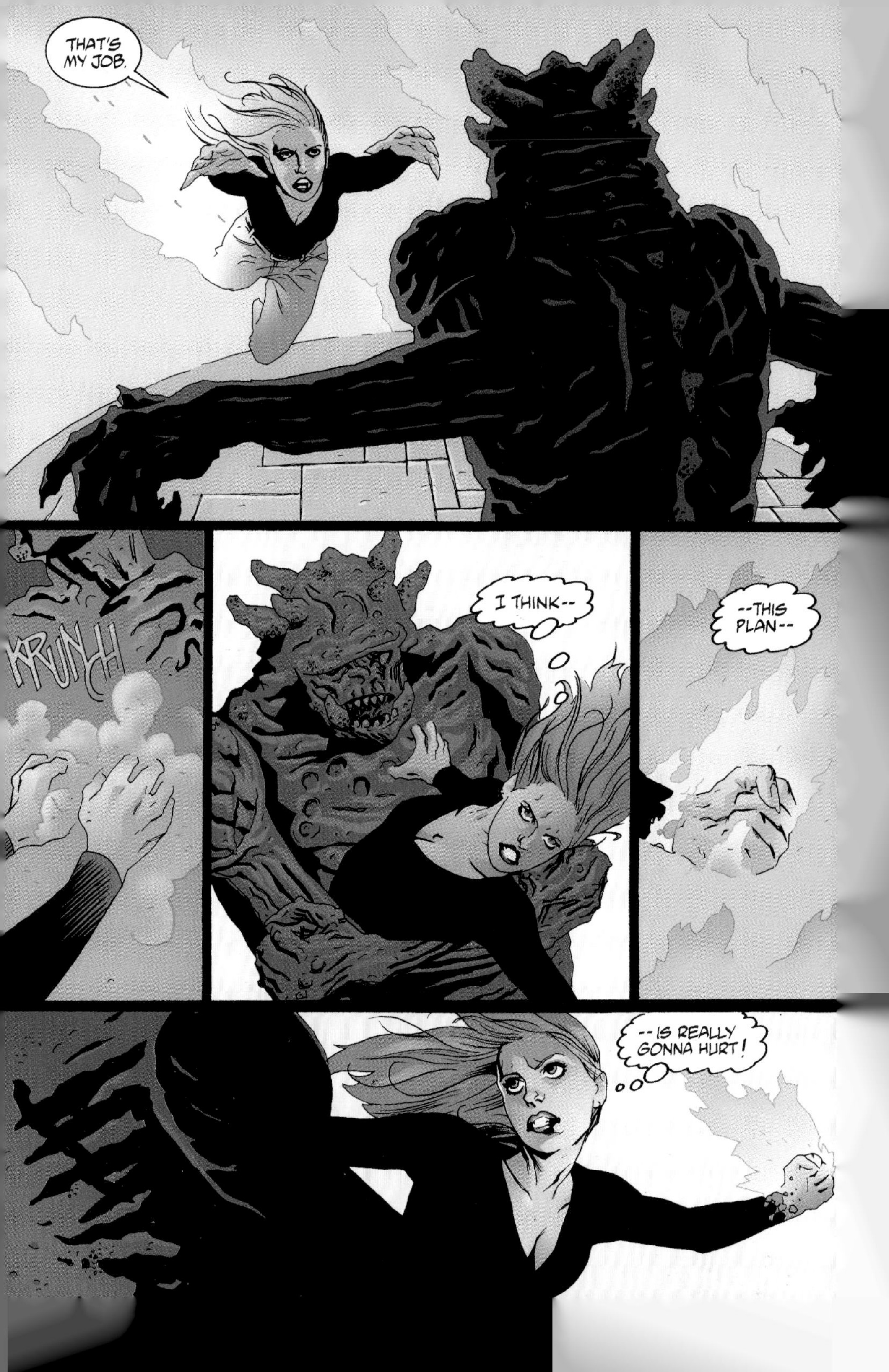
THAT'S MY JOB.
KRUNCH
I THINK--
--THIS PLAN--
--IS REALLY GONNA HURT!

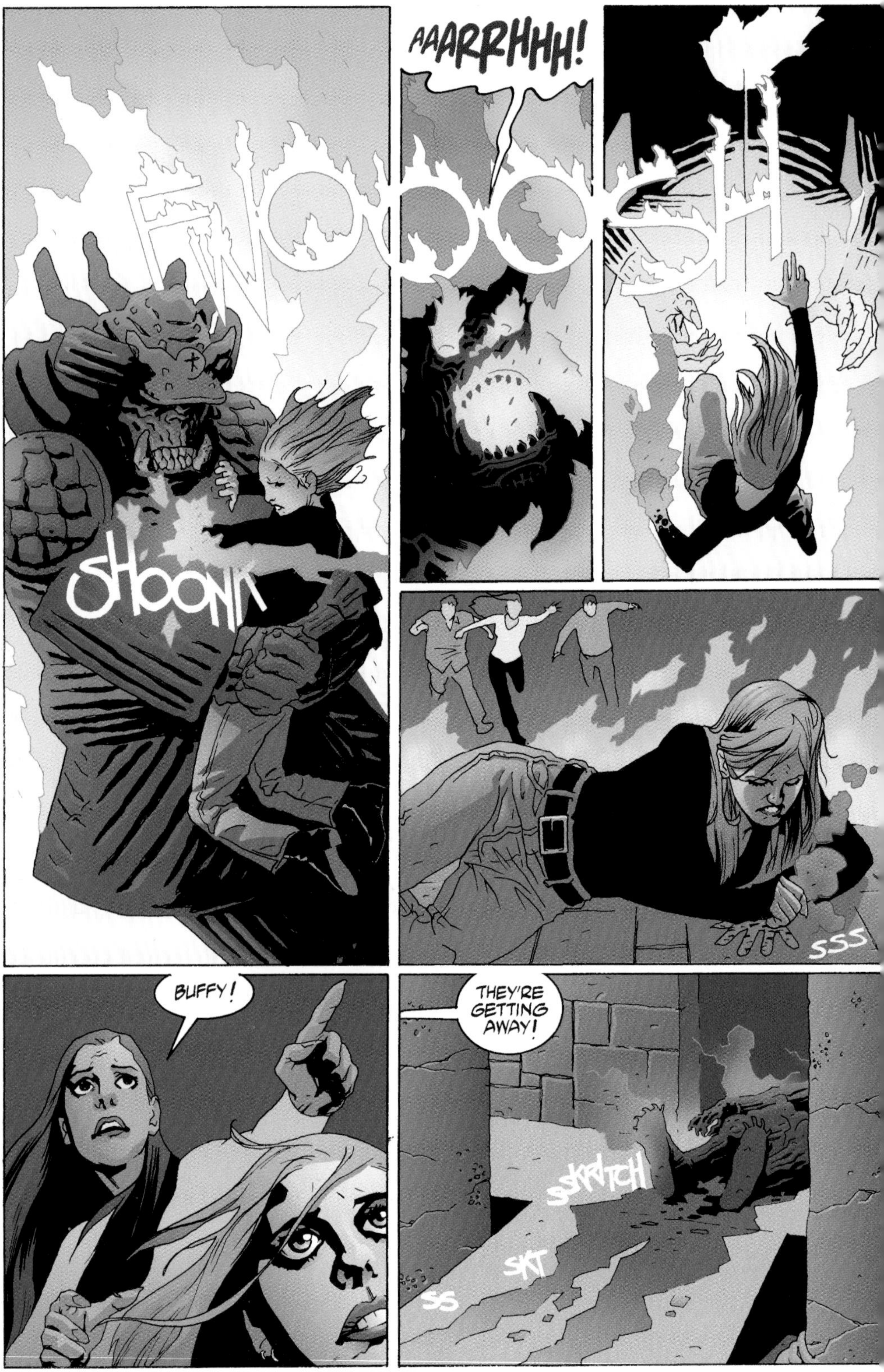
FWOOOOSH
AAARRHHH!
SHOONK
SSS
BUFFY!
THEY'RE GETTING AWAY!
SSKRRTCH
SKT
SS

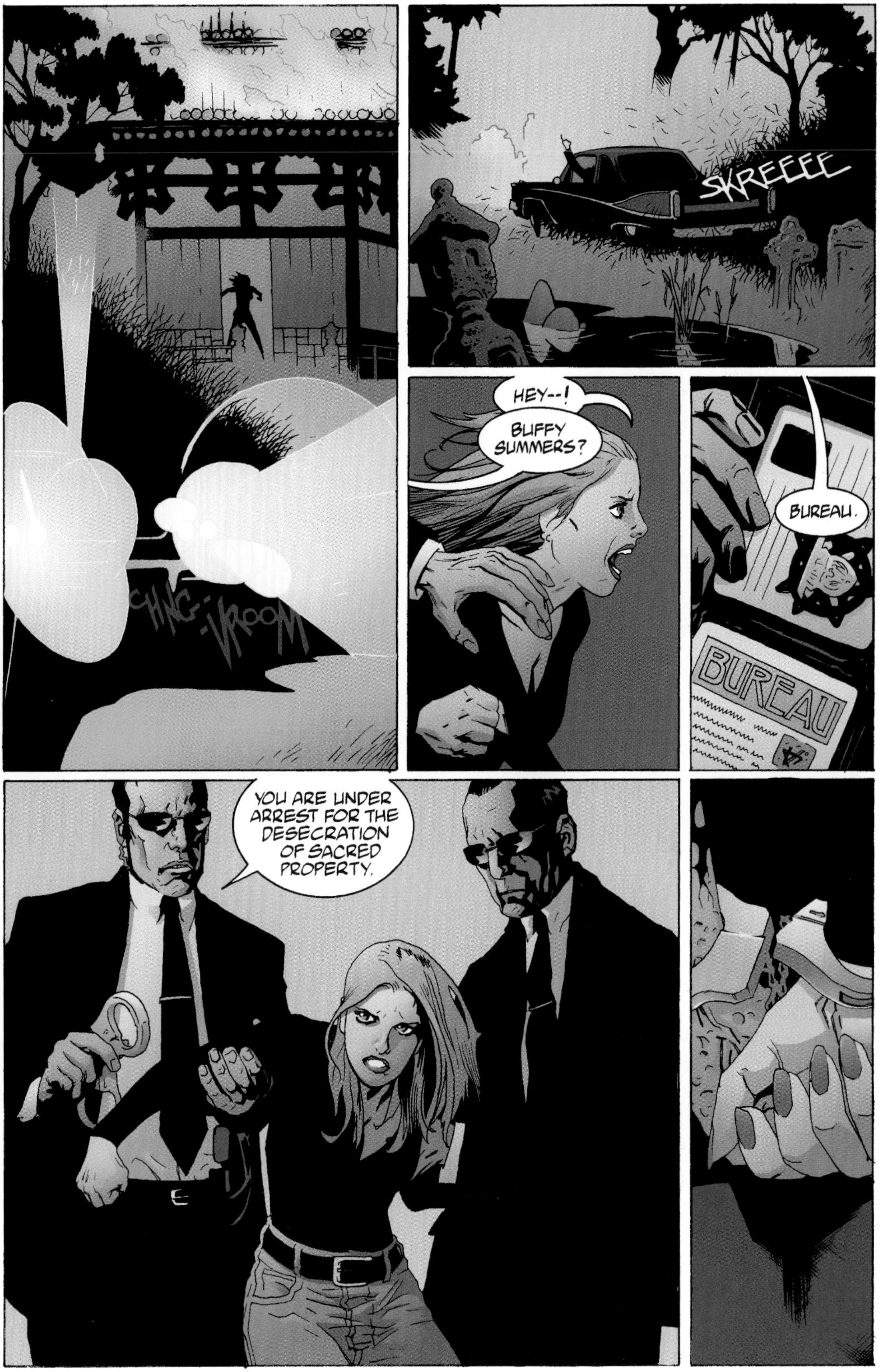
CHNG-VROOM
SKREEEE
HEY--!
BUFFY SUMMERS?
BUREAU.
BUREAU
YOU ARE UNDER ARREST FOR THE DESECRATION OF SACRED PROPERTY.

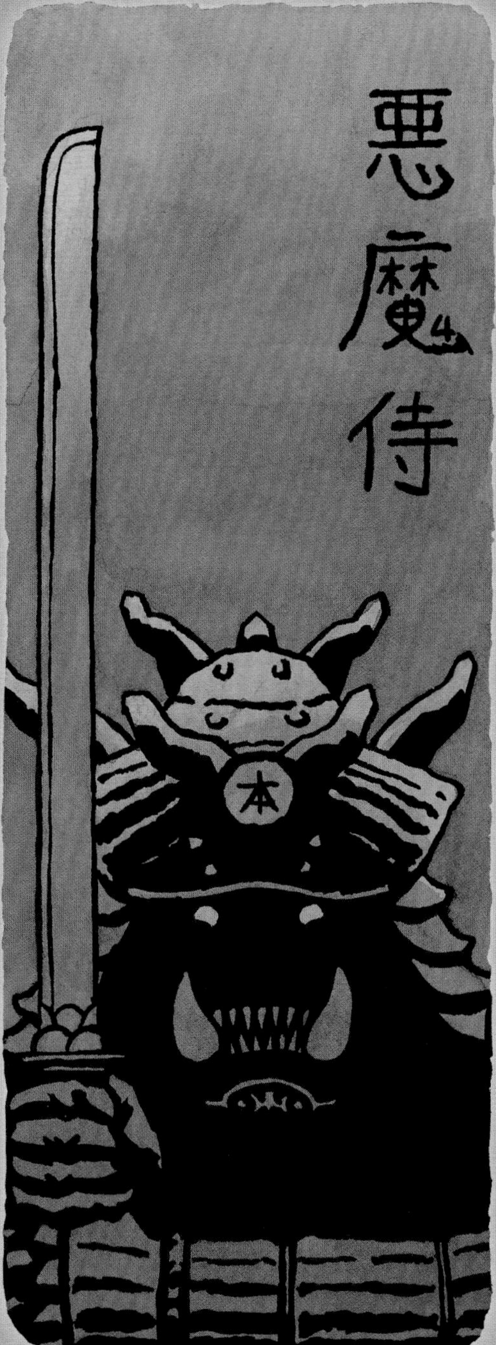
悪魔侍
本

The Seven Samurai

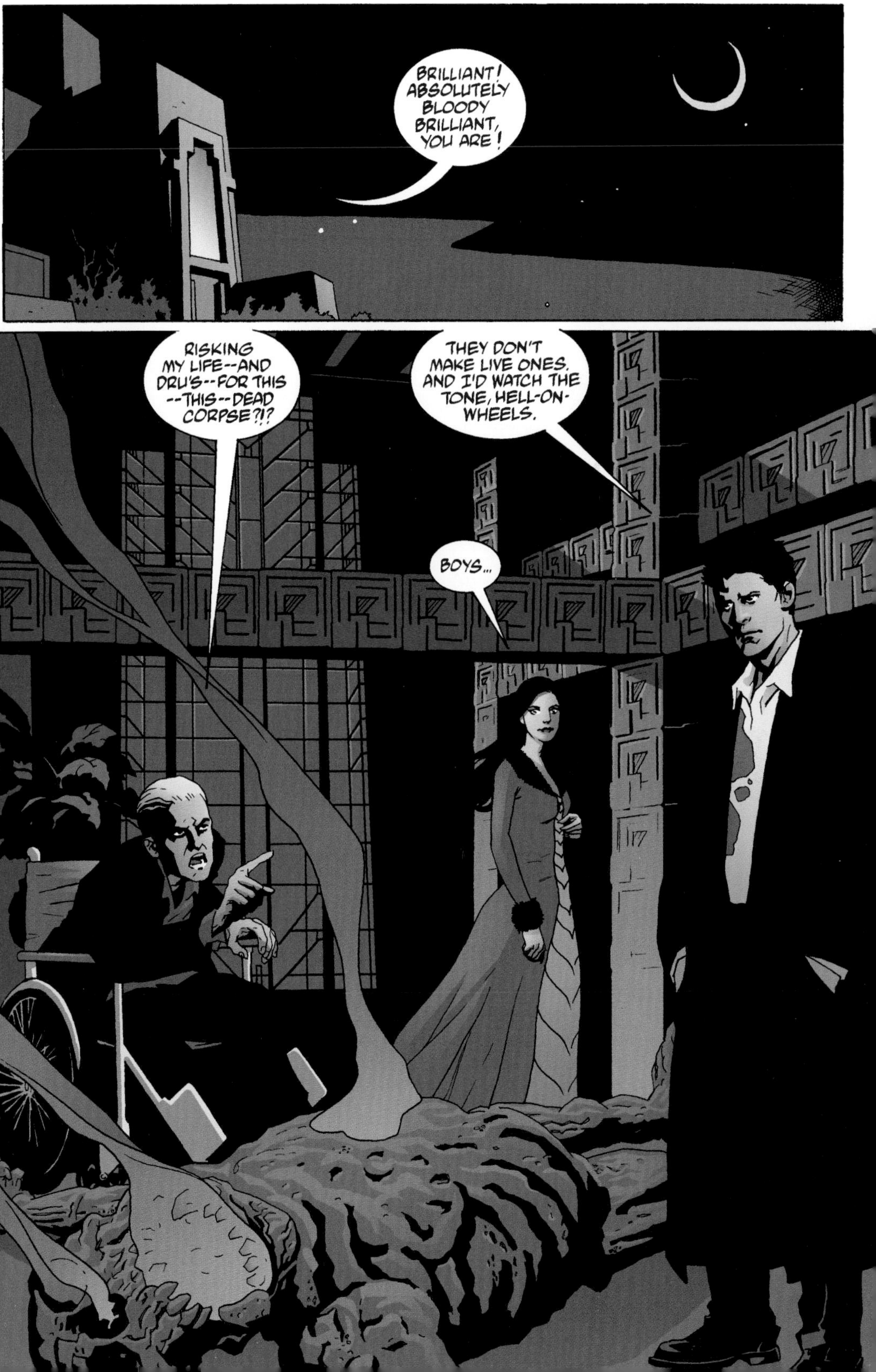
BRILLIANT! ABSOLUTELY BLOODY BRILLIANT, YOU ARE!
RISKING MY LIFE--AND DRU'S--FOR THIS --THIS--DEAD CORPSE?!?
THEY DON'T MAKE LIVE ONES. AND I'D WATCH THE TONE, HELL-ON-WHEELS.
BOYS...

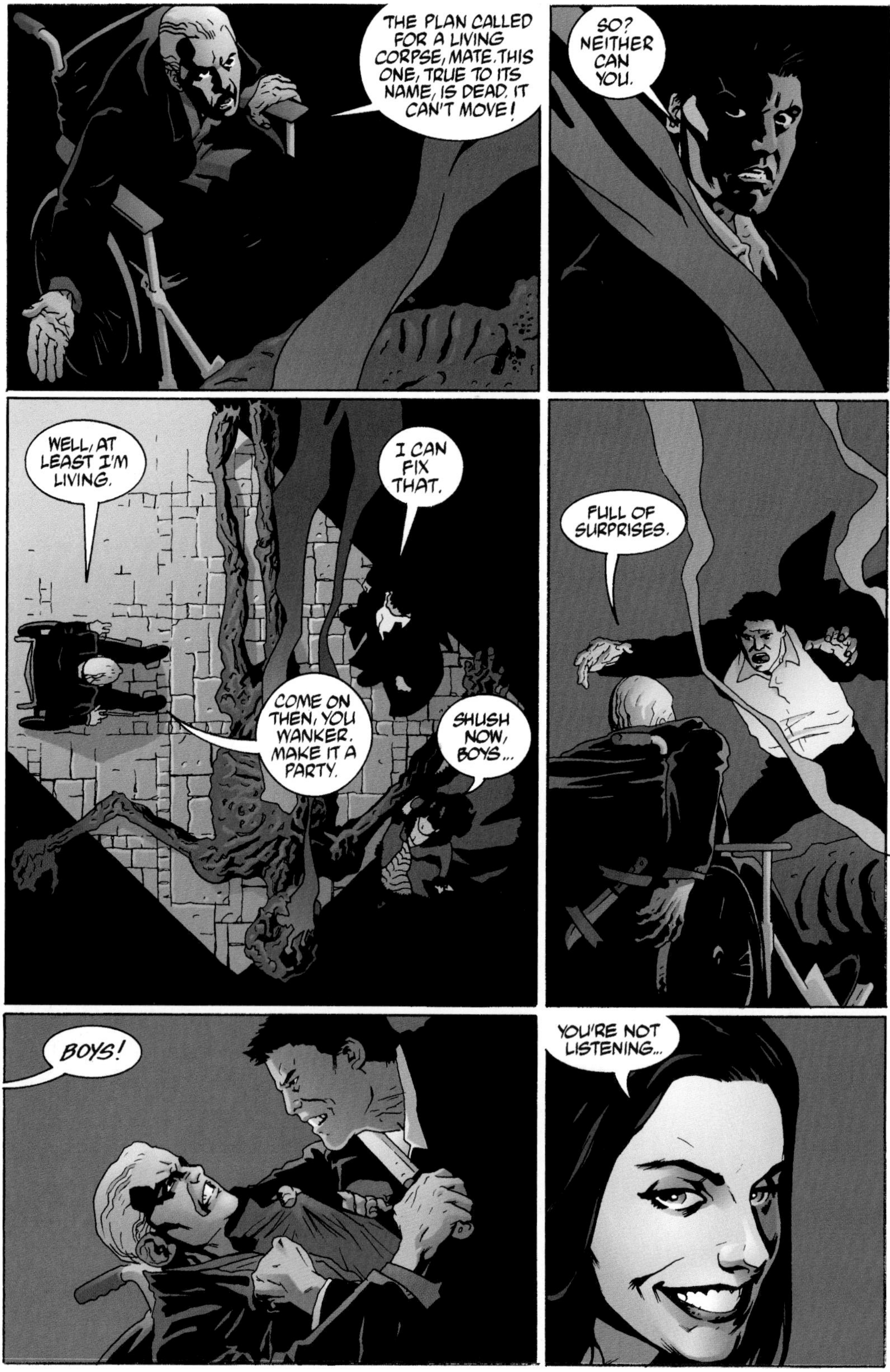
THE PLAN CALLED FOR A LIVING CORPSE, MATE. THIS ONE, TRUE TO ITS NAME, IS DEAD. IT CAN'T MOVE!
SO? NEITHER CAN YOU.
WELL, AT LEAST I'M LIVING.
I CAN FIX THAT.
COME ON THEN, YOU WANKER. MAKE IT A PARTY.
SHUSH NOW, BOYS...
FULL OF SURPRISES.
BOYS!
YOU'RE NOT LISTENING...

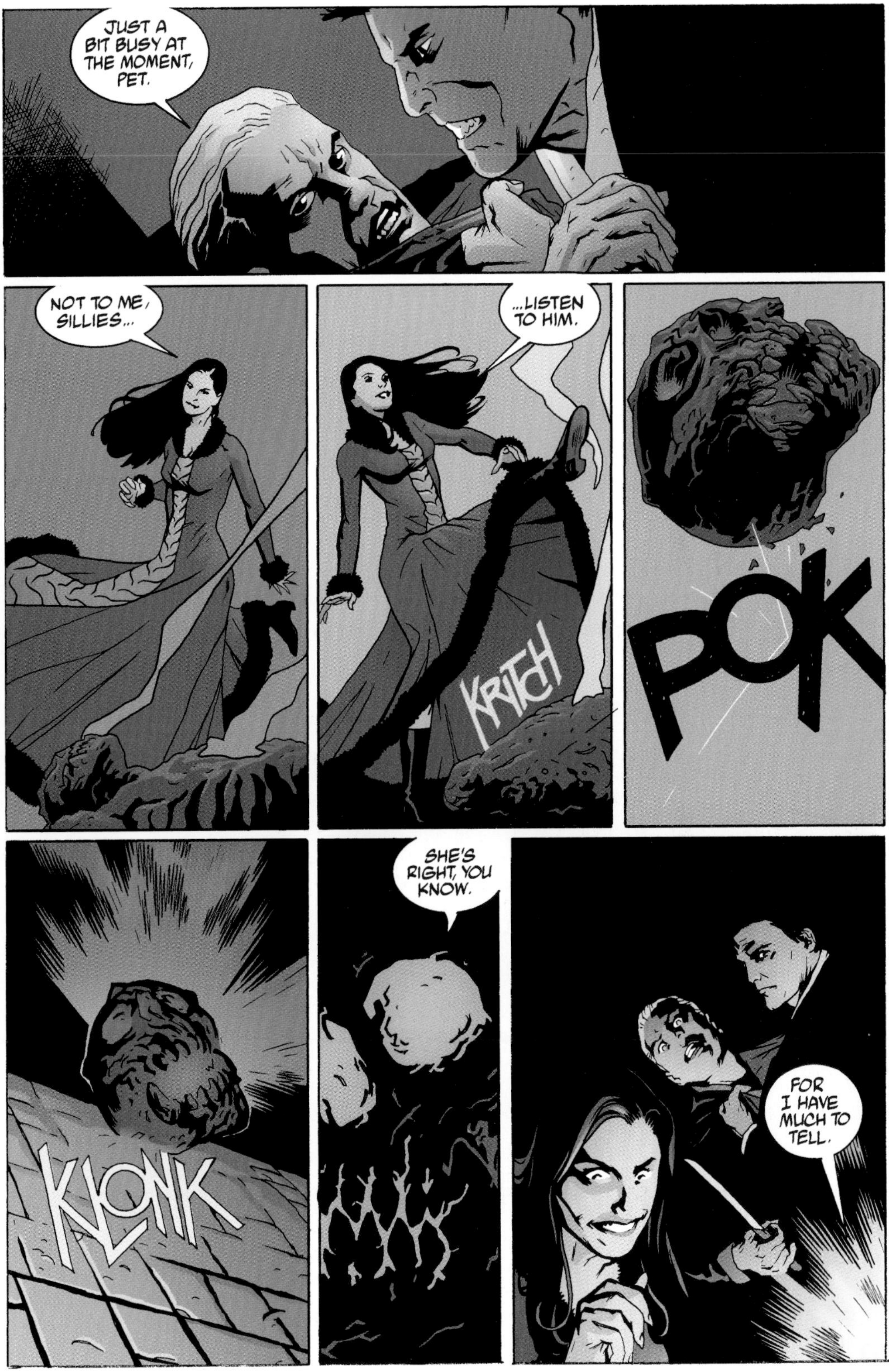
JUST A BIT BUSY AT THE MOMENT, PET.
NOT TO ME, SILLIES...
...LISTEN TO HIM.
KRITCH
POK
KLONK
SHE'S RIGHT, YOU KNOW.
FOR I HAVE MUCH TO TELL.

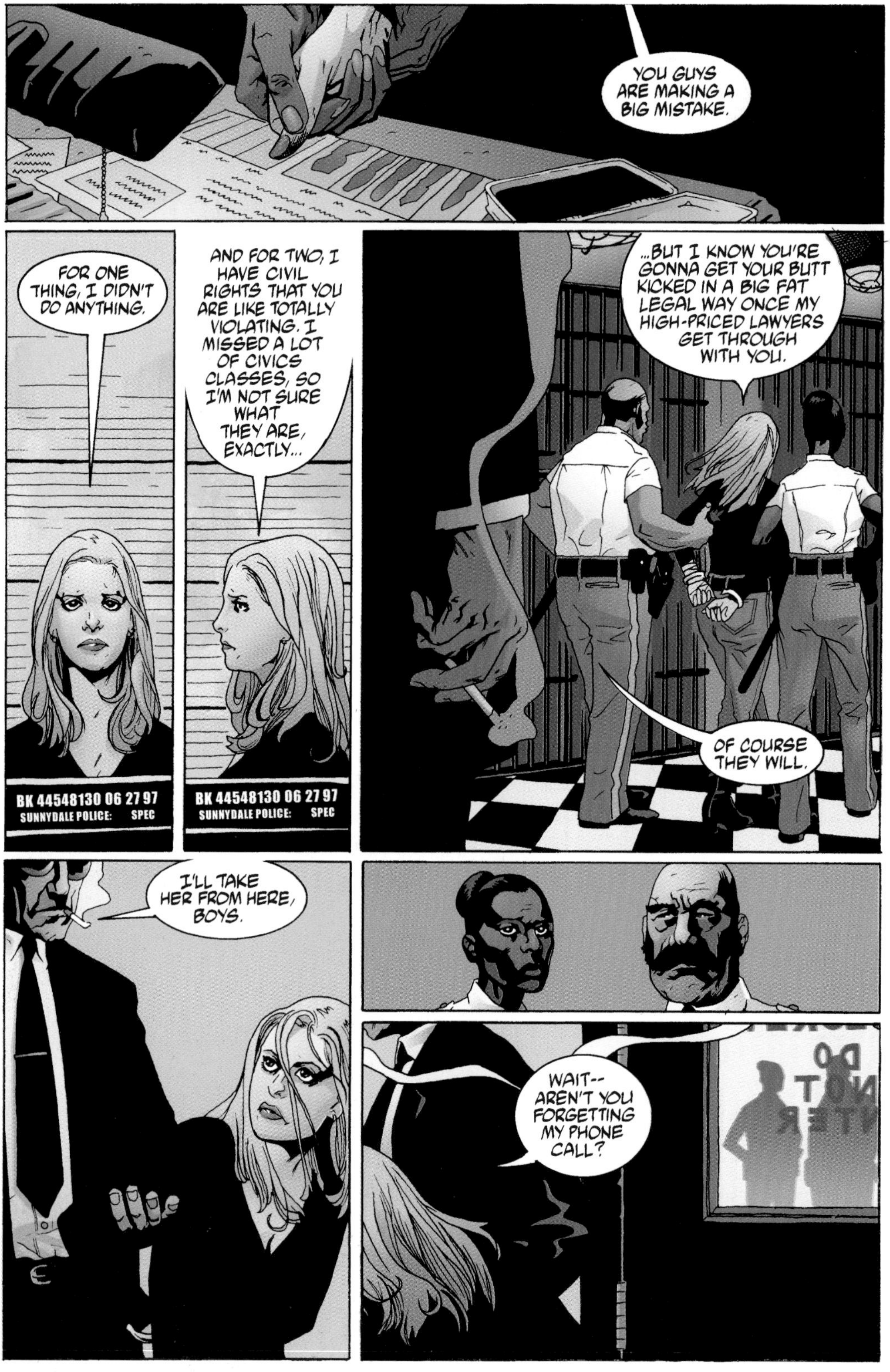
YOU GUYS ARE MAKING A BIG MISTAKE.
FOR ONE THING, I DIDN'T DO ANYTHING.
BK 44548130 06 27 97
SUNNYDALE POLICE: SPEC
AND FOR TWO, I HAVE CIVIL RIGHTS THAT YOU ARE LIKE TOTALLY VIOLATING. I MISSED A LOT OF CIVICS CLASSES, SO I'M NOT SURE WHAT THEY ARE, EXACTLY...
BK 44548130 06 27 97
SUNNYDALE POLICE: SPEC
...BUT I KNOW YOU'RE GONNA GET YOUR BUTT KICKED IN A BIG FAT LEGAL WAY ONCE MY HIGH-PRICED LAWYERS GET THROUGH WITH YOU.
OF COURSE THEY WILL.
I'LL TAKE HER FROM HERE, BOYS.
WAIT-- AREN'T YOU FORGETTING MY PHONE CALL?

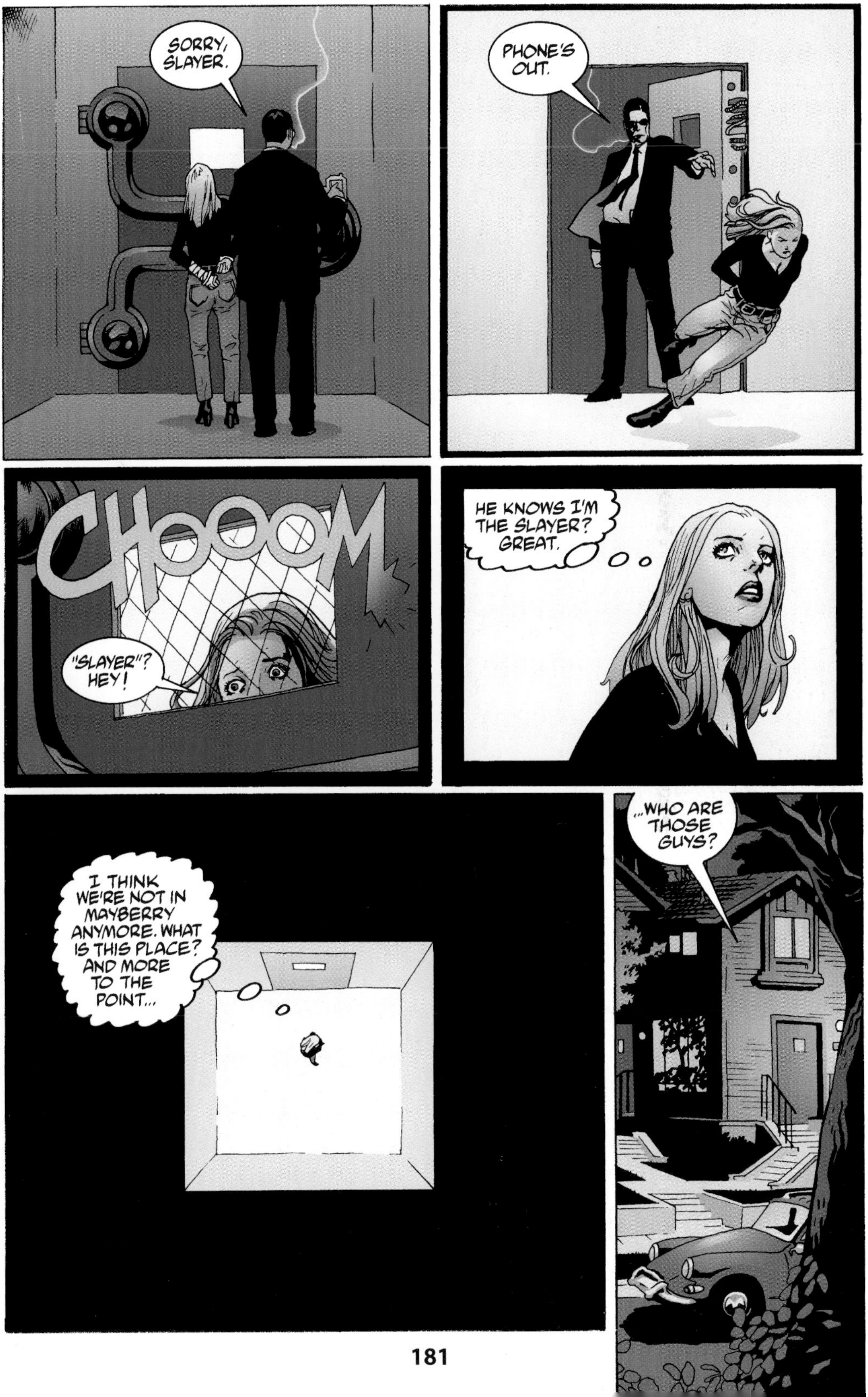
SORRY, SLAYER.
PHONE'S OUT.
CHOOOM
"SLAYER"? HEY!
HE KNOWS I'M THE SLAYER? GREAT.
I THINK WE'RE NOT IN MAYBERRY ANYMORE. WHAT IS THIS PLACE? AND MORE TO THE POINT...
...WHO ARE THOSE GUYS?

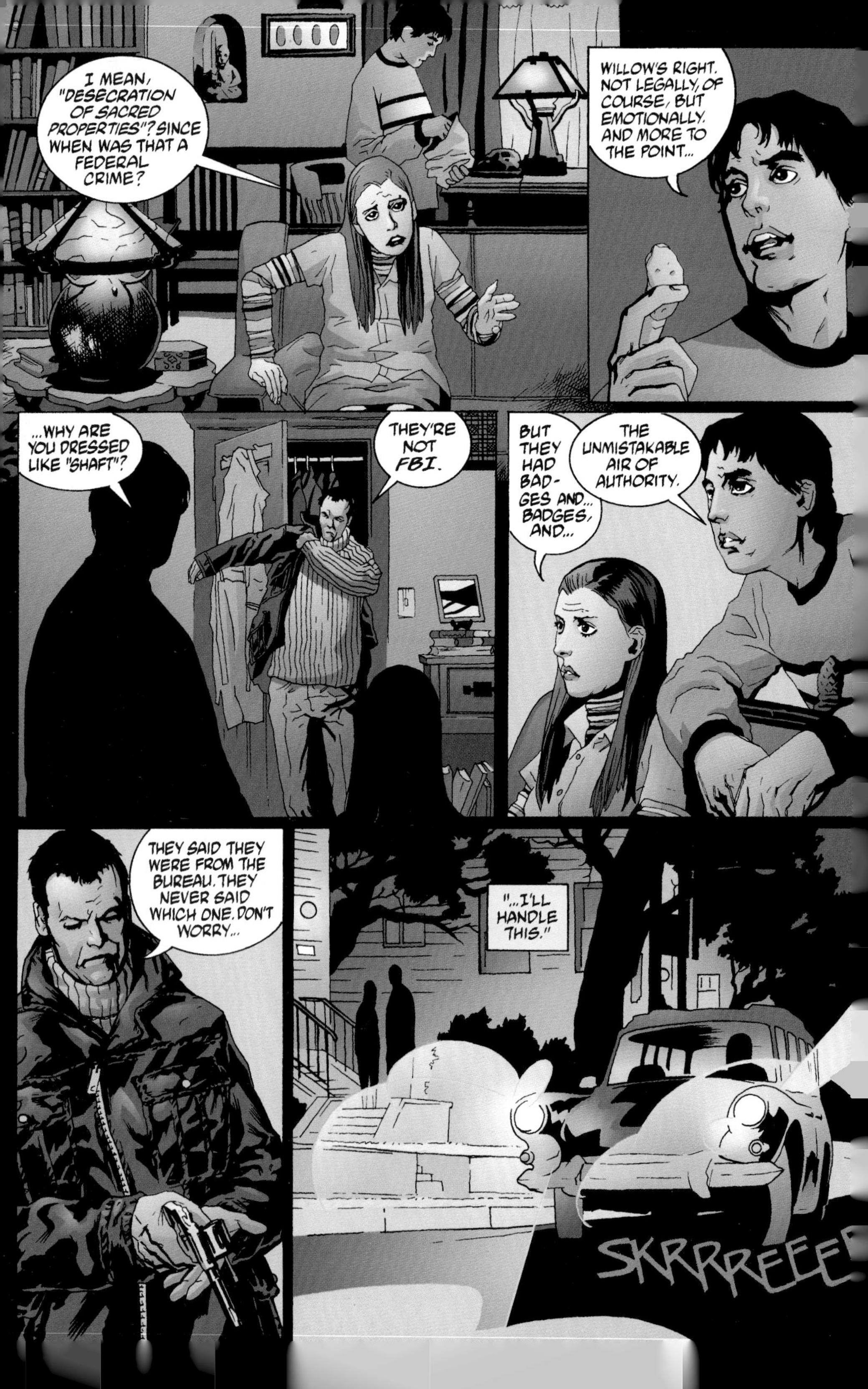

I MEAN, "DESECRATION OF SACRED PROPERTIES"? SINCE WHEN WAS THAT A FEDERAL CRIME?
WILLOW'S RIGHT. NOT LEGALLY, OF COURSE, BUT EMOTIONALLY. AND MORE TO THE POINT...
...WHY ARE YOU DRESSED LIKE "SHAFT"?
THEY'RE NOT FBI.
BUT THEY HAD BAD-GES AND... BADGES, AND...
THE UNMISTAKABLE AIR OF AUTHORITY.
THEY SAID THEY WERE FROM THE BUREAU. THEY NEVER SAID WHICH ONE. DON'T WORRY...
"...I'LL HANDLE THIS."
SKRRREEEE

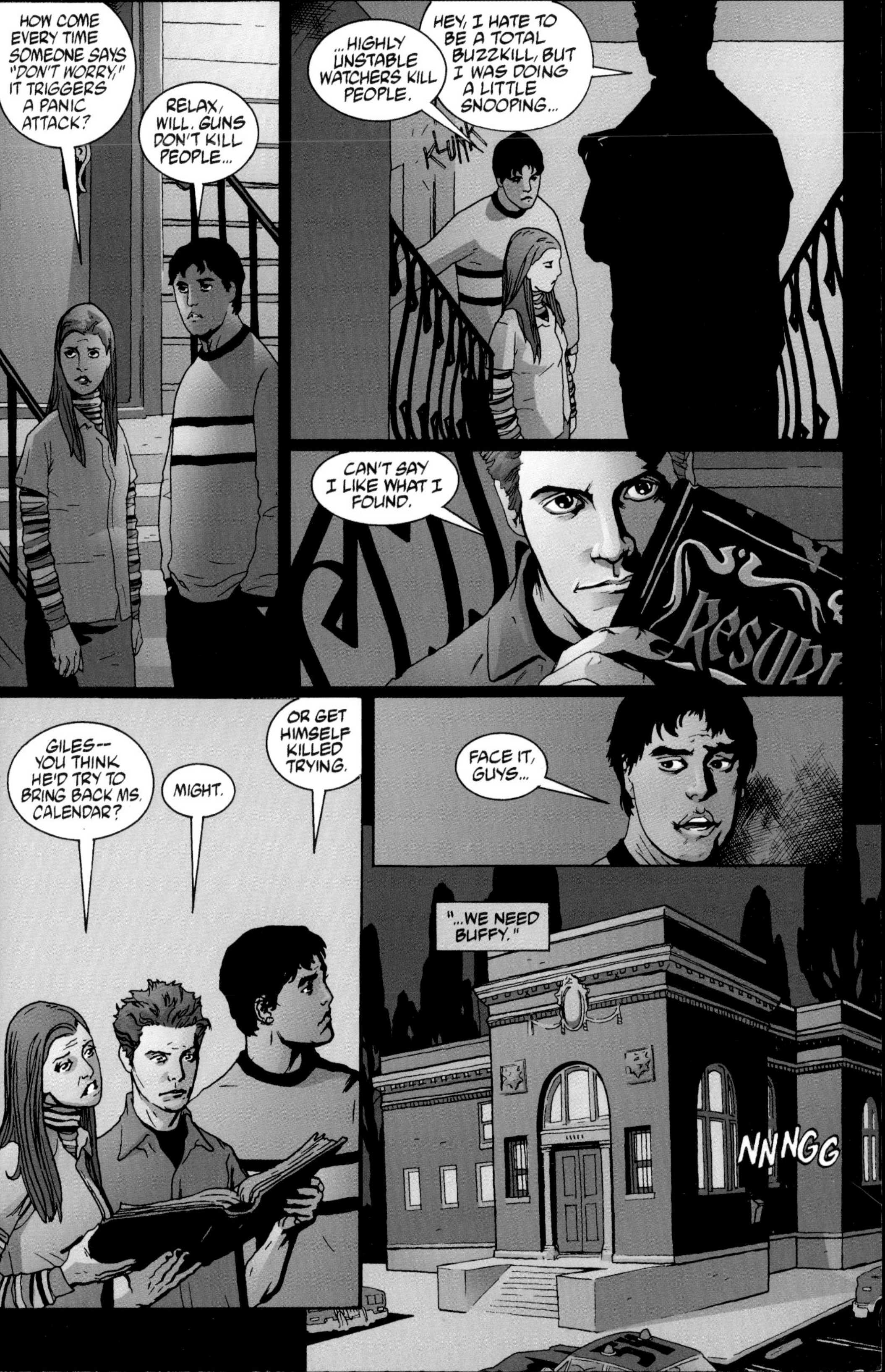
HOW COME EVERY TIME SOMEONE SAYS "DON'T WORRY," IT TRIGGERS A PANIC ATTACK?
RELAX, WILL. GUNS DON'T KILL PEOPLE...
...HIGHLY UNSTABLE WATCHERS KILL PEOPLE.
KLUNK
HEY, I HATE TO BE A TOTAL BUZZKILL, BUT I WAS DOING A LITTLE SNOOPING...
CAN'T SAY I LIKE WHAT I FOUND.
GILES-- YOU THINK HE'D TRY TO BRING BACK MS. CALENDAR?
MIGHT.
OR GET HIMSELF KILLED TRYING.
FACE IT, GUYS...
"...WE NEED BUFFY."
NNNGG

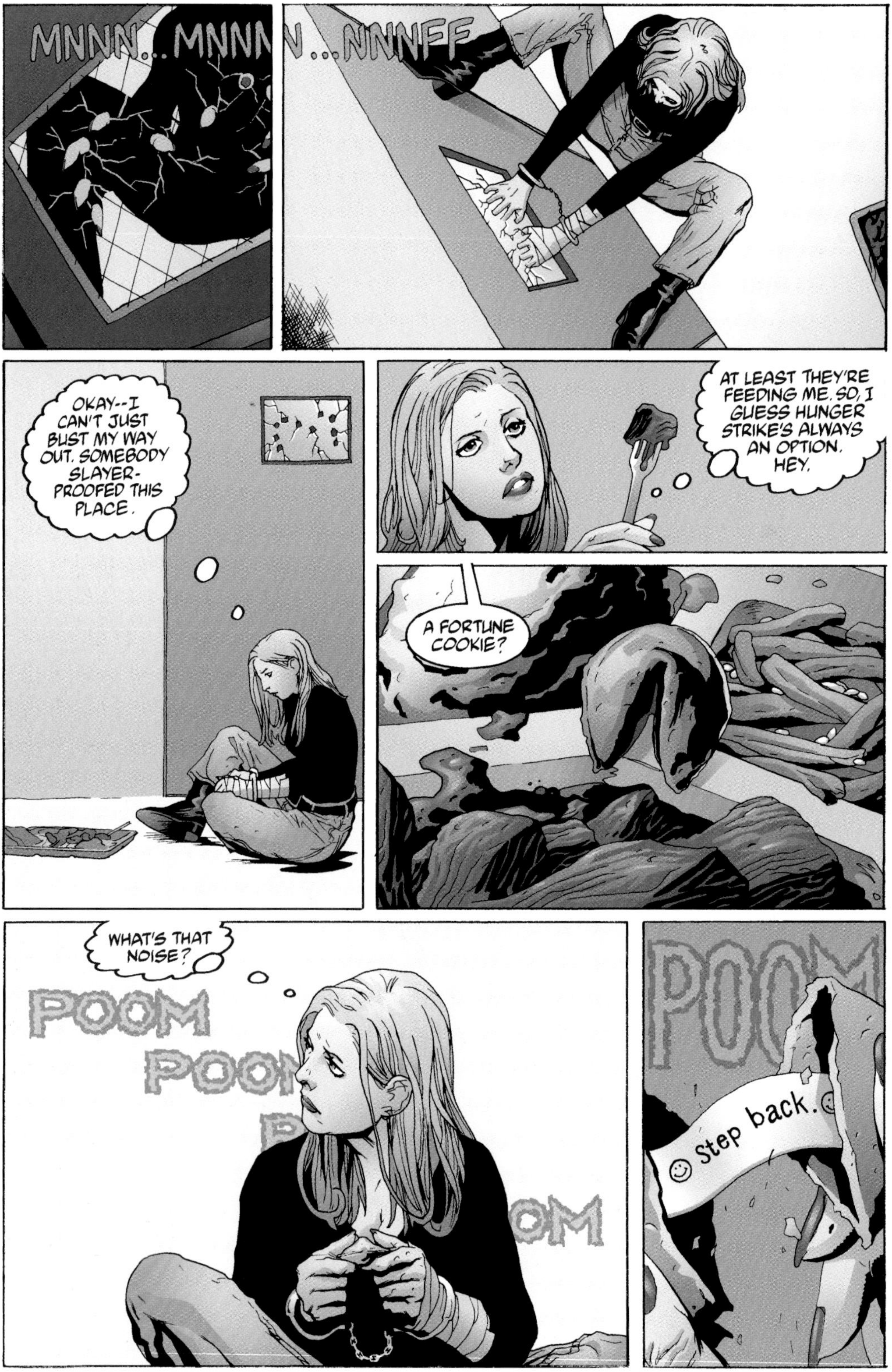
MNNN...MNNNN...NNNFF
OKAY--I CAN'T JUST BUST MY WAY OUT. SOMEBODY SLAYER-PROOFED THIS PLACE.
AT LEAST THEY'RE FEEDING ME. SO, I GUESS HUNGER STRIKE'S ALWAYS AN OPTION. HEY.
A FORTUNE COOKIE?
WHAT'S THAT NOISE?
POOM
POOM
POOM
step back.

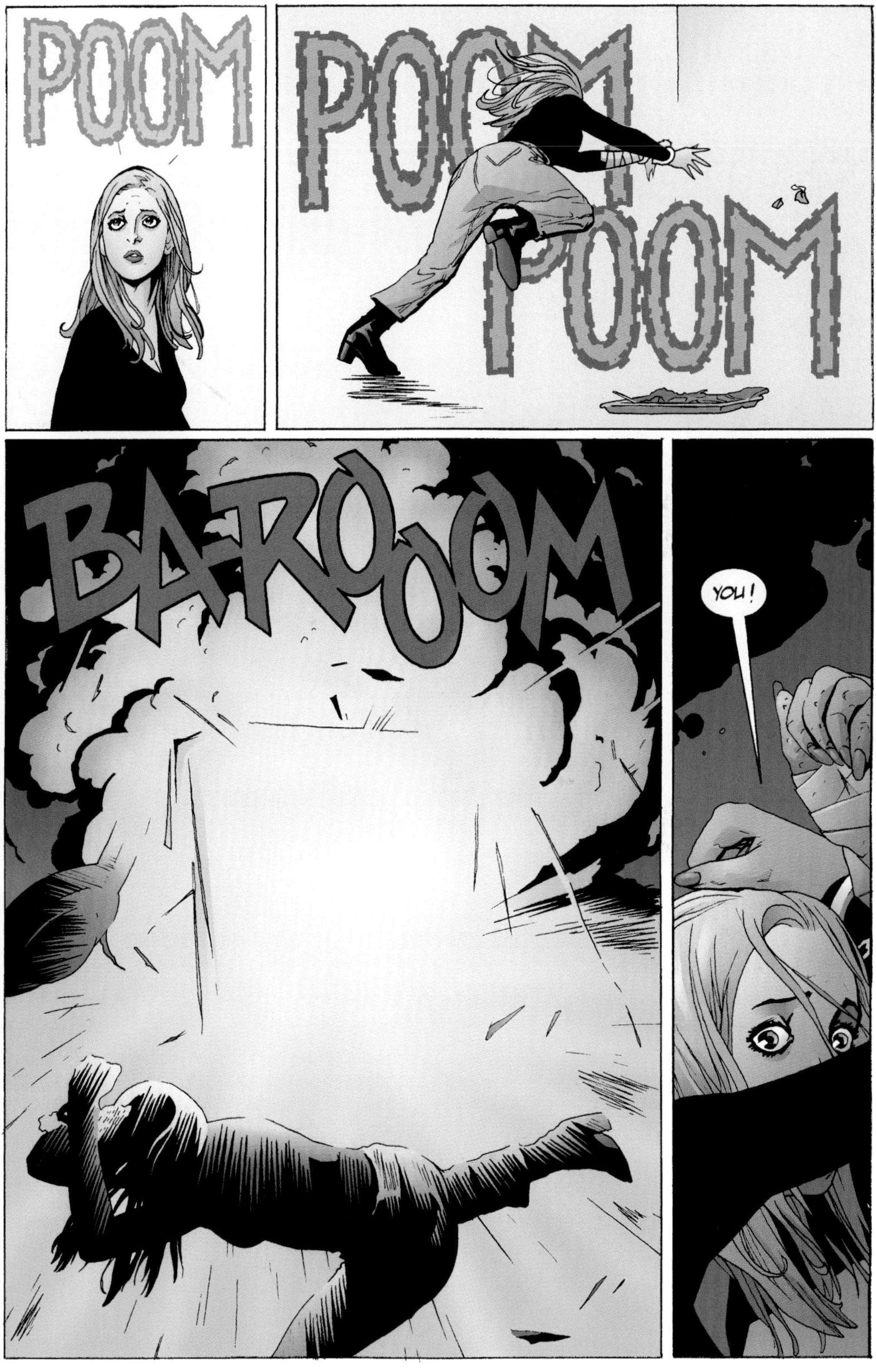
POOM
POOM
POOM
BA-ROOOOM
YOU!

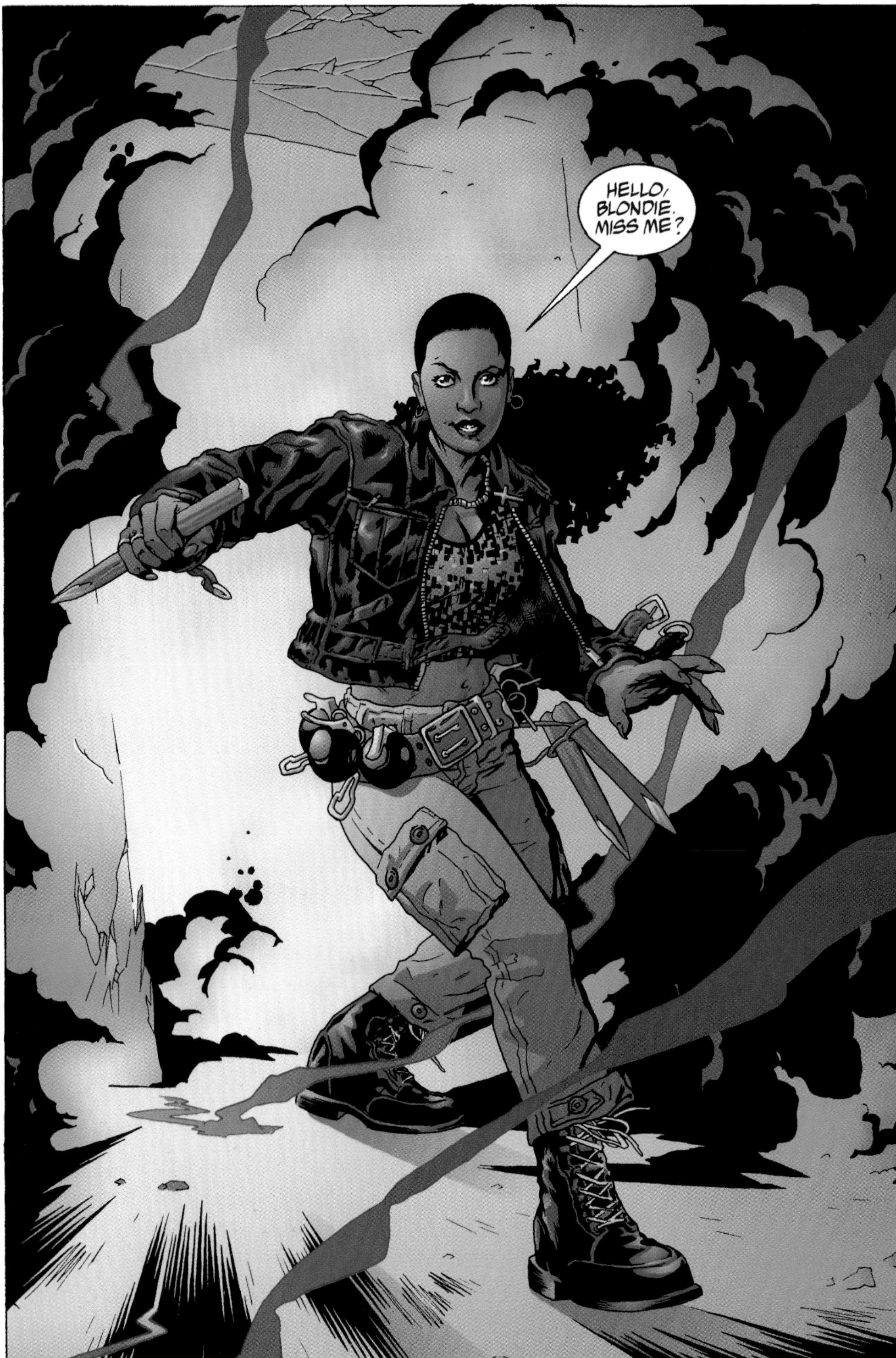
HELLO, BLONDIE. MISS ME?

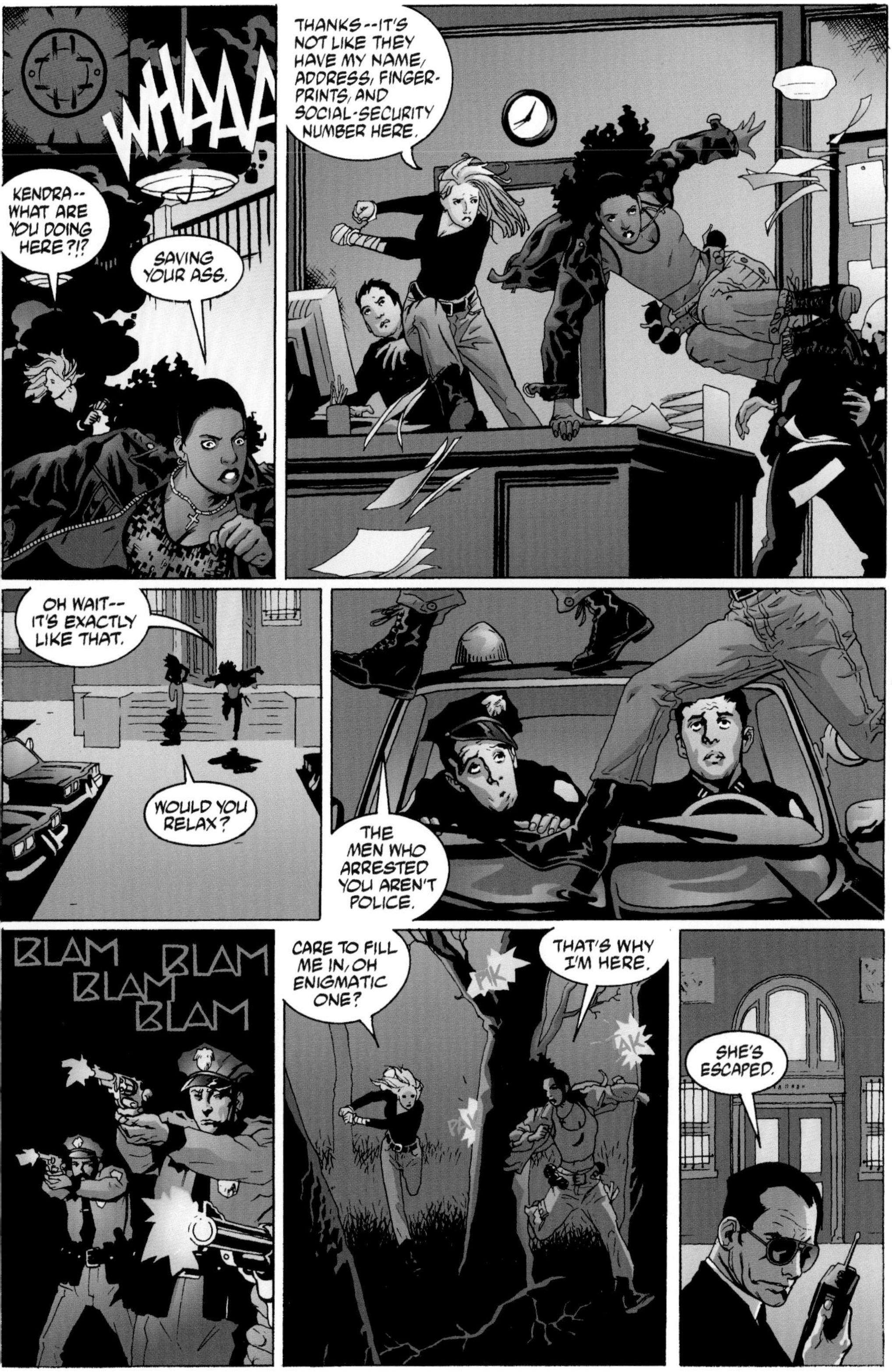
WHAAA
KENDRA-- WHAT ARE YOU DOING HERE?!?
SAVING YOUR ASS.
THANKS--IT'S NOT LIKE THEY HAVE MY NAME, ADDRESS, FINGER-PRINTS, AND SOCIAL-SECURITY NUMBER HERE.
OH WAIT-- IT'S EXACTLY LIKE THAT.
WOULD YOU RELAX?
THE MEN WHO ARRESTED YOU AREN'T POLICE.
BLAM BLAM BLAM BLAM
CARE TO FILL ME IN, OH ENIGMATIC ONE?
THAT'S WHY I'M HERE.
PIK
AK
SHE'S ESCAPED.

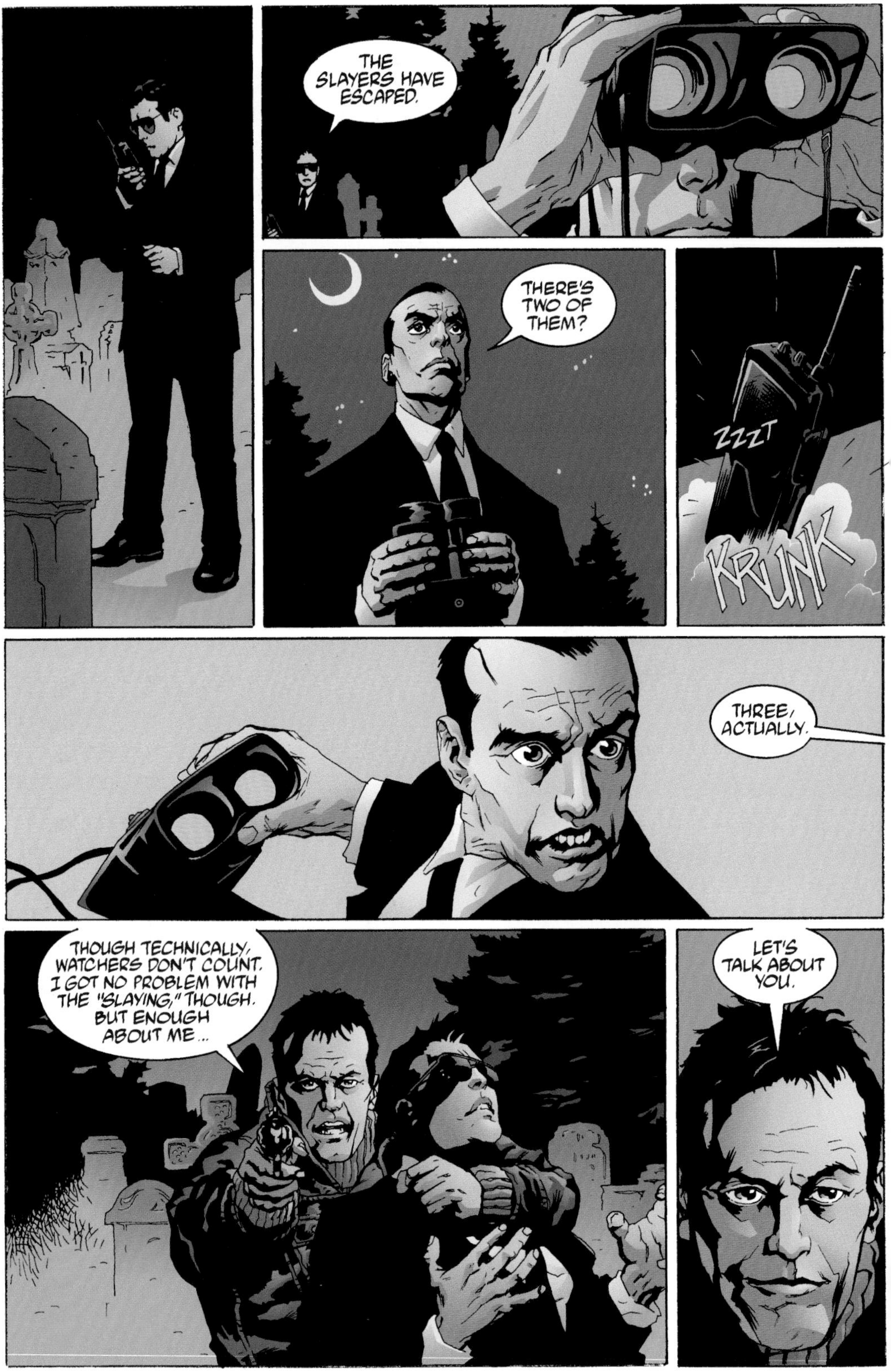
THE SLAYERS HAVE ESCAPED.
THERE'S TWO OF THEM?
ZZZT
KRUNK
THREE, ACTUALLY.
THOUGH TECHNICALLY, WATCHERS DON'T COUNT. I GOT NO PROBLEM WITH THE "SLAYING," THOUGH. BUT ENOUGH ABOUT ME...
LET'S TALK ABOUT YOU.

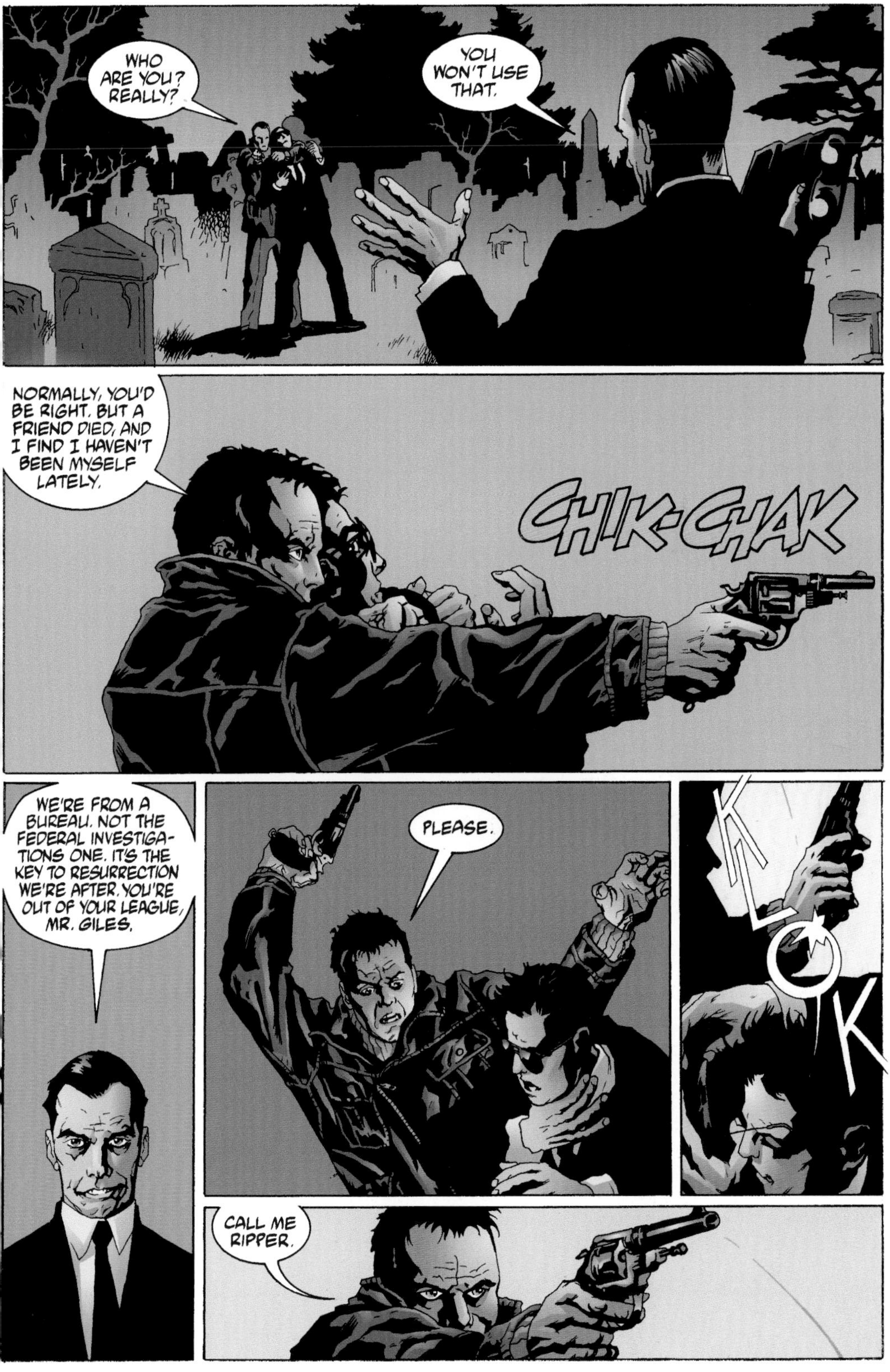
WHO ARE YOU? REALLY?
YOU WON'T USE THAT.
NORMALLY, YOU'D BE RIGHT. BUT A FRIEND DIED, AND I FIND I HAVEN'T BEEN MYSELF LATELY.
CHIK-CHAK
WE'RE FROM A BUREAU. NOT THE FEDERAL INVESTIGATIONS ONE. IT'S THE KEY TO RESURRECTION WE'RE AFTER. YOU'RE OUT OF YOUR LEAGUE, MR. GILES.
PLEASE.
KLOK
CALL ME RIPPER.

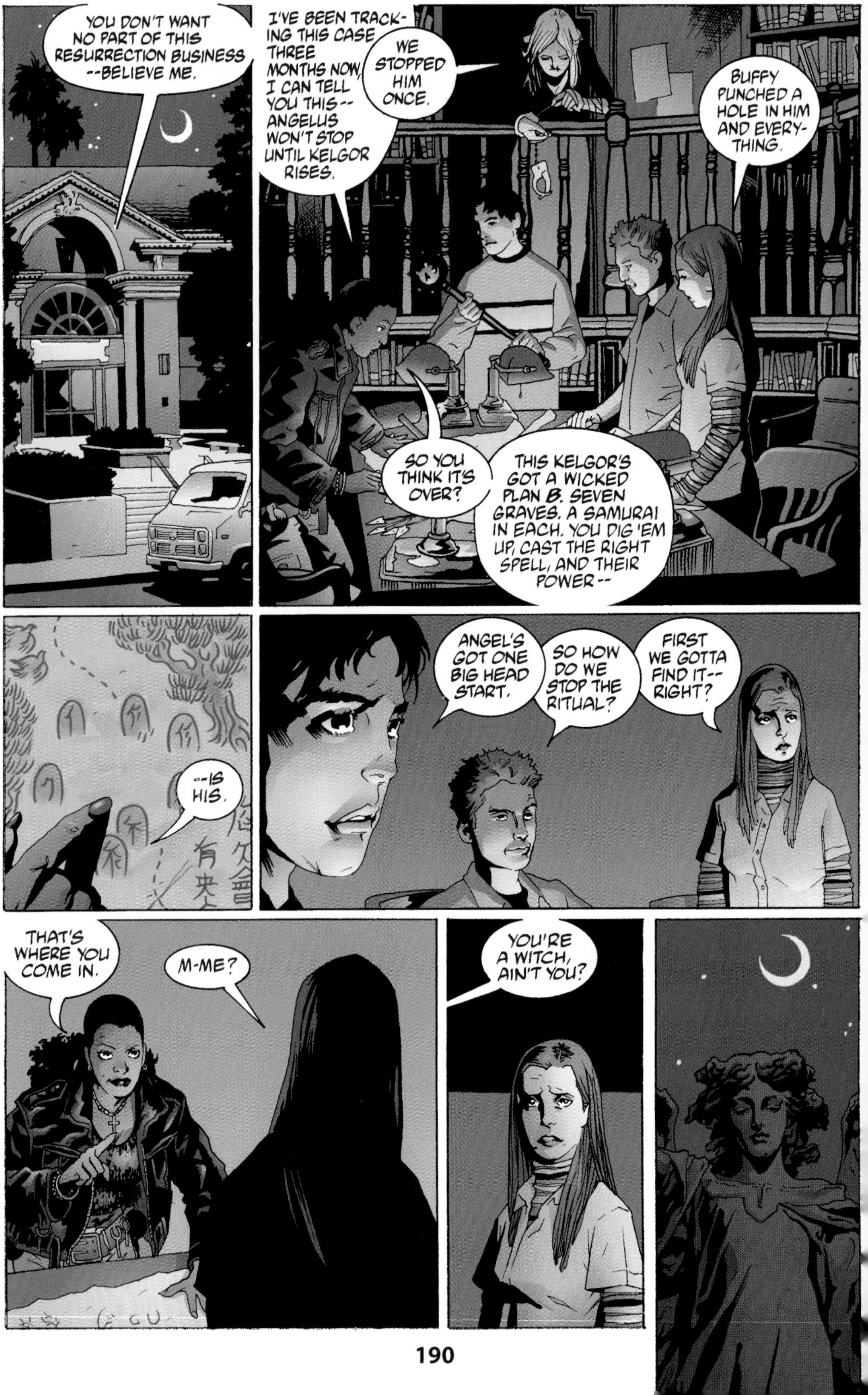
YOU DON'T WANT NO PART OF THIS RESURRECTION BUSINESS --BELIEVE ME.
I'VE BEEN TRACKING THIS CASE THREE MONTHS NOW, I CAN TELL YOU THIS-- ANGELUS WON'T STOP UNTIL KELGOR RISES.
WE STOPPED HIM ONCE.
BUFFY PUNCHED A HOLE IN HIM AND EVERYTHING.
SO YOU THINK IT'S OVER?
THIS KELGOR'S GOT A WICKED PLAN B. SEVEN GRAVES. A SAMURAI IN EACH. YOU DIG 'EM UP, CAST THE RIGHT SPELL, AND THEIR POWER--
--IS HIS.
ANGEL'S GOT ONE BIG HEAD START.
SO HOW DO WE STOP THE RITUAL?
FIRST WE GOTTA FIND IT-- RIGHT?
THAT'S WHERE YOU COME IN.
M-ME?
YOU'RE A WITCH, AIN'T YOU?

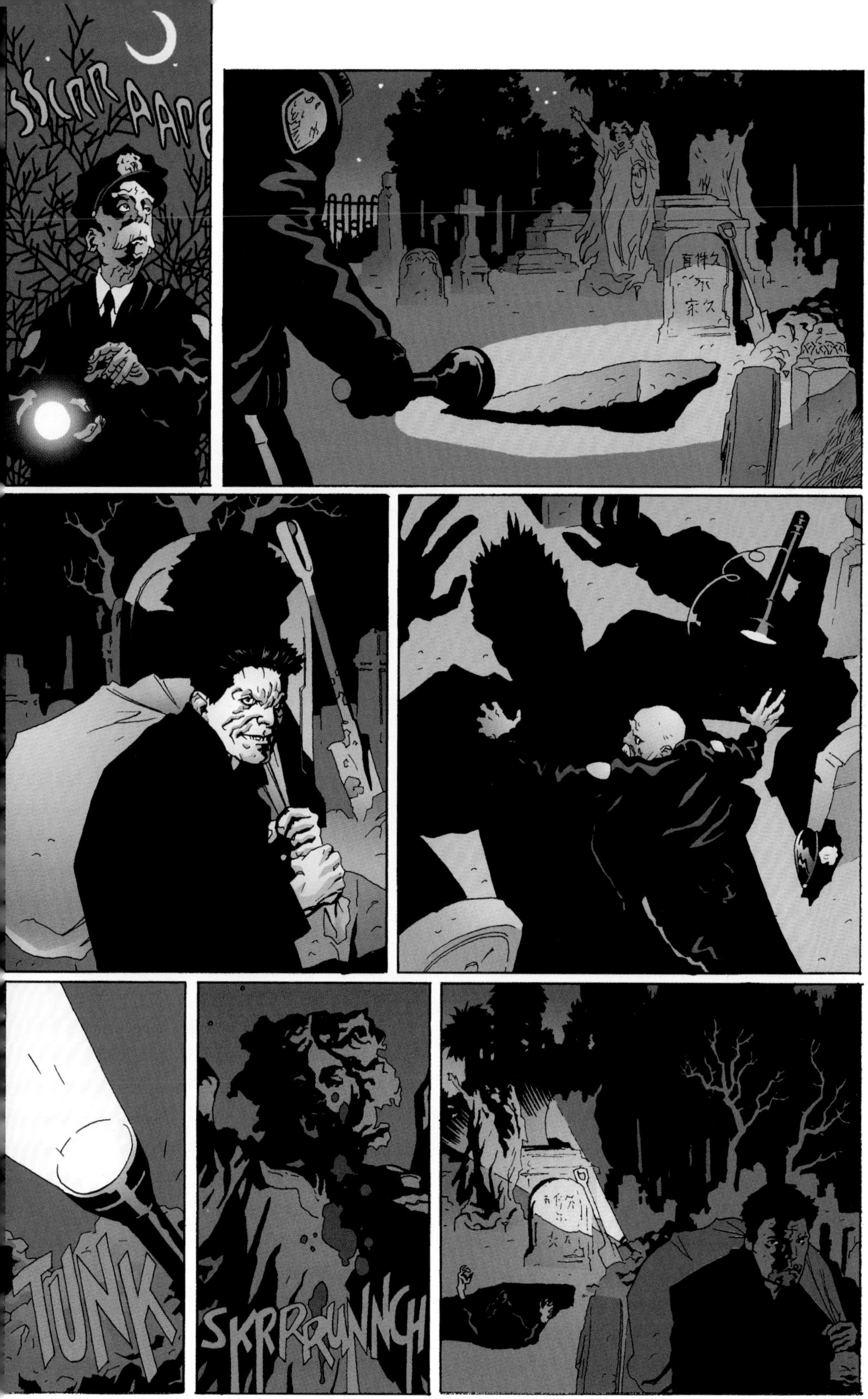
SSCRRAAPE
TUNK
SKRRRUNNCH

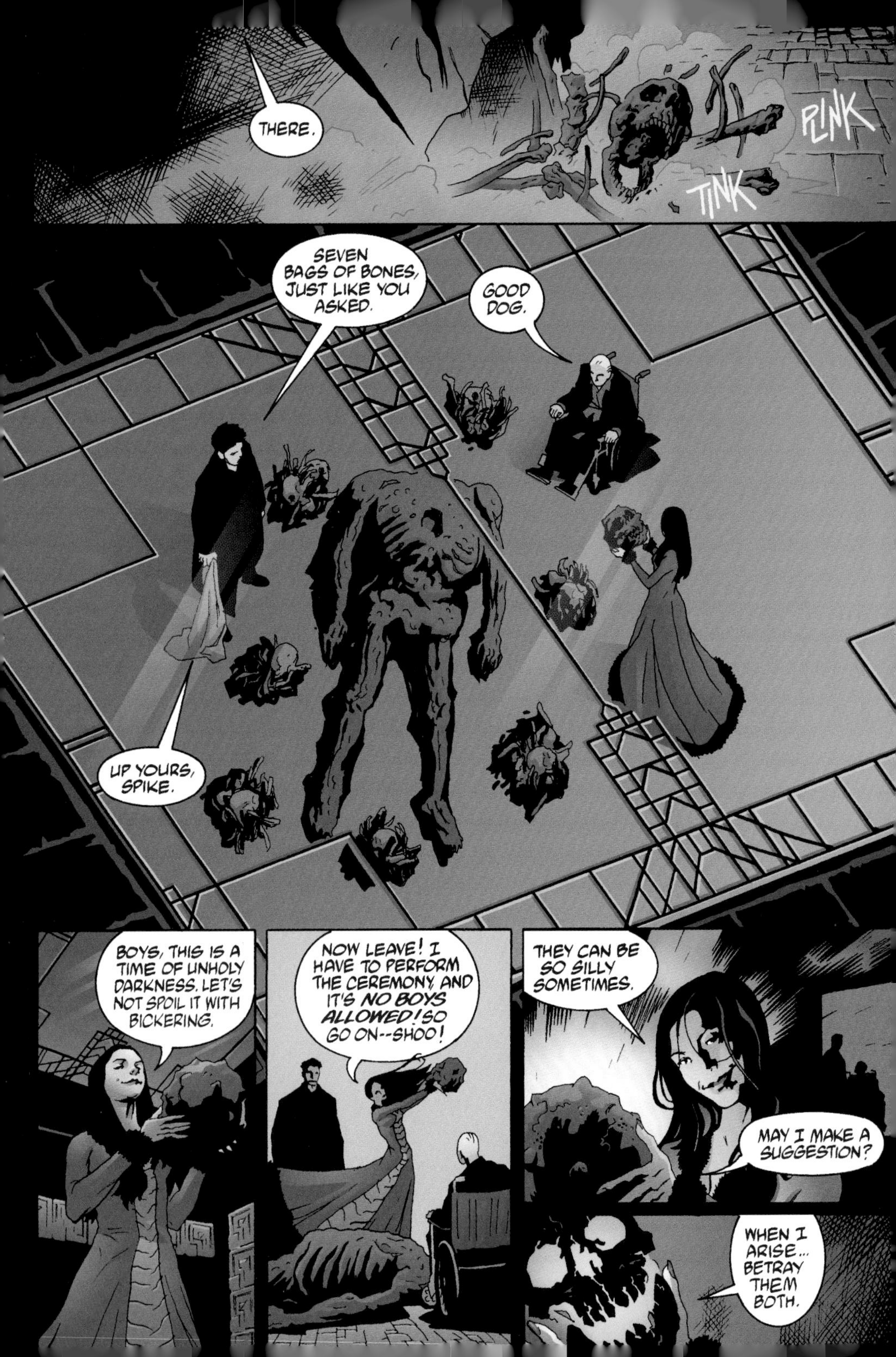
THERE.
PLINK
TINK
SEVEN BAGS OF BONES, JUST LIKE YOU ASKED.
GOOD DOG.
UP YOURS, SPIKE.
BOYS, THIS IS A TIME OF UNHOLY DARKNESS. LET'S NOT SPOIL IT WITH BICKERING.
NOW LEAVE! I HAVE TO PERFORM THE CEREMONY, AND IT'S NO BOYS ALLOWED! SO GO ON--SHOO!
THEY CAN BE SO SILLY SOMETIMES.
MAY I MAKE A SUGGESTION?
WHEN I ARISE... BETRAY THEM BOTH.

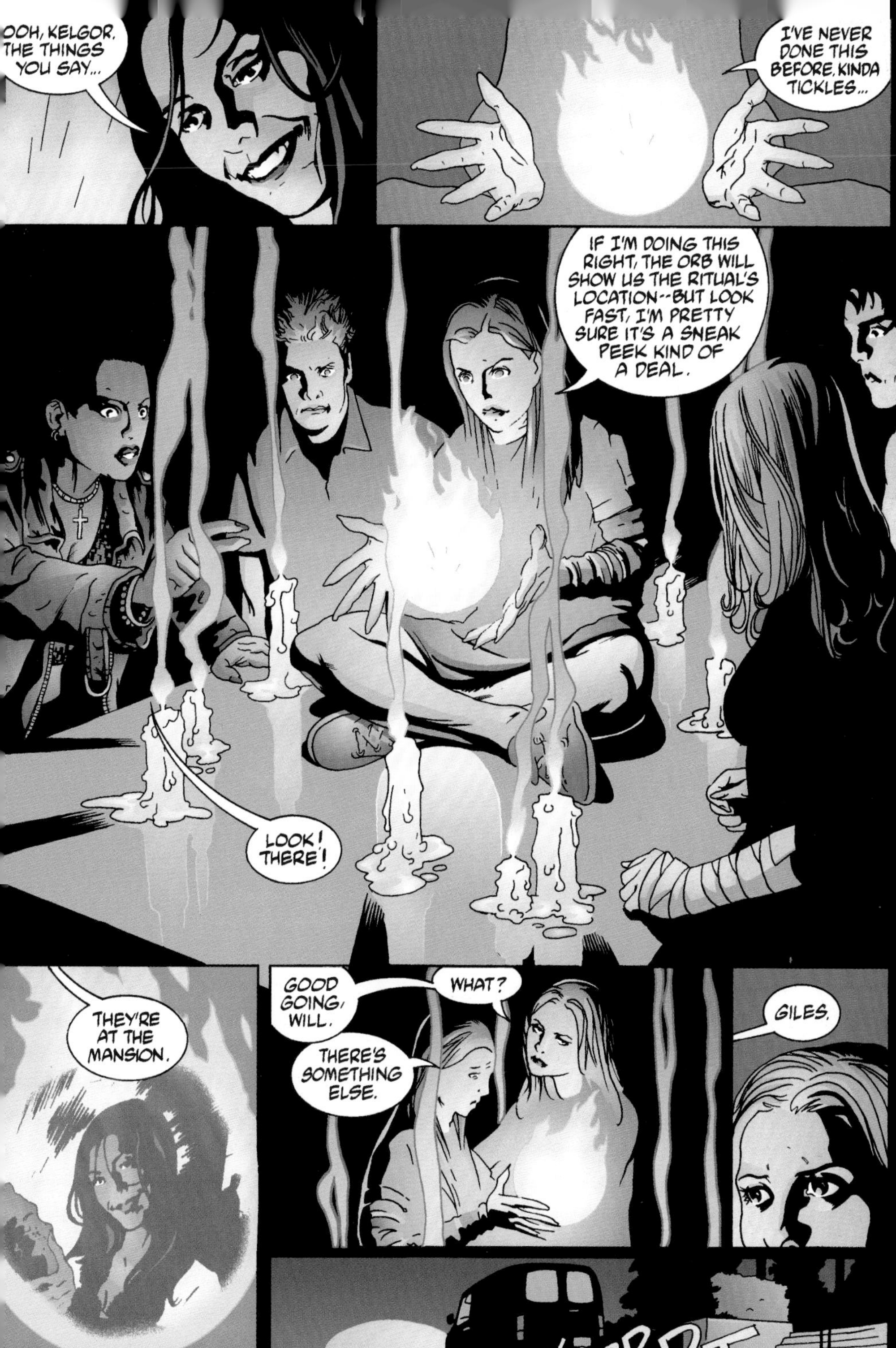
OOH, KELGOR, THE THINGS YOU SAY...
I'VE NEVER DONE THIS BEFORE, KINDA TICKLES...
IF I'M DOING THIS RIGHT, THE ORB WILL SHOW US THE RITUAL'S LOCATION--BUT LOOK FAST, I'M PRETTY SURE IT'S A SNEAK PEEK KIND OF A DEAL.
LOOK! THERE!
THEY'RE AT THE MANSION.
GOOD GOING, WILL.
WHAT?
THERE'S SOMETHING ELSE.
GILES.
SKRRRRT

SO IT BEGINS...

THE RITUAL...

...OF RESURRECTION...

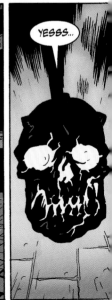

YESSS...

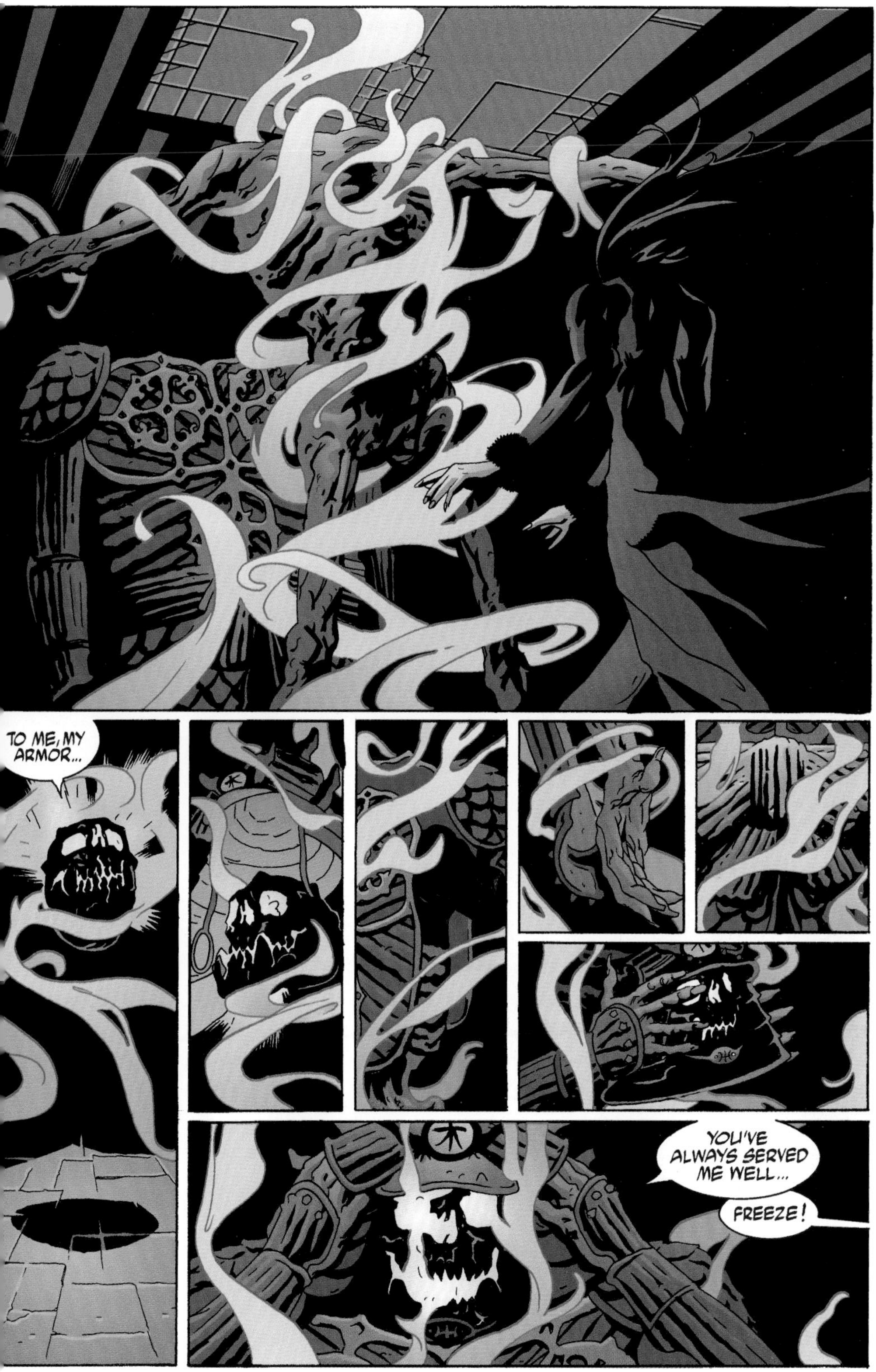
TO ME, MY ARMOR...
YOU'VE ALWAYS SERVED ME WELL...
FREEZE!

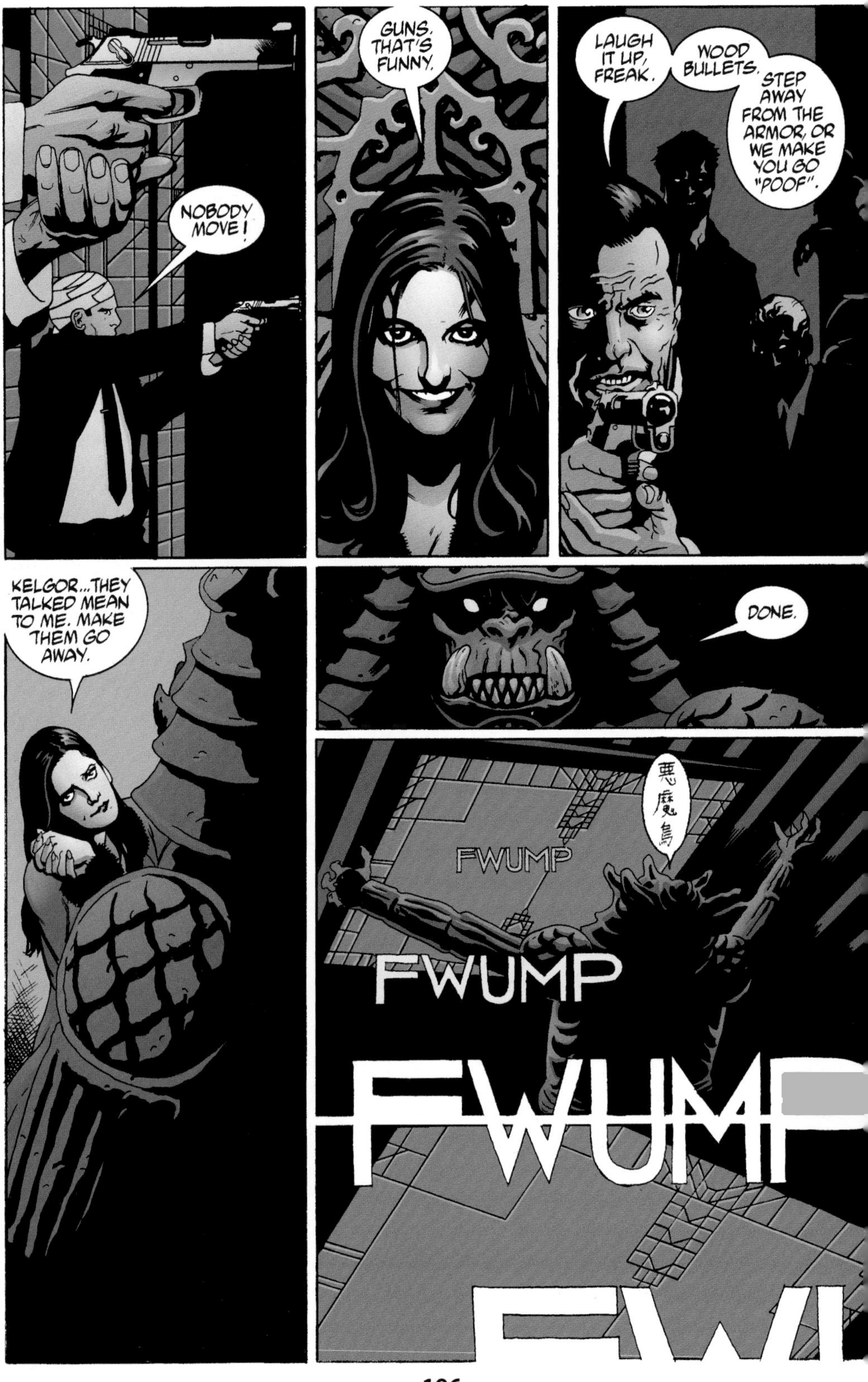
NOBODY MOVE!
GUNS. THAT'S FUNNY.
LAUGH IT UP, FREAK.
WOOD BULLETS.
STEP AWAY FROM THE ARMOR, OR WE MAKE YOU GO "POOF".
KELGOR...THEY TALKED MEAN TO ME. MAKE THEM GO AWAY.
DONE.
悪魔鳥
FWUMP
FWUMP
FWUMP

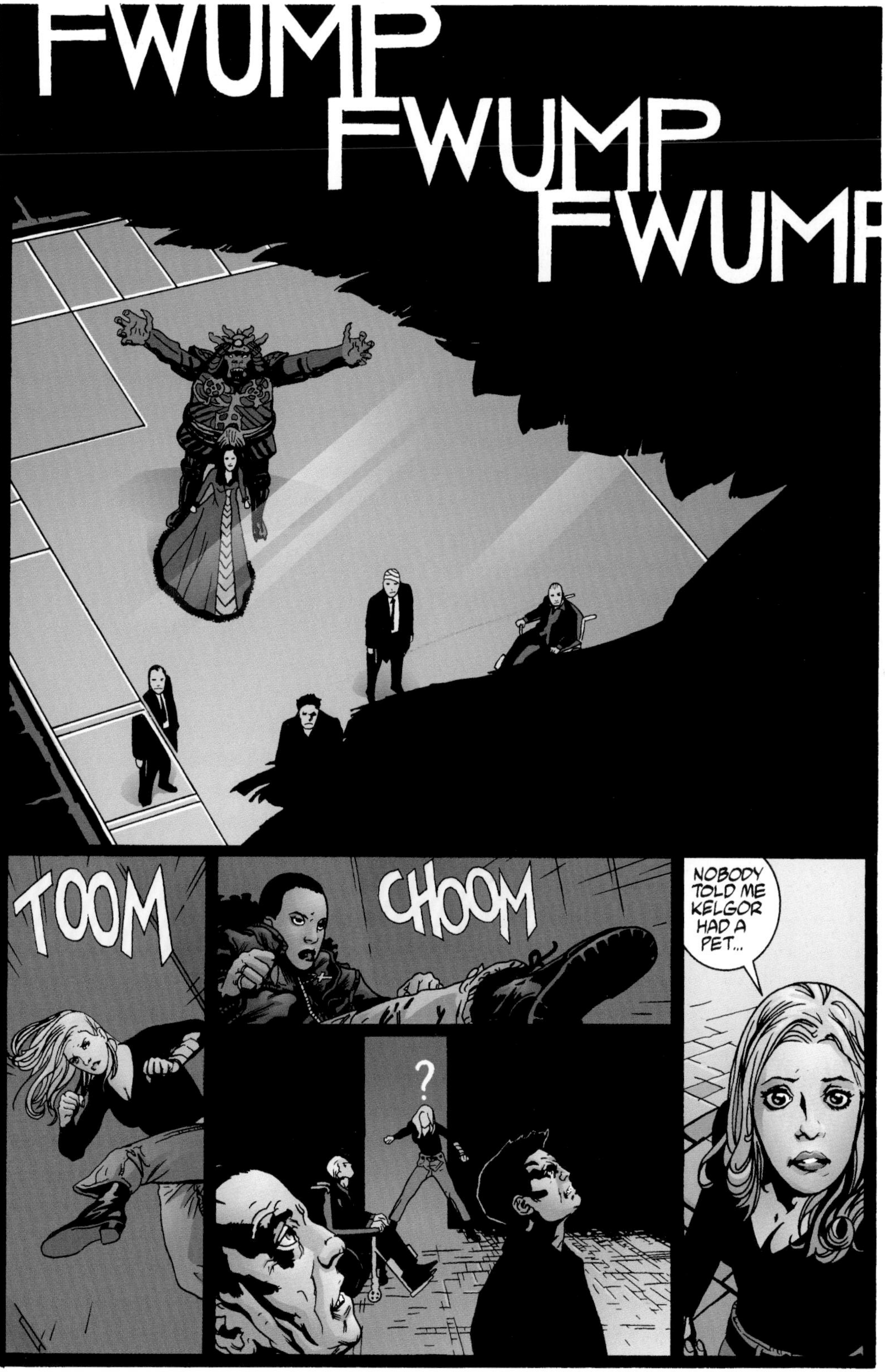
FWUMP
FWUMP
FWUMP
TOOM
CHOOM
NOBODY TOLD ME KELGOR HAD A PET...
?

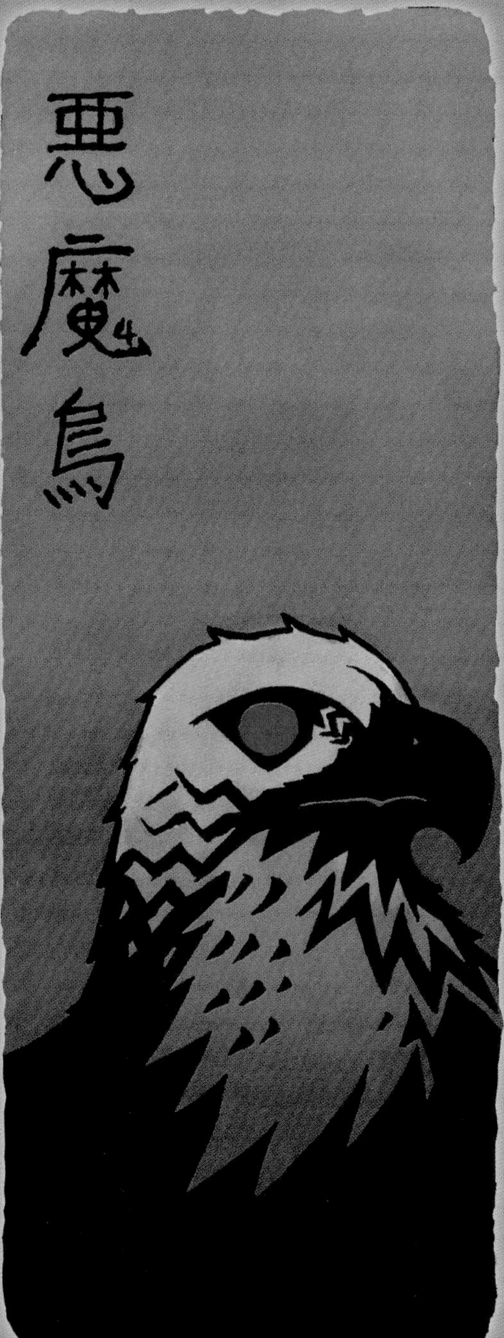
悪魔鳥

Kelgor Unbound

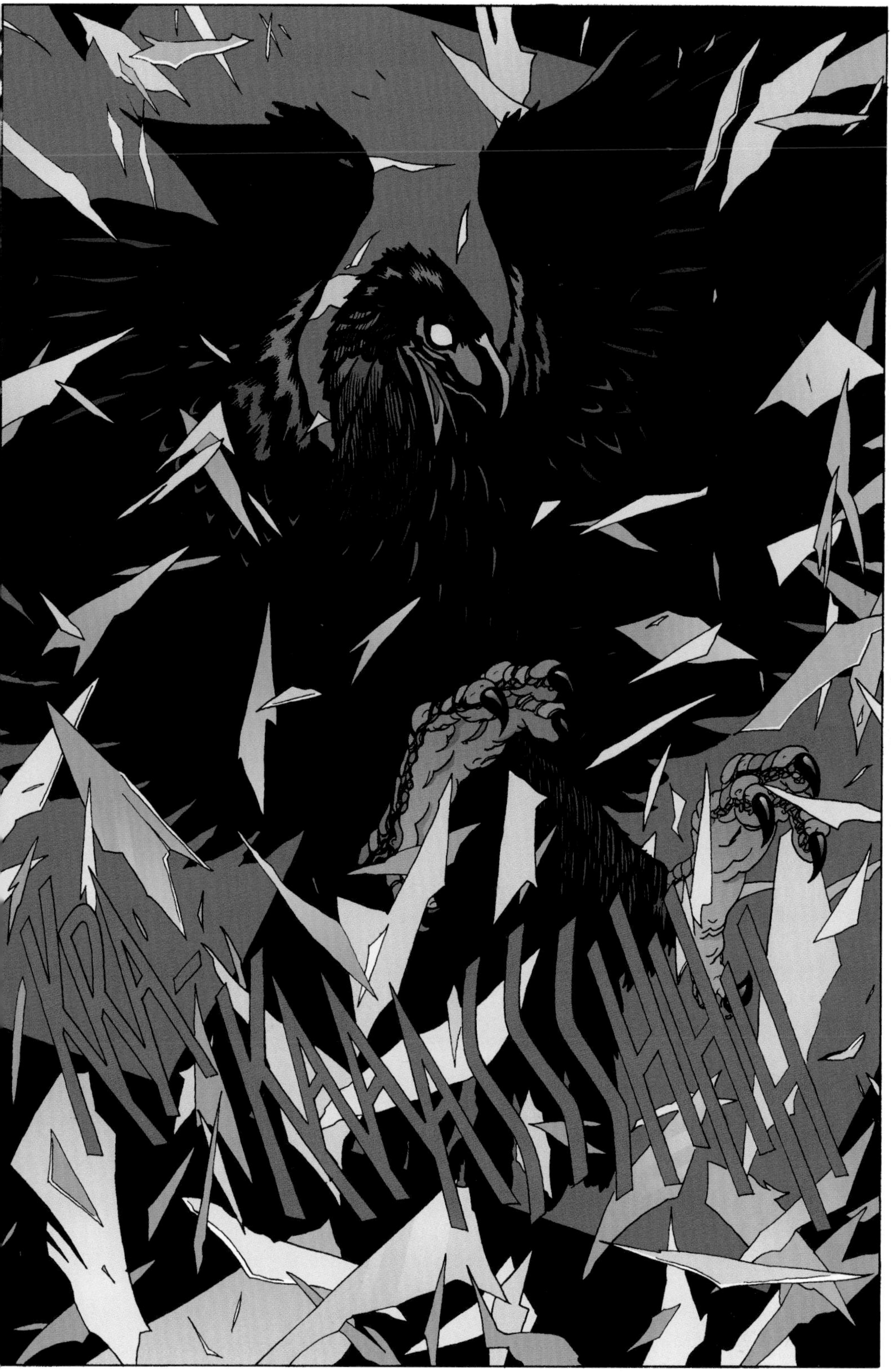
KRA-KAAASSSHHH

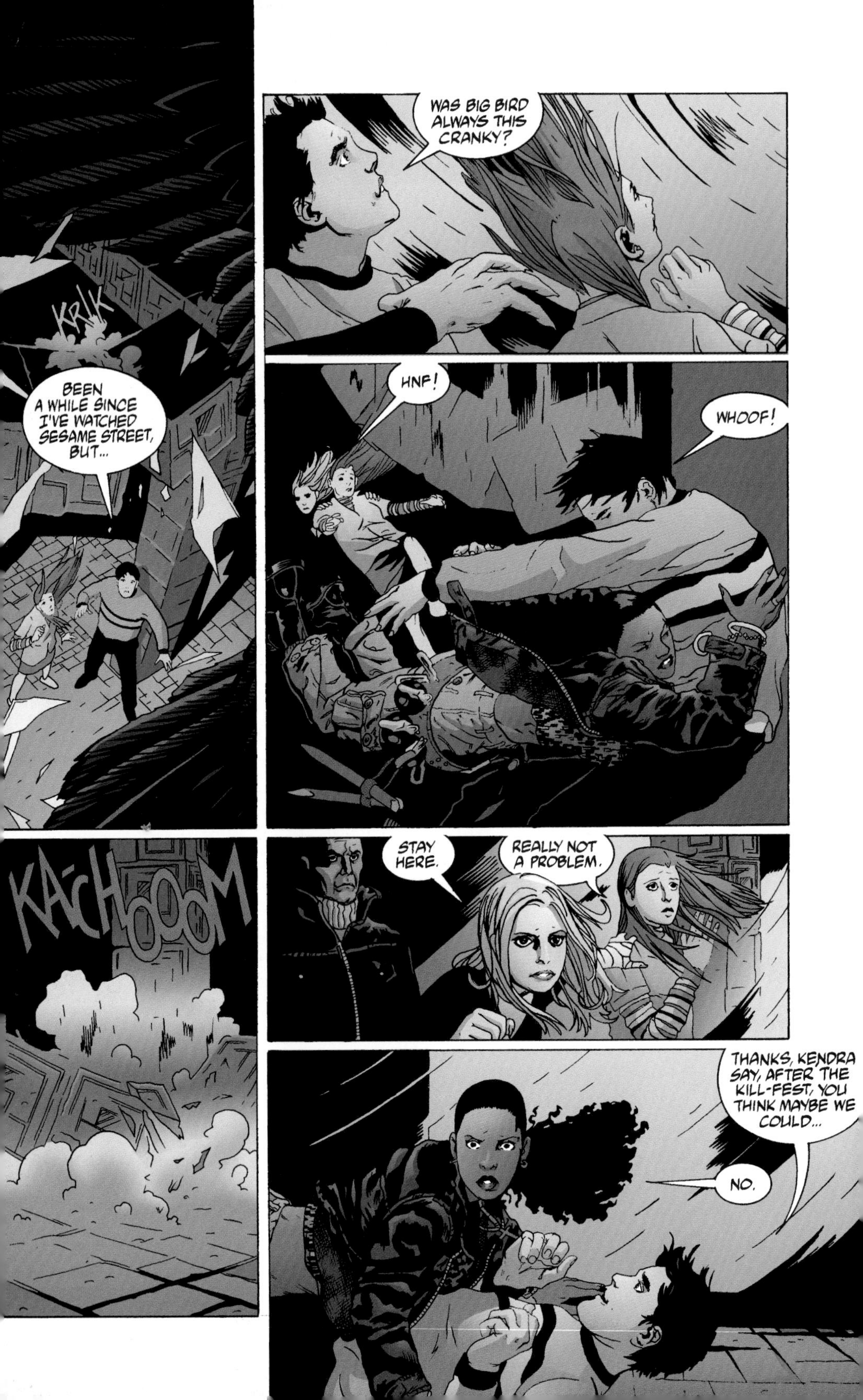

KRIK
BEEN A WHILE SINCE I'VE WATCHED SESAME STREET, BUT...
WAS BIG BIRD ALWAYS THIS CRANKY?
HNF!
WHOOF!
KA-CHOOOM
STAY HERE.
REALLY NOT A PROBLEM.
THANKS, KENDRA. SAY, AFTER THE KILL-FEST, YOU THINK MAYBE WE COULD...
NO.

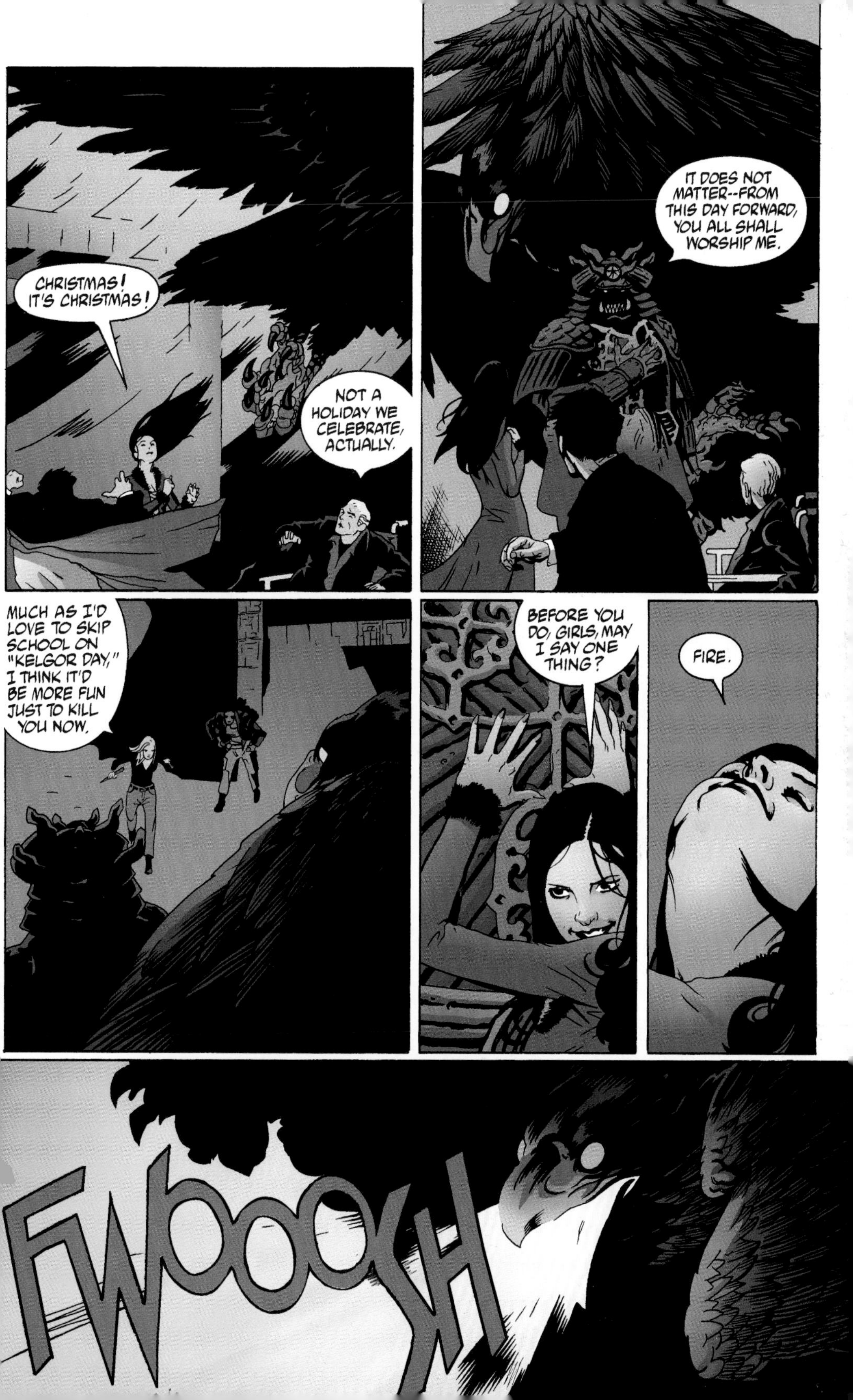
CHRISTMAS! IT'S CHRISTMAS!
NOT A HOLIDAY WE CELEBRATE, ACTUALLY.
IT DOES NOT MATTER--FROM THIS DAY FORWARD, YOU ALL SHALL WORSHIP ME.
MUCH AS I'D LOVE TO SKIP SCHOOL ON "KELGOR DAY," I THINK IT'D BE MORE FUN JUST TO KILL YOU NOW.
BEFORE YOU DO, GIRLS, MAY I SAY ONE THING?
FIRE.
FWOOOSH

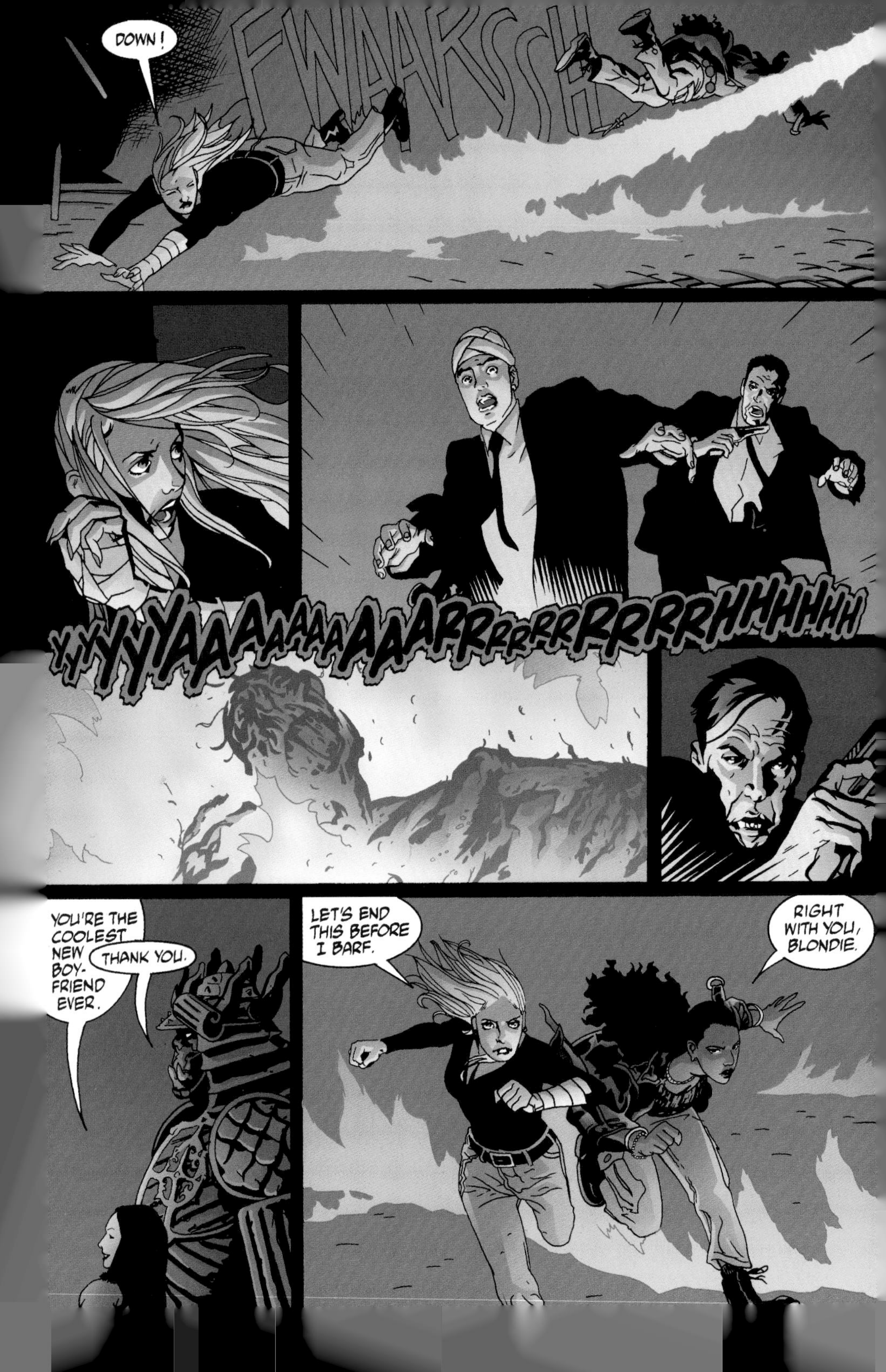
DOWN!
FWAARSCH
YYYYAAAAAAAAAAAARRRRRRRRRRRHHHHHH
YOU'RE THE COOLEST NEW BOY-FRIEND EVER.
THANK YOU.
LET'S END THIS BEFORE I BARF.
RIGHT WITH YOU, BLONDIE.

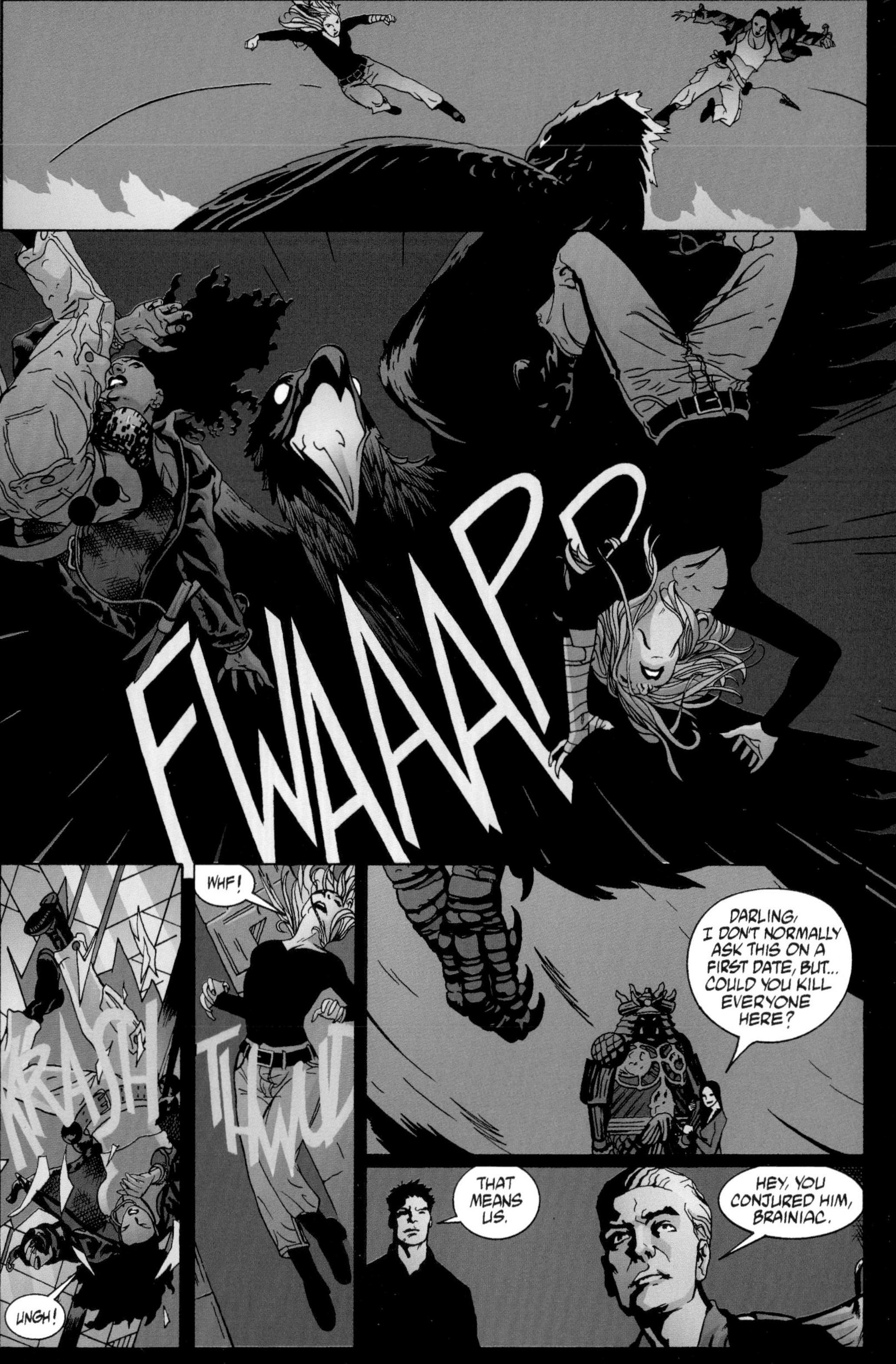
FWAAAP
KRASH
UNGH!
WHF!
THWUD
DARLING, I DON'T NORMALLY ASK THIS ON A FIRST DATE, BUT... COULD YOU KILL EVERYONE HERE?
THAT MEANS US.
HEY, YOU CONJURED HIM, BRAINIAC.

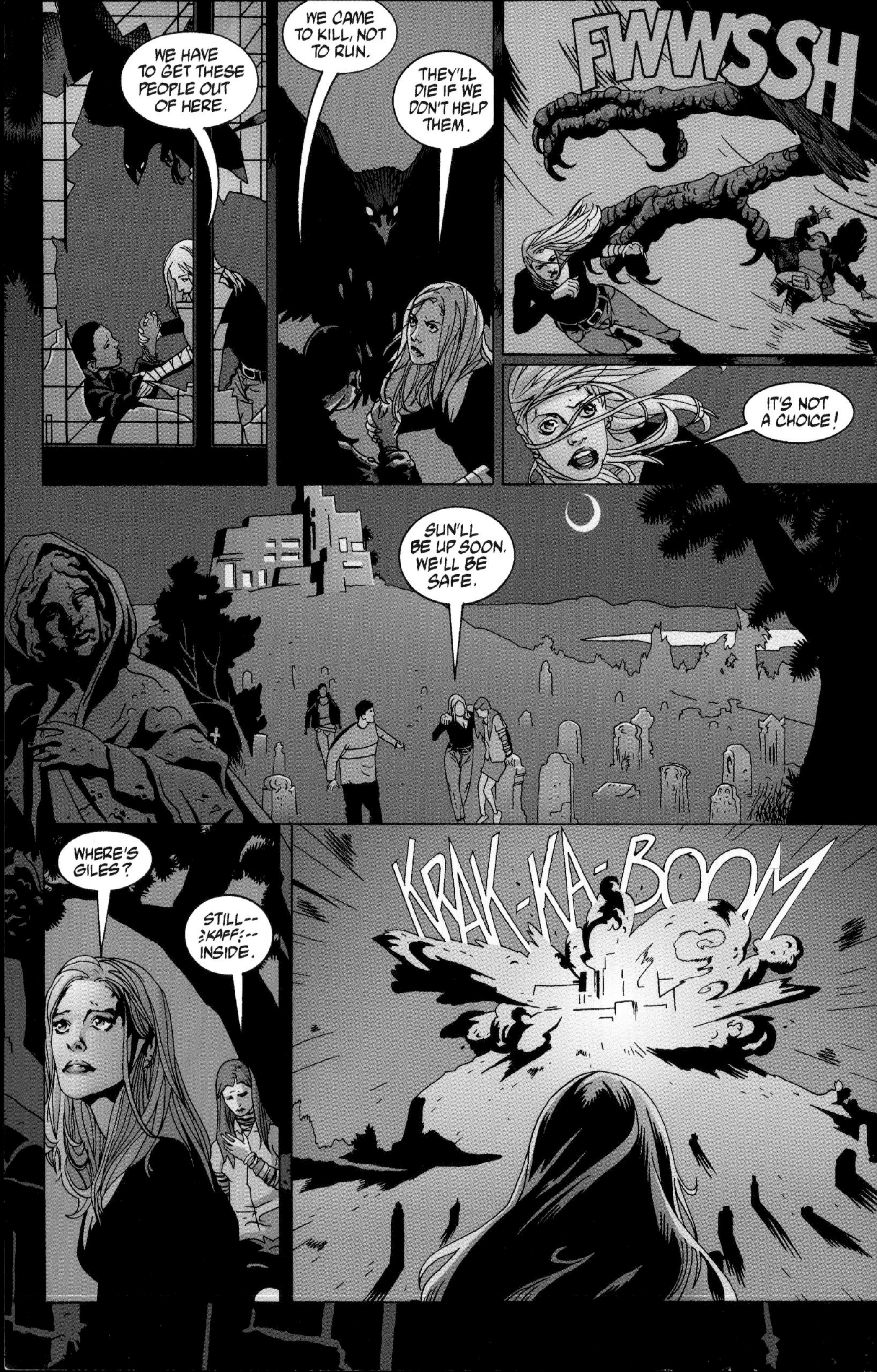

WE HAVE TO GET THESE PEOPLE OUT OF HERE.
WE CAME TO KILL, NOT TO RUN.
THEY'LL DIE IF WE DON'T HELP THEM.
FWWSSH
IT'S NOT A CHOICE!
SUN'LL BE UP SOON. WE'LL BE SAFE.
WHERE'S GILES?
STILL-- KAFF-- INSIDE.
KRAK-KA-BOOM

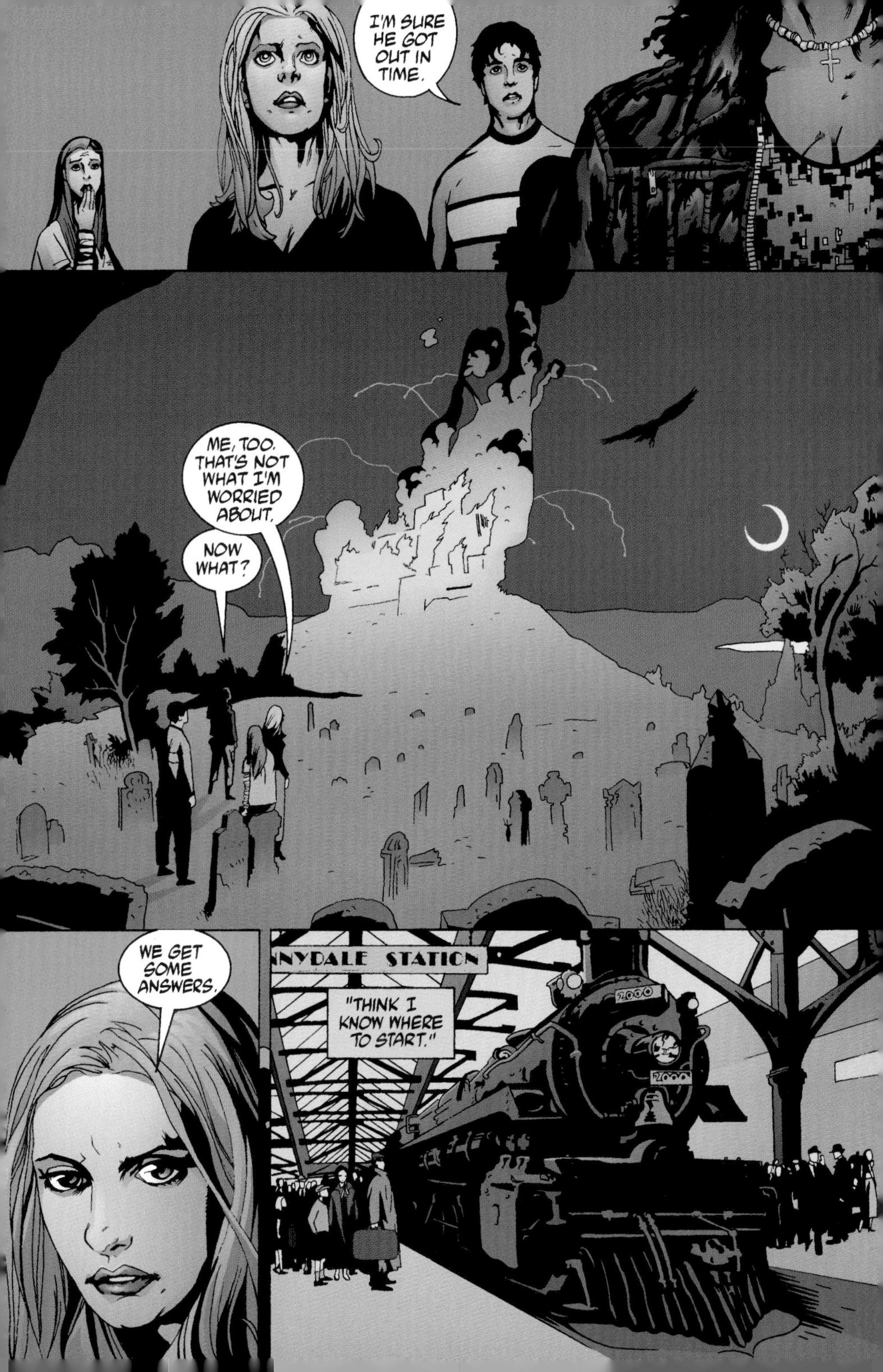
I'M SURE HE GOT OUT IN TIME.
ME, TOO. THAT'S NOT WHAT I'M WORRIED ABOUT.
NOW WHAT?
WE GET SOME ANSWERS.
NNYDALE STATION
"THINK I KNOW WHERE TO START."

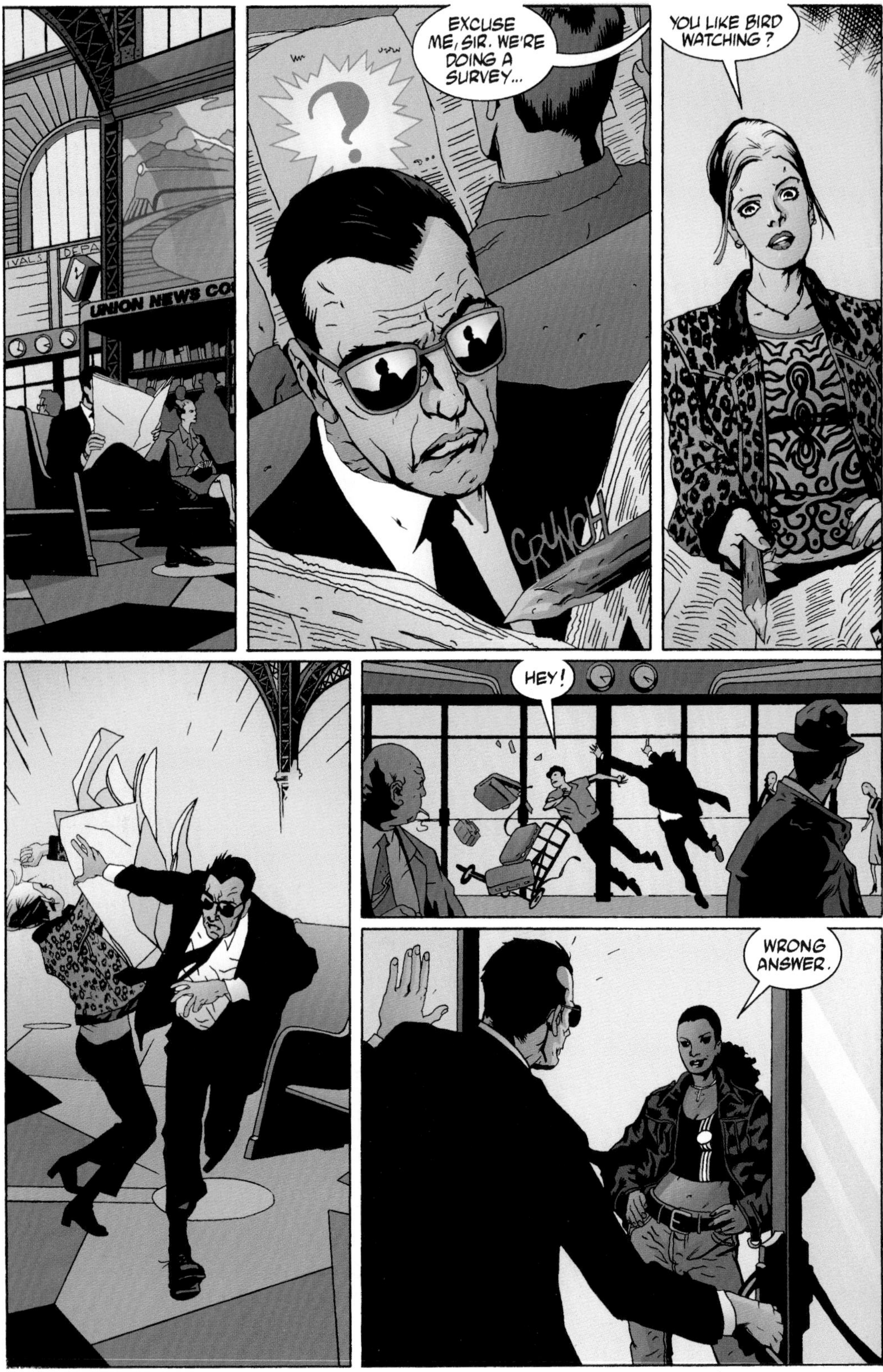

UNION NEWS CO
EXCUSE ME, SIR. WE'RE DOING A SURVEY...
YOU LIKE BIRD WATCHING?
CRUNCH
HEY!
WRONG ANSWER.

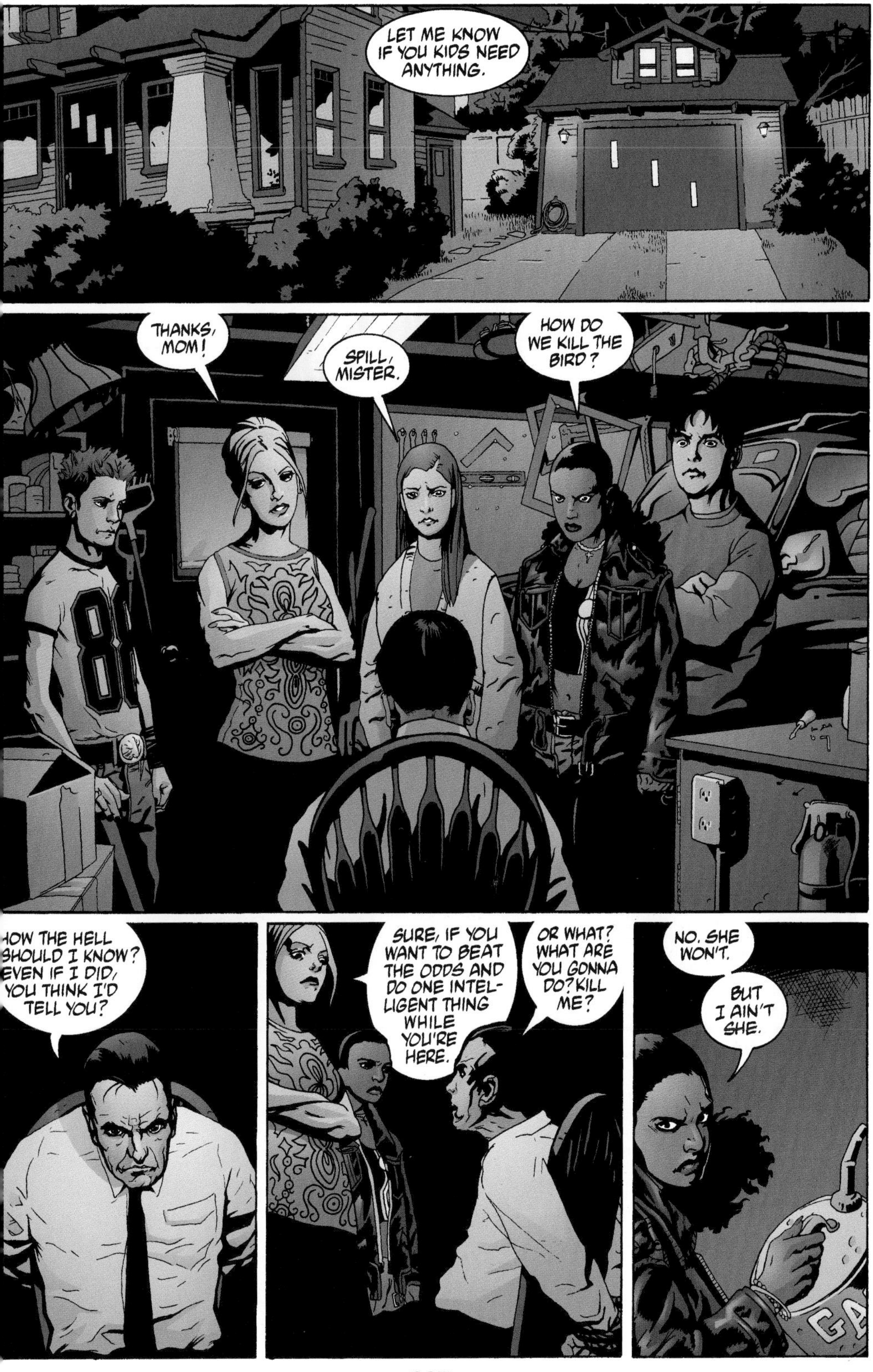
LET ME KNOW IF YOU KIDS NEED ANYTHING.
THANKS, MOM!
SPILL, MISTER.
HOW DO WE KILL THE BIRD?
HOW THE HELL SHOULD I KNOW? EVEN IF I DID, YOU THINK I'D TELL YOU?
SURE, IF YOU WANT TO BEAT THE ODDS AND DO ONE INTELLIGENT THING WHILE YOU'RE HERE.
OR WHAT? WHAT ARE YOU GONNA DO? KILL ME?
NO. SHE WON'T.
BUT I AIN'T SHE.

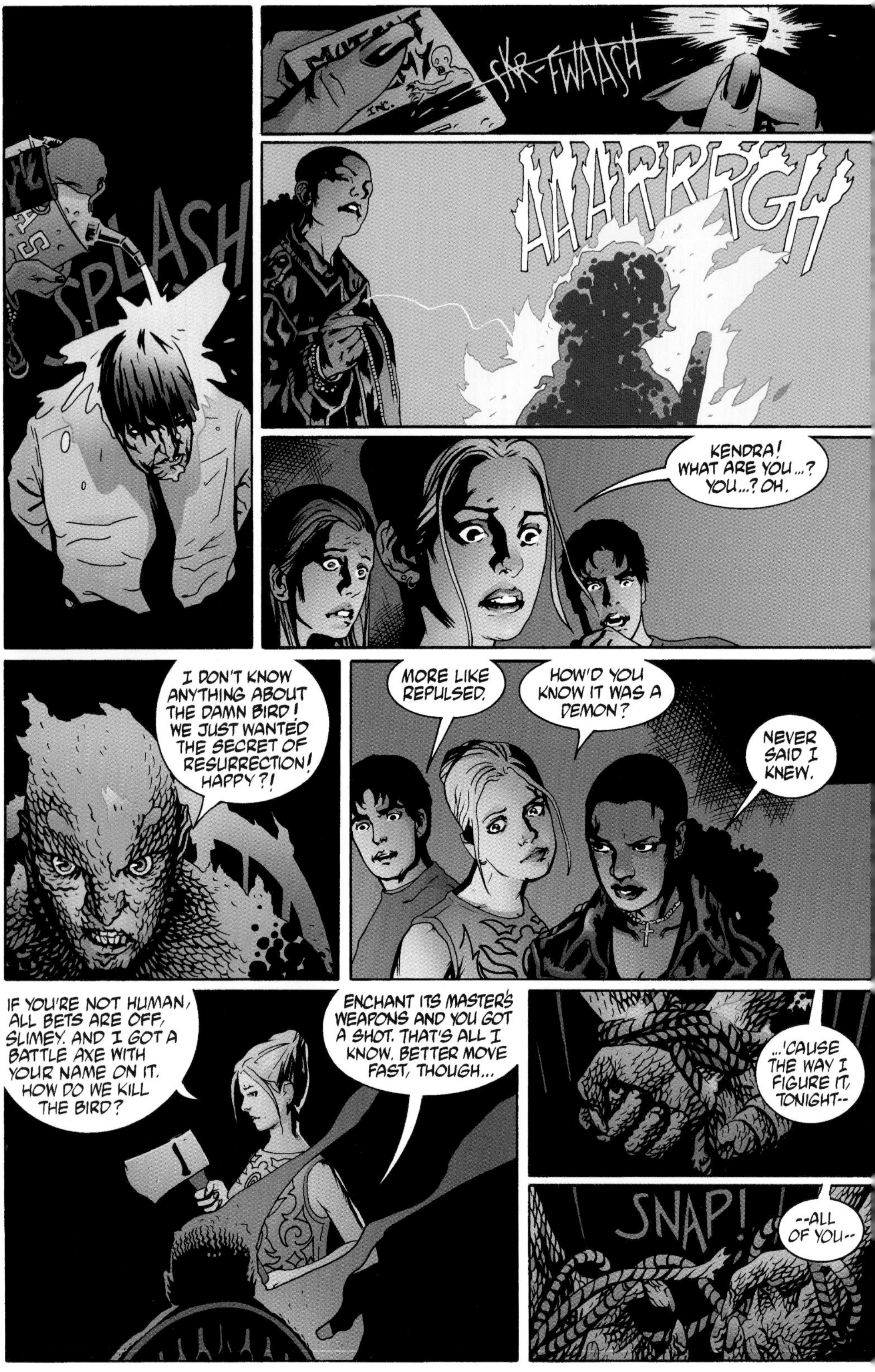
SKR-FWAASH
SPLASH
AAARRRGH
KENDRA! WHAT ARE YOU...? YOU...? OH.
I DON'T KNOW ANYTHING ABOUT THE DAMN BIRD! WE JUST WANTED THE SECRET OF RESURRECTION! HAPPY?!
MORE LIKE REPULSED.
HOW'D YOU KNOW IT WAS A DEMON?
NEVER SAID I KNEW.
IF YOU'RE NOT HUMAN, ALL BETS ARE OFF, SLIMEY. AND I GOT A BATTLE AXE WITH YOUR NAME ON IT. HOW DO WE KILL THE BIRD?
ENCHANT ITS MASTER'S WEAPONS AND YOU GOT A SHOT. THAT'S ALL I KNOW. BETTER MOVE FAST, THOUGH...
...'CAUSE THE WAY I FIGURE IT, TONIGHT--
SNAP!
--ALL OF YOU--

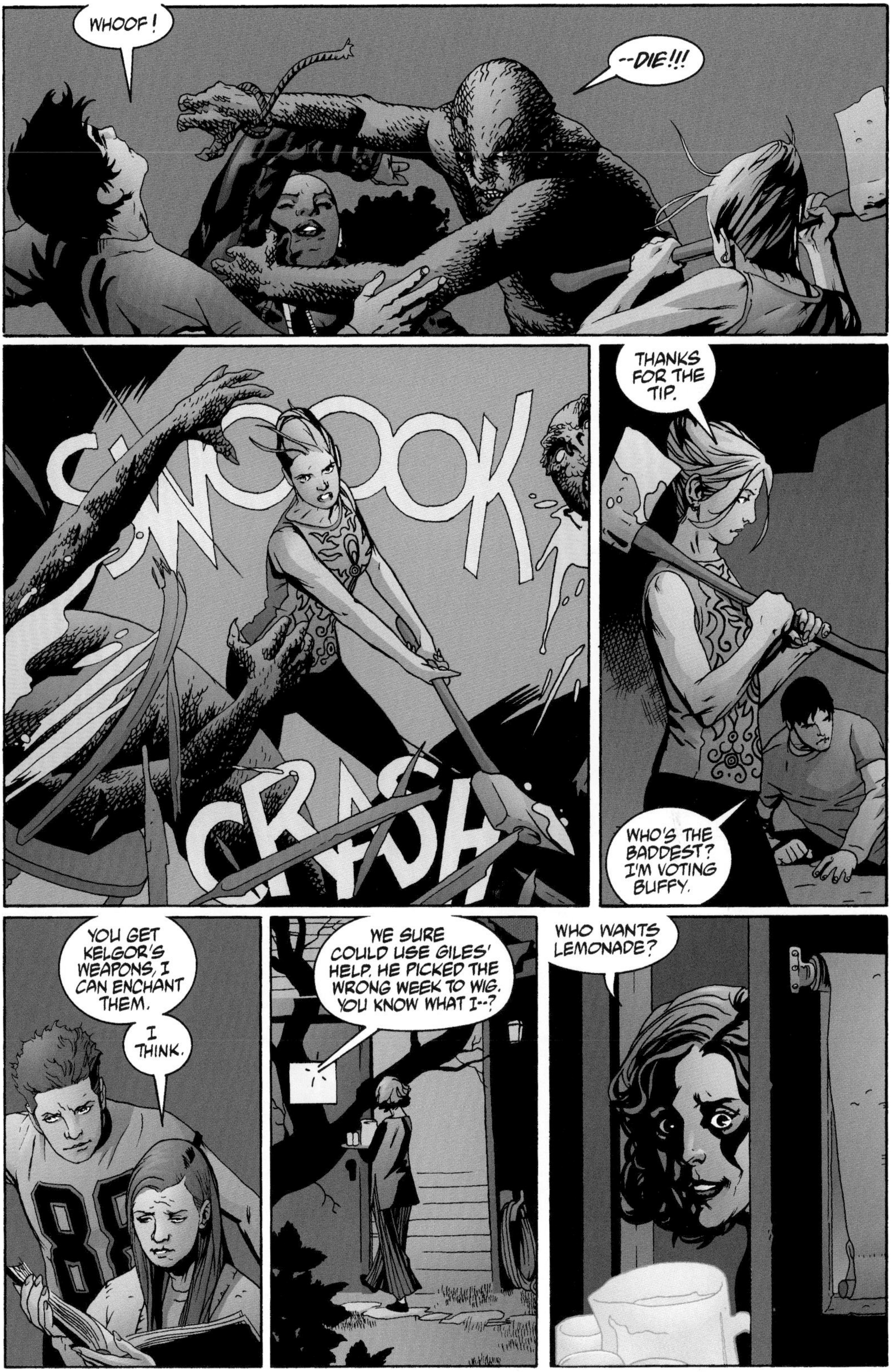
WHOOF!
--DIE!!!
SHOOOK
CRASH
THANKS FOR THE TIP.
WHO'S THE BADDEST? I'M VOTING BUFFY.
YOU GET KELGOR'S WEAPONS, I CAN ENCHANT THEM.
I THINK.
WE SURE COULD USE GILES' HELP. HE PICKED THE WRONG WEEK TO WIG. YOU KNOW WHAT I--?
WHO WANTS LEMONADE?

THANKS, MOM! WE'RE ALMOST DONE FIXING THE, um...THE...

FUEL RODS.

FEUL RODS! THEY'RE ALL FEULLY AND RODDED.

TUMP

GILES WANTS WHAT THE DEMONS WERE AFTER.

THE RESURREC- TION RITUAL? BUT WE NEED HIM IF WE WANT TO STOP KELGOR AND THE BIG SCARY BIRD.

MAYBE IF WE GET A REALLY BIG CAT...

MR. GILES HAS ABAN- DONED YOU? THAT'S A SERIOUS BREACH OF DUTY.

AND I SPEAK FOR ALL OF US WHEN I SAY, "DUH." MAYBE WE BETTER CHECK ON OUR TIGHTLY WRAPPED FRIEND.

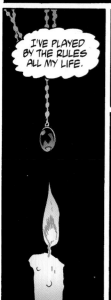

I'VE PLAYED BY THE RULES ALL MY LIFE.

I'VE GROWN TIRED OF IT.

SO TIRED...

KNOCK KNOCK

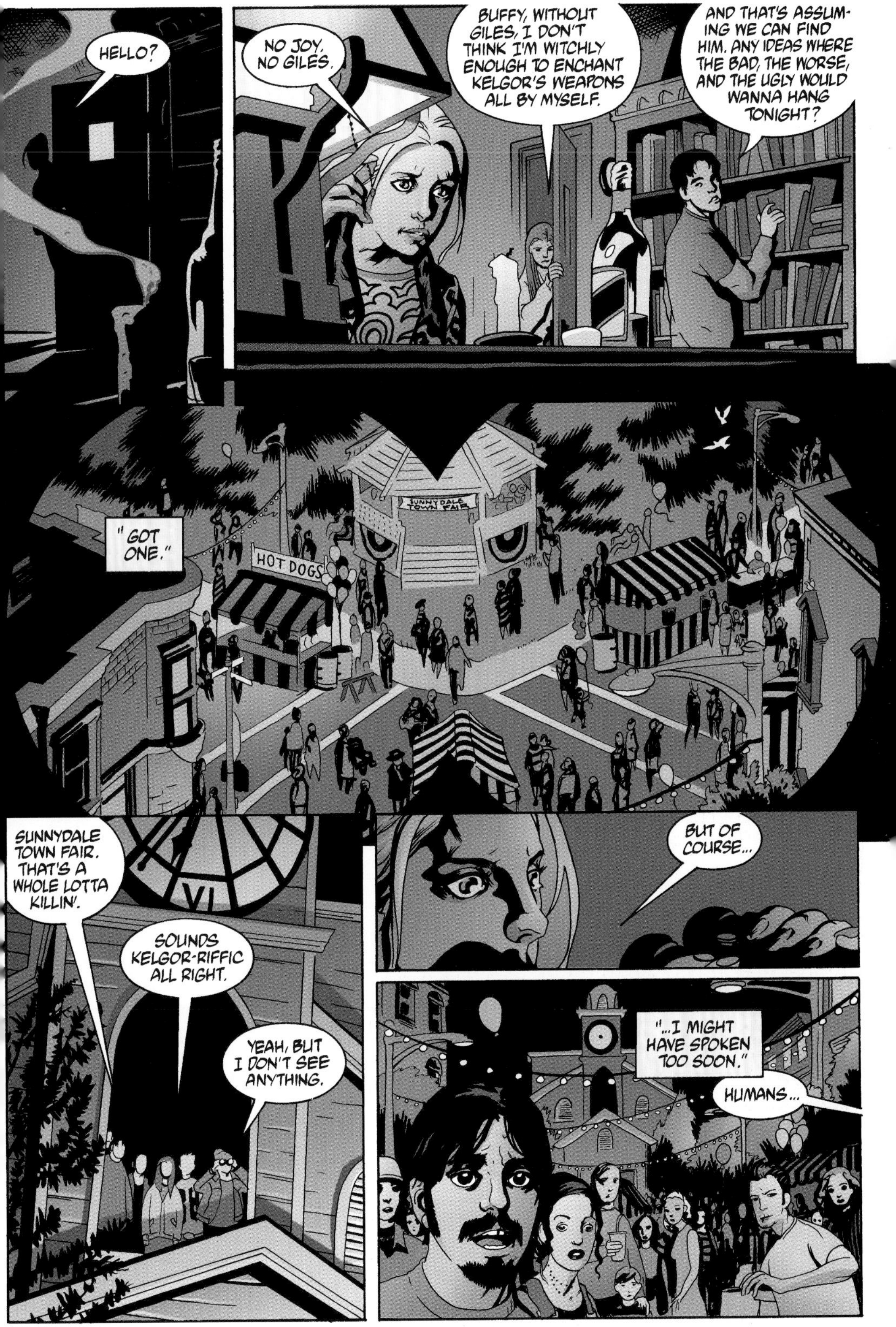
HELLO?
NO JOY. NO GILES.
BUFFY, WITHOUT GILES, I DON'T THINK I'M WITCHLY ENOUGH TO ENCHANT KELGOR'S WEAPONS ALL BY MYSELF.
AND THAT'S ASSUMING WE CAN FIND HIM. ANY IDEAS WHERE THE BAD, THE WORSE, AND THE UGLY WOULD WANNA HANG TONIGHT?
"GOT ONE."
SUNNYDALE TOWN FAIR
HOT DOGS
SUNNYDALE TOWN FAIR. THAT'S A WHOLE LOTTA KILLIN'.
SOUNDS KELGOR-RIFFIC ALL RIGHT.
YEAH, BUT I DON'T SEE ANYTHING.
BUT OF COURSE...
"...I MIGHT HAVE SPOKEN TOO SOON."
HUMANS...

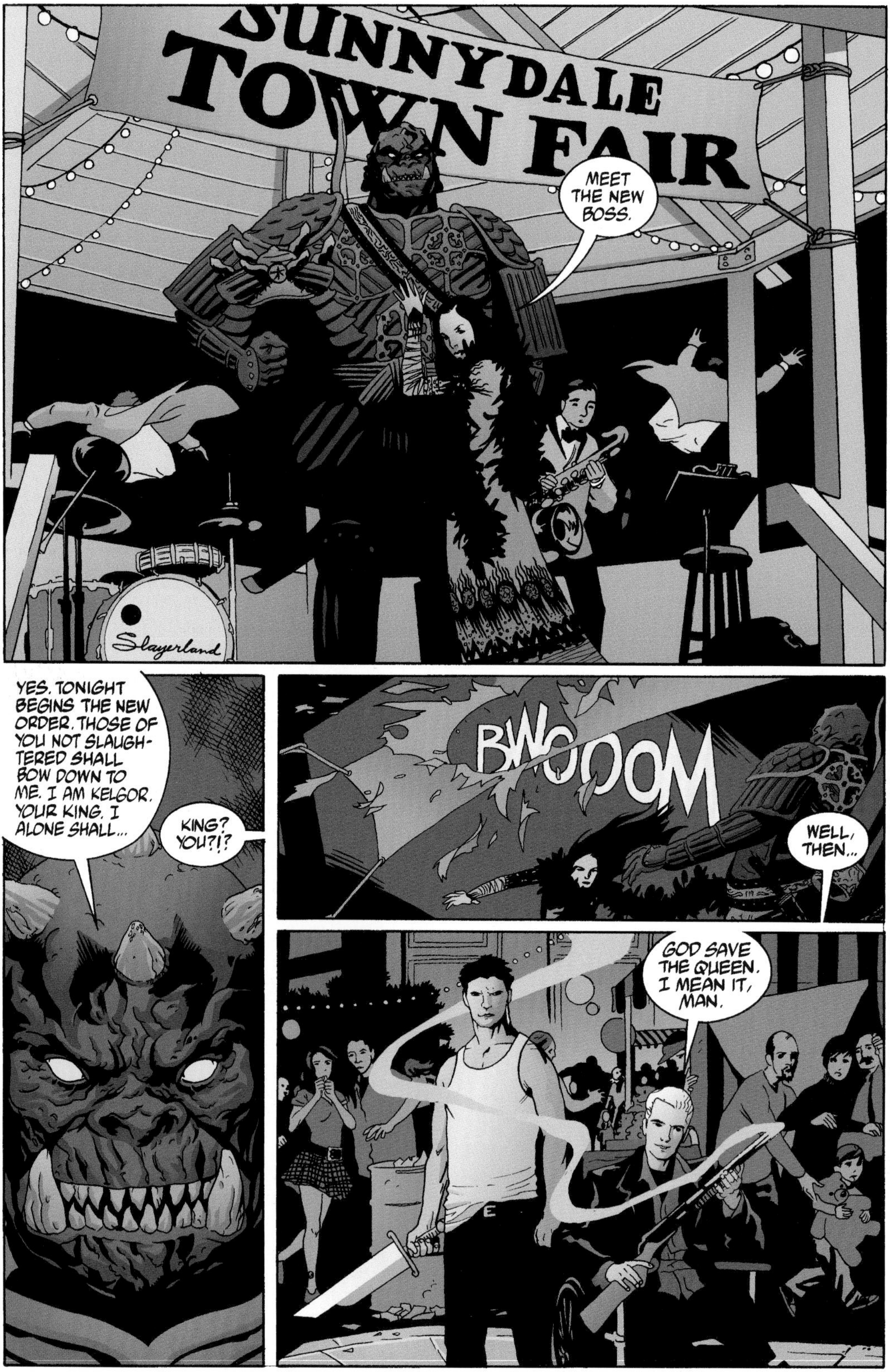
SUNNYDALE TOWN FAIR
MEET THE NEW BOSS.
Slayerland
YES. TONIGHT BEGINS THE NEW ORDER. THOSE OF YOU NOT SLAUGHTERED SHALL BOW DOWN TO ME. I AM KELGOR. YOUR KING. I ALONE SHALL...
KING? YOU?!?
BWOOOM
WELL, THEN...
GOD SAVE THE QUEEN. I MEAN IT, MAN.

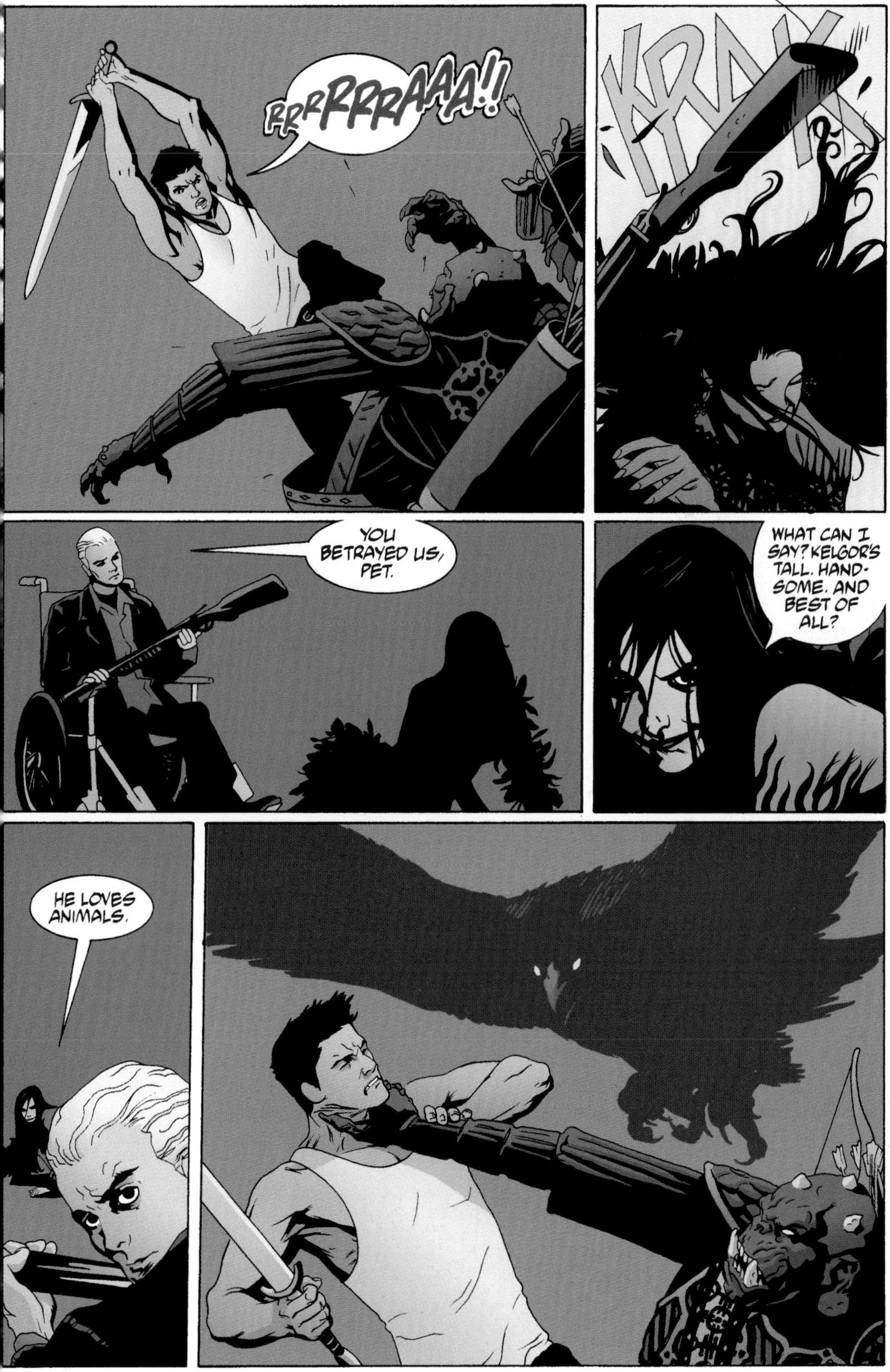
RRRRRRAAA!!
KRAK
YOU BETRAYED US, PET.
WHAT CAN I SAY? KELGOR'S TALL. HAND-SOME. AND BEST OF ALL?
HE LOVES ANIMALS.

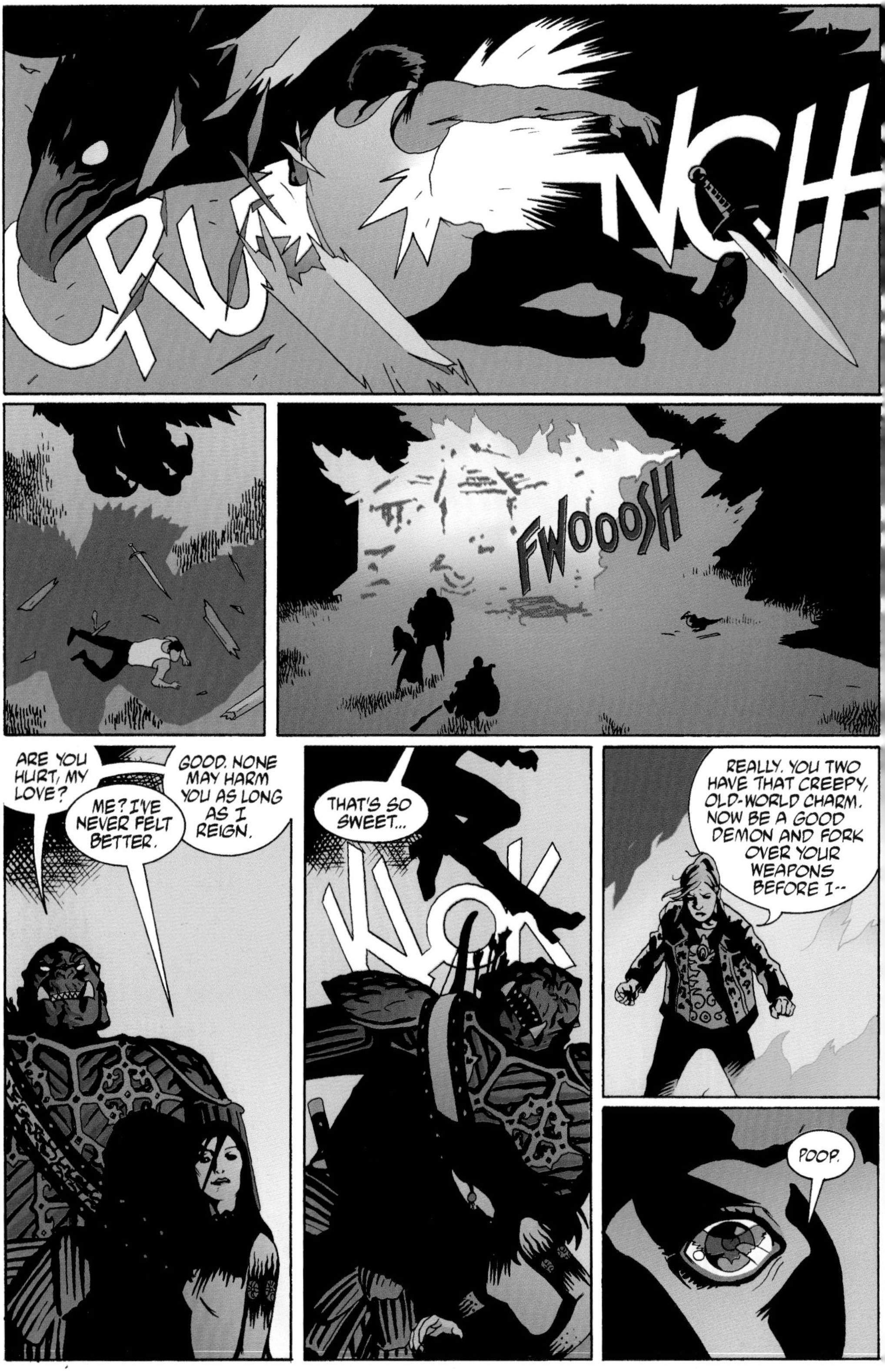
CRUNCH
FWOOOSH
ARE YOU HURT, MY LOVE?
ME? I'VE NEVER FELT BETTER.
GOOD. NONE MAY HARM YOU AS LONG AS I REIGN.
THAT'S SO SWEET...
KLOK
REALLY. YOU TWO HAVE THAT CREEPY, OLD-WORLD CHARM. NOW BE A GOOD DEMON AND FORK OVER YOUR WEAPONS BEFORE I--
POOP.

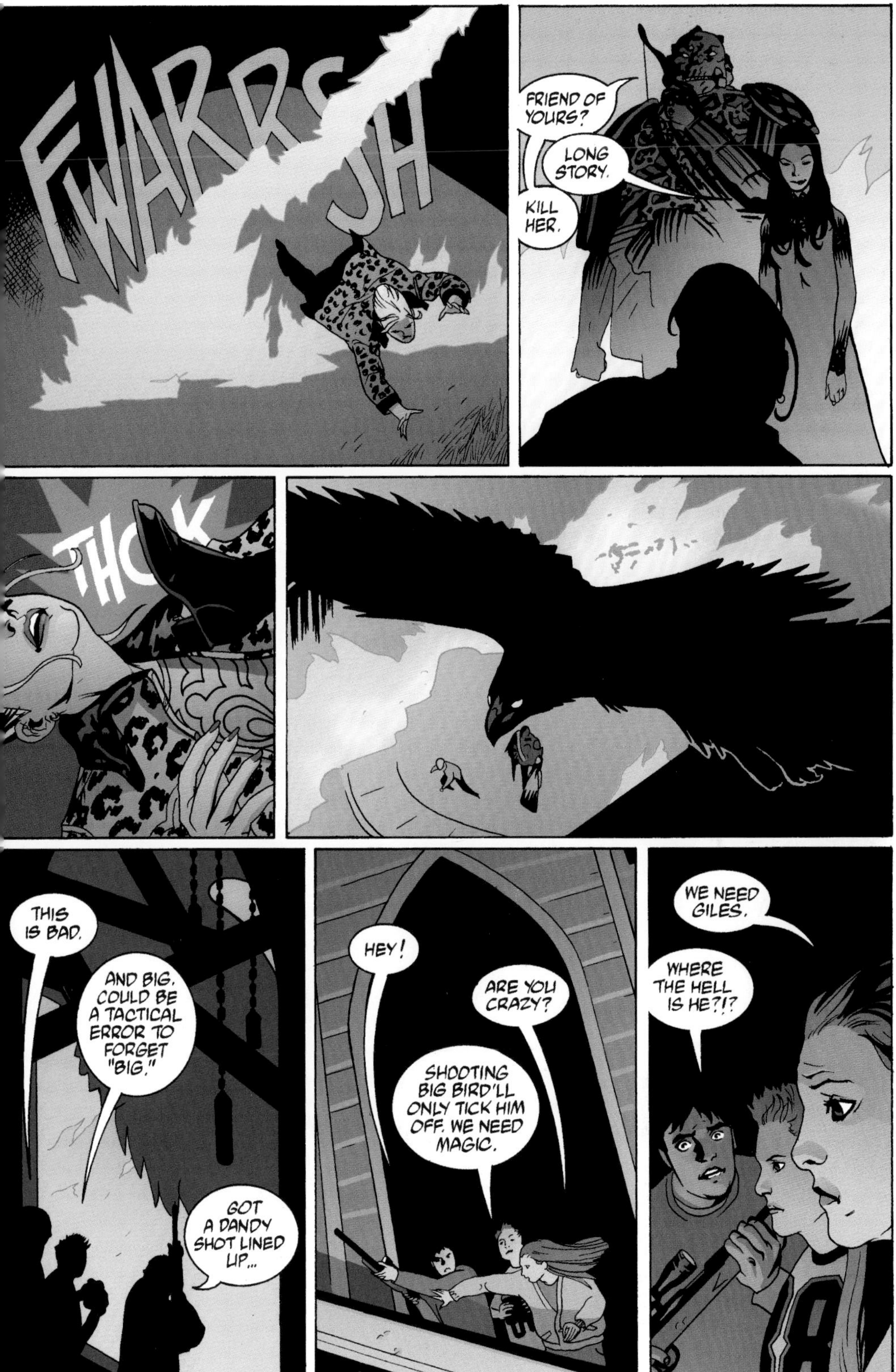
FWARRSJH
FRIEND OF YOURS?
LONG STORY.
KILL HER.
THOK
THIS IS BAD.
AND BIG. COULD BE A TACTICAL ERROR TO FORGET "BIG."
GOT A DANDY SHOT LINED UP...
HEY!
ARE YOU CRAZY?
SHOOTING BIG BIRD'LL ONLY TICK HIM OFF. WE NEED MAGIC.
WE NEED GILES.
WHERE THE HELL IS HE?!?

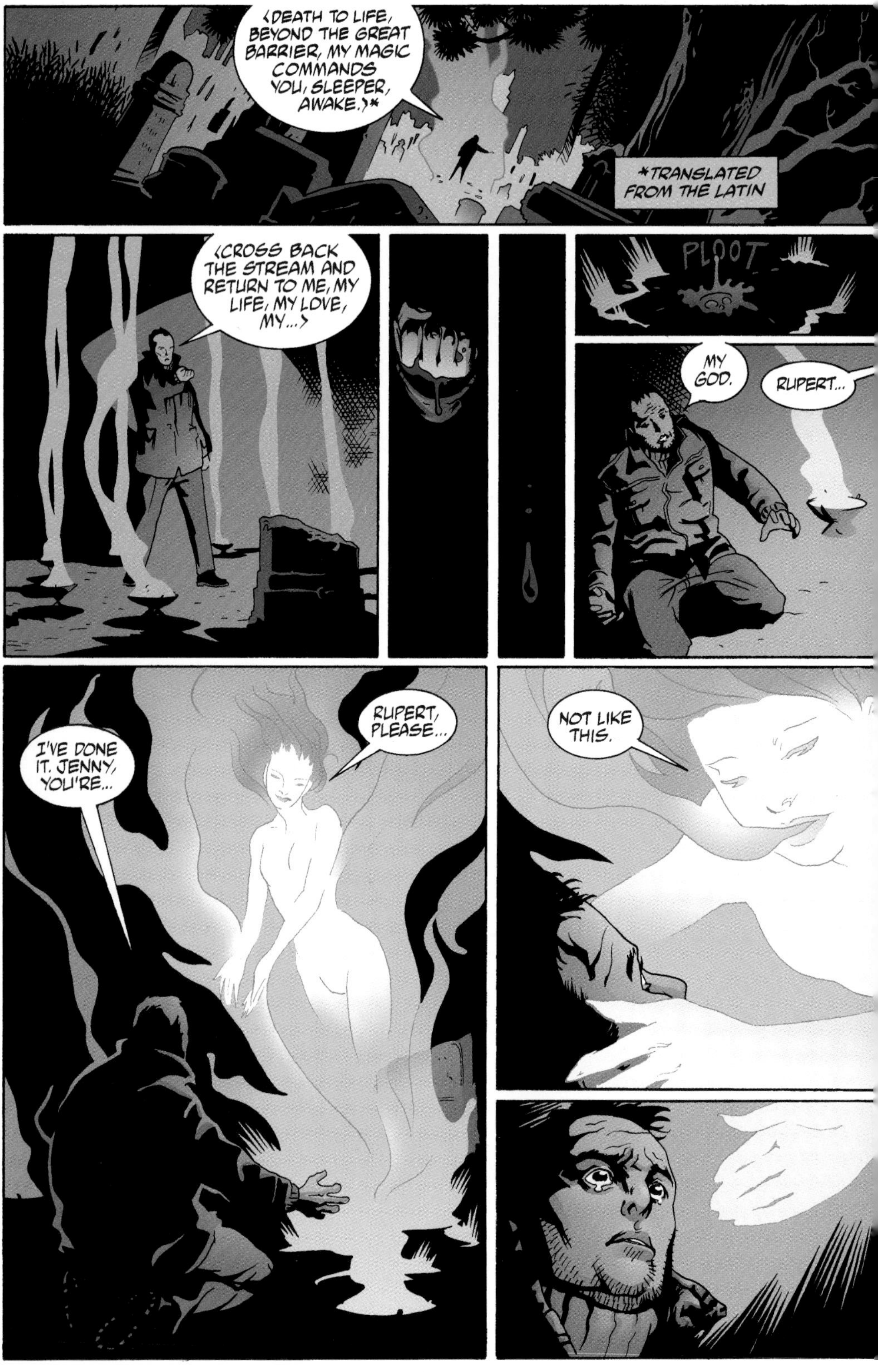
‹DEATH TO LIFE, BEYOND THE GREAT BARRIER, MY MAGIC COMMANDS YOU, SLEEPER, AWAKE.›*
*TRANSLATED FROM THE LATIN
‹CROSS BACK THE STREAM AND RETURN TO ME, MY LIFE, MY LOVE, MY...›
PLOOT
MY GOD.
RUPERT...
I'VE DONE IT. JENNY, YOU'RE...
RUPERT, PLEASE...
NOT LIKE THIS.

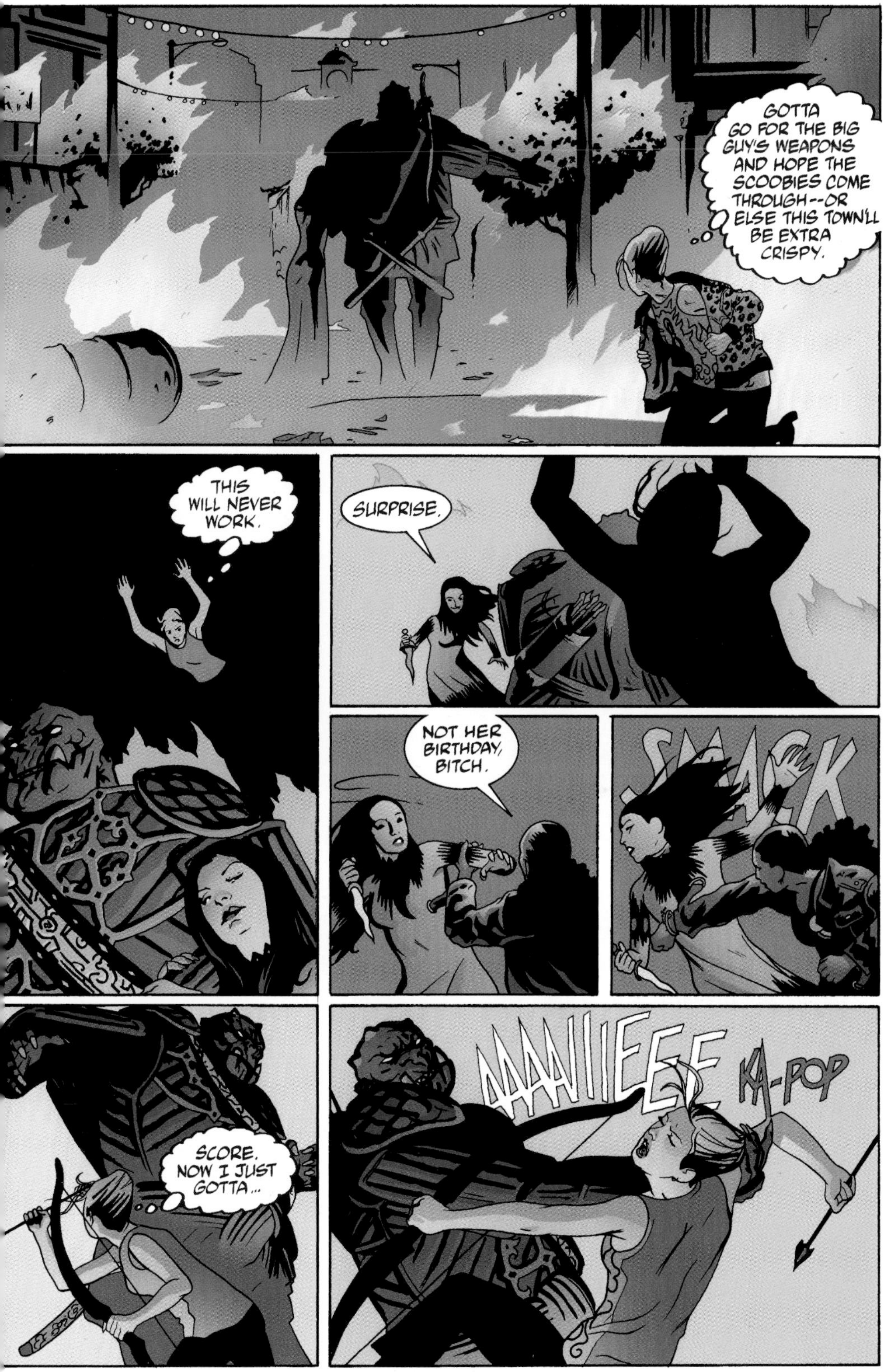
GOTTA GO FOR THE BIG GUY'S WEAPONS AND HOPE THE SCOOBIES COME THROUGH--OR ELSE THIS TOWN'LL BE EXTRA CRISPY.
THIS WILL NEVER WORK.
SURPRISE.
NOT HER BIRTHDAY, BITCH.
SMACK
SCORE. NOW I JUST GOTTA...
AAAAIIEEEE
KA-POP

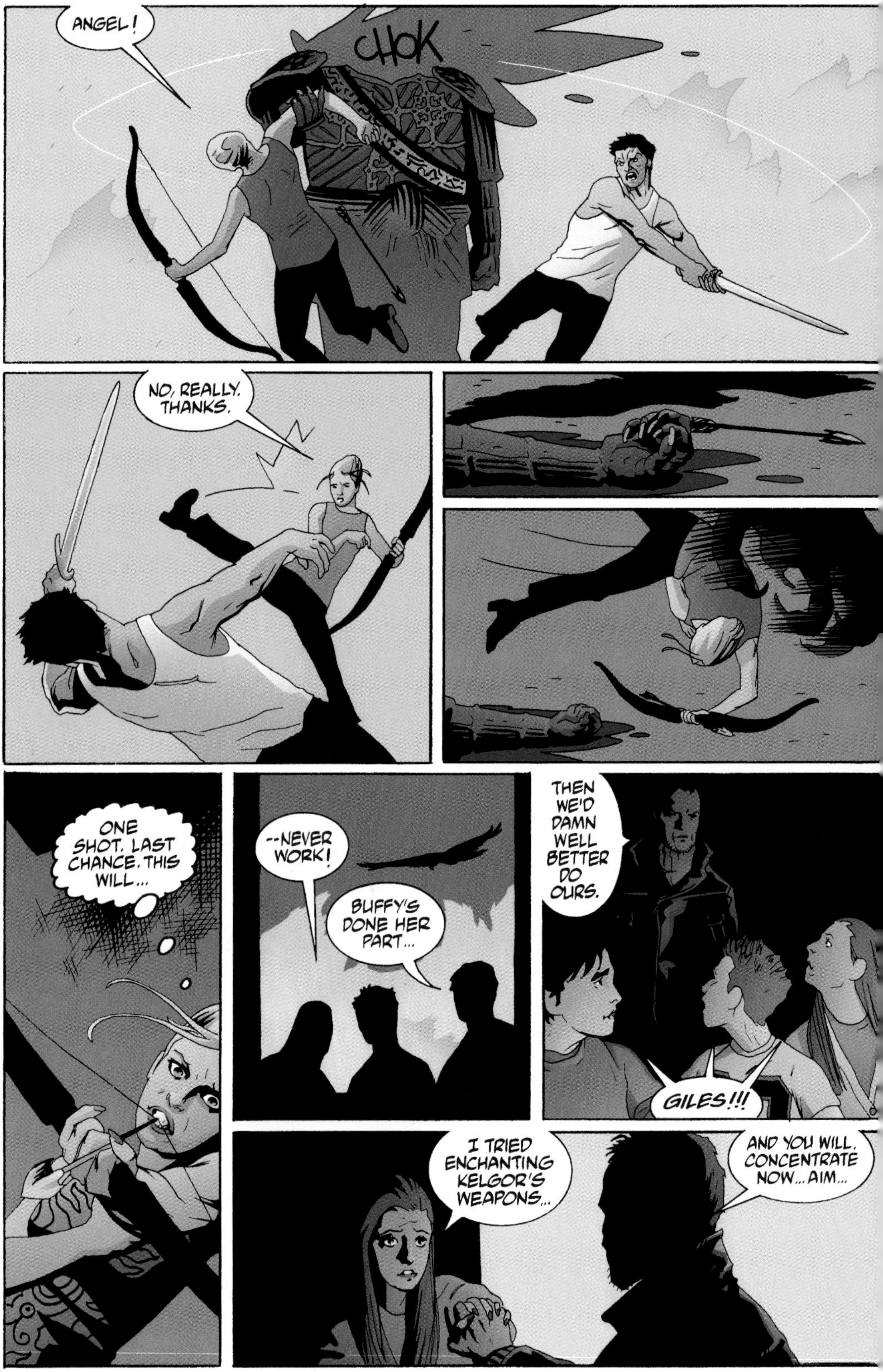
ANGEL!
CHOK
NO, REALLY. THANKS.
ONE SHOT. LAST CHANCE. THIS WILL...
--NEVER WORK!
BUFFY'S DONE HER PART...
THEN WE'D DAMN WELL BETTER DO OURS.
GILES!!!
I TRIED ENCHANTING KELGOR'S WEAPONS...
AND YOU WILL. CONCENTRATE NOW... AIM...

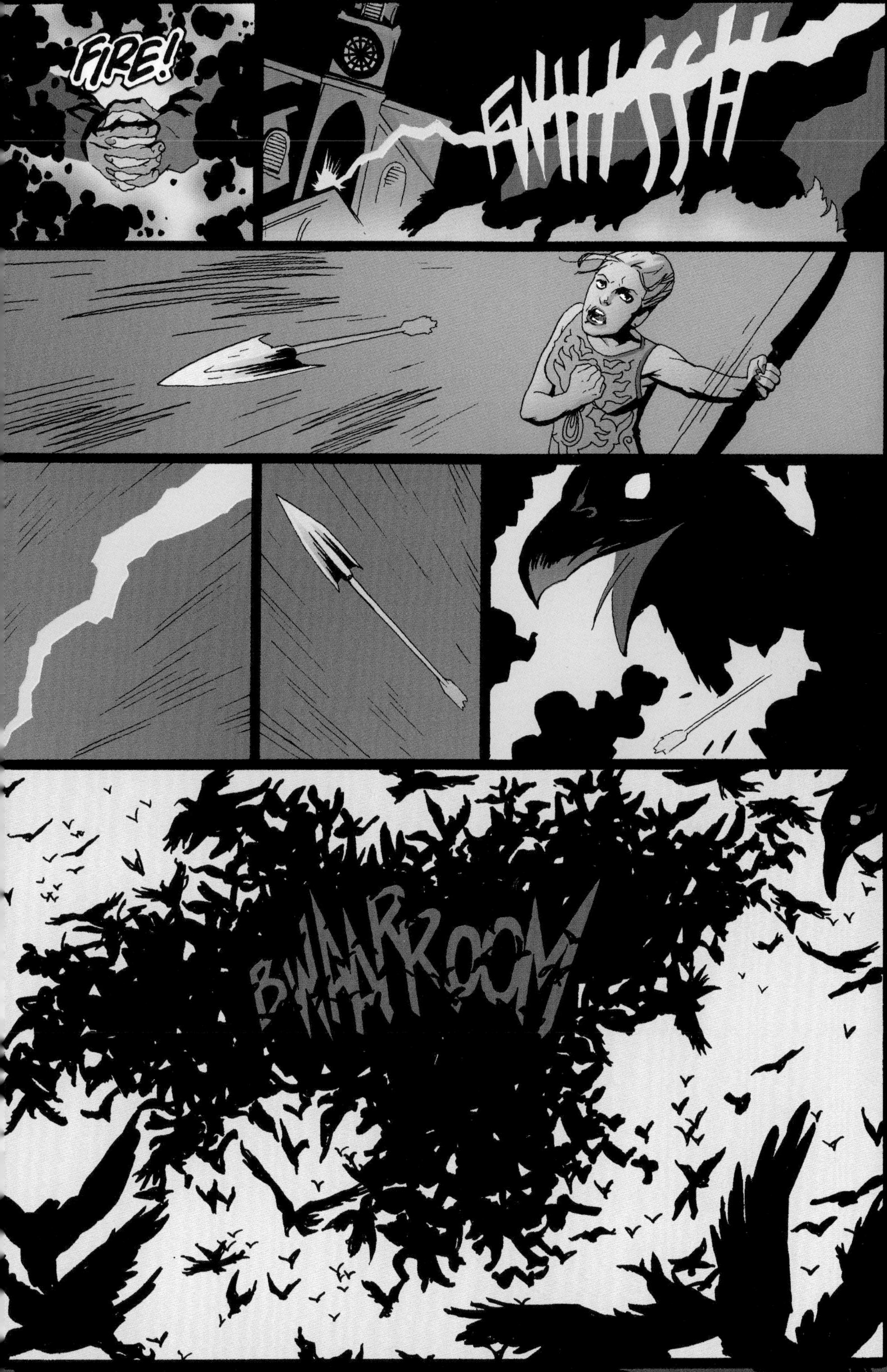
FIRE!
FWHHSSH
BWARROOM

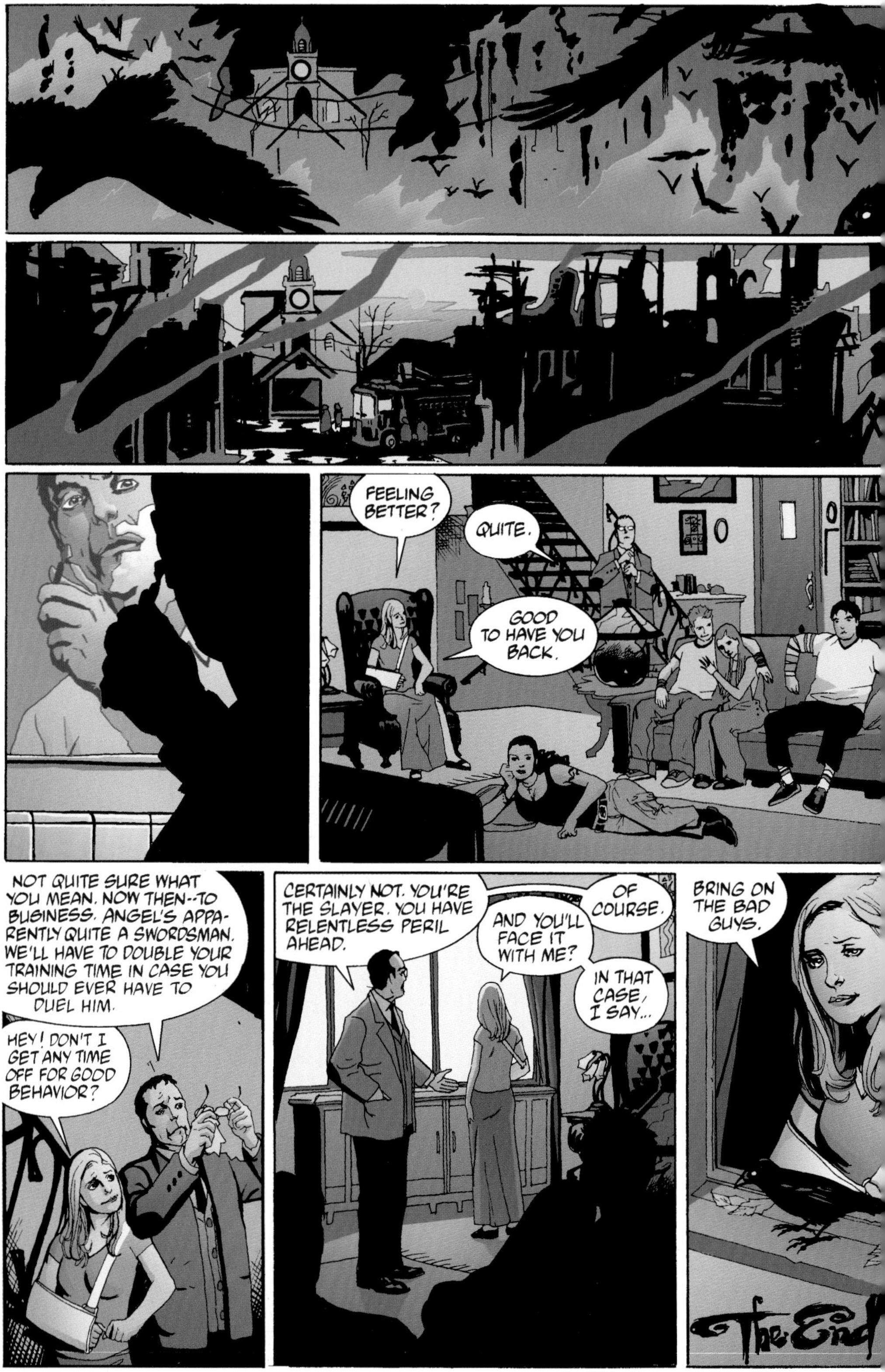
FEELING BETTER?
QUITE.
GOOD TO HAVE YOU BACK.
NOT QUITE SURE WHAT YOU MEAN. NOW THEN--TO BUSINESS. ANGEL'S APPARENTLY QUITE A SWORDSMAN. WE'LL HAVE TO DOUBLE YOUR TRAINING TIME IN CASE YOU SHOULD EVER HAVE TO DUEL HIM.
HEY! DON'T I GET ANY TIME OFF FOR GOOD BEHAVIOR?
CERTAINLY NOT. YOU'RE THE SLAYER. YOU HAVE RELENTLESS PERIL AHEAD.
AND YOU'LL FACE IT WITH ME?
OF COURSE.
IN THAT CASE, I SAY...
BRING ON THE BAD GUYS.
The End

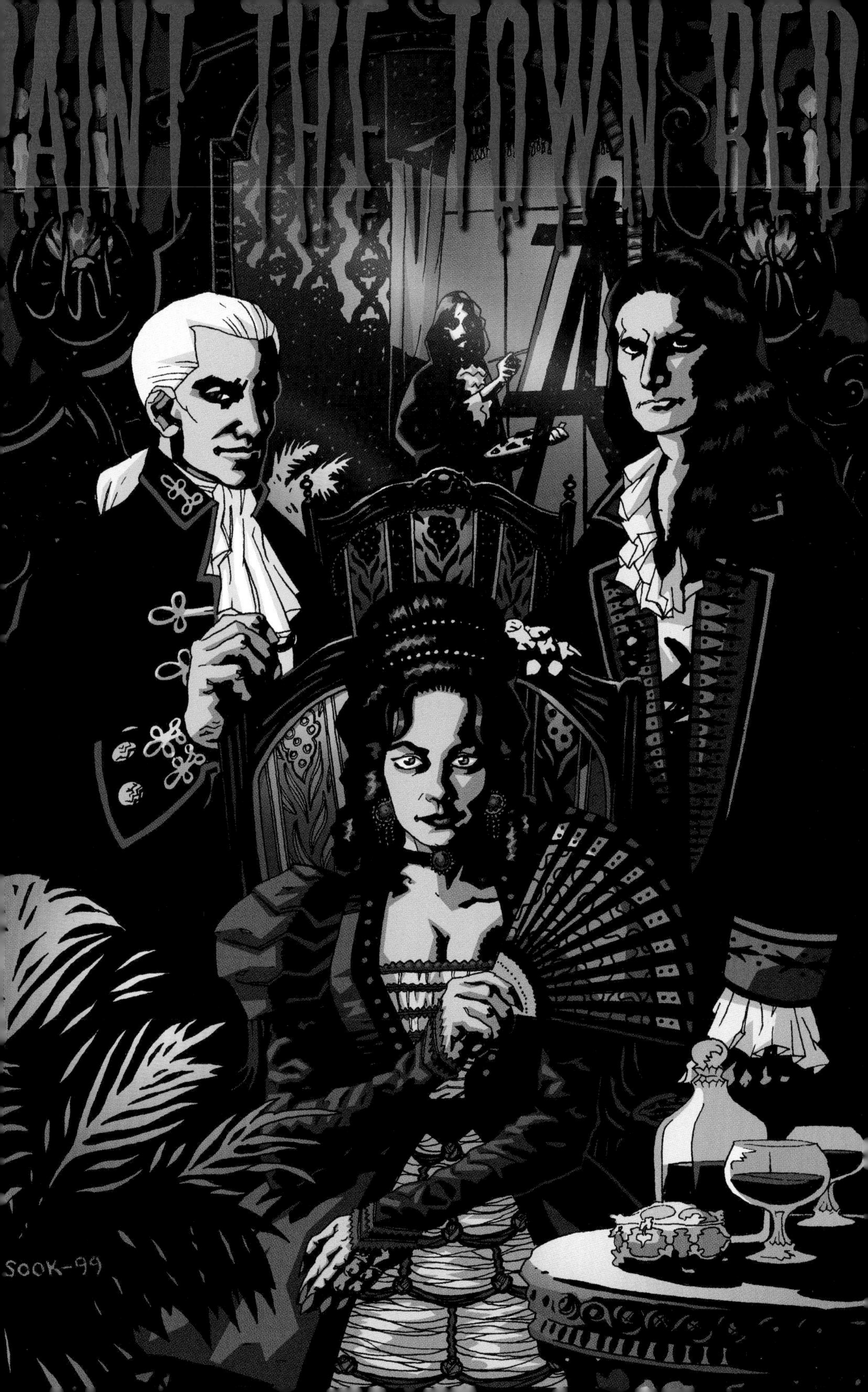
AINT THE TOWN RED
SOOK-99

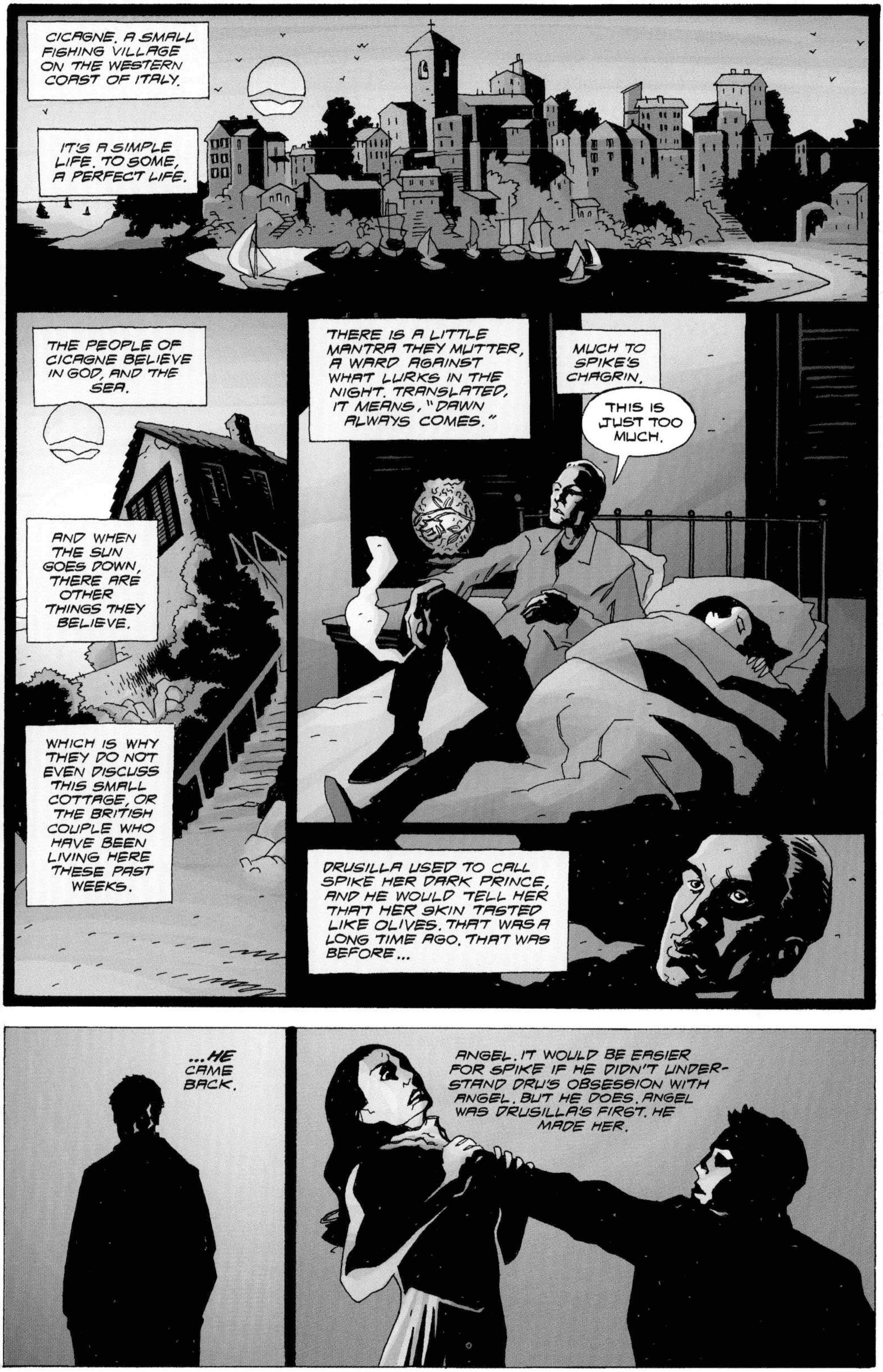
CICAGNE. A SMALL FISHING VILLAGE ON THE WESTERN COAST OF ITALY.
IT'S A SIMPLE LIFE. TO SOME, A PERFECT LIFE.
THE PEOPLE OF CICAGNE BELIEVE IN GOD, AND THE SEA.
AND WHEN THE SUN GOES DOWN, THERE ARE OTHER THINGS THEY BELIEVE.
WHICH IS WHY THEY DO NOT EVEN DISCUSS THIS SMALL COTTAGE, OR THE BRITISH COUPLE WHO HAVE BEEN LIVING HERE THESE PAST WEEKS.
THERE IS A LITTLE MANTRA THEY MUTTER, A WARD AGAINST WHAT LURKS IN THE NIGHT. TRANSLATED, IT MEANS, "DAWN ALWAYS COMES."
MUCH TO SPIKE'S CHAGRIN.
THIS IS JUST TOO MUCH.
DRUSILLA USED TO CALL SPIKE HER DARK PRINCE, AND HE WOULD TELL HER THAT HER SKIN TASTED LIKE OLIVES. THAT WAS A LONG TIME AGO. THAT WAS BEFORE...
...HE CAME BACK.
ANGEL. IT WOULD BE EASIER FOR SPIKE IF HE DIDN'T UNDERSTAND DRU'S OBSESSION WITH ANGEL. BUT HE DOES. ANGEL WAS DRUSILLA'S FIRST. HE MADE HER.

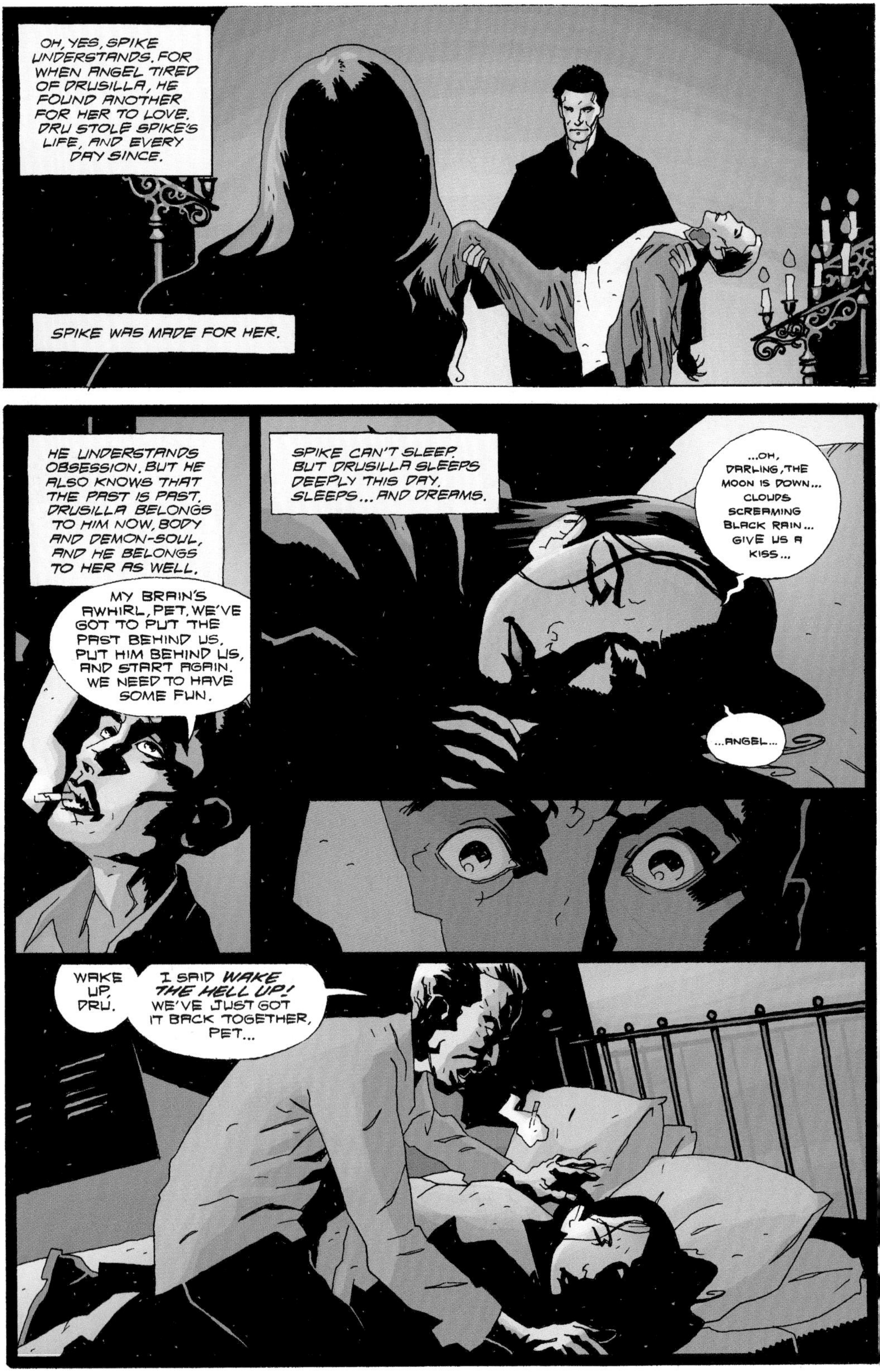
OH, YES, SPIKE UNDERSTANDS. FOR WHEN ANGEL TIRED OF DRUSILLA, HE FOUND ANOTHER FOR HER TO LOVE. DRU STOLE SPIKE'S LIFE, AND EVERY DAY SINCE.
SPIKE WAS MADE FOR HER.
HE UNDERSTANDS OBSESSION. BUT HE ALSO KNOWS THAT THE PAST IS PAST. DRUSILLA BELONGS TO HIM NOW, BODY AND DEMON-SOUL, AND HE BELONGS TO HER AS WELL.
MY BRAIN'S AWHIRL, PET. WE'VE GOT TO PUT THE PAST BEHIND US. PUT HIM BEHIND US, AND START AGAIN. WE NEED TO HAVE SOME FUN.
SPIKE CAN'T SLEEP. BUT DRUSILLA SLEEPS DEEPLY THIS DAY. SLEEPS... AND DREAMS.
...OH, DARLING, THE MOON IS DOWN... CLOUDS SCREAMING BLACK RAIN... GIVE US A KISS...
...ANGEL...
WAKE UP, DRU.
I SAID WAKE THE HELL UP! WE'VE JUST GOT IT BACK TOGETHER, PET...

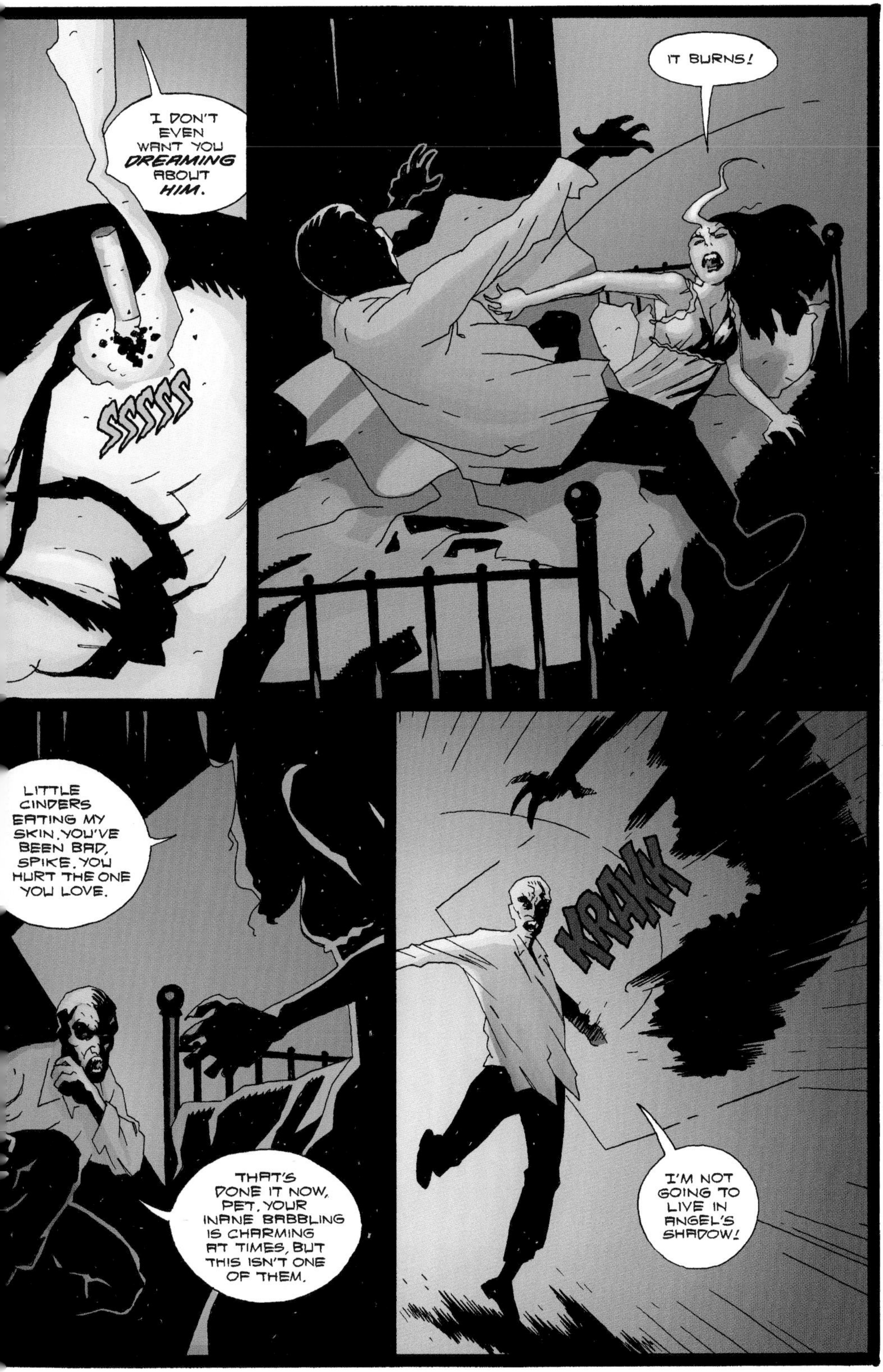
I DON'T EVEN WANT YOU DREAMING ABOUT HIM.
SSSSS
IT BURNS!
LITTLE CINDERS EATING MY SKIN. YOU'VE BEEN BAD, SPIKE. YOU HURT THE ONE YOU LOVE.
THAT'S DONE IT NOW, PET. YOUR INANE BABBLING IS CHARMING AT TIMES, BUT THIS ISN'T ONE OF THEM.
KRAKK
I'M NOT GOING TO LIVE IN ANGEL'S SHADOW!

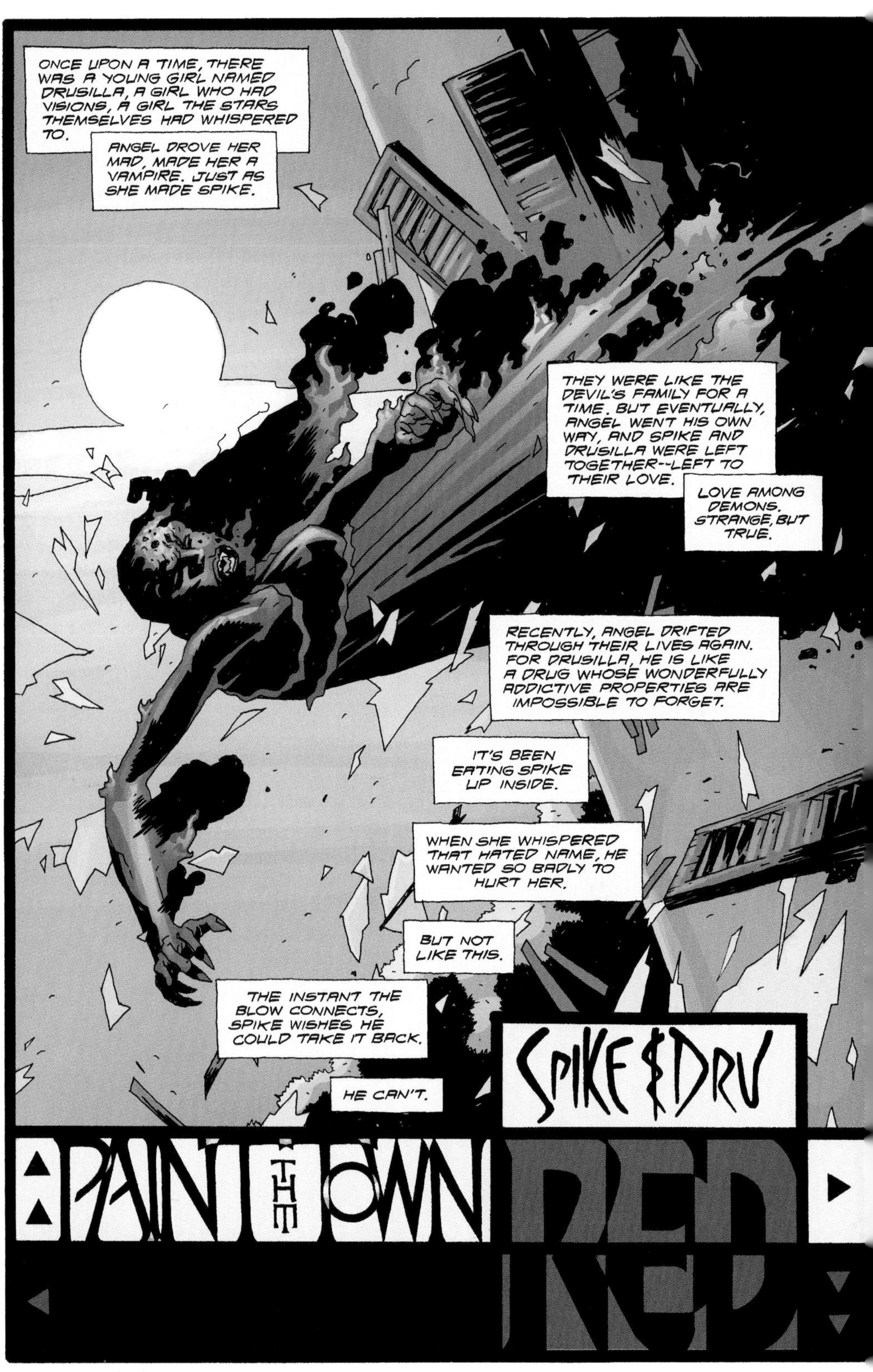
ONCE UPON A TIME, THERE WAS A YOUNG GIRL NAMED DRUSILLA, A GIRL WHO HAD VISIONS, A GIRL THE STARS THEMSELVES HAD WHISPERED TO.
ANGEL DROVE HER MAD, MADE HER A VAMPIRE. JUST AS SHE MADE SPIKE.
THEY WERE LIKE THE DEVIL'S FAMILY FOR A TIME. BUT EVENTUALLY, ANGEL WENT HIS OWN WAY, AND SPIKE AND DRUSILLA WERE LEFT TOGETHER--LEFT TO THEIR LOVE.
LOVE AMONG DEMONS. STRANGE, BUT TRUE.
RECENTLY, ANGEL DRIFTED THROUGH THEIR LIVES AGAIN. FOR DRUSILLA, HE IS LIKE A DRUG WHOSE WONDERFULLY ADDICTIVE PROPERTIES ARE IMPOSSIBLE TO FORGET.
IT'S BEEN EATING SPIKE UP INSIDE.
WHEN SHE WHISPERED THAT HATED NAME, HE WANTED SO BADLY TO HURT HER.
BUT NOT LIKE THIS.
THE INSTANT THE BLOW CONNECTS, SPIKE WISHES HE COULD TAKE IT BACK.
HE CAN'T.
SPIKE & DRU
PAINT THE TOWN RED

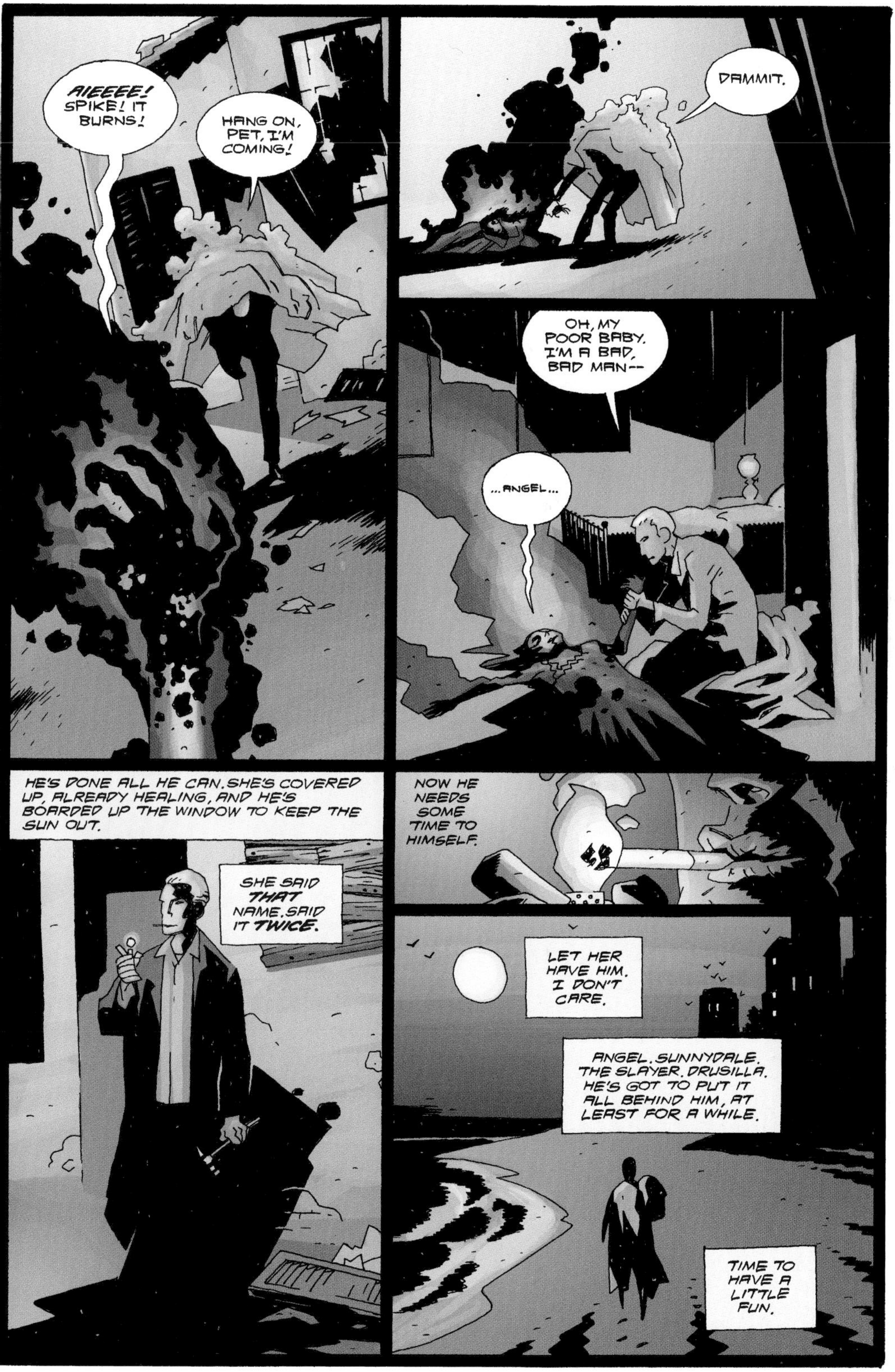
AIEEEE! SPIKE! IT BURNS!
HANG ON, PET, I'M COMING!
DAMMIT.
OH, MY POOR BABY. I'M A BAD, BAD MAN--
...ANGEL...
HE'S DONE ALL HE CAN. SHE'S COVERED UP, ALREADY HEALING, AND HE'S BOARDED UP THE WINDOW TO KEEP THE SUN OUT.
SHE SAID THAT NAME. SAID IT TWICE.
NOW HE NEEDS SOME TIME TO HIMSELF.
LET HER HAVE HIM. I DON'T CARE.
ANGEL. SUNNYDALE. THE SLAYER. DRUSILLA. HE'S GOT TO PUT IT ALL BEHIND HIM, AT LEAST FOR A WHILE.
TIME TO HAVE A LITTLE FUN.

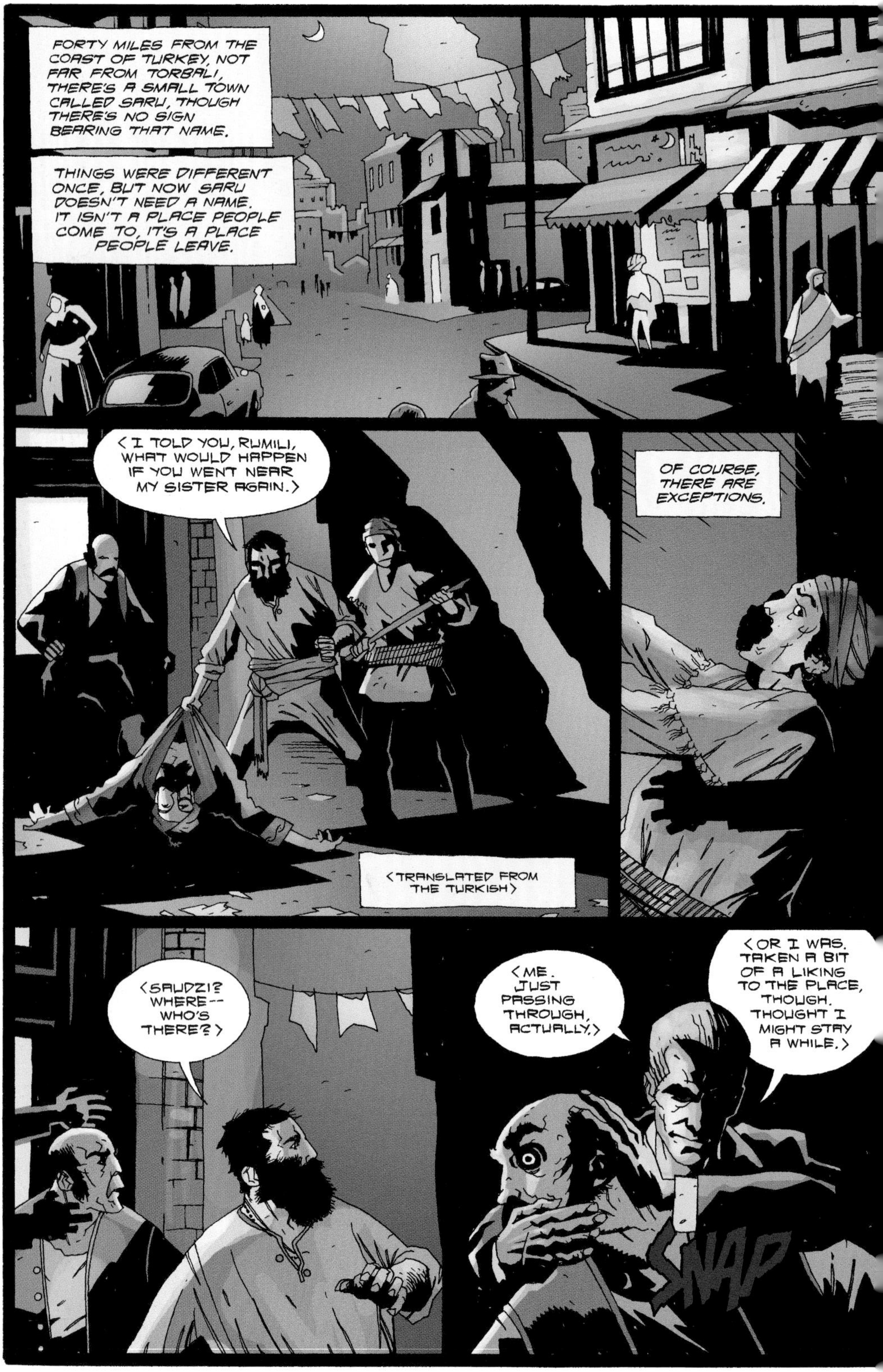
FORTY MILES FROM THE COAST OF TURKEY, NOT FAR FROM TORBALI, THERE'S A SMALL TOWN CALLED SARU, THOUGH THERE'S NO SIGN BEARING THAT NAME.
THINGS WERE DIFFERENT ONCE, BUT NOW SARU DOESN'T NEED A NAME. IT ISN'T A PLACE PEOPLE COME TO, IT'S A PLACE PEOPLE LEAVE.
<I TOLD YOU, RUMILI, WHAT WOULD HAPPEN IF YOU WENT NEAR MY SISTER AGAIN.>
<TRANSLATED FROM THE TURKISH>
OF COURSE, THERE ARE EXCEPTIONS.
<SAUDZI? WHERE-- WHO'S THERE?>
<ME. JUST PASSING THROUGH, ACTUALLY.>
<OR I WAS. TAKEN A BIT OF A LIKING TO THE PLACE, THOUGH. THOUGHT I MIGHT STAY A WHILE.>
SNAP

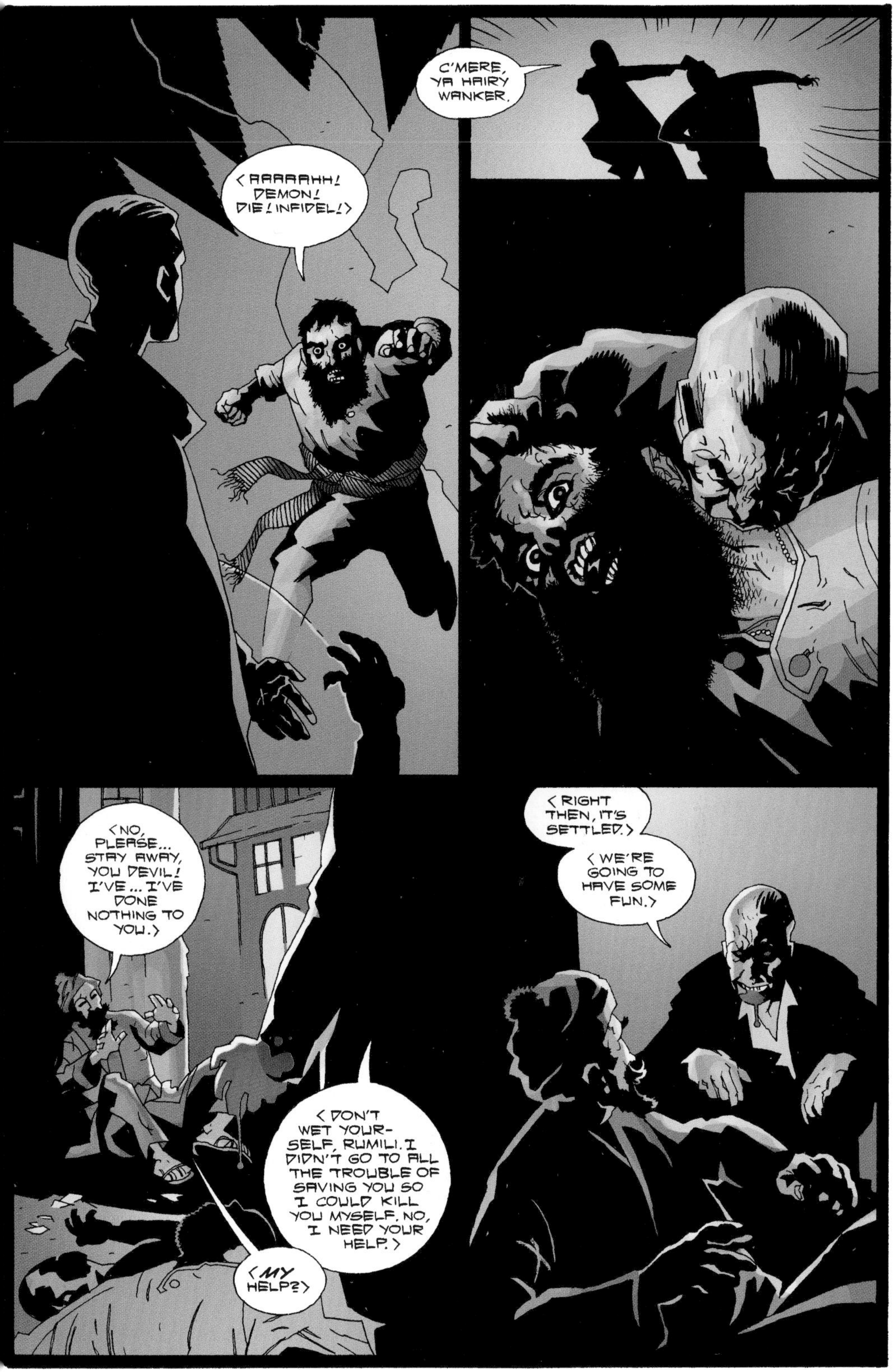
C'MERE, YA HAIRY WANKER.
< AAAAAAHH! DEMON! DIE! INFIDEL! >
<NO, PLEASE... STAY AWAY, YOU DEVIL! I'VE... I'VE DONE NOTHING TO YOU.>
< DON'T WET YOURSELF, RUMILI. I DIDN'T GO TO ALL THE TROUBLE OF SAVING YOU SO I COULD KILL YOU MYSELF. NO, I NEED YOUR HELP.>
<MY HELP?>
< RIGHT THEN, IT'S SETTLED.>
< WE'RE GOING TO HAVE SOME FUN.>

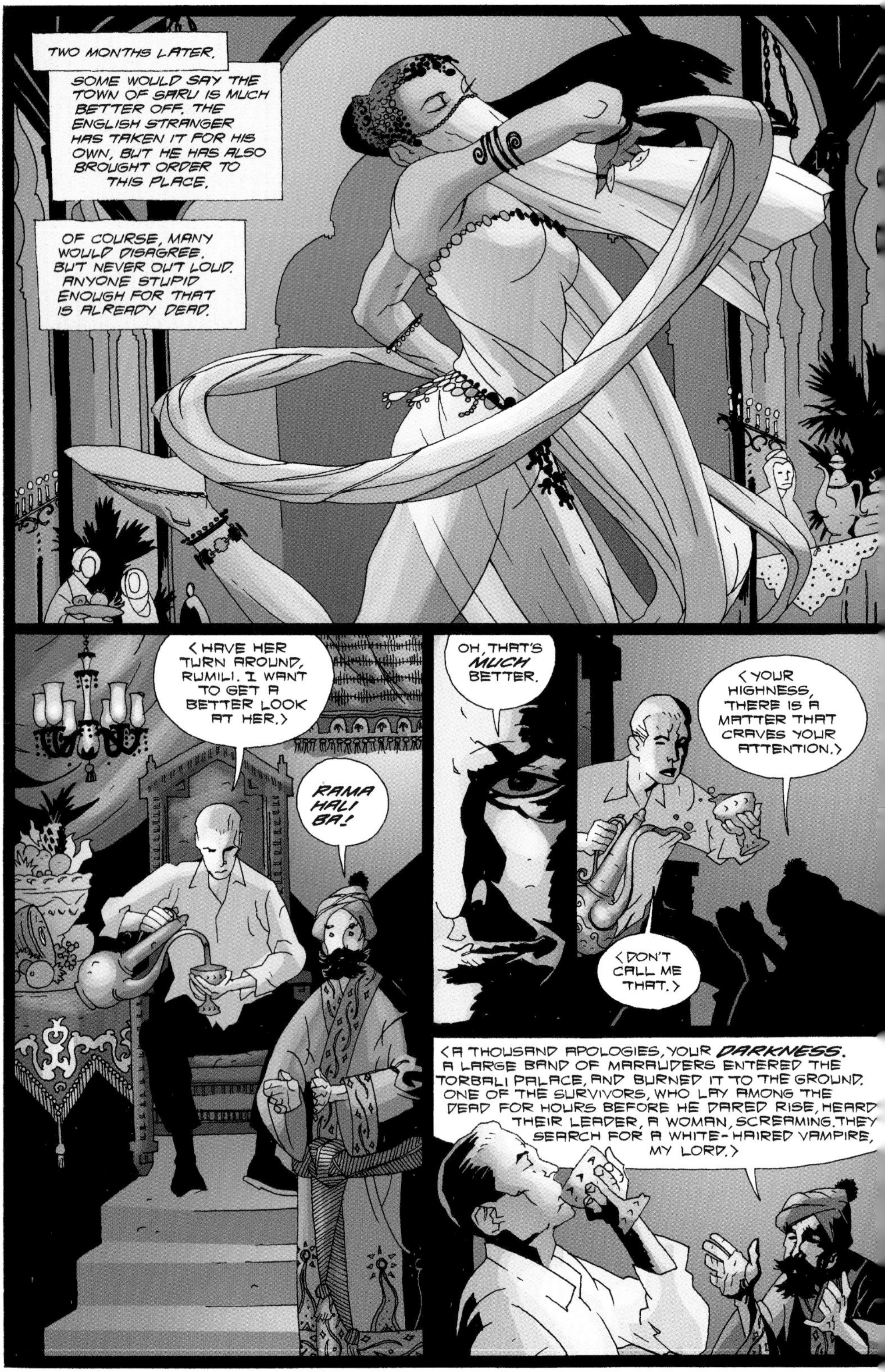
TWO MONTHS LATER.
SOME WOULD SAY THE TOWN OF SARU IS MUCH BETTER OFF. THE ENGLISH STRANGER HAS TAKEN IT FOR HIS OWN, BUT HE HAS ALSO BROUGHT ORDER TO THIS PLACE.
OF COURSE, MANY WOULD DISAGREE. BUT NEVER OUT LOUD. ANYONE STUPID ENOUGH FOR THAT IS ALREADY DEAD.
<HAVE HER TURN AROUND, RUMILI. I WANT TO GET A BETTER LOOK AT HER.>
RAMA HALI BA!
OH, THAT'S MUCH BETTER.
<YOUR HIGHNESS, THERE IS A MATTER THAT CRAVES YOUR ATTENTION.>
<DON'T CALL ME THAT.>
<A THOUSAND APOLOGIES, YOUR DARKNESS. A LARGE BAND OF MARAUDERS ENTERED THE TORBALI PALACE, AND BURNED IT TO THE GROUND. ONE OF THE SURVIVORS, WHO LAY AMONG THE DEAD FOR HOURS BEFORE HE DARED RISE, HEARD THEIR LEADER, A WOMAN, SCREAMING. THEY SEARCH FOR A WHITE-HAIRED VAMPIRE, MY LORD.>

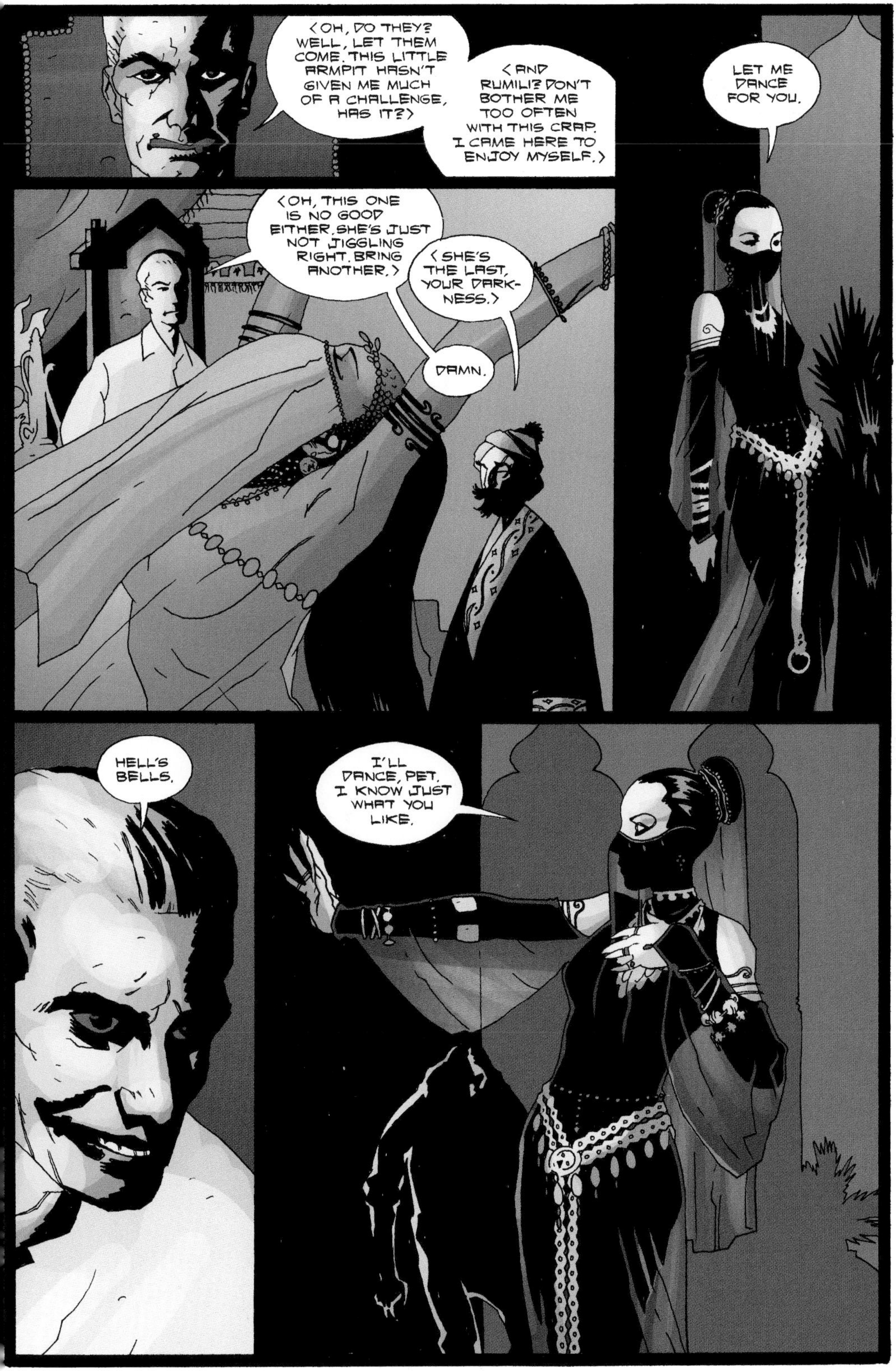

<OH, DO THEY? WELL, LET THEM COME. THIS LITTLE ARMPIT HASN'T GIVEN ME MUCH OF A CHALLENGE, HAS IT?>
<AND RUMILI? DON'T BOTHER ME TOO OFTEN WITH THIS CRAP. I CAME HERE TO ENJOY MYSELF.>
<OH, THIS ONE IS NO GOOD EITHER. SHE'S JUST NOT JIGGLING RIGHT. BRING ANOTHER.>
<SHE'S THE LAST, YOUR DARKNESS.>
DAMN.
LET ME DANCE FOR YOU.
HELL'S BELLS.
I'LL DANCE, PET. I KNOW JUST WHAT YOU LIKE.

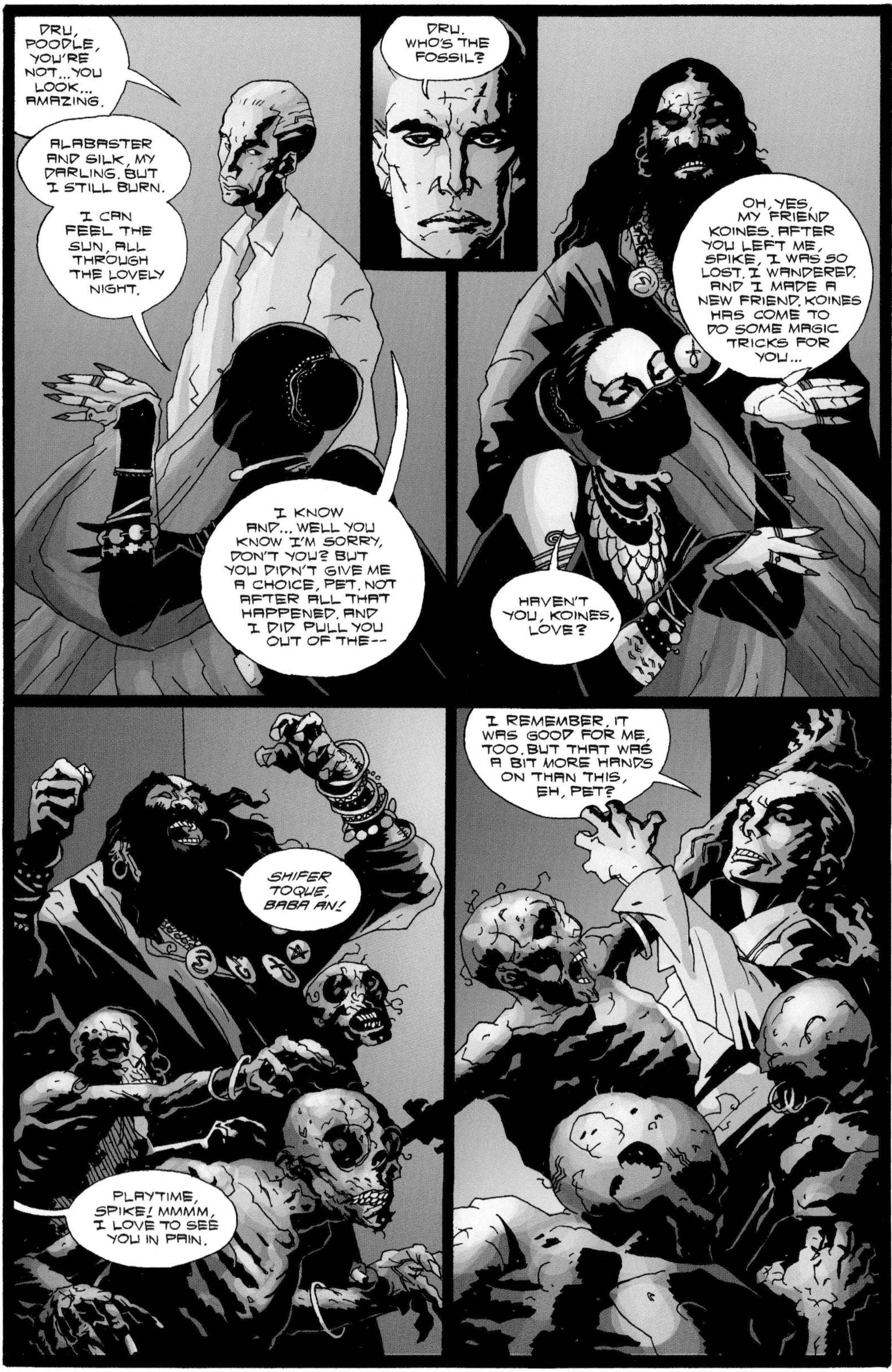
DRU, POODLE, YOU'RE NOT... YOU LOOK... AMAZING.
ALABASTER AND SILK, MY DARLING, BUT I STILL BURN.
I CAN FEEL THE SUN, ALL THROUGH THE LOVELY NIGHT.
I KNOW AND... WELL YOU KNOW I'M SORRY, DON'T YOU? BUT YOU DIDN'T GIVE ME A CHOICE, PET, NOT AFTER ALL THAT HAPPENED. AND I DID PULL YOU OUT OF THE--
DRU. WHO'S THE FOSSIL?
OH, YES, MY FRIEND KOINES. AFTER YOU LEFT ME, SPIKE, I WAS SO LOST. I WANDERED. AND I MADE A NEW FRIEND. KOINES HAS COME TO DO SOME MAGIC TRICKS FOR YOU...
HAVEN'T YOU, KOINES, LOVE?
SHIFER TOQUE, BABA AN!
PLAYTIME, SPIKE! MMMM, I LOVE TO SEE YOU IN PAIN.
I REMEMBER, IT WAS GOOD FOR ME, TOO. BUT THAT WAS A BIT MORE HANDS ON THAN THIS, EH, PET?

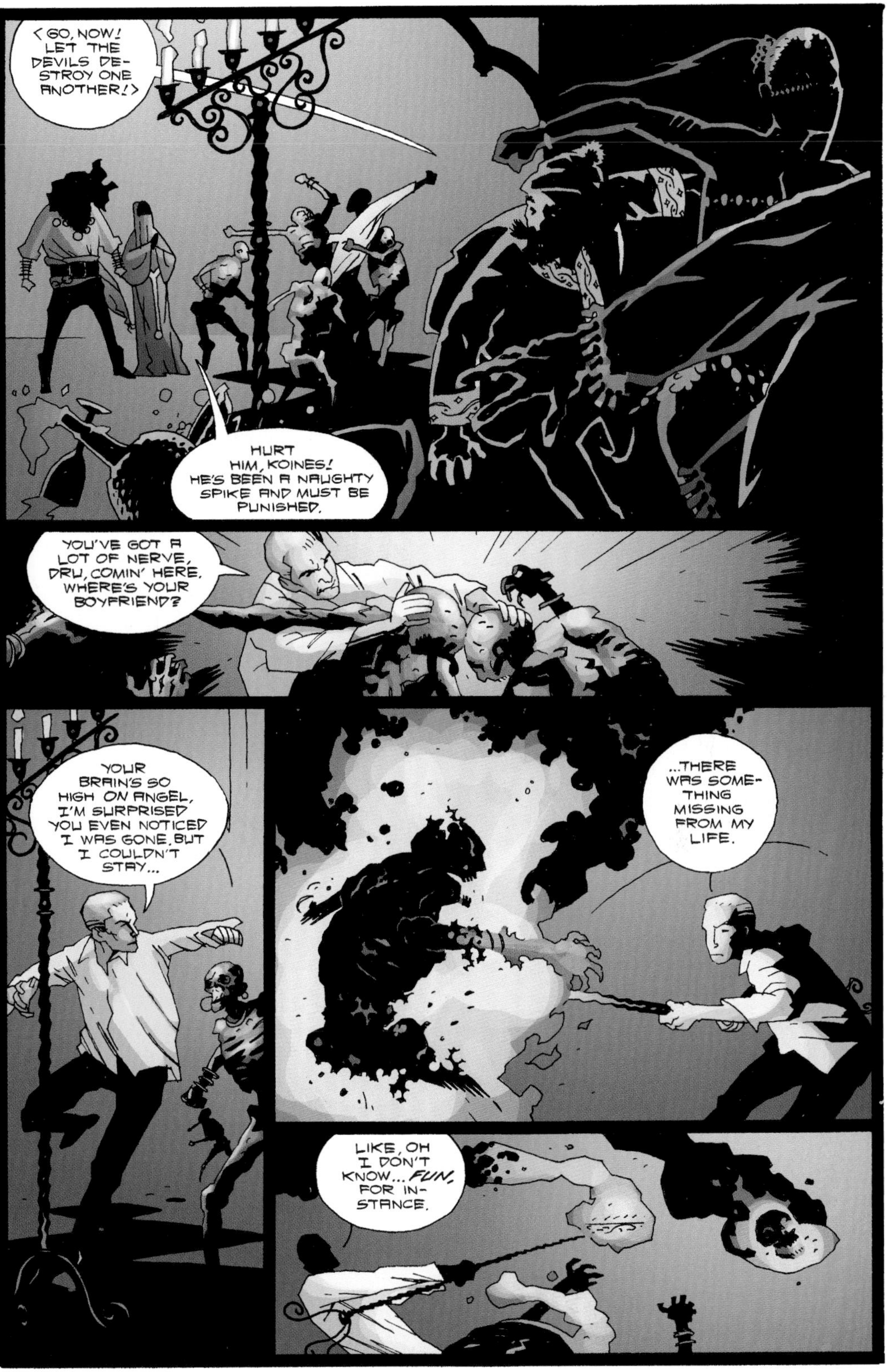
<GO, NOW! LET THE DEVILS DE-STROY ONE ANOTHER!>
HURT HIM, KOINES! HE'S BEEN A NAUGHTY SPIKE AND MUST BE PUNISHED.
YOU'VE GOT A LOT OF NERVE, DRU, COMIN' HERE. WHERE'S YOUR BOYFRIEND?
YOUR BRAIN'S SO HIGH ON ANGEL, I'M SURPRISED YOU EVEN NOTICED I WAS GONE. BUT I COULDN'T STAY...
...THERE WAS SOME-THING MISSING FROM MY LIFE.
LIKE, OH I DON'T KNOW... FUN, FOR IN-STANCE.

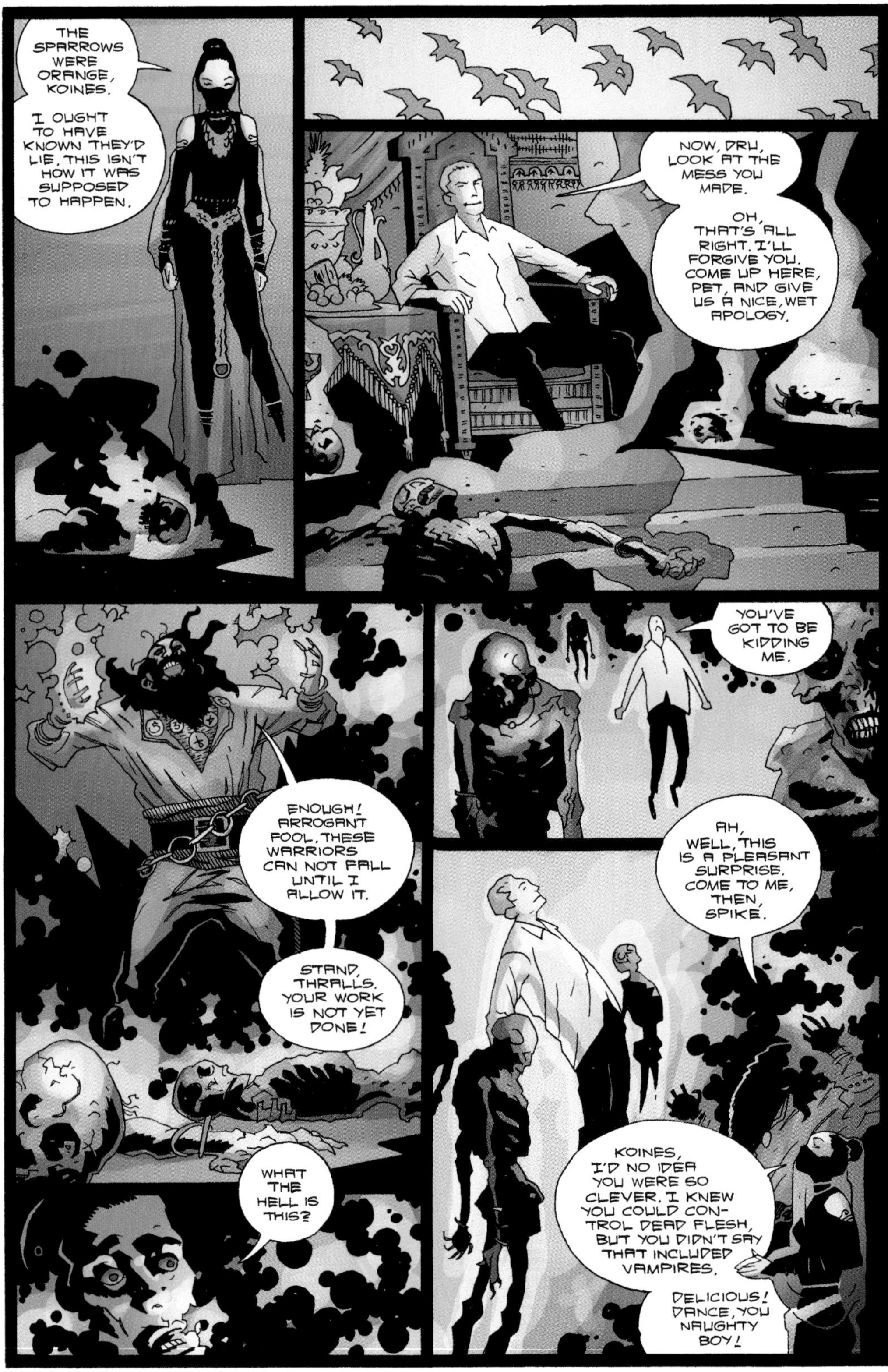
THE SPARROWS WERE ORANGE, KOINES.
I OUGHT TO HAVE KNOWN THEY'D LIE. THIS ISN'T HOW IT WAS SUPPOSED TO HAPPEN.
NOW, DRU, LOOK AT THE MESS YOU MADE.
OH, THAT'S ALL RIGHT. I'LL FORGIVE YOU. COME UP HERE, PET, AND GIVE US A NICE, WET APOLOGY.
ENOUGH! ARROGANT FOOL. THESE WARRIORS CAN NOT FALL UNTIL I ALLOW IT.
STAND, THRALLS. YOUR WORK IS NOT YET DONE!
YOU'VE GOT TO BE KIDDING ME.
AH, WELL, THIS IS A PLEASANT SURPRISE. COME TO ME, THEN, SPIKE.
WHAT THE HELL IS THIS?
KOINES, I'D NO IDEA YOU WERE SO CLEVER. I KNEW YOU COULD CONTROL DEAD FLESH, BUT YOU DIDN'T SAY THAT INCLUDED VAMPIRES.
DELICIOUS! DANCE, YOU NAUGHTY BOY!

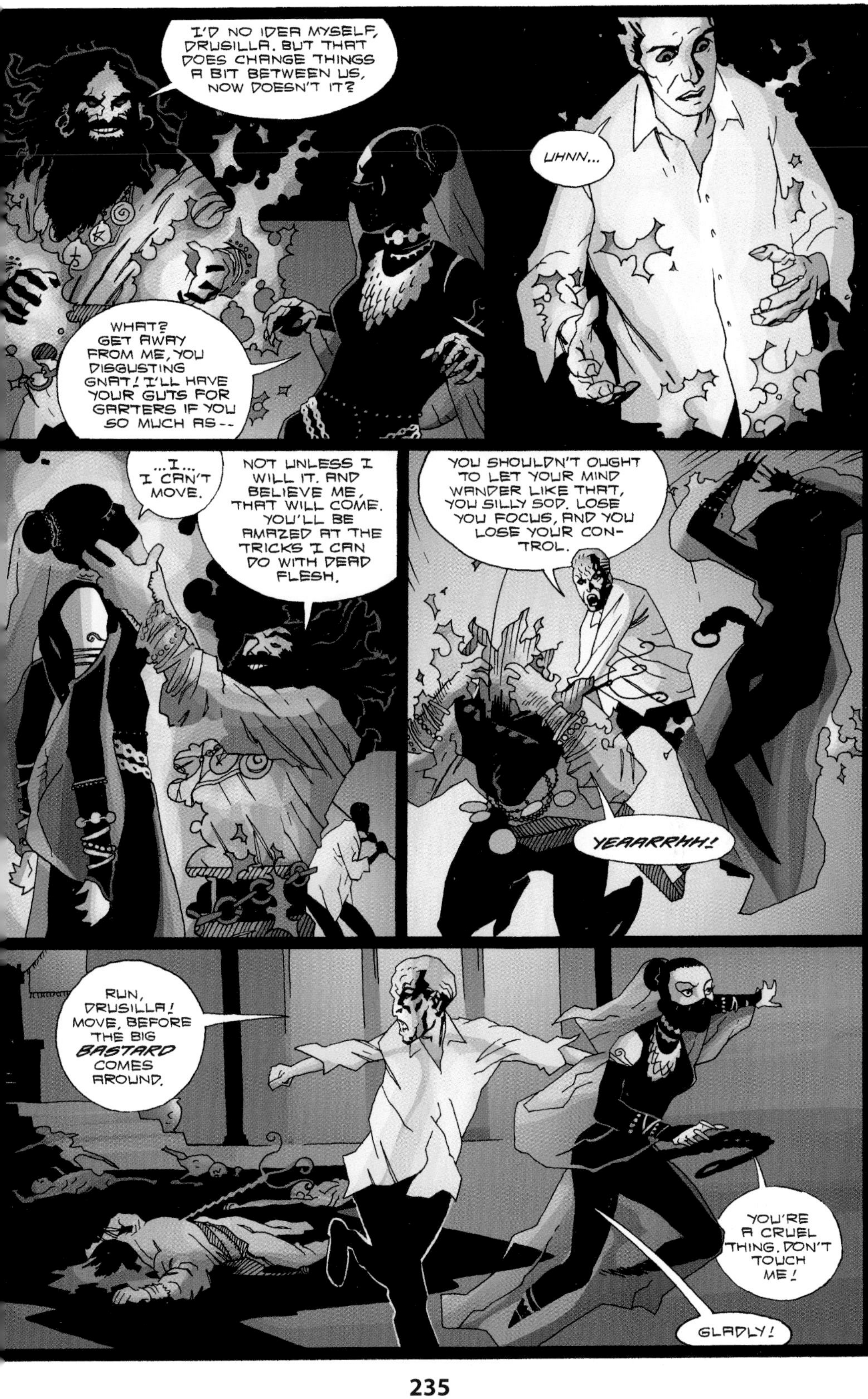
I'D NO IDEA MYSELF, DRUSILLA. BUT THAT DOES CHANGE THINGS A BIT BETWEEN US, NOW DOESN'T IT?
WHAT? GET AWAY FROM ME, YOU DISGUSTING GNAT! I'LL HAVE YOUR GUTS FOR GARTERS IF YOU SO MUCH AS--
UHNN...
...I... I CAN'T MOVE.
NOT UNLESS I WILL IT. AND BELIEVE ME, THAT WILL COME. YOU'LL BE AMAZED AT THE TRICKS I CAN DO WITH DEAD FLESH.
YOU SHOULDN'T OUGHT TO LET YOUR MIND WANDER LIKE THAT, YOU SILLY SOD. LOSE YOU FOCUS, AND YOU LOSE YOUR CONTROL.
YEAARRHH!
RUN, DRUSILLA! MOVE, BEFORE THE BIG BASTARD COMES AROUND.
YOU'RE A CRUEL THING. DON'T TOUCH ME!
GLADLY!

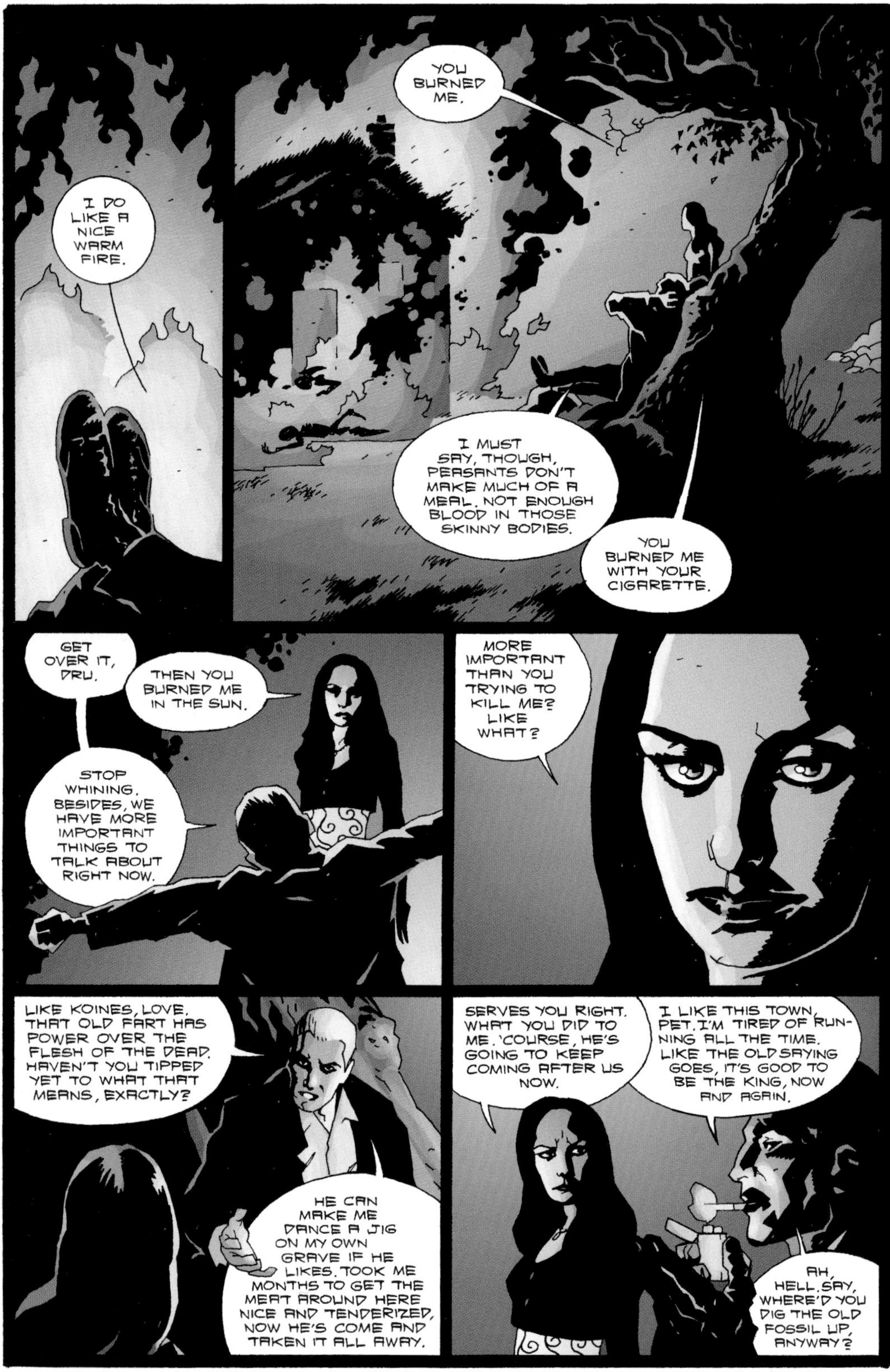
I DO LIKE A NICE WARM FIRE.
YOU BURNED ME.
I MUST SAY, THOUGH, PEASANTS DON'T MAKE MUCH OF A MEAL. NOT ENOUGH BLOOD IN THOSE SKINNY BODIES.
YOU BURNED ME WITH YOUR CIGARETTE.
GET OVER IT, DRU.
THEN YOU BURNED ME IN THE SUN.
STOP WHINING. BESIDES, WE HAVE MORE IMPORTANT THINGS TO TALK ABOUT RIGHT NOW.
MORE IMPORTANT THAN YOU TRYING TO KILL ME? LIKE WHAT?
LIKE KOINES, LOVE. THAT OLD FART HAS POWER OVER THE FLESH OF THE DEAD. HAVEN'T YOU TIPPED YET TO WHAT THAT MEANS, EXACTLY?
HE CAN MAKE ME DANCE A JIG ON MY OWN GRAVE IF HE LIKES. TOOK ME MONTHS TO GET THE MEAT AROUND HERE NICE AND TENDERIZED, NOW HE'S COME AND TAKEN IT ALL AWAY.
SERVES YOU RIGHT. WHAT YOU DID TO ME. 'COURSE, HE'S GOING TO KEEP COMING AFTER US NOW.
I LIKE THIS TOWN, PET. I'M TIRED OF RUNNING ALL THE TIME. LIKE THE OLD SAYING GOES, IT'S GOOD TO BE THE KING, NOW AND AGAIN.
AH, HELL. SAY, WHERE'D YOU DIG THE OLD FOSSIL UP, ANYWAY?

OH, I AM A CLEVER GIRL. I FOUND HIM IN A FOREST ON THE ISLAND OF CRETE.

"YOU NEEDED TO BE PUNISHED, TO BE SPANKED. I KNOW YOU DON'T LIKE TO BE SPANKED."

WELL, THERE WAS THAT *ONE* TIME.

DON'T INTERRUPT.

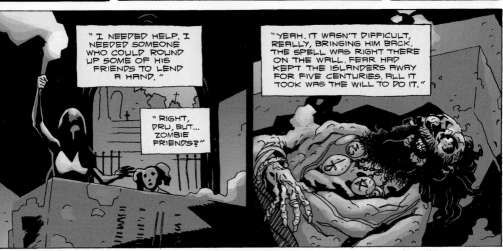

"I NEEDED HELP. I NEEDED SOMEONE WHO COULD ROUND UP SOME OF HIS FRIENDS TO LEND A HAND."

"RIGHT, DRU, BUT... ZOMBIE FRIENDS?"

"YEAH. IT WASN'T DIFFICULT, REALLY, BRINGING HIM BACK. THE SPELL WAS RIGHT THERE ON THE WALL, FEAR HAD KEPT THE ISLANDERS AWAY FOR FIVE CENTURIES. ALL IT TOOK WAS THE WILL TO DO IT."

THAT, AND THE BLOOD OF AN INNOCENT. SIMPLE AS THAT. MY OWN PET SORCERER.

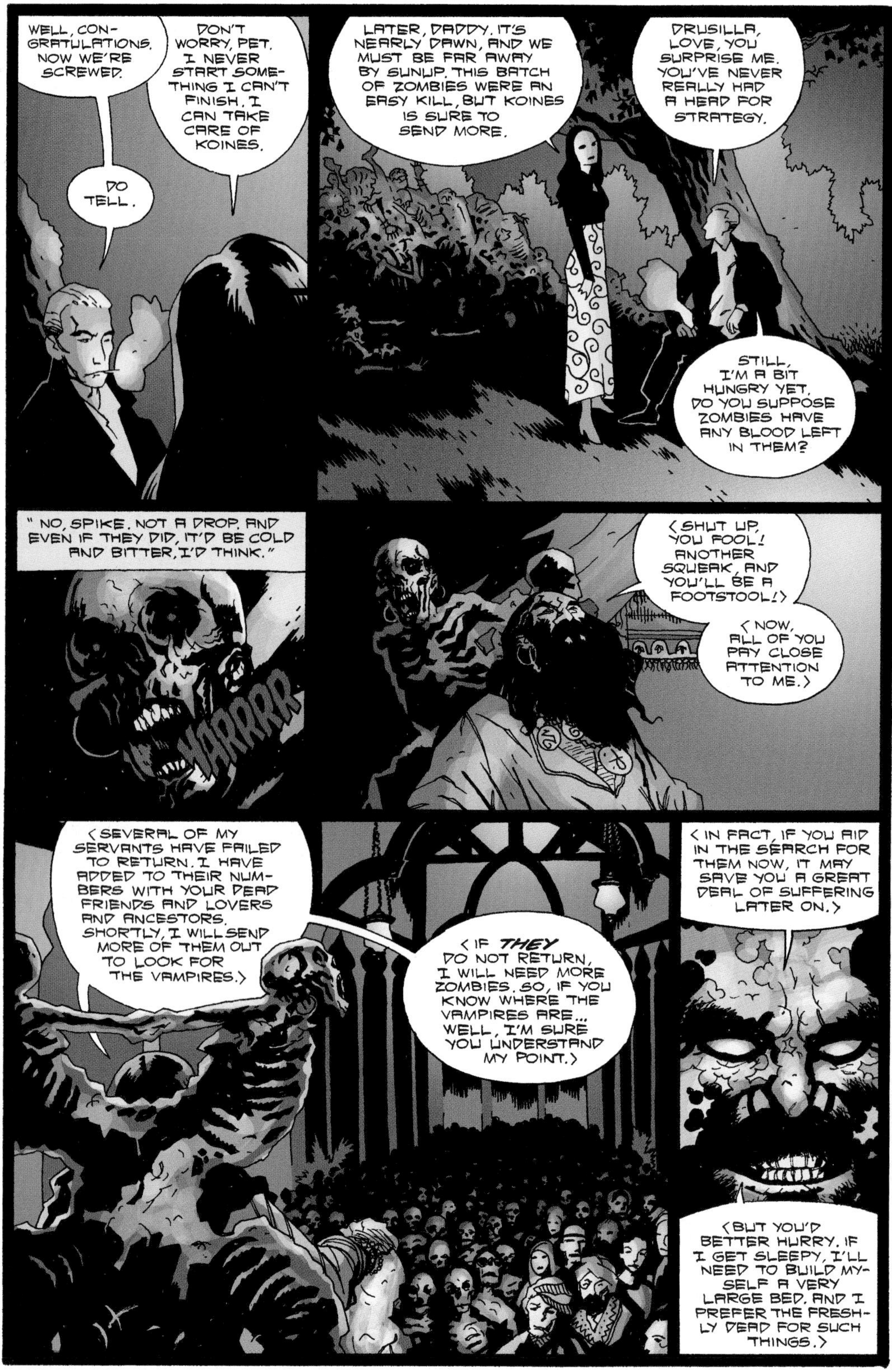
WELL, CON-GRATULATIONS. NOW WE'RE SCREWED.
DON'T WORRY, PET. I NEVER START SOME-THING I CAN'T FINISH. I CAN TAKE CARE OF KOINES.
DO TELL.
LATER, DADDY. IT'S NEARLY DAWN, AND WE MUST BE FAR AWAY BY SUNUP. THIS BATCH OF ZOMBIES WERE AN EASY KILL, BUT KOINES IS SURE TO SEND MORE.
DRUSILLA, LOVE, YOU SURPRISE ME. YOU'VE NEVER REALLY HAD A HEAD FOR STRATEGY.
STILL, I'M A BIT HUNGRY YET. DO YOU SUPPOSE ZOMBIES HAVE ANY BLOOD LEFT IN THEM?
" NO, SPIKE. NOT A DROP. AND EVEN IF THEY DID, IT'D BE COLD AND BITTER, I'D THINK."
HARRRR
< SHUT UP, YOU FOOL! ANOTHER SQUEAK, AND YOU'LL BE A FOOTSTOOL! >
< NOW, ALL OF YOU PAY CLOSE ATTENTION TO ME. >
< SEVERAL OF MY SERVANTS HAVE FAILED TO RETURN. I HAVE ADDED TO THEIR NUM-BERS WITH YOUR DEAD FRIENDS AND LOVERS AND ANCESTORS. SHORTLY, I WILL SEND MORE OF THEM OUT TO LOOK FOR THE VAMPIRES. >
< IF THEY DO NOT RETURN, I WILL NEED MORE ZOMBIES. SO, IF YOU KNOW WHERE THE VAMPIRES ARE... WELL, I'M SURE YOU UNDERSTAND MY POINT. >
< IN FACT, IF YOU AID IN THE SEARCH FOR THEM NOW, IT MAY SAVE YOU A GREAT DEAL OF SUFFERING LATER ON. >
< BUT YOU'D BETTER HURRY. IF I GET SLEEPY, I'LL NEED TO BUILD MY-SELF A VERY LARGE BED. AND I PREFER THE FRESH-LY DEAD FOR SUCH THINGS. >

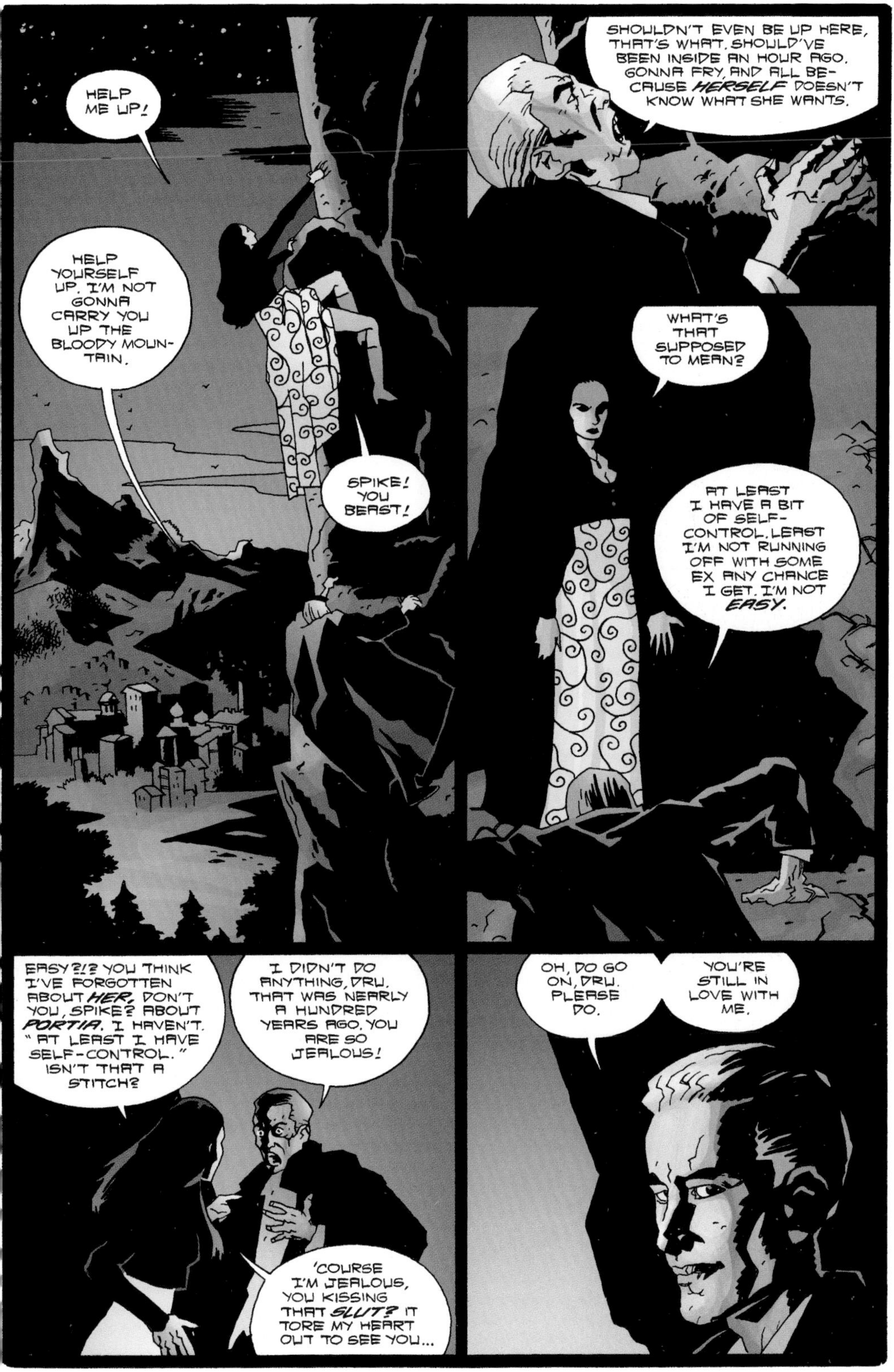
HELP ME UP!
HELP YOURSELF UP. I'M NOT GONNA CARRY YOU UP THE BLOODY MOUN-TAIN.
SPIKE! YOU BEAST!
SHOULDN'T EVEN BE UP HERE, THAT'S WHAT. SHOULD'VE BEEN INSIDE AN HOUR AGO. GONNA FRY, AND ALL BE-CAUSE HERSELF DOESN'T KNOW WHAT SHE WANTS.
WHAT'S THAT SUPPOSED TO MEAN?
AT LEAST I HAVE A BIT OF SELF-CONTROL. LEAST I'M NOT RUNNING OFF WITH SOME EX ANY CHANCE I GET. I'M NOT EASY.
EASY?!? YOU THINK I'VE FORGOTTEN ABOUT HER, DON'T YOU, SPIKE? ABOUT PORTIA. I HAVEN'T. "AT LEAST I HAVE SELF-CONTROL." ISN'T THAT A STITCH?
I DIDN'T DO ANYTHING, DRU. THAT WAS NEARLY A HUNDRED YEARS AGO. YOU ARE SO JEALOUS!
'COURSE I'M JEALOUS, YOU KISSING THAT SLUT? IT TORE MY HEART OUT TO SEE YOU...
OH, DO GO ON, DRU. PLEASE DO.
YOU'RE STILL IN LOVE WITH ME.

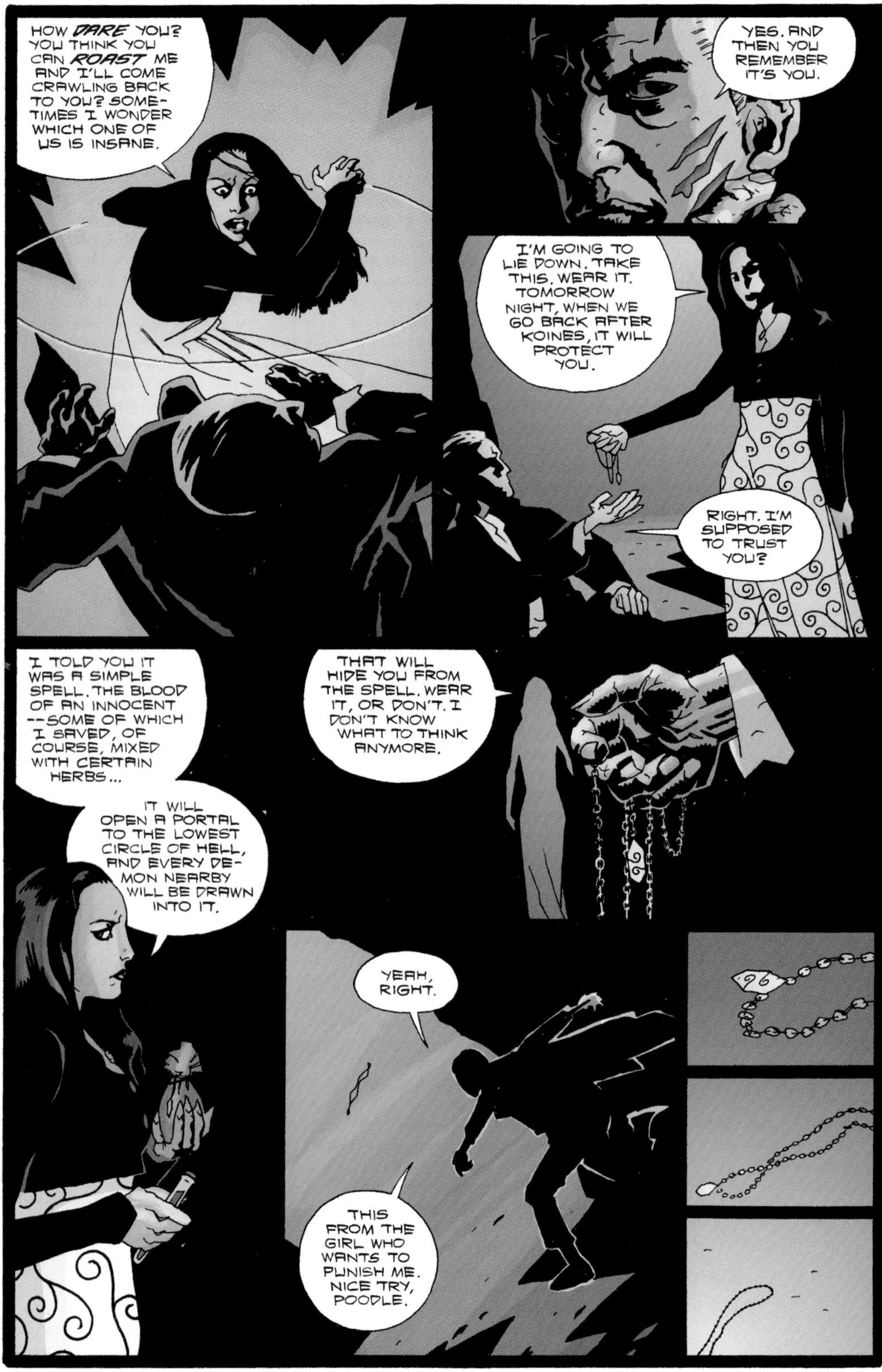
HOW DARE YOU? YOU THINK YOU CAN ROAST ME AND I'LL COME CRAWLING BACK TO YOU? SOMETIMES I WONDER WHICH ONE OF US IS INSANE.
YES. AND THEN YOU REMEMBER IT'S YOU.
I'M GOING TO LIE DOWN. TAKE THIS. WEAR IT. TOMORROW NIGHT, WHEN WE GO BACK AFTER KOINES, IT WILL PROTECT YOU.
RIGHT. I'M SUPPOSED TO TRUST YOU?
I TOLD YOU IT WAS A SIMPLE SPELL. THE BLOOD OF AN INNOCENT --SOME OF WHICH I SAVED, OF COURSE, MIXED WITH CERTAIN HERBS...
IT WILL OPEN A PORTAL TO THE LOWEST CIRCLE OF HELL, AND EVERY DEMON NEARBY WILL BE DRAWN INTO IT.
THAT WILL HIDE YOU FROM THE SPELL. WEAR IT, OR DON'T. I DON'T KNOW WHAT TO THINK ANYMORE.
YEAH, RIGHT.
THIS FROM THE GIRL WHO WANTS TO PUNISH ME. NICE TRY, POODLE.

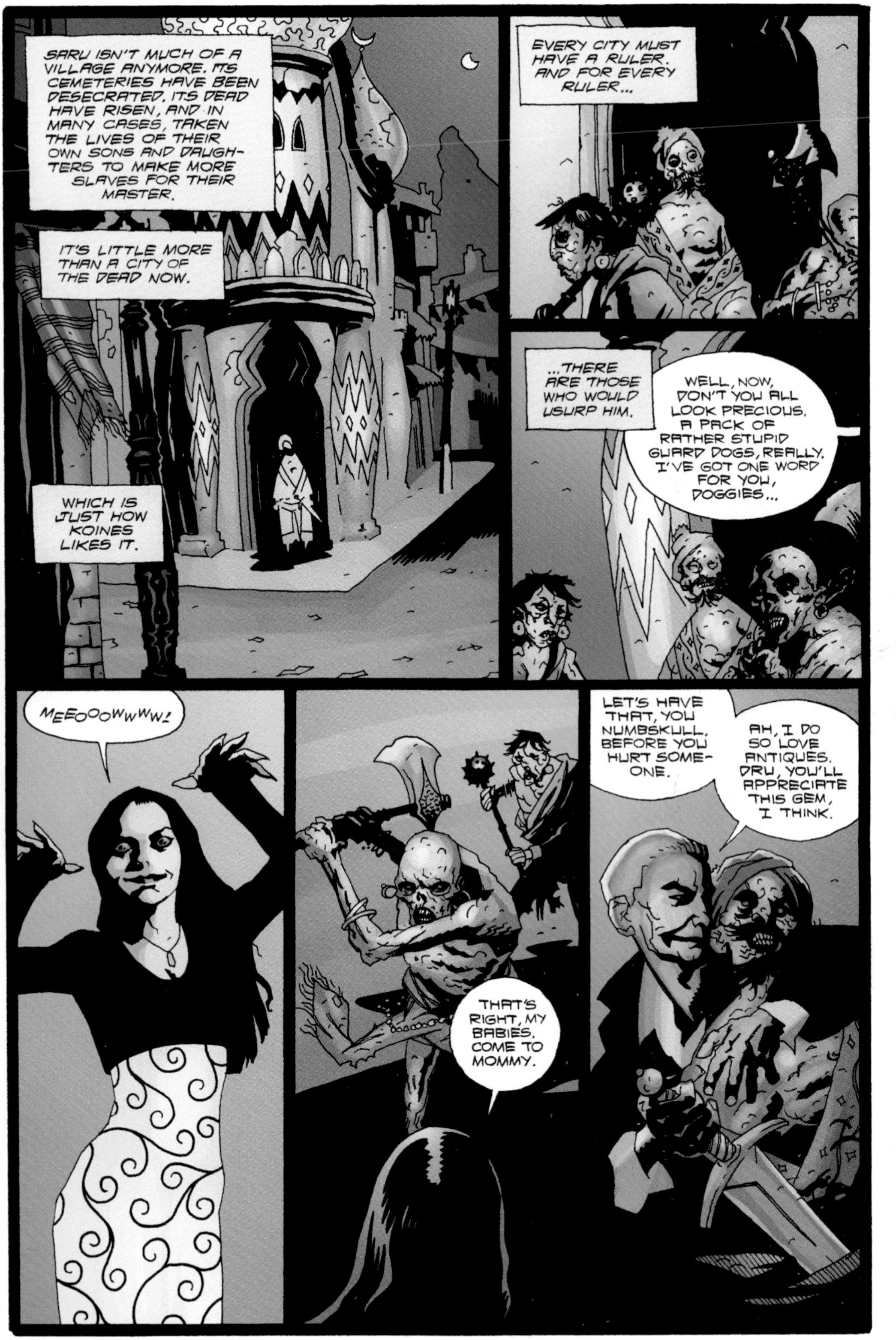
SARU ISN'T MUCH OF A VILLAGE ANYMORE. ITS CEMETERIES HAVE BEEN DESECRATED. ITS DEAD HAVE RISEN, AND IN MANY CASES, TAKEN THE LIVES OF THEIR OWN SONS AND DAUGHTERS TO MAKE MORE SLAVES FOR THEIR MASTER.
IT'S LITTLE MORE THAN A CITY OF THE DEAD NOW.
WHICH IS JUST HOW KOINES LIKES IT.
EVERY CITY MUST HAVE A RULER. AND FOR EVERY RULER...
...THERE ARE THOSE WHO WOULD USURP HIM.
WELL, NOW, DON'T YOU ALL LOOK PRECIOUS. A PACK OF RATHER STUPID GUARD DOGS, REALLY. I'VE GOT ONE WORD FOR YOU, DOGGIES...
MEEOOOWWWW!
THAT'S RIGHT, MY BABIES, COME TO MOMMY.
LET'S HAVE THAT, YOU NUMBSKULL, BEFORE YOU HURT SOMEONE.
AH, I DO SO LOVE ANTIQUES. DRU, YOU'LL APPRECIATE THIS GEM, I THINK.

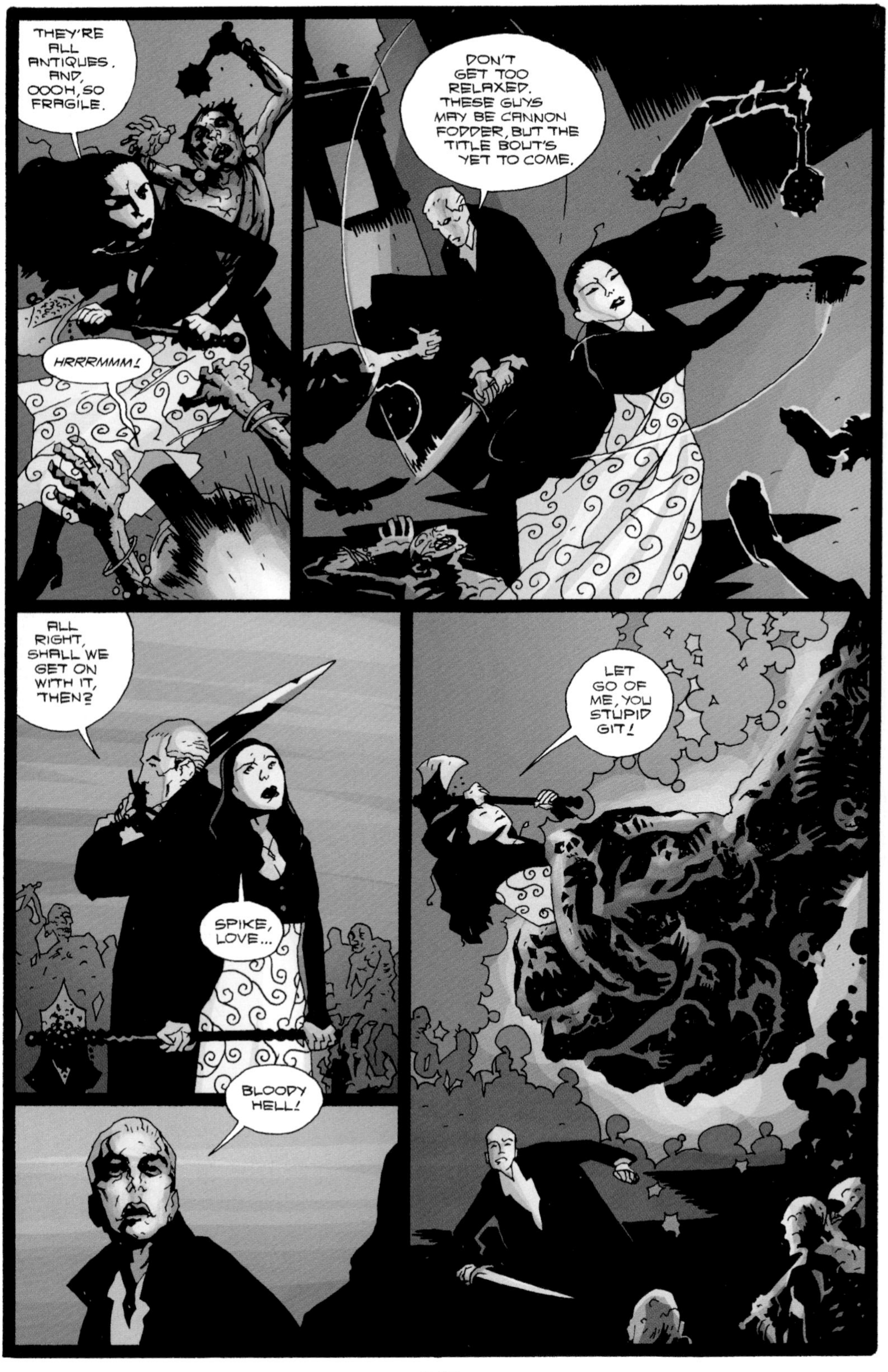
THEY'RE ALL ANTIQUES. AND, OOOH, SO FRAGILE.
HRRRMMM!
DON'T GET TOO RELAXED. THESE GUYS MAY BE CANNON FODDER, BUT THE TITLE BOUT'S YET TO COME.
ALL RIGHT, SHALL WE GET ON WITH IT, THEN?
SPIKE, LOVE...
BLOODY HELL!
LET GO OF ME, YOU STUPID GIT!

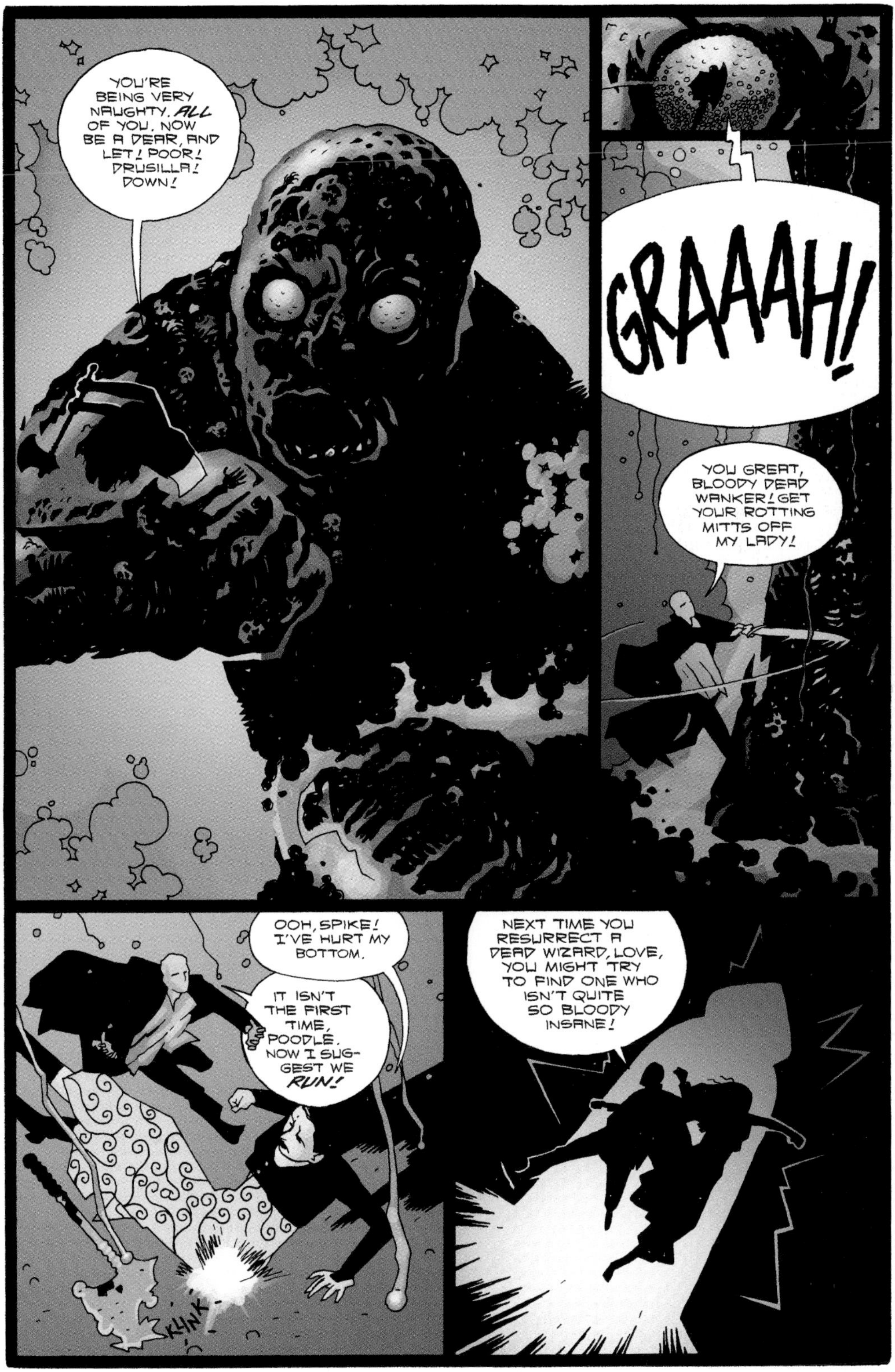
YOU'RE BEING VERY NAUGHTY. ALL OF YOU. NOW BE A DEAR, AND LET! POOR! DRUSILLA! DOWN!
GRAAAH!!
YOU GREAT, BLOODY DEAD WANKER! GET YOUR ROTTING MITTS OFF MY LADY!
OOH, SPIKE! I'VE HURT MY BOTTOM.
IT ISN'T THE FIRST TIME, POODLE. NOW I SUGGEST WE RUN!
KLINK
NEXT TIME YOU RESURRECT A DEAD WIZARD, LOVE, YOU MIGHT TRY TO FIND ONE WHO ISN'T QUITE SO BLOODY INSANE!

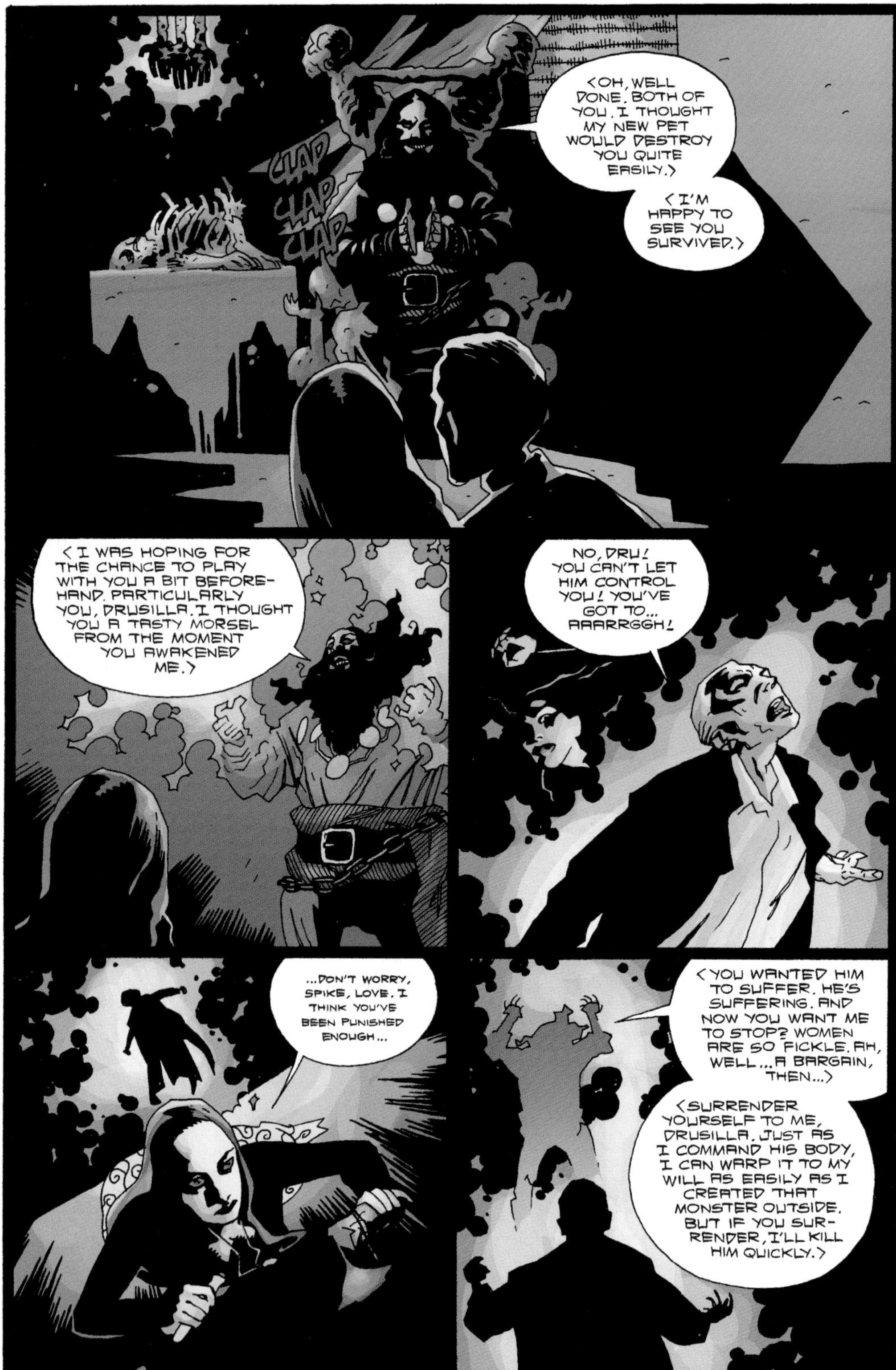
CLAP CLAP CLAP
<OH, WELL DONE. BOTH OF YOU. I THOUGHT MY NEW PET WOULD DESTROY YOU QUITE EASILY.>
<I'M HAPPY TO SEE YOU SURVIVED.>
<I WAS HOPING FOR THE CHANCE TO PLAY WITH YOU A BIT BEFORE-HAND. PARTICULARLY YOU, DRUSILLA. I THOUGHT YOU A TASTY MORSEL FROM THE MOMENT YOU AWAKENED ME.>
NO, DRU! YOU CAN'T LET HIM CONTROL YOU! YOU'VE GOT TO... AAAARRGGH!
...DON'T WORRY, SPIKE, LOVE. I THINK YOU'VE BEEN PUNISHED ENOUGH...
<YOU WANTED HIM TO SUFFER. HE'S SUFFERING. AND NOW YOU WANT ME TO STOP? WOMEN ARE SO FICKLE. AH, WELL... A BARGAIN, THEN...>
<SURRENDER YOURSELF TO ME, DRUSILLA. JUST AS I COMMAND HIS BODY, I CAN WARP IT TO MY WILL AS EASILY AS I CREATED THAT MONSTER OUTSIDE. BUT IF YOU SUR-RENDER, I'LL KILL HIM QUICKLY.>

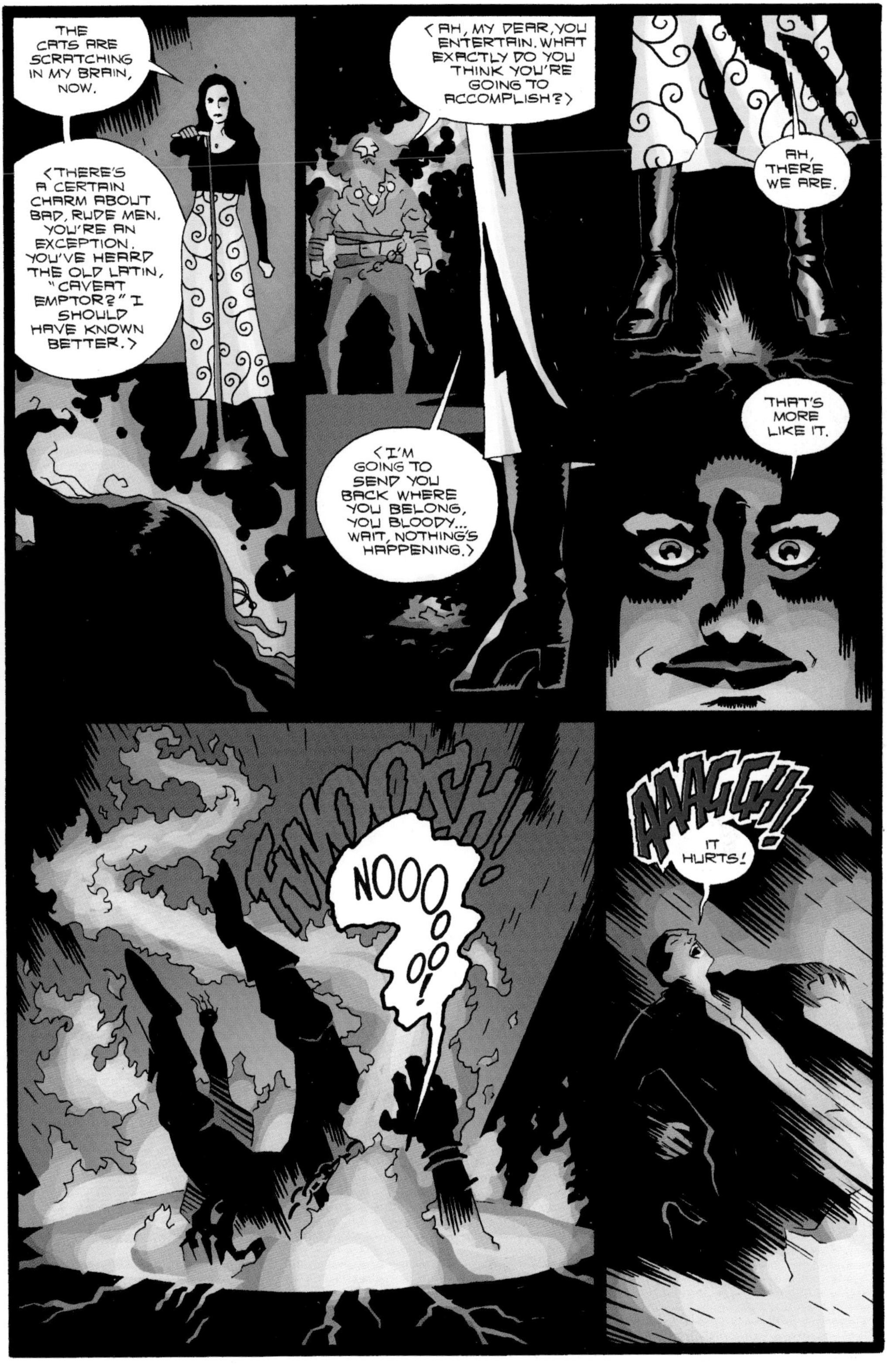
THE CATS ARE SCRATCHING IN MY BRAIN, NOW.
<THERE'S A CERTAIN CHARM ABOUT BAD, RUDE MEN. YOU'RE AN EXCEPTION. YOU'VE HEARD THE OLD LATIN, "CAVEAT EMPTOR?" I SHOULD HAVE KNOWN BETTER.>
<AH, MY DEAR, YOU ENTERTAIN. WHAT EXACTLY DO YOU THINK YOU'RE GOING TO ACCOMPLISH?>
<I'M GOING TO SEND YOU BACK WHERE YOU BELONG, YOU BLOODY... WAIT, NOTHING'S HAPPENING.>
AH, THERE WE ARE.
THAT'S MORE LIKE IT.
FWOOOSH!
NOOOooooo!
AAAGGH!
IT HURTS!

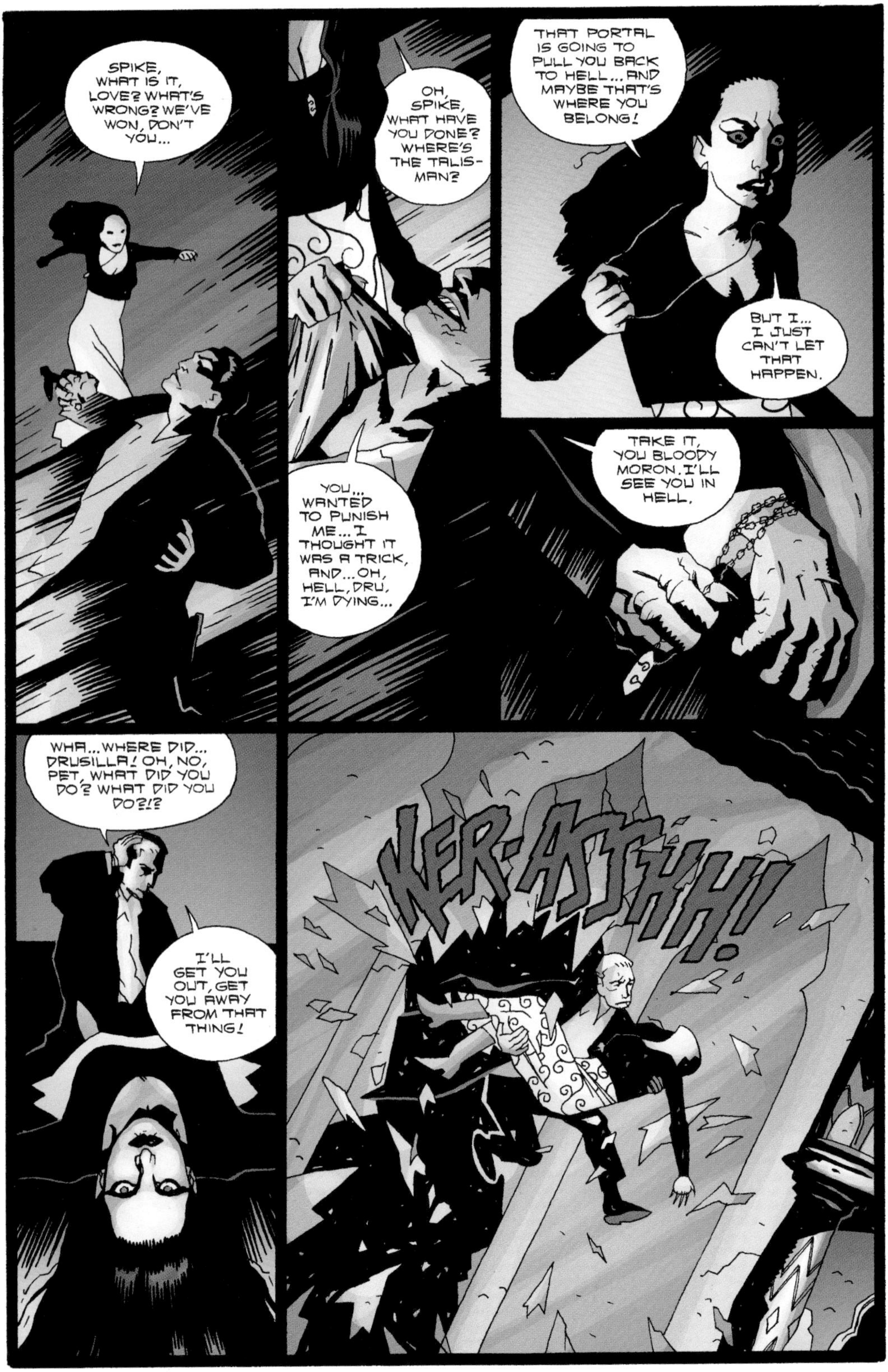
SPIKE, WHAT IS IT, LOVE? WHAT'S WRONG? WE'VE WON, DON'T YOU...
OH, SPIKE, WHAT HAVE YOU DONE? WHERE'S THE TALIS-MAN?
YOU... WANTED TO PUNISH ME... I THOUGHT IT WAS A TRICK, AND... OH, HELL, DRU, I'M DYING...
THAT PORTAL IS GOING TO PULL YOU BACK TO HELL... AND MAYBE THAT'S WHERE YOU BELONG!
BUT I... I JUST CAN'T LET THAT HAPPEN.
TAKE IT, YOU BLOODY MORON. I'LL SEE YOU IN HELL.
WHA... WHERE DID... DRUSILLA! OH, NO, PET, WHAT DID YOU DO? WHAT DID YOU DO?!?
I'LL GET YOU OUT, GET YOU AWAY FROM THAT THING!
KER-ASHH!

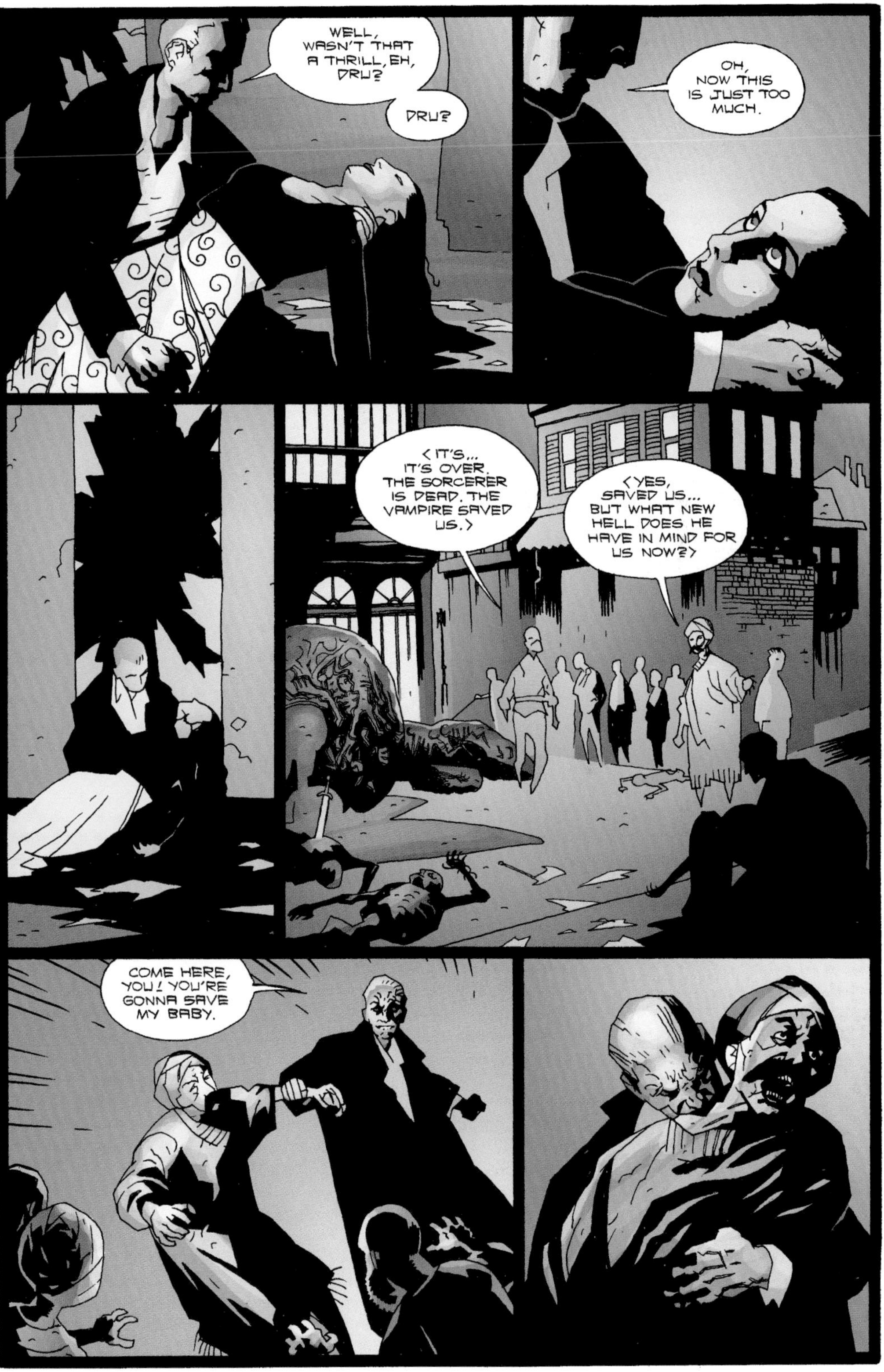
WELL, WASN'T THAT A THRILL, EH, DRU?
DRU?
OH, NOW THIS IS JUST TOO MUCH.
< IT'S... IT'S OVER. THE SORCERER IS DEAD. THE VAMPIRE SAVED US. >
<YES, SAVED US... BUT WHAT NEW HELL DOES HE HAVE IN MIND FOR US NOW?>
COME HERE, YOU! YOU'RE GONNA SAVE MY BABY.

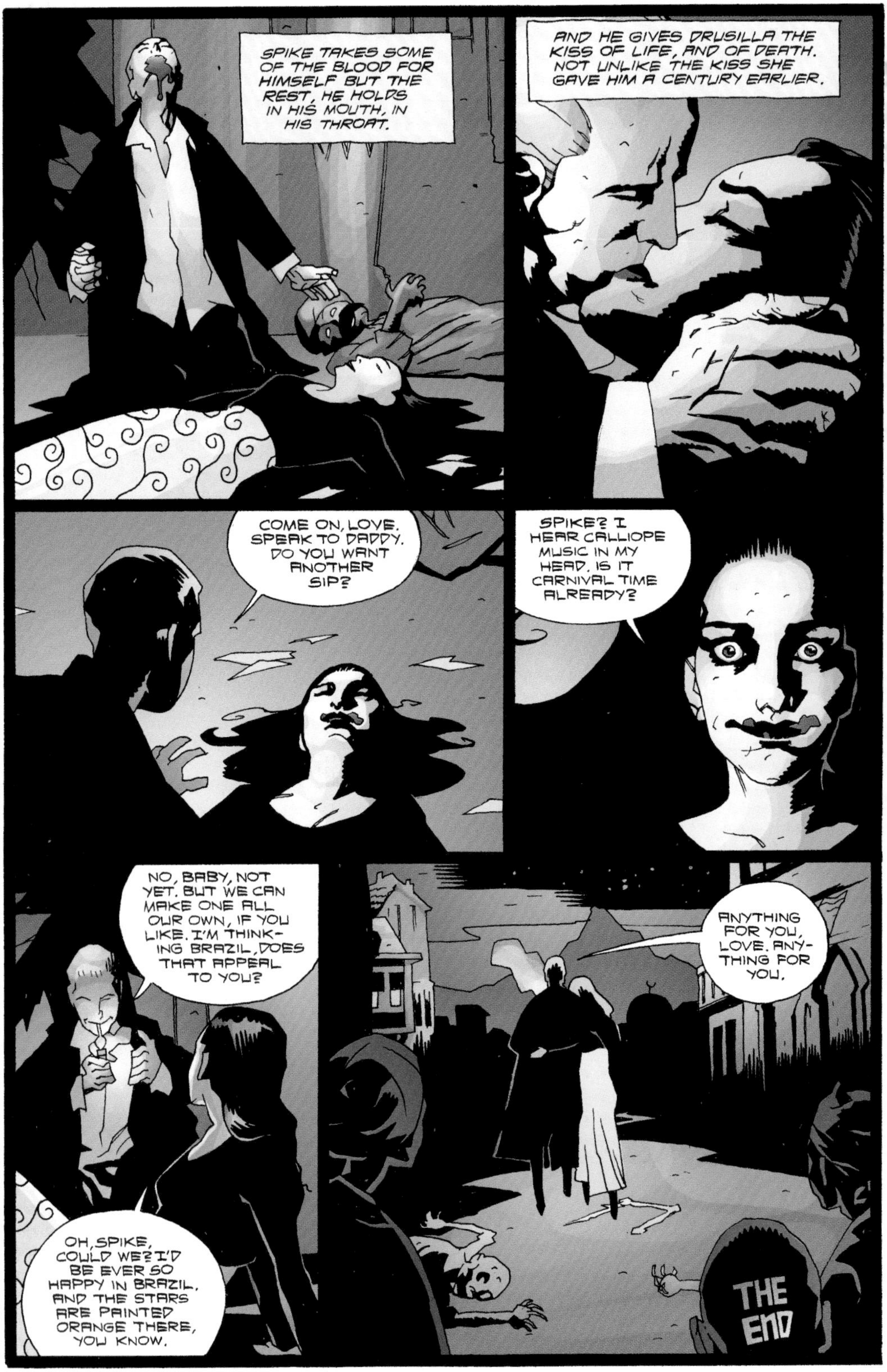
SPIKE TAKES SOME OF THE BLOOD FOR HIMSELF BUT THE REST, HE HOLDS IN HIS MOUTH, IN HIS THROAT.
AND HE GIVES DRUSILLA THE KISS OF LIFE, AND OF DEATH. NOT UNLIKE THE KISS SHE GAVE HIM A CENTURY EARLIER.
COME ON, LOVE. SPEAK TO DADDY. DO YOU WANT ANOTHER SIP?
SPIKE? I HEAR CALLIOPE MUSIC IN MY HEAD. IS IT CARNIVAL TIME ALREADY?
NO, BABY, NOT YET. BUT WE CAN MAKE ONE ALL OUR OWN, IF YOU LIKE. I'M THINKING BRAZIL, DOES THAT APPEAL TO YOU?
OH, SPIKE, COULD WE? I'D BE EVER SO HAPPY IN BRAZIL. AND THE STARS ARE PAINTED ORANGE THERE, YOU KNOW.
ANYTHING FOR YOU, LOVE. ANYTHING FOR YOU.
THE END

THE DUST WALTZ

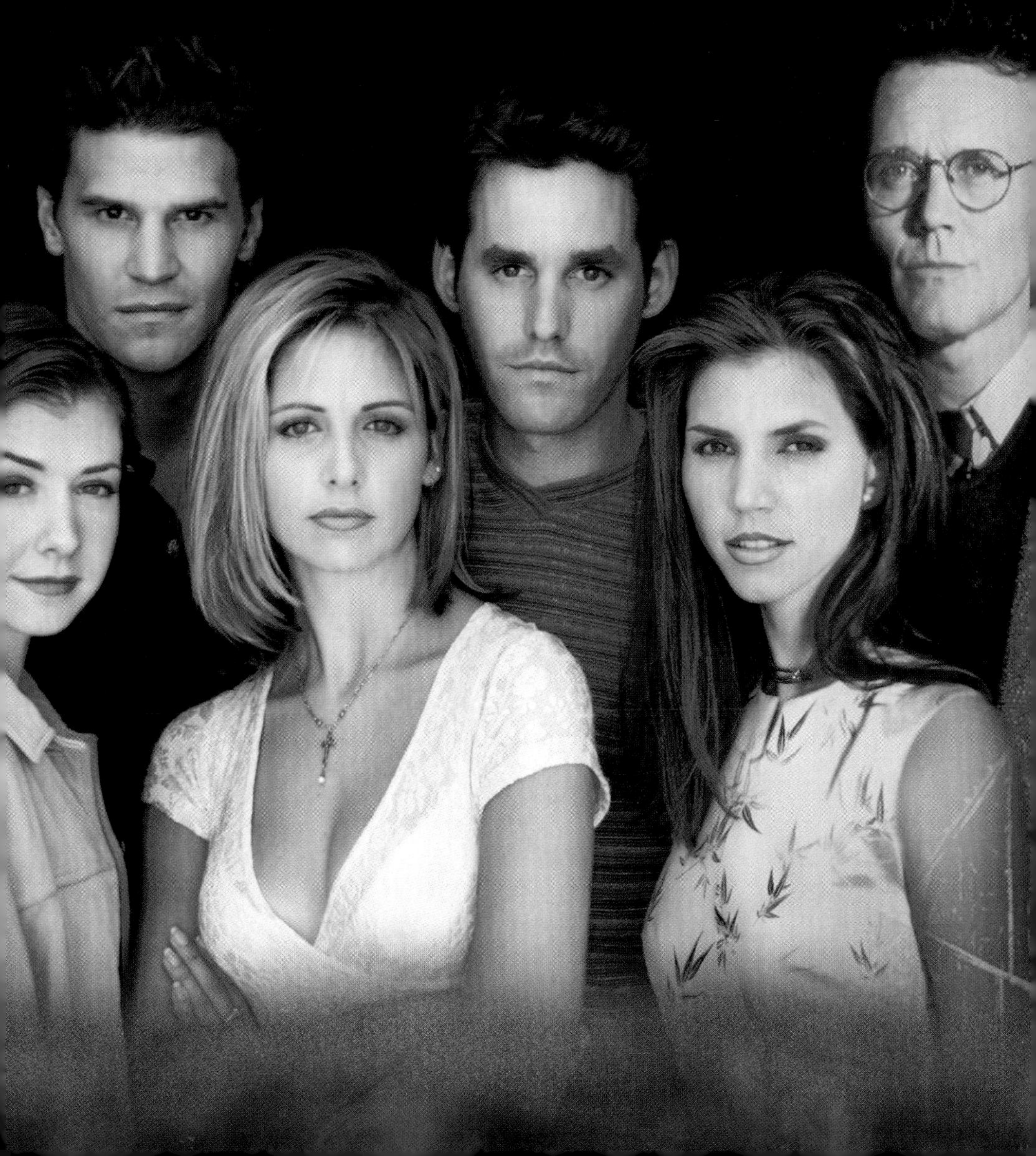

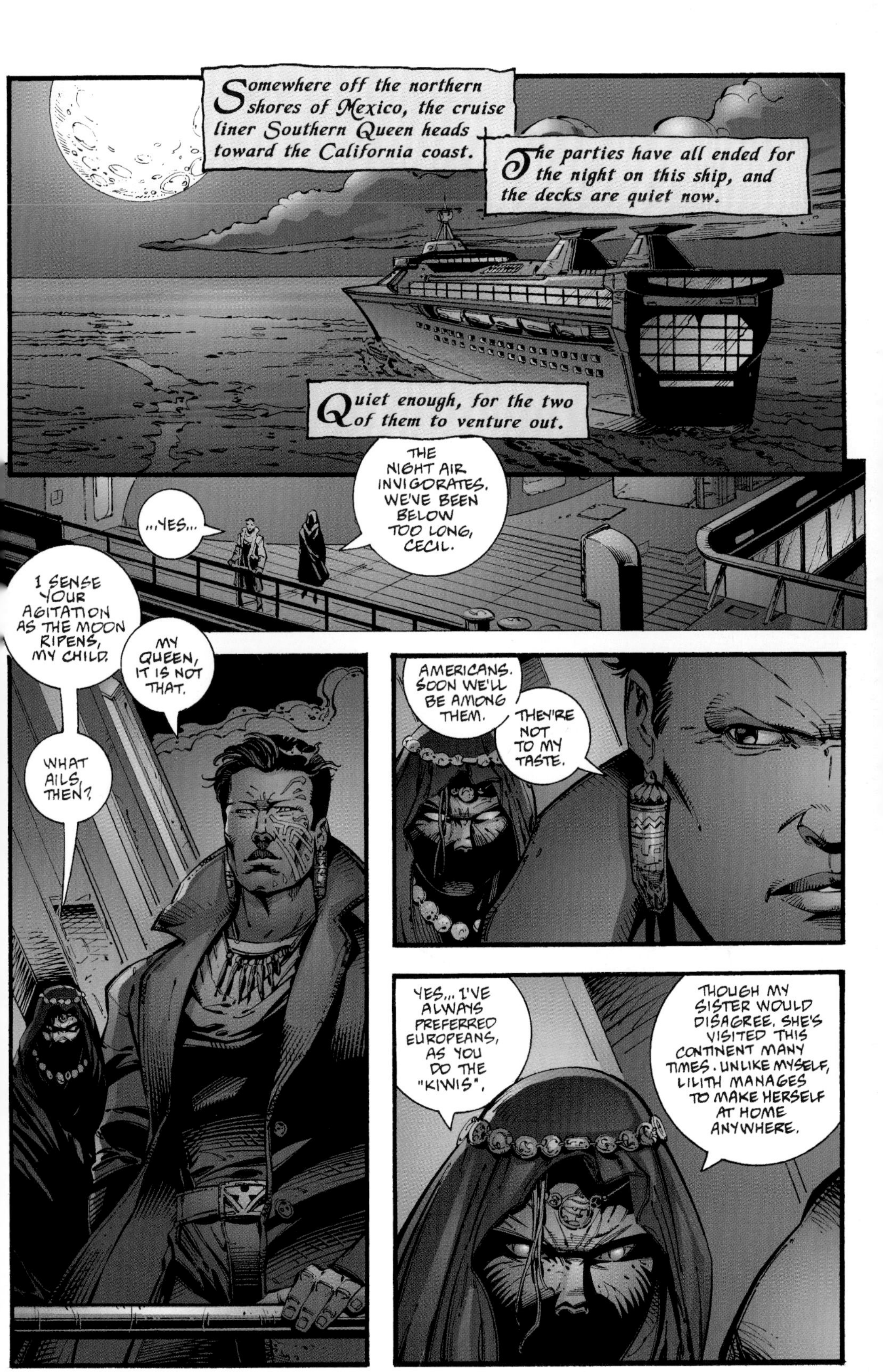
Somewhere off the northern shores of Mexico, the cruise liner Southern Queen heads toward the California coast.
The parties have all ended for the night on this ship, and the decks are quiet now.
Quiet enough, for the two of them to venture out.
THE NIGHT AIR INVIGORATES. WE'VE BEEN BELOW TOO LONG, CECIL.
...YES...
I SENSE YOUR AGITATION AS THE MOON RIPENS, MY CHILD.
MY QUEEN, IT IS NOT THAT.
WHAT AILS, THEN?
AMERICANS. SOON WE'LL BE AMONG THEM.
THEY'RE NOT TO MY TASTE.
YES... I'VE ALWAYS PREFERRED EUROPEANS, AS YOU DO THE "KIWIS".
THOUGH MY SISTER WOULD DISAGREE. SHE'S VISITED THIS CONTINENT MANY TIMES. UNLIKE MYSELF, LILITH MANAGES TO MAKE HERSELF AT HOME ANYWHERE.

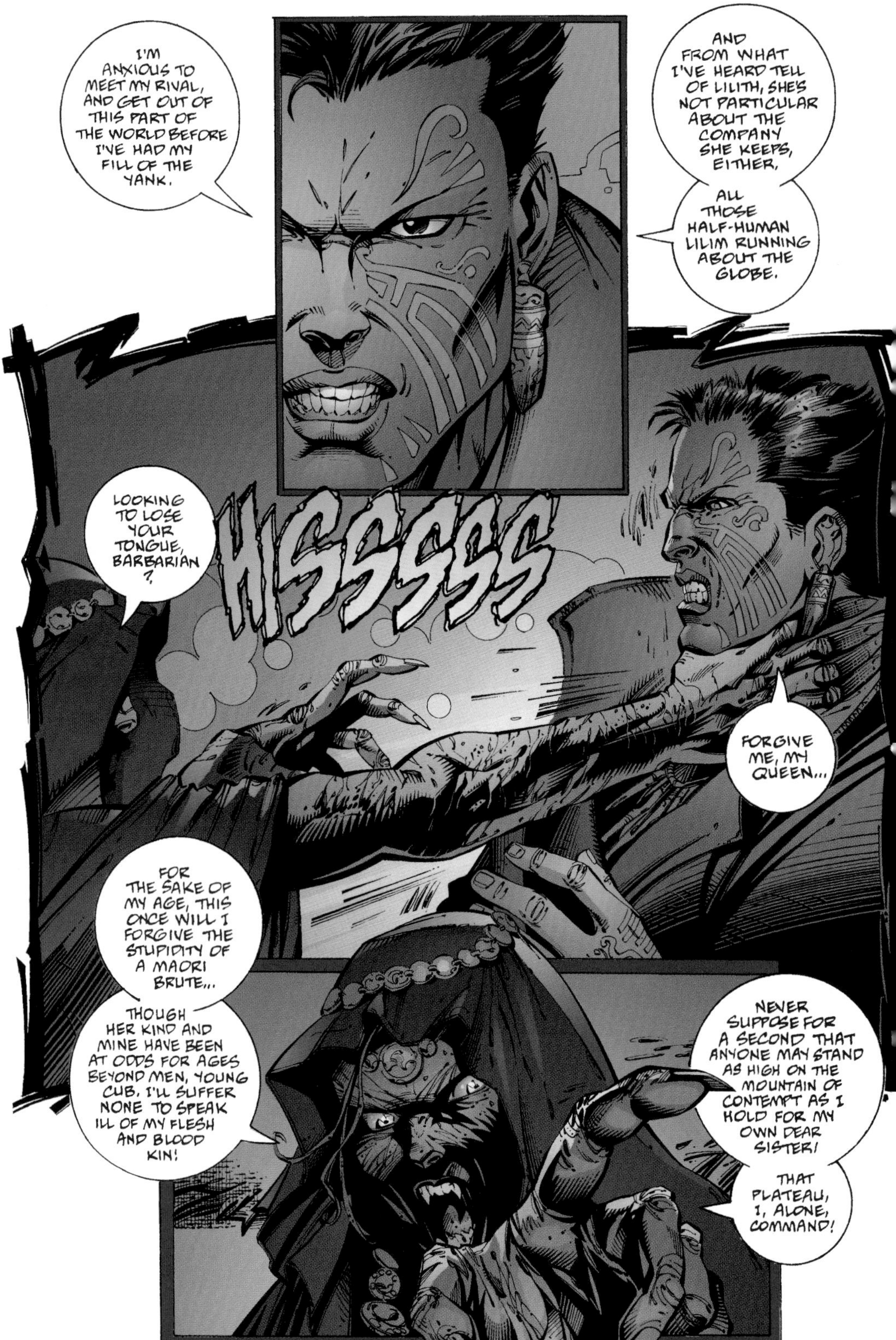
I'M ANXIOUS TO MEET MY RIVAL, AND GET OUT OF THIS PART OF THE WORLD BEFORE I'VE HAD MY FILL OF THE YANK.
AND FROM WHAT I'VE HEARD TELL OF LILITH, SHE'S NOT PARTICULAR ABOUT THE COMPANY SHE KEEPS, EITHER.
ALL THOSE HALF-HUMAN LILIM RUNNING ABOUT THE GLOBE.
LOOKING TO LOSE YOUR TONGUE, BARBARIAN?
HSSSSS
FORGIVE ME, MY QUEEN...
FOR THE SAKE OF MY AGE, THIS ONCE WILL I FORGIVE THE STUPIDITY OF A MAORI BRUTE...
THOUGH HER KIND AND MINE HAVE BEEN AT ODDS FOR AGES BEYOND MEN, YOUNG CUB, I'LL SUFFER NONE TO SPEAK ILL OF MY FLESH AND BLOOD KIN!
NEVER SUPPOSE FOR A SECOND THAT ANYONE MAY STAND AS HIGH ON THE MOUNTAIN OF CONTEMPT AS I HOLD FOR MY OWN DEAR SISTER!
THAT PLATEAU, I, ALONE, COMMAND!

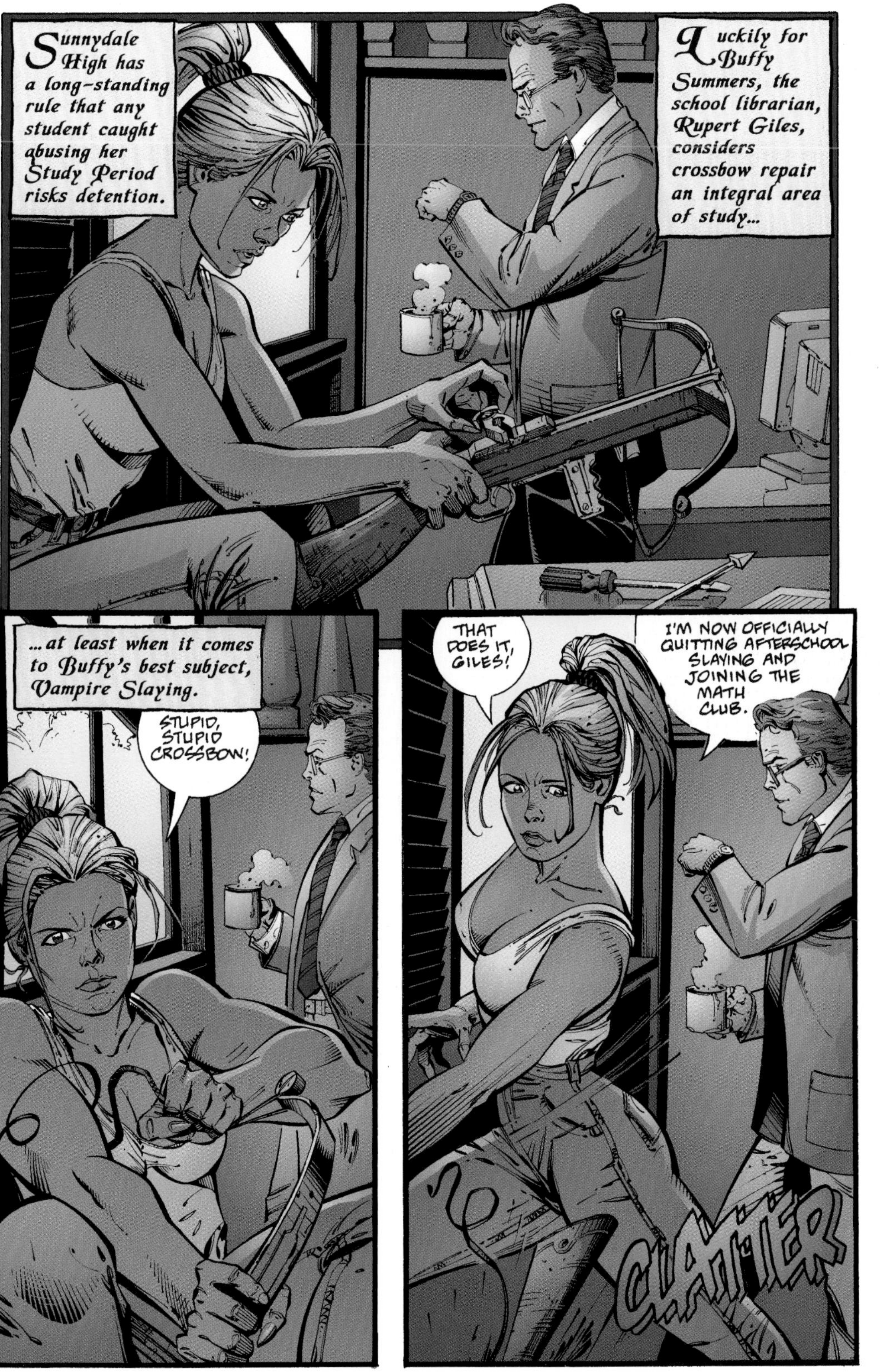
Sunnydale High has a long-standing rule that any student caught abusing her Study Period risks detention.
Luckily for Buffy Summers, the school librarian, Rupert Giles, considers crossbow repair an integral area of study...
...at least when it comes to Buffy's best subject, Vampire Slaying.
STUPID, STUPID CROSSBOW!
THAT DOES IT, GILES!
I'M NOW OFFICIALLY QUITTING AFTERSCHOOL SLAYING AND JOINING THE MATH CLUB.
CLATTER

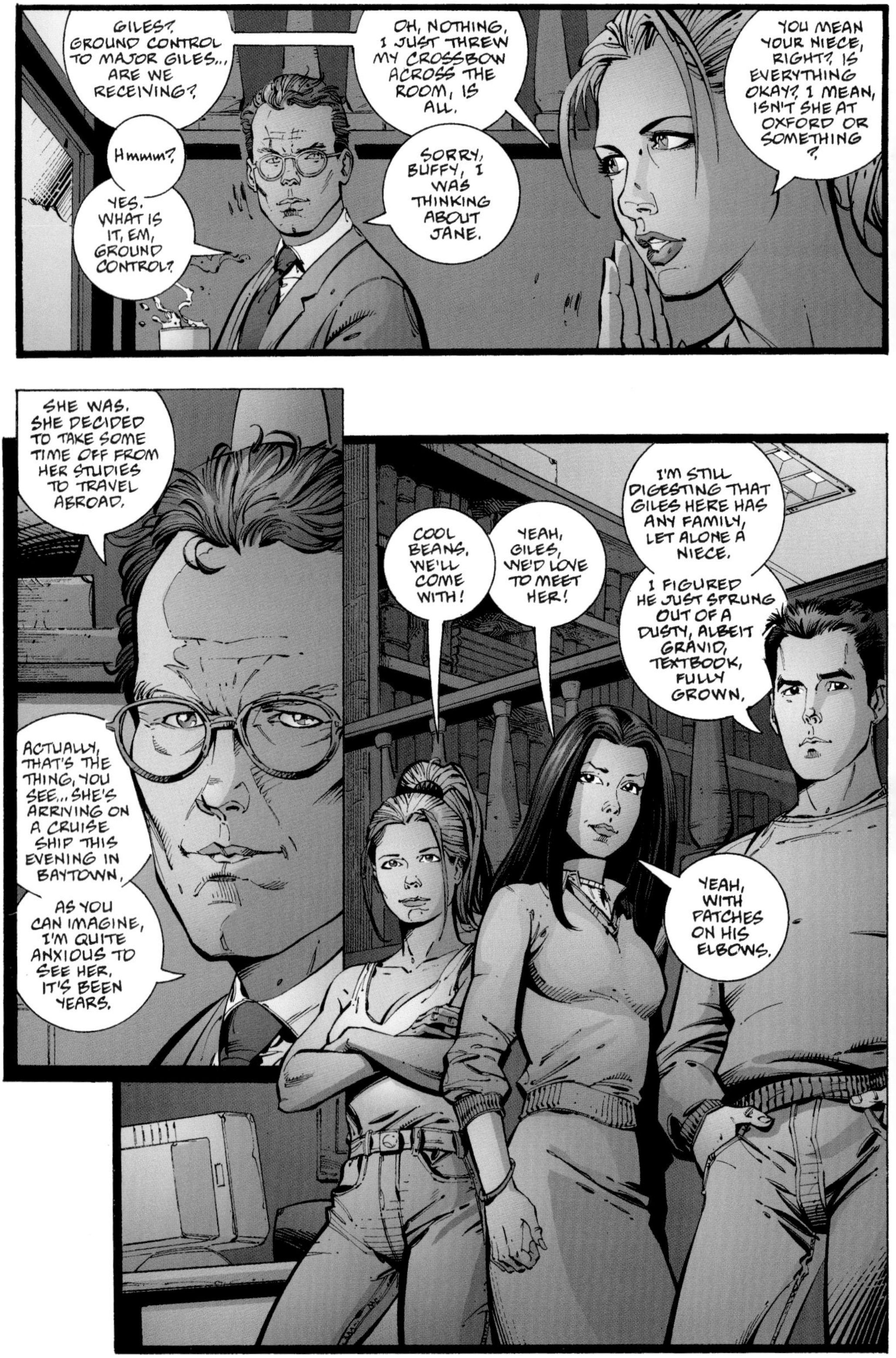

GILES? GROUND CONTROL TO MAJOR GILES... ARE WE RECEIVING?
Hmmm?
YES. WHAT IS IT, EM, GROUND CONTROL?
OH, NOTHING, I JUST THREW MY CROSSBOW ACROSS THE ROOM, IS ALL.
SORRY, BUFFY, I WAS THINKING ABOUT JANE.
YOU MEAN YOUR NIECE, RIGHT? IS EVERYTHING OKAY? I MEAN, ISN'T SHE AT OXFORD OR SOMETHING?
SHE WAS. SHE DECIDED TO TAKE SOME TIME OFF FROM HER STUDIES TO TRAVEL ABROAD.
I'M STILL DIGESTING THAT GILES HERE HAS ANY FAMILY, LET ALONE A NIECE.
I FIGURED HE JUST SPRUNG OUT OF A DUSTY, ALBEIT GRAVID, TEXTBOOK, FULLY GROWN.
YEAH, WITH PATCHES ON HIS ELBOWS.
ACTUALLY, THAT'S THE THING, YOU SEE... SHE'S ARRIVING ON A CRUISE SHIP THIS EVENING IN BAYTOWN.
AS YOU CAN IMAGINE, I'M QUITE ANXIOUS TO SEE HER. IT'S BEEN YEARS.
COOL BEANS, WE'LL COME WITH!
YEAH, GILES, WE'D LOVE TO MEET HER!

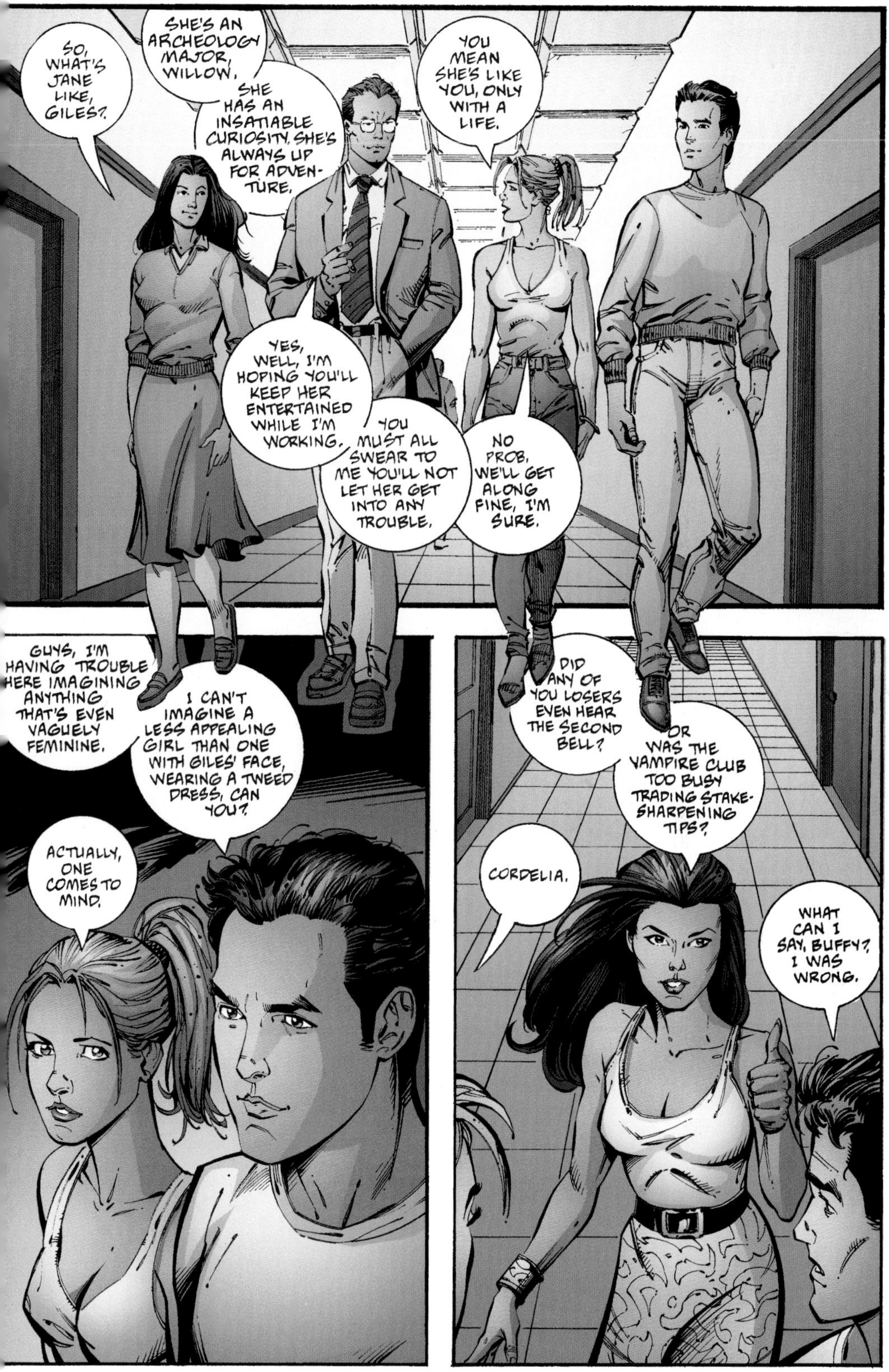
SO, WHAT'S JANE LIKE, GILES?
SHE'S AN ARCHEOLOGY MAJOR, WILLOW.
SHE HAS AN INSATIABLE CURIOSITY. SHE'S ALWAYS UP FOR ADVEN-TURE.
YOU MEAN SHE'S LIKE YOU, ONLY WITH A LIFE.
YES, WELL, I'M HOPING YOU'LL KEEP HER ENTERTAINED WHILE I'M WORKING.
YOU MUST ALL SWEAR TO ME YOU'LL NOT LET HER GET INTO ANY TROUBLE.
NO PROB. WE'LL GET ALONG FINE, I'M SURE.
GUYS, I'M HAVING TROUBLE HERE IMAGINING ANYTHING THAT'S EVEN VAGUELY FEMININE.
I CAN'T IMAGINE A LESS APPEALING GIRL THAN ONE WITH GILES' FACE, WEARING A TWEED DRESS, CAN YOU?
ACTUALLY, ONE COMES TO MIND.
DID ANY OF YOU LOSERS EVEN HEAR THE SECOND BELL?
OR WAS THE VAMPIRE CLUB TOO BUSY TRADING STAKE-SHARPENING TIPS?
CORDELIA.
WHAT CAN I SAY, BUFFY? I WAS WRONG.

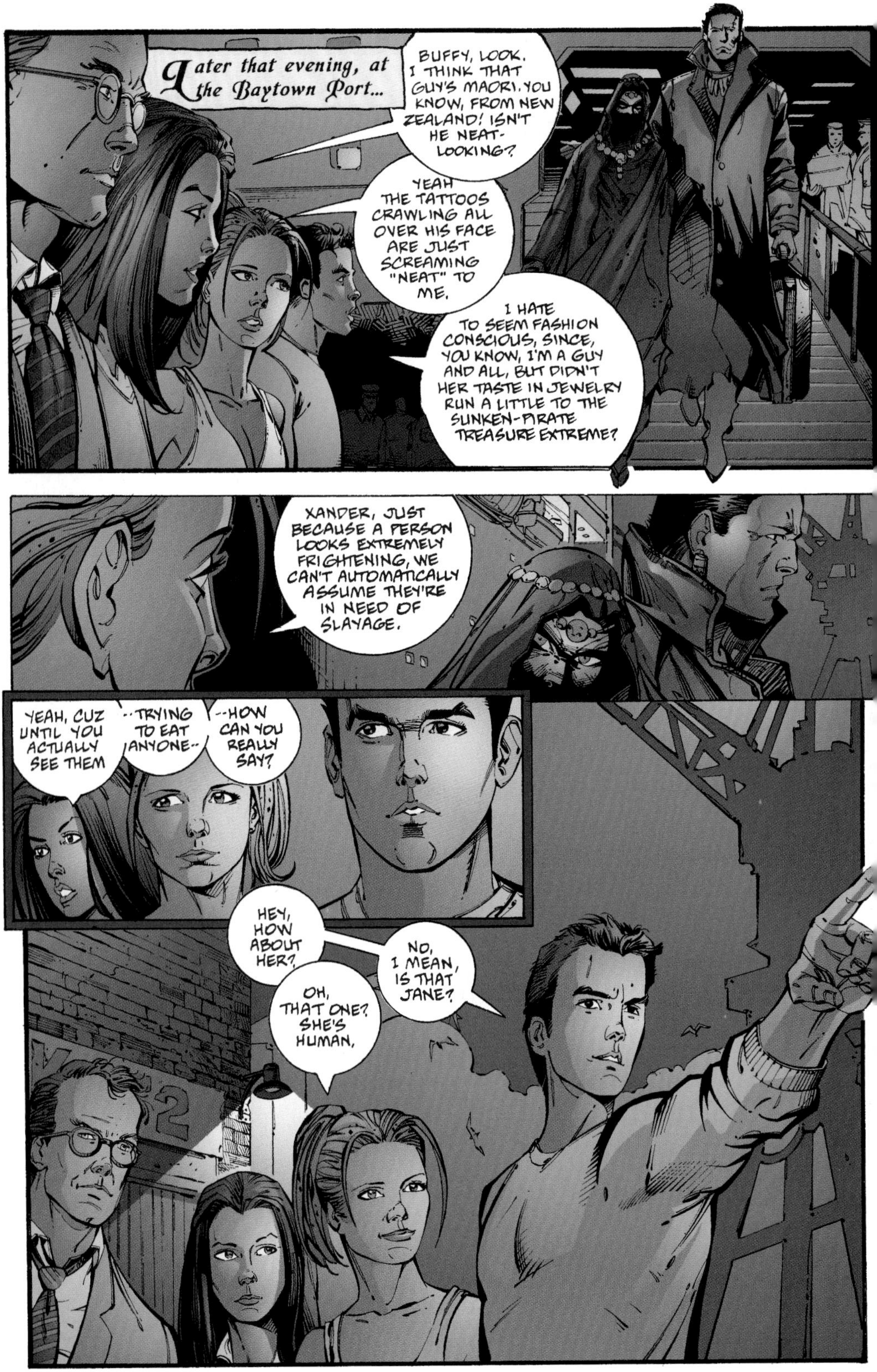
Later that evening, at the Baytown Port...
BUFFY, LOOK. I THINK THAT GUY'S MAORI. YOU KNOW, FROM NEW ZEALAND! ISN'T HE NEAT-LOOKING?
YEAH THE TATTOOS CRAWLING ALL OVER HIS FACE ARE JUST SCREAMING "NEAT" TO ME.
I HATE TO SEEM FASHION CONSCIOUS, SINCE, YOU KNOW, I'M A GUY AND ALL, BUT DIDN'T HER TASTE IN JEWELRY RUN A LITTLE TO THE SUNKEN-PIRATE TREASURE EXTREME?
XANDER, JUST BECAUSE A PERSON LOOKS EXTREMELY FRIGHTENING, WE CAN'T AUTOMATICALLY ASSUME THEY'RE IN NEED OF SLAYAGE.
YEAH, CUZ UNTIL YOU ACTUALLY SEE THEM
--TRYING TO EAT ANYONE--
--HOW CAN YOU REALLY SAY?
HEY, HOW ABOUT HER?
NO, I MEAN, IS THAT JANE?
OH, THAT ONE? SHE'S HUMAN.

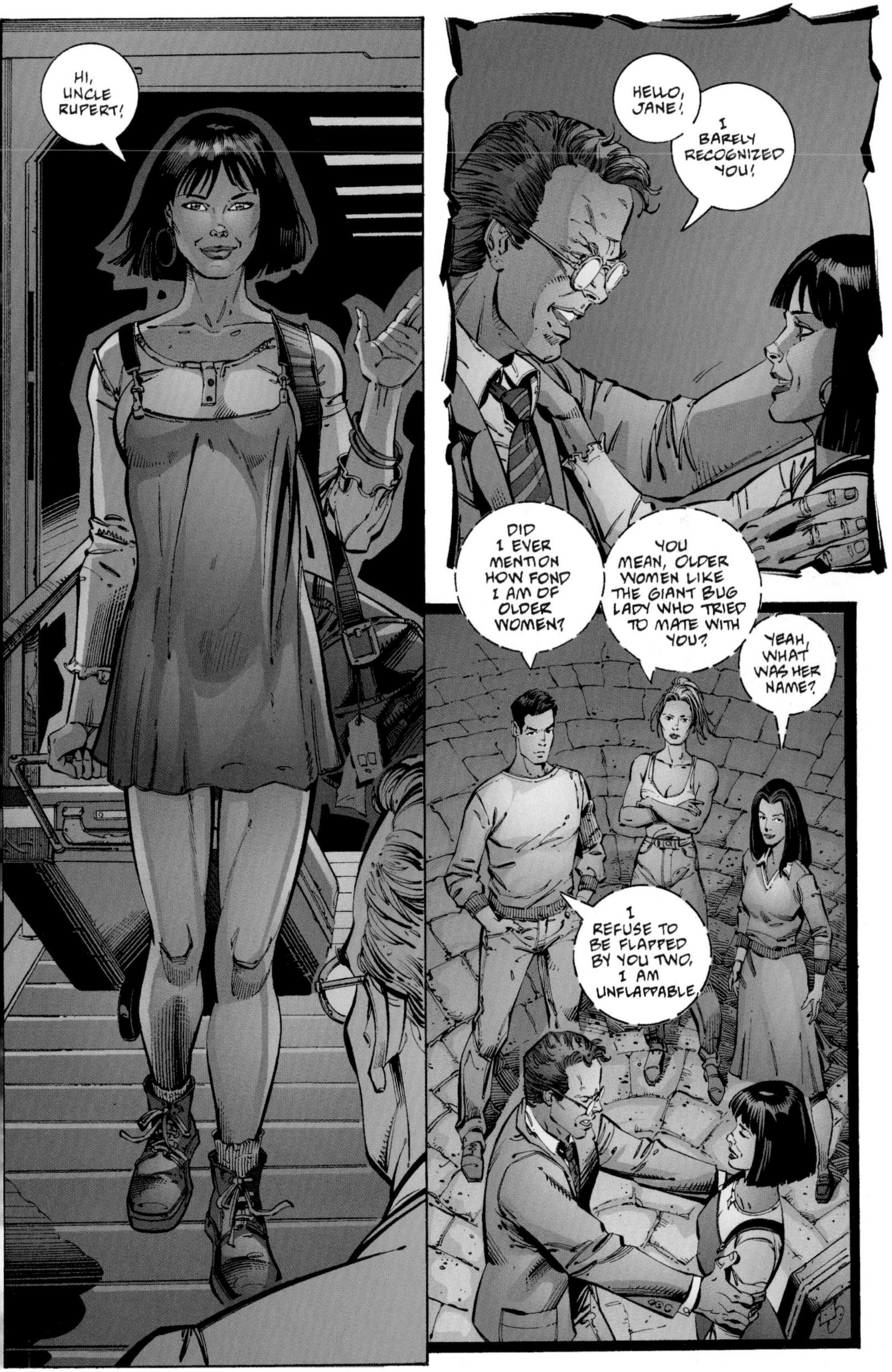
HI, UNCLE RUPERT!
HELLO, JANE!
I BARELY RECOGNIZED YOU!
DID I EVER MENTION HOW FOND I AM OF OLDER WOMEN?
YOU MEAN, OLDER WOMEN LIKE THE GIANT BUG LADY WHO TRIED TO MATE WITH YOU?
YEAH, WHAT WAS HER NAME?
I REFUSE TO BE FLAPPED BY YOU TWO, I AM UNFLAPPABLE.

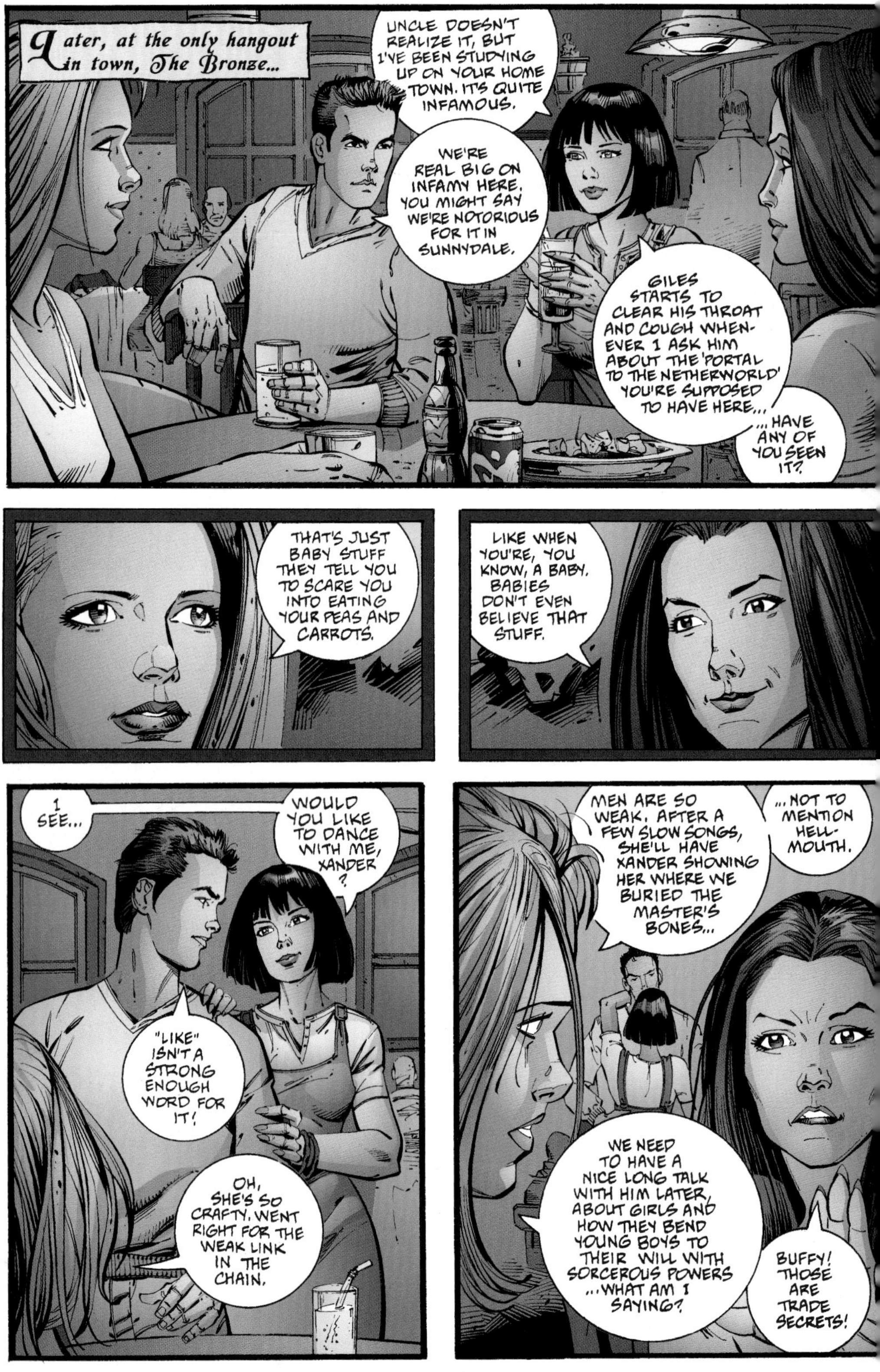
Later, at the only hangout in town, The Bronze...
UNCLE DOESN'T REALIZE IT, BUT I'VE BEEN STUDYING UP ON YOUR HOME TOWN. IT'S QUITE INFAMOUS.
WE'RE REAL BIG ON INFAMY HERE. YOU MIGHT SAY WE'RE NOTORIOUS FOR IT IN SUNNYDALE.
GILES STARTS TO CLEAR HIS THROAT AND COUGH WHEN-EVER I ASK HIM ABOUT THE 'PORTAL TO THE NETHERWORLD' YOU'RE SUPPOSED TO HAVE HERE...
...HAVE ANY OF YOU SEEN IT?
THAT'S JUST BABY STUFF THEY TELL YOU TO SCARE YOU INTO EATING YOUR PEAS AND CARROTS.
LIKE WHEN YOU'RE, YOU KNOW, A BABY. BABIES DON'T EVEN BELIEVE THAT STUFF.
I SEE...
WOULD YOU LIKE TO DANCE WITH ME, XANDER?
"LIKE" ISN'T A STRONG ENOUGH WORD FOR IT!
OH, SHE'S SO CRAFTY. WENT RIGHT FOR THE WEAK LINK IN THE CHAIN.
MEN ARE SO WEAK. AFTER A FEW SLOW SONGS, SHE'LL HAVE XANDER SHOWING HER WHERE WE BURIED THE MASTER'S BONES...
...NOT TO MENTION HELL-MOUTH.
WE NEED TO HAVE A NICE LONG TALK WITH HIM LATER, ABOUT GIRLS AND HOW THEY BEND YOUNG BOYS TO THEIR WILL WITH SORCEROUS POWERS ...WHAT AM I SAYING?
BUFFY! THOSE ARE TRADE SECRETS!

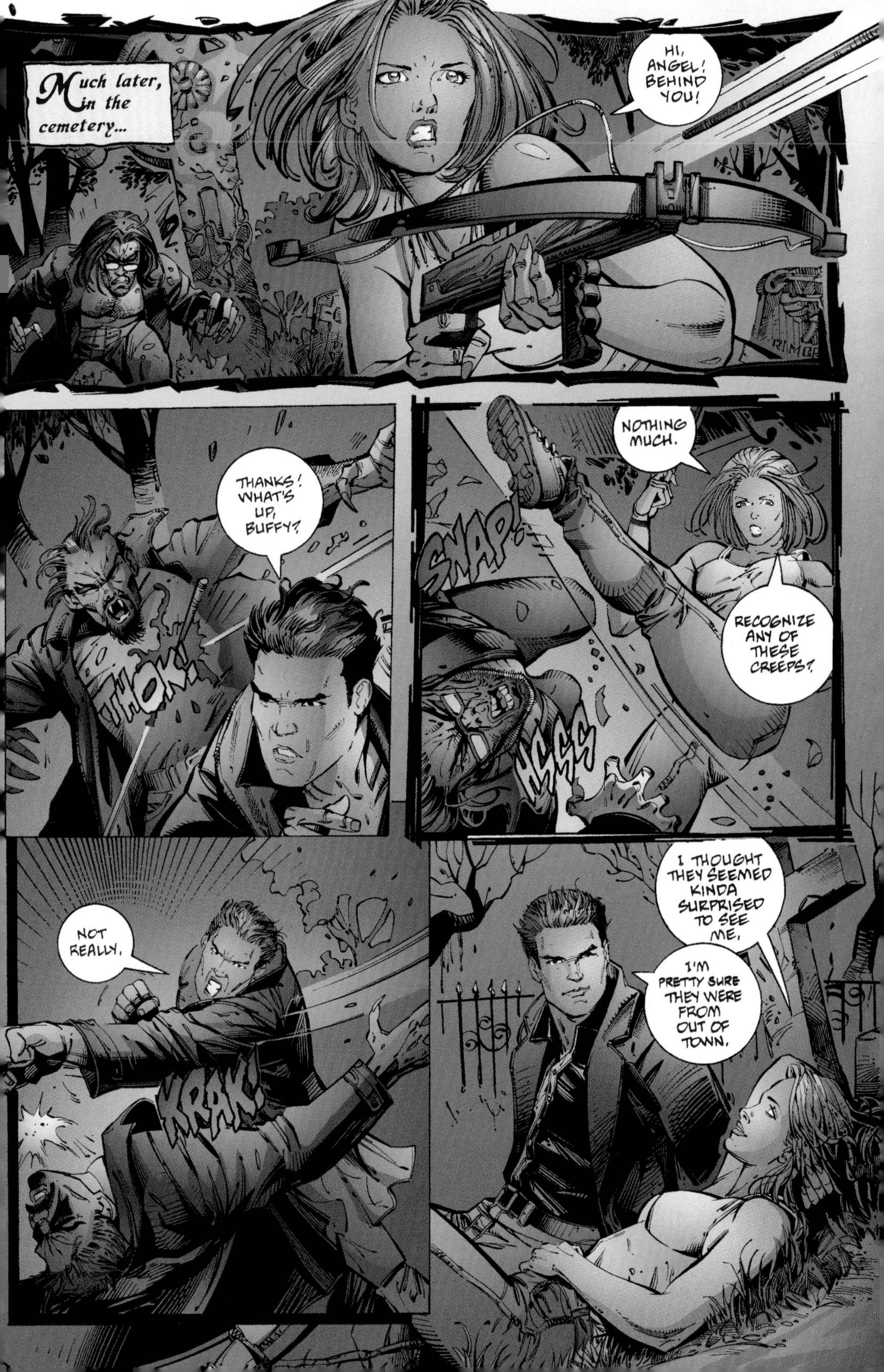
Much later, in the cemetery...
HI, ANGEL! BEHIND YOU!
THANKS! WHAT'S UP, BUFFY?
THOK!
NOTHING MUCH.
SNAP!
RECOGNIZE ANY OF THESE CREEPS?
HSSS
NOT REALLY.
KRAK!
I THOUGHT THEY SEEMED KINDA SURPRISED TO SEE ME.
I'M PRETTY SURE THEY WERE FROM OUT OF TOWN.

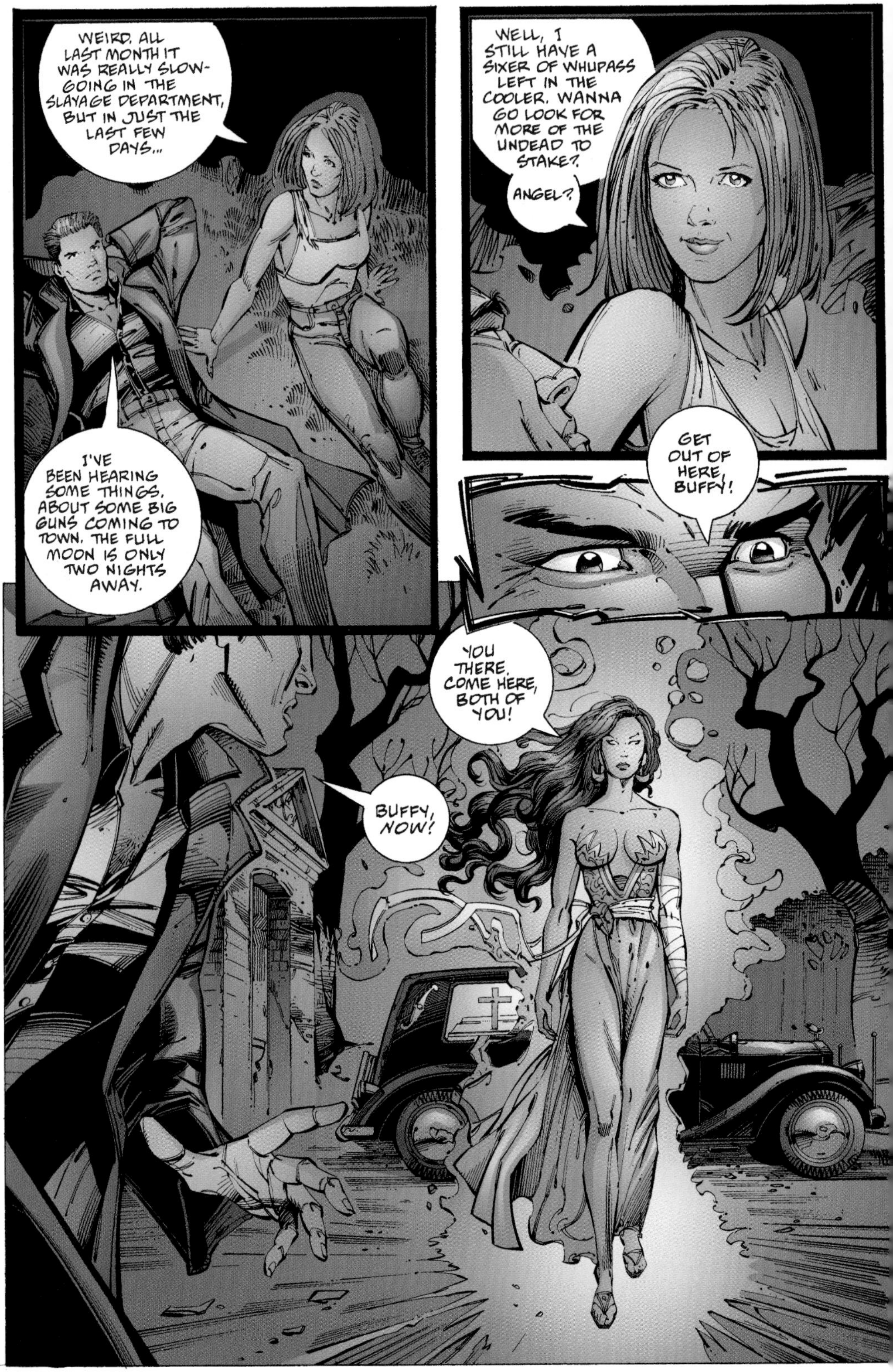
WEIRD. ALL LAST MONTH IT WAS REALLY SLOW-GOING IN THE SLAYAGE DEPARTMENT, BUT IN JUST THE LAST FEW DAYS...
I'VE BEEN HEARING SOME THINGS. ABOUT SOME BIG GUNS COMING TO TOWN. THE FULL MOON IS ONLY TWO NIGHTS AWAY.
WELL, I STILL HAVE A SIXER OF WHUPASS LEFT IN THE COOLER. WANNA GO LOOK FOR MORE OF THE UNDEAD TO STAKE?
ANGEL?
GET OUT OF HERE, BUFFY!
YOU THERE. COME HERE, BOTH OF YOU!
BUFFY, NOW!

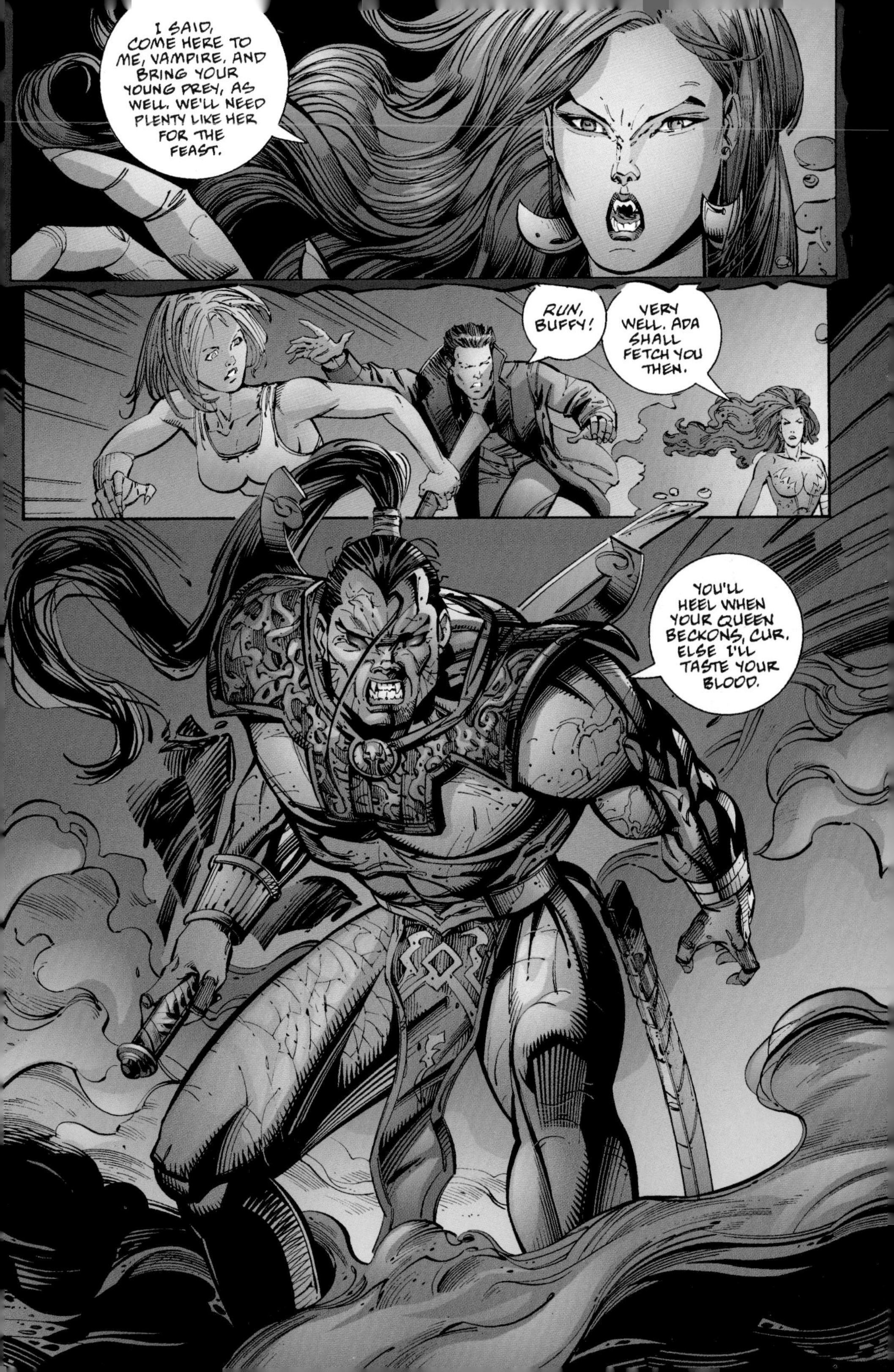
I SAID, COME HERE TO ME, VAMPIRE, AND BRING YOUR YOUNG PREY, AS WELL. WE'LL NEED PLENTY LIKE HER FOR THE FEAST.
RUN, BUFFY!
VERY WELL. ADA SHALL FETCH YOU THEN.
YOU'LL HEEL WHEN YOUR QUEEN BECKONS, CUR, ELSE I'LL TASTE YOUR BLOOD.

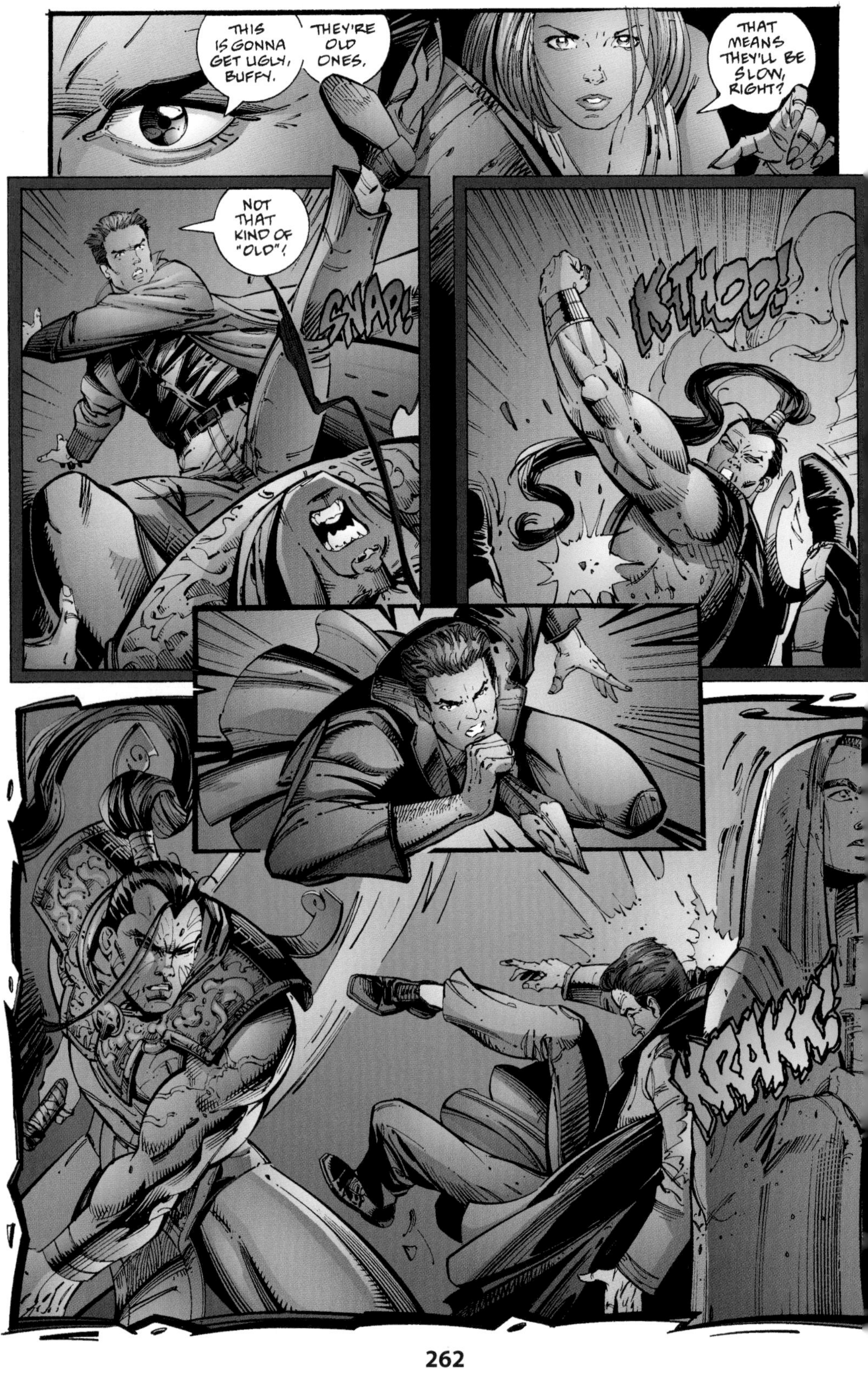
THIS IS GONNA GET UGLY, BUFFY.
THEY'RE OLD ONES.
THAT MEANS THEY'LL BE SLOW, RIGHT?
NOT THAT KIND OF "OLD"!
SNAP!
K-THOO!
KRAKK!

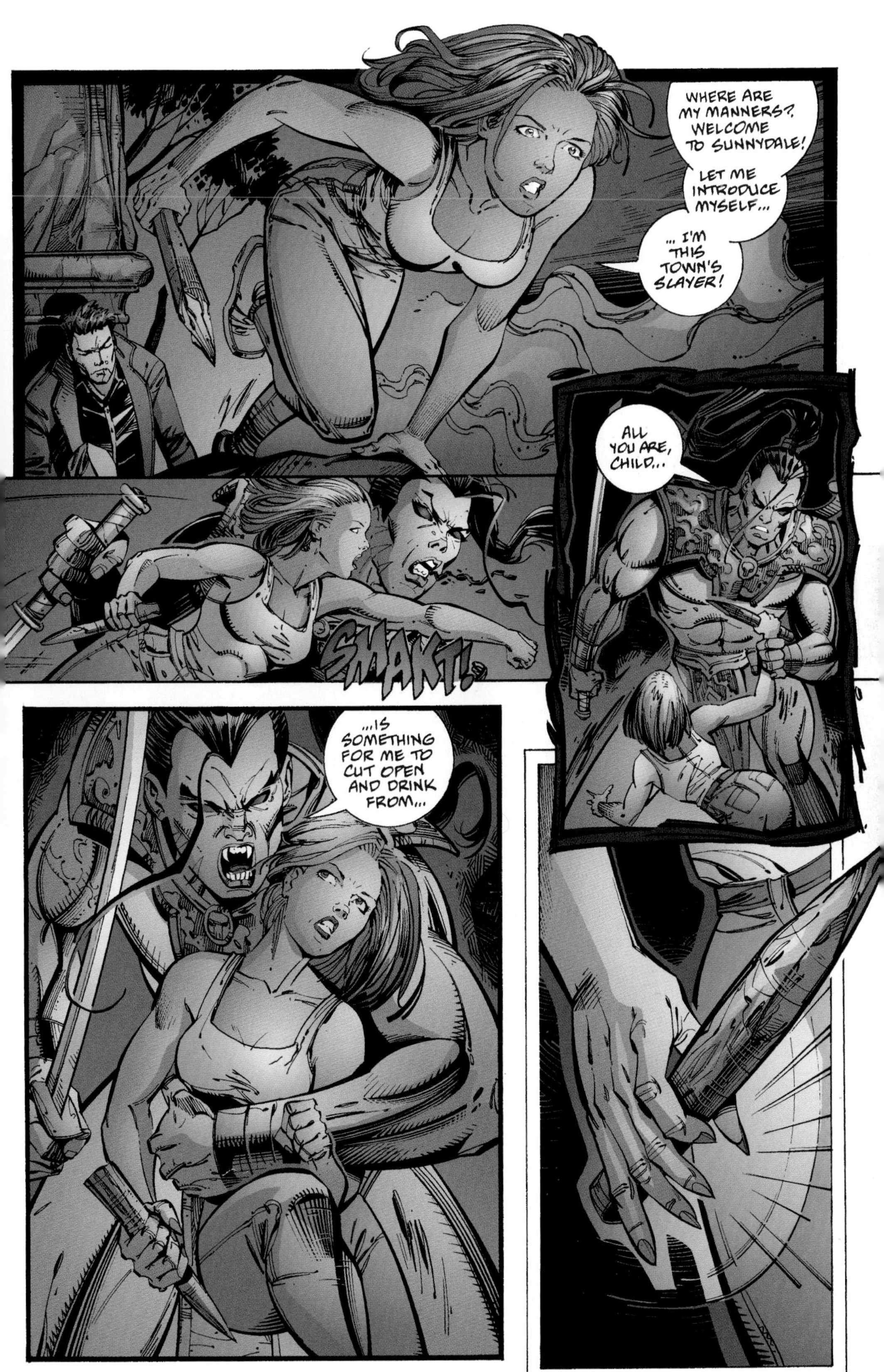
WHERE ARE MY MANNERS? WELCOME TO SUNNYDALE!
LET ME INTRODUCE MYSELF...
... I'M THIS TOWN'S SLAYER!
ALL YOU ARE, CHILD...
SMAKT!
...IS SOMETHING FOR ME TO CUT OPEN AND DRINK FROM...

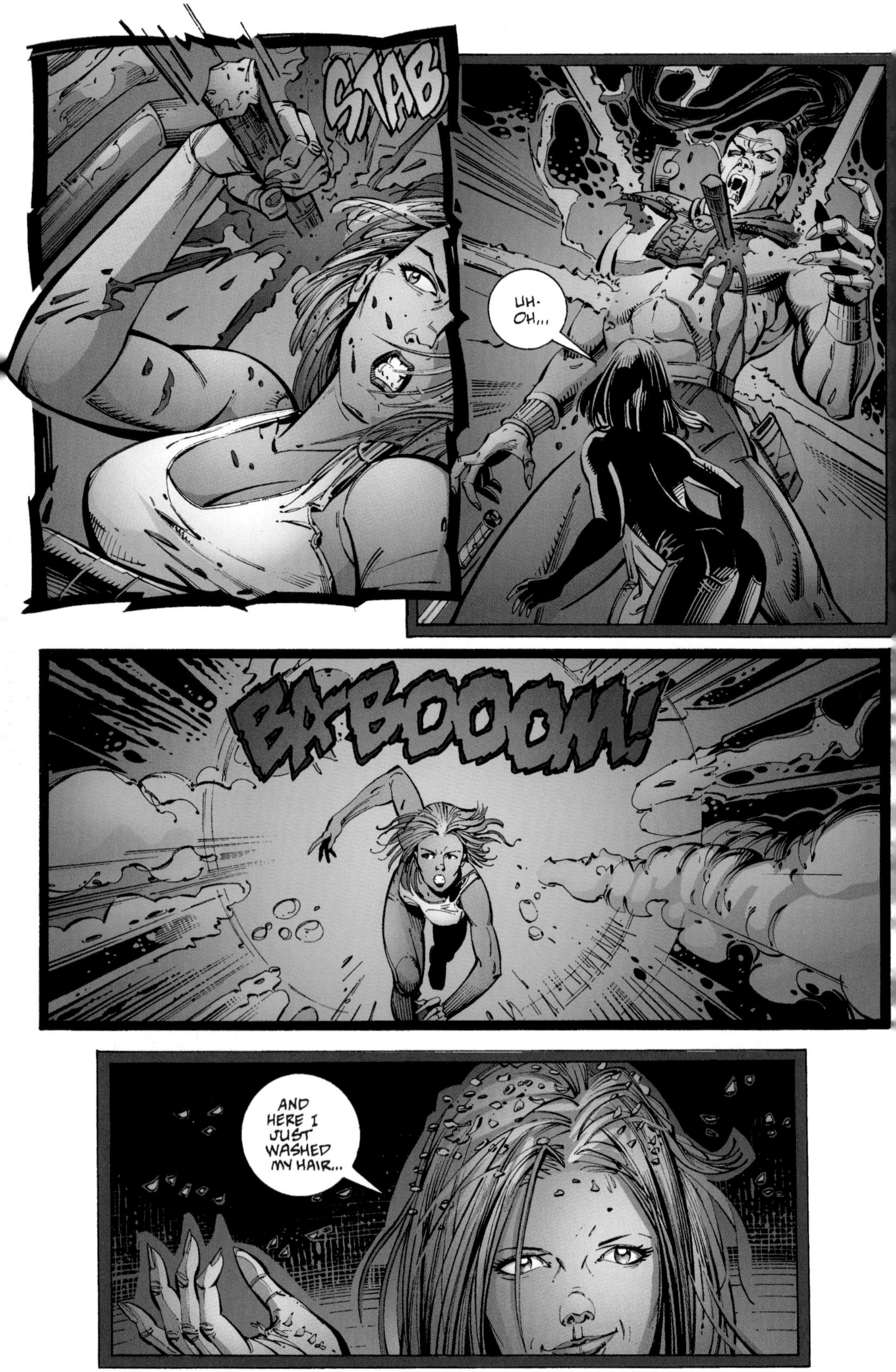
STAB!
UH-OH...
BA-BOOOM!
AND HERE I JUST WASHED MY HAIR...

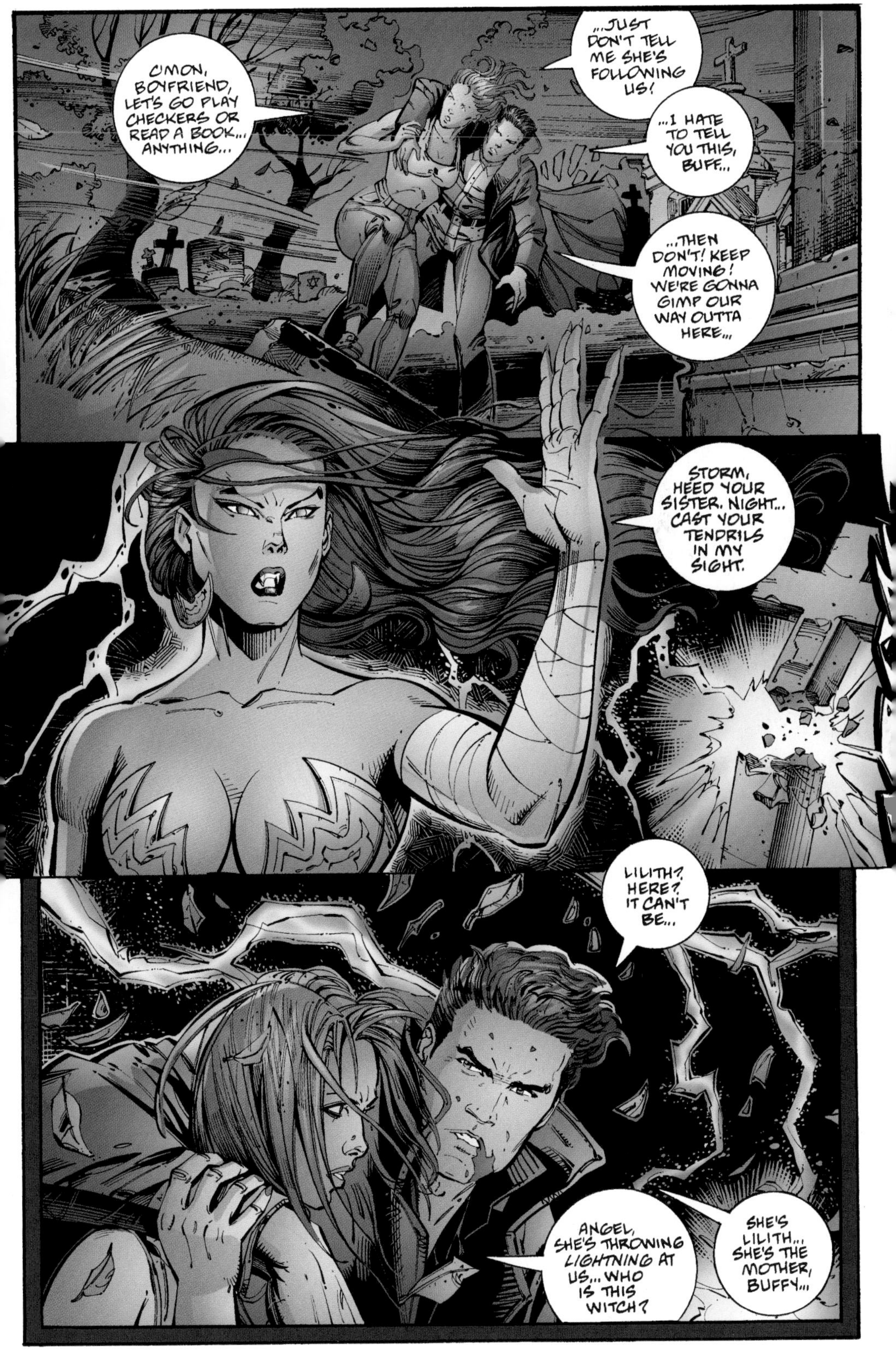
C'MON, BOYFRIEND, LET'S GO PLAY CHECKERS OR READ A BOOK... ANYTHING...
...JUST DON'T TELL ME SHE'S FOLLOWING US!
...I HATE TO TELL YOU THIS, BUFF...
...THEN DON'T! KEEP MOVING! WE'RE GONNA GIMP OUR WAY OUTTA HERE...
STORM, HEED YOUR SISTER, NIGHT... CAST YOUR TENDRILS IN MY SIGHT.
LILITH? HERE? IT CAN'T BE...
ANGEL, SHE'S THROWING LIGHTNING AT US... WHO IS THIS WITCH?
SHE'S LILITH... SHE'S THE MOTHER, BUFFY...

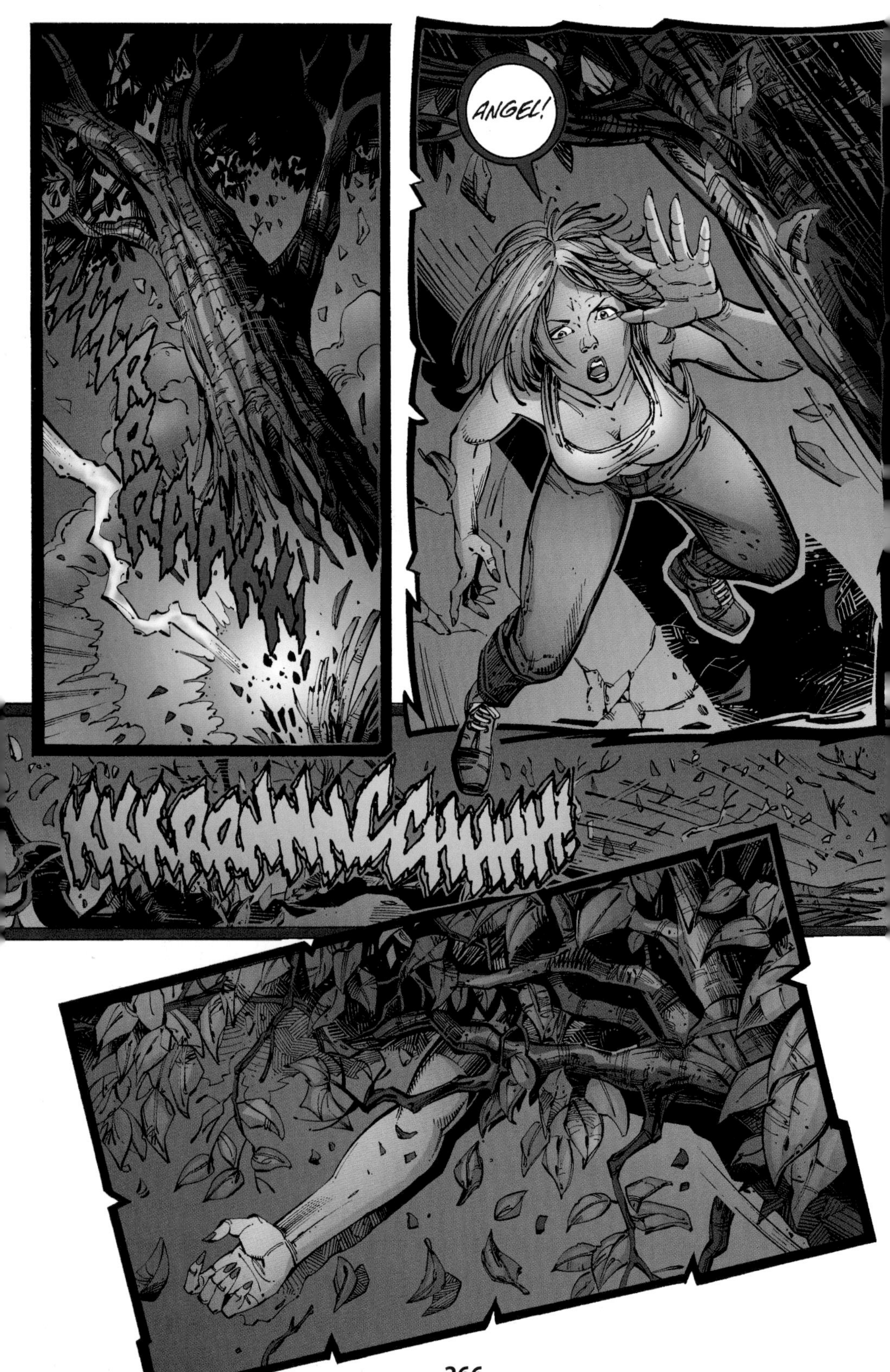
ANGEL!

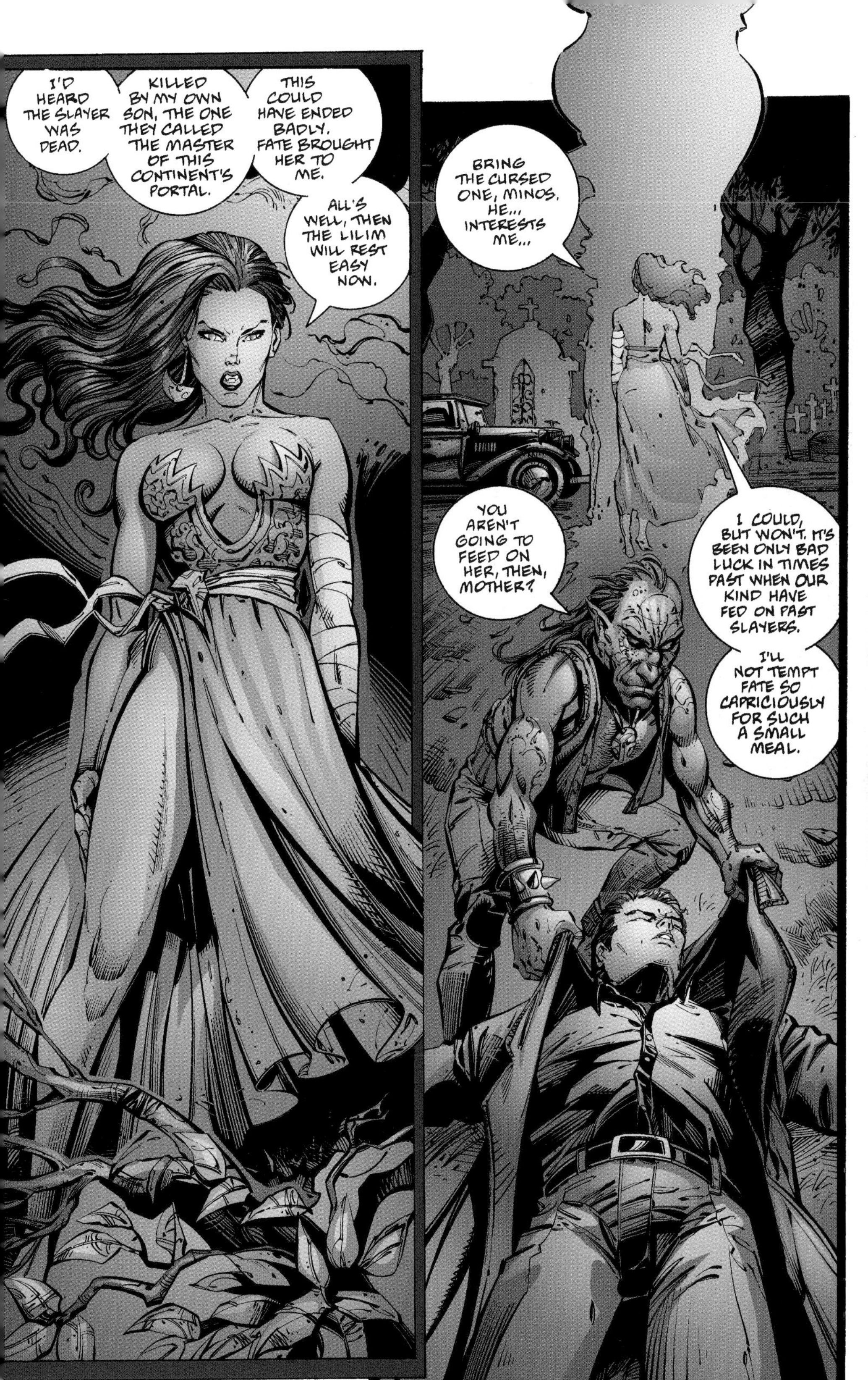
I'D HEARD THE SLAYER WAS DEAD.
KILLED BY MY OWN SON, THE ONE THEY CALLED THE MASTER OF THIS CONTINENT'S PORTAL.
THIS COULD HAVE ENDED BADLY. FATE BROUGHT HER TO ME.
ALL'S WELL, THEN THE LILIM WILL REST EASY NOW.
BRING THE CURSED ONE, MINOS. HE... INTERESTS ME...
YOU AREN'T GOING TO FEED ON HER, THEN, MOTHER?
I COULD, BUT WON'T. IT'S BEEN ONLY BAD LUCK IN TIMES PAST WHEN OUR KIND HAVE FED ON PAST SLAYERS.
I'LL NOT TEMPT FATE SO CAPRICIOUSLY FOR SUCH A SMALL MEAL.

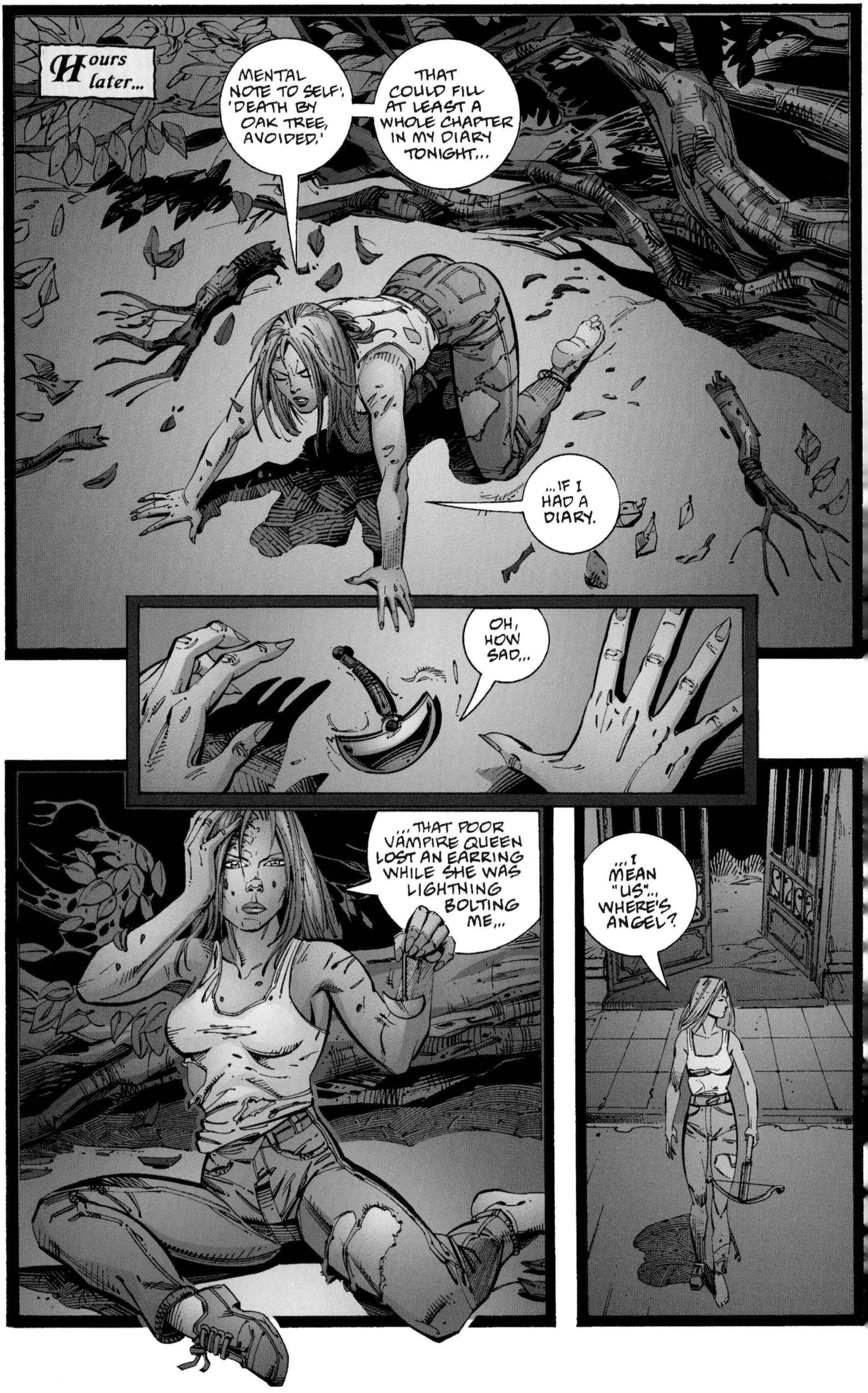
Hours later...
MENTAL NOTE TO SELF: 'DEATH BY OAK TREE, AVOIDED.'
THAT COULD FILL AT LEAST A WHOLE CHAPTER IN MY DIARY TONIGHT...
...IF I HAD A DIARY.
OH, HOW SAD...
...THAT POOR VAMPIRE QUEEN LOST AN EARRING WHILE SHE WAS LIGHTNING BOLTING ME...
...I MEAN "US"... WHERE'S ANGEL?

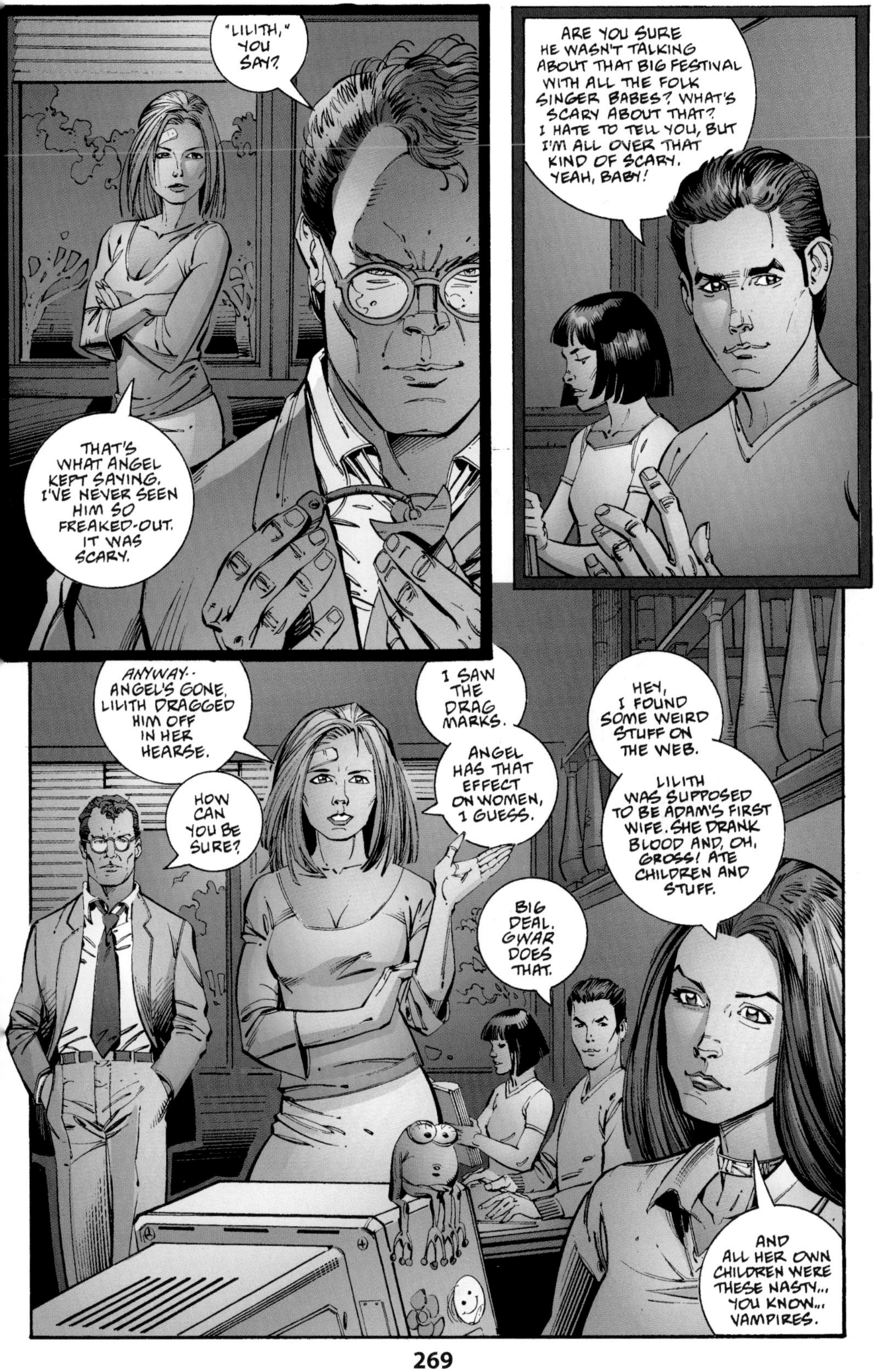

"LILITH," YOU SAY?
THAT'S WHAT ANGEL KEPT SAYING. I'VE NEVER SEEN HIM SO FREAKED-OUT. IT WAS SCARY.
ARE YOU SURE HE WASN'T TALKING ABOUT THAT BIG FESTIVAL WITH ALL THE FOLK SINGER BABES? WHAT'S SCARY ABOUT THAT? I HATE TO TELL YOU, BUT I'M ALL OVER THAT KIND OF SCARY. YEAH, BABY!
ANYWAY.. ANGEL'S GONE. LILITH DRAGGED HIM OFF IN HER HEARSE.
HOW CAN YOU BE SURE?
I SAW THE DRAG MARKS.
ANGEL HAS THAT EFFECT ON WOMEN, I GUESS.
HEY, I FOUND SOME WEIRD STUFF ON THE WEB.
LILITH WAS SUPPOSED TO BE ADAM'S FIRST WIFE. SHE DRANK BLOOD AND, OH, GROSS! ATE CHILDREN AND STUFF.
BIG DEAL. GWAR DOES THAT.
AND ALL HER OWN CHILDREN WERE THESE NASTY... YOU KNOW... VAMPIRES.

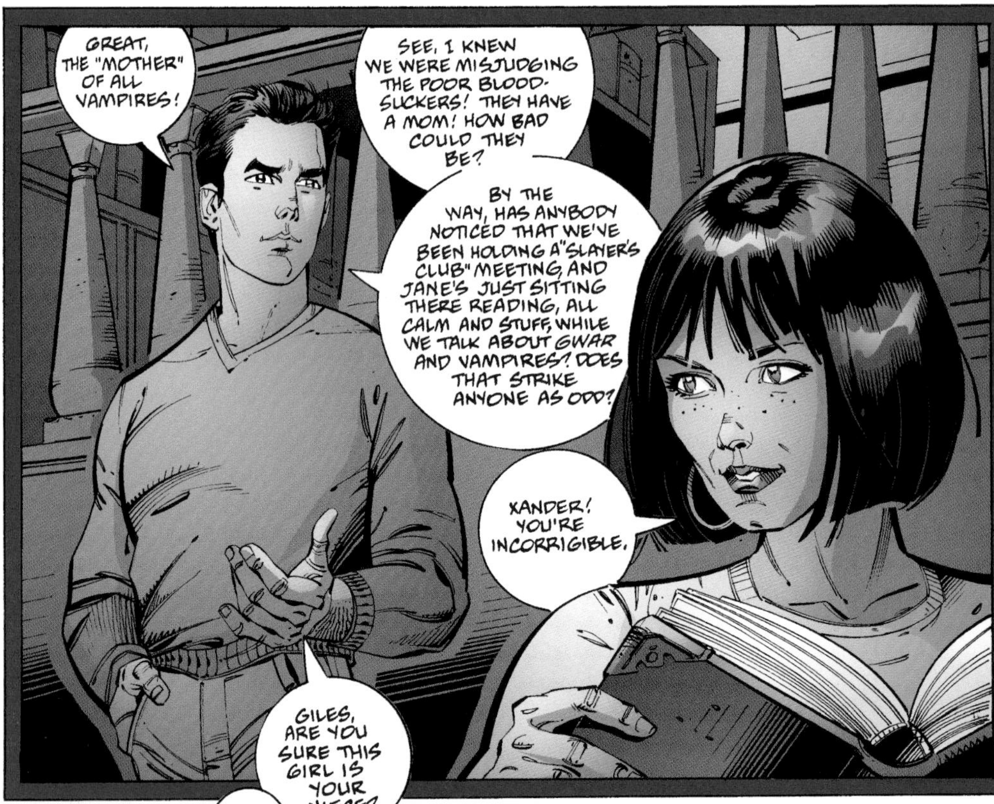
GREAT, THE "MOTHER" OF ALL VAMPIRES!
SEE, I KNEW WE WERE MISJUDGING THE POOR BLOOD-SUCKERS! THEY HAVE A MOM! HOW BAD COULD THEY BE?
BY THE WAY, HAS ANYBODY NOTICED THAT WE'VE BEEN HOLDING A "SLAYER'S CLUB" MEETING, AND JANE'S JUST SITTING THERE READING, ALL CALM AND STUFF, WHILE WE TALK ABOUT GWAR AND VAMPIRES? DOES THAT STRIKE ANYONE AS ODD?
XANDER! YOU'RE INCORRIGIBLE.
GILES, ARE YOU SURE THIS GIRL IS YOUR NIECE?

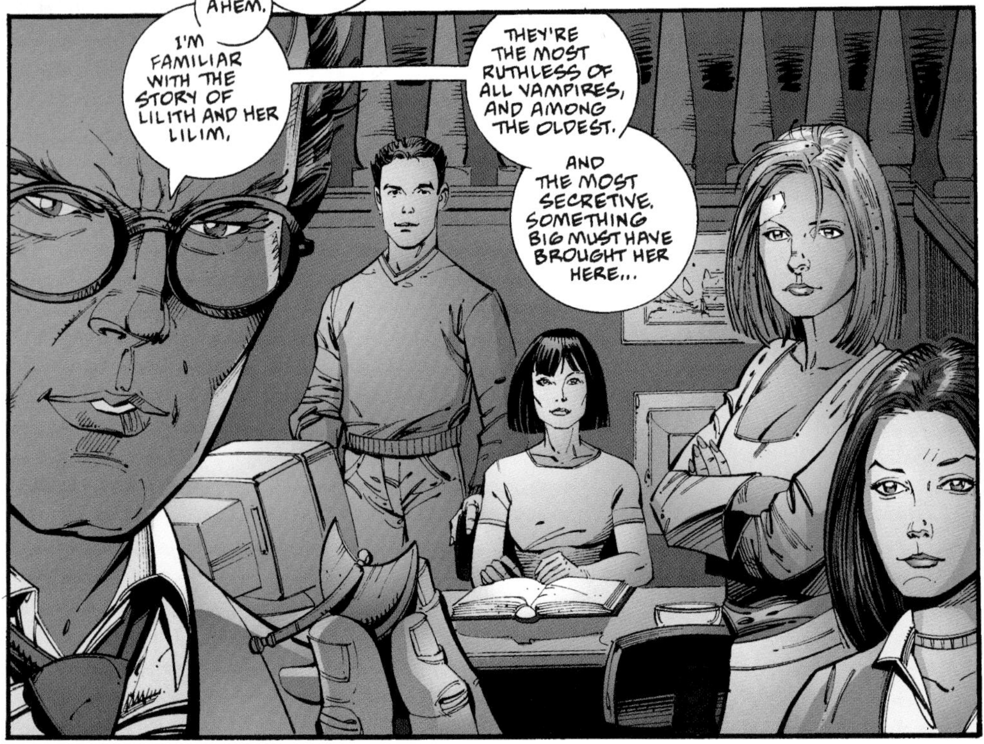
AHEM.
I'M FAMILIAR WITH THE STORY OF LILITH AND HER LILIM,
THEY'RE THE MOST RUTHLESS OF ALL VAMPIRES, AND AMONG THE OLDEST.
AND THE MOST SECRETIVE. SOMETHING BIG MUST HAVE BROUGHT HER HERE...

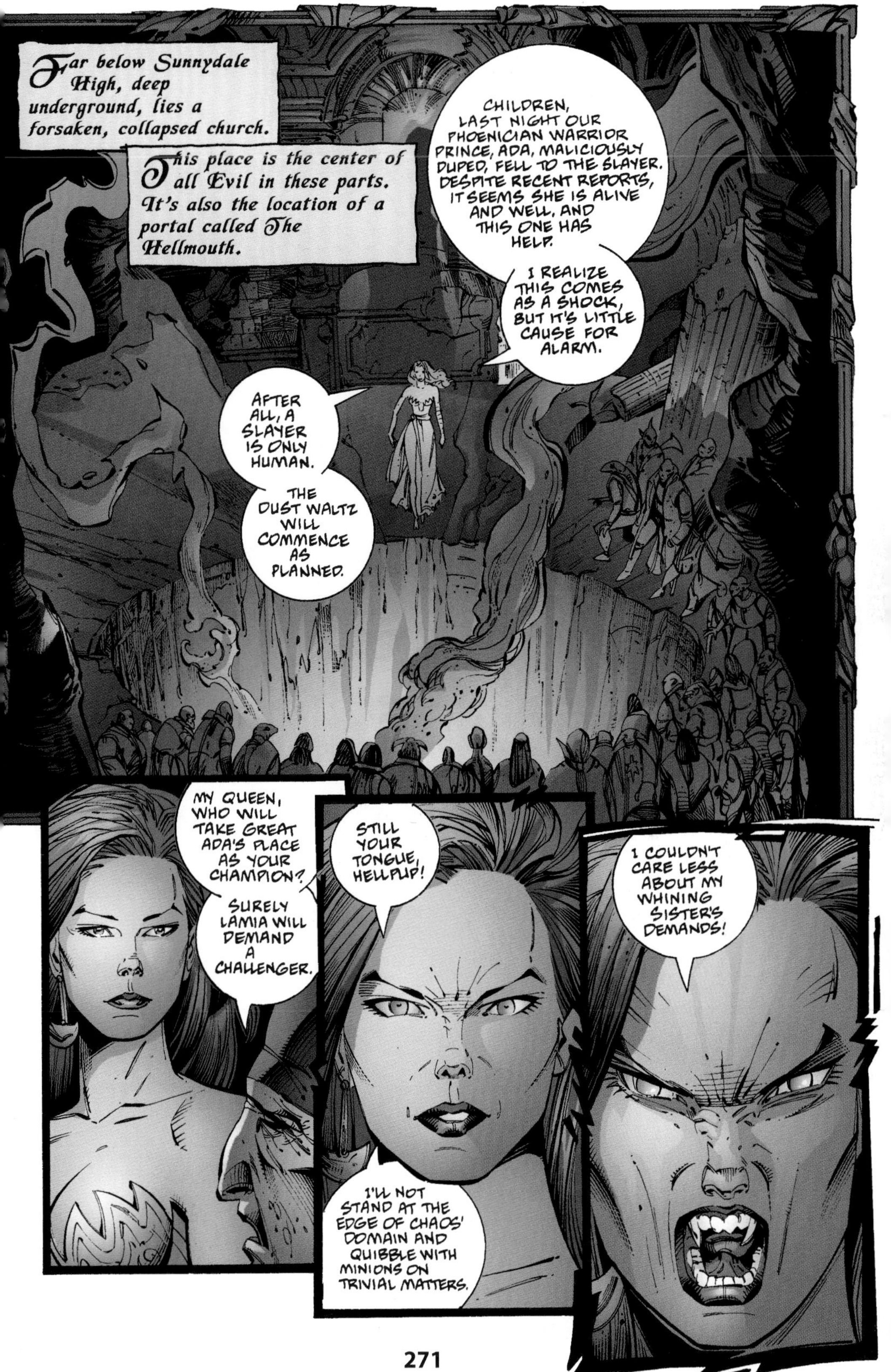
Far below Sunnydale High, deep underground, lies a forsaken, collapsed church.
This place is the center of all Evil in these parts. It's also the location of a portal called The Hellmouth.
CHILDREN, LAST NIGHT OUR PHOENICIAN WARRIOR PRINCE, ADA, MALICIOUSLY DUPED, FELL TO THE SLAYER. DESPITE RECENT REPORTS, IT SEEMS SHE IS ALIVE AND WELL, AND THIS ONE HAS HELP.
I REALIZE THIS COMES AS A SHOCK, BUT IT'S LITTLE CAUSE FOR ALARM.
AFTER ALL, A SLAYER IS ONLY HUMAN.
THE DUST WALTZ WILL COMMENCE AS PLANNED.
MY QUEEN, WHO WILL TAKE GREAT ADA'S PLACE AS YOUR CHAMPION?
SURELY LAMIA WILL DEMAND A CHALLENGER.
STILL YOUR TONGUE, HELLPUP!
I'LL NOT STAND AT THE EDGE OF CHAOS' DOMAIN AND QUIBBLE WITH MINIONS ON TRIVIAL MATTERS.
I COULDN'T CARE LESS ABOUT MY WHINING SISTER'S DEMANDS!

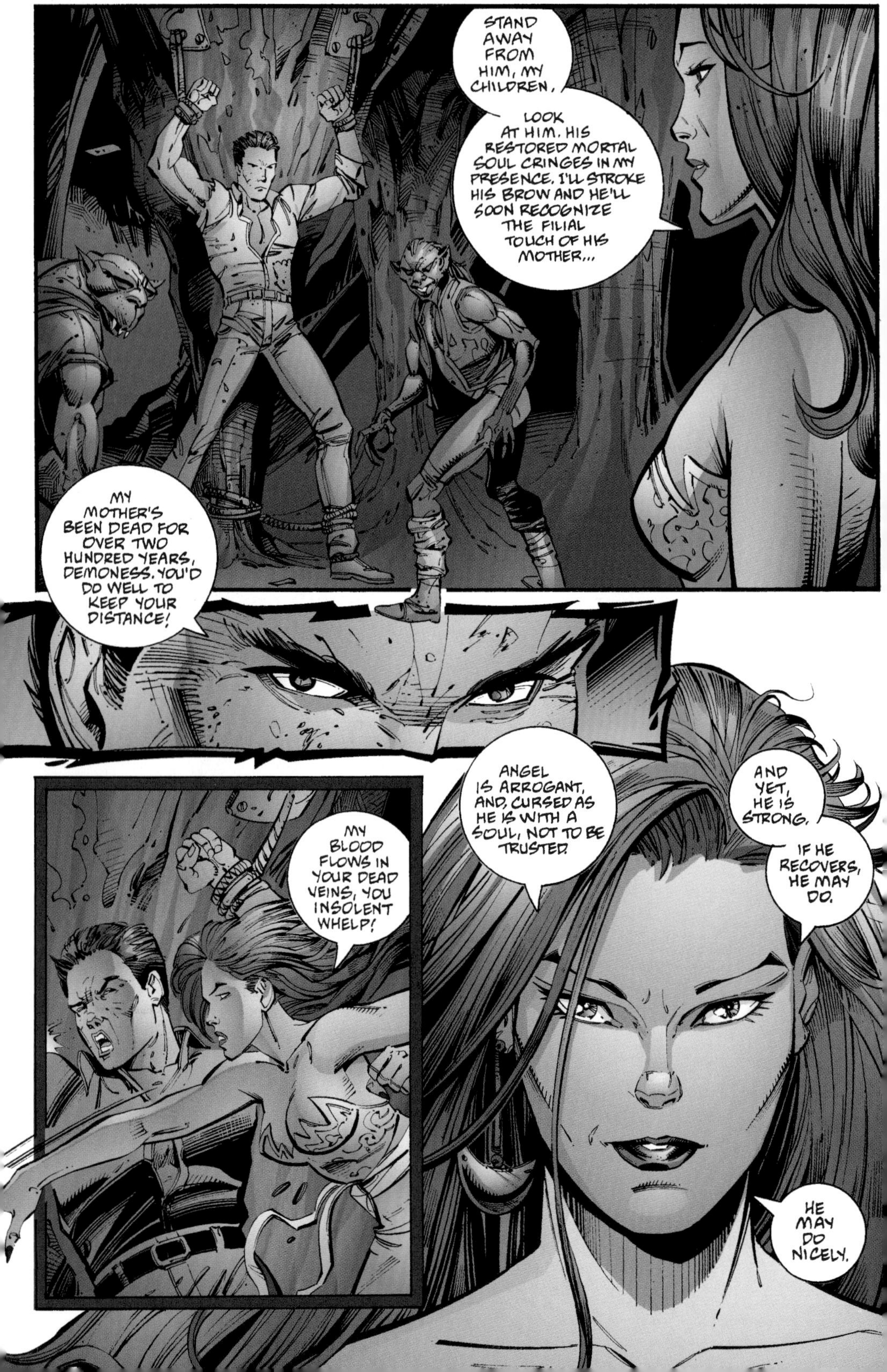
STAND AWAY FROM HIM, MY CHILDREN.
LOOK AT HIM. HIS RESTORED MORTAL SOUL CRINGES IN MY PRESENCE. I'LL STROKE HIS BROW AND HE'LL SOON RECOGNIZE THE FILIAL TOUCH OF HIS MOTHER...
MY MOTHER'S BEEN DEAD FOR OVER TWO HUNDRED YEARS, DEMONESS. YOU'D DO WELL TO KEEP YOUR DISTANCE!
MY BLOOD FLOWS IN YOUR DEAD VEINS, YOU INSOLENT WHELP!
ANGEL IS ARROGANT, AND, CURSED AS HE IS WITH A SOUL, NOT TO BE TRUSTED.
AND YET, HE IS STRONG.
IF HE RECOVERS, HE MAY DO.
HE MAY DO NICELY.

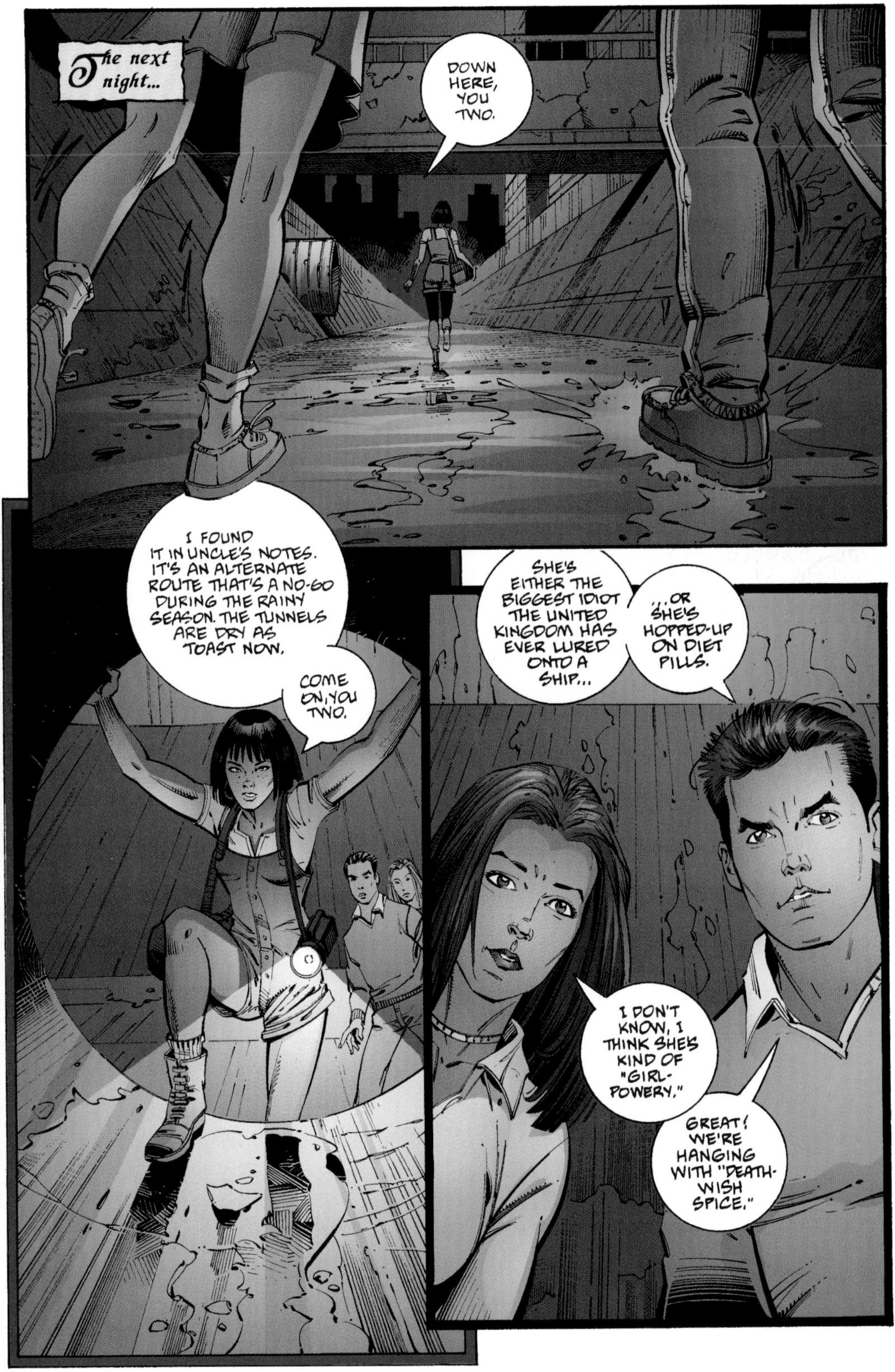
The next night...
DOWN HERE, YOU TWO.
I FOUND IT IN UNCLE'S NOTES. IT'S AN ALTERNATE ROUTE THAT'S A NO-GO DURING THE RAINY SEASON. THE TUNNELS ARE DRY AS TOAST NOW.
COME ON, YOU TWO.
SHE'S EITHER THE BIGGEST IDIOT THE UNITED KINGDOM HAS EVER LURED ONTO A SHIP...
...OR SHE'S HOPPED-UP ON DIET PILLS.
I DON'T KNOW, I THINK SHE'S KIND OF "GIRL-POWERY."
GREAT! WE'RE HANGING WITH "DEATH-WISH SPICE."

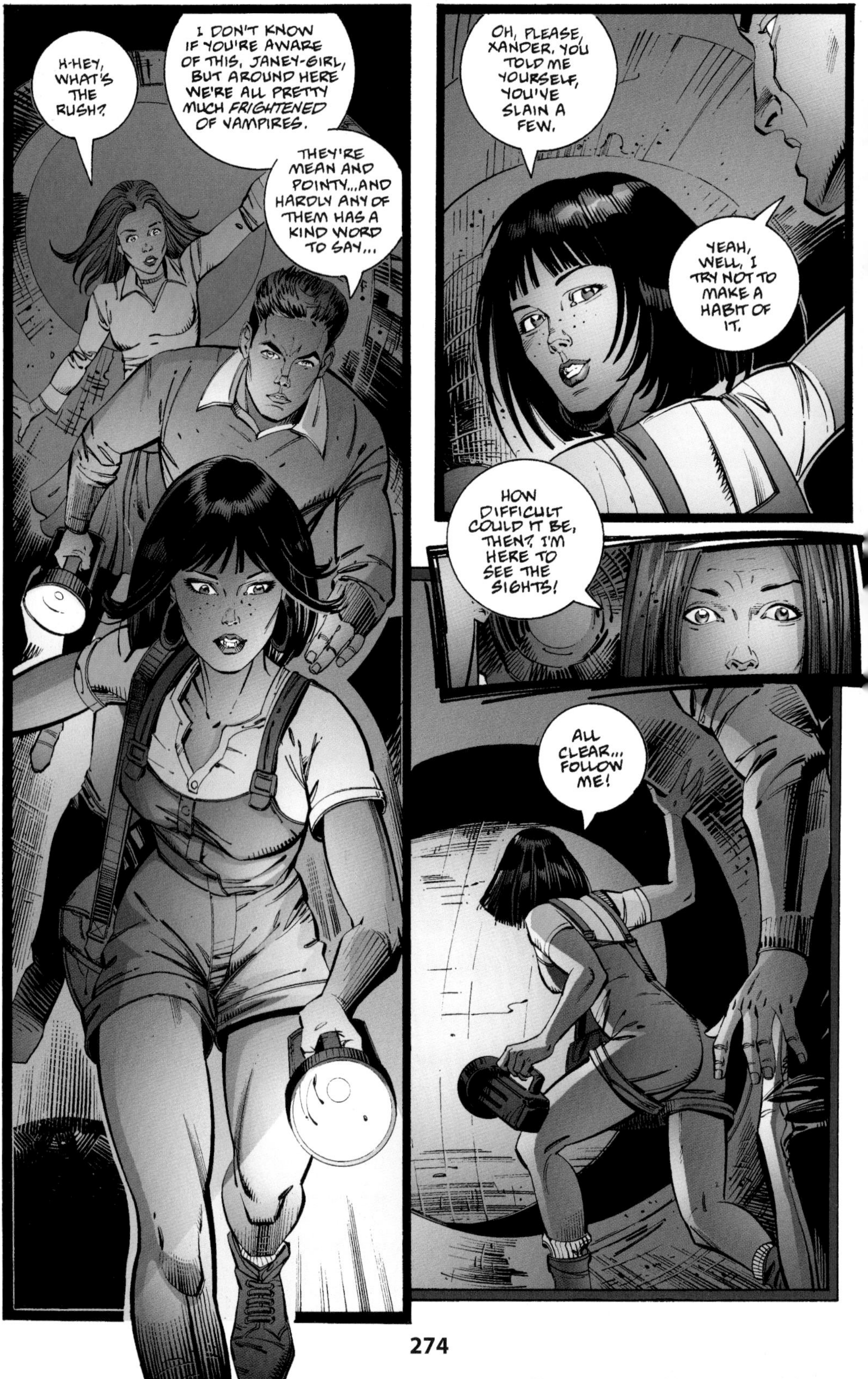
H-HEY, WHAT'S THE RUSH?
I DON'T KNOW IF YOU'RE AWARE OF THIS, JANEY-GIRL, BUT AROUND HERE WE'RE ALL PRETTY MUCH *FRIGHTENED* OF VAMPIRES.
THEY'RE MEAN AND POINTY... AND HARDLY ANY OF THEM HAS A KIND WORD TO SAY...
OH, PLEASE, XANDER. YOU TOLD ME YOURSELF, YOU'VE SLAIN A FEW.
YEAH, WELL, I TRY NOT TO MAKE A HABIT OF IT.
HOW DIFFICULT COULD IT BE, THEN? I'M HERE TO SEE THE SIGHTS!
ALL CLEAR... FOLLOW ME!

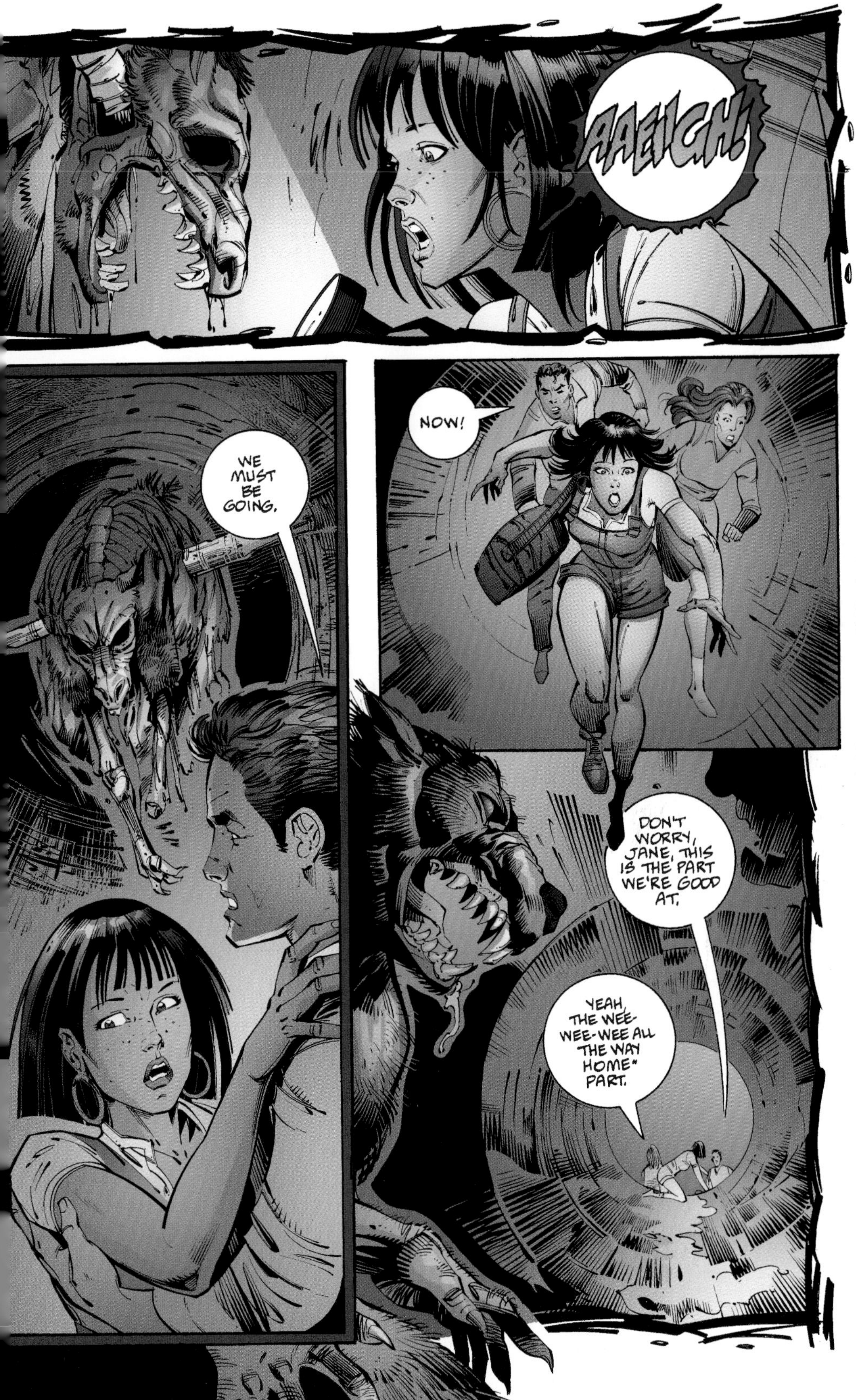
AAEIGH!
WE MUST BE GOING.
NOW!
DON'T WORRY, JANE, THIS IS THE PART WE'RE GOOD AT.
YEAH, THE WEE-WEE-WEE ALL THE WAY HOME" PART.

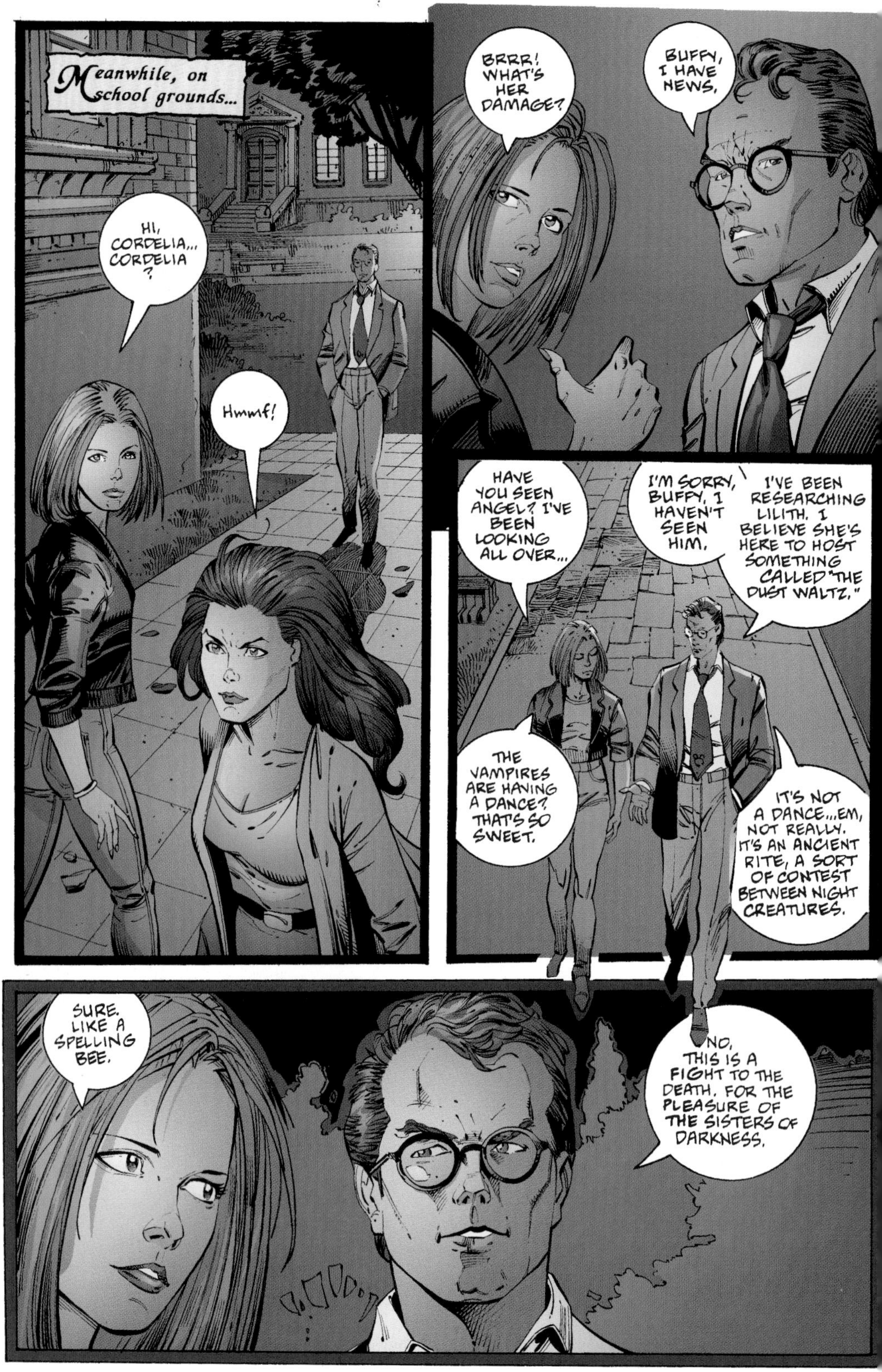
Meanwhile, on school grounds...
HI, CORDELIA... CORDELIA?
Hmmf!
BRRR! WHAT'S HER DAMAGE?
BUFFY, I HAVE NEWS.
HAVE YOU SEEN ANGEL? I'VE BEEN LOOKING ALL OVER...
I'M SORRY, BUFFY, I HAVEN'T SEEN HIM.
I'VE BEEN RESEARCHING LILITH. I BELIEVE SHE'S HERE TO HOST SOMETHING CALLED "THE DUST WALTZ."
THE VAMPIRES ARE HAVING A DANCE? THAT'S SO SWEET.
IT'S NOT A DANCE...EM, NOT REALLY. IT'S AN ANCIENT RITE, A SORT OF CONTEST BETWEEN NIGHT CREATURES.
SURE. LIKE A SPELLING BEE.
NO, THIS IS A FIGHT TO THE DEATH. FOR THE PLEASURE OF THE SISTERS OF DARKNESS.

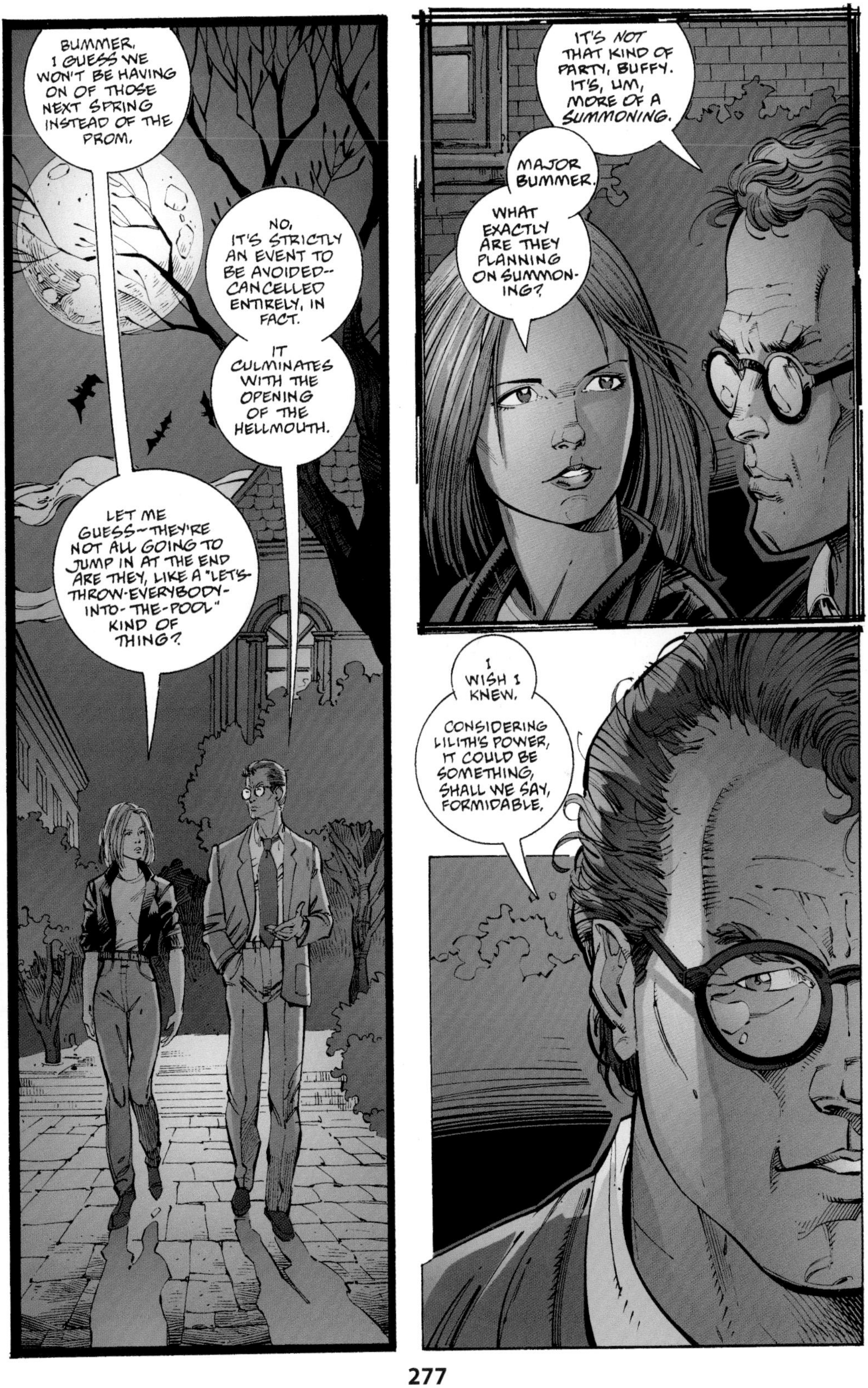
BUMMER. I GUESS WE WON'T BE HAVING ON OF THOSE NEXT SPRING INSTEAD OF THE PROM.
NO, IT'S STRICTLY AN EVENT TO BE AVOIDED--CANCELLED ENTIRELY, IN FACT.
IT CULMINATES WITH THE OPENING OF THE HELLMOUTH.
LET ME GUESS--THEY'RE NOT ALL GOING TO JUMP IN AT THE END ARE THEY, LIKE A "LET'S-THROW-EVERYBODY-INTO-THE-POOL" KIND OF THING?
IT'S NOT THAT KIND OF PARTY, BUFFY. IT'S, UM, MORE OF A SUMMONING.
MAJOR BUMMER.
WHAT EXACTLY ARE THEY PLANNING ON SUMMONING?
I WISH I KNEW.
CONSIDERING LILITH'S POWER, IT COULD BE SOMETHING, SHALL WE SAY, FORMIDABLE.

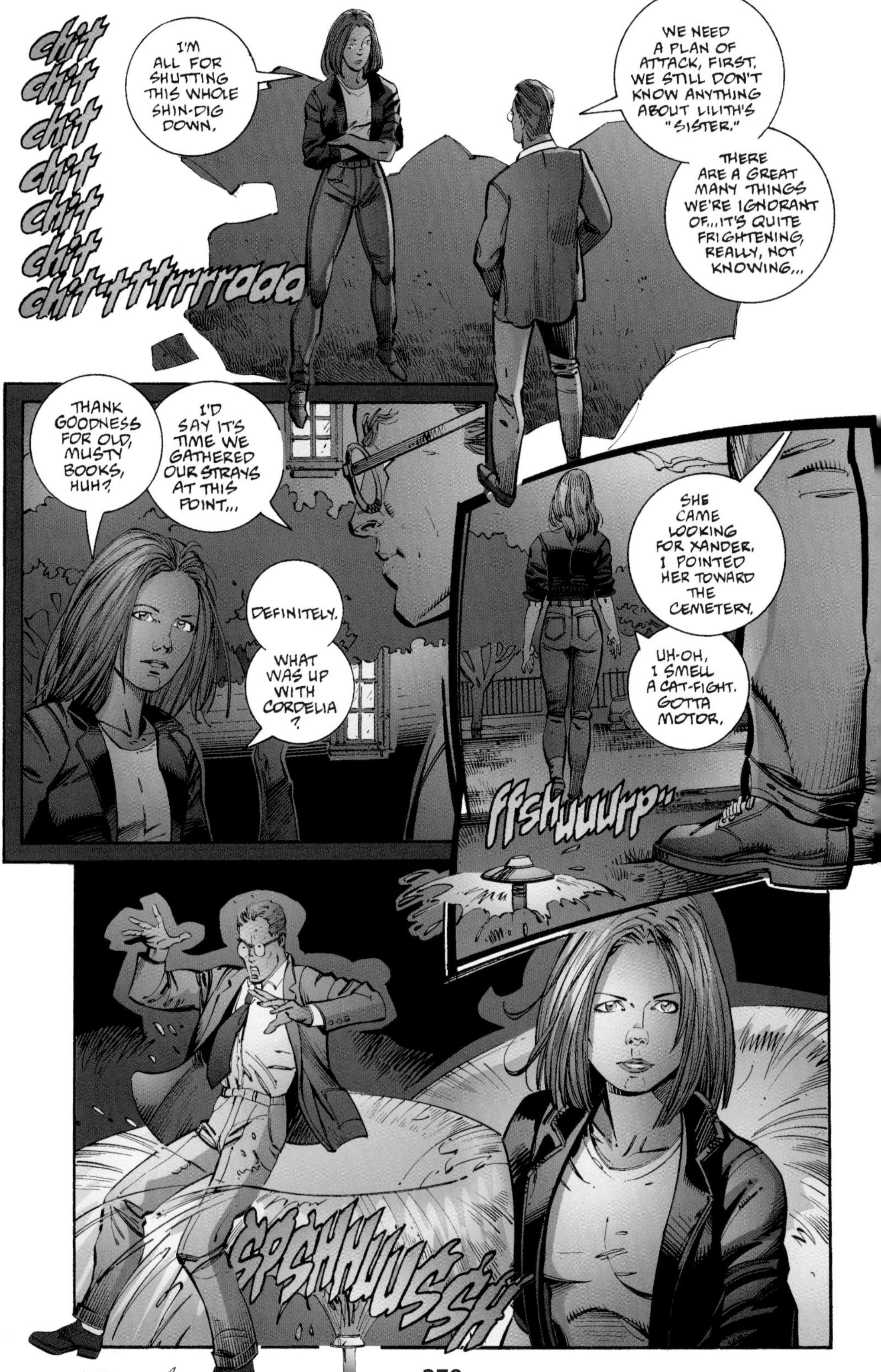
chit chit chit chit chit chit chit-tttrrrraaa
I'M ALL FOR SHUTTING THIS WHOLE SHIN-DIG DOWN.
WE NEED A PLAN OF ATTACK, FIRST. WE STILL DON'T KNOW ANYTHING ABOUT LILITH'S "SISTER."
THERE ARE A GREAT MANY THINGS WE'RE IGNORANT OF... IT'S QUITE FRIGHTENING, REALLY, NOT KNOWING...
THANK GOODNESS FOR OLD, MUSTY BOOKS, HUH?
I'D SAY IT'S TIME WE GATHERED OUR STRAYS AT THIS POINT...
DEFINITELY.
WHAT WAS UP WITH CORDELIA?
SHE CAME LOOKING FOR XANDER. I POINTED HER TOWARD THE CEMETERY.
UH-OH, I SMELL A CAT-FIGHT. GOTTA MOTOR.
ffshuuurp
SPSHHUUSSH

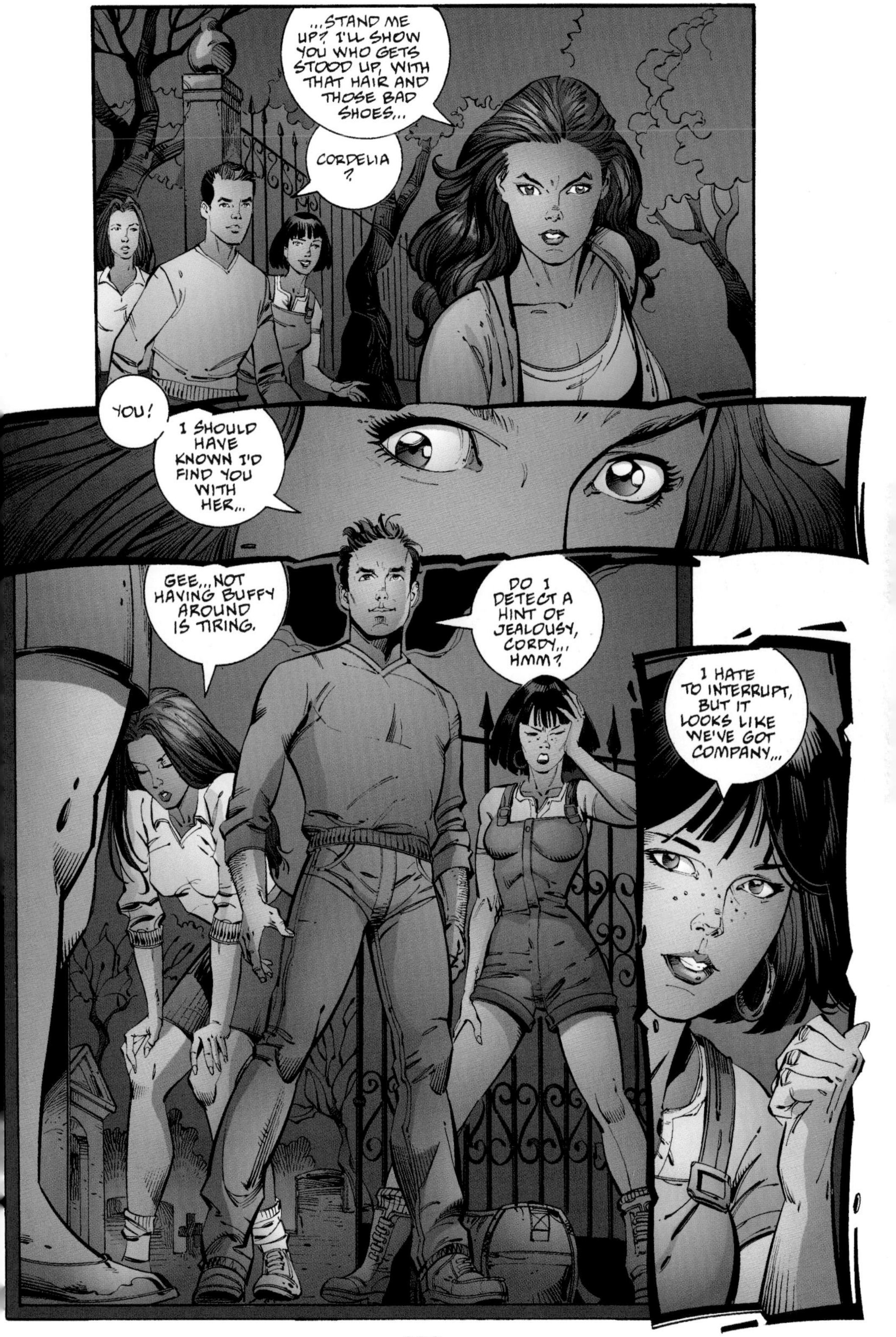
...STAND ME UP? I'LL SHOW YOU WHO GETS STOOD UP, WITH THAT HAIR AND THOSE BAD SHOES...
CORDELIA?
YOU!
I SHOULD HAVE KNOWN I'D FIND YOU WITH HER...
GEE... NOT HAVING BUFFY AROUND IS TIRING.
DO I DETECT A HINT OF JEALOUSY, CORDY... HMM?
I HATE TO INTERRUPT, BUT IT LOOKS LIKE WE'VE GOT COMPANY...

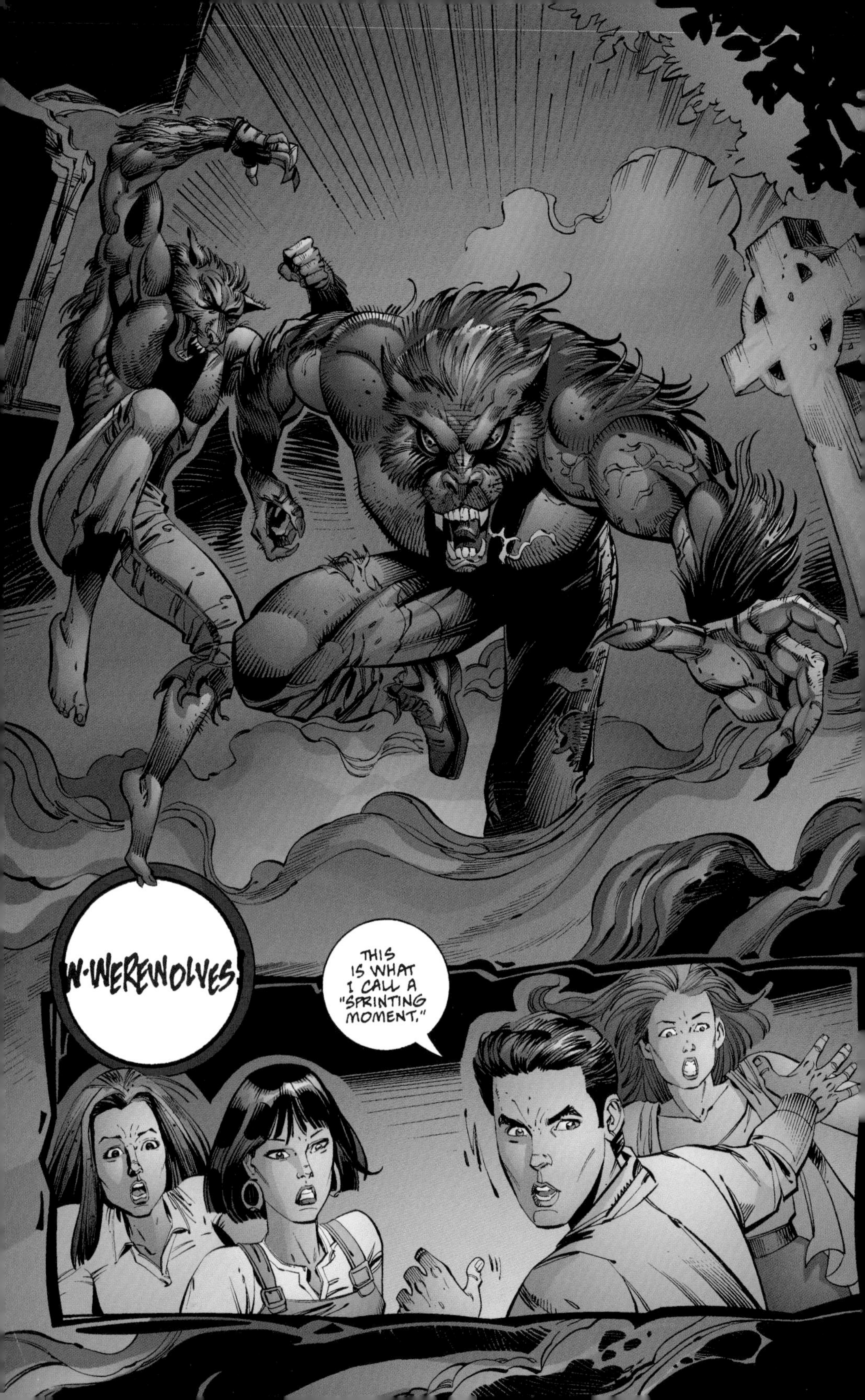
W-WEREWOLVES!
THIS IS WHAT I CALL A "SPRINTING MOMENT."

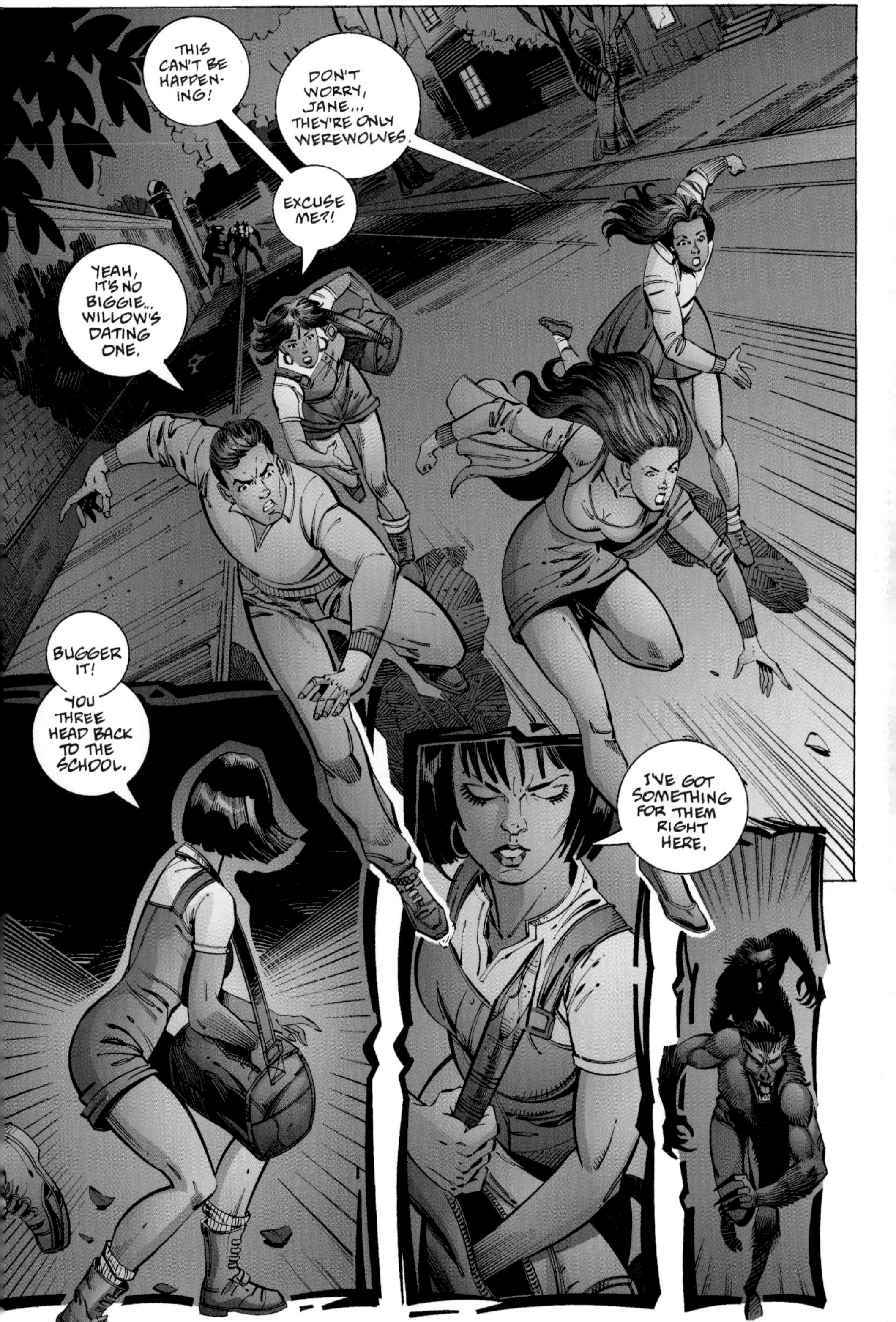
THIS CAN'T BE HAPPEN-ING!
DON'T WORRY, JANE... THEY'RE ONLY WEREWOLVES.
EXCUSE ME?!
YEAH, IT'S NO BIGGIE... WILLOW'S DATING ONE.
BUGGER IT!
YOU THREE HEAD BACK TO THE SCHOOL.
I'VE GOT SOMETHING FOR THEM RIGHT HERE.

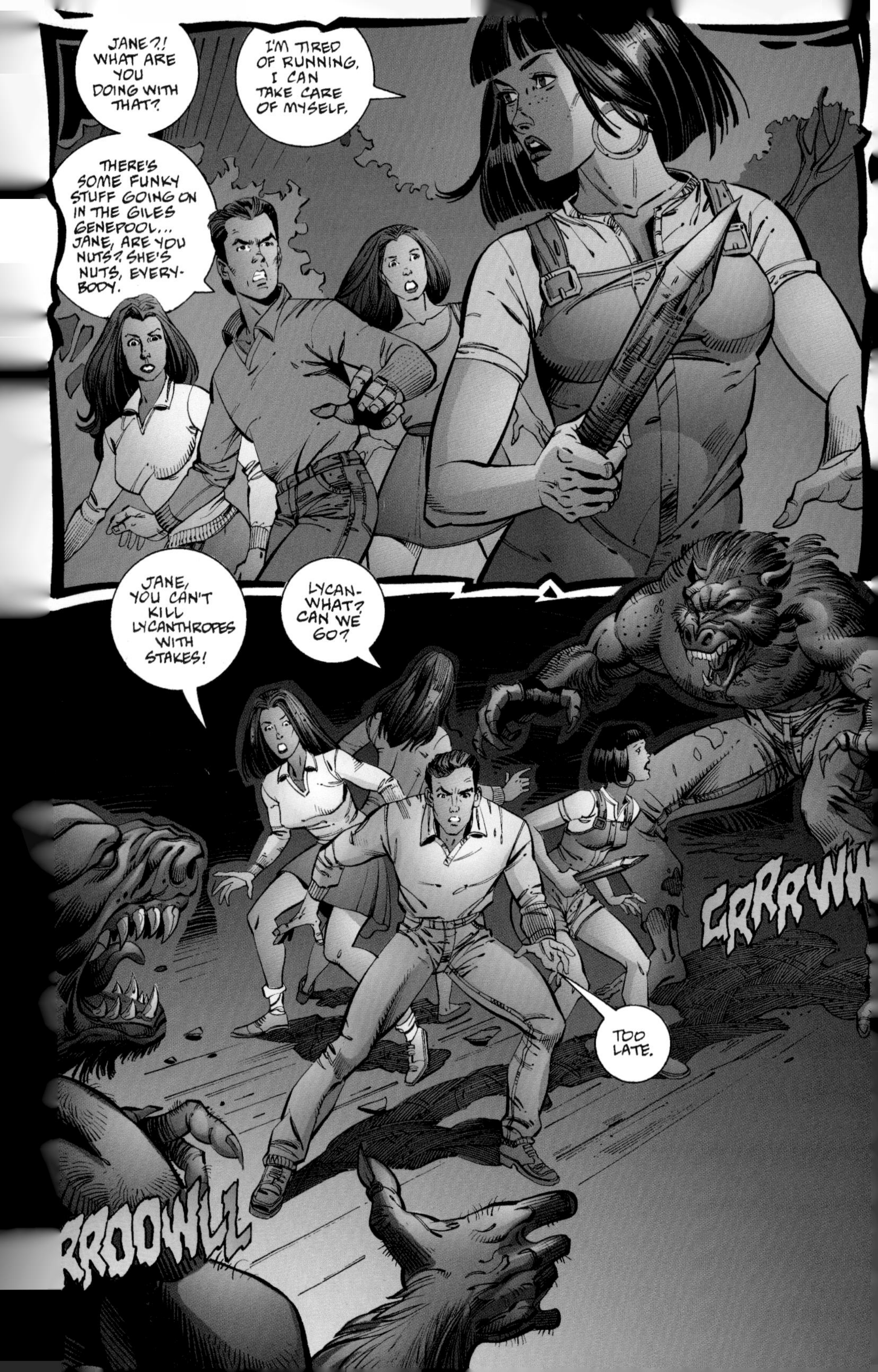

JANE?! WHAT ARE YOU DOING WITH THAT?
I'M TIRED OF RUNNING. I CAN TAKE CARE OF MYSELF.
THERE'S SOME FUNKY STUFF GOING ON IN THE GILES GENEPOOL... JANE, ARE YOU NUTS? SHE'S NUTS, EVERYBODY.
JANE, YOU CAN'T KILL LYCANTHROPES WITH STAKES!
LYCAN-WHAT? CAN WE GO?
GRRRWH
TOO LATE.
RROOWLL

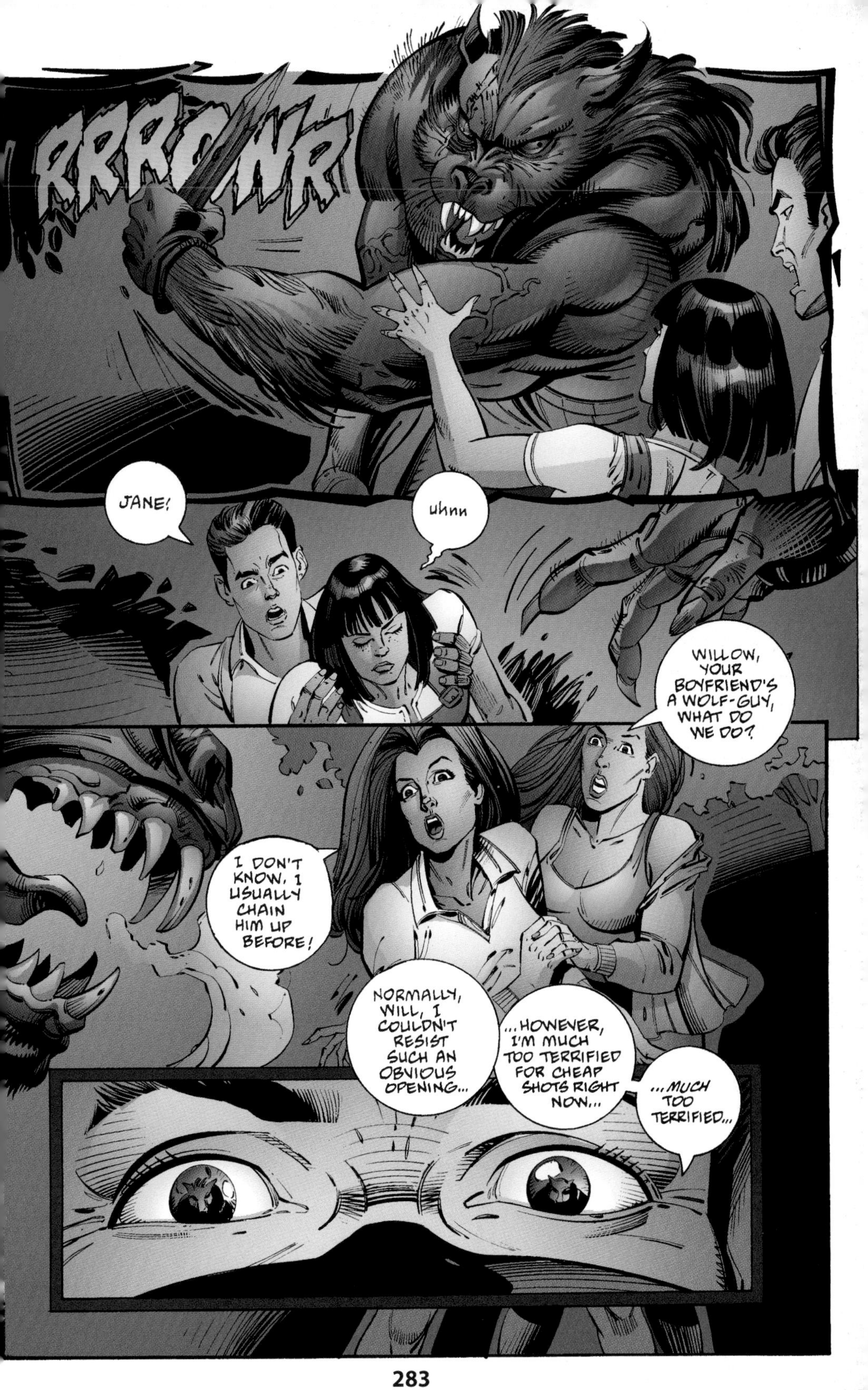
RRROWR
JANE!
uhnn
WILLOW, YOUR BOYFRIEND'S A WOLF-GUY, WHAT DO WE DO?
I DON'T KNOW. I USUALLY CHAIN HIM UP BEFORE!
NORMALLY, WILL, I COULDN'T RESIST SUCH AN OBVIOUS OPENING...
...HOWEVER, I'M MUCH TOO TERRIFIED FOR CHEAP SHOTS RIGHT NOW...
...MUCH TOO TERRIFIED...

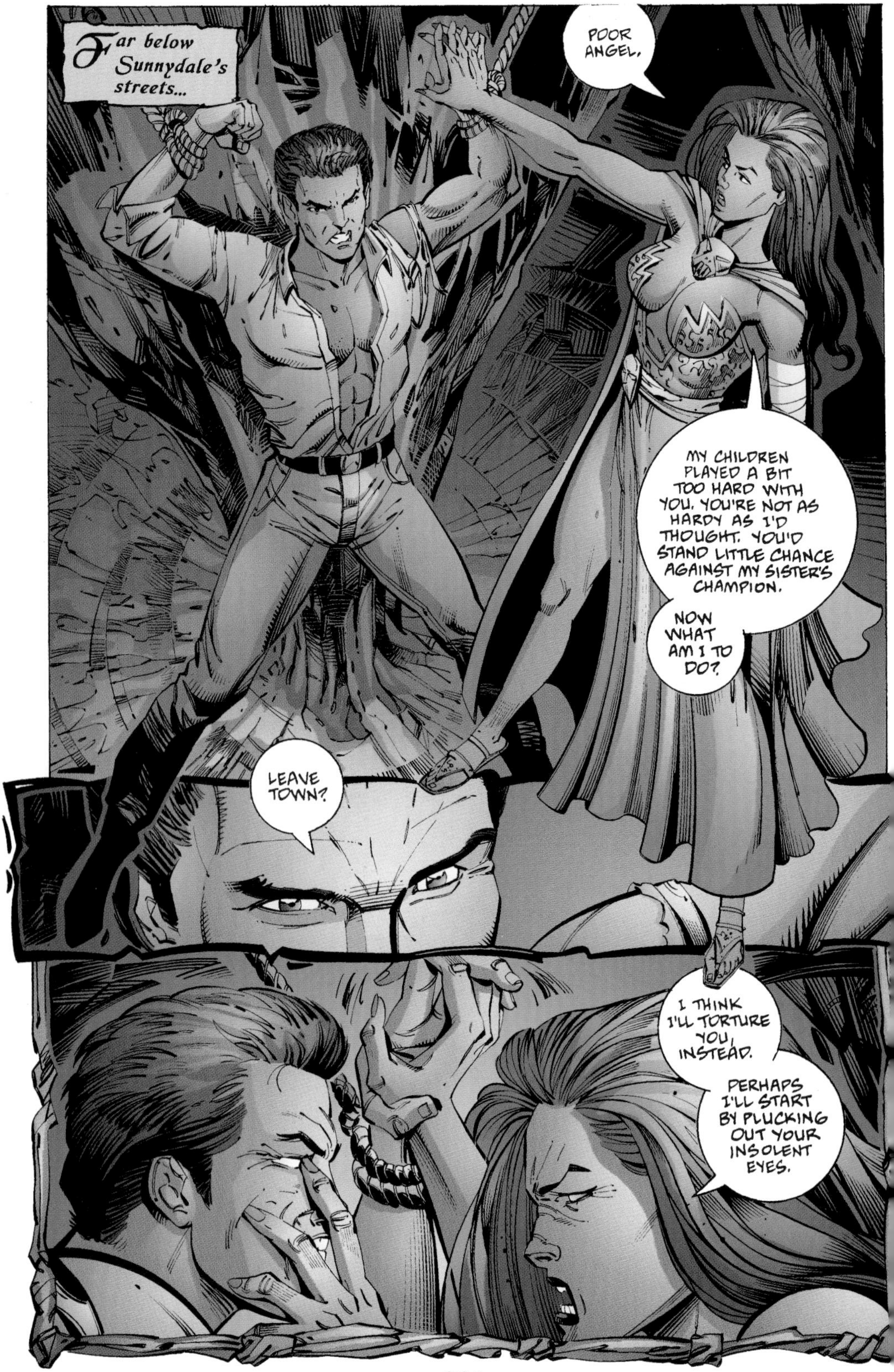
Far below Sunnydale's streets...
POOR ANGEL,
MY CHILDREN PLAYED A BIT TOO HARD WITH YOU. YOU'RE NOT AS HARDY AS I'D THOUGHT. YOU'D STAND LITTLE CHANCE AGAINST MY SISTER'S CHAMPION.
NOW WHAT AM I TO DO?
LEAVE TOWN?
I THINK I'LL TORTURE YOU, INSTEAD.
PERHAPS I'LL START BY PLUCKING OUT YOUR INSOLENT EYES.

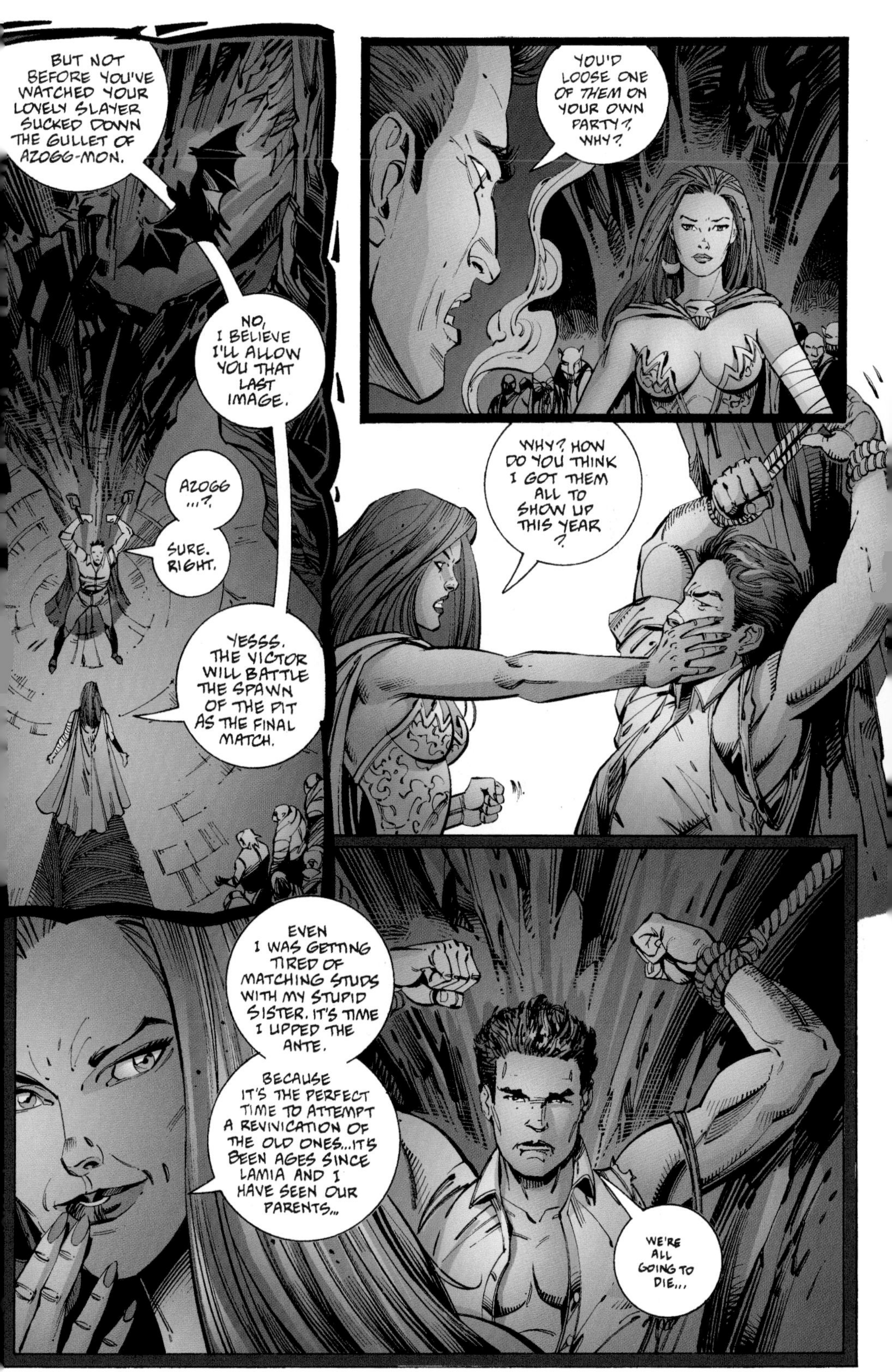

BUT NOT BEFORE YOU'VE WATCHED YOUR LOVELY SLAYER SUCKED DOWN THE GULLET OF AZOGG-MON.
NO, I BELIEVE I'LL ALLOW YOU THAT LAST IMAGE.
AZOGG ...?
SURE. RIGHT.
YESSS. THE VICTOR WILL BATTLE THE SPAWN OF THE PIT AS THE FINAL MATCH.
YOU'D LOOSE ONE OF THEM ON YOUR OWN PARTY? WHY?
WHY? HOW DO YOU THINK I GOT THEM ALL TO SHOW UP THIS YEAR?
EVEN I WAS GETTING TIRED OF MATCHING STUDS WITH MY STUPID SISTER. IT'S TIME I UPPED THE ANTE.
BECAUSE IT'S THE PERFECT TIME TO ATTEMPT A REVIVICATION OF THE OLD ONES...IT'S BEEN AGES SINCE LAMIA AND I HAVE SEEN OUR PARENTS...
WE'RE ALL GOING TO DIE...

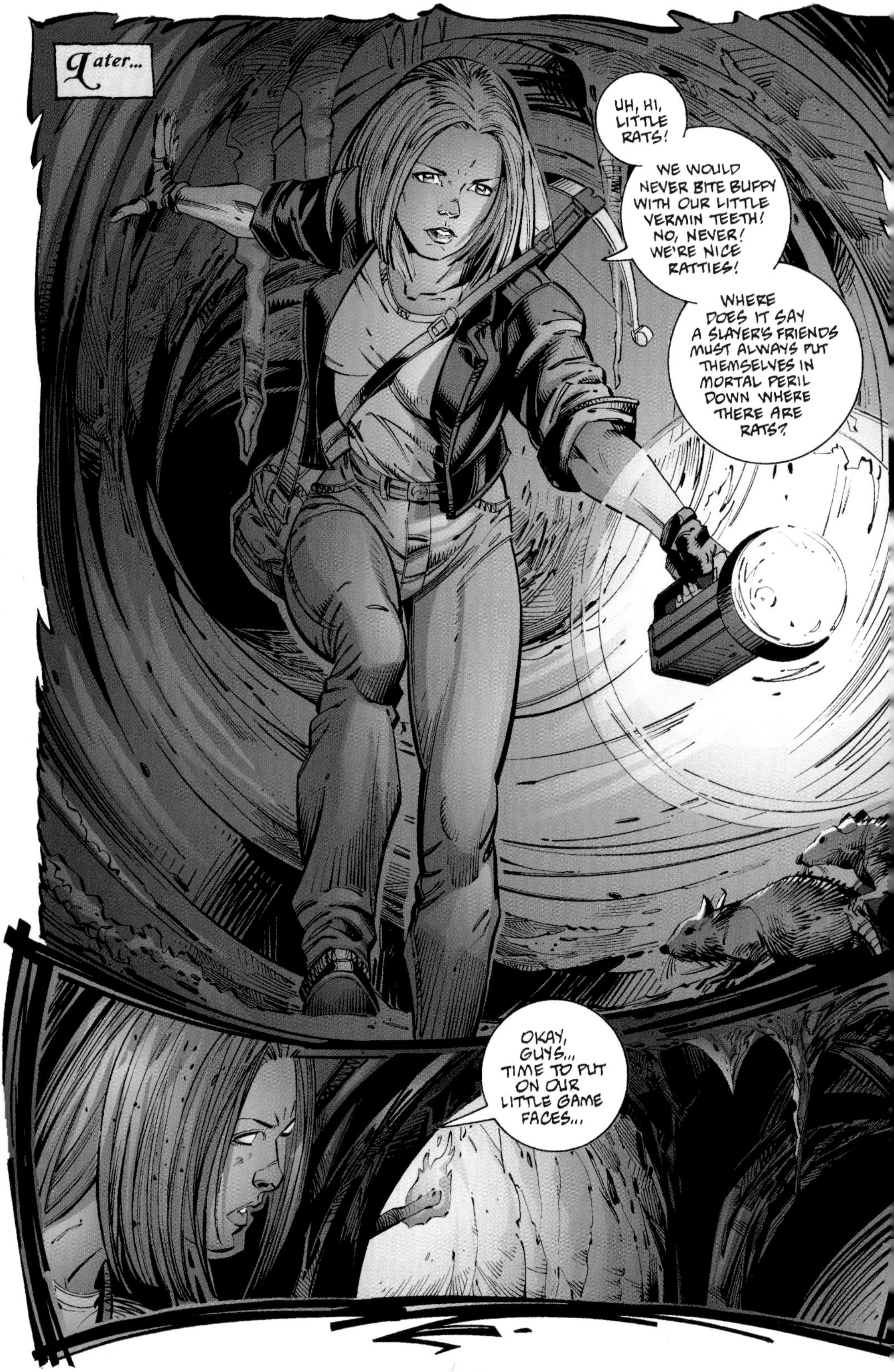
Later...
UH, HI, LITTLE RATS!
WE WOULD NEVER BITE BUFFY WITH OUR LITTLE VERMIN TEETH! NO, NEVER! WE'RE NICE RATTIES!
WHERE DOES IT SAY A SLAYER'S FRIENDS MUST ALWAYS PUT THEMSELVES IN MORTAL PERIL DOWN WHERE THERE ARE RATS?
OKAY, GUYS... TIME TO PUT ON OUR LITTLE GAME FACES...

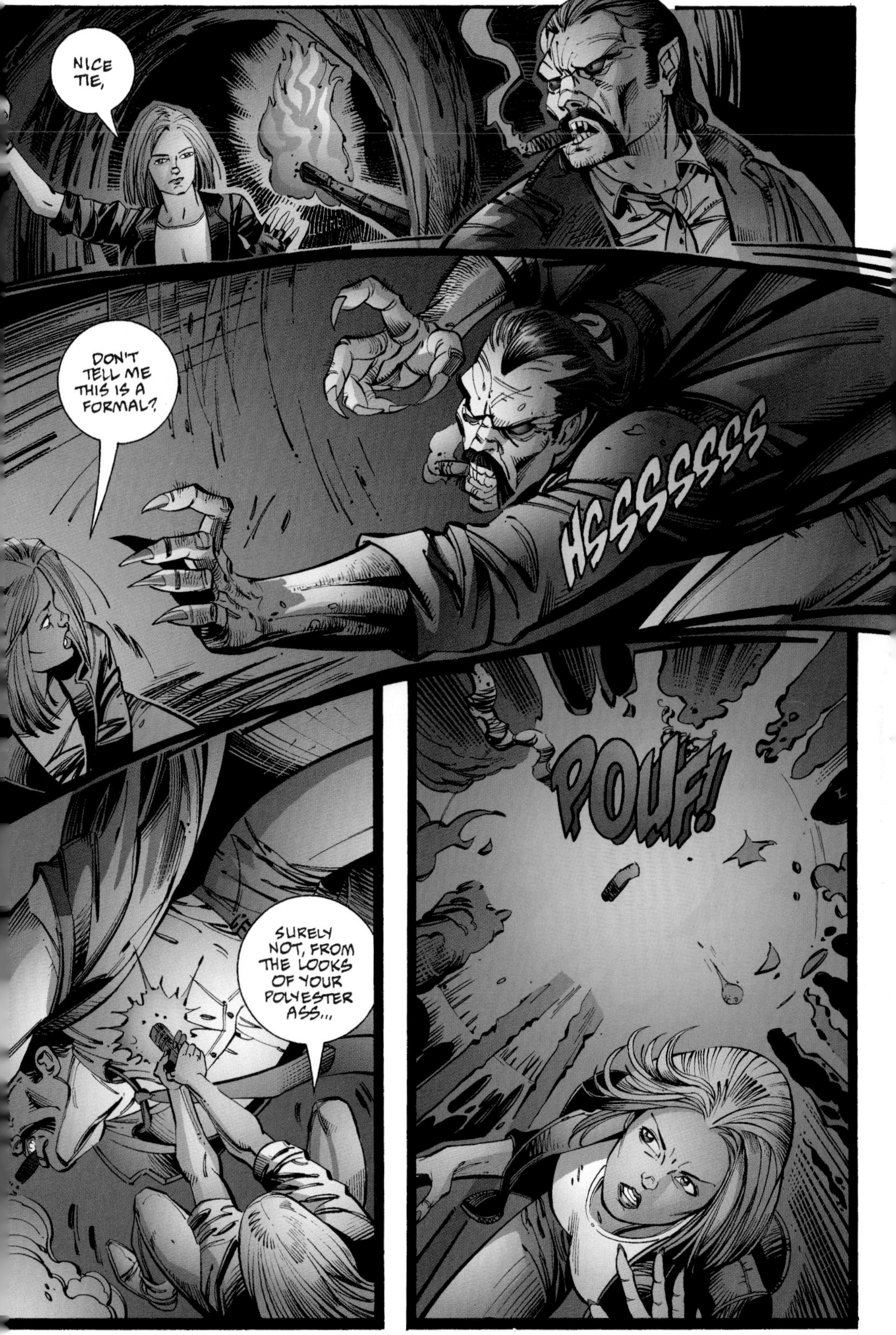
NICE TIE,
DON'T TELL ME THIS IS A FORMAL?
HSSSSSSS
SURELY NOT, FROM THE LOOKS OF YOUR POLYESTER ASS...
POUF!

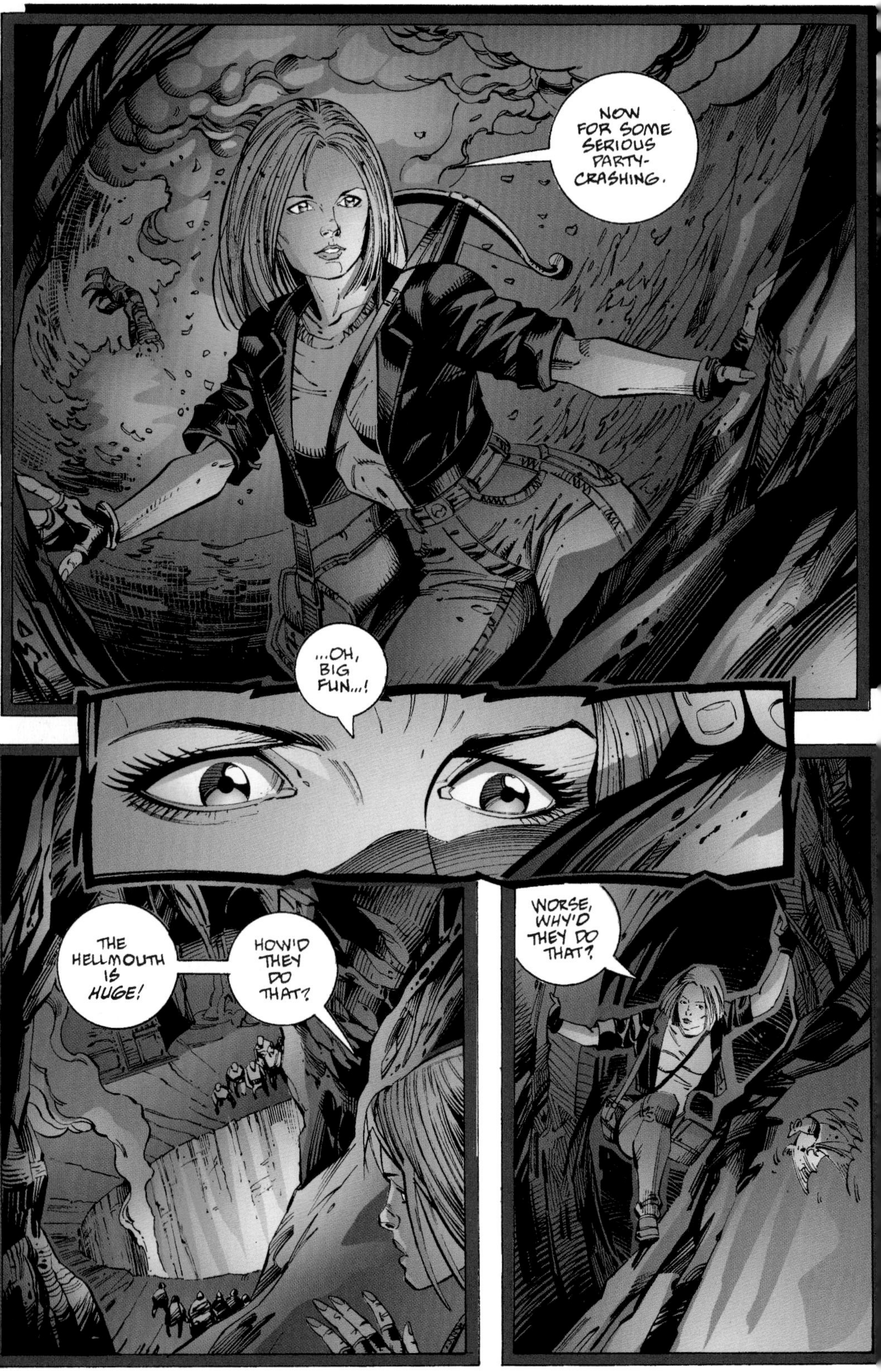
NOW FOR SOME SERIOUS PARTY-CRASHING.
...OH, BIG FUN...!
THE HELLMOUTH IS HUGE!
HOW'D THEY DO THAT?
WORSE, WHY'D THEY DO THAT?

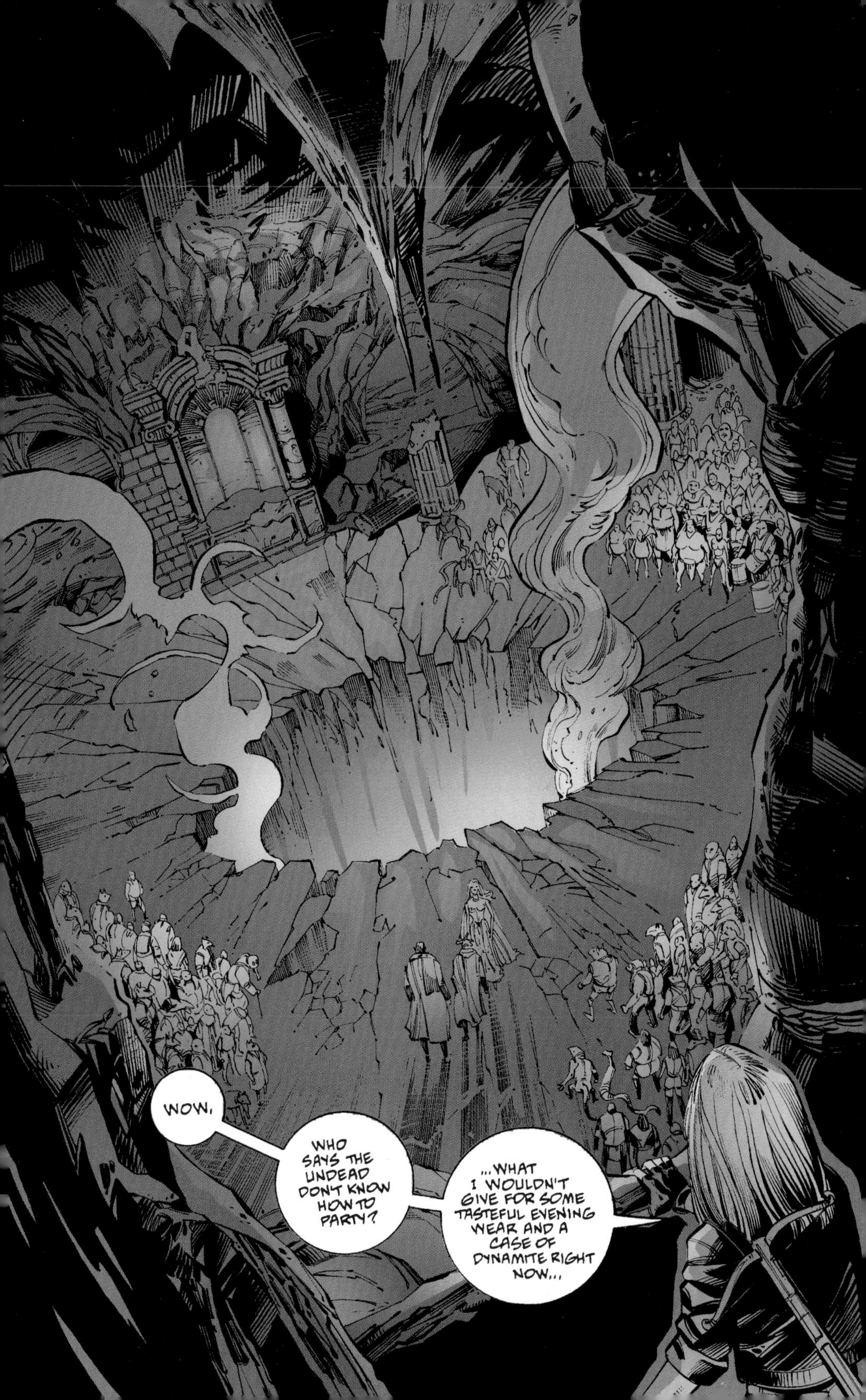
WOW.
WHO SAYS THE UNDEAD DON'T KNOW HOW TO PARTY?
...WHAT I WOULDN'T GIVE FOR SOME TASTEFUL EVENING WEAR AND A CASE OF DYNAMITE RIGHT NOW...

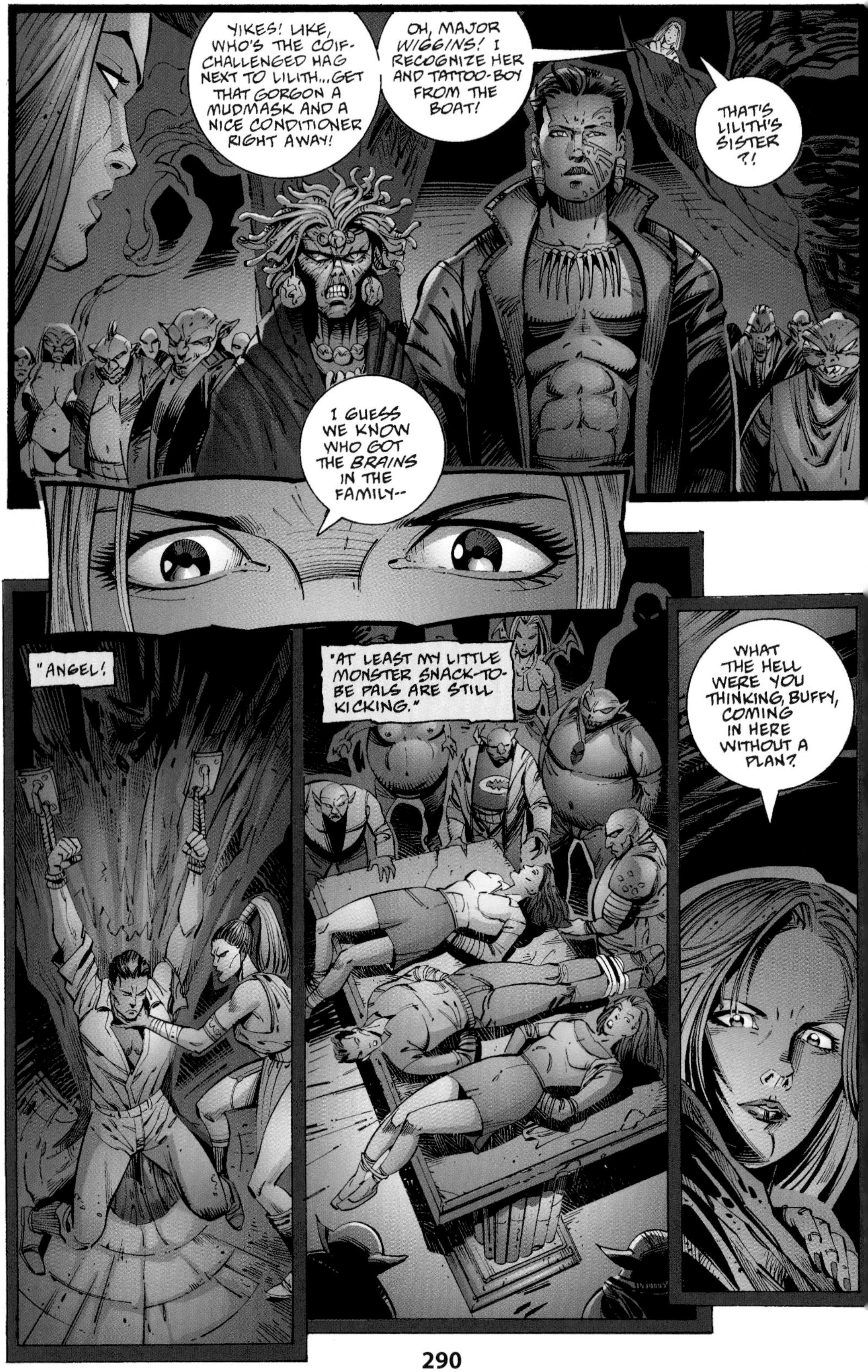
YIKES! LIKE, WHO'S THE COIF-CHALLENGED HAG NEXT TO LILITH...GET THAT GORGON A MUDMASK AND A NICE CONDITIONER RIGHT AWAY!
OH, MAJOR WIGGINS! I RECOGNIZE HER AND TATTOO-BOY FROM THE BOAT!
THAT'S LILITH'S SISTER ?!
I GUESS WE KNOW WHO GOT THE BRAINS IN THE FAMILY--
"ANGEL!
"AT LEAST MY LITTLE MONSTER SNACK-TO-BE PALS ARE STILL KICKING."
WHAT THE HELL WERE YOU THINKING, BUFFY, COMING IN HERE WITHOUT A PLAN?

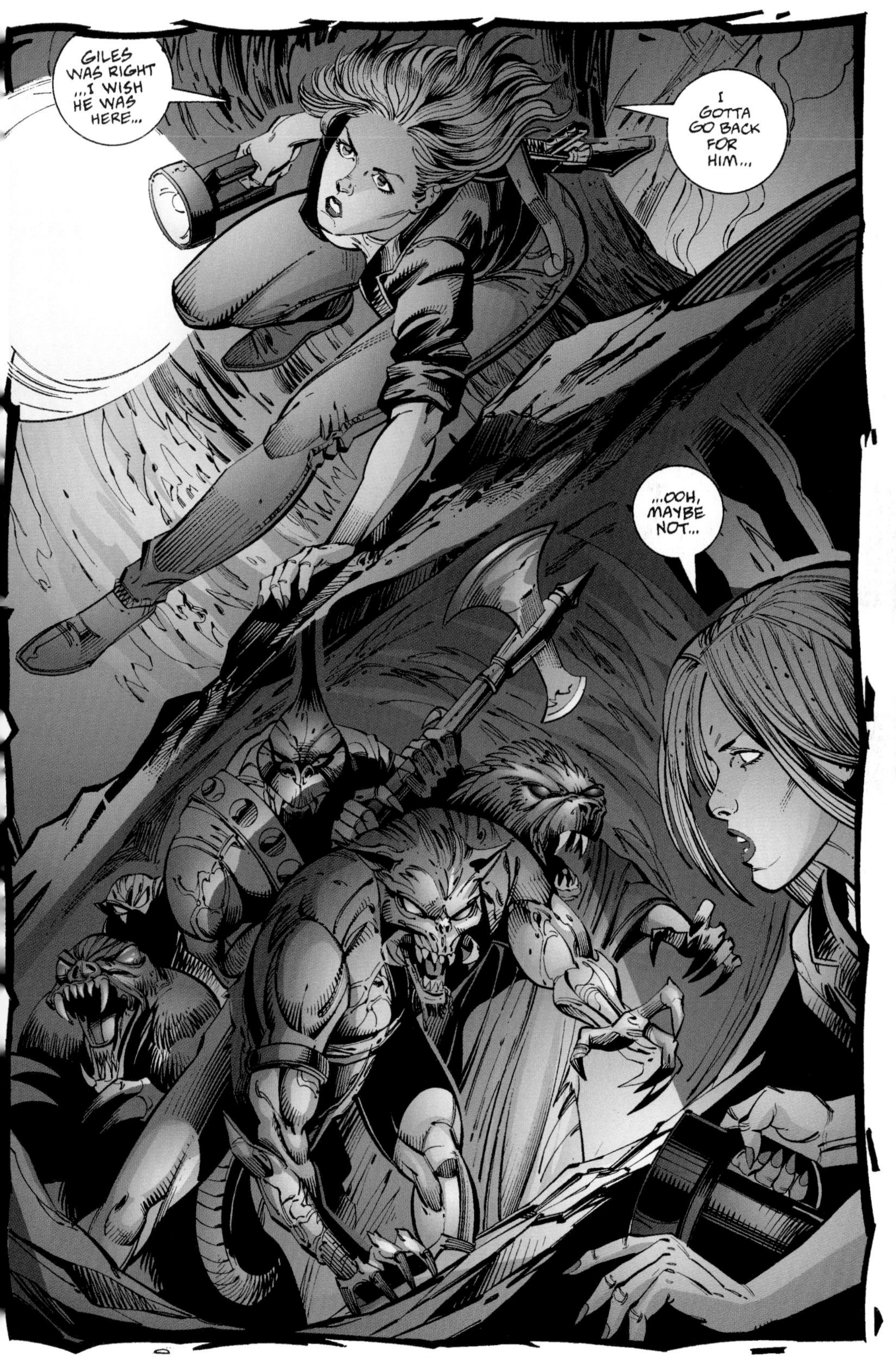
GILES WAS RIGHT ...I WISH HE WAS HERE...
I GOTTA GO BACK FOR HIM...
...OOH, MAYBE NOT...

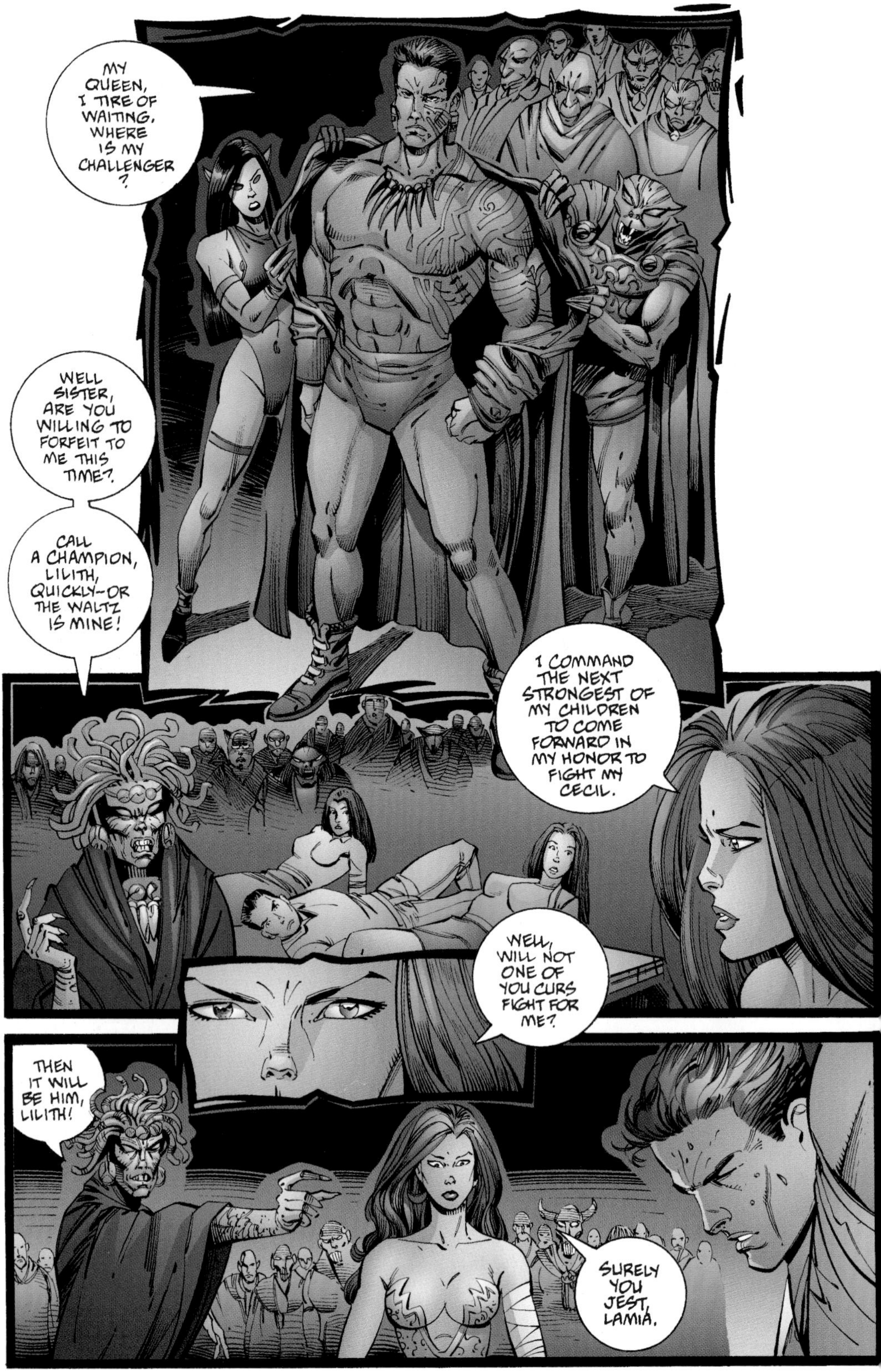

MY QUEEN, I TIRE OF WAITING. WHERE IS MY CHALLENGER?
WELL SISTER, ARE YOU WILLING TO FORFEIT TO ME THIS TIME?
CALL A CHAMPION, LILITH, QUICKLY--OR THE WALTZ IS MINE!
I COMMAND THE NEXT STRONGEST OF MY CHILDREN TO COME FORWARD IN MY HONOR TO FIGHT MY CECIL.
WELL, WILL NOT ONE OF YOU CURS FIGHT FOR ME?
THEN IT WILL BE HIM, LILITH!
SURELY YOU JEST, LAMIA.

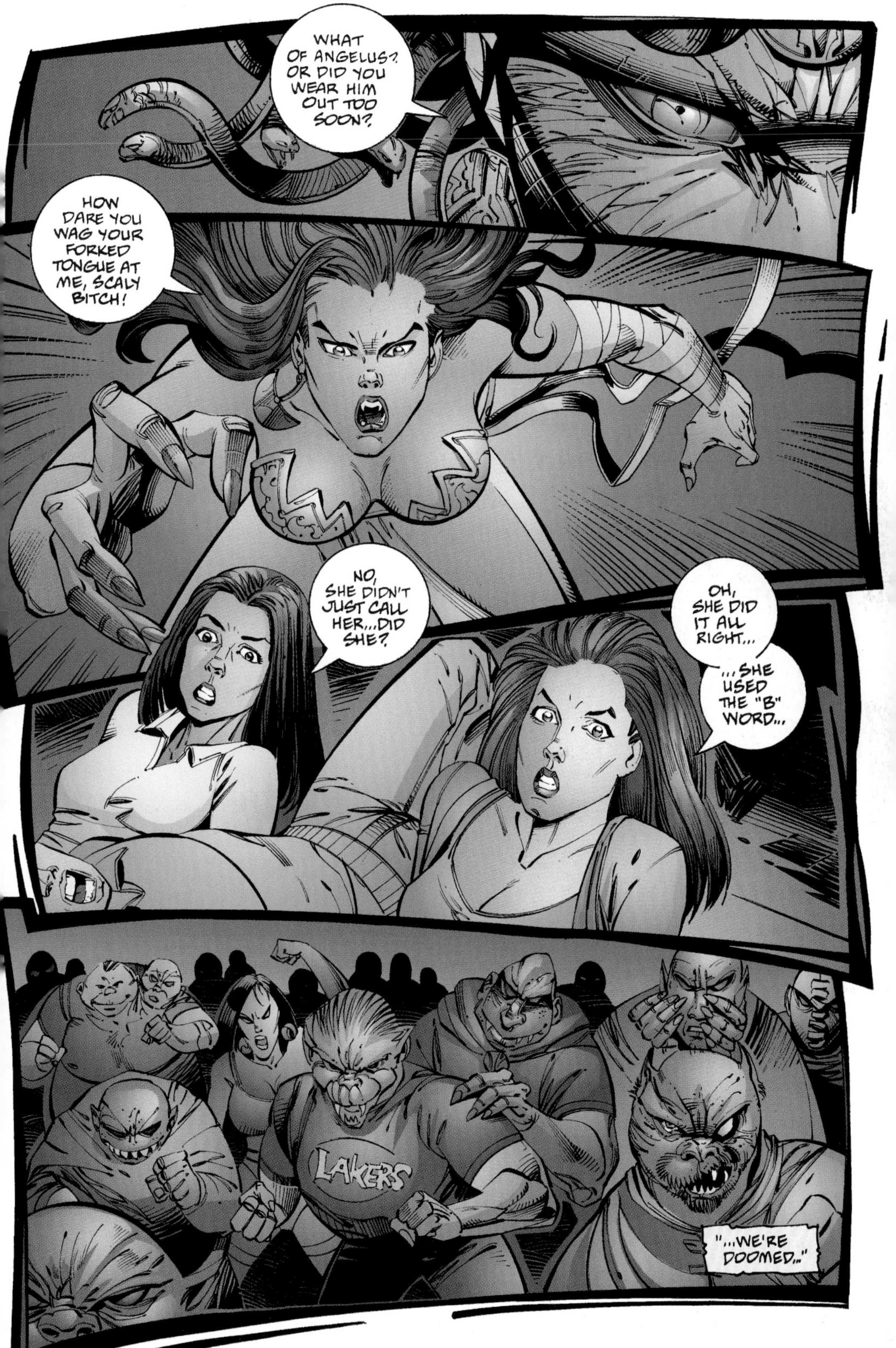
WHAT OF ANGELUS? OR DID YOU WEAR HIM OUT TOO SOON?
HOW DARE YOU WAG YOUR FORKED TONGUE AT ME, SCALY BITCH!
NO, SHE DIDN'T JUST CALL HER...DID SHE?
OH, SHE DID IT ALL RIGHT...
...SHE USED THE "B" WORD...
LAKERS
"...WE'RE DOOMED..."

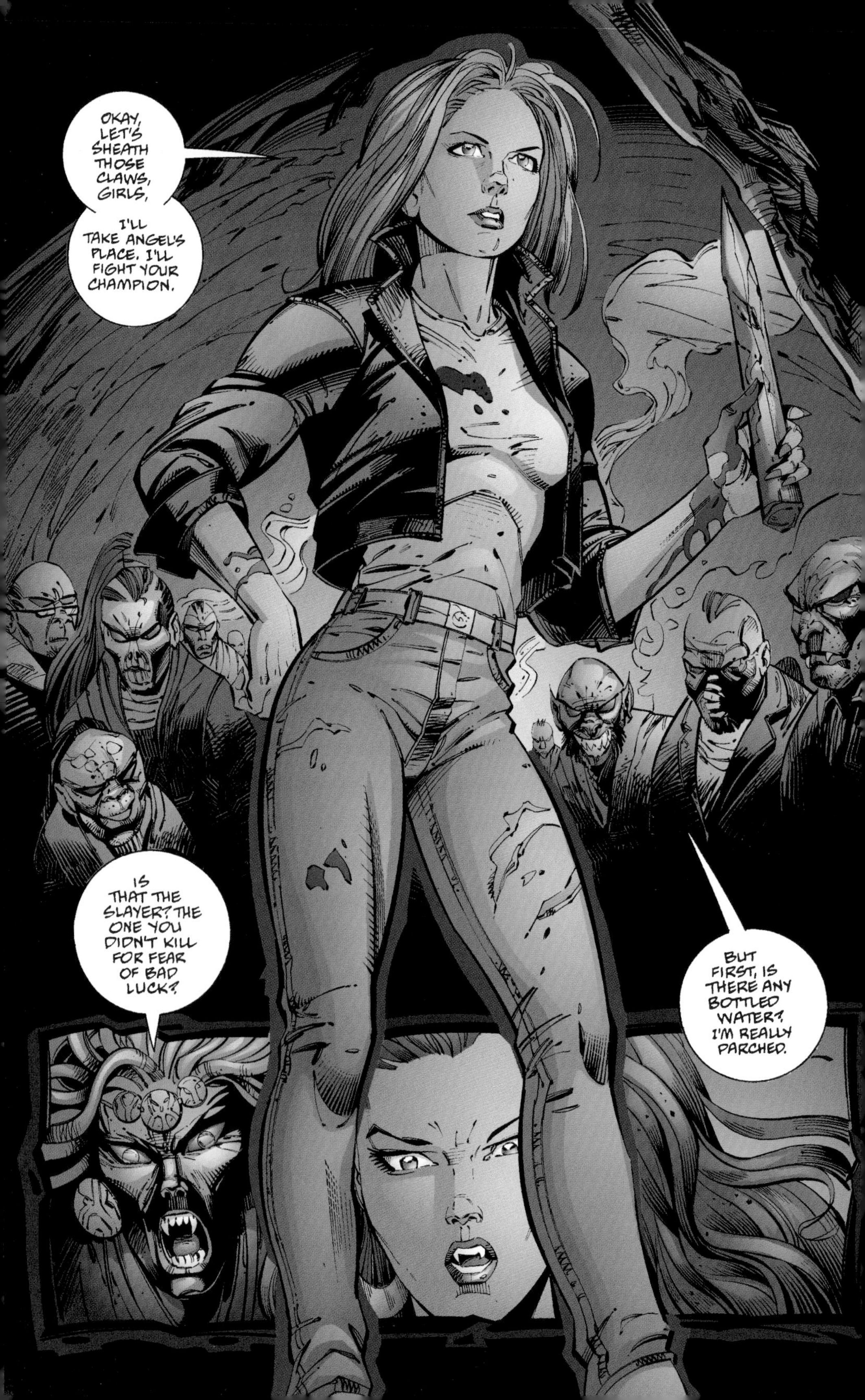
OKAY, LET'S SHEATH THOSE CLAWS, GIRLS,
I'LL TAKE ANGEL'S PLACE. I'LL FIGHT YOUR CHAMPION.
IS THAT THE SLAYER? THE ONE YOU DIDN'T KILL FOR FEAR OF BAD LUCK?
BUT FIRST, IS THERE ANY BOTTLED WATER? I'M REALLY PARCHED.

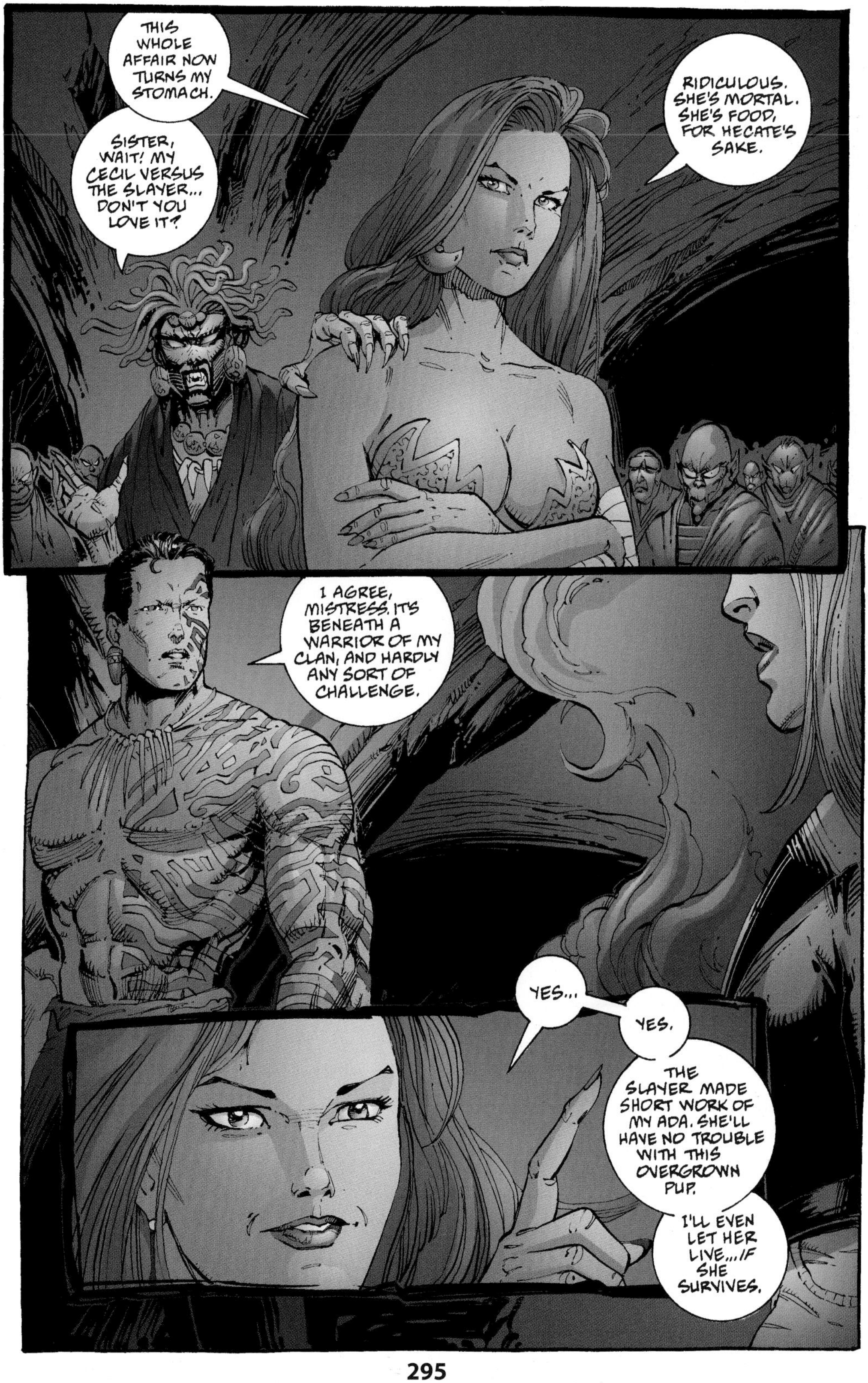
THIS WHOLE AFFAIR NOW TURNS MY STOMACH.
SISTER, WAIT! MY CECIL VERSUS THE SLAYER... DON'T YOU LOVE IT?
RIDICULOUS. SHE'S MORTAL. SHE'S FOOD, FOR HECATE'S SAKE.
I AGREE, MISTRESS. IT'S BENEATH A WARRIOR OF MY CLAN, AND HARDLY ANY SORT OF CHALLENGE.
YES...
YES.
THE SLAYER MADE SHORT WORK OF MY ADA. SHE'LL HAVE NO TROUBLE WITH THIS OVERGROWN PUP.
I'LL EVEN LET HER LIVE... IF SHE SURVIVES.

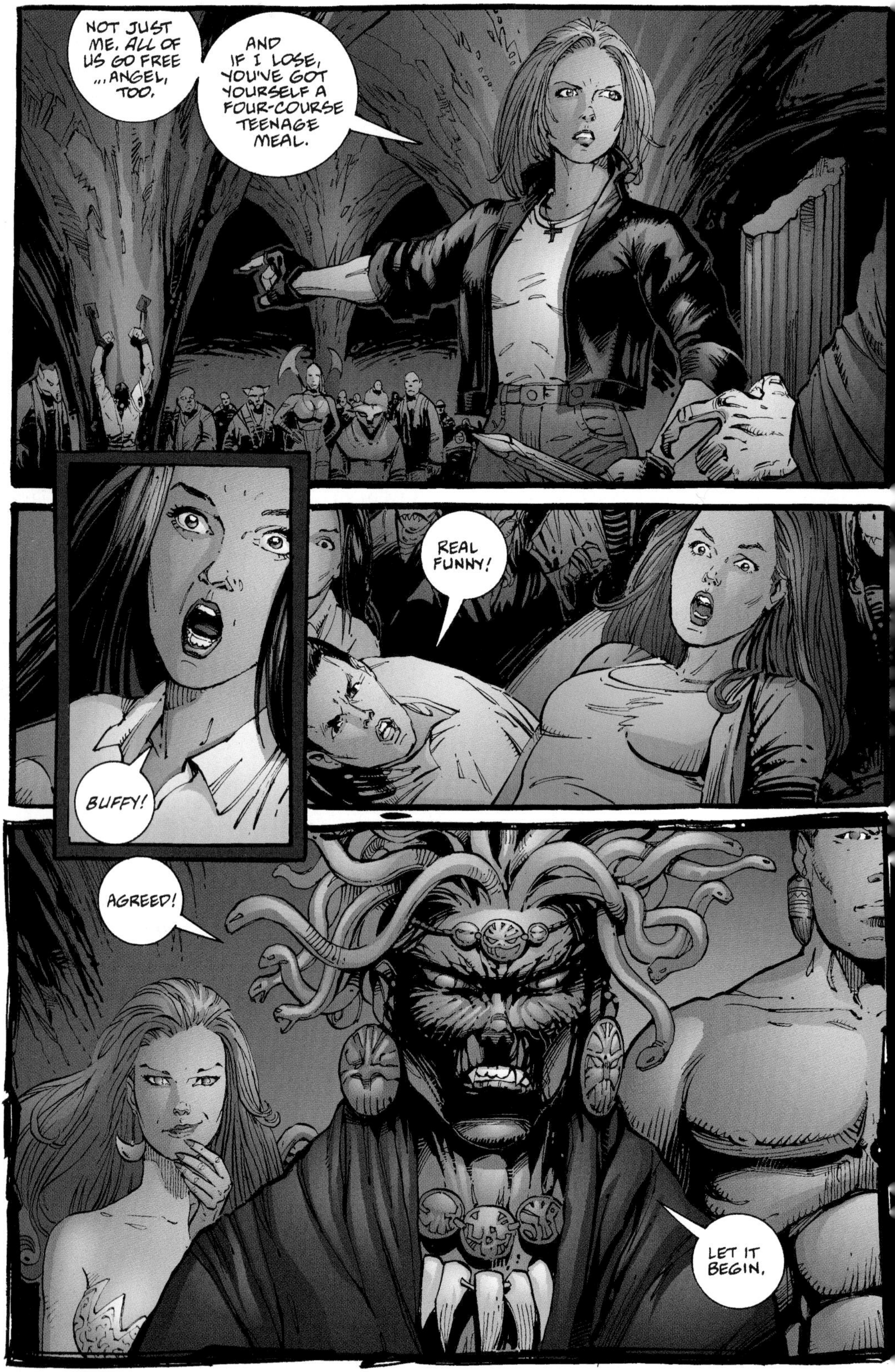
NOT JUST ME. ALL OF US GO FREE ...ANGEL, TOO.
AND IF I LOSE, YOU'VE GOT YOURSELF A FOUR-COURSE TEENAGE MEAL.
BUFFY!
REAL FUNNY!
AGREED!
LET IT BEGIN.

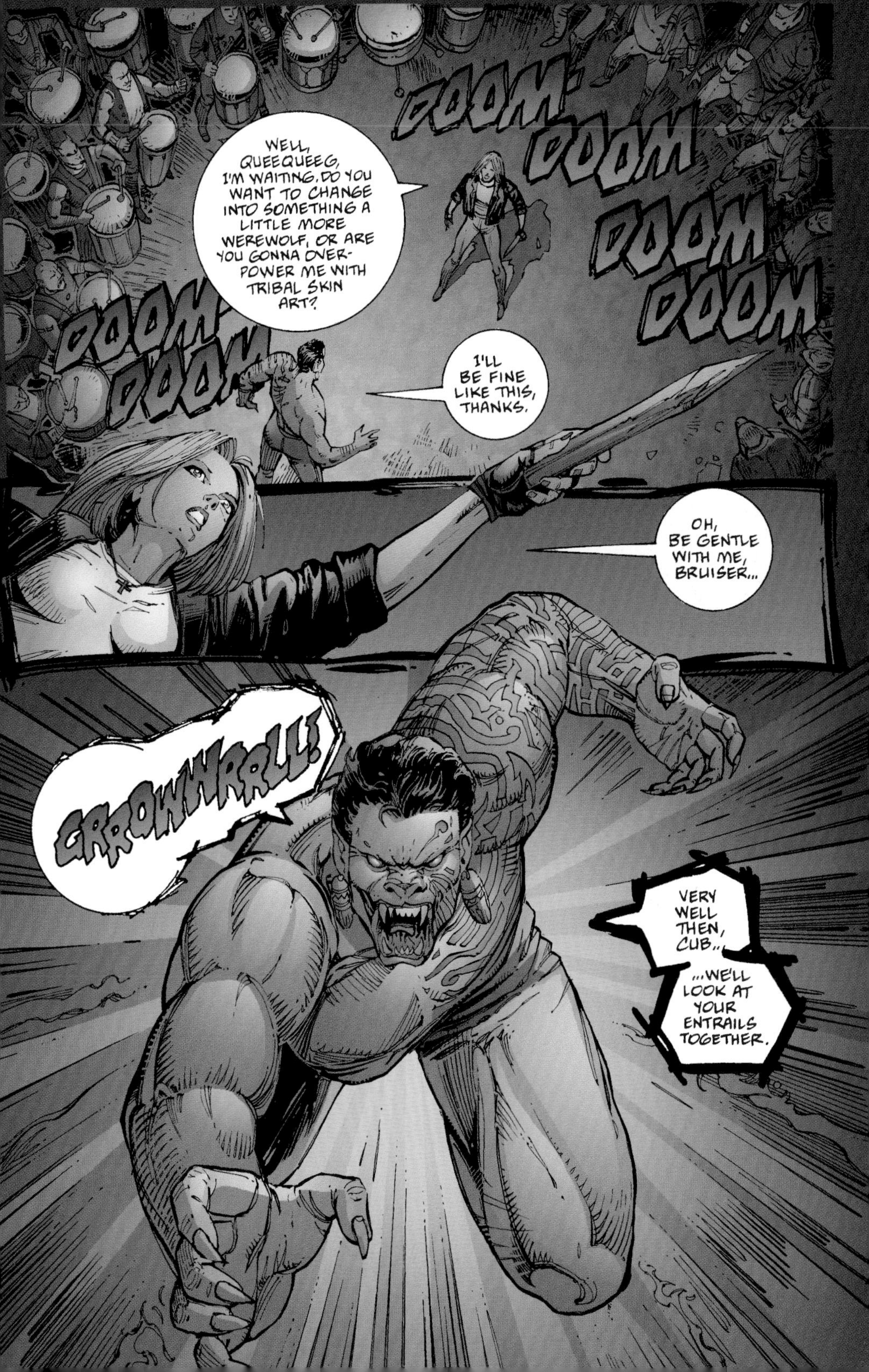
DOOM-DOOM
DOOM DOOM
WELL, QUEEQUEEG, I'M WAITING. DO YOU WANT TO CHANGE INTO SOMETHING A LITTLE MORE WEREWOLF, OR ARE YOU GONNA OVER-POWER ME WITH TRIBAL SKIN ART?
DOOM-DOOM
I'LL BE FINE LIKE THIS, THANKS.
OH, BE GENTLE WITH ME, BRUISER...
GRROWWRRLL!
VERY WELL THEN, CUB...
...WE'LL LOOK AT YOUR ENTRAILS TOGETHER.

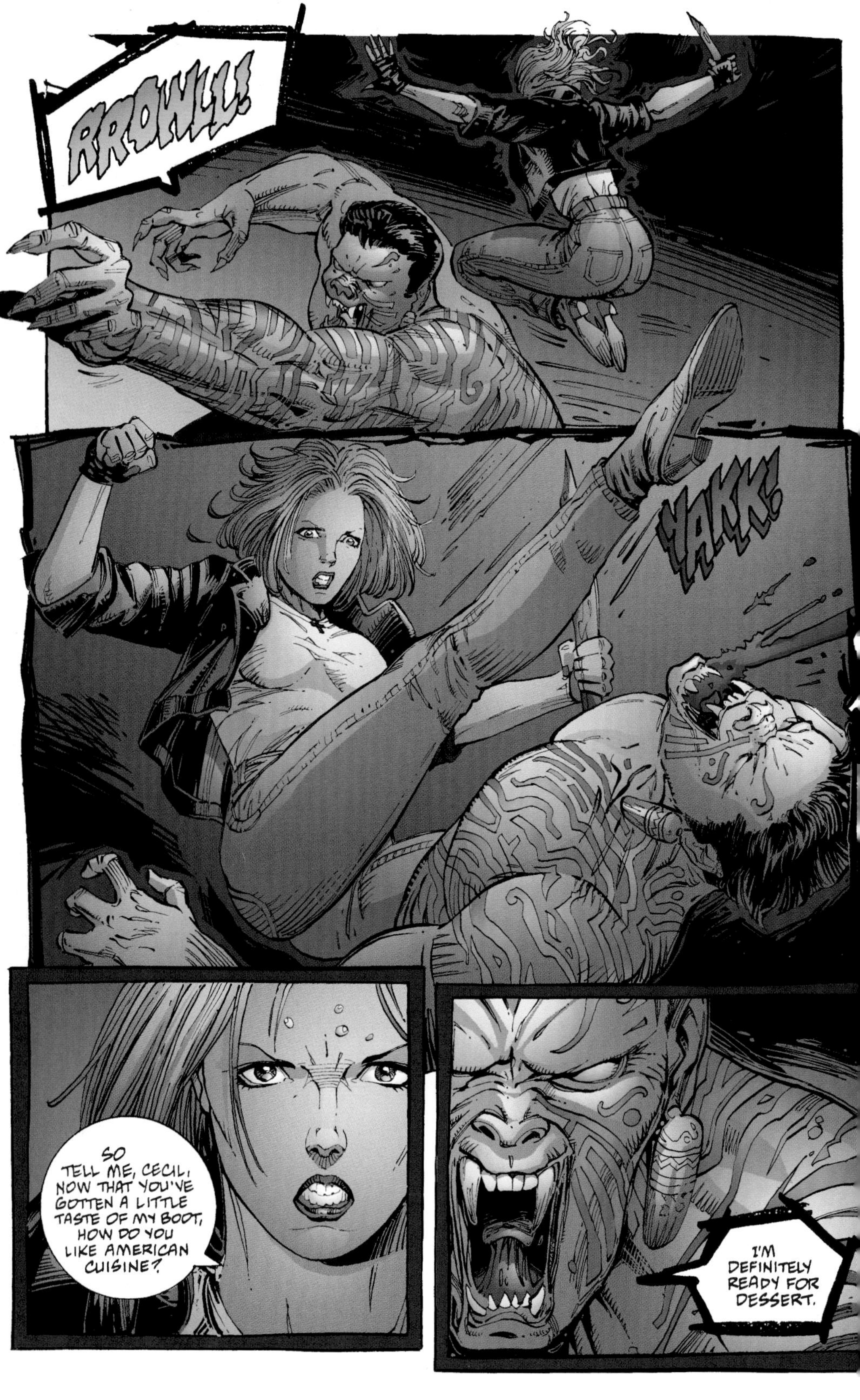
RROWLL!
YAKK!
SO TELL ME, CECIL, NOW THAT YOU'VE GOTTEN A LITTLE TASTE OF MY BOOT, HOW DO YOU LIKE AMERICAN CUISINE?
I'M DEFINITELY READY FOR DESSERT.

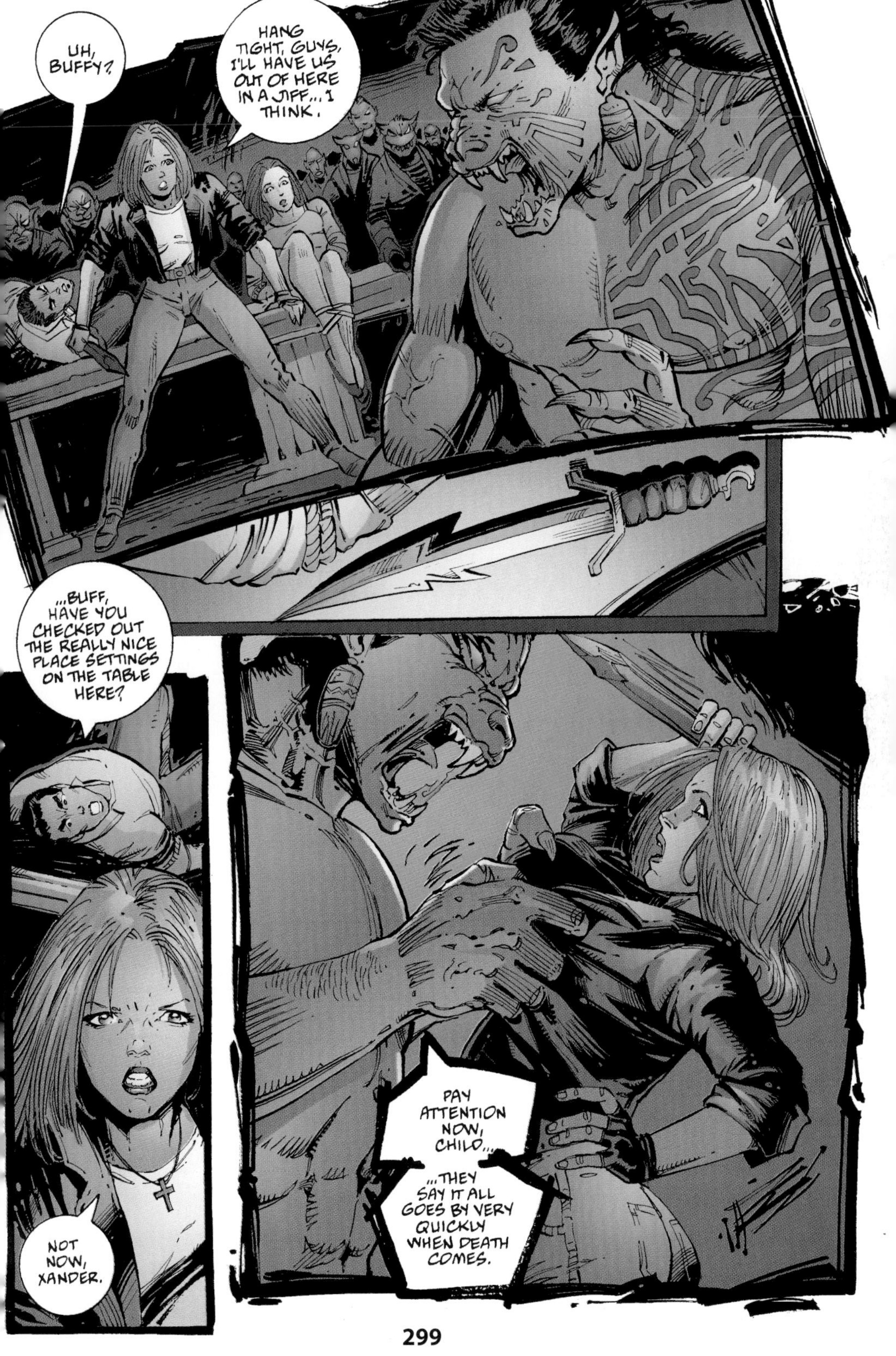
UH, BUFFY?
HANG TIGHT, GUYS, I'LL HAVE US OUT OF HERE IN A JIFF... I THINK.
...BUFF, HAVE YOU CHECKED OUT THE REALLY NICE PLACE SETTINGS ON THE TABLE HERE?
NOT NOW, XANDER.
PAY ATTENTION NOW, CHILD...
...THEY SAY IT ALL GOES BY VERY QUICKLY WHEN DEATH COMES.

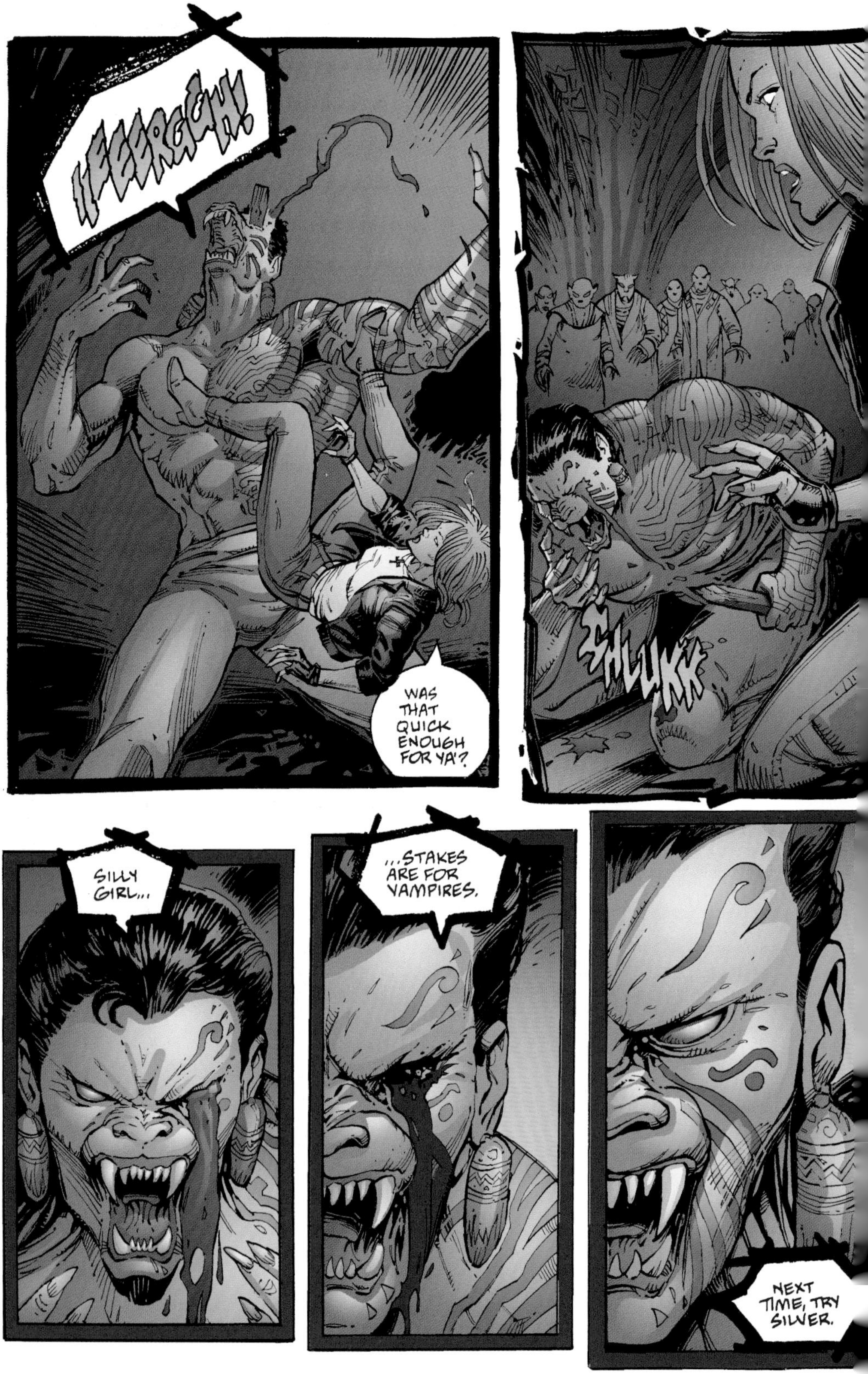
IIEEERGGH!
WAS THAT QUICK ENOUGH FOR YA'?
SHLUKK
SILLY GIRL...
...STAKES ARE FOR VAMPIRES.
NEXT TIME, TRY SILVER.

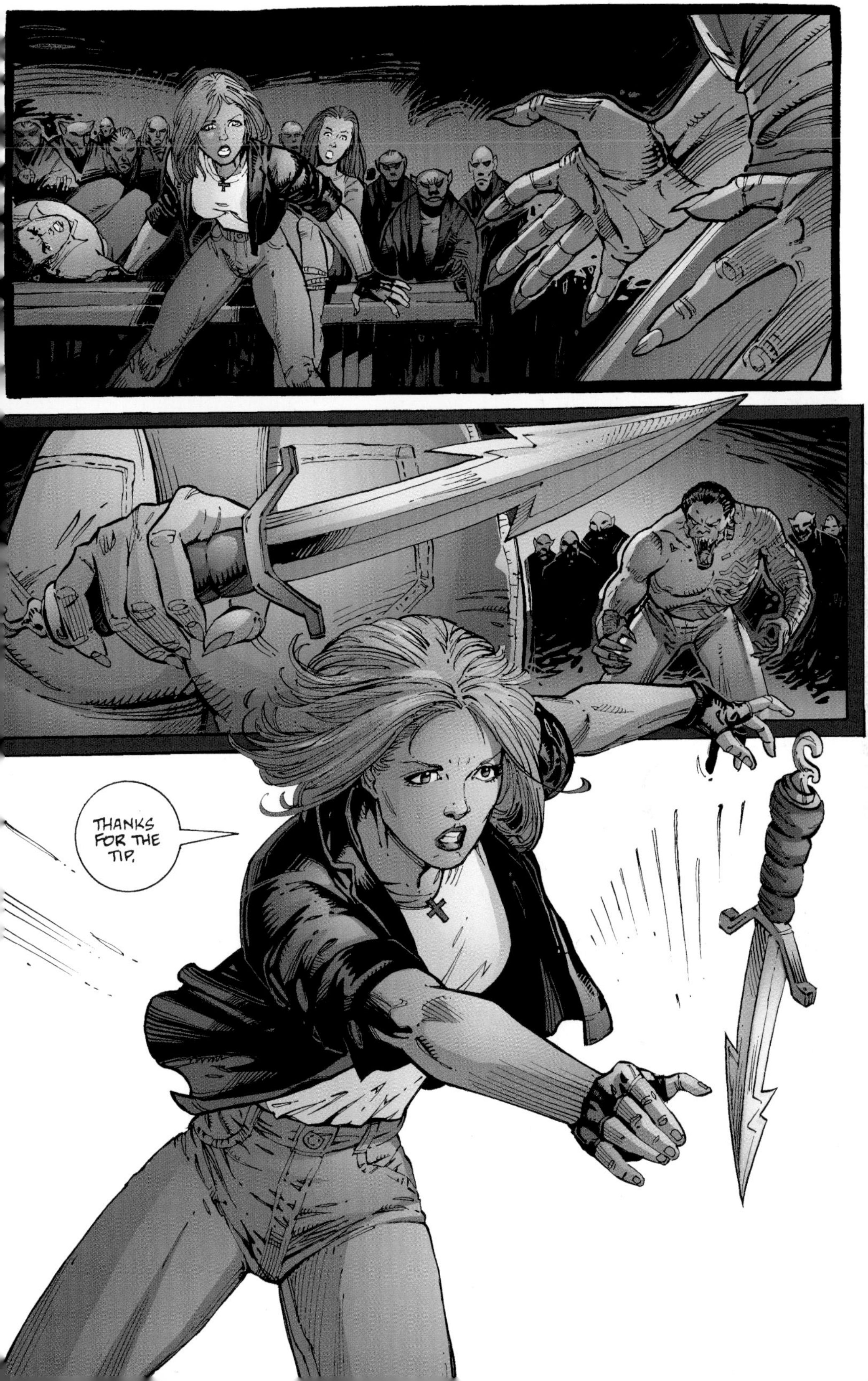
THANKS FOR THE TIP.

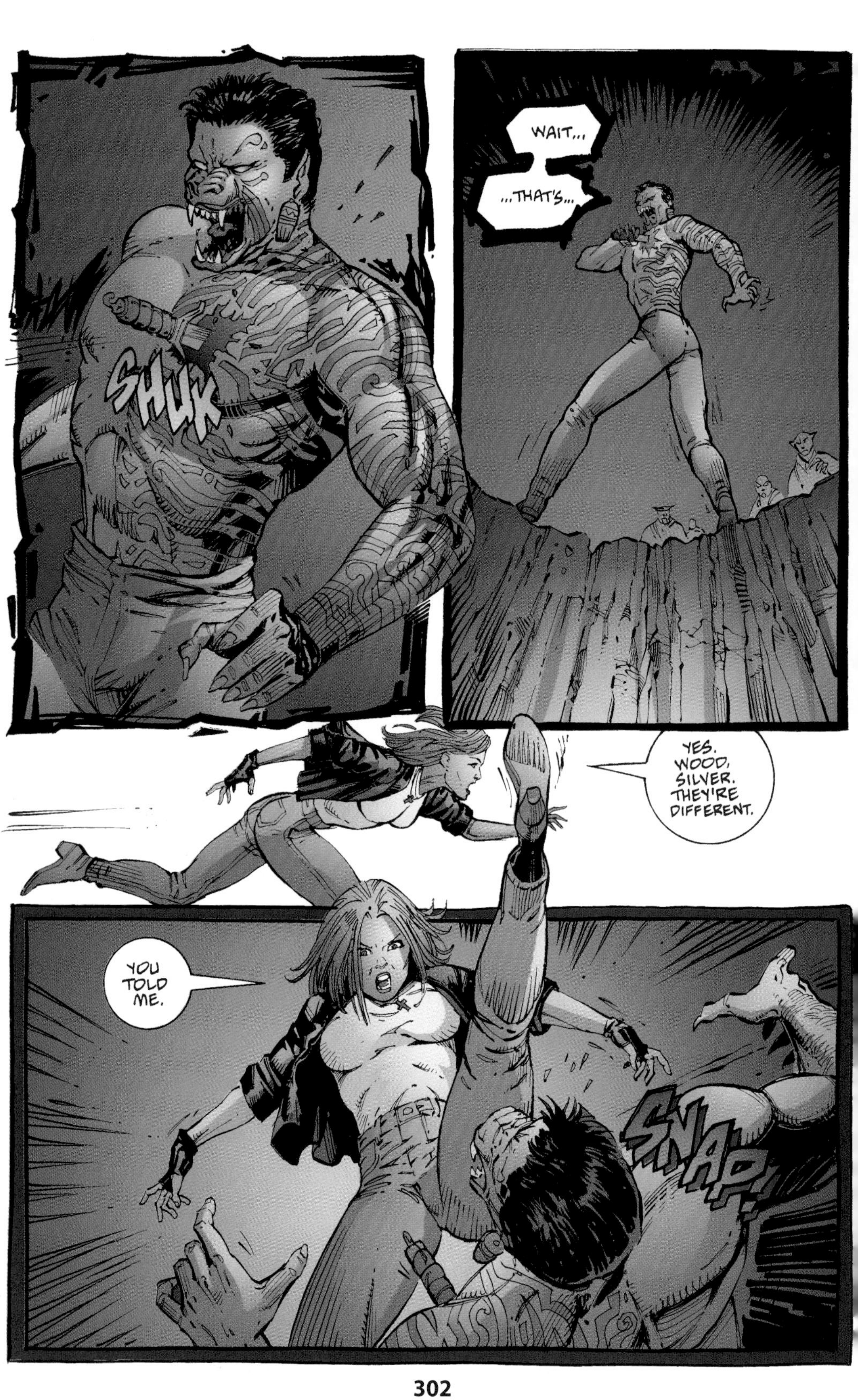
SHUK
WAIT...
...THAT'S...
YES. WOOD, SILVER. THEY'RE DIFFERENT.
YOU TOLD ME.
SNAP

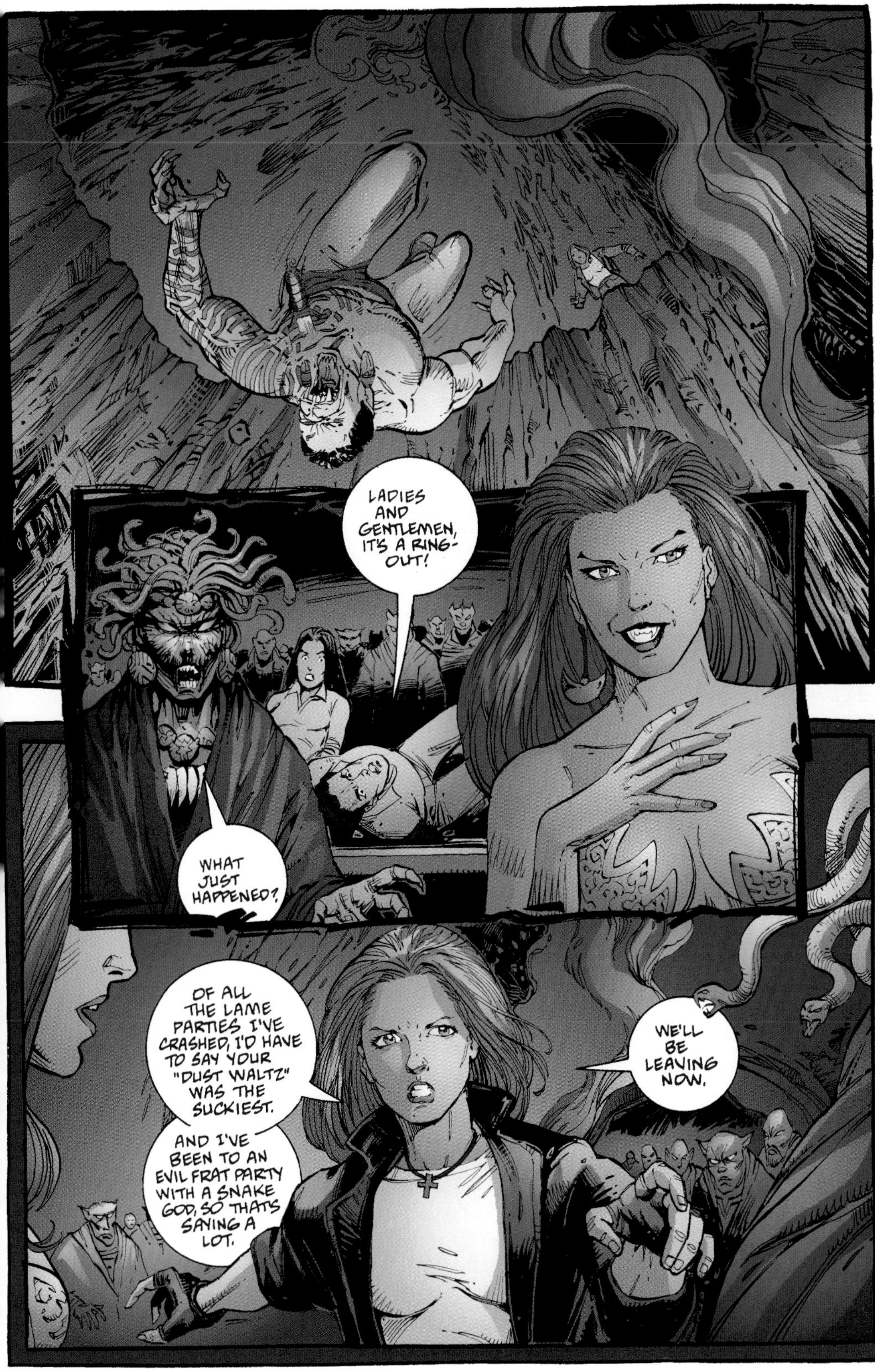

LADIES AND GENTLEMEN, IT'S A RING-OUT!
WHAT JUST HAPPENED?
OF ALL THE LAME PARTIES I'VE CRASHED, I'D HAVE TO SAY YOUR "DUST WALTZ" WAS THE SUCKIEST.
AND I'VE BEEN TO AN EVIL FRAT PARTY WITH A SNAKE GOD, SO THAT'S SAYING A LOT.
WE'LL BE LEAVING NOW.

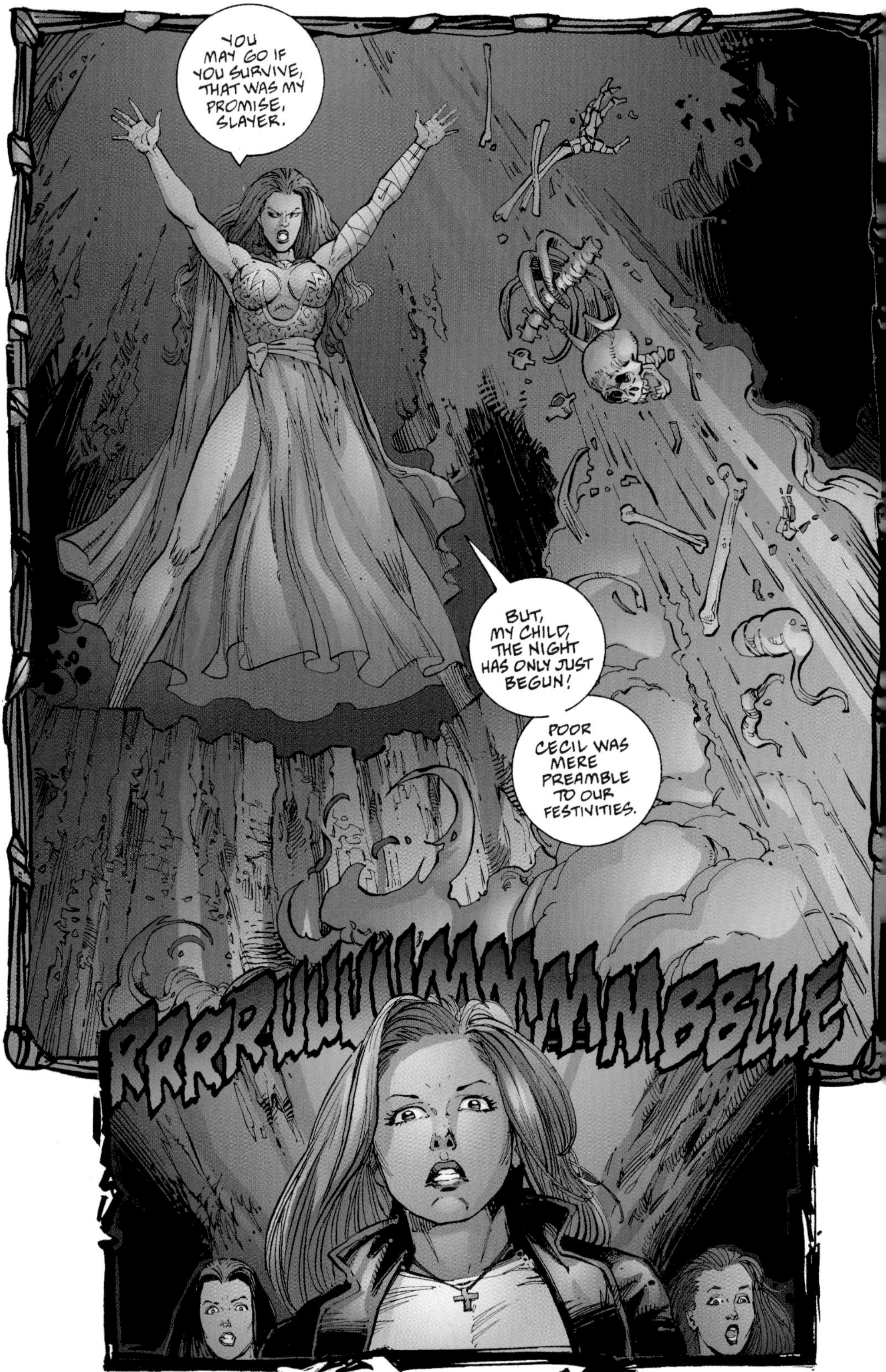
YOU MAY GO IF YOU SURVIVE, THAT WAS MY PROMISE, SLAYER.
BUT, MY CHILD, THE NIGHT HAS ONLY JUST BEGUN!
POOR CECIL WAS MERE PREAMBLE TO OUR FESTIVITIES.
RRRRUUUMMMMBBLLE

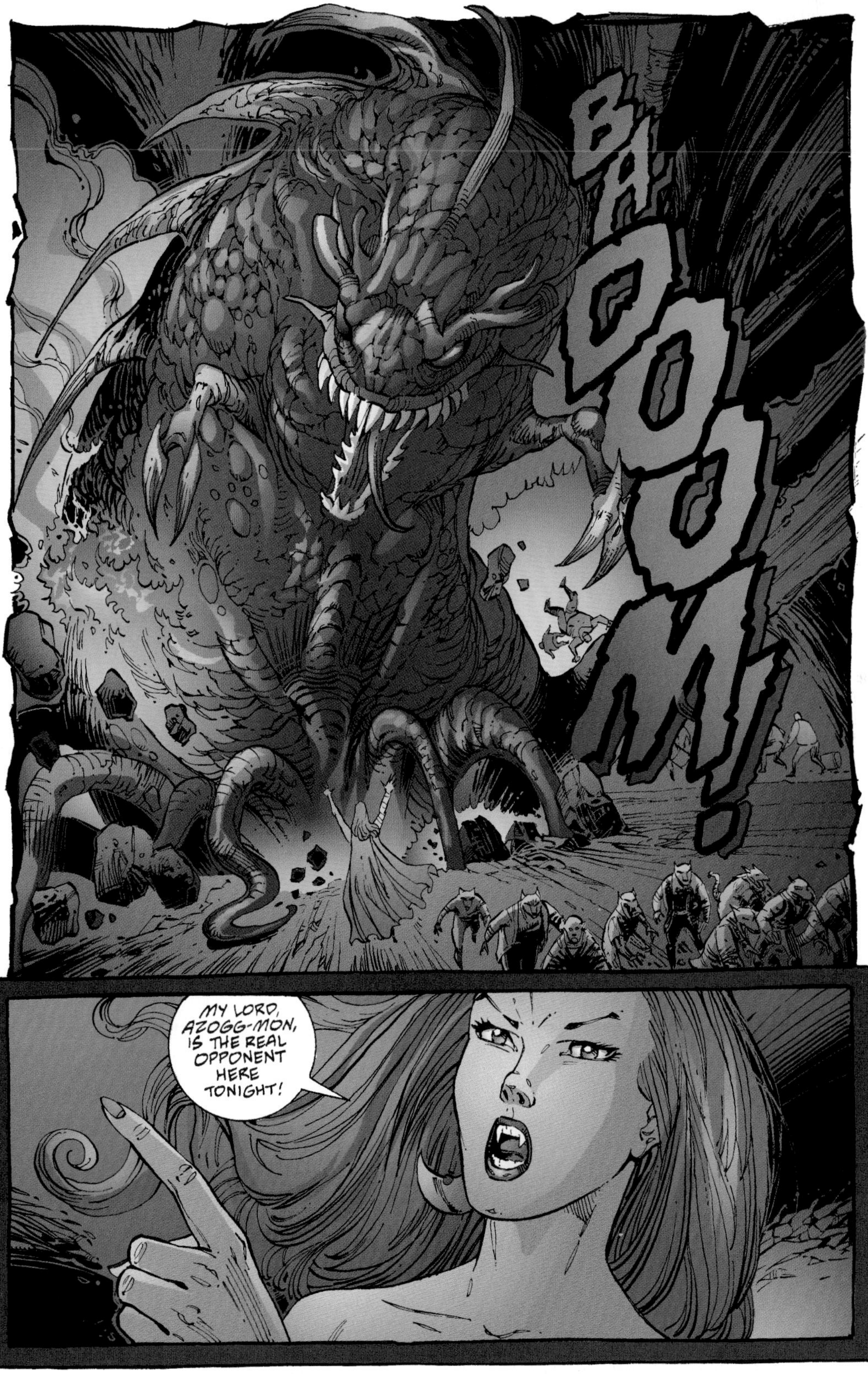
BA-DOOM!
MY LORD, AZOGG-MON, IS THE REAL OPPONENT HERE TONIGHT!

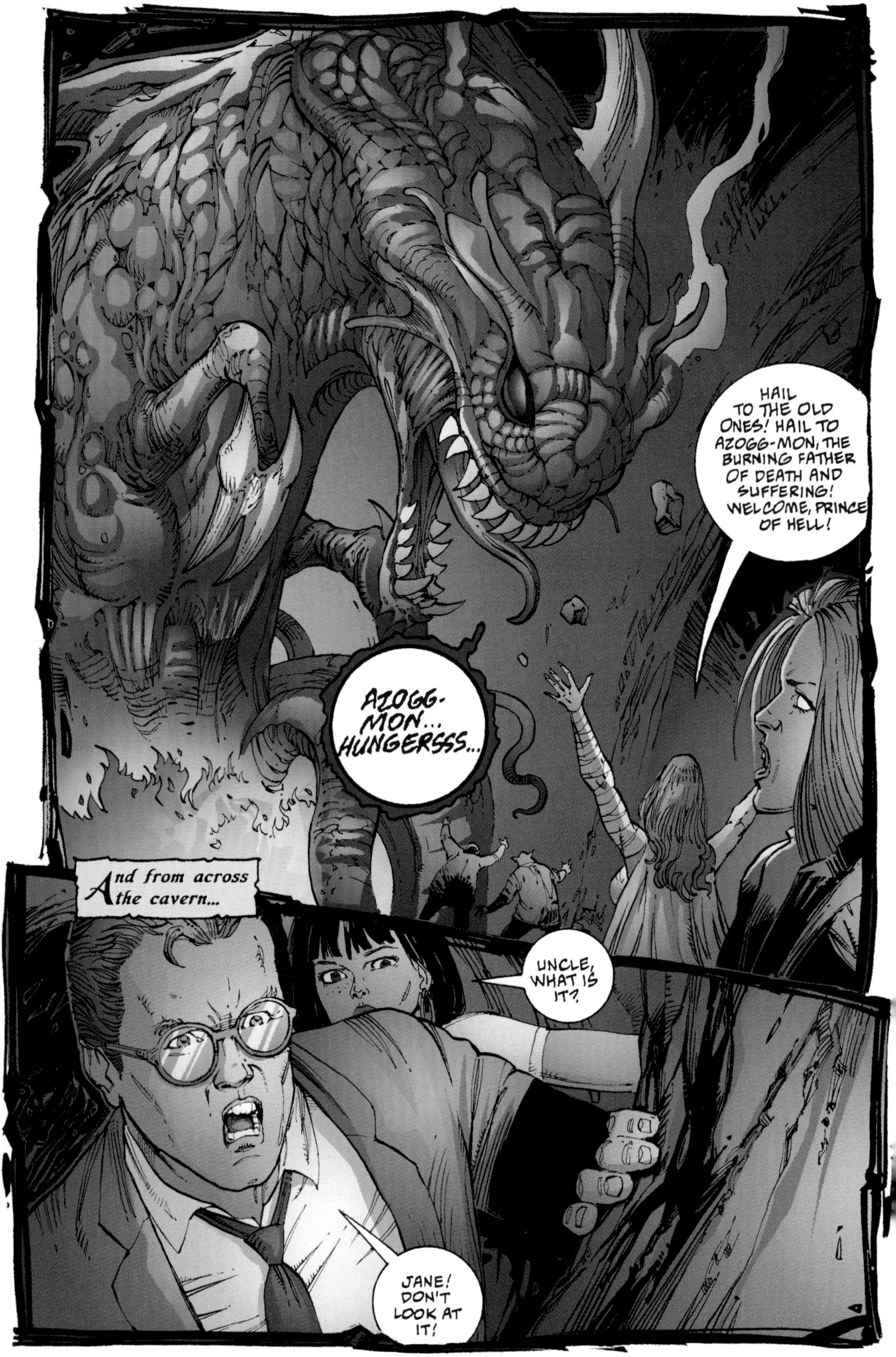
HAIL TO THE OLD ONES! HAIL TO AZOGG-MON, THE BURNING FATHER OF DEATH AND SUFFERING! WELCOME, PRINCE OF HELL!
AZOGG-MON... HUNGERSSS...
And from across the cavern...
UNCLE, WHAT IS IT?
JANE! DON'T LOOK AT IT!

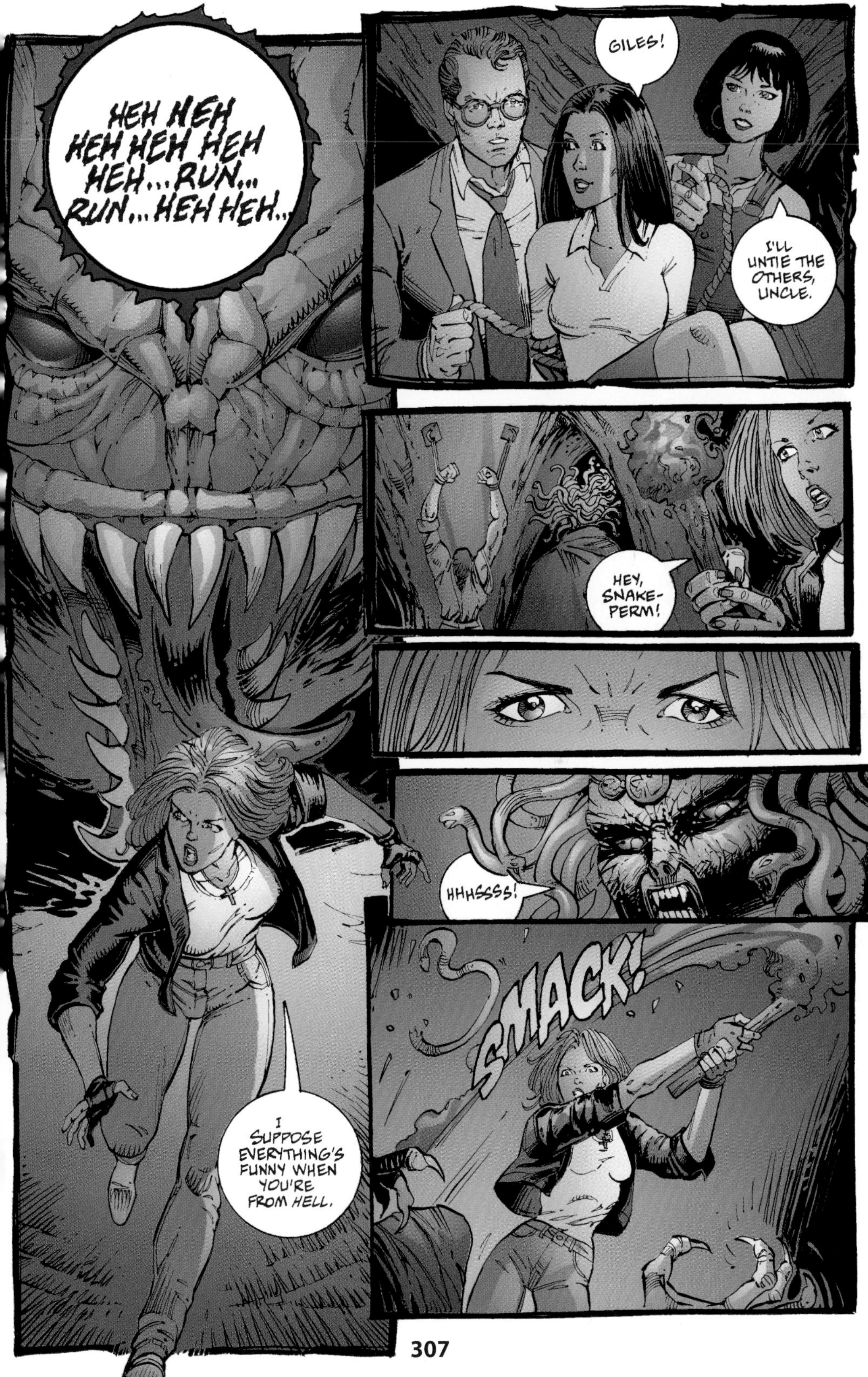
HEH HEH HEH HEH HEH HEH...RUN... RUN...HEH HEH...
GILES!
I'LL UNTIE THE OTHERS, UNCLE.
HEY, SNAKE-PERM!
HHHSSSS!
I SUPPOSE EVERYTHING'S FUNNY WHEN YOU'RE FROM *HELL*.
SMACK!

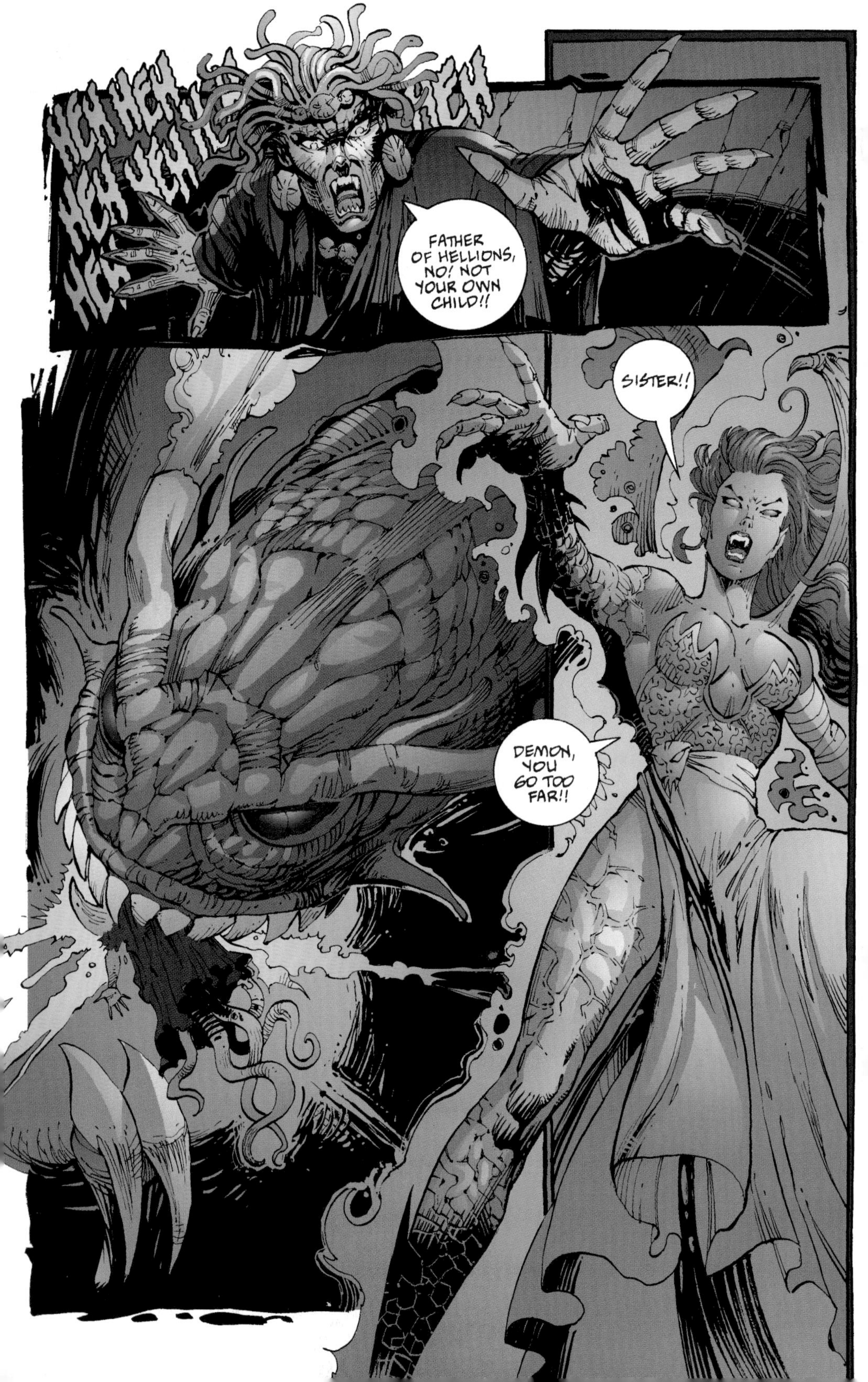
FATHER OF HELLIONS, NO! NOT YOUR OWN CHILD!!
SISTER!!
DEMON, YOU GO TOO FAR!!

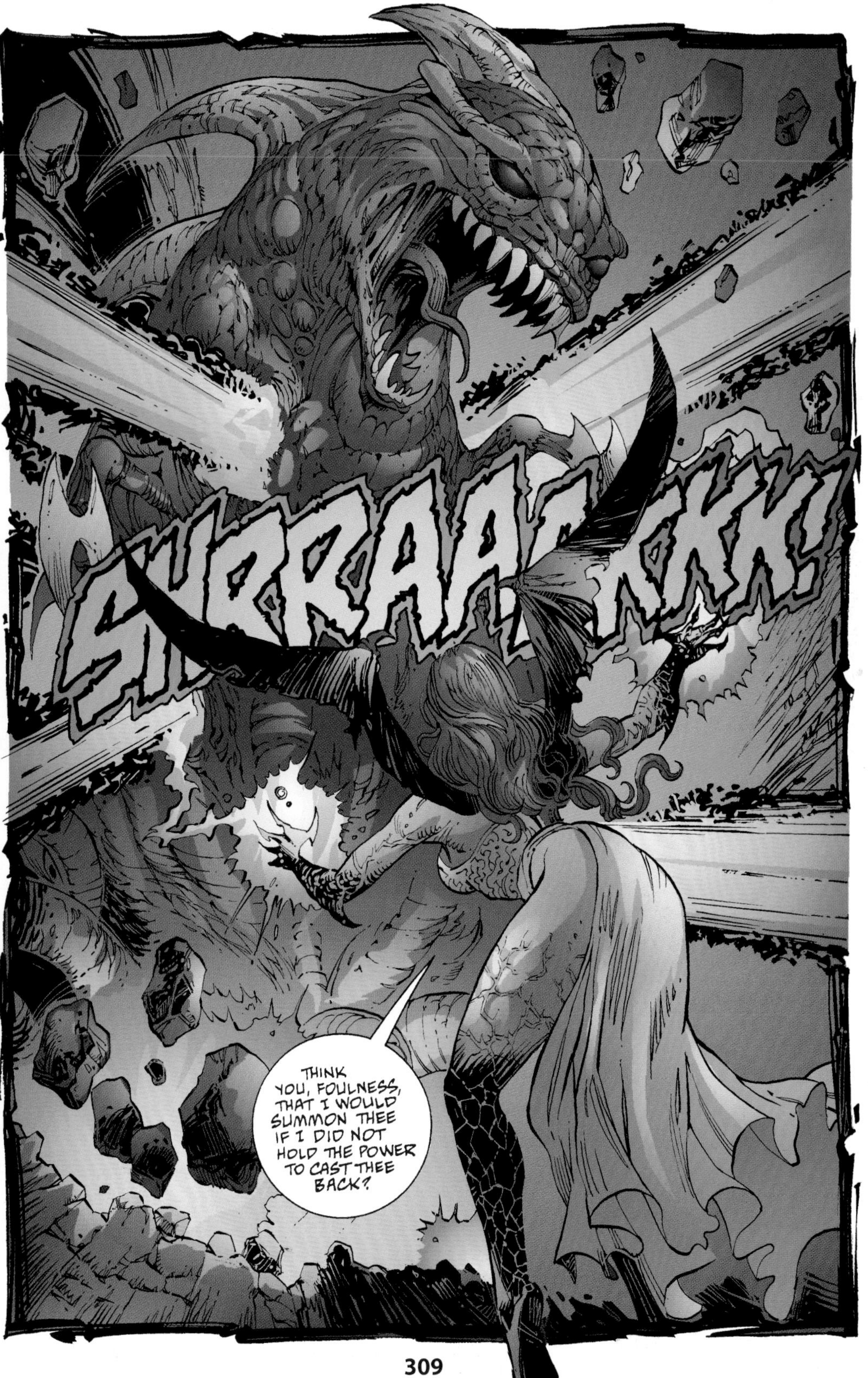
THINK YOU, FOULNESS, THAT I WOULD SUMMON THEE IF I DID NOT HOLD THE POWER TO CAST THEE BACK?

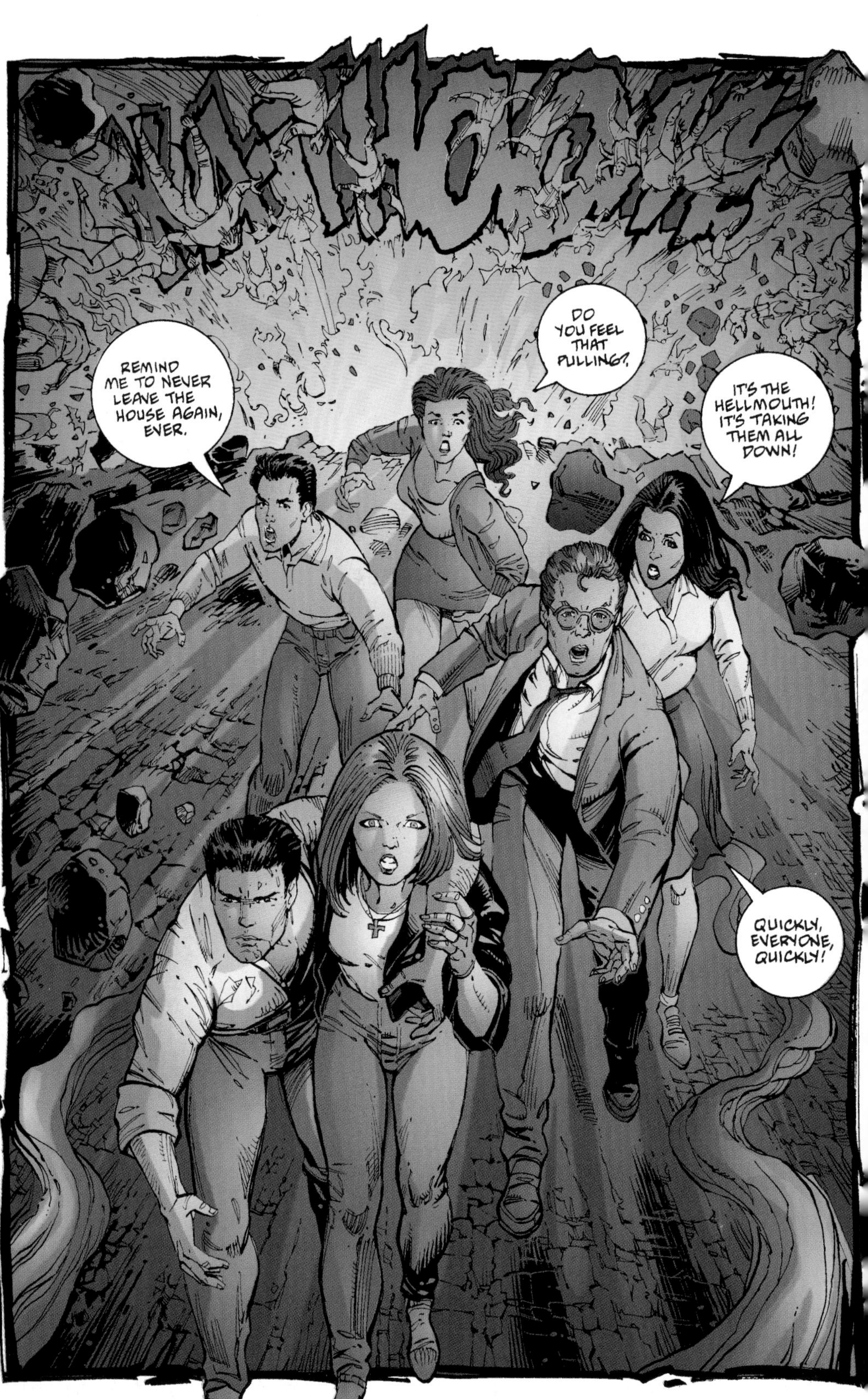
REMIND ME TO NEVER LEAVE THE HOUSE AGAIN, EVER.
DO YOU FEEL THAT PULLING?
IT'S THE HELLMOUTH! IT'S TAKING THEM ALL DOWN!
QUICKLY, EVERYONE, QUICKLY!

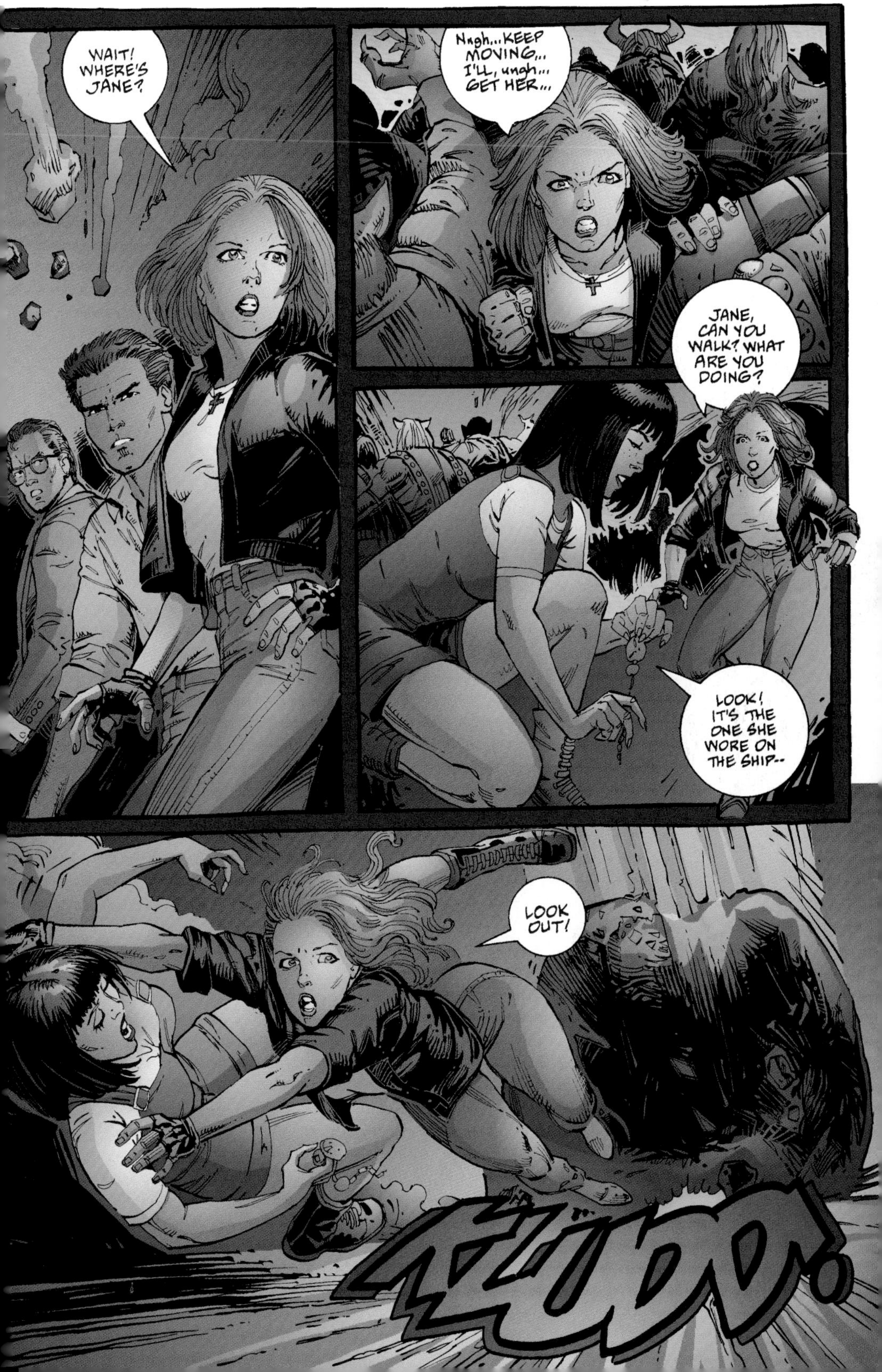
WAIT! WHERE'S JANE?
Nngh... KEEP MOVING... I'LL, ungh... GET HER...
JANE, CAN YOU WALK? WHAT ARE YOU DOING?
LOOK! IT'S THE ONE SHE WORE ON THE SHIP--
LOOK OUT!

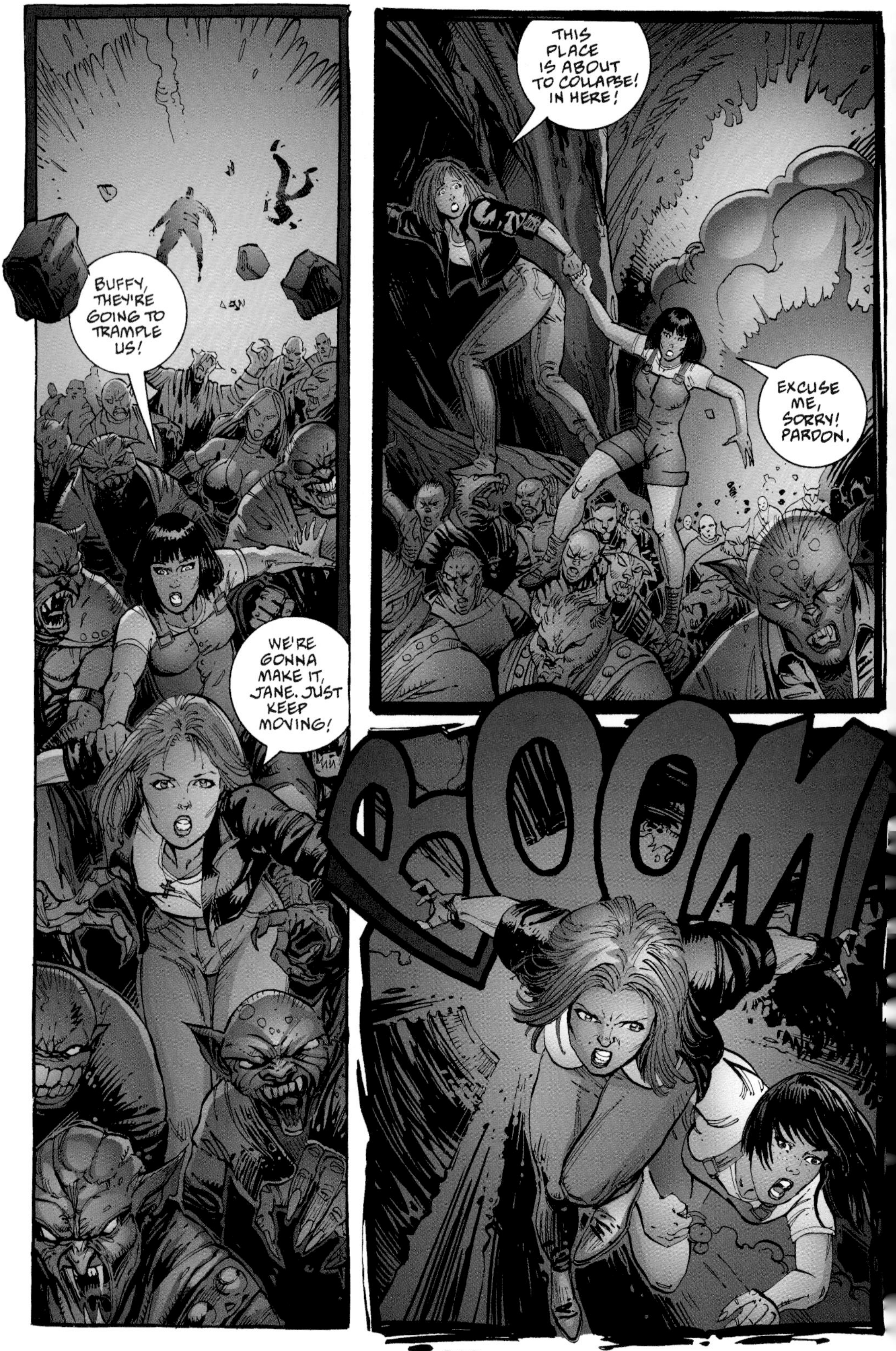
BUFFY, THEY'RE GOING TO TRAMPLE US!
WE'RE GONNA MAKE IT, JANE. JUST KEEP MOVING!
THIS PLACE IS ABOUT TO COLLAPSE! IN HERE!
EXCUSE ME, SORRY! PARDON.
BOOM

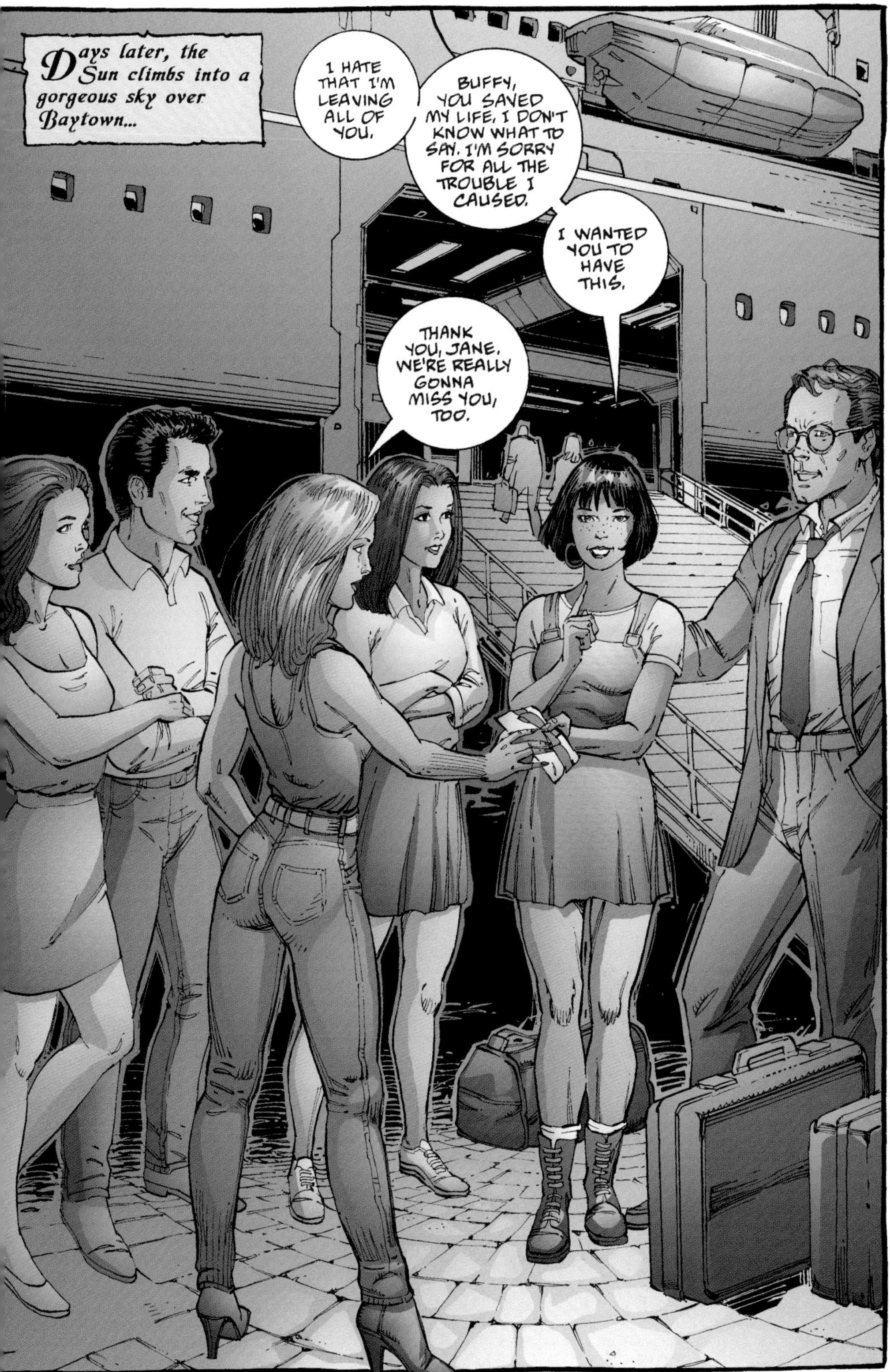
Days later, the Sun climbs into a gorgeous sky over Baytown...
I HATE THAT I'M LEAVING ALL OF YOU.
BUFFY, YOU SAVED MY LIFE. I DON'T KNOW WHAT TO SAY. I'M SORRY FOR ALL THE TROUBLE I CAUSED.
I WANTED YOU TO HAVE THIS.
THANK YOU, JANE. WE'RE REALLY GONNA MISS YOU, TOO.

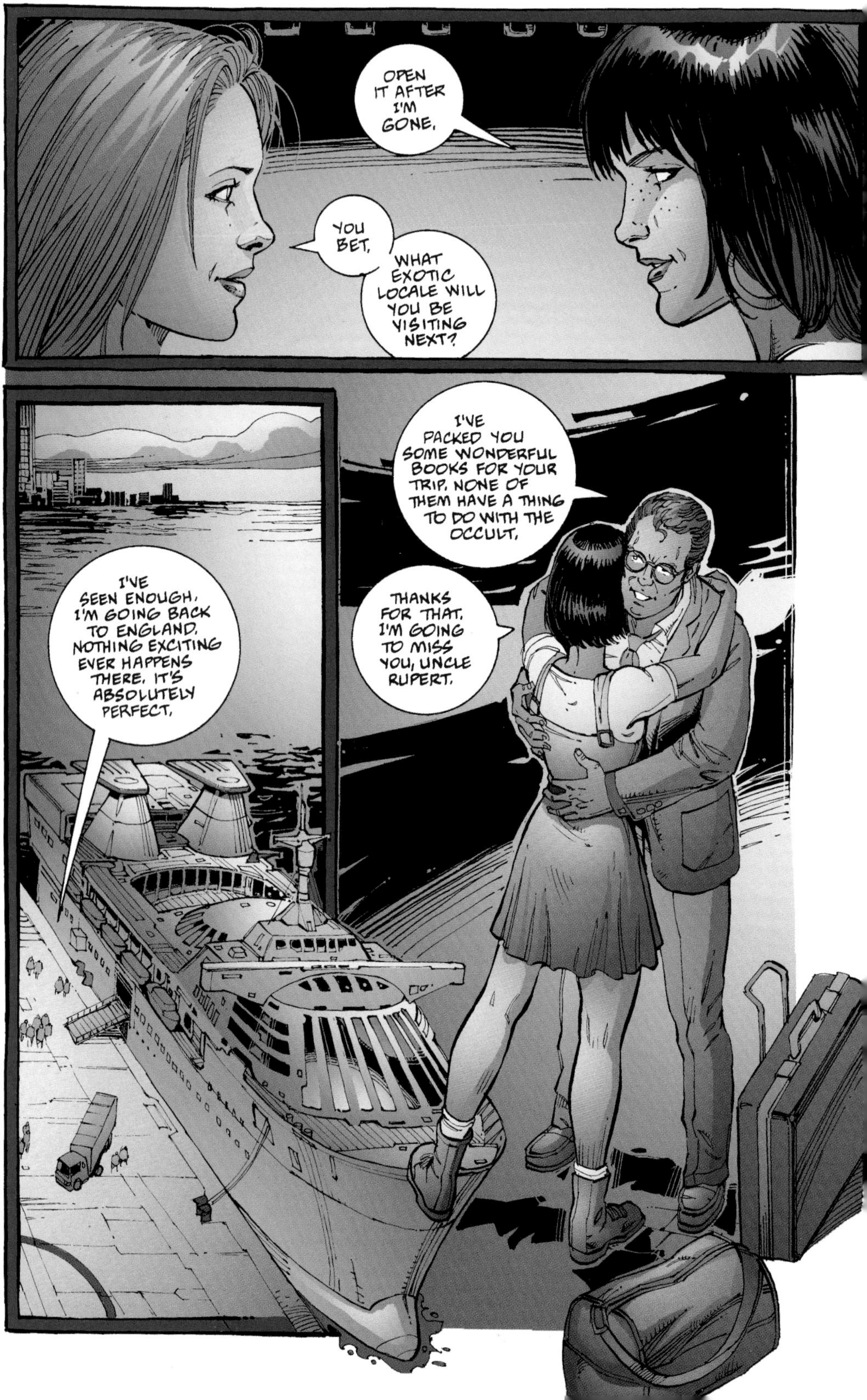
OPEN IT AFTER I'M GONE.
YOU BET.
WHAT EXOTIC LOCALE WILL YOU BE VISITING NEXT?
I'VE PACKED YOU SOME WONDERFUL BOOKS FOR YOUR TRIP. NONE OF THEM HAVE A THING TO DO WITH THE OCCULT.
THANKS FOR THAT. I'M GOING TO MISS YOU, UNCLE RUPERT.
I'VE SEEN ENOUGH. I'M GOING BACK TO ENGLAND. NOTHING EXCITING EVER HAPPENS THERE. IT'S ABSOLUTELY PERFECT.

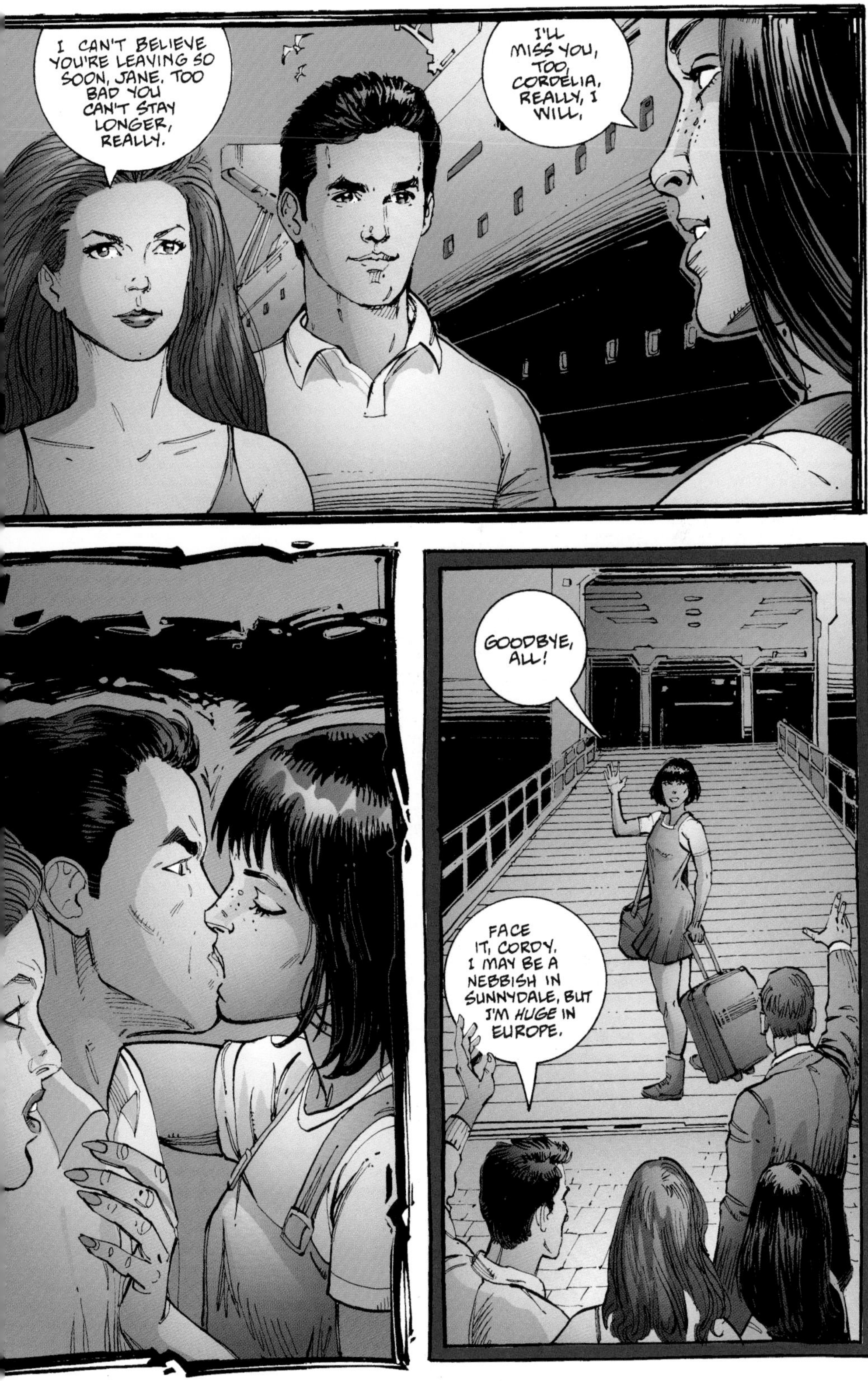
I CAN'T BELIEVE YOU'RE LEAVING SO SOON, JANE. TOO BAD YOU CAN'T STAY LONGER, REALLY.
I'LL MISS YOU, TOO, CORDELIA. REALLY, I WILL.
GOODBYE, ALL!
FACE IT, CORDY. I MAY BE A NEBBISH IN SUNNYDALE, BUT I'M *HUGE* IN EUROPE.

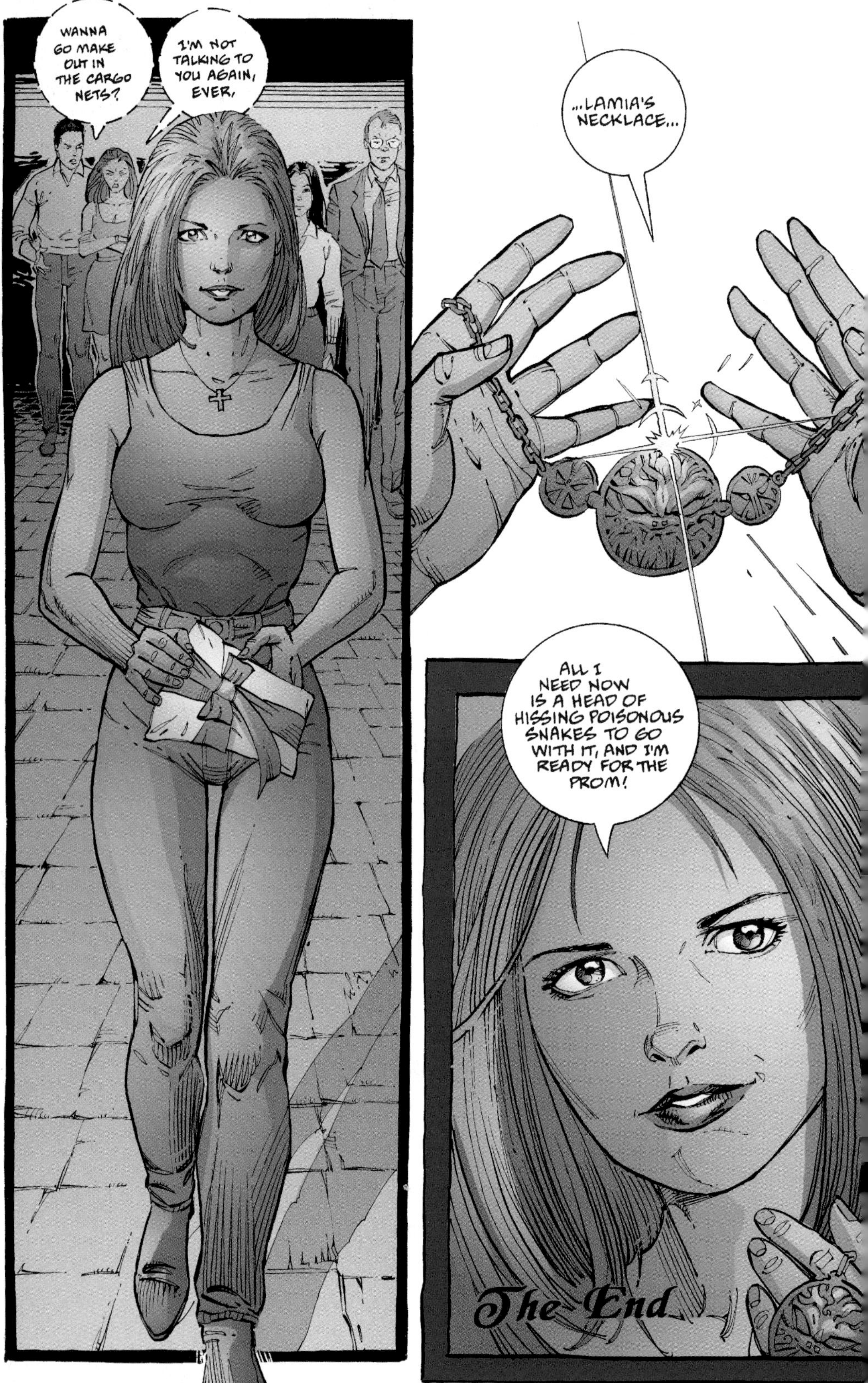
WANNA GO MAKE OUT IN THE CARGO NETS?
I'M NOT TALKING TO YOU AGAIN, EVER.
...LAMIA'S NECKLACE...
ALL I NEED NOW IS A HEAD OF HISSING POISONOUS SNAKES TO GO WITH IT, AND I'M READY FOR THE PROM!
The End

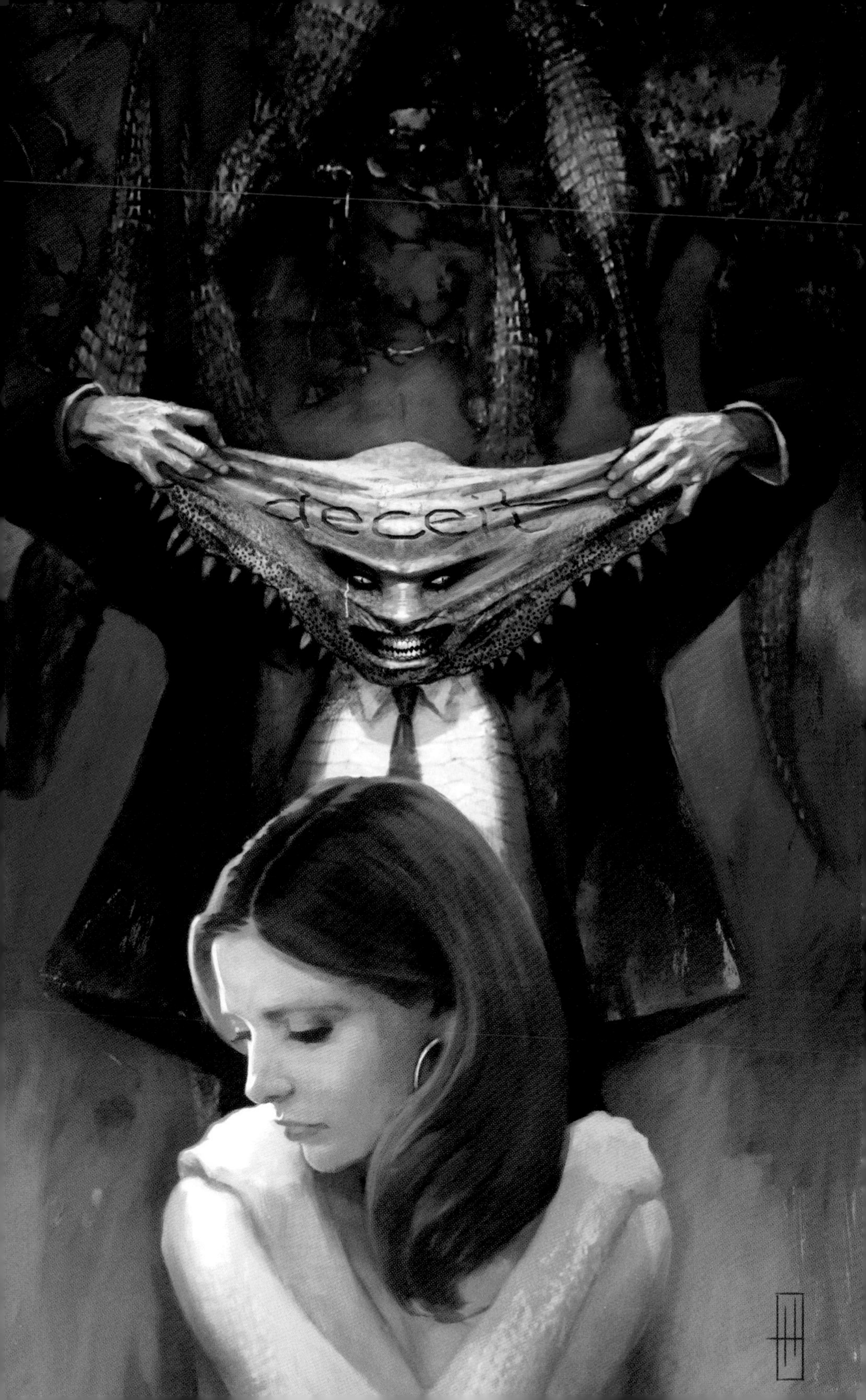
deceit

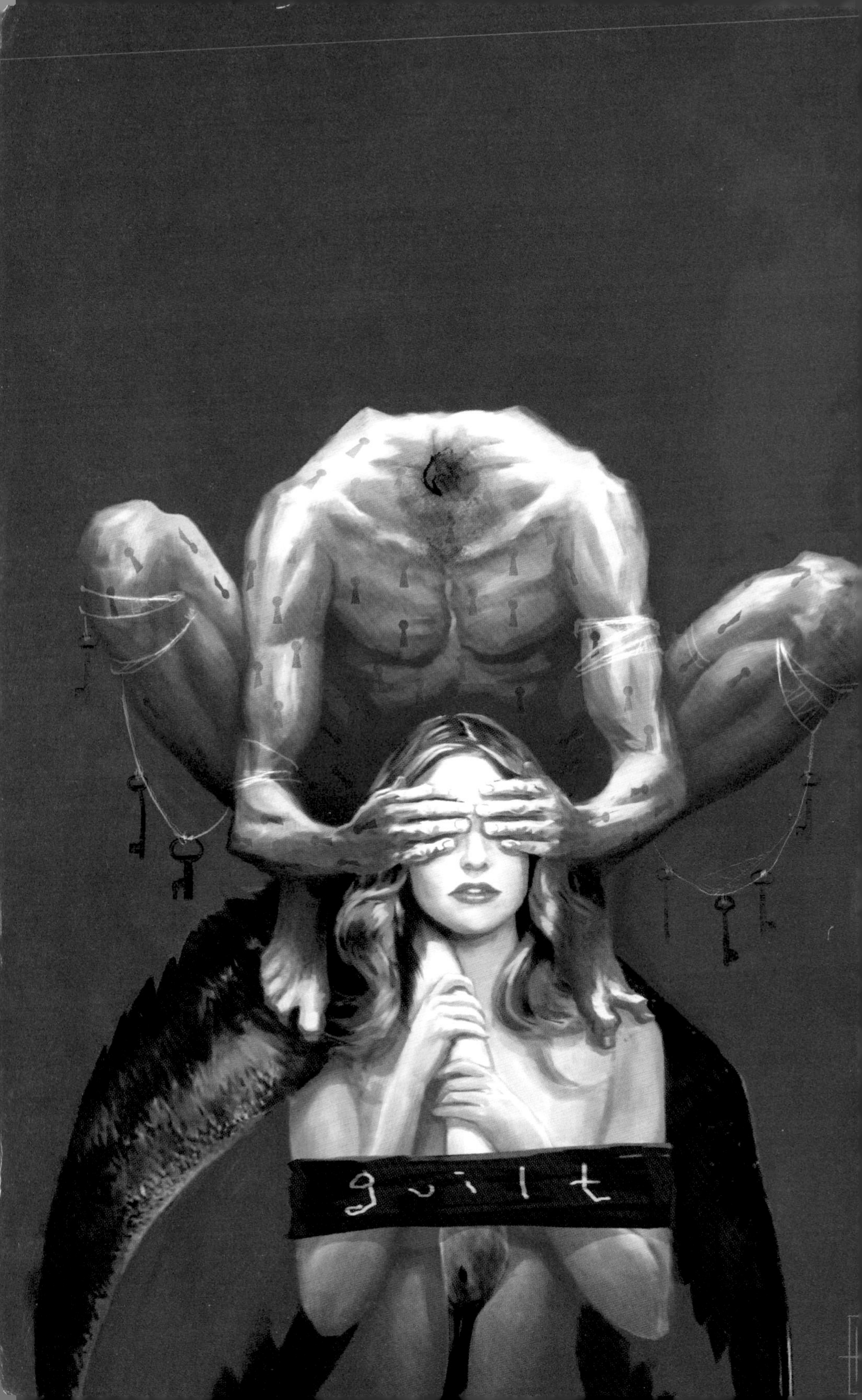
guilt

ALSO FROM JOSS WHEDON AND THE BUFFYVERSE!

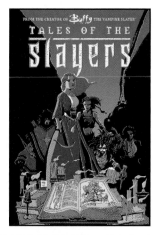

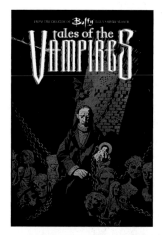

FROM THE CREATOR OF Buffy THE VAMPIRE SLAYER
TALES OF THE
slayers

BUFFY THE VAMPIRE SLAYER: TALES OF THE SLAYERS

Joss Whedon, Leinil Francis Yu, Tim Sale, Brett Matthews, and others

Buffy Summers is only the latest in a long line of women who have battled vampires, demons, and other forces of evil as the Slayer. Now, hear the stories behind other Slayers, past and future, told by the writers of the hit television show and illustrated by some of the most acclaimed artists in comics.

ISBN-10: 1-56971-605-6 / ISBN-13: 978-1-56971-605-2

$14.95

tales of the
VAMPIRES

BUFFY THE VAMPIRE SLAYER: TALES OF THE VAMPIRES

Joss Whedon, Brett Matthews, Cameron Stewart, Tim Sale, and others

The creator of Buffy the Vampire Slayer reunites with the writers from his hit TV show for a frightening look into the history of vampires. Illustrated by some of comics' greatest artists, the stories span medieval times to today, including Buffy's rematch with Dracula, and Angel's ongoing battle with his own demons.

ISBN-10: 1-56971-749-4 / ISBN-13: 978-1-56971-749-3

$15.95

joss whedon
karl moline
andy owens
FRAY

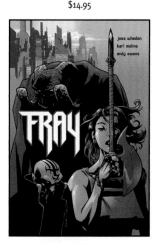

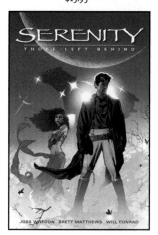

FRAY

Joss Whedon, Karl Moline, and Andy Owens

In a future Manhattan so poisoned it doesn't notice the monsters on its streets, it's up to a gutter punk named Fray to unite a fallen city against a demonic plot to consume mankind. But will this girl who thought she had no future embrace her destiny—as the first Vampire Slayer in centuries—in time?

ISBN-10: 1-56971-751-6 / ISBN-13: 978-1-56971-751-6

$19.95

SERENITY
THOSE LEFT BEHIND
JOSS WHEDON BRETT MATTHEWS WILL CONRAD

SERENITY: THOSE LEFT BEHIND

Joss Whedon, Brett Matthews, Will Conrad, and Adam Hughes

Joss Whedon, creator of Buffy the Vampire Slayer and scribe of Marvel's *Astonishing X-Men*, unveils a previously unknown chapter in the lives of his favorite band of space brigands in this comics prequel of the *Serenity* feature film, bridging the gap from Whedon's cult-hit TV show *Firefly*.

ISBN-10: 1-59307-449-2 / ISBN-13: 978-1-59307-449-4

$9.95

AVAILABLE AT YOUR LOCAL COMICS SHOP OR BOOKSTORE! • To find a comics shop in your area, call 1-888-266-4226. For more information or to order direct visit darkhorse.com or call 1-800-862-0052 Mon.-Fri. 9 A.M. to 5 P.M. Pacific Time *Prices and availability subject to change without notice

DARK HORSE COMICS *drawing on your nightmares*
darkhorse.com

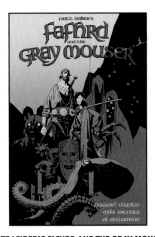

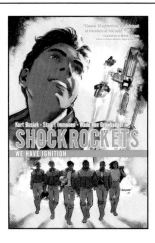

FRITZ LEIBER'S FAFHRD AND THE GRAY MOUSER
Howard Chaykin and Mike Mignola
Since their first appearance in 1939, Fritz Leiber's Fafhrd and the Gray Mouser have ranked among the most beloved characters in fantasy. Their rollicking adventures in the land of Nehwon have influenced the work of some of the best in modern fantasy, including Michael Moorcock, Terry Pratchett, and countless others.
ISBN-10: 1-59307-713-0 / ISBN-13: 978-1-59307-713-6
$19.95

SHOCKROCKETS: WE HAVE IGNITION
Kurt Busiek, Stuart Immonen, and Wade Von Grawbadger
In the wake of a devastating alien war, Earth is protected by the Shockrockets—a squadron of aerial fighters built from a fusion of alien and human technology and piloted by the best Earth has to offer. Now they face a deadly challenge as the military genius who saved the planet makes an all-out attempt at global domination.
ISBN-10: 1-59307-129-9 / I SBN-13: 978-1-59307-129-5
$14.95

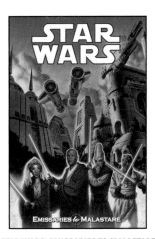

STAR WARS: EMISSARIES TO MALASTARE
Timothy Truman, Tom Lyle, Jan Duursema, and John Nadeau
Half of the Jedi High Council travel to the exotic world of Malastare to negotiate a peace treaty between two of that planet's warring factions. But the whole affair is being manipulated by a secret, third party out to assassinate the Jedi! This story features many familiar characters from *The Phantom Menace* and continues the ongoing adventures that bridge the gap between *Episodes I* and *II*!
ISBN-10: 1-56971-545-9 / ISBN-13: 978-1-56971-545-1
$15.95

SAMURAI: HEAVEN AND EARTH VOLUME 1
Ron Marz and Luke Ross
Beginning in feudal Japan in 1704, *Samurai: Heaven & Earth* follows Shiro, a lone samurai warrior sworn to be reunited with the love of his life who has been spirited away by his enemies. His pursuit of Yoshiko will carry him farther than he could have imagined—from his native Japan to the sprawling empire of China, across Europe, and finally to Paris itself!
ISBN-10: 1-59307-388-7 / ISBN-13: 978-1-59307-388-6
$14.95

AVAILABLE AT YOUR LOCAL COMICS SHOP OR BOOKSTORE! • To find a comics shop in your area, call 1-888-266-4226.
For more information or to order direct visit darkhorse.com or call 1-800-862-0052 Mon.-Fri. 9 A.M. to 5 P.M. Pacific Time
*Prices and availability subject to change without notice

DARK HORSE BOOKS